THE HISTORY OF
SIR RICHARD CALMADY

THE HISTORY OF
SIR RICHARD CALMADY

A ROMANCE

BY

LUCAS MALET

METHUEN & CO.

36 ESSEX STREET W.C.

LONDON

1901

CONTENTS

BOOK I

THE CLOWN

BOOK II

THE BREAKING OF DREAMS

CONTENTS

BOOK III

LA BELLE DAME SANS MERCI

BOOK IV

A SLIP BETWIXT CUP AND LIP

BOOK V

RAKE'S PROGRESS

BOOK VI

THE NEW HEAVEN AND THE NEW EARTH

CONTENTS

THE HISTORY OF
SIR RICHARD CALMADY

BOOK I
THE CLOWN

CHAPTER I

ACQUAINTING THE READER WITH A FAIR DOMAIN AND
THE MAKER THEREOF

IN that fortunate hour of English history, when the cruel
sights and haunting insecurities of the Middle Ages had
passed away, and while, as yet, the fanatic zeal of Puritanism
had not cast its blighting shadow over all merry and pleasant
things, it seemed good to one Denzil Calmady, esquire, to
build himself a stately red-brick and freestone house upon the
southern verge of the great plateau of moorland which ranges
northward to the confines of Windsor Forest and eastward to
the Surrey Hills. And this he did in no vainglorious spirit,
with purpose of exalting himself above the county gentlemen,
his neighbours, and showing how far better lined his pockets
were than theirs. Rather did he do it from an honest love of
all that is ingenious and comely, and as the natural outgrowth of
an inquiring and philosophic mind. For Denzil Calmady, like
so many another son of that happy age, was something more
than a mere wealthy country squire, breeder of beef and brewer
of ale. He was a courtier and traveller; and, if tradition
speaks truly, a poet, who could praise his mistress's many
charms, or wittily resent her caprices, in well-turned verse. He
was a patron of art, having brought back ivories and bronzes
from Italy, pictures and china from the Low Countries, and

enamels from France. He was a student, and collected the
many rare and handsome, leather-bound volumes telling of
curious arts, obscure speculations, half-fabulous histories,
voyages, and adventures, which still constitute the almost
unique value of the Brockhurst library. He might claim to
be a man of science, moreover—of that delectable old-world
science which has no narrow-minded quarrel with miracle or
prodigy, wherein angel and demon mingle freely, lending a
hand unchallenged to complicate the operations both of nature
and of grace—a science which, even yet, in perfect good faith,
busied itself with the mysteries of the Rosy Cross, mixed
strange ingredients into a possible Elixir of Life, ran far afield
in search for the Philosopher's Stone, gathered herbs for the
confection of simples during auspicious phases of the moon,
and beheld in comet and meteor awful forewarnings of public
calamity or of Divine Wrath.

From all of which it may be premised that when, like the
wise king, of old, in Jerusalem, Denzil Calmady "builded him
houses, made him gardens and orchards, and planted trees
in them of all kind of fruits," when he "made him pools
of water to water therewith the wood that bringe forth trees,"
when he "gathered silver and gold, and the treasure of pro-
vinces," and got him singers, and players of musical instruments,
and "the delights of the sons of men,"—he did so that, having
tried and sifted all these things, he might, by the exercise of a
ripe and untrammelled judgment, decide what amongst them is
illusory and but a passing show, and what—be it never so
small a remnant—has in it the promise of eternal subsistence,
and therefore of vital worth; and that, having so decided and
thus gained an even mind, he might prepare serenely to take
leave of the life he had dared so largely to live.

Commencing his labours at Brockhurst during the closing
years of the reign of Queen Elizabeth, Denzil Calmady completed them in 1611 with a royal house-warming. For the
space of a week, during the autumn of that year,—the last autumn,
as it unhappily proved, that graceful and scholarly prince was
fated to see,—Henry, Prince of Wales, condescended to be his
guest. He was entertained at Brockhurst—as contemporary
records inform the curious—with "much feastinge and many
joyous masques and gallant pastimes," including "a great slay-
inge of deer and divers beastes and fowl in the woods and coverts
thereunto adjacent." It is added, with unconscious irony, that
his host, being a "true lover of all wild creatures, had caused a
fine bear-pit to be digged beyond the outer garden wall to the

west." And that, on the Sunday afternoon of the Prince's visit, there "was held a most mighty baitinge," to witness which "many noble gentlemen of the neighbourhood did visit Brockhurst and lay there two nights."

Later it is reported of Denzil Calmady, who was an excellent churchman,—suspected even, notwithstanding his little turn for philosophy, of a greater leaning towards the old Mass-Book than towards the modern Book of Common Prayer,—that he notably assisted Laud, then Bishop of St. David's, in respect of certain delicate diplomacies. Laud proved not ungrateful to his friend; who, in due time, was honoured with one of King James's newly instituted baronetcies, not to mention some few score, seedling, Scotch firs, which, taking kindly to the light, moorland soil, increased and multiplied exceedingly and sowed themselves broadcast over the face of the surrounding country.

And, save for the vigorous upgrowth of those same fir trees, and for the fact that bears and bear-pit had long given place to racehorses and to a great square of stable-buildings in the hollow lying back from the main road across the park, Brockhurst was substantially the same, in the year of grace 1842, when this truthful history actually opens, as it had been when Sir Denzil's workmen set the last tier of bricks of the last twisted chimney-stack in its place. The grand, simple masses of the house—Gothic in its main lines, but with much of Renaissance work in its details—still lent themselves to the same broad effects of light and shadow, as it crowned the southern and western sloping hillside amid its red-walled gardens and pepper-pot summer-houses, its gleaming ponds and watercourses, its hawthorn dotted paddocks, its ancient avenues of elm, of lime, and oak. The same panellings and tapestries clothed the walls of its spacious rooms and passages. The same quaint treasures adorned its fine Italian cabinets. The same air of large and generous comfort pervaded it. As the child of true lovers is said to bear through life, in a certain glad beauty of person and of nature, witness to the glad hour of its conception, so Brockhurst, on through the accumulating years, still bore witness to the fortunate historic hour in which it was planned.

Yet, since in all things material and mortal there is always a little spot of darkness, a germ of canker, at least the echo of a cry of fear—lest life being too sweet, man should grow proud to the point of forgetting he is, after all, but a pawn upon the board, but the sport and plaything of destiny and the vast purposes of God—all was not quite well with Brockhurst. At a given moment of time, the diabolic element had of necessity

intruded itself.   And, in the chronicles of this delightful
dwelling-place, even as in those of Eden itself, the angels are
proven not to have had things altogether their own gracious
way.

The pierced stone parapet, which runs round three sides of
the house and constitutes architecturally one of its most noteworthy features, is broken in the centre of the north front by a
tall, stepped and sharply pointed, gable, flanked on either hand
by slender, four-sided pinnacles.   From the niche in the said
gable, arrayed in sugarloaf hat, full doublet and trunk hose,
his head a trifle bent so that the tip of his pointed beard rests
on the pleatings of his marble ruff, a carpenter's rule in his right
hand, Sir Denzil Calmady gazes meditatively down.   Delicate,
coral-like tendrils of the Virginian creeper, which covers the
house walls and strays over the bay-windows of the Long Gallery
below, twine themselves yearly about his ankles and his square-
toed shoes.   The swallows yearly attempt to fix their grey, mud
nests against the flutings of the scallop-shell canopy sheltering
his bowed head ; and are yearly ejected by cautious gardeners,
armed with imposing array of ladders and conscious of no
little inward reluctance to face the dangers of so aërial a
height.

And here, it may not be unfitting to make further mention
of that same little spot of darkness, germ of canker, echo of the
cry of fear, that had come to mar the fair records of Brockhurst.
For very certain it was that among the varying scenes, moving
merry or majestic, upon which Sir Denzil had looked down
during the two and a quarter centuries of his sojourn in the
lofty niche of the northern gable, there was one his eyes had
never yet rested upon—one matter, and that a very vital one, to
which, had he applied his carpenter's rule, the measure of it must
have proved persistently and grievously short.

Along the straight walks, across the smooth lawns, and
beside the brilliant flower-borders of the formal gardens, he
had seen generations of babies toddle and stagger, with gurglings
of delight, as they clutched at glancing bird or butterfly far out
of reach.   He had seen healthy, clean-limbed, boisterous lads
and dainty, little maidens laugh and play, quarrel, kiss, and be
friends again.   He had seen ardent lovers—in glowing June
twilights, while the nightingales shouted from the laurels, or
from the coppices in the park below—driven to the most
desperate straits, to visions of cold poison, of horse-pistols,
of immediate enlistment, or the consoling arms of Betty the
housemaid, by the coquetries of some young lady captivating

in powder and patches, or arrayed in the high-waisted, agreeably-revealing costume which our grandmothers judged it not improper to wear in their youth. He had seen husband and wife, too, wandering hand in hand at first, tenderly hopeful and elate. And then, sometimes, as the years lengthened,—growing somewhat sated with the ease of their high estate,—he had seen them hand in hand no longer, waxing cold and indifferent, debating even, at moments, reproachfully whether they might not have invested the capital of their affections to better advantage elsewhere.

All this, and much more, Sir Denzil had seen, and doubtless measured, for all that he appeared so immovably calm and apart. But that which he had never yet seen was a man of his name and race, full of years and honours, come slowly forth from the stately house to sun himself, morning or evening, in the comfortable shelter of the high, red-brick, rose-grown, garden walls.—Looking the while, with the pensive resignation of old age, at the goodly, wide-spreading prospect. Smiling again over old jokes, warming again over old stories of prowess with horse and hound, or rod and gun. Feeling the eyes moisten again at the memory of old loves, and of those far-away first embraces which seemed to open the gates of paradise and create the world anew ; at remembrances of old hopes too, which proved still-born, and of old distresses, which often enough proved still-born likewise,—the whole of these simplified now, sanctified, the tumult of them stilled, along with the hot, young blood which went to make them, by the kindly torpor of increasing age and the approaching footsteps of greatly reconciling Death.

For Sir Denzil's male descendants, one and all,—so says tradition, so say too the written and printed family records, the fine monuments in the chancel of Sandyfield church, and more than one tombstone in the yew-shaded churchyard,—have displayed a disquieting incapacity for living to the permitted "threescore years and ten"— let alone fourscore—and dying decently, in ordinary, commonplace fashion, in their beds. Mention is made of casualties surprising in number and variety ; and not always, it must be owned, to the moral credit of those who suffered them. It is told how Sir Thomas, grandson of Sir Denzil, died miserably of gangrene, caused by a tear in the arm from the antler of a wounded buck. How his nephew Zachary —who succeeded him—was stabbed, during a drunken brawl, in an eating-house in the Strand. How the brother of the said Zachary, a gallant, young soldier, was killed at the battle of Ramillies in 1706. Duelling, lightning during a summer storm, even the blue-brown waters of the Brockhurst Lake, in turn claim a victim. Later it is told how a second Sir Denzil, after hard fighting to save his purse, was shot by highwaymen on Bagshot Heath, when riding with a couple of servants—not notably distinguished, as it would appear, for personal valour — from Brockhurst up to town.

Lastly comes Courtney Calmady, who, living in excellent repute until close upon sixty, seemed destined by Providence to break the evil chain of the family fate. But he too goes the way of all flesh, suddenly enough, after a long run with the hounds, owing to the opening of a wound, received when he was little more than a lad, at the taking of Frenchtown under General Proctor, during the second American war. So he too died, and they buried him with much honest mourning, as befitted so kindly and honourable a gentleman; and his son Richard—of whom more hereafter—reigned in his stead.

CHAPTER II

GIVING THE VERY EARLIEST INFORMATION OBTAINABLE OF THE HERO OF THIS BOOK

IT happened in this way, towards the end of August 1842. In the grey of the summer evening, as the sunset faded and the twilight gathered, spreading itself tenderly over the pastures and cornfields,—over the purple-green glooms of the fir forest— over the open moors, whose surface is scored for miles by the turf-slane of the cottager and squatter—over the clear, brown streams that trickle out of the pink and emerald mosses of the peat-bogs, and gain volume and vigour as they sparkle away by woodside, and green-lane, and village street — and over those secret, bosky places, in the heart of the great common-lands, where the smooth, white stems and glossy foliage of the self-sown hollies spring up between the roots of the beech trees, where plovers cry, and stoat and weazel lurk and scamper, while the old poacher's lean, ill-favoured, rusty-coloured lurcher picks up a shrieking hare, and where wandering bands of gypsies—those lithe, onyx-eyed children of the magic East—still pitch their dirty, little, fungus-like tents around the camp fire,—as the sunset died and the twilight thus softly widened and deepened, Lady Calmady found herself, for the first time during all the long summer day, alone.

For, though no royal personage had graced the occasion with his presence, nor had bears suffered martyrdom to promote questionably amiable mirth, Brockhurst, during the past week, had witnessed a series of festivities hardly inferior to those which marked Sir Denzil's historic house-warming. Young Sir Richard Calmady had brought home his bride, and it was but fitting the whole countryside should see her. So all and sundry received generous entertainment according to their degree.—Labourers, tenants, school-children. Weary old-age from Pennygreen poorhouse, taking its pleasure of cakes and ale half suspiciously in the broad sunshine. The leading shopkeepers of Westchurch, and their humbler brethren from Farley Row. All the country gentry too.—Lord and Lady Fallowfeild and a goodly company from Whitney Park, Lord Denier and a large contingent from Grimshott Place, the Cathcarts of Newlands, and many more persons of undoubted consequence—specially perhaps in their own eyes. Not to mention a small army of local clergy — who ever display a touching alacrity in attending festivals, even those of a secular character—with camp-followers, in the form of wives and families, galore.

And now, at last, all was over,—balls, sports, theatricals, dinners—the last, in the case of the labourers, with the unlovely adjunct of an ox roasted whole. Even the final garden-party, designed to include such persons as it was, socially speaking, a trifle difficult to place—Image, owner of the big Shotover brewery, for instance, who was shouldering his way so vigorously towards fortune and a seat on the bench of magistrates ; the younger members of the firm of Goteway & Fox, solicitors of Westchurch ; Goodall, the Methodist miller from Parson's Holt, and certain sporting yeoman farmers with their comely womankind—even this final entertainment, with all its small triumphs and heart-burnings, flutterings of youthful inexperience, aspirations, condescensions, had gone, like the rest of the week's junketings, to swell the sum of things accomplished, of all that which is past and done with and will never come again.

Fully an hour ago, Dr. Knott, under plea of waiting cases, had hitched his ungainly, thick-set figure into his high gig.

"Plenty of fine folks, eh, Timothy?" he said to the ferret-faced groom beside him, as he gathered up the reins, and the brown mare, knowing the hand on her mouth, laid herself out to her work. "Handsome young couple as anybody need wish to see. Not much business doing there for me, I fancy, unless it lies in the nursery line."

"Say those Brockhurst folks mostly dies airly though,"
remarked Timothy, with praiseworthy effort at professional
encouragement.

"Eh! so you've heard that story too, have you?"—and John
Knott drew the lash gently across the hollow of the mare's back.

"This 'ere Sir Richard's the third baronet I've a-seen, and I
bean't so very old neither."

The doctor looked down at the spare little man with a certain
snarling affection, as he said:—"Oh no! I'm not kept awake o'
nights by the fear of losing you, Timothy.   Your serviceable old
carcass 'll hang together for a good while yet."—Then his rough
eyebrows drew into a line, and he stared thoughtfully down the
long space of the clean gravel road under the meeting branches
of the lime trees.

The Whitney *char à bancs* had driven off but a few minutes
later, to the admiration of all beholders; yet not, it must be
admitted, without a measure of inward perturbation on the part
of that noble charioteer, Lord Fallowfeild.   Her Ladyship was
constitutionally timid, and he was none too sure of the behaviour
of his leaders in face of the string of very miscellaneous vehicles
waiting to take up.   However, the illustrious party happily got
off without any occasion for Lady Fallowfeild's screaming.
Then the ardour of departure became universal, and in broken
procession the many carriages, phætons, gigs, traps, pony-chaises
streamed away from Brockhurst House, north, south, and east,
and west.

Lady Calmady had bidden her guests farewell at the side-door
opening on to the terrace, before they passed through the house
to the main entrance in the south front.   Last to go, as he had
been first to come, was that worthy person, Thomas Caryll, the
rector of Sandyfield.   Mild, white-haired, deficient in chin, he
had a natural leaning towards women in general, and towards
those of the upper classes in particular.   Katherine Calmady's
radiant youth, her courtesy, her undeniable air of distinction, and
a certain gracious gaiety which belonged to her, had, combined
with unaccustomed indulgence in claret cup, gone far to turn
the good man's head during the afternoon.   Regardless of the
slightly flustered remonstrances of his wife and daughters, he
lingered, expending himself in innocently confused compliment,
supplemented by prophecies regarding the blessings destined to
descend upon Brockhurst and the mother parish of Sandyfield
in virtue of Lady Calmady's advent.

But at length he also departed.   Katherine waited, her eyes
full of laughter, until Mr. Caryll's footsteps died away on the

stone quarries of the great hall within. Then she gently drew the heavy door to, and stepped out on to the centre of the terrace. The grass slopes of the park—dotted with thorn trees and beds of bracken,—the lime avenue running along the ridge of the hill, the ragged edge of the fir forest to the east, and the mass of the house, all these were softened to a vagueness—as the landscape in a dream—by the deepening twilight. An immense repose pervaded the whole scene. It affected Katherine to a certain seriousness. Social excitements and responsibilities, the undoubted success that had attended her maiden essay as hostess during the past week, shrank to trivial proportions. Another order of emotion arose in her. She became sensible of a necessity to take counsel with herself.

She moved slowly along the terrace, paused in the arcaded garden-hall at the end of it—the carven stone benches and tables of which showed somewhat ghostly in the dimness—to put off her bonnet and push back the lace scarf from her shoulders. An increasing solemnity was upon her. There were things to think of—things deep and strange. She must needs place them, make an effort, anyhow, to do so. And, in face of this necessity, came an instinct to rid herself of all small impeding conventionalities even in the matter of dress. For there was in Katherine that inherent desire of harmony with her surroundings, that natural sense of fitness, which—given certain technical aptitudes —goes to make a great dramatic artist. But, since in her case such technical aptitudes were either non-existent or wholly latent, it followed that, save in nice questions of private honour, she was quite the least self-conscious and self-critical of human beings. Now, as she passed out under the archway on to the square lawn of the troco-ground, bare-headed, in her pale dress, a sweet seriousness filling all her mind, even as the sweet, summer twilight filled all the valley and veiled the gleaming surface of the Long Water far below, she felt wholly in sympathy with the aspect and sentiment of the place. Indeed it appeared to her, just then, that the four months of her marriage, the five months of her engagement, even the twenty-two years which made up all the sum of her earthly living, were a prelude merely to the present hour and to that which lay immediately ahead.

Yet the prelude had, in truth, been a pretty enough piece of music. Katherine's experience had but few black patches in it as yet. Furnished with a fair and healthy body, with fine breeding, with a character in which the pride and grit of her North Country ancestry were tempered by the poetic instincts and quick

wit which came to her with her mother's Irish blood, Katherine
Ormiston started better furnished than most to play the great
game that all are bound to play—whether they will or no—with
fate.   Mrs. Ormiston, still young and beloved, had died in bringing this, her only daughter, into the world ; and her husband had
looked somewhat coldly upon the poor baby in consequence.
There was an almost misanthropic vein in the autocratic land-
owner and iron-master. He had three sons already, and therefore
found but little use for this woman-child. So, while pluming
himself on his clear judgment and unswerving reason, he resented,
most unreasonably, her birth, since it took his wife from him.
Such is the irony of things, forever touching man on the raw,
proving his weakness in that he holds his strongest point !   In
fact, however, Katherine suffered but slightly from the poor
welcome that greeted her advent in the grey, many-towered house
upon the Yorkshire coast. For her great-aunt, Mrs. St. Quentin,
speedily gathered the small creature into her still beautiful arms,
and lavished upon it both tenderness and wealth, along—as it
grew to a companionable age—with the wisdom of a mind ripened
by wide acquaintance with men and with public affairs.   Mrs.
St. Quentin—famous in Dublin, London, Paris, as a beauty and
a wit—had passed her early womanhood amid the tumult of great
events.   She had witnessed the horrors of the Terror, the
splendid amazements of the First Empire ; and could still count
among her friends and correspondents, politicians and literary
men of no mean standing. A legend obtains that Lord Byron
sighed for her—and in vain. For, as Katherine came to know
later, this woman had loved once, daringly, finally, yet without
scandal—though the name of him whom she loved, and who
loved her, was not, it must be owned, St. Quentin.   And
perhaps it was just this, this hidden and somewhat tragic
romance, which kept her so young, so fresh ; kept her unworldly,
though moving so freely in the world ; had given her that exquisite sense of relative values and that knowledge of the heart,
which leads, as the divine Plato has testified, to the highest and
most reconciling philosophy.

Thus, the delicately brilliant old lady and the radiant young
lady lived together delightfully enough, spending their winters
in Paris in a pretty apartment in the rue de Rennes—shared with
one Mademoiselle de Mirancourt, whose friendship with Mrs.
St. Quentin dated from their schooldays at the convent of the
Sacré Cœur. Spring and autumn found Katherine and her
great-aunt in London. While, in summer, there was always a
long visit to Ormiston Castle, looking out from the cliff-edge

upon the restless North Sea. Lovers came in due course. For
over and above its own shapeliness—which surely was reason
enough—Katherine's hand was well worth winning from the
worldly point of view. She would have money; and Mrs. St.
Quentin's influence would count for much in the case of a great-
nephew-by-marriage who aspired to a parliamentary or diplomatic
career. But the lovers also went, for Katherine asked a great
deal—not so much of them, perhaps, as of herself. She had
taken an idea, somehow, that marriage, to be in the least satisfactory, must be based on love ; and that love, worth the name, is
an essentially two-sided business. Indirectly the girl had learnt
much on this difficult subject from her great-aunt; and with
characteristic directness had agreed with herself to wait till her
heart was touched, if she waited a lifetime—though of exactly
in what either her heart, or the touching of it, consisted she was
deliciously innocent as yet.

And then, in the summer of 1841, Sir Richard Calmady came
to Ormiston. He and her brother Roger had been at Eton
together. Katherine remembered him, years ago, as a well-bred
and courteously contemptuous schoolboy, upon whose superior
mind, small female creatures—busy about dolls, and victims of
the athletic restrictions imposed by petticoats—made but slight
impression. Latterly Sir Richard's name had come to be one to
conjure with in racing circles, thanks to the performances of
certain horses bred and trained at the Brockhurst stables ; though
some critics, it is true, deplored his tendency to neglect the
older and more legitimate sport of flat-racing in favour of
steeple-chasing. It was said he aspired to rival the long list of
victories achieved by Mr. Elmore's Gaylad and Lottery, and the
successes of Peter Simple the famous grey. This much
Katherine had heard of him from her brother. And, having
her naughty turns—as what charming woman has not?—had set
him down as probably a rough sort of person, notwithstanding his
wealth and good connections, a kind of gentleman-jockey, upon
whom it would be easy to take a measure of pretty revenge for
his boyish indifference to her existence. But the meeting and
the young man, alike, turned out quite other than she had anticipated. For she found a person as well furnished in all polite
and social arts as herself, with no flavour of the stable about him.
She had reckoned on one whose scholarship would carry him no
further than a few stock quotations from Horace, and whose
knowledge of art would begin and end with a portrait of himself
presented by the members of a local hunt. Therefore it was
a little surprising — possibly a little mortifying to her — to

hear him talking over obscure passages in Spenser's *Faerie Queene* with Mrs. St. Quentin, before the end of the dinner, and nicely apprising the relative merits of the water-colour sketches, by Turner, that hung on either side the drawing-room fireplace.

Nor did Katherine's surprises end here. An unaccountable something was taking place within her, that opened up a whole new range of emotion. She, the least moody of young women, had strange fluctuations of temper, finding herself buoyantly happy one hour, the next pensive, filled with timidity and self-distrust — not to mention little fits of gusty anger, and purposeless jealousy which took her, hurting her pride shrewdly. She grew anxiously solicitous as to her personal appearance. This dress would not please her nor that. The image of her charming, oval face and well-set head ceased to satisfy her. Surely a woman's hair should be either positively blond or black, not this undeterminate brown, with warm lights in it? She feared her mouth was not small enough, the lips too full and curved for prettiness. She wished her eyes less given to change, under their dark lashes, from clear grey-blue to a nameless colour, like the gloom of the pools of a woodland stream, as her feelings changed from gladness to distress. She feared her complexion was too bright, and then not bright enough. And, all the while, a certain shame possessed her that she should care at all about such trivial matters; for life had grown suddenly larger and more august. Books she had read, faces she had watched a hundred times, the vast horizon looking eastward over the unquiet sea, all these gained a new value and meaning which at once enthralled her and agitated her thought.

Sir Richard Calmady stayed a fortnight at Ormiston. And the two ladies crossed to Paris earlier, that autumn, than was their custom. Katherine was not in her usual good health, and Mrs. St. Quentin desired change of air and scene on her account. She took Mademoiselle de Mirancourt into her confidence, hinting at causes for her restlessness and wayward, little humours unacknowledged by the girl herself. Then the two elder women wrapped Katherine about with an atmosphere of—if possible—deeper tenderness than before; mingling sentiment with their gaiety, and gaiety with their sentiment, and the delicate respect which refrains from question with both.

One keenly bright, October afternoon Richard Calmady called in the rue de Rennes. It appeared he had come to Paris with the intention of remaining there for an indefinite period. He called again and yet again, making himself charming—a touch of deference tempering his natural suavity—alike to his hostesses and to such of their guests as he happened to meet. It was the fashion of fifty years ago to conduct affairs, even those of the heart, with a dignified absence of precipitation. The weeks passed, while Sir Richard became increasingly welcome in some of the very best houses in Paris.—And Katherine? It must be owned Katherine was not without some heartaches, which she proudly tried to deny to herself and conceal from others. But eventually—it was on the morning after the ball at the British Embassy—the man spoke and the maid answered, and the old order changed, giving place to new, in the daily life of the pretty apartment of the rue de Rennes.

About five months later the marriage took place in London; and Sir Richard and Lady Calmady started forth on a wedding journey of the old-fashioned type. They travelled up the Rhine, and posted, all in the delicious, early summer weather, through Northern Italy, as far as Florence. They returned by Paris. And there, Mrs. St. Quentin watching—in almost painful anxiety —to see how it fared with her recovered darling, was wholly satisfied, and gave thanks. For she perceived that, in this case at least, marriage was no legal, conventional connection leaving the heart emptier than it found it—the bartering of precious freedom for a joyless bondage—an obligation, weary in the present, and hopeless of alleviation in the future, save by the reaching of that far-distant, heavenly country, concerning which it is comfortably assured us "that there they neither marry nor are given in marriage." For the Katherine who came back to her was at once the same, and yet another Katherine—one who carried her head more proudly and stepped as though she was mistress of the whole fair earth, but whose merry wit had lost its little edge of sarcasm, whose sympathy was quicker and more in-stinctive, whose voice had taken fuller and more caressing tones, and in whose sweet eyes sat a steady content good to see. Then, suddenly, Mrs. St. Quentin began to feel her age as she had never, consciously, felt it before; and to be very willing to fold her hands and recite her *Nunc Dimittis*. For, in looking on the faces of the bride and bridegroom, she had looked once again on the face of Love itself, and had stood within the court of the temple of that Uranian Venus whose unsullied glory is secure here and hereafter, since to her it is given to discover to her worshippers the innermost secret of existence, thereby fencing them forever against the plagues of change, delusion, and decay. Love began gently to loosen the cords of life, and to draw Lucia St. Quentin home—home to that dear dwelling-place which, as we fondly trust—since God Himself is Love—is reserved for all true lovers beyond the grave and Gates of Death. Thus one flower falls as another opens, and to-day, however sweet, is only won across the corpse of yesterday.

And it was some perception of just this—the ceaseless push of event following on event, the ceaseless push of the yet unborn struggling to force the doors of life—which moved Katherine to seriousness, as she stood alone on the smooth expanse of the troco-ground, in the soft, all-covering twilight, at the close of the day's hospitality.

On her right the house, and its delicate, twisted chimneys, showed dark against the fading rose of the western sky. The air, rich with the fragrance of the red-walled gardens behind her, —with the scent of jasmine, heliotrope and clove carnations, ladies-lilies and mignonette, — was stirred, now and again, by wandering winds, cool from the spaces of the open moors. While, as the last roll of departing wheels died out along the avenues, the voices of the woodland began to reassert themselves. Wild-fowl called from the alder-fringed Long Water. Night-hawks churred as they beat on noiseless wings above the beds of bramble and bracken. A cock pheasant made a most admired stir and keckling in seeing his wife and brood to roost on the branches of one of King James's age-old Scotch firs.

And this sense of nature coming back to claim her own, to make known her eternal supremacy, now that the fret of man's little pleasuring had passed, was very grateful to Katherine Calmady. Her soul cried out to be free, for a time, to contemplate, to fully apprehend and measure, its own happiness. It needed to stand aside, so that the love given and all given with that love—even these matters of house and gardens, of men-servants and maid-servants, of broad acres, all the poetry, in short, of great possessions—might be seen in perspective. For Katherine had that necessity—in part intellectual, in part practical, and common to all who possess the gift for rule—to resist the confusing importunity of detail, and to grasp intelligently the Whole, which alone gives to detail coherence and purpose. Her mind was not one—perhaps unhappily—which is contented to merely play with bricks, but which demands the plan of the building into which those bricks should grow. And she wanted, just now, to lay hold of the plan of the fair building of her own life. And to this end the solitude, the evening quiet, the restful unrest of the forest and its wild creatures, should surely have ministered. She moved forward and sat on the broad, stone balustrade which, topping the buttressed masonry that supports it above the long downward slope of the park, encloses the troco-ground on the south.

The landscape lay drowned in the mystery of the summer night. And Katherine, looking out into it, tried to think clearly, tried to range the many new experiences of the last few months and to reckon with them. But her brain refused to work obediently to her will. She felt strangely hurried for all the surrounding quiet.

One train of thought, which she had been busy enough by day and honestly sleepy enough at night to keep at arm's length during this time of home-coming and entertaining, now invaded and possessed her mind—filling it at once with a new and overwhelming movement of tenderness yet, for all her high courage, with a certain fear. She cried out for a little space of liberty, a little space in which to take breath. She wanted to pause, here in the fulness of her content. But no pause was granted her. She was so happy, she asked nothing more. But something more was forced upon her. And so it happened that, in realising the ceaseless push of event on event, the ceaseless dying of dear to-day in the service of unborn to-morrow, her gentle seriousness touched on regret.

How long she remained lost in such pensive reflections Lady Calmady could not have said. Suddenly the terrace door slammed. A moment later a man's footsteps echoed across the flags of the garden-hall.

"Katherine," Richard Calmady called, somewhat imperatively, "Katherine, are you there?"

She turned and stood watching him as he came rapidly across the turf.

"Yes, I am here," she said. "Do you want me?"

"Do I want you?" he answered curtly. "Don't I always want you?"

A little sob rose in her throat—she knew not why, for, hearing the tone of his voice, her sadness was strangely assuaged.

"I could not find you," he went on. "And I got into an absurd state of panic—sent Roger in one direction, and Julius in another, to look for you."

"Whereupon Roger, probably, posted down to the stables, and Julius up to the chapel to search. Where the heart dwells there the feet follow. Meanwhile, you came straight here and found me yourself."

"I might have known I should do that."

The importunate thought returned upon Katherine, and with it a touch of her late melancholy.

"Ah! one knows nothing for certain when one is frightened," she said. She moved closer to him, holding out her hand. "Here," she continued, "you are a little too shadowy, too unsubstantial, in this light, Dick. I would rather make more sure of your presence."

Richard Calmady laughed very gently. Then the two stood silent, looking out over the dim valley, hand in hand.—The scent of the gardens was about them. Moving lights showed through the many windows of the great house. The water-fowl called sleepily. The churring of the night-hawks was continuous, soothing as the hum of a spinning-wheel. Somewhere, away in the Warren, a fox barked. In the eastern sky, the young moon began to climb above the ragged edge of the firs.—When they spoke again it was very simply, in broken sentences, as children speak. The poetry of their relation to one another and the scene about them were too full of meaning, too lovely, to call for polish of rhetoric, or pointing by epigram.

"Tell me," Katherine said, "were you satisfied? Did I entertain your people prettily?"

"Prettily? You entertained them as they had never been entertained before—like a queen—and they knew it. But why did you stay out here alone?"

"To think—and to look at Brockhurst."

"Yes, it's worth looking at now," he said. "It was like a body wanting a soul till you came."

"But you loved it?" Katherine reasoned.

"Oh yes! because I believed the soul would come some day. Brockhurst, and the horses, and the books, all helped to make the time pass while I was waiting."

"Waiting for what?"

"Why, for you, of course, you dear, silly sweet! Haven't I always been waiting for you—just precisely and wholly you, nothing more or less — all through my life, all through all conceivable and inconceivable lives, since before the world began?"

Katherine's breath came with a fluttering sigh. She let her head fall back against his shoulder. Her eyes closed involuntarily. She loved these fond exaggerations—as what woman does not who has had the good fortune to hear them? They pierced her with a delicious pain. And—perhaps therefore, perhaps not unwisely—she believed them true.

"Are you tired?" he asked presently.

Katherine looked up smiling, and shook her head.

"Not too tired to be up early to-morrow morning and come out with me to see the horses galloped? Sultan will give you no trouble. He is well-seasoned and merely looks on at things in general with intelligent interest, goes like a lamb and stands like a rock."

While her husband was speaking Katherine straightened herself up, and moved a little from him though still holding his hand. Her languor passed, and her eyes grew large and black.

"I think, perhaps, I had better not go to-morrow, Dick," she said slowly.

"Ah! you are tired, you poor dear! No wonder, after the week's work you have had. Another day will do just as well. Only I want you to come out sometimes in the first blush of the morning, before the day has had time to grow common-place, while the gossamers are still hung with dew, and the mists are in hollows, and the horses are heady from the fresh air and the light. You will like it all, Kitty. It is rather inspiring. But it will keep. To-morrow I'll let you rest in peace."

"Oh no! it is not that," Katherine said quickly.—The importunate thought was upon her again, clamouring, not only to be recognised, but fairly owned to and permitted to pass the doors of speech. And a certain modesty made her shrink from this. To know something in the secret of your own heart, to tell it, thereby making it a hard, concrete fact, outside yourself, over which, in a sense, you cease to have control, are two such very different matters! Katherine trembled on the edge of her confession; though that to be confessed was, after all, but the natural crown of her love.

"I think I ought not to ride now—for a time, Dick." All the blood rushed into her face and throat, and then ebbed, leaving her very white in the growing darkness.—"You have given me a child," she said.

2

CHAPTER III

TOUCHING MATTERS CLERICAL AND CONTROVERSIAL

BROCKHURST had rarely appeared more blessed by spacious sunshine and stately cheerfulness than during the remaining weeks of that summer. A spirit of unclouded serenity possessed the place, both indoors and out. If rain fell, it was only at night. And this, as so much else, Julius March noted duly in his diary.

For that was the period of elaborate private chronicles, when persons of intelligence and position still took themselves, their doings, and their emotions, with most admired seriousness. Natural science, the great leveller, had hardly stepped in as yet. Therefore it was that already Julius's diary ran into many stout, manuscript volumes, each in turn soberly but richly bound, with silver clasp and lock complete, so soon as its final page was written. Begun when he first went up to Oxford, some thirteen years earlier, it formed an intimate history of the influences of the Tractarian Movement upon a scholarly mind and delicately spiritual nature. At the commencement of his Oxford career he had come into close relations with some of the leaders of the movement. And the conception of an historic church, endowed with mystic powers,—conveyed through an unbroken line of priests from the age of the apostles — the orderly round of vigil, fast, and festival, the secret, introspective joys of penance and confession, the fascinations of the strictly religious life as set before him in eloquent public discourse or persuasive private conversation,—had combined to kindle an imagination very insufficiently satisfied by the lean spiritual meats offered it during an Evangelical childhood and youth. Julius yielded himself up to his instructors with passionate self-abandon. He took orders, and remained on at Oxford—being a fellow of his college—working earnestly for the cause he had so at heart. Eventually he became a member of the select band of disciples that dwelt, uncomfortably, supported by visions of reactionary reform at once austere and beneficent, in the range of disused stable-buildings at Littlemore.

Of the storm and stress of this religious war, its triumphs, its defeats, its many agitations, Julius's diaries told with a deep, if chastened, enthusiasm. His was a singularly pure nature, unmoved by the primitive desires which usually inflame young blood. Ideas heated him; while the lust of the eye and the pride of life left him almost scornfully cold. He strove earnestly, of course, to bring the flesh into subjection to the spirit; which was, calmly considered, a slight waste of time, since the said flesh showed the least possible inclination towards revolt. The earlier diaries contain pathetic exaggerations of the slightest indiscretion. Innocent and virtuous persons have ever been prone to such little manias of self-accusation! Later, the flesh did assert itself, though in a hardly licentious manner. Oxford fogs and damp, along with plain living and high thinking, acting upon a constitution naturally far from robust, produced a commonplace but most disabling nemesis in the form of colds, coughs, and chronic asthma. Julius did not greatly care. He was in that exalted frame of mind in which martyrdom, even by phthisis or bronchial affections, is immeasurably preferable to no martyrdom at all. Perhaps fortunately his relations, and even his Oxford friends, took a quite other view of the matter, and insisted upon his using all legitimate means to prolong his life.

Julius left Oxford with intense regret. It was the Holy City of the Tractarian Movement; and at this moment the progress of that Movement was the one thing worth living for, if live indeed he must. He went forth bewailing his exile and enforced idleness, as a man bewails the loss of the love of his youth. For a time he travelled in Italy and in the south of France. On his return to England he went to stay with his friend and cousin, Sir Richard Calmady. Brockhurst House had always been extremely congenial to him. Its suites of handsome rooms, the inlaid, marble chimneypieces of which reach up to the frieze of the heavily-moulded ceilings, its wide passages and stairways, their carved balusters and newel-posts, the treasures of its library—now overflowing the capacity of the two rooms originally designed for them, and filling ranges of bookcases between the bay-windows of the Long Gallery which runs the whole length of the first floor from east to west, the chapel in the southern wing, its richly furnished altar and the glories of its famous, stained-glass windows—all these were very grateful to his taste. While the light, dry, upland air and near neighbourhood of the fir forest eased the physical discomforts from which, at times, he still suffered shrewdly.

He found the atmosphere of the place both soothing and steadying. And of precisely this he stood sorely in need just now. For it must be admitted that a change had come over the spirit of Julius March's great, ecclesiastical dream. Absence from Oxford and foreign travel had tended at once to widen

and modify his thought. He had seen the Tractarian Movement from a distance, in due perspective. He had also seen
Catholicism at close quarters. He had realised that the logical
consequence of the teaching of the former could be nothing less
than unqualified submission to the latter. On his return to
England he learned that more than one of his Oxford friends
was arriving, reluctantly, at the same conclusion. Then there
arose within him the fiercest struggle his gentle nature had ever
yet known. He was torn by the desire to go forward, risking
all, with those whom he reverenced; yet was restrained by a
sense of honour. For there was, in Julius, a strain of obstinate,
almost fanatic, loyalty. To the Anglican Church he had pledged
himself. Through her ministry he had received illumination.
To the work of her awakening he had given all his young
enthusiasm. How then could he desert her? Her rites might
be maimed. The scandal of schism might tarnish her fair
fame. Accusations of sloth and lukewarmness might not un-
justly be preferred against her. All this he admitted. And it
was very characteristic of the man that, just because he did
admit it, he remained within her fold.

Yet the decision was dislocating to all his thought, even as
the struggle had been. It left him bruised. It cruelly shook
his self-confidence. For he was not one of those persons upon
whom the shipwreck of long-cherished hopes and purposes
have a stimulating effect, filling them merely with a buoyant
satisfaction at the opportunity afforded them of beginning all
over again! Julius was oppressed by the sense of a great
failure. The diaries of this period are but sorrowful reading.
He believed he should go softly all his days; and, from a certain
point of view, in this he was right.

And it was here that Sir Richard Calmady intervened. He
had watched his cousin's struggle, had accepted its reality,
sympathising through friendship rather than through moral or
intellectual agreement. For he was one of those fortunate
mortals who, while possessing a strong sense of God, have but
small necessity to define Him. Many of Julius's keenest agonies
appeared to him subjective, a matter of words and phrases.
Yet he respected them, out of the sincere regard he bore the
man who suffered them. He did more. He tried a practical
remedy. Courteously, as one asking rather than conferring a
favour, he invited Julius to remain at Brockhurst, on a fair
stipend, as domestic chaplain and librarian.

"In the fulness of your generosity towards me you are
creating a costly sinecure," Julius had remonstrated.

"Not in the least. I am selfishly trying to secure myself a most welcome companion, by asking you to undertake a very modest cure of souls and to catalogue my books, when you might be filling some important post and qualifying for a bishopric."

Julius had shaken his head sadly enough. "The high places of the Church are not for me," he said, "neither are her great adventures."

Thus did Julius March, somewhat broken both in health and spirit, become a carpet-priest. The trumpet blasts of controversy reached him as echoes merely, while his days passed in peaceful, if pensive, monotony. He read prayers morning and evening to the assembled household in the chapel; reduced the confusion of the library shelves, doing a fair amount of study, both secular and theological, during the process; rode with his cousin on fine afternoons to distant farms, by high-banked lanes in the lowland, or across the open moors; visited the lodges, or the keepers' and gardeners' cottages within the limits of the park, on foot. Now and again he took a service, or preached a sermon, for good Mr. Caryll of Sandyfield, in whose amiable mind instinctive admiration of those, even distantly, related to persons of wealth and position jostled an equally instinctive terror of Mr. March's "well-known Romanising tendencies." And in that there was, surely, a touch of the irony of fate! Lastly, Julius did his utmost to exercise an influence for good over the twenty and odd boys at the racing stables — an unpromising generation at best, the majority of whom, he feared, accepted his efforts for their moral and spiritual welfare with the same somewhat brutish philosophy with which they accepted Tom Chifney, the trainer's rough-and-ready system of discipline, and the thousand and one vagaries of the fine-limbed, queer-tempered horses which were at once the glory and torment of their young lives.

Things had gone on thus for rather more than a year, when Richard Calmady married. Julius was perhaps inclined, beforehand, to underrate the importance of that event. He was singularly innocent, so far, of the whole question of woman. He had no sisters. At Oxford he had lived exclusively among men, while the Tractarian Movement had offered a sufficient outlet to all his emotion. The severe and exquisite verses of the "Lyra Apostolica" fitly expressed the passions of his heart. To the Church, at once his mother and his mistress, he had wholly given his first love. He had gone so far, indeed, in a rapture of devotion one Easter Day, during the celebration of the Holy Eucharist, as to impose upon himself a vow of lifelong celibacy. This he did—let it be added—without either the sanction or knowledge of his spiritual advisers. The vow, therefore, remained unwitnessed and unratified, but he held it inviolable nevertheless. And it lay but lightly upon him, joyfully almost—rather as a ridding of himself of possible perturbations and obsessions, than as an act of most austere self-renunciation. In his ignorance he merely went forward with an increased freedom of spirit. All of which is set down, not without underlying pathos, in the diary of that date.

And that freedom of spirit remained by him, notwithstanding his altered circumstances. It even served—indirectly, since none knew the fact of his self-dedication save himself—as a basis of pleasant intercourse with the women of his own social standing whom he now met. It served him thus in respect of Lady Calmady, who accepted him as a member of her new household with charming kindliness, treating him with a gentle solicitude born of pity for his far from robust health and for the mental struggles which she understood him to have passed through.

Many persons, it must be owned, described Julius as remarkably ugly. But he did not strike Katherine thus. His heavy, black hair, beardless face and sallow skin—rendered dull and colourless, his features thickened, though not actually scarred, by small-pox which he had had as a child,—his sensitive mouth, and the questioning expression of his short-sighted, brown eyes, reminded her of a fifteenth-century, Florentine portrait that had always challenged her attention when she passed it in the vestibule of a certain obscure, yet aristocratic, Parisian hotel, on the left bank—well understood—of the Seine.

The man of the portrait was narrow-chested, clothed in black. So was Julius March. He had long-fingered, finely shaped hands. So had Julius. He gave her the impression of a person endowed with a capacity of prolonged and silent self-sacrifice. So did Julius. She wondered about his story. For Julius, at least—little as she or he then suspected it—the deepest places of the story still lay ahead.

CHAPTER IV

RAISING PROBLEMS WHICH IT IS THE PURPOSE OF THIS
HISTORY TO RESOLVE

IT was not without a movement of inward thanksgiving that, the festivities connected with Sir Richard and Lady Calmady's home-coming being over, Julius March returned to his labours in the Brockhurst library. Humanity at first hand, whatever its social standing or its pursuits, was, in truth, always slightly disturbing to him. He felt more at home when dealing with conclusions than with the data that go to build up those conclusions, with the thoughts of men printed and bound, than with the urgent raw material from which those thoughts arise. Revelation, authority—these were still his watchwords. And, in face of them, even the harmless spectacle of a country neighbourhood at play, let alone the spectacle of the human comedy generally, is singularly confusing.

He sought the soothing companionship of books with even heightened relief one fair morning some three weeks later. For Mrs. St. Quentin and Mademoiselle de Mirancourt had arrived at Brockhurst the day previously, and Julius had been sensible of certain perturbations of mind in meeting these two ladies, one of whom was a devout Catholic by inheritance and personal conviction, while the other, though nominally a member of his own communion, was known to temper her religion with a wide, if refined, philosophy. Conversation had drifted towards serious subjects in the course of the evening, and Mrs. St. Quentin had admitted, with a playful deprecation of her dear friend's rigid religious attitude, that no one creed, no one system, offered an adequate solution of the infinite mystery and complexity of life— as she knew it. The serene adherence of one charming and experienced woman to an authority which he had rejected, the almost equally serene indifference on the part of the other to the revelation he held as absolute and final, troubled Julius. Small wonder then, that early, after a solitary breakfast, he retired upon the society of the odd volumes cluttering the shelves of the Long Gallery, that he sorted, arranged, catalogued, grateful for that dulling of thought which mechanical labour brings with it.

But fate was malicious, and elected to make a sport of Julius this morning. Unexpectedly importunate human drama obtruded itself, the deep places of the story—such as, in the innocence of his ascetic refinement, he had never dreamed of—began to reveal themselves.

He had climbed the wide, carpeted steps of the library ladder and seated himself on the topmost one, at right angles to a topmost shelf the contents of which he proposed to investigate, duster and notebook in hand. The vast perspective of the gallery lengthened out before him, cool, faint-tinted, full of a diffused and silvery light. The self-coloured, unpainted panelling of the walls and bookcases—but one shade warmer in tone than that of the stone mullions and transoms of the lofty windows—gave an indescribable delicacy of effect to the atmosphere of the room. Through the many-paned, leaded lights of the eastern bay, the sunshine—misty, full of dancing notes—streamed in obliquely, bringing into quaint prominence of light and shadow a very miscellaneous collection of objects.—A marble Buddha, benign of aspect, his right hand raised in blessing, seated cross-legged upon the many-petalled lotus. A pair of cavalier's jack-boots, standing just below, most truculent and ungainly of foot-gear, wooden, hinged, leather-covered. A trophy of Polynesian spears, shields, and canoe paddles. A bronze Antinous, seductive of bearing and dainty of limb, but roughened by green rust. A collection of old sporting-prints, softly coloured, covering a bare space of wall, beneath a moose skull, from the broad flat antlers of which hung a pair of Canadian snow-shoes. Along the inside wall of the great room, placed at regular intervals, were consol tables bearing tall, oriental jars and huge bowls of fine porcelain, filled with potpourri; so that the scent of dried rose-leaves, bay, verbena, and many spices impregnated the air. The place was, in short, a museum. Whatever of strange, grotesque, and curious, Calmadys of past generations had collected in their wanderings, by land and sea, found lodgment here. It was a home of half-forgotten histories, of valorous deeds grown dim through the lapse of years; a harbour of refuge for derelict gods, derelict weapons, derelict volumes, derelict instruments which had once discoursed sweet enough music, but the fashion of which had now passed away. The somewhat obsolete sentiment of the place harmonised with the thin, silvery light and the thin sweetness of spices and dead roses which pervaded it. It seemed to smile, as with the pitying tolerance of the benign image of Buddha, upon the heat and flame, the untempered scarlet and purple of the fleeting procession of individual lives, that had ministered to its furnishing. For how much vigorous endeavour, now over and done with, never to be recalled, had indeed gone to supply the furnishing of that room!

—And, after all, is not the most any human creature dare hope for the more or less dusty corner of some such museum shelf at last? The passion of the heart testified to by some battered trinket, the sweat of the brain by some maggot-eaten manuscript, the agony of death, at best, by some round shot turned up by the ploughshare? And how shall anyone dare complain of this, since have not empires before now only been saved from oblivion by a few buried potsherds, and whole races of mankind by childish picture-scratchings on a reindeer bone? *Tout lasse, tout passe, tout casse.* The individual—his arts, his possessions, his religion, his civilisation —is always as an envelope, merely, to be torn asunder and cast away. Nothing subsists, nothing endures, but life itself, endlessly self-renewed, endlessly one, through all the endless divergencies of its manifestations. And, as Julius March was to find, hide from it, deny it, strive to elude it as we may, the recognition of just that is bound to grip us sooner or later and hold us with a fearful and dominating power from which there is no escape.

Meanwhile, his occupation was tranquil enough, comfortably remote, as it seemed, from all such profound and disquieting matters. For the top shelf proved not very prolific of interest. One book after another, examined and rejected as worthless, was dropped—with a reproachful flutter of pages and final thud —into the capacious paper-basket standing on the floor below. Then, at the far end of the said shelf, he came unexpectedly upon a collection of those quaint chap-books which commanded so wide a circulation during the eighteenth century.

Julius, with the true bibliophile's interest in all originals, examined his find carefully. The tattered and dogs-eared, little volumes, coarsely printed and embellished by a number of rough, square woodcuts, had, he knew, a distinct value. He soon perceived that they formed a very representative selection. He glanced at The famous History of Guy of Warwick; at that of Sir Bevis of Southampton; at Joaks upon Joaks, a lively work regarding the manners and customs of the aristocracy at the period of the Restoration; at the record of the amazing adventures of that lusty serving-wench, Long Meg of Westminster; and at that refreshing piece of comedy known as Merry Tales concerning the Sayings and Doings of the Wise Men of Gotham.

Finally, hidden behind the outstanding frame of the book-case, he discovered four tiny volumes tied together with a rusty, black ribbon. A heavy coating of dust lay upon them. A large spider, moreover, darted from behind them. Dust clung un-

pleasantly to its hairy and ill-favoured person.   It was a matter
of principle with Julius never to take life; yet instinctively he
drew back his hand from the books in disgust.

"*Araignée du matin, chagrin,*" he said, involuntarily, while he
watched the insect make good its escape over the top of the
bookcase.

Then he flicked uneasily at the little parcel with his duster,
causing a cloud of grey atoms to float up and out into the room.
Julius was perhaps absurdly open to impressions.   It took him
some seconds to recover from his sense of repulsion and to
untie the rusty ribbon around the little books.   They all proved
to be ragged and imperfect copies of the same work.   The
woodcuts in them were splotched with crude colour.   The title
page was printed in assorted type—here a line of Roman capitals,
there one in italics or old English letters.   The inscription,
consequently, was difficult to decipher, causing him to hold the
tattered page very close to his short-sighted eyes.   It ran thus—

"Setting forth a true and particular account of the dealings
of Sir Thomas Calmady with the Forester's Daughter and the
bloudy death of her Only Child.   To which is added her
Prophecy and Curse."

Julius had been standing, so as to reach the length of the
shelf.   Now he sat down on the top step of the ladder again.
A whole rush of memories came upon him.   He remembered
vaguely how, long ago, in his childhood, he had heard legends
of this same curse.   Staying here at Brockhurst as a baby-child
with his mother, maids had hinted at it, gossiping over the
nursery fire at night; and his mind, irresistibly attracted, even
then, by the supernatural, had been filled at once by desperate
curiosity and by panic fear.   He paused, thinking back, singularly moved, as one on the edge of the satisfaction of long-
desired knowledge, yet slightly contemptuous, both of his own
emotion and of the rather vulgar means by which that knowledge
promised to be obtained.

The shafts of sunshine fell more obliquely across the eastern
end of the gallery.   Benign Buddha had passed into shadow;
while a painting by Velasquez, standing on an easel near by,
caught the light, starting into arresting reality.   It represented a
hideous and mis-shapen dwarf, holding a couple of graceful greyhounds in a leash—an unhappy creature who had made sport for
the household of some Castilian grandee, and whose gorgeous
garments were ingeniously designed to emphasise the physical
degradation of his contorted body.   This painting, appearing to

Julius too painful for habitual contemplation, had, at his request, been removed from his study downstairs to its present station. Just now he fancied it looked forth at him queerly insistent. At this distance he could distinguish little more than a flare of scarlet and cloth-of-gold, and the white of the hounds' flanks and bellies, under the strong sunlight.   But he knew the picture in all its details ; and was oppressed by the remembrance of tragic eyes in a brutal face, eyes that protested dumbly against cruelty inflicted by nature and by mankind alike.   He, Julius, was not, so he feared, quite guiltless in this matter.   For had there not been a savour of cruelty in his ejection of the portrait of this unhappy being from his peaceful study ?

And thinking of this his discomfort augmented.   He was assailed by an unreasoning nervousness of something malign, something sinister, about to befall or to become known to him.

"*Araignée du matin, chagrin,*" he repeated involuntarily.

He laid the four little chap-books back hastily behind the outstanding woodwork of the bookshelf, descended the steps, walked the length of the gallery, and leaning against one of the stone mullions of the great, eastern bay-window looked out of the wide-open casement.

The prospect was, indeed, reassuring enough.   The softly-green square of the troco-ground, the brilliant beds and borders of the brick-walled gardens, the grey flags of the great terrace —its row of little orange trees, heavy with flower and fruit, set in blue painted tubs—lay below him in a blaze of August sunshine.   From the direction of the Long Water in the valley, Richard Calmady rode up, between the thorn trees and the beds of bracken, across the turf slopes of the park.   It was a joy to see him ride.   The rider and horse were one in vigour and in the repose which comes of vigour—a something classic in the natural beauty and sympathy of rider and of horse.   Half-way up the slope Richard swerved, turned towards the house, sat looking up, hat in hand, while Katherine stood at the edge of the terrace looking down, speaking with him.   The warm breeze fluttered her full, muslin skirts, rose and white, and the white lace of her parasol.   The rich tones of her voice and the ring of her laughter came up to Julius, as he leant against the stone mullion, along with the droning of innumerable bees, and the cooing of the pink-footed pigeons—that bowed to one another, spreading their tails, drooping their wings amorously, upon the broad, grey string-course running along the house-front just beneath.   Mademoiselle de Mirancourt, a small, neat, grey and black figure, was beside Katherine, and, now and again, he heard the pretty staccato of her foreign speech. Then Richard Calmady rode onward, turning half round in the saddle, looking up for a moment at the woman he loved. His horse broke into a canter, bearing him swiftly in and out of the shadow of the glistening, domed oaks and ancient, stag-headed, Spanish chestnuts which crowned the ascent, and on down the long, softly-shaded vista of the lime avenue. While Camp, the bull-dog, who had lain panting in the bracken, streaked like a white flash up the hillside in pursuit of his well-beloved master.

And Julius March moved away from the open window with a sigh. Yet what, after all, of malign or sinister was perceptible, conceivable even, in respect of this glorious morning and these happy people—unless, as he reflected, something of pathos is of necessity ever resident in all beauty, all happiness, the world being sinful, and existence so prolific of pain and melancholy happenings? So he went back, climbed the library steps again, and taking the little bundle of chap-books from their dusty resting-place, set himself, in a somewhat penitential spirit, to master their contents. If the occupation was distasteful to him, the more wholesome to pursue it! So, supplying the deficiencies of torn or defaced pages by reference to another of the copies, he arrived by degrees at a clear understanding of the whole matter. The story was set forth in rhyming doggerel. The poet was not blessed with a gift of melody or of style. Absence of scansion tortured the ear. Coarseness of diction offended the taste. And yet, as he read on, Julius reluctantly admitted that the cruel tale gained credibility and moral force from the very homeliness of the language in which it was chronicled.

Thus Julius learned how, during the closing years of the Commonwealth, the young royalist gentleman, Sir Thomas Calmady, dwelling in enforced seclusion at Brockhurst, relieved the tedium of country life by indulgence in divers amours. He was large-hearted, apparently, and could not see a comely face without attempting intimate acquaintance with the possessor of it. Among other damsels distinguished by his attentions was his head forester's handsome daughter, whom, under reiterated promise of marriage, he seduced. In due time she bore him a child, ideally beautiful, according to the poet of the chap-book, blessed with "red-gold hair and eyes of blue," and many charms of infantile healthfulness. And yet, notwithstanding the noble looks of her little son, the forester's daughter still remained unwed. For just now came the Restoration, and, along with it, a notable change in the outlook of Sir Thomas Calmady and many another lusty, young gallant; since the event in question not only restored Charles the Second to the arms of his devoted subjects, but restored such loyal gentlemen to the by no means too strait-laced society of town and court. Thence, some few years later, Sir Thomas—amiably willing in all things to oblige his royal master—brought home a bride, whose rank and wealth, according to the censorious chap-book, were extensively in excess of her youth and virtue.

Julius lingered a little in contemplation of the quaint wood-cut representing the arrival of this lady at Brockhurst. Clothed in a bottle-green bodice — very generously *décolletée*—her head adorned by a portentous erection of coronet and feathers, a sanguine dab of colour on her cheek, she craned a skinny neck out of the window of the family coach. Apparently she was engaged in directing the movements of persons—presumably foot-men—clad in canary-coloured coats and armed with long staves. With these last, they treated a female figure, in blue, to, as it seemed, sadly rough usage. And the context informed Julius, in jingling verse, how that poor Hagar, the forester's daughter, in-conveniently defiant of custom and of common sense, had stoutly refused to be cast forth into the social wilderness, along with her small Ishmael and a few pounds sterling as price of her honour and content, until she had stood face to face with Sarah, the safely church-wed, if none too reputable, wife. It informed him, further, how the said small Ishmael—whether alarmed by the violence of my lady's men-servants, or wanting merely, childlike, to welcome his returning father—ran to the coach door and clambered on the step; whence, thanks to a vicious thrust — so declares the chap-book — from "the painted Jezebel within," he fell, while the horses plunging forward caused the near hind wheel of the heavy, lumbering vehicle to pass over his legs, almost severing them from his body just above the knee.

Thereupon—and here the homely language of the gutter poet rose to a level of rude eloquence—the outraged mother, holding the mangled and dying child in her arms, cursed the man who had brought this ruin upon her—cursed him and his descendants, to the sixth and seventh generation, good and bad alike. Declaring, moreover, that as judgment on his perfidy and lust, no owner of Brockhurst should reach the life limit set by the Psalmist, and die quiet and

christianly in his bed, until a somewhat portentous event
should have taken place.—Namely, until, as the jingling rhyme
set forth :—

> "—a fatherless babe to the birth shall have come,
> Of brother or sister shall he have none,
> But red-gold hair and eyes of blue
> And a foot that will never know stocking or shoe.
> If he opens his purse to the lamenter's cry,
> Then the woe shall lift and be laid for aye."

Julius March, his spare, black figure crouched together, sat
on the top step of the library ladder musing. His first movement had been one of refined and contemptuous disgust.
Sensuality, and the tragedies engendered by it, were so wholly
foreign to his nature and mental outlook, that it was difficult
to him to reckon with them seriously and admit the very actual
and permanent part which they play, and always have played, in the
great drama of human life.   It distressed, it, in a sense, annoyed
him that the legend of Brockhurst, which had caused him
elaborate imaginative terrors during his childhood, should belong
to this gross and vulgar order of history.   Yet indubitably—as
he reluctantly admitted—each owner of Brockhurst had, very
certainly, found death in the midst of life, and that according
to some rather brutal and bloody pattern. This might, of
course, be judged the result of merest coincidence. Had he
leisure and opportunity to search them out, he could find, no
doubt, plausible explanation of the majority of cases.   Only
that fact of persistent violence, persistent accident, did remain.
It stared him in the face, so to speak, defiant of denial. And
the deduction, consequent upon it, stared him in the face likewise. He was constrained to confess that the first clause of
the deeply-wronged mother's prediction had found ample
fulfilment.—Julius paused, shifted his position uneasily, somewhat fearful of the conclusions of his own reasoning.

For how about the second clause of that same prediction?
How about the advent of that strange Child of Promise, who preordained in his own flesh to bear the last and heaviest stroke at
the hands of retributive justice, should, rightly bearing it, bring
salvation both to himself and to his race? Behind the coarse
and illiterate presentment of the chap-book, Julius began
dimly to apprehend a somewhat majestic moral and spiritual
tragedy, a tragedy of vicarious suffering crowned by triumphant
emancipation. Thus has God, as he reflected with a self-con-
demnatory emotion of humility, chosen the base things of the

world and those which are despised—yea, and the things which are not, to bring to nought the things which are!—His heart, hungry of all martyrdom, all saintly doings, went forth to welcome the idea. But then, he asked himself almost awed, in this sceptical, rationalistic age, are such semi-miraculous moral examples still possible? And answered, with strong exultation— as one finding practical justification of a long, though silently, cherished conviction—yes, that even now, nineteen centuries after the death of that divine Saving Victim to whose service he had devoted his life and the joys of his manhood, such nobly sad and strange happenings may still be.

And, even while he thus answered, his eyes were drawn involuntarily to the portrait of the unsightly dwarf, painted by Velasquez. The broad shaft of sunlight had crept backward, away from it, leaving the canvas unobtrusive, no longer harshly evident either in violence of colour or grotesqueness of form. It had become part of the great whole merely, modulated to gracious harmony with the divers objects surrounding it, and, like them, softly overlaid by a diffused and silvery light.

CHAPTER V

IN WHICH JULIUS MARCH BEHOLDS THE VISION OF THE NEW LIFE

HE was aroused from these austere, yet, to him, inspiring reflections by the click of an opening door and the sound of women's voices. Mademoiselle de Mirancourt paused on the threshold, one hand raised in quick admiration, the other resting on Lady Calmady's arm.

"But this is superb!" she cried gaily. "Your charming King Richard, *Cœur d'Or*, has given you a veritable palace to inhabit!"

"Ah yes! King Richard has indeed given me a palace to live in. But, better still, he has given me his dear heart of gold in which to hide the life of my heart for ever and a day."

Katherine's words came triumphantly, more as song than as speech. She caught the elder woman's upraised hand gently and kissed it, looking her, meanwhile, full in the face.—"I am happy, very, very happy, best and dearest," she said. "And it is so delicious to be happy."

" Ah, my child, my beautiful child ! " Mademoiselle de Mirancourt cried.

There were tears in her pretty, patient eyes. For if youth
finds age pathetic with the obvious pathos of spent body, and
of tired mind which has ceased to greatly hope, how far more
deeply pathetic does age, from out its sad and settled wisdom,
find poor, gallant youth and all its still unbroken trust in the
beneficence of destiny, its unbroken faith in the enchantments
of earth !

Meanwhile, Julius March—product as he was of an arbitrary
system of thought and training, and by so much divorced from
the natural instincts of youth and age alike, the confident joy of
the one, the mature acquiescence of the other—in overhearing
this brief conversation suffered embarrassment amounting almost
to shame. For not only Katherine's words, but the vital gladness of her voice, the sweet exuberance of her manner as she
bent, in all her spotless bravery of white and rose, above the
elder woman's hand and kissed it, came to him as a revelation
before which he shrank with a certain fearful modesty. Julius
had read of love in the poets, of course. But, in actual fact, he
had never wooed a woman, nor heard from any woman's lips the
language of intimate devotion. The cold embraces of the Church
—a church, as he too often feared, rendered barren by schism
and heresy—were the only embraces he had ever suffered.
Things read of and things seen, moreover, are singularly different
in power. And so he trembled now at the mystery of human
love, actual and concrete, here close beside him. He was,
indeed, moved to the point of losing his habitual suavity of
demeanour. He rose hastily and descended the library steps,
forgetful of the handful of chap-books, which fell in tattered and
dusty confusion upon the floor.

Katherine looked round. Until now she had been unobservant
of his presence, innocent of other audience than the old friend,
to whom it was fitting enough to confide dear secrets. For an
instant she hesitated, embarrassed too, her pride touched to
annoyance, at having laid bare the treasures of her heart thus
unwittingly. She was tempted to retreat through the still open
door, into the library, and leave the review of the Long Gallery
and its many relics to a more convenient season. But it was
not Katherine's habit to run away, least of all from the consequences of her own actions. And her sense of justice compelled
her to admit that, in this case, the indiscretion—if indiscretion
indeed there was—lay with her, in not having seen poor Julius ;
rather than with him, in having overheard her little outburst. So

she called to him in friendly greeting, and came swiftly towards him down the length of the great room.

And Julius stood waiting for her, leaning against the frame of the library ladder—a spare, black figure, notably at variance with the broad glory of sunshine and colour reigning out of doors.

His usually quick instinct of courtesy was in abeyance, shaken, as he still was, and confused by the revelation that had just come to him. He looked at Lady Calmady with a new and agitated understanding. She made so fair a picture that he could only gaze dumbly at it. Tall in fact, Katherine was rendered taller by the manner—careless of passing fashion—in which her hair was dressed. The warm, brown mass of it, rolled up and back from her forehead, showed all the perfect oval of her face. Tender, lovely, smiling, her blue-brown eyes soft and lustrous, with a certain wondering serenity in their depths, there was yet something majestic about Katherine Calmady. No poor or unworthy line marred the nobility of her face or figure. The dark, arched eyebrows, the well-chiselled and slightly aquiline nose, the firm chin and throat, the shapely hands, all denoted harmony and completeness of development, and promised a reserve of strength, ready to encounter and overcome if danger were to be met. Years afterwards the remembrance of Katherine as he just then saw her would return upon Julius, as prophetic of much. Quailing in spirit, still reluctant, in his asceticism, to comprehend and reckon with her personality in the fulness of its present manifestation, he answered her at random and with none of the pause and playful evasiveness usual to his speech.

"I am very glad we have found you," Katherine said frankly. "I was afraid, by the fact of your not coming to breakfast, that you were overtired. We talked late last night. Did we weary you too much?"

"Existence in itself is vexatiously wearisome at times—at least to feeble persons, like myself."

Katherine's smile faded. She looked at him with charming solicitude.

"Ah! you are not well," she declared. "Go out and enjoy the sunshine. Leave all those stupid books. Go," she repeated, "order one of the horses. Go and meet Richard. He has gone over to look at the new lodge. You could ride all the way through the east woods in the cool.—See, I will put these tidy."

And, as she spoke, Katherine stooped to pick up the

3

scattered chap-books from the ground. But, in the last few moments, while looking at her, yet further understanding had overtaken Julius March. Not only the mystery of human love, but the mystery of dawning motherhood had come close to him. And he put Lady Calmady aside with a determination of authority somewhat surprising.

"No, no, pardon me! They are dusty, they will soil your hands. You must not touch those books," he said.

Katherine straightened herself up. Her face was slightly flushed, her expression full of kindly amusement.

"Dear Julius, you are very imperative. Surely I may make my hands dirty, once in a way, in a good cause? They will wash, you know, just as well as your own, after all."

"A thousand times better. Still, I will ask you not to touch those books. I have valid reasons. For one, an evil beast in the form of a spider has dwelt among them. I disturbed it and it fled, looking as though it had grown old in trespasses and sins. It seemed to me a thing of ill omen."

He tried to steady himself, to treat the matter lightly. Yet his speech struck Katherine as hurried and anxious, out of all proportion to the matter in hand.

"Poor thing—and you killed it? Yet it couldn't help being ugly, I suppose," she answered, not without a touch of malice.

Julius was on his knees, his long, thin fingers gathering up the tattered pages, ranging them into a bundle, tying them together with the tag of rusty, black ribbon aforesaid. For an unreasoning, fierce desire was upon him—very alien to his usual gentle attitude of mind—to shield this beautiful woman from all acquaintance with the foul story set forth in those little books. To shield her, indeed, from more than merely that. For a vague presentiment possessed him that she might, in some mysterious way, be intimately involved in the final development of that same story which, though august, was so full of suffering, so profoundly sad. Meanwhile, in his excitement, he replied, less to her gently mocking question than to the importunities of his own thought.

"No," he said, "I let it go. I begin to fear it is useless to attempt to take short-cuts to the extinction of what is evil. It does not cease, but merely changes its form. Unwillingly I have learned that. No violent death is possible to things evil."

Julius rose to his feet.

"They must go on," he continued, "till, in the merciful providence of God, their term is reached, till their power is exhausted, till they have worn themselves out."

Lady Calmady turned and moved thoughtfully towards the far end of the room, where the sunshine still slanted in through the open casements of the bay-window, and where the delicate, little, spinster lady stood awaiting her. Amorous pigeons cooed below on the string-course. Bees droned sleepily against the glass.

"But," she said, in gentle remonstrance, "that is a rather terrible doctrine, Julius. Surely it is not quite just; for it would seem to leave us almost hopelessly at the mercy of the wrong-doing of others."

"Yes, but are we not, just that—all of us at the mercy of the wrong-doing of others?—The courageous forever suffering for the cowardly, the wise for the ignorant and brutish, the just for the unjust? Is not this, perhaps, the very deepest lesson of our religion?"

"Oh no, no!" Katherine cried incredulously. "There is something at once deeper and more comforting than that. Remember, in the beginning, when God created all things and reviewed His handiwork, He pronounced it very good."

Julius was recovering his suavity. The little packet of chap-books rested safely in the pocket of his coat.

"But that was a long time ago," he said, smiling.

They reached the bay-window. Katherine took her old friend's hand once again and laid it caressingly upon her arm.

"Pardon me for keeping you waiting, dearest," she said. "Julius is in fault. He will argue with me about the date of the creation, and that takes time. He declares it was so long ago that everything has had time to grow very old and go very wrong. But, indeed, he is mistaken. Agree with me, tell him he is mistaken! The world is deliciously young yet. It was only made a little over twenty-two years ago. I must know, for I came into it then. And I found it all as new as I was myself, and a thousand times prettier — quite adorably gay, adorably fresh."

Katherine's voice sank, grew fuller in tone. She gazed out over the brilliant garden to the woodland shimmering in the noontide heat. Then she looked at Julius March, her eyes and lips eloquent with joyous conviction.

"Indeed, I think, God makes His whole creation over again for each one of us, it is so beautiful. As in the beginning, so now," she said; "behold it is very good — ah yes! who can doubt that—it is very good!"

"Amen. To you may it ever so continue," Julius murmured, bowing his head.

That evening there was a dinner party at Brockhurst. Lord Denier brought his handsome second wife. She was a Hellard, and took the judge *faute de mieux*, so said the wicked world, rather late in life. The Cathcarts of Newlands and their daughter Mary came; and Roger Ormiston too, who, being off duty, had run down from London for a few days' partridge shooting, bringing with him his cousin Colonel St. Quentin—invalided home, to his own immense chagrin, in the midst of the Afghan war. On the terrace, after dinner, for the night was warm enough for the whole company to take coffee out of doors, Lady Calmady—incited thereunto by her brother—had persuaded Mary Cathcart to sing, accompanying herself on her guitar. The girl's musical gifts were of no extraordinary order, but her young contralto was true and sweet. The charm of the hour and the place, moreover, was calculated to heighten the effect of the Jacobite songs and old-world love-ditties which she selected.

Roger Ormiston unquestionably found her performance sufficiently moving. But then the girl's frank manner, her warm, gipsy-like colouring, and the way in which she could sit a horse, moved him also ; had done so, indeed, ever since he first saw her, as quite a child, some eight or nine years ago, on one of his earliest visits to Brockhurst, fighting a half-broken, Welsh pony that refused at a grip by the roadside. The little maiden, her face pale, for once, from concentration of purpose, had forced the pony over the grip. Then, slipping out of the saddle, she coaxed and kissed the rough, unruly, little beast, with tears of apology for the hard usage to which she had been obliged to subject it. So stout, yet so tender, a heart, struck Roger as an excellent thing in woman. And now, listening to the full, rounded notes and thrumming of the guitar strings, in the evening quiet under the stars, he wished, remorsefully, that he had never been guilty of any pleasant sins, that his record was cleaner, his tastes less expensive, that he was a better fellow all round, in short, than he was, because, then, perhaps—

And Julius March, too, found the singing somewhat agitating, though to him the personality of the singer was of small account. Another personality, and a train of feeling evoked by certain new aspects of it, had pursued him all the day long. Katherine, mindful of her somewhat outspoken divergence of opinion from his, in the morning, had been particularly thoughtful of his pleasure and entertainment. At dinner she directed the conversation upon subjects interesting to him, and had thereby made him talk more unreservedly than was his wont. Not even the most saintly of human beings is wholly indifferent to social success. Julius was conscious of a stirring of the blood, of a subdued excitement. These sensations were pleasurable. But his training had taught him to distrust pleasurable sensations as too often the offspring of very questionable parentage. And, while Mary Cathcart's voice still breathed upon the fragrant night air, he, standing on the outskirts of the listening company, slipped away unperceived.

His study, a long, narrow room occupying, with his bedroom, the ground floor of the chapel wing of the house, struck chill as he entered it. Above the range of pigeon-holes and little drawers, forming the back of the writing-table, two candles burned on either side of a bronze *pietà*, which Julius had brought back with him from Rome. On the broad slab of the table below were the many quires of foolscap forming the library catalogue, neatly numbered and lettered; while his diary lay open upon the blotting-pad, ready for the chronicle of the past day's events. Beside it was the packet of chap-books, still tied together with their tag of rusty ribbon.

It was Julius March's habit to exchange his coat for a cassock in the privacy of his study. He did so now, and knotted a black cord about his waist. Let no one underrate the sustaining power of costume, whether it take the form of ballet-skirt or monk's frock. Human nature is but a weak thing at best, and needs outward and visible signs, not only to support its faith in its deity, but even its faith in its own poor self! Of persons of sensitive temperament and limited experience, such as Julius, this is particularly true. Putting off his secular garment, as a rule he could put off secular thoughts as well. Beneath the severe and scanty folds of the cassock there was small space for remembrance of the pomp and glory of this perishing world. At least he hoped so. To-night, importuned as he had been by scenes and emotions quite other than ecclesiastical, Julius literally sought refuge in his cassock. It represented "port after stormy seas,"—home, after travel in lands altogether foreign.

He took St. Augustine's *De Civitate Dei* from its place in the bookshelves lining one side of the room. There should be peace to the soul, surely, emancipation from questioning of transitory things, in reading of the City of God? But, alas, his attention strayed. That sense of subdued excitement was upon him yet. He thought of the conversation at dinner, of brilliant speeches he might have made, of the encouragement of Katherine's smiling eyes and sympathetic speech, of the scene in the gallery that morning, of Mary Cathcart's old-time love-ditties.

The City of God was far off. All these were things very near at hand. Notwithstanding the scanty folds of the cassock, they importuned him still.

Pained at his own lack of poise and seriousness, Julius returned the volume of St. Augustine to its place, and, sitting down at the writing-table prepared to chronicle the day's events. Perhaps by putting a statement of them on paper he could rid himself of their all too potent influence. But his thought was tumultuous, words refused to come in proper order and sequence; and Julius abhorred that erasures should mar the symmetry of his pages. Impatiently he pushed the diary from him. Clearly it, like the City of God, was destined to wait.

The guests had departed. He had heard the distant calling of voices in friendly farewell, the rumble of departing wheels. The night was very soft and mild. He would go out and walk the grey flags of the terrace, till this unworthy restlessness gave place to reason and calm.

Passing along the narrow passage, he opened the door on to the garden-hall. And there paused. The hall itself, and the inner side of the carven arches of the arcade, were in dense shadow. Beyond stretched the terrace bathed in moonlight, which glittered on the polished leaves of the little orange trees, on the leaded panes of the many windows, and strangely transmuted the colours of the range of pot-flowers massed beneath them along the base of the house. It was a fairy world upon which Julius looked forth. Nor did it need suitable inhabitants. Pacing slowly down the centre of the terrace came Richard and Katherine Calmady, hand in hand. Tall, graceful, strong in the perfection of their youth and of their great devotion, amid that ethereal brightness, they seemed as two heroic figures—immortal, fairy lovers moving through the lovely wonder of that fairyland. As they drew near, Katherine stopped, leant—with a superb abandon —back against her husband, resting her hand on his shoulder, drew his arm around her waist for support, drew his face down to her upturned face until their lips met, while the moonlight played upon the jewels on her bare arms and neck and gleamed softly on the surface of her white, satin dress.

To true lovers the longest kiss is all too sadly short—a thing brief almost in proportion to its sweetness. But to Julius March, watching from the blackness of the doorway, it seemed a whole eternity before Richard Calmady raised his head. Then Julius turned and fled down the passage and back into the chill study, where the candles burned on either side the image of the Virgin Mother cradling the dead Christ upon her knee.

Gentle persons, breaking from the lines of self-restraint, run to a curious violence in emotion. All day long, shrink from it, ignore it, as he might, a moral storm had been brewing. Now it broke. Not from those two lovers did Julius turn thus in amazement and terror; but from just that from which it is impossible for anyone to turn in actual fact—namely from himself. He was appalled by the narrowness of his own past outlook; appalled by the splendour of that heritage which, by his own act, he had forfeited. The cassock ceased, indeed, to be a refuge, the welcome livery of home and rest. It had become a prison-suit, a badge of slavery, against which his whole being rebelled. For the moment—happily violence is shortlived, only for a very little while do even the gentlest persons "see red"—asceticism appeared to him as a blasphemy against the order of nature and of nature's God. His vow of perpetual chastity, made with so passionate an enthusiasm, for the moment appeared to him an act of absolutely monstrous vanity and self-conceit. In his stupid ignorance he had tried to be wiser than his Maker, preferring the ordinances of man to the glad and merciful purposes of God. In so doing had he not, only too possibly, committed the unpardonable sin, the sin against the Holy Ghost?

Poor Julius, his thought had indeed run almost humorously mad! Yet it was characteristic of the man that the breaking of his self-imposed bonds never occurred to him. Made in ignorance, unwitnessed though his vow might be, it remained inviolable. He never, even in this most heated hour of his trial, doubted that.

Stretching out his arms, he clenched his hands in anguish of spirit. The sacerdotal pride, the subjective joys of self-consecration, the mental luxury of feeling himself different from others, singled out, set apart,—all the Pharisee, in short, in Julius March, —was sick to death. He had supposed he was living to God—and now it appeared to him he had lived only to himself. He had trusted God too little, had come near reckoning the great natural laws — which, after all, must be of God's ordering — common and unclean. Katherine was right. The eternal purpose is joy, not sorrow; youth and health, not age and decay; thankful acceptance, not fastidious rejection and fear. Katherine—yes, Katherine—and there the young man's wild tirade stopped—

He flung himself down in front of the writing-table, leaning his elbows on it, pressing his face upon his folded arms. For in good truth, what did it all amount to? Not outraged laws of nature, not sins against the Holy Ghost; but just simply this, that the common fate had overtaken him.   He loved a woman, and in so loving had, at last, found himself.

The most vital experiences are beyond language.   When Julius looked up, his eyes rested upon the bronze *pietà*, age-old witness to the sanctity of motherhood and of suffering alike. His face was wet with tears.   He was faint and weak ; yet a certain calm had come to him.   He no longer quarrelled — though his attitude towards them was greatly changed—either with his priestly calling or his rashly made vow.   Not as sources of pride did he now regard them ; but as searching discipline to be borne humbly and faithfully, to the honour—as he prayed— both of earthly and heavenly love.   He loved Katherine, but he loved her husband, and that with the fulness of a loyal and equal friendship.   And so no taint was upon his love, of this he felt assured.   Indeed, he asked nothing better than that things might continue as they were at Brockhurst ; and that he might continue to warm his hands a little—only a little—in the dear sunshine of Richard and Katherine Calmady's perfect love.

As Julius rose, his knees gave under him.   He rested both hands heavily on the table, looked down, saw the unsightly packet of dirty chap-books.   Again, and almost with a cry, he prayed that things might continue as they were at Brockhurst.

"Give peace in my time, O Lord!" he said.   Then he wrapped up the little bundle carefully, sealed and labelled it, and locked it away in one of the table-drawers.

Thus, kneeling before the image of the stricken Mother and the dead Christ, did Julius March behold the Vision of the New Life.   But the page of his diary, on which surely a matter of so great importance should have been duly chronicled, remains to this day a blank.

CHAPTER VI

ACCIDENT OR DESTINY, ACCORDING TO YOUR HUMOUR

ON the 18th of October that year, St. Luke's day, a man died, and this was the manner of his passing.

There was nothing more to be done.   Dr. Knott had gone out of the red drawing-room on the ground floor into the tapestry-hung dining-room next door, which struck cold as the small hours drew on towards the dawn.   And Julius March, after reciting the prayer in which the Anglican Church commends the souls of her departing children to the merciful keeping of the God who gave them, had followed him. The doctor was acutely distressed. He hated to lose a patient. He also hated to feel emotion. It made him angry. Moreover, he was intolerant of the presence of the clergy and of their ministrations in sick-rooms. He greeted poor Julius rather snarlingly.

"So your work's through as well as mine," he said. "No disrespect to your cloth, Mr. March, but I'm not altogether sorry. I daresay I'm a bit of a heathen; but I can't help fancying the dying know more of death, and the way to meet it, than any of us can teach them."

A group of men-servants stood about the open door, at the farther end of the room, with Iles, the steward, and Mr. Tom Chifney, the trainer from the racing-stables. The latter advanced a little and, clearing his throat, inquired huskily :—

"No hope at all, doctor?"

"Hope?" he returned impatiently.—The lamp on the great bare dining-table burned low, and John Knott's wide mouth, conical skull and thick, ungainly person looked ogreish, almost brutal in the uncertain light.—"There never was a grain of hope from the first, except in Sir Richard's fine constitution. He is as sound as only a clean-living man of thirty can be,—I wish there were a few more like him, though your beastly diseases do put money into my pocket,—that offered us a bare chance, and we were bound to act on that chance"—his loose lips worked into a bitterly humorous smile—"and torture him. Well, I've seen a good many men under the knife before now, and I tell you I never saw one who bore himself better. Men and horses alike, it's breeding that tells when it comes to the push. You know that, eh, Chifney?"

In the red drawing-room, where the drama of this sad night centred, Roger Ormiston had dropped into a chair by the fireside, his head sunk on his chest and his hands thrust into his pockets. He was very tired, very miserable. A shocking thing had happened, and, in some degree, he held himself responsible for that happening. For was it not he who had been so besotted with the Clown, and keen about its training? Therefore the young man cursed himself, after the manner of his kind ; and cursed his luck too, in that, if this thing was to happen, it had not happened to him instead of to Richard Calmady.

Mrs. Denny, the housekeeper, had retired to a straight-backed chair stationed against the wall. She sat there, waiting till the next call should come for her skilful nursing, upright, her hands folded upon her silk apron, her attitude a model of discreet and self-respecting repose. Mrs. Denny knew her place, and had a considerable capacity for letting other persons know theirs. She ruled the large household with unruffled calm. But, to-night, even her powers of self-control were heavily taxed; and though she carried her head high, she could not help tears coursing slowly down her cheeks, and falling sadly to the detriment of the goffered frills of her white, lawn crossover.

And Richard Calmady, meanwhile, lay still and very fairly peaceful upon the narrow, camp bed in the middle of the room. He had lain there, save during one hour,—the memory of which haunted Katherine with hideous and sickening persistence,—ever since Tom Chifney, the head-lad from the stables and a couple of grooms, had carried him in, on a hurdle, from the steeple-chase course four days ago.

The crimson-covered chairs and sofas, and other furniture of the large square room, had been pushed back against the walls in a sort of orderly confusion, leaving a broad passage-way between the doors at either end, and a wide vacant space round the bed. At the head of this stood a high, double-shelved what - not, bearing medicine bottles, cups, basins, rolled bandages, dressings of rag and lint, a spirit-lamp over which simmered a vessel containing vinegar, and a couple of shaded candles in a tall, branched, silver candlestick. The light from these fell, in intersecting circles, upon the white bed, upon the man's brown, close-curled hair, upon his handsome face—drawn and sharpened by suffering — and its rather ghastly three days' growth of beard.

It fell, too, upon Katherine, as she sat facing her husband, the side of her large easy-chair drawn up parallel to the side of the bed.

Silently, unlooked for, as a thief in the night, the end of Katherine's fair world had come. There had been no time for forethought or preparation. At one step she had been called upon to pass from the triumph to the terror of mortal life. But she was a valiant creature, and her natural courage was reinforced by the greatness of her love. She met the blow standing, her brain clear, her mind strong to help. Only once had she faltered—during the hideous hour when she waited, pacing the dining-room in the dusk, four evenings back. For, after consultation with Dr. Jewsbury and Mr. Thoms of Westchurch, John Knott had told her—with a gentleness and delicacy a little surprising in so hard-bitten a man—that, owing to the shattered condition of the bone, amputation of the right leg was imperative. He added that, only too probably, the left would have eventually to go too. They must operate, he said, and operate immediately. Katherine had pleaded to be present; but Dr. Knott was obdurate.

"My dear lady, you don't know what you ask," he said. "As you love him, let him be. If you are there it will just double the strain. He'd suffer for you as well as himself. Believe me he will be far best alone."

It must be remembered that in 1842 anæsthetics had not robbed the operating-room of half its horrors. The victim went to execution wide-awake, with no mercy of deadened senses and dulled brain. And so Katherine had paced the dining-room, hearing at intervals, through the closed doors, the short peremptory tones of the surgeons, fearing she heard more and worse sounds than those. They were hurting him, sorely, sorely, dismembering and disfiguring the dear, living body which she loved. A tempest of unutterable woe swept over her. Breaking fiercely away from her brother and Denny—who strove to comfort her—she beat her poor, lovely head against the wall. But that, so far, had been her one moment of weakness. Since then she had fought steadily, with a certain lofty cheerfulness, for the life she so desired to save. The horror of the second operation had been spared her; but only because it might but too probably hasten, rather than retard, the approaching footsteps of death. Mortification had set in, in the bruised and mangled limb forty-eight hours ago. And now the scent of death was in the air. The awful presence drew very near. Yet only when doctor and priest alike rose and went, when her brother moved away, and even the faithful housekeeper stepped back from the bedside, did Katherine's mind really grasp the truth. Her well-beloved lay dying; and human tenderness, human skill, be they never so great, ceased to avail.

She was worn by the long vigil. Her face was colourless. Yet perhaps Katherine's beauty had never been more rare and sweet than as she sat there, leaning a little forward in the eagerness of her watchfulness. The dark circles about her eyes made them look very large and sombre. The corners of her mouth turned down and her under-lip quivered now and then, giving her expression a childlike piteousness of appeal. There was no trace of disorder in her appearance. Her white dressing-gown and all its pretty ribbons and laces were spotlessly fresh. Her hair was carefully dressed as usual—high at the back, showing the nape of her neck, her little ears, and the noble poise of her head.　Katherine was not one of those women who appear to imagine that slovenliness is the proper exponent of sorrow.

Still, for all her high courage, as the truth came home to her, her spirit began to falter for the second time.　It is comparatively easy to endure while there is something to be done ; but it is almost intolerable, specially to the young when life is strong in them, merely to sit by and wait.　Katherine's overwrought nerves began to play cruel tricks upon her, carrying her back in imagination to that other hideous hour of waiting, in the dining-room, four evenings ago.　Again she seemed to hear the short, peremptory tones of the surgeons, and those worse things—the stifled groan of one in the extremity of physical anguish, and the grate of a saw.　These maddened her with pity, almost with rage.　She feared that now, as then, she might lose her self-mastery and do some wild and desperate thing.　She tried to keep her attention fixed on the quick, irregular rise and fall of the linen sheet expressing the broad, full curve of the young man's chest, as he lay flat on his back, his eyes closed, but whether in sleep or in unconsciousness she did not know.　As long as the sheet rose and fell he was alive at all events, still with her.　But she was too exhausted for any sustained effort of will.　And her glance wandered back to, and followed with agonised comprehension, the formless, motionless elevation and depression of that same sheet towards the foot of the bed.

The air of the room seemed to grow more oppressive, the silence to deepen, and with it the terrible tension of her mind increased.　Suddenly she started to her feet.　The logs burning in the grate had fallen together with a crash, sending a rush of ruddy flame and an innumerable army of hurrying sparks up the wide chimney.　All the mouldings of the ceiling—all the crossing bars and sinuous lines of the richly-worked pattern, all the depending bosses and roses of it, all the foliations of the deep cornice—sprang into bold relief, outlined, splashed, and stained with living scarlet.　And this universal redness of carpet, curtains, furniture, and now of ceiling, even of white-draped bed, suggested to Katherine's distracted fancy another thing—unseen, yet known during her other hour of waiting—namely blood.

Roused by the crash of the falling logs and the rustle of Katherine's garments as she sprang up, Richard Calmady opened his eyes.　For a few seconds his glance wavered in vague distress and perplexity.　Then, as fuller consciousness returned of how it all was with him, with a slight lifting of the eyebrows his glance steadied upon Katherine and he smiled.

"Ah! my poor Kitty," he whispered, "it takes a long time, doesn't it, this business of dying?"

Katherine's evil fancies vanished. As soon as the demand for action came she grew calm and sane. The ceiling and sheets were white again and her mind was clear.

"Are you easy, my dearest?" she asked. "In less pain?"

"No," he said, "no, I'm not in pain. But everything seems to sink away from me, and I float right out. It's all dream and mist—except—except just now your face."

Katherine's lips quivered too much for speech. She moved swiftly across to the what-not at the head of the bed. If he did not suffer, there could be no selfishness, surely, in trying to keep death at bay for a little space yet? But, alas, with what grotesquely paltry and inadequate weapons are all—even the most gallant—reduced to fighting death at the last! Here, on the one hand, a half wine glass of champagne in a china feeding-cup, with a teapot-like spout to it, or a few spoonfuls of jelly, backed by the passion of a woman's heart. And, on the other hand, ranged against this pitiful display of absurdly limited resources,—as the hosts of the Philistines against the little army of Israel, — resistless laws of nature, incalculably far-reaching forces, physical and spiritual, the interminable progression of cause and effect!

Denny joined Lady Calmady at the table. The two women held brief consultation. Then the housekeeper went round to the farther side of the bed, and slipping her arm under the pillows gently raised Richard's head and shoulders, while Katherine, kneeling beside him, held the spout of the feeding-cup to his lips.

"Must I? I don't think I can manage it," he said, drawing away slightly and closing his eyes.

But Katherine persisted.

"Oh! try to drink it," she pleaded, "never mind how little —only try. Help me to keep you here just as long as I can."

The young man's glance steadied on to her once again, and his eyes and lips smiled the same faint, wholly gracious smile.

"All right, my beloved," he said. "A little higher, Denny, please."

Not without painful effort and a choking contraction of the throat, he swallowed a few drops. But the greater part of the draught spilt out sideways, and would have dribbled down on to the pillows had not Katherine held her handkerchief to his mouth.

Ormiston, who had been standing at the foot of the bed in the hope of rendering some assistance, ground his teeth together with a half-audible imprecation, and went slowly over to the fireplace again. He had supposed himself as miserable as he well could be before. But this incident of the feeding-cup was the climax, somehow. It struck him as an intolerable humiliation and outrage that Richard Calmady, splendid fellow as he was, gifted, high-bred gentleman, should, of all men, come to this sorry pass! He was filled with impotent fury. And was it this pass, indeed, he asked himself, to which every human creature must needs come one day? Would he, Roger Ormiston, one day, find himself thus weak and broken, his body—now so lively a source of various enjoyment—degraded into a pest-house, a mere dwelling-place of suffering and corruption? The young man gripped the high, narrow mantelshelf with both hands and pressed his forehead down between them. He really had not the nerve to watch what was going forward over there any longer. It was too painful. It knocked all the manhood out of him. But for very shame, before those two calm, devoted women, he would have broken down and wept.

Presently Richard's voice reached him, feeble yet uncomplaining.

"I am so sorry, but you see it's no use, Kitty. The machinery won't work. Let me lie flat again, Denny, please. That's better, thanks."

Then after a few moments of laboured breathing, he added :—

"You mustn't trouble any more, it only disappoints you. We have just got to submit to fact, my beloved. I've taken my last fence."

Ormiston's shoulders heaved convulsively as he leaned his forehead against the cold, marble edge of the chimneypiece. His brother-in-law's words brought the whole dreadful picture up before him. Oh! that cursed slip and fall, that struggling, plunging, frenzied horse!—And how the horse had plunged and struggled, good God! It seemed as though Chifney, the grooms, all of them, would never get hold of it or draw Richard out from beneath the pounding hoofs. And then Ormiston went over his own share in the business again, lamenting, blaming himself. Yet what more natural, after all, than that he should have set his affections on the Clown? Chifney believed in the horse too—a five-year-old brother of Touchstone, resembling, in his black-brown skin and intelligent, white-reach face, that celebrated horse, and inheriting — less enviable distinction—the high shoulders and withers of his sire Camel. If the Clown did not make a name, Captain Ormiston had sworn, by all the gods of sport, he would never judge a horse again. And, Heaven help us, was this the ghastly way the Clown's name was to be made, then?

The room grew very quiet again, save for a strange gurgling, rattling sound Richard Calmady made, at times, in breathing. Mrs. Denny had retired beyond the circle of firelight. And Katherine, having drawn her chair a little farther forward so that the foot of the bed might be out of sight, sat holding her husband's hand, softly caressing his wrist and palm with her finger-tips. Soon the slow movement of her fingers ceased, while she felt, in quick fear, for the fluttering, intermittent pulse. Richard's breathing had become more difficult. He moved his head restlessly and plucked at the sheet with his right hand. It was a little more than flesh and blood could bear.

Katherine called to him softly under her breath :—" Richard, Dick, my darling !"

" All right, I'm coming."

He opened his eyes wide, as in sudden terror.

"Oh ! I say, though, what's happened? Where am I ? "

Katherine leant down, kissed his hand, caressed it.

" Here, my dearest," she said, "at home, at Brockhurst, with me."

" Ah yes !" he said, "of course, I remember, I'm dying." He waited a little space, and then, turning his head on the pillow so as to have a better view of her, spoke again :— " I was floating right out—the under-tow had got me—it was sucking me down into the deep sea of mist and dreams. I was so nearly gone—and you brought me back."

" But I wanted you so—I wanted you so," Katherine cried, smitten with sudden contrition. " I could not help it. Do you mind ? "

" You silly sweet, could I ever mind coming back to you ? " he asked wistfully. " Don't you suppose I would much rather stay here at Brockhurst, at home, with you—than sink away into the unknown ? "

" Ah ! my dear," she said, swaying herself to and fro in the misery of tearless grief.

" And yet I have no call to complain," he went on. " I have had thirty years of life and health. It is not a small thing to have seen the sun, and to have rejoiced in one's youth. And I have had you "—his face hardened and his breath came short —"you, most enchanting of women."

" My dear! my dear !" Katherine cried, again bowing her head.

" God has been so good to me here that—I hope it is not presumptuous—I can't be much afraid of what is to follow. The best argument for what will be, is what has been. Don't you think so?"

"But you go and I stay," she said. "If I could only go too, go with you."

Richard Calmady raised himself in the bed, looked hard at her, spoke as a man in the fulness of his strength.

"Do you mean that? Would you come with me if you could—come through the deep sea of mist and dreams, to whatever lies beyond?"

For all answer Katherine bent lower, her face suddenly radiant, notwithstanding its pallor. Sorrow was still so new a companion to her that she would dare the most desperate adventures to rid herself of its hateful presence. Her reason and moral sense were in abeyance, only her poor heart spoke. She laid hold of her husband's hands and clasped them about her throat.

"Let us go together, take me," she prayed. "I love you, I will not be left. Closer, Dick, closer!"

"Thank God, I am strong enough even yet!" he said fiercely, while his jaw set, and his grasp tightened somewhat dangerously upon her throat. Katherine looked into his eyes and laughed. The blood was tingling through her veins.

"Ah! dear love," she panted, "if you knew how delicious it is to be a little hurt!"

But her ecstasy was shortlived, as ecstasy usually is. Richard Calmady unclasped his hands and dropped back against the pillows, putting her away from him with a certain authority.

"My beloved one, do not tempt me," he said. "We must remember the child. The devil of jealousy is very great, even when one lies, as I do now, more than half dead."—He turned his head away, and his voice shook. "Ten years hence, twenty years hence, you will be as beautiful—more so, very likely—than ever. Other men will see you, and I"—

"You will be just what you were and always have been to me," Katherine interrupted. "I love you, and shall love."

She answered bravely, taking his hand again and caressing it, while he looked round and smiled at her. But she grew curiously cold. She shivered, and had a difficulty in controlling her speech. Her new companion, Sorrow, refused to be tricked and to leave her, and the breath of sorrow is as sharp as a wind blowing over ice.

"You have made me perfectly content," Richard Calmady said presently. "There is nothing I would have changed. No hour of day—or night—ah, my God! my God!—which I could ask to have otherwise." He paused, fighting a sob which rose in his throat. "Still you are quite young "—

"So much the worse for me," Katherine said.

"Oh! I don't know about that," he put in quietly. "Anyhow, remember that you are free, absolutely and unconditionally free. I hold a man a cur who, in dying, tries to bind the woman he loves."

Katherine shivered. Despair had possession of her.

"Why reason about it?" she asked. "Don't you see that to be bound is the only comfort I shall have left?"

"My poor darling," Richard Calmady almost groaned.

His own helplessness to help her cut him to the quick. Wealth, and an inherent graciousness of disposition, had always made it so simple to be of service and of comfort to those about him. It was so natural to rule, to decide, to alleviate, to give little trouble to others and take a good deal of trouble on their behalf, that his present and final incapacity in any measure to shield even Katherine, the woman he worshipped, amazed him. Not pain, not bodily disfigurement,—though he recoiled, as every sane being must, from these,—not death itself, tried his spirit so bitterly as his own uselessness. All the pleasant, kindly activities of common intercourse were over. He was removed alike from good deeds and from bad. He had ceased to have part or lot in the affairs of living men. The desolation of impotence was upon him.

For a little time he lay very still, looking up at the firelight playing upon the mouldings of the ceiling, trying to reconcile himself to this. His mind was clear, yet, except when actually speaking, he found it difficult to keep his attention fixed. Images, sensations, began to chase each other across his mental field of vision; and his thought, though definite as to detail, grew increasingly broken and incoherent, small matters in unseemly fashion jostling great. He wondered concerning those first steps of the disembodied spirit, when it has crossed the threshold of death; and then, incontinently, he passed to certain time-honoured jokes and impertinent follies at Eton, over which he, and Roger, and Major St. Quentin, had laughed a hundred times. They amused him greatly even yet. But he could not linger with them. He was troubled about the attics of the new lodge, now in building at the entrance to the east woods. The windows were too small, and he disliked that blind, north gable. There were letters to be answered too. Lord Fallowfeild wanted to know about something—he could not remember what— Fallowfeild's inquiries had a habit of being vague. And

4

through all these things—serious or trivial—a terrible yearning over Katherine and her baby—the new, little, human life which was his own life, and which yet he would never know or see. And through all these things also, the perpetual, heavy ache of those severed nerves and muscles, flitting pains in the limb of which, though it was gone, he had not ceased to be aware.—He dozed off, and mortal weakness closed down on him, floating him out and out into vague spaces. And then suddenly, once more, he felt a horse under him and gripped it with his knees. He was riding, riding, whole and vigorous, with the summer wind in his face, across vast, flowering pastures towards a great light on the far horizon, which streamed forth, as he knew, from the throne of Almighty God.

Choking, with the harsh rattle in his throat, he awoke to the actual and immediate—to the familiar, square room and its crimson furnishings, to Katherine's sweet, pale face and the touch of her caressing fingers, to someone standing beside her, whom he did not immediately recognise. It was Roger—Roger worn with watching, grown curiously older. But a certain exhilaration, born of that strange ride, remained by Richard Calmady. Both ache of body and distress of mind had abated. He felt a lightness of spirit, an eagerness, as of one setting forth on a promised journey, who—not unlovingly, yet with something of haste—makes his dispositions before he starts.

"Look here, darling," he said, "you'll let the stables go on just as usual. Chifney will take over the whole management of them. You can trust him implicitly. And—that is you, Roger, isn't it?—you'll keep an eye on things, won't you, so that Kitty shall have no bother? I should like to know nothing was changed at the stables. They've been a great hobby of mine, and if—if the baby is a boy, he may take after me and care for them. Make him ride straight, Roger. And teach him to love sport for its own sake, dear old man, as a gentleman should, not for the money that may come out of it."

He waited, struggling for breath, then his hand closed on Katherine's.

"I must go," he said. "You'll call the boy after me, Kitty, won't you? I want there to be another Richard Calmady. My life has been very happy, so, please God, the name will bring luck."

A spasm took him, and he tried convulsively to push off the sheet. Katherine was down on her knees, her right arm under his head, while with her left hand she stripped the bedclothes away from his chest and bared his throat.

"Denny, Denny!" she cried, "come—tell me—is this death?"

And Ormiston, impelled by an impulse he could hardly have explained, crossed the room, dragged back the heavy curtains, and flung one of the casements wide open.

The soft light of autumn dawn flowed in through the great mullioned window, quenching the redness of fire and candles, spreading, dim and ghostly, over the white dress and bowed head of the woman, over the narrow bed and the form of the maimed and dying man. The freshness of the morning air, laden with the soothing murmur of the fir forest swaying in the breath of a mild, westerly breeze, laden too with the moist fragrance of the moorland,—of dewy grass, of withered bracken and fallen leaves,—flowed in also, cleansing the tainted atmosphere of the room. While, from the springy turf of the green ride—which runs eastward, parallel to the lime avenue—came the thud and suck of hoofs, and the voices of the stable boys, as they rode the long string of dancing, snorting racehorses out to the training ground for their morning exercise.

Richard Calmady opened his eyes wide.

"Ah, it's daylight!" he cried, in accents of joyfulness. "I am glad. Kiss me, my beloved, kiss me.—You dear—yes, once more. I have had such a queer night. I dreamt I had been fearfully knocked about somehow, and was crippled, and in pain. It is good to wake, and find you, and know I'm all right after all. God keep you, my dearest, you and the boy. I am longing to see him—but not just now—let Denny bring him later. And tell them to send Chifney word I shall not be out to see the gallops this morning. I really believe those dreams half frightened me. I feel so absurdly used up. And then—Kitty, where are you?—put your arms round me and I'll go to sleep again."

He smiled at her quite naturally and stroked her cheek.

"My sweet, your face is all wet and cold!" he said. "Make Richard a good boy. After all that is what matters most—Julius will help you—Ah! look at the sunrise—why—why"—

An extraordinary change passed over him. To Katherine it seemed like the upward leap of a livid flame. Then his head fell back and his jaw dropped.

CHAPTER VII

MRS. WILLIAM ORMISTON SACRIFICES A WINE GLASS TO FATE

MRS. ST. QUENTIN'S health became increasingly fragile that autumn ; and the weight of the sorrow which had fallen upon Brockhurst bowed her to the earth.   Her desire was to go to Lady Calmady, wrap her about with tenderness and strengthen her in patience.   But, though the spirit was willing, the flesh was weak. Daily she assured Mademoiselle de Mirancourt that she was better, that she would be able to start for England in the course of the next week.   Yet day after day, week after week, passed by, and still the two ladies lingered in the pretty apartment of the rue de Rennes.   Day by day, and week by week, moreover, the elder lady grew more feeble, left her bed later in the morning, sought it earlier at night, finally resigned the attempt to leave it at all.   The keepers of Lucia St. Quentin's house of life trembled, desire—even of gentle ministries—began to fail, the sound of the grinding was low.   Yet neither she, nor her lifelong friend, nor her doctor, nor the few intimate ac-quaintances who were still privileged to visit her, admitted that she would never set forth on that journey to England at all, but only on that quite other journey,—upon which Richard Calmady had already set forth in the fulness of his manhood,—and upon which, the manifold uncertainties of human existence notwith-standing, we are, each one of us, so perfectly certain to set forth at last.   Silently they agreed with her to treat her increasing weakness with delicate stoicism, to speak of it—if at all—merely as a passing indisposition, so allowing no dreary, lamentable element to obtrude itself. Sad Mrs. St. Quentin might be, bitterly sad at heart, perplexed by the rather incomprehensible dealings of God with man.   Yet, to the end, she would remain charming, gently gay even, both out of consideration for others and out of a fine self-respect, since she held it the mark of a cowardly and ignoble nature to let anything squalid appear in her attitude towards grief, old age, or death.

But Brockhurst she would never see again.   The way was too great for her.   And so it came about that when Lady Calmady's child was born, towards the end of the following March, no more staid and responsible woman-creature of her family was at hand to support her than that lively, young lady, her brother, William Ormiston's wife.

Meanwhile, the parish of Sandyfield rejoiced. Thomas Caryll, the rector, had caused the church bells to be rung immediately on receipt of the good news; while he selected, as text for his Sunday-morning sermon, those words, usually reserved to another and somewhat greater advent—"For unto us a child is born, unto us a son is given." Good Mr. Caryll was innocent of the remotest intention of profanity. But his outlook was circumscribed, his desire to please abnormally large, and his sense of relative values slight. While that Lady Calmady should give birth to a son and heir was, after all, a matter of no small moment —locally considered at all events.

Brockhurst House rejoiced also, yet it did so not without a measure of fear. For there had been twenty-four hours of acute anxiety regarding Katherine Calmady. And even now, on the evening of the second day, although Dr. Knott declared himself satisfied both as to her condition and that of the baby, an air of mystery surrounded the large, state bedroom—where she lay, white and languid, slowly feeling her way back to the ordinary conditions of existence—and the nursery next door. Mrs. Denny, who had taken possession by right divine of long and devoted service, not only did not encourage, but positively repulsed visitors. Her ladyship must not be disturbed. She, the nurse, the baby, in turn, were sleeping. According to Denny the god of sleep reigned supreme in those stately, white-panelled chambers, looking away, across the valley and the long lines of the elm avenue, to the faint blue of the chalk downs rising against the southern sky.

John Knott had driven over, for the second time that day, in the windy March sunset. He fell in very readily with Mrs Ormiston's suggestion that he should remain to dinner. That young lady's spirits were sensibly on the rise. It is true that she had wept copiously at intervals while her sister-in-law's life appeared to be in danger—keeping at the same time as far from the sick-room as the ample limits of Brockhurst House allowed, and wishing herself a thousand and one times safe back in Paris, where her devoted and obedient husband occupied a subordinate post at the English Embassy. But Mrs. Ormiston's tears were as easily stanched as set flowing. And now, in her capacity of hostess, with three gentlemen—or rather "two and a half, for you can't," as she remarked, "count a brother-in-law for a whole one"—as audience, she felt remarkably cheerful. She had been over to Newlands during the afternoon, and insisted on Mary Cathcart returning with her. Mrs. Ormiston was a Desmolyns. The Cathcarts are distantly connected with that family. And, when the girl had protested that this was hardly a suitable moment for a visit to Brockhurst, Charlotte Ormiston had replied, with that hint of a brogue which gave her ready speech its almost rollicking character :—

"But, my dear child, propriety demands it. I depart myself to-morrow. And, now that we're recovering our tone, I daren't be left with such a houseful of men on my hands any longer. While we were tearing our hair over poor Kitty's possible demise, and agonising as to the uncertain sex of the baby, it did not matter. But now even that dear creature, Saint Julius, is beginning to pick up, and looks less as if his diet was mouldy peas and his favourite plaything a cat-o'-nine-tails. Scourge?—Yes, of course, but it's all the same in the application of the instrument, you know. And then in your secret soul, Mary dear," she added, not unkindly, "there's no denying it's far from obnoxious to you to spend a trifle of time in the society of Roger."

Mrs Ormiston carried her point. It may be stated, in passing, that this sprightly, young matron was brilliantly pretty, though her facial angle might be deemed too acute, leaving somewhat to be desired in the matter of forehead and of chin. She was plump, graceful, and neat waisted. Her skin was exquisitely white and fine, and a charming colour flushed her cheeks under excitement. Her hair was always untidy, her hairpins displaying abnormal activity in respect of escape and independent action. Her eyes were round and very prominent, suggestive of highly-polished, brown agates. She was not the least shy or averse to attracting attention. She laughed much, and practised, as prelude to her laughter, an impudently, coquettish, little stare.—And that, finally, as he sat on her right at dinner, her rattling talk and lightness of calibre generally struck John Knott as rather cynically inadequate to the demands made by her present position. Not that he underrated her good-nature or was insensible to her personal attractions. But the doctor was in search of an able coadjutor just then, blessed with a steady brain and a tongue skilled in tender diplomacies. For there were trying things to be said and done, and he needed a woman of a fine spirit to do and say them aright.

"Head like an eft," he said to himself, as course followed course and, while bandying compliments with her, he watched and listened. "As soon set a harlequin to lead a forlorn hope. Well it's to be trusted her husband's some use for her—that's more than I have anyhow, so the sooner we see her off the premises the better. Suppose I shall have to fall back on Ormiston. Bit of a rake, I expect, though in looks he is so curiously like that beautiful, innocent, young thing upstairs. Wonder how he'll take it? No mistake, it's a facer!"

Dr. Knott settled himself back squarely in his chair and pushed his cheese-plate away from him, while his shaggy eyebrows drew together as he fixed his eyes on the young man at the head of the table.

"A facer!" he repeated to himself. "Yes, the ancients knew what they were about in these awkward matters. The modern conscience is disastrously anæmic."

Although it looks on the terrace, the dining-room at Brockhurst is among the least cheerful of the living rooms. The tapestry with which it is hung—representing French hunting scenes, each panel set in a broad border pattern of birds, fruits and leaves, interspersed with classic urns and medallions—is worked in neutral tints of brown, blue, and grey. The chimney-piece, reaching the whole height of the wall, is of liver-coloured marble. At the period in question, it was still the fashion to dine at the modestly early hour of six; and, the spring evenings being long, the curtains had been left undrawn, so that the dying daylight without and the lamplight within contended rather mournfully for mastery, while a wild, south-easterly wind, breaking in gusts against the house front, sobbed at the casements and made a loose pane, here and there, click and rattle.

And it was in the midst of a notably heavy gust, when dessert had been served and the servants had left the room, that Captain Ormiston leaned across the table and addressed his sister-in-law.

The young soldier had been somewhat gloomy and silent during dinner. He was vaguely anxious about Lady Calmady. The news of Mrs. St. Quentin was critical, and he cherished a very true affection for his great-aunt. Had she not been his confidante ever since his first term at Eton? Had she not, moreover, helped him on several occasions when creditors displayed an incomprehensibly foolish pertinacity regarding payment for goods supplied? He was burdened too by a prospective sense of his own uncommon righteousness. For, during the past five months while he had been on leave at Brockhurst, assisting Katherine to master the details of the very various business of the estate, Ormiston had revised his position and decided on heroic measures of reform. He would rid himself of debt, forswear expensive London habits, and those many pleasant iniquities which every great city offers liberally to such handsome, fine gentlemen as himself. He actually proposed, just so soon as Katherine could conveniently spare him, to decline from the splendid inactivity of the Guards, upon the hard work of some line regiment under orders for foreign service. Ormiston was quite affected by contemplation of his own good resolutions. He appeared to himself in a really pathetic light. He would like to have told Mary Cathcart all about it and have claimed her sympathy and admiration. But then, she was just precisely the person he could not tell, until the said resolutions had, in a degree at all events, passed into accomplished fact! For—as not infrequently happens—it was not so much a case of being off with the old love before being on with the new, as of being off with the intermediate loves, before being on with the old one again. To announce his estimable future, was, by implication at all events, to confess a not wholly estimable past. And so Roger Ormiston, sitting that night at dinner beside the object of his best and most honest affections, proved but poor company; and roused himself, not without effort, to say to his sister-in-law :—

" It's about time to perform the ceremony of the evening, isn't it, Charlotte, and drink that small boy's health ? "

" By all manner of means. I'm all for the observance of ancient forms and ceremonies. You can never be sure how much mayn't lie at the bottom of them, and it's best to be on the safe side of the unseen powers. You'll agree to that now, Mr. March, won't you ? "—She took a grape skin from between her neat teeth and flicked it out on to her plate.—" So, for myself," she went on, " I curtsey nine times to the new moon, though the repeated genuflexion is perniciously likely to give me the backache ; touch my hat in passing to the magpies ; wish when I behold a piebald ; and bless my neighbour devoutly if he sneezes."

At the commencement of this harangue she met her brother-in-law's rather depreciative scrutiny with her bold little stare—in his present mood Ormiston found her vivacity tedious, though he was usually willing enough to laugh at her extravagancies—then she whipped Julius in with a side glance, and concluded with her round eyes set on Dr. Knott's rough-hewn and weather-beaten countenance.

" I'm afraid you are disgracefully superstitious, Mrs. Ormiston," the latter remarked.

She was a feather-headed chatterbox, he reflected, but her chatter served to occupy the time. And the doctor was by no means anxious the time should pass too rapidly. He felt slightly self-contemptuous ; but in good truth he would be glad to put away some few glasses of sound port before administering the aforementioned facer to Captain Ormiston.

"Superstitious?" she returned. "Well, I trust my superstition is not chronic, but nicely intermittent like all the rest of my many virtues. Charity begins at home, you know, and I would not like to keep any of the poor, dear creatures on guard too long for fear of tiring them out. But I give every one of them a turn, Dr. Knott, I assure you."

"And that's more than most of us do," he said, smiling rather savagely. "The majority of my acquaintance have a handsome power of self-restraint in the practice of virtue."

"And I'm the happy exception! Well, now, that's an altogether pretty speech," Mrs. Ormiston cried, laughing. "But to return to the matter in hand, to this hero of a baby— I dote on babies, Dr. Knott. I've one of my own of six months old, and she's a charming child I assure you."

"I don't doubt that for an instant, having the honour of knowing her mother. Couldn't be otherwise than charming if she tried," the doctor said, reaching out his hand again to the decanter.

Mrs. Ormiston treated him to her little stare, and then looked round the table, putting up one plump, bare arm as she pushed in a couple of hairpins.

"Ah! but she's a real jewel of a child," she said audaciously. "She's the comfort of my social existence. For she doesn't resemble me in the least, and therefore my reputation's everlastingly safe, thanks to her. Why, before the calumniating thought has had time to arise in your mind, one look in that child's face will dissipate it, she's so entirely the image of her father."

There was a momentary silence, but for the sobbing of the gale and rattling of the casements. Then Captain Ormiston broke into a rather loud laugh. Even if they sail near the wind, you must stand by the women of your family.

"Come, that will do, I think, Charlotte," he said. "You won't beat that triumphant bull in a hurry."

"But, my dear boy, so she is. Even at her present tender age, she's the living picture of your brother William."

"Oh, poor William!" Roger said hastily.

He turned to Mary Cathcart. The girl had blushed up to the roots of her crisp, black hair. She did not clearly understand the other woman's speech, nor did she wish to do so. She was admirably pure-minded. But, like all truly pure-minded persons, she carried a touchstone that made her recoil, directly and instinctively, from that which was of doubtful quality. The twinkle in Dr. Knott's grey eyes, as he sipped his port, still more the tone of Roger Ormiston's laugh, she did understand some-

how. And this last jarred upon her cruelly. It opened the
flood-gates of doubt which Mary—like so many another woman
in respect of the man she loves—had striven very valiantly to
keep shut. All manner of hints as to his indiscretions, all
manner of half-told tales as to his debts, his extravagance, which
rumour had conveyed to her unwilling ears, seemed suddenly to
gather weight and probability, viewed in the moral light—so
to speak—of that laugh. Great loves mature and deepen under
the action of sorrow and the necessity to forgive; yet it is a
shrewdly bitter moment, when the heart of either man or woman
first admits that the god of its idolatry has, after all, feet of but
very common clay. Her head erect, her eyes moist, Mary
turned to Julius March and asked him of the welfare of a certain
labourer's family that had lately migrated from Newlands to
Sandyfield. But Ormiston's voice broke in upon the inquiries
with a determination to claim her attention.

"Miss Cathcart," he said, "forgive my interrupting you. I
can tell you more about the Spratleys than March can. They're
all right. Iles has taken the man on as carter at the home-farm,
and given the eldest boy a job with the woodmen. I told him
to do what he could for them as you said you were interested
in them. And now, please, I want you to drink my small
nephew's health."

The girl pushed forward her wine glass without speaking,
and, as he filled it, Ormiston added in a lower tone :—

"He, at all events, unlike some of his relations, is guiltless
of foolish words or foolish actions. I don't pretend to share
Charlotte's superstitions, but some people's good wishes are
very well worth having."

Unwillingly Mary Cathcart raised her eyes. Her head was
still carried a little high and her cheeks were still glowing. Her
god might not be of pure gold throughout—such gods rarely are,
unfortunately—yet she was aware she still found him a very
worshipful kind of deity.

"Very well worth having," he repeated. "And so I should
like that poor, little chap to have your good wishes, Miss Cathcart.
Wish him all manner of nice things, for his mother's sake as well
as his own. There's been a pretty bad run of luck here lately,
and it's time it changed. Wish him better fortune than his forefathers. I'm not superstitious, as I say, but Richard Calmady's
death scared one a little. Five minutes beforehand it seemed
so utterly improbable. And then one began to wonder if there
could be any truth in the old legend. And that was ugly, you
know."

Dr. Knott glanced at the speaker sharply. — "Oh! that occurred to you, did it?" he said.

"Bless me! why, it occurred to everybody!" Ormiston answered impatiently. "Some idiot raked the story up, and it was canvassed from one end of the county to the other last autumn till it made me fairly sick."

"Poor boy!" cried Mrs. Ormiston. "And what is this wonderful story that so nauseates him, Dr. Knott?"

"I'm afraid I can't tell you," the doctor answered slowly. A nervous movement on the part of Julius March had attracted his attention. "I have never managed to get hold of the story as a whole, but I should like to do so uncommonly."

Julius pushed back his chair, and groped hurriedly for the dinner-napkin which had slipped to the ground from his knees. The subject of the conversation agitated him. The untidy, little chap-books, tied together with the tag of rusty ribbon, had lain undisturbed in the drawer of his library table ever since the—to him—very memorable evening, when, kneeling before the image of the stricken Mother and the dead Christ, he had found the man's heart under the priest's cassock and awakened to newness of life. Much had happened since then; and Julius had ranged himself, accepting, open-eyed, the sorrows and alleviations of the fate he had created for himself. But to-night he was tired. The mental and emotional strain of the last few days had been considerable. Moreover, John Knott's presence always affected him. The two men stood, indeed, at opposing poles of thought—the one spiritual and ideal, the other material and realistic. And, though he struggled against the influence, the doctor's rather brutal common sense and large knowledge of physical causes, gained a painful ascendency over his mind at close quarters. Knott, it must be owned, was slightly merciless to his clerical acquaintances. He loved to bait them, to impale them on the horns of some moral or theological dilemma. And it was partly with this purpose of harrying and worrying that he continued now :—

"Yes, Mrs. Ormiston, I should like to hear the story just as much as you would. And—it strikes me, if he pleased, Mr. March could tell it to us. Suppose you ask him to!"

Promptly the young lady fell upon Julius, regardless of Ormiston's hardly concealed displeasure.

"Oh! you bad man, what are you doing," she cried, "trying to conceal thrilling family legends from the nearest relatives? Tell us all about it, if you know, as Dr. Knott declares you do. I dote on terrifying stories—don't you, Mary?—that send the cold shivers all down my back. And if they deal with the history of my nearest and dearest, why, there's an added charm to them. Now, Mr. March, we're all attention. Stand and deliver, and make it all just as bad as you can."

"I am afraid I am not an effective *improvisatore*," he replied. "And the subject, if you will pardon my saying so, seems to me too intimate for mirth. A curse is supposed to rest on this place. The owners of Brockhurst die young and by violent means."

"We know that already, and look to you to tell us something more, Mr. March," Dr. Knott said dryly.

Julius was slightly nettled at the elder man's tone and manner. He answered with an accentuation of his usual refinement of enunciation and suavity of manner.

"There is a term to the curse—a saviour who, according to the old prediction, has the power, should he also have the will, to remove it altogether."

"Oh, really, is that so? And when does this saviour put in an appearance?" the doctor asked again.

"That is not revealed."

Julius would very gladly have said nothing further. But Dr. Knott's expression was curiously intent and compelling as he sat fingering the stem of his wine glass. All the ideality of Julius's nature rose in revolt against the half-sneering rationalism he seemed to read in that expression. Mrs. Ormiston, who had an hereditary racial appreciation of anything approaching a fight, turned her round eyes first on one speaker and then on the other provokingly, inciting them to more declared hostilities, while she bit her lips in the effort to avoid spoiling sport by untimely laughter or speech.

"But unhappily," Julius proceeded, yielding under protest to these opposing forces, "the saviour comes in so questionable a shape, that I fear, whenever the appointed time may be, his appearance will only be welcomed by the discerning few."

"That's a pity," Dr. Knott said. He paused a minute, passed his hand across his mouth.—"Still, if we are to believe the Bible, and other so-called sacred histories, it's been the way of saviours from the beginning to try the faith of ordinary mortals by presenting themselves under rather queer disguises."—He paused again, drawing in his wide lips, moistening them with his tongue. "But since you evidently know all about it, Mr. March, may I make bold to inquire in what special form of fancy dress the saviour in question is reported as likely to present himself?"

"He comes as a child of the house," Julius answered, with

dignity. " A child who in person—if I understand the wording of the prophecy aright—is half angel, half monster."

John Knott opened his mouth as though to give passage to some very forcible exclamation. Thought better of it and brought his jaws together with a kind of grind. His heavy figure seemed to hunch itself up as in the recoil from a blow.

"Curious," he said quietly. Yet Julius, looking at him, could have fancied that his weather-beaten face went a trifle pale.

But Mrs. Ormiston, in the interests of a possible fight, had contained herself just as long as was possible. Now she clapped her hands, and broke into a little scream of laughter.

"That's just the most magnificently romantic thing I ever heard!" she cried. "Come now, this requires further investigation. What's our baby like, Dr. Knott? I've seen nothing but an indistinguishable mass of shawls and flannels. Have we, by chance, got an angelic monstrosity upstairs without being aware of it?"

"Charlotte!" Roger Ormiston called out sternly. The young man looked positively dangerous. "This conversation has gone quite far enough. I agree with March, it may all be stuff and nonsense, not worth a second thought, still it isn't a thing to joke about."

"Very well, dear boy, be soothed then," she returned, making a little grimace and putting her head on one side coquettishly. "I'll be as solemn as nine owls. But you must excuse a momentary excitement. It's all news to me, you know. I'd no notion Katherine had married into such a remarkable family. I'm bound to learn a little more. Do you believe it's possible at all, Dr. Knott, now tell me?"

"The fulfilment of prophecy is rather a wide and burning question to embark on," he said. "With Captain Ormiston's leave, I think we'd better go back to the point we started from and drink the little gentleman's health. I have my patient to see again, and it is getting rather late."

The lady addressed, laughed, held up her glass, and stared round the table with a fine air of bravado, looking remarkably pretty.

"Fire away, Roger, dear fellow," she said. "We're loaded, and ready."

Thus admonished, Ormiston raised his glass too. But his temper was not of the sweetest, just then, he spoke forcedly.

"Here's to the boy," he said; "good luck, and good health,

and," he added hastily, "please God he'll be a comfort to his mother."

"Amen," Julius said softly.

Dr. Knott contemplated the contents of his glass, for a moment, whether critically or absently it would have been difficult to decide. But all the harshness had gone out of his face, and his loose lips worked into a smile pathetic in quality.

"To the baby.—And I venture to add a clause to your invocation of that heartless jade, Dame Fortune. May he never lack good courage and good friends. He will need both."

Julius March set down his wine untasted. He had received a very disagreeable impression.

"Come, come, it appears to me, we are paying these honours in a most lugubrious spirit," Mrs. Ormiston broke in. "I wish the baby a long life and a merry one, in defiance of all prophecies and traditions belonging to his paternal ancestry. Go on, Mr. March, you're shamefully neglecting your duty. No heel taps."

She threw back her head, showing the whole of her white throat, drained her glass and then flung it over her shoulder. It fell on the black, polished boards, beyond the edge of the carpet, shivered into a hundred pieces, that lay glittering, like scattered diamonds in the lamplight. For the day had died altogether. Fleets of dark, straggling cloud chased each other across spaces of pallid sky, against the earthward edge of which dusky tree-tops strained and writhed in the force of the tearing gale.

Mrs. Ormiston rose, laughing, from her place at table.

"That's the correct form," she said, "it ensures the fulfilment of the wish. You ought all to have cast away your glasses regardless of expense. Come, Mary, we will remove ourselves. Mind and bid me good-bye before you go, Dr. Knott, and report on Lady Calmady. It's probably the last time you'll have the felicity of seeing me. I'm off at cock-crow to-morrow morning."

CHAPTER VIII

ENTER A CHILD OF PROMISE

AFTER closing the door behind the two ladies, Ormiston paused by the near window and gazed out into the night. The dinner had been, in his opinion, far from a success. He feared his relation to Mary Cathcart had retrograded rather than progressed. He wished his sister-in-law would be more correct in speech and behaviour. Then he held the conversation had been in bad taste. The doctor should have abstained from pressing Julius with questions. He assured himself, again, that the story was not worth a moment's serious consideration; yet he resented its discussion. Such discussion seemed to him to tread hard on the heels of impertinence to his sister, to her husband's memory, and to this boy, born to so excellent a position and so great wealth. And the worst of it was that, like a fool, he had started the subject himself!

"The wind's rising," he remarked at last. "You'll have a rough drive home, Knott."

"It won't be the first one. And my beauty's of the kind which takes a lot of spoiling."

The answer did not please the young man. He sauntered across the room and dropped into his chair, with a slightly insolent demeanour.

"All the same, don't let me detain you," he said, "if you prefer seeing Lady Calmady at once and getting off."

"You don't detain me," Dr. Knott answered. "I'm afraid it's just the other way about and that I must detain you, Captain Ormiston, and that on rather unpleasant business."

Julius March had risen to his feet. "You—you have no fresh cause for anxiety about Lady Calmady?" he said hurriedly.

The doctor glanced up at the tall, spare, black figure and dark, sensitive face with a half-sneering, half-pitying smile.

"Oh no, no!" he replied; "Lady Calmady's going on splendidly. And it is to guard, just as far as we can, against cause for anxiety later, that I want to speak to Captain Ormiston now. We've got to be prepared for certain contingencies. Don't you go, Mr. March. You may as well hear what I've to say. It will interest you particularly, I fancy, after one or two things you have told us to-night!"

"Sit down, Julius, please."—Ormiston would have liked to maintain that same insolence of demeanour, but it gave before an apprehension of serious issues. He looked hard at the doctor, cudgelling his brains as to what the latter's enigmatic speech might mean—divined, put the idea away as inadmissible, returned to it, then said angrily:—"There's nothing wrong with the child, of course?"

Dr. Knott turned his chair sideways to the table and shaded his face with his thick, square hand.

"Well, that depends on what you call wrong," he slowly replied.

"It's not ill?" Ormiston said.

"The baby's as well as you or I—better, in fact, than I am, for I am confoundedly touched up with gout.   Bear that in mind, Captain Ormiston—that the child is well, I mean, not that I am gouty.   I want you to definitely remember that, you and Mr. March."

"Well, then, what on earth is the matter?" Ormiston asked sharply.   "You don't mean to imply it is injured in any way, deformed?"

Dr. Knott let his hand drop on the table.   He nodded his head.   Ormiston perceived, and it moved him strangely, that the doctor's eyes were wet.

"Not deformed," he answered.   "Technically you can hardly call it that, but maimed."

"Badly?"

"Well, that's a matter of opinion.   You or I should think it bad enough, I fancy, if we found ourselves in the same boat." He settled himself back in his chair.—"You had better understand it quite clearly," he continued, "at least as clearly as I can put it to you.   There comes a point where I cannot explain the facts but only state them.   You have heard of spontaneous amputation?"

Across Ormiston's mind came the remembrance of a litter of puppies he had seen in the sanctum of the veterinary surgeon of his regiment.   A lump rose in his throat.

"Yes, go on," he said.

"It is a thing that does not happen once in most men's experience.   I have only seen one case before in all my practice and that was nothing very serious.   This is an extraordinary example.   I need not remind you of Sir Richard Calmady's accident and the subsequent operation?"

"Of course not—go on," Ormiston repeated.

"In both cases the leg is gone from here," the doctor continued, laying the edge of his palm across the thigh immediately above the knee.   "The foot is there—that is the amazing part of it—and, as far as I can see, is well formed and of the normal size, but so embedded in the stump that I cannot discover whether the ankle-joint and bones of the lower leg exist in a contracted form or not."

Ormiston poured himself out a glass of port.   His hand shook so that the lip of the decanter chattered against the lip of the glass.   He gulped down the wine and, getting up, walked the length of the room and back again.

"God in heaven," he murmured, "how horrible !   Poor Kitty, how utterly horrible !—Poor Kitty."

For the baby, in his own fine completeness, he had as yet no feeling but one of repulsion.

"Can nothing be done, Knott?" he asked at last.

"Obviously nothing."

"And it will live?"

"Oh! bless you, yes! ' It'll live fast enough if I know a healthy infant when I see one. And I ought to know 'em by now. I've brought them into the world by dozens for my sins."

"Will it be able to walk?"

"Umph — well — shuffle," the doctor answered, smiling savagely to keep back the tears.

The young man leaned his elbows on the table, and rested his head on his hands. All this shocked him inexpressibly—shocked him almost to the point of physical illness. Strong as he was he could have fainted, just then, had he yielded by ever so little. And this was the boy whom they had so longed for then! The child on whom they had set such fond hopes, who was to be the pride of his young mother, and restore the so rudely shaken balance of her life! This was the boy who should go to Eton, and into some crack regiment, who should ride straight, who was heir to great possessions!

"The saviour has come, you see, Mr. March, in as thorough-paced a disguise as ever saviour did yet," John Knott said cynically.

"He had better never have come at all!" Ormiston put in fiercely, from behind his hands.

"Yes—very likely—I believe I agree," the doctor answered. "Only it remains that he has come, is feeding, growing, stretching, and bellowing too, like a young bull-calf, when anything doesn't suit him. He is here, very much here, I tell you. And so we have just got to consider how to make the best of him, both for his own sake and for Lady Calmady's. And you must understand he is a splendid, little animal, clean skinned and strong, as you would expect, being the child of two such fine young people. He is beautiful,—I am old fashioned enough, perhaps scientific enough, to put a good deal of faith in that notion,—beautiful as a child only can be who is born of the passion of true lovers."

He paused, looking somewhat mockingly at Julius.

"Yes, love is an incalculably great, natural force," he continued. "It comes uncommonly near working miracles at times, unconscious and rather deplorable miracles. In this case it has worked strangely against itself—at once for irreparable injury and for perfection. For the child is perfect, is superb, but for the one thing."

5

"Does my sister know?" Ormiston asked hoarsely.

"Not yet; and, as long as we can keep the truth from her, she had better not know. We must get her a little stronger, if we can, first. That woman, Mrs. Denny, is worth her weight in gold, and her weight's not inconsiderable. She has her wits about her, and has contrived to meet all difficulties so far."

Ormiston sat in the same dejected attitude.

"But my sister is bound to know before long."

"Of course. When she is a bit better she'll want to have the baby to play with, dress and undress it and see what the queer little being is made of. It's a way young mothers have, and a very pretty way too. If we keep the child from her she will grow suspicious, and take means to find out for herself, and that won't do. It must not be. I won't•be responsible for the consequences. So as soon as she asks a definite question, she must have a definite answer."

The young man looked up quickly.

"And who is to give the answer?" he said.

"Well, it rests chiefly with you to decide that. Clearly she ought not to hear this thing from a servant. It is too serious. It needs to be well told—the whole kept at a high level, if you understand me. Give Lady Calmady a great part and she will play it nobly. Let this come upon her from a mean, wet-nurse, hospital-ward sort of level, and it may break her. What we have to do is to keep up her pluck. Remember we are only at the beginning of this business yet. In all probability there are many years ahead. Therefore this announcement must come to Lady Calmady from an educated person, from an equal, from somebody who can see all round it. Mrs. Ormiston tells me she leaves here to-morrow morning?"

"Mrs. Ormiston is out of the question anyhow," Roger exclaimed rather bitterly.

Here Julius March, who had so far been silent, spoke, and, in speaking, showed what manner of spirit he was of. The doctor agitated him, treated him, moreover, with scant courtesy. But Julius put this aside. He could afford to forget himself in his desire for any possible mitigation of the blow which must fall on Katherine Calmady. And, listening to his talk, he had, in the last quarter of an hour, gained conviction not only of this man's ability, but of his humanity, of his possession of the peculiar gentleness which so often, mercifully, goes along with unusual strength. As the coarse-looking hand could soothe, touching delicately, so the hard intellect and rough tongue could, he believed, modulate themselves to very consoling and inspiring tenderness of thought and speech.

"We have you, Dr. Knott," he said. "No one, I think, could better break this terrible sorrow to Lady Calmady, than yourself."

"Thank you—you are generous, Mr. March," the other answered cordially; adding to himself :—"Got to revise my opinion of the black coat. Didn't quite deserve that after the way you've badgered him, eh, John Knott?"

He shrugged his big shoulders a little shamefacedly.

"Of course, I'd do my best," he continued. "But you see ten to one I shan't be here at the moment. As it is, I have neglected lingering sicknesses and sudden deaths, hysterical girls, croupy children, broken legs, and all the other pretty little amusements of a rather large practice, waiting for me. Suppose I happen to be twenty miles away on the far side of Westchurch, or seeing after some of Lady Fallowfeild's numerous progeny engaged in teething or measles? Lady Calmady might be kept waiting, and we cannot afford to have her kept waiting in this crisis."

"I wish to God my aunt, Mrs. St. Quentin, was here!" Ormiston exclaimed. "But she is not, and won't be, alas !"

"Well, then, who remains?"

As the doctor spoke he pressed his fingers against the edge of the table, leaned forward, and looked keenly at Ormiston. He was extremely ugly just then, ugly as the weather-worn gargoyle on some mediæval church tower, but his eyes were curiously compelling.

"Good heavens! you don't mean that I've got to tell her?" Ormiston cried.

He rose hurriedly, thrust his hands into his pockets, and walked a little unsteadily across to the window, crunching the shining pieces of Mrs. Ormiston's sacrificial wine glass under foot. Outside the night was very wild. In the colourless sky stars reeled among the fleets of racing cloud. The wind hissed up the grass slopes and shouted among the great trees crowning the ridge of the hill. The prospect was not calculated to encourage. Ormiston turned his back on it. But hardly more encouraging was the sombre, grey-blue-walled room. The vision of all that often returned to him afterwards in very different scenes—the tall lamps, the two men, so strangely dissimilar in appearance and temperament, sitting on either side the dinner-table with its fine linen and silver, wines and fruits, waiting silently for him to speak.

"I can't tell her," he said, "I can't. Damn it all, I tell you,

Knott, I daren't. Think what it will be to her! Think of being told that about your own child!"—Ormiston lost control of himself. He spoke violently. "I'm so awfully fond of her and proud of her," he went on. "She's behaved so splendidly ever since Richard's death, laid hold of all the business, never spared herself, been so able and so just. And now the baby coming, and being a boy, seemed to be a sort of let up, a reward to her for all her goodness. To tell her this horrible thing will be like doing her some hideous wrong. If her heart has to be broken, in common charity don't ask me to break it."

There was a pause. He came back to the table and stood behind Julius March's chair.

"It's asking me to be hangman to my own sister," he said.

"Yes, I know it is a confoundedly nasty piece of work. And it's rough on you, very rough. Only, you see, this hanging has to be put through — there's the nuisance. And it is just a question whether your hand won't be the lightest after all."

Again silence obtained, but for the rush and sob of the gale against the great house.

"What do you say, Julius?" Ormiston demanded at last.

"I suppose our only thought is for Katherine—for Lady Calmady?" he said. "And in that case I agree with Dr. Knott."

Roger took another turn to the window, stood there awhile struggling with his natural desire to escape from so painful an embassy.

"Very well, if you are not here, Knott, I undertake to tell her," he said at last. "Please God, she mayn't turn against me altogether for bringing her such news. I'll be on hand for the next few days, and—you must explain to Denny that I am to be sent for whenever I am wanted. That's all—I suppose we may as well go now, mayn't we?"

Julius knelt at the faldstool, without the altar rails of the chapel, till the light showed faintly through the grisaille of the stained-glass windows and outlined the spires and carven canopies of the stalls. At first his prayers were definite, petitions for mercy and grace to be outpoured on the fair, young mother and her, seemingly, so cruelly afflicted child; on himself, too, that he might be permitted to stay here, and serve her through the difficult future. If she had been sacred before, Katherine was doubly sacred to him now. He bowed himself, in reverential awe, before the thought of her martyrdom. How would her proud and naturally joyous spirit bear the bitter pains of it? Would it make, eventually, for evil or for good? And then—the ascetic within him asserting itself, notwithstanding the widening of outlook produced by the awakening of his heart—he was overtaken by a great horror of that which we call matter; by a revolt against the body, and those torments and shames, mental, moral, and physical, which the body brings along with it. Surely the dualists were right? It was unregenerate, a thing, if made by God, yet wholly fallen away from grace and given over to evil, this fleshly envelope wherein the human soul is seated, and which, even in the womb, may be infected by disease or rendered hideous by mutilation? Then, as the languor of his long vigil overcame him, he passed into an ecstatic contemplation of the state of that same soul after death, clothed with a garment of incorruptible and enduring beauty, dwelling in clear, luminous spaces, worshipping among the ranks of the redeemed, beholding its Lord God face to face.

John Knott, meanwhile, after driving home beneath the reeling stars, through the roar of the forest and shriek of the wind across the open moors, found an urgent summons awaiting him. He spent the remainder of that night, not in dreams of paradise and of spirits redeemed from the thraldom of the flesh, but in increasing the population of this astonishing planet, by assisting to deliver a scrofulous, half-witted, shrieking servant-girl of twins—illegitimate—in the fusty atmosphere of a cottage garret, right up under the rat-eaten thatch.

CHAPTER IX

IN WHICH KATHERINE CALMADY LOOKS ON HER SON

MORE than a week elapsed before Ormiston was called upon to redeem his promise. For Lady Calmady's convalescence was slow. An apathy held her, which was tranquillising rather than tedious. She was glad to lie still and rest. She found it very soothing to be shut away from the many obligations of active life for a while; to watch the sunlight, on fair days, shift from east by south to west, across the warm fragrant room; to see the changing clouds in the delicate, spring sky, and the slow-dying crimson and violet of the sunset; to hear the sudden hurry of falling rain, the subdued voices of the women in the adjoining nursery, and, sometimes, the lusty protestations of her baby when—as John Knott had put it—"things didn't suit him." She felt a little jealous of the comely, young wet-nurse, a little desirous to be more intimately acquainted with this small, new Richard Calmady, on whom all her hopes for the future were set. But, immediately, she was very submissive to the restrictions laid by Denny and the doctor upon her intercourse with the child. She only stood on the threshold of motherhood as yet. While the inevitable exhaustion, following on the excitement of her spring and summer of joy, her autumn of bitter sorrow, and her winter of hard work, asserted itself now that she had time and opportunity for rest.

The hangings and coverlet of the great, ebony, half-tester bed were lined with rose silk, and worked, with many coloured worsteds on a white ground, in the elaborate Persian pattern so popular among industrious ladies of leisure in the reign of good Queen Anne. It may be questioned whether the parable, wrought out with such patience of innumerable stitches, was closely comprehensible or sympathetic to the said ladies ; since a particularly wide interval, both of philosophy and practice, would seem to divide the temper of the early eighteenth century from that of the mystic East. Still the parable was there, plain to whoso could read it ; and not—perhaps rather pathetically—without its modern application.

The Powers of Evil, in the form of a Leopard, pursue the soul of man, symbolised by a Hart, through the Forest of This Life. In the midst of that same forest stands an airy, domed pavilion, in which—if so be it have strength and fleetness to reach it—the panting, hunted creature may, for a time, find security and repose. Above this resting-place the trees of the forest interlace their spreading branches, loaded with amazing leaves and fruit ; while companies of rainbow-hued birds, standing very upright upon nothing in particular, entertain themselves by holding singularly indigestible looking cherries and mulberries in their yellow beaks.

And so, Katherine, resting in dreamy quiet within the shade of the embroidered curtains, was even as the Hart pasturing in temporary security before the quaint pavilion. The mark of her bereavement was upon her sensibly still—would be so until the end. Often in the night, when Denny had at last left her, she would wake suddenly and stretch her arms out across the vacant space of the wide bed, calling softly to the beloved one who could give no answer, and then, recollecting, would sob herself again to sleep. Often, too, as Ormiston's step sounded through the Chapel-Room when he came to pay her those short, frequent visits, bringing the clean freshness of the outer air along with him, Katherine would look up in a wondering gladness, cheating herself for an instant with unreasoning delight—look up, only to know her sorrow, and feel the knife turn in the wound. Nevertheless these days made, in the main, for peace and healing. On more than one occasion she petitioned that Julius March should come and read to her, choosing, as the book he should read from, Spenser's *Faerie Queene*. He obeyed, in manner calm, in spirit deeply moved. Katherine spoke little. But her charm was great, as she lay, her eyes changeful in colour as a moorland stream, listening to those intricate stanzas, in which the large hope, the pride of honourable deeds, the virtue, the patriotism, the masculine fearlessness, the ideality, the fantastic imagination, of the English Renaissance so nobly finds voice. They comforted her mind, set by instinct and training to welcome all splendid adventures of romance, of nature, and of faith. They carried her back, in dear remembrance, to the perplexing and enchanting discoveries which Richard Calmady's visit to Ormiston Castle—the many-towered, grey house looking eastward across the unquiet sea—had brought to her. And specially did they recall to her that first evening—even yet she grew hot as she thought of it—when the supposed gentleman-jockey, whom she had purposed treating with gay and reducing indifference, proved not only fine scholar and fine gentleman, but absolute and indisputable master of her heart.

Dr. Knott came to see her, too, almost daily—rough, tender-hearted, humorous, dependable, never losing sight, in his intercourse with her, of the matter in hand, of the thing which immediately is.

Thus did these three men, each according to his nature and capacity, strive to guard the poor Hart, pasturing before the quaint pavilion, set—for its passing refreshment—in the midst of the Forest of This Life, and to keep, just so long as was possible, the pursuing Leopard at bay. Nevertheless the Leopard gained, despite of their faithful guardianship — which was inevitable, the case standing as it did.

For one bright afternoon, about three o'clock, Mrs. Denny arrived in the gun-room, where Ormiston sat smoking, while talking over with Julius the turf-cutting claims of certain squatters on Spendle Flats—arrived, not to summon the latter to further readings of the great Elizabethan poet, but to say to the former:—

"Will you please come at once, sir? Her ladyship is sitting

up. She is a little difficult about the baby—only, you know, sir, if I can say it with all respect, in her pretty, teasing way. But I am afraid she must be told."

And Roger rose and went — sick at heart. He would rather have faced an enemy's battery, vomiting out shot and shell, than gone up the broad, stately staircase, and by the silent, sunny passage-ways, to that fragrant, white-panelled room.

On the stands and tables were bowls full of clear-coloured, spring flowers — early primrose, jonquil, and narcissus. A wood-fire burned upon the blue-and-white tiled hearth. And on the sofa, drawn up at right angles to it, Katherine sat, wrapped in a grey, silk dressing-gown bordered with soft, white fur. She flushed slightly as her brother came in, and spoke to him with an air of playful apology.

"I really don't know why you should have been dragged up here, just now, dear old man! It is some fancy of Denny's. I'm afraid in the excess of her devotion she makes me rather a nuisance to you. And now, not contented with fussing about me, she has taken to being absurdly mysterious about the baby"—

She stopped abruptly. Something in the young man's expression and bearing impressed her, causing her to stretch out her hands to him in swift fear and entreaty.

"Oh, Roger!" she cried, "Roger—what is it?"

And he told her, repeating, with but a few omissions, the statement made to him by the doctor ten days ago. He dared not look at her while he spoke, lest seeing her should unnerve him altogether.

Katherine was very still. She made no outcry. Yet her very stillness seemed to him the more ominous, and the horror of the recital grew upon him. His voice sounded to him unnaturally loud and harsh in the surrounding quiet. Once her silken draperies gave a shuddering rustle—that was all.

At last it was over. At last he dared to look at her. The colour and youthful roundness had gone out of her face. It was grey as her dress, fixed and rigid as a marble mask. Ormiston was overcome with a consuming pity for her and with a violence of self-hatred. Hangman, and to his own sister —in truth, it seemed to him to have come to that! He knelt down in front of her, laying hold of both her knees.

"Kitty, can you ever forgive me for telling you this?" he asked hoarsely.

Even in this extremity Katherine's inherent sweetness asserted

itself. She would have smiled, but her frozen lips refused. Her
eyelids quivered a little and closed.

"I have nothing to forgive you, dear," she said. "Indeed,
it is good of you to tell me, since—since so it is."

She put her hands upon his shoulders, gripping them fast,
and bowed her head. The little flames crackled, dancing among
the pine logs, and the silk of her dress rustled as her bosom rose
and fell.

"It won't make you ill again?" Roger asked anxiously.

Katherine shook her head.

"Oh no!" she said, "I have no more time for illness. This
is a thing to cure, as a cautery cures—to burn away all idleness
and self-indulgent, sick-room fancies. See, I am strong, I
am well."

She stood up, her hands slipping down from Ormiston's
shoulders and steadying themselves on his hands as he too
rose. Her face was still ashen, but purpose and decision had
come into her eyes.

"Do this for me," she said, almost imperiously. "Go to
Denny, tell her to bring me the baby. She is to leave him with
me. And tell her, as she loves both him and me,—as she values
her place here at Brockhurst,—she is not to speak."

As he looked at her Ormiston turned cold. She was terrible
just then.

"Katherine," he said quickly, "what on earth are you going
to do?"

"No harm to my baby in any case—you need not be alarmed.
I am quite to be trusted. Only I cannot be reasoned with or
opposed, still less condoled with or comforted, yet. I want my
baby, and I must have him, here, alone, the doors shut—locked
if I please."—Her lips gave, the corners of her mouth drooped.
And watching her Ormiston swore a little under his breath.—
"We have something to say to each other, the baby and I," she
went on, "which no one else may hear. So do what I ask you,
Roger. And come back—I may want you—in about an hour,
if I do not send for you before."

Alone with her child, Lady Calmady moved slowly across
and bolted both the nursery and the Chapel-Room doors. Then
she drew a low stool up in front of the fire and sat down, laying
the infant upon her lap. It was a delicious, dimpled creature,
with a quantity of silky, golden-brown hair, that curled in a tiny
crest along the top of its head. It was but half awake yet, the
rounded cheeks pink with the comfort of food and slumber.
And as the beautiful, young mother, bending that set, ashen

face of hers above it, laid the child upon her knees, it stretched, clenching soft, baby fists and rubbing them into its blue eyes.

Katherine unwrapped the shawls, and took off one small garment after another—delicate gossamer - like things of fine flannel, lawn and lace, such as women's fingers linger over in the making with tender joy. Once her resolution failed her. She wrapped the half-dressed child in its white shawls again, rose from her place and walked over to the sunny window, carrying it in the hollow of her arm—it staring up, meanwhile, with the strange wonder of baby eyes, and cooing, as though holding communication with gracious presences haunting the moulded ceiling above. Katherine gazed at it for a few seconds. But the little creature's serene content, its absolute unconsciousness of its own evil fortune, pained her too greatly. She went back, sat down on the stool again, and completed the task she had set herself.

Then, the baby lying stark naked on her lap, she studied the fair, little face, the pencilled eyebrows and fringed eyelids—dark like her own,—the firm, rounded arms, the rosy-palmed hands, their dainty fingers and finger-nails, the well-proportioned and well-nourished body, without smallest mark or blemish upon it, sound, wholesome, and complete. All these she studied long and carefully, while the dancing glow of the firelight played over the child's delicate flesh, and it extended its little arms in the pleasant warmth, holding them up, as in act of adoration, towards those gracious unseen presences, still, apparently, hovering above the flood of instreaming sunshine against the ceiling overhead. Lastly she turned her eyes, with almost dreadful courage, upon the mutilated, malformed limbs, upon the feet—set right up where the knee should have been, thus dwarfing the child by a fourth of his height. She observed them, handled, felt them. And, as she did so, her mother-love, which, until now, had been but a part and consequence—since the child was his gift, the crown and outcome of their passion, his and hers—of the great love she bore her husband, became distinct from that, an emotion by itself, heretofore unimagined, pervasive of all her being. It had none of the sweet self - abandon, the dear enchantments, the harmonising sense of safety and repose, which that earlier passion had. This was altogether different in character, and made quite other demands on mind and heart. For it was fierce, watchful, anxious, violent with primitive instinct; the roots of it planted far back in that unthinkable remoteness of time, when the fertile womb of the great Earth Mother began to bring forth the first blind, simple forms of those countless generations of living creatures which, slowly differentiating themselves, slowly developing, have peopled this planet from that immeasurable past to the present hour. Love between man and woman must be forever young, even as Eros, Cupid, Krishna, are forever youthful gods. But mother-love is of necessity mature, majestic, ancient, from the stamp of primal experience which is upon it.

And so, at this juncture, realising that which her motherhood meant, her immaturity, her girlhood, fell away from Katherine Calmady. Her life and the purpose of it moved forward on another plane.

She bent down and solemnly kissed the unlovely, shortened limbs, not once or twice but many times, yielding herself up with an almost voluptuous intensity to her own emotion. She clasped her hands about her knees, so that the child might be enclosed, over-shadowed, embraced on all sides, by the living defences of its mother's love. Alone there, with no witnesses, she brooded over it, crooned to it, caressed it with an insatiable hunger of tenderness.

"And yet, my poor pretty, if we had both died, you and I, ten days ago," she murmured, "how far better! For what will you say to me when you grow older—to me who have brought you, without any asking or will of yours, into a world in which you must always be at so cruel a disadvantage? How will you bear it all when you come to face it for yourself, and I can no longer shield you and hide you away as I can do now? Will you have fortitude to endure, or will you become sour, vindictive, misanthropic, envious? Will you curse the hour of your birth?"

Katherine bowed her proud head still lower.

"Ah! don't do that, my darling," she prayed in piteous entreaty, "don't do that. For I will share all your trouble, do share it even now, beforehand, foreseeing it, while you still lie smiling unknowing of your own distress. I shall live through it many times, by day and night, while you live through it only once. And so you must be forbearing towards me, my dear one, when you come"—

She broke off abruptly, her hands fell at her sides, and she sat rigidly upright, her lips parted, staring blankly at the dancing flames.

In repeating Dr. Knott's statement Ormiston had purposely abstained from all mention of Richard Calmady's accident and its tragic sequel. He could not bring himself to speak to Katherine of that. Until now, dominated by the rush of her emotion, she had only recognised the bare terrible fact of the baby's crippled condition, without attempting to account for it. But, now, suddenly the truth presented itself to her. She understood that she was herself, in a sense, accountable—that the greatness of her love for the father had maimed the child.

As she realised the profound irony of the position, a blackness of misery fell upon Katherine. And then, since she was of a strong, undaunted spirit, an immense anger possessed her, a revolt against nature which could work such wanton injury, and against God, who, being all-powerful, could sit by and permit it so to work. All the foundations of faith and reverence were, for the time being, shaken to the very base.

She gathered the naked baby up against her bosom, rocking herself to and fro in a paroxysm of rebellious grief.

"God is unjust!" she cried aloud. "He takes pleasure in fooling us. God is unjust!"

CHAPTER X

THE BIRDS OF THE AIR TAKE THEIR BREAKFAST

ORMISTON'S first sensation on re-entering his sister's room was one of very sensible relief. For Katherine leaned back against the pink, brocade cushions in the corner of the sofa, with the baby sleeping peacefully in her arms. Her colour was more normal too, her features less masklike and set. The cloud which had shadowed the young man's mind for nearly a fortnight lifted. She knew—therefore, he argued, the worst must be over. It was an immense gain that this thing was fairly said. Yet, as he came nearer and sat down on the sofa beside her, Ormiston, who was a keen observer both of horses and women, became aware of a subtle change in Katherine. He was struck—he had never noticed it before—by her likeness to her—and his—father, whose stern, high-bred, clean-shaven face and rather inaccessible bearing and manner impressed his son, even to this day, as somewhat alarming. People were careful not to trifle with old Mr. Ormiston. His will was absolute in his own house, with his tenants, and in the great iron-works— almost a town in itself—which fed his fine fortune. While from his equals—even from his fellow-members of that not overreverent or easily impressible body, the House of Commons—he required and received a degree of deference such as men yield only to an unusually powerful character. And there was now just such underlying energy in Katherine's expression. Her eyes were dark, as a clear, midnight sky is dark, her beautiful lips compressed, but with concentration of purpose not with weakness of sorrow. The force of her motherhood had awakened in Katherine a latent, titanic element. Like "Prometheus Bound," chained to the rock, torn, her spirit remained unquelled. For good or evil—as the event should prove—she defied the gods.

And something of all this—though he would have worded it very differently in the vernacular of passing fashion—Ormiston perceived. She was unbroken by that which had occurred, and for this he was thankful. But she was another woman to her who had greeted him in pretty apology an hour ago. Yet, even recognising this, her first words produced in him a shock of surprise.

"Is that horse, the Clown, still at the stables?" she asked.

Ormiston thrust his hands into his pockets, and, sitting on the edge of the sofa with his knees apart, stared down at the carpet. The mention of the Clown always cut him, and raised in him a remorseful anger.—Yes she was like his father, going straight to the point, he thought. And, in this case, the point was acutely painful to him personally. Ormiston's moral courage had been severely taxed, and he had a fair share of the selfishness common to man. It was all very well, but he wished to goodness she had chosen some other subject than this. Yet he must answer.

"Yes," he said; "Willy Taylor has been leading the gallops for the two-year-olds on him for the last month."—He paused. "What about the Clown?"

"Only that I should be glad if you would tell Chifney he must find some other horse to lead the gallops."

Ormiston turned his head.

"I see—you wish the horse sold," he said, over his shoulder.

Katherine looked down at the sleeping baby, its round head, crowned by that delicious crest of silky hair, cuddled in against her breast. Then she looked in her brother's eyes full and steadily.

"No," she answered. "I don't want it sold. I want it shot —by you, here, to-night."

"By Jove!" the young man exclaimed, rising hastily and standing in front of her.

Katherine gazed up at him, and held the child a little closer to her breast.

"I have been alone with my baby. Don't you suppose I see how it has come about?" she asked.

"Oh, damn it all!" Ormiston cried. "I prayed at least you might be spared thinking of that."

He flung himself down on the sofa again—while the baby clenching its tiny fist, stretched and murmured in its sleep—and bowed himself together, resting his elbows on his knees and his chin in his hands.

"I'm at the bottom of it. It's all my fault," he said. "I am haunted by the thought of that day and night, for, if ever one man loved another, I loved Richard. And yet if I hadn't been so cursedly keen about the horse all this might never have happened. Oh! if you only knew how often I've wished myself dead since that ghastly morning. You must hate me, Kitty. You've cause enough. Yet how the deuce could I foresee what would come about?"

For the moment Katherine's expression softened. She laid her left hand very gently on his bowed head.

"I could never hate you, dear old man," she said. "You are innocent of Richard's death. But this last thing is different."— Her voice became fuller and deeper in tone. "And whether I am equally innocent of his child's disfigurement, God only knows—if there is a God, which perhaps, just now, I had better doubt, lest I should blaspheme too loudly, hoping my bitter words may reach His hearing."

Yet further disturbed in the completeness of its comfort, as it would seem, by the seriousness of her voice, the baby's mouth puckered. It began to fret. Katherine rose and stood rocking it, soothing it—a queenly, young figure in her clinging grey and white draperies, which the instreaming sunshine touched, as she moved, to a delicate warmth of colour.

"Hush, my pretty lamb," she crooned—and then softly yet fiercely to Ormiston :—"You understand, I wish it. The Clown is to be shot."

"Very well," he answered.

"Sleep—what troubles you, my precious," she went on. "I want it done, now, at once.—Hush, baby, hush.—The sun shall not go down upon my wrath, because my wrath shall be some-what appeased before the sunset."

Katherine swayed with a rhythmic motion, holding the baby a little away from her in her outstretched arms.

"Tell Chifney to bring the horse up to the square lawn, here, right in front of the house.—Hush, my kitty sweet.—He is to bring the horse himself. None of the stable boys or helpers are to come. It is not to be an entertainment, but an execution. I wish it done quietly."

"Very well," Ormiston repeated. He hesitated, strong protest rising to his lips, which he could not quite bring himself to utter. Katherine, the courage and tragedy of her anger, dominated him as she moved to and fro in the sunshine soothing her child.

"You know it's a valuable horse?" he remarked, at last, tentatively.

"So much the better. You do not suppose I should care to take that which costs me nothing? I am quite willing to pay.— Sleep, my pet, so—is that better?—I do not propose to defraud —hush, baby darling, hush—Richard's son of any part of his inheritance. Tell Chifney to name a price for the Clown, an outside price. He shall have a cheque to-morrow, which he is to enter with the rest of the stable accounts.—Now go, please. We understand each other clearly, and it is growing late.—Poor honey love, what vexes you?—You will shoot the Clown, here, before sunset. And, Roger, it must lie where it falls to-night. Let some of the men come early to-morrow, with a float. It is to go to the kennels."

Ormiston got up, shaking his shoulders as though to rid himself of some encumbering weight. He crossed to the fire-place and kicked the logs together.

"I don't half like it," he said. "I tell you I don't. It seems such a cold-blooded butchery. I can't tell if it's wrong or right. It seems merciless. And it is so unlike you, Kitty, to be merciless."

He turned to her as he spoke, and Katherine—her head erect, her eyes full of the sombre fire of her profound alienation and revolt—drew her hand slowly down over the fine lawn and lace of the baby's long, white robe, and held it flat against the soles of the child's hidden feet.

"Look at this," she said. "Remember, too, that the delight of my life has gone from me, and that I am young yet. The years will be many—and Richard is dead. Has much mercy been shown to me, do you think?"

And the young man seeing her, knowing the absolute sincerity of her speech, felt a lump rise in his throat. After all, when you have acted hangman to your own sister, as he reasoned, it is but a small matter to act slaughterman to a horse.

"Very well," he answered, huskily enough. "It shall be as you wish, Kitty. Only go back to the sofa, and stay there, please. If I think you are watching, I can't be quite sure of

myself. Something may go wrong, and we don't want a scene
which will make talk. This is a business which should be got
through as quickly and decently as possible."

The sun was but five minutes high and no longer brightened
the southern house-front, though it spread a ruddy splendour
over the western range of gables, and lingered about the stacks
of slender, twisted chimneys, and cast long, slanting shadows
across the lawns and carriage drives, before Lady Calmady's
waiting drew to a close. From the near trees of the elm avenue,
and from the wood overhanging the pond below the terraced
kitchen-gardens, came the singing of blackbirds and thrushes—
whether raised as evening hymn in praise of their Creator, or as
love-song each to his mate, who shall say? Possibly as both,
since in simple minds—and that assuredly is matter for thankfulness—earthly and heavenly affections are bounded by no harsh
dividing line. The chorus of song found its way in at the
windows of Katherine's room—fresh as the spring flowers which
filled it, innocent of hatred and wrong as the face of the now
placid baby, his soft cheeks flushed with slumber, as he nestled
in against his mother's bosom.

Indeed a long time had passed. Twice Denny had looked in
and, seeing that quiet reigned, had noiselessly withdrawn. For
Katherine, still physically weak, drained, moreover, by the greatness of her recent emotion, her senses lulled to rest by the warm
contact and even breathing of the child, had sunk away into a
dreamless sleep.

The questioning neigh of a stallion, a scuffle of horse hoofs,
footsteps approaching round the corner of the house, passing
across the broad, gravelled, carriage sweep and on to the turf,
aroused her. And these sounds were so natural, full of vigorous
outdoor life and the wholesome gladness of it, that for a moment
she came near repentance of her purpose. But then feeling, as
he rested on her arm, her baby's shortened, malformed limbs, and
thinking of her well-beloved dying, maimed and spent, in the
fulness of his manhood, her face took on that ashen pallor again
and all relenting left her. There was a satisfaction of wild
justice in the act about to be consummated. And Katherine
raised herself from the pink, brocade cushions and sat erect,
her lips parted in stern excitement, her forehead contracted in the
effort to hear, her eyes fixed on the wide, carven, ebony bed and
its embroidered hangings. The poor Hart had, indeed, ceased
to pasture in reposeful security before the quaint pavilion, set—
for its passing refreshment—in the midst of the Forest of This
Life. Now it fled, desperate, by crooked, tangled ways, over

rocks, through briars, while Care, the Leopard, followed hard behind.

First Roger Ormiston's voice reached her in brief direction, and the trainer's in equally brief reply. The horse neighed again —a sound strident and virile, the challenge of a creature of perfect muscle, hot desire, and proud, quick-coursing blood. Afterwards, an instant's pause, and Chifney's voice again—"So-ho—my beauty—take it easy—steady there, steady, good lad "— and the slap of his open hand on the horse's shoulder straightening it carefully into place. While, behind and below all this, in sweet incongruous undertone of uncontrollable joy, arose the carolling of the blackbirds and thrushes praising, according to their humble powers, God, life, and love.

Finally, as climax of the drama, the sharp report of a pistol, ringing out in shattering disturbance of the peace of the fair spring evening, followed by a dead silence, the birds all scared and dumb—a silence so dead, that Katherine Calmady held her breath, almost awed by it, while the hissing and crackling of the little flames upon the hearth seemed to obtrude as an indecent clamour. This lasted a few seconds. Then the noise of a plunging struggle and the muffled thud of something falling heavily upon the turf.

Dr. Knott had been up all night. But his patient, Lord Denier's second coachman, would pull through right enough, so he started on his homeward journey in a complacent frame of mind. He reckoned it would save him a couple of miles, let alone the long hill from Farley Row up to Spendle Flats, if on his way back from Grimshott he went by Brockhurst House. It is stretching a point, he admitted, to drive under even your neighbour's back windows at five o'clock in the morning. But the doctor being himself unusually amiable, was inclined to accredit others with a like share of good temper. Moreover, the natural man in him cried increasingly loudly for food and bed.

John Knott was not given to sentimental rhapsodies over the beauties of nature. Like other beauties she had her dirty enough moods, he thought. Still, in his own half-snarling fashion, he dearly loved this forest country in which he had been born and bred, while he was too keen a sportsman to be unobservant of any aspect of wind and weather, any movement of bird or beast. With the collar of his long, drab driving-coat turned up about his ears, and the stem of a well-coloured, meerschaum pipe between his teeth, he sat huddled together in the high, swinging gig, with Timothy, the weasel-faced, old groom, by his side. while the pageant of the opening day unfolded itself

6

before his somewhat critical gaze. He noted that it would be
fine, though windy. In the valley, over the Long Water, spread
beds of close, white mist. The blue of the upper sky was
crossed by curved winrows of flaky, opalescent cloud. In
the east, above the dusky rim of the fir woods on the edge
of the high-lying tableland, stretched a blinding blaze of rose-
saffron, shading through amber into pale primrose-colour above.
The massive house-front, and the walls fencing the three sides
of the square enclosure before it, with the sexagonal, pepper-pot
summer-houses at either corner, looked pale and unsubstantial in
that diffused, unearthly light. At the head of the elm avenue,
passing through the high, wrought-iron gates and along the
carriage drive which skirts the said enclosure,—the great, square
grass plot on the right hand, the red wall of the kitchen-gardens
on the left,—Dr. Knott had the reins nearly jerked out of his
hand. The mare started and swerved, grazing the off wheel
against the brickwork, and stopped, her head in the air, her
ears pricked, her nostrils dilated showing the red.

"Hullo, old girl, what's up? Seen a ghost?" he said,
drawing the whip quietly across the hollow of her back.

But the mare only braced herself more stiffly, refusing to
move, while she trembled and broke into a sudden sweat. The
doctor was interested and looked about him. He would first
find out the cause of her queer behaviour, and give her a good
dressing down afterwards if she deserved it.

The smooth, slightly up-sloping lawn was powdered with
innumerable dewdrops. In the centre of it, neck outstretched,
the fine legs doubled awkwardly together, the hind quarters and
barrel rising, as it lay on its side, in an unshapely lump, grey
from the drenching dew, was a dead horse. Along the top of
the farther wall a smart and audacious party of jackdaws had
stationed themselves, with much ruffling of grey, neck feathers,
impudent squeakings and chatter. While a pair of carrion crows
hopped slowly and heavily about the carcass, flapping up with a
stroke or two of their broad wings in sudden suspicion, then
settling down again nearer than before.

"Go to her head, Timothy, and get her by as quietly as you
can. I'll be after you in a minute, but I'm bound to see what
the dickens they've been up to here."

As he spoke Dr. Knott hitched himself down from off the gig.
He was cramped with sitting, and moved forward awkwardly,
his footsteps leaving a track of dark irregular patches upon the
damp grass. As he approached, the jackdaws flung themselves
gleefully upward from the wall, the sun glinting on their glossy

plumage as they circled and sailed away across the park. But the crow, who had just begun work in earnest, stood his ground notwithstanding the warning croak of his more timid mate. He grasped the horse's skull with his claws, and tore away greedily at the fine skin about the eye-socket with his strong, black beak.

"How's this, my fine gentleman, in too much of a hurry this morning to wait for the flavour to get into your meat?" John Knott said, as the bird rose sullenly at last. "Got a small hungry family at home, I suppose, crying 'give, give.' Well, that's taught better men than you, before now, not to be too nice, but to snatch at pretty well anything they can get."

He came close and stood looking meditatively down at the dead racehorse—recognised its long, white-reach face, the colour and make of it, while his loose lips worked with a contemptuous yet pitying smile.

"So that's the way my lady's taken it, has she?" he said presently. "On the whole I don't know that I'm sorry. In some cases much benefit unquestionably is derivable from letting blood. This shows she doesn't mean to go under, if I know her, and that's a mercy, for that poor, little beggar, the baby's sake."

He turned and contemplated the stately façade of the house. The ranges of windows, blind with closed shutters and drawn curtains, in the early sunshine gave off their many panes a broad dazzle of white light.

"Poor, little beggar," he repeated, "with his forty thousand a year and all the rest of it. Such a race to run and yet so badly handicapped!"

He stooped down, examined the horse, found the mark of the bullet.

"Contradictory beings, though, these dear women," he went on. "So fanciful and delicate, so sensitive you're afraid to lay a finger on them. So unselfish, too, some of them, they seem too good for this old rough and tumble of a world. And yet touch 'em home, and they'll show an unscrupulous savagery of which we coarse brutes of men should be more than half ashamed. God Almighty made a little more than He bargained for when He made woman. She must have surprised Him pretty shrewdly, one would think, now and then since the days of the apple and the snake."

He moved away up the carriage drive, following Timothy, the sweating, straining mare, and swinging gig. The carrion crow flapped back, with a croak, and dropped on the horse's skull again. Hearing that bodeful sound the doctor paused a moment, knocking the ashes out of his pipe, and looked round at the bird and its ugly work set as foreground to that pure glory of the sunrise, and the vast and noble landscape, misty valley, dewy grassland, far-ranging hillside crowned with wood.

"The old story," he muttered, "always repeating itself! And it strikes one as rather a wasteful, clumsy contrivance, at times. Life forever feeding on death—death forever breeding life."

Thus ended the Clown, own brother to Touchstone, race-horse of merry name and mournful memory, paying the penalty of wholly involuntary transgressions. From which ending another era dated at Brockhurst, the most notable events of which it is the purpose of the ensuing pages duly to set forth.

BOOK II

THE BREAKING OF DREAMS

CHAPTER I

RECORDING SOME ASPECTS OF A SMALL PILGRIM'S PROGRESS

I T is an ill wind that blows nobody good, says the comfortable
proverb. Which would appear to be but another manner
of declaring that the law of compensation works permanently in
human affairs. All quantities, material and immaterial alike, are,
of necessity, stable ; therefore the loss or defect of one participant
must—indirectly, no doubt, yet very surely—make for the gain
of some other. As of old, so now, the blood of the martyrs is
the seed of the Church.

Julius March would, how gladly, have been among the
martyrs ! But the lot fell otherwise. And—always admitting
the harshness of the limitations he had imposed on himself—
the martyrdom of those he held dearest, did, in fact, work to
secure him a measure of content that had otherwise been
unattainable. The twelve years following the birth of Lady
Calmady's child were the most fruitful of his life. He filled a
post no other person could have filled ; one which, while satisfying
his religious sense and priestly ideal of detachment, appeased the
cravings of his heart and developed the practical man in him.
The contemplative and introspective attitude was balanced by an
active and objective one. For he continued to live under his
dear lady's roof, seeing her daily and serving her in many
matters. He watched her, admiring her clear yet charitable
judgment and her prudence in business. He bowed in reverence
before her perfect singleness of purpose. He was almost
appalled apprehending, now and then, the secret abysses of
her womanhood, the immensity of her self-devotion, the swing
of her nature from quick, sensitive shrinking to almost impious

pride.   Man is the outcome of the eternal common sense;
woman that of some moment of divine folly.   Meanwhile the
ways of true love are many, and Julius March, thus watching
his dear lady, discovered, as other elect souls have discovered
before him, that the way of chastity and silence, notwithstanding
its very constant heartache, is by no means among the least
sweet.   The entries in his diaries of this period are intermittent,
concise, and brief—naturally enough, since the central figure of
Julius's mental picture had ceased, happily for him, to be Julius
himself.

And, not only Katherine's sorrows, but the unselfish action
of another woman, went to make Julius March's position at
Brockhurst tenable.   A few days after Ormiston's momentous
interview with his sister, news came of Mrs. St. Quentin's death.
She had passed hence peacefully in her sleep.   Knowledge of
the facts of poor, little Dickie Calmady's ill-fortune had been
spared her.   For it would be more satisfactory—so Mademoiselle
de Mirancourt had remarked, not without a shade of irony—that
if Lucia St. Quentin must learn the sad fact at all, she should
learn it where *le bon Dieu* Himself would be at hand to explain
matters, and so, in a degree, set them right.

Early in April Mademoiselle de Mirancourt had gathered
together her most precious possessions and closed the pretty
apartment in the rue de Rennes.   It had been a happy halting-
place on the journey of life.   It was haunted by well-beloved
ghosts.   It cost her not a little to bid it, the neighbouring church
of the St. Germain des Près, where she had so long worshipped,
and her little *coterie* of intimate friends, farewell.   Yet she set
forth, taking with her Henriette, the hard-featured, old, Breton
maid, and *Monsieur Pouf*, the grey, Persian cat,—he protesting
plaintively from within a large, Manilla basket,—and thus accompanied, made pilgrimage to Brockhurst.   And when Katherine,
all the lost joys of her girlhood assailing her at sight of her
lifelong friend, had broken down for once, and, laying her
beautiful head on the elder woman's shoulder, had sobbed out
a question as to when this visit must end, Marie de Mirancourt
had answered :—

"That, most dear one, is precisely as you shall see fit to
decide.   It need not end till I myself end, if you so please."

And when Katherine, greatly comforted yet fearing to be
over-greedy of comfort, had reasoned with her, reminding her of
the difference of climate, the different habits of living in that gay,
little, Paris home and this great, English country-house ; reminding her, further, of her so often and fondly expressed desire to

retire from the world while yet in the complete possession of her
powers and prepare for the inevitable close within the calm
and sacred precincts of the convent—the other replied almost
gaily :—

"Ah, my child! I have still a naughty little spirit of experiment in me which defies the barbarities of your climate.   While
as to the convent, it has beckoned so long—let it beckon still!
It called first when my *fiancé* died,—God rest his soul,—worn
out by the hardships he endured in the war of La Vendée, and
I put from me, forever, all thought of marriage.   But then my
mother, an emigrant here in London, claimed all my care.   It
called me again when she departed, dear saintly being.   But
then there were my brother's sons—orphaned by the guillotine—
to place.   And when I had established them honourably, our
beloved Lucia turned to me, with her many enchantments and
exquisite tragedy of the heart.   And, now, in my old age I come
to you—whom I receive from her as a welcome legacy—to
remain just so long as I am not a burden to you.   Second
childhood and first should understand one another.   We will
play delightful games together, the dear baby and I.   So let the
convent beckon.   For the convent is perhaps, after all, but an
impatient grasping at the rest of paradise, before that rest is
fairly earned.   I have a good hope that, after all, we give ourselves most acceptably to God in thus giving ourselves to His
human creatures."

Thus did Marie de Mirancourt, for love's sake, condemn
herself to exile, thereby rendering possible—among other things
—Julius's continued residence at Brockhurst.   For Captain
Ormiston had held true to his resolve of scorning the delights
of idleness, the smiles of ladies more fair and kind than wise,
and all those other pleasant iniquities to which idleness inclines
the young and full-blooded, of bidding farewell to London and
Windsor, and proceeding to "live laborious days" in some far
country.   He had offered to remain indefinitely with Katherine
if she needed him.   But she refused.   Let him be faithful to the
noble profession of arms and make a name for himself therein.

"Brockhurst has ceased to be a place for a soldier," she
said.   "Leave it to women and priests!"   And then, repenting
of the bitterness of her speech, she added :—"Really there is
not more work than I can manage, with Julius to help me at
times.   Iles is a good servant if a little tediously pompous, and
Chifney must see to the stables."—Lady Calmady paused, and
her face grew hard.   But for her husband's dying request, she
would have sold every horse in the stud, razed the great square

of buildings to the ground and made the site of it a dunghill.—
"Work is a drug to deaden thought. So it is a kindness to let
me have plenty of it, dear old man. And I fear, even when the
labour of each day is done, and Dickie is safe asleep,—poor
darling,—I shall still have more than enough of time for thought,
for asking those questions to which there seems no answer, and
for desires, vain as they are persistent, that things were somehow,
anyhow, other than they are!"

Therefore it came about that a singular quiet settled down
on Brockhurst—a quiet of waiting, of pause, rather than of
accomplishment. But Julius March, for reasons aforesaid, and
Mademoiselle de Mirancourt, in virtue of her unclouded faith
in the teachings of her Church,—which assures its members of
the beneficent purpose working behind all the sad seeming of
this world,—alike rejoiced in that. A change of occupations
and of interests came naturally with the change of the seasons,
with the time to sow and reap, to plant saplings, to fell timber,
to fence, to cut copsing, to build or rebuild, to receive rents or
remit them, to listen to many appeals, to readjust differences, to
feed game or to shoot it, to bestow charity of meat and fuel, to
haul ice in winter to the ice-house from the lake. But beyond
all this there was little of going or coming at Brockhurst. The
magnates of the countryside called at decent intervals, and at
decent intervals Lady Calmady returned their civilities. But
having ceased to entertain, she refused to receive entertainment.
She shut herself away in somewhat jealous seclusion, defiant of
possibly curious glances and pitying tongues. Before long her
neighbours, therefore, came to raise their eyebrows a little in
speaking of her, and to utter discreet regrets that Lady Calmady,
though handsome and charming when you met her, was so very
eccentric, adding:—"Of course everyone knows there is something very uncomfortable about the little boy!" Then would
follow confidences as to the disastrous results of popish influences
and Romanising tendencies, and an openly expressed conviction
—more especially on the part of ladies blessed with daughters
of marriageable age—that it would have been so very much
better for many people if the late Sir Richard Calmady had
looked nearer home for a bride.

But these comments did not affect Katherine. In point of
fact they rarely reached her ears. Alone among her neighbours,
Mary Cathcart, of the crisp, black hair and gipsy-like complexion,
was still admitted to some intimacy of intercourse. And the
girl was far too loyal either to bring in gossip or to carry it out.
Brockhurst held the romance of her heart. And, notwithstand-

ing the earnest wooing—as the years went on—of more than
one very eligible gentleman, Brockhurst continued to hold it.

Meanwhile the somewhat quaint fixed star around which
this whole system of planets, large and small, very really re-
volved, shone forth upon them all with a cheerful enough light.
For Dickie by no means belied the promise of his babyhood.
He was a beautiful and healthy little boy, with a charming
brilliance of colouring, warm and solid in tone. He had his
mother's changeful eyes, though the blue of them was brighter
than hers had now come to be. He had her dark eyebrows
and eyelashes too, and her finely curved lips. While he bore
likeness to his father in the straight, square-tipped nose and
the close-fitting cap of bright, brown hair with golden stains in
it, growing low in short curling locks on the broad forehead and
the nape of the neck—expressing the shape of the head very
definitely, and giving it something of antique nobility and grace.

And the little lad's appearance afforded, in these pleasant
early days at all events, fair index to his temperament. He was
gay-natured, affectionate, intelligent, full of a lively yet courteous
curiosity, easily moved to laughter, almost inconveniently fearless
and experimental ; while his occasional thunderbursts of passion
cleared off quickly into sunshine and blue sky again. For as yet
the burden of deformity rested upon him very lightly. He associated hardly at all with other children, and so had but scant
occasion to measure his poor powers of locomotion against their
normal ones. Lady Fallowfeild it is true, in obedience to suggestions on the part of her kindly lord and master, offered
tentatively to import a carriage-load—little Ludovic Quayle was
just the same age as Dickie—from the Whitney nurseries to
spend the day at Brockhurst.

"Good fellow, Calmady. I liked Calmady," Lord Fallowfeild had said to her. His conversation, it may be observed,
was nothing if not interjectional.—"Pretty woman, Lady Calmady — terrible thing for her being left as she is. Always
shall regret Calmady. Very sorry for her. Always have been
sorry for a pretty woman in trouble. Ought to see something
of her, my dear. The two estates join, and, as I always have
said, it's a duty to support your own class. Can't expect the
masses to respect you unless you show them you're prepared to
stand by your own class. Just take some of the children over to
see Lady Calmady. Pretty children, do her good to see them.
Rode uncommonly straight did Calmady. Terribly upsetting
thing his funeral. Never shall forget it. Always did like
Calmady—good fellow, Calmady. Nasty thing his death."

But Katherine's pen was fertile in excuses to avoid the invasion from Whitney. Lady Fallowfeild's small brains and large domestic complacency were too trying to her. And that noble lady, it must be owned, was secretly not a little glad to have her advances thus firmly, though gently, repulsed. For she was alarmed at Lady Calmady's reported acquaintance with foreign lands and with books; added to which her simple mind harboured much grisly though vague terror concerning the Roman Church. Picture all her brood of little Quayles incontinently converted into little monks and nuns with shaven heads! How such sudden conversion could be accomplished Lady Fallowfeild did not presume to explain. It sufficed her that "everybody always said Papists were so dreadfully clever and unscrupulous you never could tell what they might not do next."

Once, when Dickie was about six years old, Colonel St. Quentin brought his young wife and two little girls to stay at Brockhurst. Katherine had a great regard for her cousin, yet the visit was never repeated. On the flat poor Dick could manage fairly well, his strangely shod feet travelling laboriously along in effort after rapidity; his hands hastily outstretched now and again to lay hold of door-jamb or table-edge, since his balance was none of the securest. But in that delightfully varied journey from the nursery, by way of his mother's bedroom, the Chapel-Room next door, the broad stair-head,—with its carven balusters, shiny oak flooring, and fine landscapes by Claude and Hobbema,—the state drawing-room and libraries, to that America of his childish dreams, that country of magnificent distances and large possibility of discovery, the Long Gallery, he was speedily distanced by the three-year-old Betty, let alone her six-year-old sister Honoria, a tall, slim, little maiden, daintily high-bred of face and fleet of foot as a hind. This was bad enough. But the stairways afforded yet more afflicting experiences. The descent of even the widest and shallowest flights presented matter of insuperable difficulty, while the ascent was only to be achieved by recourse to all-fours, against the ignominy of which mode of progression Dickie's soul revolted. And so the little boy concluded that he did not care much about little girls. And confided to his devoted play-fellow Clara—Mrs. Denny's niece and sometime second still-room maid, now promoted, on account of her many engaging qualities, to be Dickie's special attendant—that:—

"They went so quick, they always left him behind, and it was not nice to be left behind, and it was very rude of them to do it; didn't Clara think so?"

And Clara, as in duty and affection bound, not without additional testimony in a certain dimness of her pretty, honest, brown eyes, did indeed very much think so.   It followed, therefore, that Dickie saw the St. Quentin family drive away, nurses and luggage complete, quite unmoved.   And returned, with satisfaction and renewed self-confidence, to the exclusive society of all those dear, grown-up people—gentle and simple—who were never guilty of leaving him behind—to that of Camp, the old, white bull-dog, and young Camp, his son and heir, who, if they so far forgot themselves as to run away, invariably ran back again and apologised, fawning upon him and pushing their broad, ugly, kindly muzzles into his hands—and to that of *Monsieur Pouf,* the grey Persian cat, who, far from going too quickly, displayed such majestic deliberation of movement and admirable dignity of waving fluffed tail, that it required much patient coaxing on Dickie's part ever to make him leave his cushion by the fire and go at all.

But, with the above-mentioned exception, the little boy's self-content suffered but slight disturbance.   He took himself very much for granted.   He was very curious of outside things, very much amused.   Moreover, he was king of a far from contemptible kingdom ; and in the blessed ignorance of childhood —that finds pride and honour in things which a wider and sadder knowledge often proves far from glad or glorious—it appeared to him not unnatural that a king should differ, even to the point of some slightly impeding disabilities, from the rank and file of his obedient and devoted subjects.   For Dickie, happily for him, was as yet given over to that wholly pleasant vanity, the aristocratic idea.   The rough justice of democracy, and the harsh breaking of all purely personal and individualistic dreams that comes along with it, for him, was not just yet.

And Richard's continued and undismayed acquiescence in his physical misfortune was fostered, indirectly, by the captivating poetry of myth and legend with which his mind was fed. He had an insatiable appetite for stories, and Mademoiselle de Mirancourt was an untiring *raconteuse.*   On Sunday afternoons upon the terrace, when the park lay bathed in drowsy sunshine and sapphire shadows haunted the under edge of the great woods, the pretty, old lady—her eyes shining with gentle laughter, for Marie de Mirancourt's faith had reached the very perfect stage in which the soul dares play, even as lovers play, with that it holds most sacred—would tell Dickie the fairy tales of her Church.   Would tell him of blessed St. Francis and of Poverty, his sweet, sad bride ; of his sermon to

the birds dwelling in the oak groves along Tiber valley ; of the
mystic stigmata, marking as with nail-prints his hands and feet,
and of that indomitable love towards all creatures, which found,
alike in the sun in heaven and the heavy - laden ass, brothers
and friends. Or she would tell him of that man of mighty
strength and stature, St. Christopher, who, in the stormy
darkness, — yielding to its reiterated entreaties,—set forth to
bear the little child across the wind-swept ford.   How he
staggered, in midstream, amazed and terrified under the awful
weight of that, apparently so light, burden; to learn, on
struggling ashore at last, that he had borne upon his shoulder
no mortal infant, but the whole world and the eternal maker
of it, Christ Himself.

These and many another wonder tale of Christian miracle did
she tell to Dickie—he squatting on a rug beside her, resting his
curly head against her knees, while the pink-footed pigeons
hurried hither and thither, picking up the handfuls of barley he
scattered on the flags, and the peacocks sunned themselves with
a certain worldly and disdainful grace on the hand-rails of the
grey balustrades, and young Camp, after some wild skirmish in
search of sport, flung himself down panting, his tongue lolling
out of his grinning jaws, by the boy's side.

And Katherine, putting aside her cares as regent of Dickie's
kingdom and the sorrow that lay so chill against her heart,
would tell him stories too, but of a different order of sentiment
and of thought.   For Katherine was young yet, and her stories
were gallant—since her own spirit was very brave—or merry,
because it delighted her to hear the boy laugh.   And often, as
he grew a little older, she would sit with her arm round him, in
the keen, winter twilights before the lamps were lit, on the broad,
cushioned bench of the oriel window in the Chapel - Room.
Outside, the stars grew in number and brightness as the dusk
deepened.   Within, the firelight played over the white-panelled
walls, revealing fitfully the handsome faces of former Calmadys
—shortlived, passing hence all unsated with the desperate joys
of living — painted by Vandyke and Sir Peter Lely, or by
Romney and Sir Joshua.   Then she would tell him not only of
Aladdin, of Cinderella, and time-honoured Puss-in-Boots, but
of Merlin the great enchanter, and of King Arthur and his
company of noble knights.   And of the loves of Sigurd the
Niblung and Brunhilda the wise and terrible queen, and of their
lifelong sorrow, and of the fateful treasure of fairy gold which
lies buried beneath the rushing waters of the Rhine.   Or she
would tell him of those cold, clear, far-off times in the northern

sojourning places of our race—tell him of the cow Audhumla, alone in the vast plain at the very beginning of things, licking the stones crusted over with hoar frost and salt, till, on the third day, there sprung from them a warrior named Bur, the father of Bör, the father of Odin, who is the father of all the gods. She would tell him of wicked Loki too, the deceiver and cunning plotter against the peace of heaven. And of his three evil children—here Dickie would, for what reason he knew not, always feel his mother hold him more closely, while her voice took a deeper tone—Fenrir the wolf, who, when Thor sought to bind him, bit off the brave god's right hand; and Jörmungand the Midgard serpent, who, tail in mouth, circles the world; and Hela, the pale queen, who reigns in Niflheim over the dim kingdoms of the dead. And of Baldur the bright-shining god, joy of Asgard, slain in error by Höder his blind twin-brother, for whom all things on earth—save one—weep, and will weep, till in the last days he comes again. And of All-Father Odin himself, plucking out his right eye and bartering it for a draught of wisdom-giving water from Mirmir's magic well. Again, she would tell him of the End—which it must be owned frightened Dickie a little, so that he would stroke her cheek, and say softly: —"But, mummy, you really are sure, aren't you, it won't happen for a good while yet?"—Of Ragnarök, the Twilight of the Gods, of the Fimbul winter, and cheerless sun and hurrying, blood-red moon, and all the direful signs which must needs go before the last great battle between good and evil.

And through all of these stories, of Christian and heathen origin alike, Richard began dimly, almost unconsciously, to trace, recurrent as a strain of austere music, the idea—very common to ages less soft and fastidious than our own—of payment in self-restraint and labour, or in actual bodily pain, loss, or disablement, for all good gained and knowledge won.

He found the same idea again when, under the teaching of Julius March, he began reading history, and when his little skill in Greek and Latin carried him as far as the easier passages of the classic poets. Dick was a very apt, if somewhat erratic and inaccurate, scholar. His insatiable curiosity drove him forward. He scurried, in childish fashion by all short-cuts available, to get at the heart of the matter—a habit of mind detestable to pedants, since to them the letter is the main object, not the spirit. Happily Julius was ceasing to be a pedant, even in matters ecclesiastical. He loved the little boy, the mingled charm and pathos of whose personality held him as with a spell. With untiring patience he answered, to the best of his ability,

Dickie's endless questions, of how and why. And, perhaps, he learned even more than he taught, under this fire of cross-examination. He had never come intimately in contact with a child's mind before; and Dickie's daring speculations and suggestions opened up very surprising vistas at times. The boy was a born adventurer, a gaily audacious sceptic moreover, notwithstanding his large swallow for romance, until his own morsel of reason and sense of dramatic fitness were satisfied.

And so, having once apprehended that idea of payment, he searched for justification of it instinctively in all he saw and read. He found it again in the immortal story of the siege of Troy, and in the long wanderings and manifold trials of that most experimental of philosophers, the great Ulysses. He found it too in more modern and more authentic history—in the lives of Galileo and Columbus, of Sir Walter Raleigh and many another hero and heroine, of whom, because of some unusual excellence of spirit or attainment, their fellow-men, and, as it would seem, the very gods themselves, have grown jealous, not enduring to witness a beauty rivalling or surpassing their own.

The idea was all confused as yet, coloured by childish fancies, instinctive merely, not realised. Yet it occupied a very actual place in the little boy's mind. He lingered over it silently, caressing it, returning to it again and again in half-frightened delight. It lent a fascination, somewhat morbid perhaps, to all ill-favoured and unsightly creatures—to blind-worms and slow-moving toads, to trapped cats, and dusty, dis-abled, winter flies; to a winged sea-gull, property of Bushnell, one of the under-gardeners, that paced, picking up loathsome living in the matter of slugs and snails, about the cabbage beds, all the tragedy of its lost power of flight and of the freedom of the sea in its wild, pale eyes.

It further provoked Dickie to expend his not incon-siderable gift of draughtsmanship in the production of long processions of half-human monsters of a grotesque and essentially uncomfortable character. He scribbled these upon all avail-able pieces of paper, including the fly-leaves of Todhunter's Arithmetic, and of his Latin and Greek primers. In an evil hour, for the tidiness of his school books, he came across the ballad of "Aiken-Drum," with its rather terrible mixture of humour, realism, and pathos. From thenceforth for some weeks — though he adroitly avoided giving any direct account of the origin of these grisly, imaginative freaks—many margins were adorned, or rather defaced, by fancy portraits of that "foul and stalwart ghaist" the Brownie of Badnock.

So did Dickie dwell, through all his childhood and the early years of youth, in the dear land of dreams, petted, considered, sheltered with perhaps almost cruel kindness, from the keen winds of truth that blow forever across the world.   Which winds, while causing all to suffer, and bringing death to the weak and fearful, to the lovers of lies and the makers of them, go in the end to strengthen the strong who dare face them, and fortify these in the acceptance of the only knowledge really worth having—namely the knowledge that romance is no exclusive property of the past, or eternal life of the future, but that both these are here, immediately and actually, for whoso has eyes to see and courage to possess.

The fairest dreams are true.   Yet it is so ordered that to know that we must awake from them.   And the awakening is an ugly process enough, too often.   When Dickie was about thirteen, the awakening began for him.   It came in time-honoured forms—those of horses and of a woman.

CHAPTER II

IN WHICH OUR HERO IMPROVES HIS ACQUAINTANCE WITH
MANY THINGS—HIMSELF INCLUDED

IT came about in this wise.   Roger Ormiston was expected at Brockhurst, after an absence of some years.   He had served with distinction in the Sikh war; and had seen fighting on the grand scale in the battles of Sobraon and Chillianwallah.   Later the restless genius of travel had taken hold on him, leading him far eastward into China, and northward across the Himalayan snows.   He had dwelt among strange peoples and looked on strange gods.   He had hunted strange beasts, moreover, and learnt their polity and their ways.   He had seen the bewildering fecundity of nature in the tropic jungle, and her barren and terrible beauty in the out-stretch of the naked desert.   And the thought of all this set Dickie's imagination on fire.   The return of Roger Ormiston was, to him, as the return of the mighty Ulysses himself.

For a change was coming over the boy.   He began to weary of fable and cry out for fact.   He had just entered his fourteenth year.   He was growing fast; and, but for that dwarfing deformity, would have been unusually tall, graceful and well-proportioned.   But along with this increase of stature had come a listlessness and languor which troubled Lady Calmady. The boy was sweet-tempered enough, had his hours, indeed, of overflowing fun and high spirits. Still he was restless and tired easily of each occupation in turn. He developed a disquieting relish for solitude. And took to camping-out on one of the broad window-seats of the Long Gallery, in company with volumes of Captain Cook's and Hakluyt's voyages, old-time histories of sport and natural history; not to mention Robinson Crusoe and the merry if but doubtfully decent pages of Geoffrey Gambado. And his mother noted, not without a sinking of the heart, that the window-seat which in his solitary moods Dickie most frequented was precisely that one of the eastern bay which commanded—beyond the smooth, green expanse and red walls of the troco-ground—a good view of the grass ride, running parallel with the lime avenue, along which the horses from the racing-stables were taken out and back, morning and evening, to the galloping ground. Then fears began to assail Katherine that the boy's childhood, the content and repose of it, were nearly past. Small wonder that her heart should sink!

On the day of her brother's return, Katherine, after rather anxious search, so found Richard. He was standing on the book-strewn window-seat. He had pushed open the tall narrow casement and leaned out. The April afternoon was fitfully bright. A rainbow spanned the landscape, from the Long Water in the valley to the edge of the forest crowning the tableland. Here and there showers of rain fell, showing white against huge masses of purple cloud piled up along the horizon.

And as Katherine drew near, threading her way carefully between the Chinese cabinets, oriental jars, and many quaint treasures furnishing the end of the great room, she saw that, along the grass ride, some twenty racehorses came streeling homeward in single file—a long line of brown, chestnut, black, and of the raw yellows and scarlets of horse-clothing, against the delicate green of springing turf and opening leaves. Beside them, clad in pepper-and-salt mixture breeches and gaiters complete, Mr. Chifney pricked forward soberly on his handsome grey cob. The boys called to one another now and then, admonished a fretful horse breaking away from the string. One of them whistled shrilly a few bars of that popular but un-distinguished tune—"Pop goes the weasel." And Richard craned far out, steadying himself against the stone mullion on either side with uplifted hands, heedless alike of his mother's presence and of the heavy drops of rain which splattered in at the open casement.

"Dickie, Dickie," Katherine called, in swift anxiety. "Be careful. You will fall."

She came close, putting her arm round him.—"You reckless darling," she went on; "don't you see how dangerous the least slip would be?"

The boy stood upright and looked round at her. His blue eyes were alight. All the fitful brightness, all the wistful charm, of the April evening was in his face.

"But it's the only place where I can see them, and they're such beauties," he said. "And I want to see them so much. You know we always miss them somehow, mummy, when we go out."

Katherine was off her guard. Three separate strains of feeling influenced her just then. First, her growing recognition of the change in Richard, of that passing away of childhood which could not but make for difficulty and, in a sense, for pain. Secondly, the natural excitement of her brother's home-coming, disturbing the monotony of her daily life, bringing, along with very actual joy, memories of a past, well-beloved yet gone beyond recall. Lastly, the practical and immediate fear that Dickie had come uncommonly near tumbling incontinently out of the window. And so, being moved, she held the boy tightly and answered rather at random, thereby provoking fate.

"Yes, my dearest, I know we always miss them somehow when we go out. It is best so. But do pray be more careful with these high windows."

"Oh! I'm all right—I'm careful enough."—His glance had gone back to where the last of the horses passed out of sight behind the red wall of the gardens. "But why is it best so? Ah! they're gone!" he exclaimed.

Katherine sat down on the window-seat, and Richard, clinging to the window-ledge, while she still held him, lowered himself into a sitting position beside her.

"Thank you, mummy," he said. And the words cut her. They came so often in each day, and always with the same little touch of civil dignity. The courtesy of Richard's recognition of help given, failed to comfort her for the fact that help was so constantly required. Lady Calmady's sense of rebellion arose and waxed strong whenever she heard those thanks.

"Mother," he went on, "I want to ask you something. You won't mind?"

"Do I ever mind you questioning me?" Yet she felt a certain tightening about her heart.

"Ah, but this is different! I've wanted to for a long while,

7

but I did not know if I ought—and yet I did not quite like to ask Auntie Marie or Julius. And, of course, one doesn't speak to the servants about anything of that sort."

Richard's curly head went up with a fine, little air of pride as he said the last few words. His mother smiled at him. There was no doubt as to her son's breeding.

"Well, what then?" she said.

"I want to know—you're sure you don't mind—why you dislike the horses, and never go to the stables or take me there? If the horses are wrong, why do we keep them? And if they're not wrong, why, mother, don't you see, we may enjoy them, mayn't we?"

He flushed, looking up at her, spoke coaxingly, merrily, a trifle embarrassed by his own temerity, yet keen to prove his point and acquire possession of this so coveted joy.

Katherine hesitated. She was tempted to put aside his question with some playful excuse. And yet, where was the use? The question must inevitably be answered one day, and Katherine, as had been said, was moved just now, dumbness of long habit somewhat melted. Perhaps this was the appointed time. She drew her arm from around the boy and took both his hands in hers.

"My dearest," she said, "our keeping the horses is not wrong. But—one of the horses killed your father."

Richard's lips parted. His eyes searched hers.

"But how?" he asked presently.

"He was trying it at a fence, and it came down with him—and trampled him."

There was a pause. At last the boy asked rather breathlessly:—"Was he killed then, mother, at once?"

It had been Katherine's intention to state the facts simply, gravely, and without emotion. But to speak of these things, after so long silence, proved more trying than she had anticipated. The scene in the red drawing-room, the long agony of waiting and of farewell, rose up before her after all these years with a vividness and poignancy that refused to be gainsaid.

"No," she answered, "he lived four days. He spoke to me of many things he wished to do. And—I have done them all, I think. He spoke to me of you"—— Katherine closed her eyes. "The boy might care for the stables. The boy must ride straight." For the moment she could not look at Richard, knowing that which she must see. The irony of those remembered words appeared too great.—"But he suffered," she went on brokenly, "he suffered—ah! my dear"——

"Mummy, darling mummy, don't look like that!" Dickie cried. He wrenched his hands from her grasp and threw his arms impulsively about her neck. "Don't—it hurts me. And —and, after all," he added, reasoningly, consolingly, "it wasn't one of these horses you know. They've never done anybody any harm. It was an accident. There must always be accidents sometimes, mustn't there? And then, you see, it all happened long, long ago. It must have, for I don't remember anything about it. It must have happened when I was a baby."

"Alas, no!" Katherine exclaimed, wrung by the pathos of his innocent egoism; "it happened even before then, my dearest, before you were born."

With the unconscious arrogance of childhood, Richard had, so far, taken his mother's devotion very much as a matter of course. He had never doubted that he was, and always had been, the inevitable centre of all her interests. So, now, her words and her bearing, bringing—in as far as he grasped them—the revelation of aspects of her life quite independent of his all-important, little self, staggered him. For the first time poor Dickie realised that even one's own mother, be she never so devoted, is not her child's exclusive and wholly private property, but has a separate existence, joys and sorrows apart. Instinctively he took his arms from about her neck and backed away into the angle of the window-seat, regarding her with serious and somewhat startled attention. And, doing so, he for the first time realised consciously something more, namely the greatness of her beauty.

For the years had dealt kindly with Katherine Calmady. Not the great sorrows of life, or its great sacrifices, but fretfulness, ignoble worries, sordid cares, are that which draw lines upon a woman's face and harshen her features. At six and thirty Lady Calmady's skin was smooth and delicate, her colour still clear and softly bright. Her hair, though somewhat darker than of old, was abundant. Still she wore it rolled up and back from her forehead, showing the perfect oval of her face. Her eyes, too, were darker; and the expression of them had become profound—the eyes of one who has looked on things which may not be told and has chosen her part. Her bosom had become a little fuller; but the long, inward curve of her figure below it to the round and shapely waist, and the poise of her rather small hips, were lithe and free as ever. While there was that enchanting freshness about her which is more than the mere freshness of youth or of physical health—which would seem, indeed, to be the peculiar dowry of those women who, having once known love in all its completeness and its strength, of choice live ever afterwards in perfect chastity of act and thought.

And a perception not only of the grace of her person, as she sat sideways on the window-seat in her close-fitting, grey gown, with its frilled lace collar and ruffles at the wrists, came to Richard now. He perceived something of this more intimate and subtle charm which belonged to her. He was enthralled by the clear sweetness, as of dewy grass newly turned by the scythe, which always clung about her, and by the whispering of her silken garments when she moved. A sudden reverence for her came upon him, as though, behind her gracious and so familiar figure, he apprehended that which belonged to a region superior, almost divine. And then he was seized—it is too often the fate of worshippers—with jealousy of that past of hers of which he had been, until now, ignorant. And yet another emotion shook him, for, in thus realising and differentiating her personality, he had grown vividly, almost painfully, conscious of his own.

He turned away, laying his cheek against the stone window-ledge, while the drops of a passing scud of rain beat in on his hot face.

"Then—then my father never saw me," he exclaimed vehemently. And, after a moment's pause, added:—"I am glad of that—very glad."

"Ah! But, my dearest," Lady Calmady cried, bewildered and aghast, "you don't know what you are saying—think !"

Richard kept his face to the splashing rain.

"I don't want to say anything wrong; but," he repeated, "I am glad."

He turned to her, his lips quivering a little, and a desolate expression in his eyes, which told Katherine, with only too bitter assurance, that his childhood and the repose of it were indeed over and gone.

She held out her arms to him in silent invitation, and drew the dear curly head on to her bosom.

"You're not displeased with me, mummy?"

"Does this seem as if I was displeased?" she asked.

Then they sat silent once more, Katherine swaying a little as she held him, soothing him almost as in his baby days.

"I won't lean out of the window again," he said presently, with a sigh of comfort. "I promise that."

"There's a darling. But I am afraid we must go. Uncle Roger will be here soon."

The boy raised his head.

"Mother," he said quickly, "will you send Clara, please, to put away these books? And may I have Winter to fetch me? I—I'm tired. If you don't mind? I don't care to walk."

Yet, since happily at thirteen Richard's moods were still as many and changeful as the aspects of that same April day, he enjoyed some royally unclouded hours before he—most unwillingly—retired to bed that night. For, on close acquaintance, the great Ulysses proved a very satisfactory hero. Roger Ormiston's character had consolidated. It was to some purpose that he had put away the pleasant follies of his youth. He looked out now with a coolness and patience, born of wide experience, upon men and upon affairs. He had ceased to lose either his temper or his head. Acquiescing with undismayed and cheerful common sense in the fact that life, as we know it, is but a sorry business, and that rough things must of necessity be done and suffered every day, he had developed an active—though far from morbidly sentimental—compassion for the individual, man and beast alike. Not that Colonel Ormiston formulated all that, still less held forth upon it. He was content, as is so many another Englishman, to be a dumb and practical philosopher—for which those who have lived with philosophers of the eloquent sort will unquestionably give thanks, knowing, to their sorrow, how often handsome speech is but a cloak to hide incapacity of honest doing.

And so, after dinner, under plea of an imperative need of cigars, Ormiston had borne Dickie off to the Gun-Room; and there, in the intervals of questioning him a little about his tastes and occupations, had told him stories many and great. For he wanted to get hold of the boy and judge of what stuff he was made. Like all sound and healthy-minded men he had an inherent suspicion of the abnormal. He could not but fear that persons unusually constituted in body must be the victims of some corresponding crookedness of spirit. But as the evening drew on he became easy on this point. Whatever Richard's physical infirmity, his nature was wholesome enough. Therefore when, at close upon ten o'clock, Lady Calmady arrived in person to insist that Dickie must go, there and then, straight to bed, she found a pleasant scene awaiting her.

The square room was gay with lamplight and firelight, which brought into strong relief the pictures of famous horses and trophies of old-time weapons—matchlocks, basket-handled swords, and neat, silver-hilted rapiers, prettiest of toys with which to pink your man—that decorated its white-panelled walls.

Ormiston stood with his back to the fire, one heel on the fender, his broad shoulders resting against the high chimney-piece, his head bent forward as he looked down, in steady yet kindly scrutiny, at the boy. His face was tanned by the sun and wind of the long sea voyage—people still came home from India by the Cape—till his hair and moustache showed pale against his bronzed skin. And to Richard, listening and watching from the deep arm-chair drawn up at right angles to the hearth, he appeared as a veritable demigod, master of the secrets of life and death—beheld, moreover, through an atmosphere of fragrant tobacco-smoke, curiously intoxicating to unaccustomed nostrils. Dickie had tucked himself into as small a space as possible, to make room for young Camp, who lay outstretched beside him. The bull-dog's great underhung jaw and pendulous, wrinkled cheeks rested on the arm of the chair, as he stared and blinked rather sullenly at the fire—moved and choked a little, slipping off unwillingly to sleep, to wake with a start, and stare and blink once more. The embroidered *couvre-pieds*, which Dickie had spread across him gathering the top edge of it up under the front of his Eton jacket, offered luxurious bedding. But Camp was a typical conservative, slow-witted, stubborn against the ingress of a new idea. This tall, somewhat masterful stranger must prove himself a good man and true—according to bull-dog understanding of those terms—before he could hope to gain entrance to that faithful, though narrow heart.

Ormiston meanwhile, finely contemptuous of canine criticism, greeted his sister cheerily.

"You're bound to give us a little law to-night, Kitty," he said, holding out his hand to her. "We won't break rules and indulge in unbridled license as to late hours again, will we, Dick? But, you see, we've both been doing a good deal, one way or another, since we last met, and there were arrears of conversation to make up."—He smiled very charmingly at Lady Calmady, and his fingers closed firmly on her hand.—"We've been getting on famously, notwithstanding our long separation." He looked down at Richard again.—"Fast friends, already, and mean to remain so, don't we, old chap?"

Thereupon Lady Calmady's soul received much comfort. Her pride was always on the alert, fiercely sensitive concerning Richard. And the joy of this meeting had, till now, an edge of jealous anxiety to it. If Roger did not take to the boy, then—deeply though she loved him—Roger must go. For the same elements were constant in Katherine Calmady. Not all the discipline of thirteen years had tamed the hot blood in her which made her order out the Clown for execution.   But as Ormiston spoke, her face softened, her eyes grew luminous and smiled back at him with an exquisite gladness.   The soft gloom of her black, velvet dress emphasised the warm, golden whiteness of her bare shoulders and arms.   Ormiston seeing her just then, understanding something of the drama of her thought, was moved from his habitual cool indifference of bearing.

"Katherine," he said, "do you know you take one rather by surprise?   Upon my word you're more beautiful than ever."

And Richard's clear voice rang out eagerly from the depths of the big chair:—

"Yes—yes—isn't she, Uncle Roger—isn't she—delicious?"

The man's smile broadened almost to laughter.

"You young monkey," he said very gently; "so you have discovered that fact already have you?   Well, so much the better.   It's a safe basis to start from; don't you think so, Kitty?"

But Lady Calmady drew away her hand.   The blood had rushed into her face and neck.   Her beauty, now for so long, had seemed a negligible quantity, a thing that had out-lasted its need and use—since he who had so rejoiced in it was dead. What is the value of ever so royal a crown when the throne it represents has fallen to ruin?   And yet, being very much a woman, those words of praise came altogether sweetly to Katherine from the lips of her brother and her son.   She moved away, embarrassed, not quite mistress of herself, sat down on the arm of Richard's chair, leaned across him and patted the bull-dog—who raised his heavy head with a grunt, and slapped Dickie smartly in the stomach with his tail, by way of welcome.

"You dear foolish creatures," she said, "pray talk of something more profitable.   I am growing old, and, in some ways, I am rather thankful for it.   All the same, Dickie, darling, you positively must and shall go to bed."

But Colonel Ormiston interrupted her.   He spoke with a trace of hesitation, turning to the fireplace and flicking the ash off the end of his cigar.

"By the bye, Katherine, how's Mary Cathcart?   Have you seen her lately?"

"Yes, last week."

"Then she's not gone the way of all flesh and married?"

"No," Lady Calmady answered.   She bent a little lower, tracing out the lines on the dog's wrinkled forehead with her finger.—"Several men have asked her to marry.   But there is only one man in the world, I fancy, whom Mary would ever care to marry—poor Camp, did I tickle you?—and he, I believe, has not asked her yet."

"Ah! there," Ormiston exclaimed quickly, "you are mistaken."

"Am I?" Katherine said. "I have great faith in Mary. I suppose she was too wise to accept even him, being not wholly convinced of his love."

Lady Calmady raised her eyes. Ormiston looked very keenly at her. And Richard, watching them, felt his breath come rather short with excitement, for he understood that his mother was speaking in riddles. He observed, moreover, that Colonel Ormiston's face had grown pale for all its sunburn.

"And so," Katherine went on, "I think the man in question had better be quite sure of his own heart before he offers it to Mary Cathcart again."

Ormiston flung his half-smoked cigar into the fire. He came and stood in front of Richard.

"Look here, old chap," he said, "what do you say to our driving over to Newlands to-morrow? You can set me right if I've forgotten any of the turns in the road, you know. And you and Miss Cathcart are great chums, aren't you?"

"Mother, may I go?" the boy asked.

Lady Calmady kissed his forehead.

"Yes, my dearest," she said. "I will trust you and Uncle Roger to take care of each other for once. You may go."

The immediate consequence of all which was, that Richard went to bed that night with a brain rather dangerously active and eyes rather dangerously bright. So that when sleep at last visited him, it came burdened with dreams, in which the many impressions and emotions of the day took altogether too lively a part, causing him to turn restlessly to and fro, and throw his arms out wide over the cool, linen sheets and pillow.

For there was a new element in Dickie's dreams to-night— namely a recurrent distress of helplessness and incapacity of movement, and therefore of escape, in the presence of some on-coming, multitudinous terror. He was haunted, moreover, by a certain stanza of the ballad of Chevy Chase. It had given him a peculiar feeling, sickening yet fascinating, ever since he could remember first to have read it, a feeling which caused him to dread reading it beforehand, yet made him turn back to it again and again. And, to-night, sometimes Richard was himself, sometimes his personality seemed merged in that of Witherington, the crippled fighting-man, of whose maiming, and deadly courage, that stanza tells. And the battle was long and fierce, as, from out a background of steeple-shaped, honey-combed rocks and sparse trees with large, golden leaves—like those on the panels of the great, lacquered cabinets in the Long Gallery—innumerable hordes of fanatic Chinamen poured down on him, a hideous bedizenment of vermilion war-devils painted on their blue tunics and banners and shields. And he, Richard,—or was it he, Witherington? — alone facing them all, — they countless in number, always changing yet always the same. From under their hard, upturned hats, a peacock feather erect in each, the cruel, oblique-eyed, impassive faces stared at him. They pressed him back and back against the base of a seven-storied pagoda, the wind-bells of which jangled far above him from the angles of its tiers of fluted roofs. And the sky was black and polished. Yet it was broad, glaring daylight, every object fearfully distinct. And he was fixed there, unable to get away because—yes, of course, he was Witherington, so there was no need of further explanation of that inability of escape.

And still, at the same time, he could see Chifney on the handsome, grey cob, trotting soberly along the green ride, beside the long string of racehorses coming home from exercise. The young leaves were fragile and green now, not sparse and metallic, and the April rain splashed in his face. He tried to call out to Tom Chifney, but the words died in his throat.—If they would only put him on one of those horses ! He knew he could ride, and so be safe and free. He called again. That time his voice came. They must hear. Were they not his own servants, after all, and his own horses—or would be soon, when he was grown up ? But neither the trainer, nor the boys so much as turned their heads ; and the living ribbon of brown and chestnut swept on and away out of sight. No one would heed him ! No one would hearken to his cry !

Once his mother and some man, whom he knew yet did not know, passed by him hand in hand. She wore a white dress, and smiled with a look of ineffable content. Her companion was tall, gracious in bearing and movement, but unsubstantial, a luminous shadow merely. Richard could not see his face. Yet he knew the man was of near kin to him. And to them he tried to speak. But it was useless. For now he was not Richard any more. He was not even Witherington, the crippled fighting-man of the Chevy Chase ballad. He was—he was the winged sea-gull, with wild, pale eyes, hiding—abject yet fierce—among the vegetable beds in the Brockhurst kitchen-gardens, and picking up loathsome provender of snails and slugs. Roger Ormiston, calm, able, kindly, yet just a trifle insolent, cigar in mouth, sauntered up and looked at the bird, and it crawled away among the cabbages ignominiously, covered with the shame of its incompleteness and its fallen estate.

And then from out the honey-combed rocks, under the black, polished sky, the blue-tunicked Chinamen swept down on Richard again with the maddening horror of infinite number. They crushed in upon him, nearer and nearer, pressing him back against the wall of that evil pagoda. The air was hot and musky with their breath and thick with the muffled roar of their countless footsteps. And they came right in on him, trampling him down, suffocating, choking him with the heat of them and the dead weight.

Shouting aloud—as it seemed to him—in angry terror, the boy woke. He sat up trembling, wet with perspiration, bewildered by the struggle and the wild phantasmagoria of his dream. He pulled open the neck of his night-shirt, leaned his head against the cool, brass rail of the back of the bedstead, while he listened with growing relief to the rumble of the wind in the chimney, and the swish of the rain against the casements, and watched the narrow line of light under the door of his mother's room.

Yes, he was Richard Calmady, after all,—here in his own sheltered world, among those who had loved and served him all his life. Nothing hurtful could reach him here, nothing of which he need be afraid. There was no real meaning in that ugly dream.

And then Dickie paused a moment, still sitting up in the warm darkness, pressing his hands down on the mattress on either side to keep himself from slipping. For involuntarily he recalled the feeling which had prompted his declaration that he was glad his father had never seen him ; recalled his unwillingness to walk, lest he should meet Ormiston unexpectedly ; recalled the instinct which, even during that glorious time in the Gun-Room, had impelled him to keep the embroidered *couvre-pieds* carefully over his legs and feet. And, recalling these things, poor Dickie arrived at conclusions regarding himself which he had happily avoided arriving at before. For they were harsh conclusions, causing him to cower down in the bed, and bury his face in the pillows to stifle the sound of the tearing sobs which would come.

Alas ! was there not only too real a meaning in that same ugly dream and that shifting of personality ? He understood, while his body quivered with the anguish of it, that he had more

in common with, and was nearer—far nearer—to the maimed
fighting-man of the old ballad, even to the poor sea-gull robbed
of its power of flight, than to all those dear people whose business
in life it seemed to pet and amuse him, and to minister to his
every want—to the handsome soldier uncle, whose home-coming
had so excited him, to Julius March, his indulgent tutor, to
Mademoiselle de Mirancourt, his delightful companion, to Clara,
his obedient playfellow, to brown-eyed Mary Cathcart, and even
to his lovely mother herself!

Thus did the bitter winds of truth, which blow forever across
the world, first touch Richard Calmady, cutting his poor boyish
pride as with a whip.   But he was very young.   And the young,
mercifully, know no such word as the inevitable; so that the
wind of truth is ever tempered for them—the first smart of it
over—by the sunshine of ignorant and unlimited hope.

CHAPTER III

CONCERNING THAT WHICH, THANK GOD, HAPPENS ALMOST EVERY DAY

THE merry, spring sky was clear, save in the south where a
vast perspective of dappled cloud lay against it, leaving
winding rivers of blue here and there, as does ribbed sand for
the incoming tide.   As the white gate of the inner park—the
grey, unpainted palings ranging far away to right and left—swung
to behind them, and Henry, the groom, after a smart run,
clambered up into his place again beside Camp on the back
seat of the double dog-cart, Richard's spirits rose.   Ahead
stretched out the long vista of that peculiar glory of Brockhurst,
its avenue of Scotch firs.   The trunks of them, rough-barked
and purple below, red, smooth, and glistering above, shot up
some thirty odd feet—straight as the pillars of an ancient temple
—before the branches, sweeping outward and downward, met,
making a whispering, living canopy overhead, through which the
sunshine fell in tremulous shafts upon the shining coats and
gleaming harness of the horses, upon Ormiston's clear-cut,
bronzed face and upright figure, and upon the even, straw-
coloured gravel of the road.   The said road is raised by about three
feet above the level of the land on either side.   On the left, the
self-sown firs grow in close ranks.   The ground below them is
bare but for tussocks of coarse grass and ruddy beds of fallen fir

needles. On the right, the fir wood is broken by coppices of silver-stemmed birches, and spaces of heather—which shows a purple-brown against the grey of the reindeer moss out of which it springs. Tits swung and frolicked among the tree-tops, and a jay flew off noisily with a flash of azure wing-coverts and volley of harsh, discordant cries.

The rapid movement, the moist, pungent odour of the woodland, the rhythmical trot of the horses, the rattle of the splinter-bar chains as the traces slackened going downhill, above all the presence of the man beside him, were pleasantly stimulating to Richard Calmady. The boy was still a prey to much innocent enthusiasm. It appeared to him, watching Ormiston's handling of the reins and whip, there was nothing this man could not do, and do skilfully, yet all with the same easy unconcern. Indeed the present position was so agreeable to him that Dickie's spirits would have risen to an unusual height, but for a certain chastening of the flesh in the shape of the occasional pressure of a broad strap against his middle, which brought him unwelcome remembrance of recent discoveries it was his earnest desire to ignore, still better to forget.

For just at starting there had been a rather bad moment. Winter, having settled him on the seat of the dog-cart, was preparing to tuck him in with many rugs, when Ormiston said :—

"Look here, dear old chap, I've been thinking about this, and upon my word you don't seem to me very safe. You see this is a different matter to your donkey-chair, or the pony-carriage. There's no protection at the side, and if the horses shied or anything—well, you'd be in the road. And I can't afford to spill you the first time we go out together, or there'd be a speedy end of all our fun."

Richard tried to emulate his uncle's cool indifference, and take the broad strap as a matter of course. But he was glad the tongue of the buckle slipped so directly into place; and that Henry's attention was engaged with the near horse, which fretted at standing; and that Leonard, the footman, was busy making Camp jump up at the back; and that his mother, who had been watching him from the lowest of the wide steps, turned away and went up to the flight to join Julius March standing under the grey arcade. As the horses sprang forward, clattering the little pebbles of the drive against the body of the carriage, and swung away round the angle of the house, Katherine came swiftly down the steps again smiling, kissing her hand to him. Still, the strap hurt—not poor Dickie's somewhat ill-balanced body, to which in truth it lent an agreeable sense of security, but his, just then, all too sensitive mind.   So that, notwithstanding a fine assumption of gaiety, as he kissed his hand in return, he found the dear vision of his mother some-what blurred by foolish tears which he had resolutely to wink away.

But now that disquieting incident was left nearly ten minutes behind.   The last park gate and its cluster of mellow - tinted, thatched cottages was past.   Not only out-of-doors and all the natural exhilaration of it, but the spectacle of the world beyond the precincts of the park—into which world he, in point of fact, so rarely penetrated—wooed him to interest and enjoyment. To Dickie, whose life through his mother's jealous tenderness and his own physical infirmity had been so singularly circum-scribed, there was an element, slightly pathetic, of discovery and adventure in this ordinary, afternoon drive.

He did not want to talk.   He was too busy simply seeing— everything food for those young eyes and brain so greedy of incident and of beauty.   He sat upright and stared at the pass-ing show.—At the deep lane, its banks starred with primroses growing in the hollows of the gnarled roots of oaks and ash trees. At Sandyfield rectory, deep-roofed, bow-windowed, the red walls and tiles of it half smothered in ivy and cotoneaster.   At the low, squat-towered, Georgian church, standing in its acre of close-packed graveyard, which is shadowed by yew trees and by the clump of three enormous Scotch firs in the rectory garden adjoining.   At the Church Farm, just beyond—a square white house, the slated roofs of it running up steeply to a central block of chimneys, it having, in consequence, somewhat the effect of a monster extinguisher.   At the rows of pale, wheat stacks, raised on granite staddles ; at the prosperous barns, yards, and stables, built of wood on brick foundations, that surround it, presenting a mass of rich, solid colour and of noisy, crowded, animal life.   At the fields, plough and pasture, marked out by long lines of hedgerow trees, broken by coppices—these dashed with tenderest green—stretching up and back to the dark, purple-blue range of the moorland.   At scattered cottages, over the gates of whose gardens gay with daffodils and polyanthus, groups of little girls and babies, in flopping sun- bonnets and scanty lilac pinafores, stared back at the passing carriage, and then bobbed the accustomed curtsey.   In the said groups were no boys, save of infant years.   The boys were away shepherding, or to plough, or bird-minding.   For as yet education was free indeed—in the sense that you were free to take it, or leave it, as suited your pocket and your fancy.

Richard stared too at the pleasant, furze-dotted commons, spinning away to right and left as the horses trotted sharply onward—commons whereon meditative donkeys endured rather than enjoyed existence, after the manner of their kind; and prodigiously large families of yellow-grey goslings streeled after the flocks of white geese, across spaces of fresh sprung grass around shallow ponds, in which the blue and dapple of the sky were reflected. He stared at Sandyfield village too—a straight street of detached houses, very diverse in colour and in shape, standing back, for the most part, amid small orchards and gardens that slope gently up from the brook, which last, backed, here by a row of fine elms, there by one of Lombardy poplars, borders the road. Three or four shops, modest in size as they are ambitious in the variety of objects offered for sale in them, advance their windows boldly. So does the yellow-washed inn, the Calmady arms displayed upon its swinging sign-board. A miller's tented waggon, all powdery with flour, and its team of six horses, brave with brass harness and bells, a timber-carriage, and a couple of spring-carts, were drawn up on the half-moon of gravel before the porch; while, from out the open door, came a sound of voices and odour of many pipes and much stale beer.

And Richard had uninterrupted leisure to bestow on all this seeing, for his companion, Colonel Ormiston, was pre-occupied and silent. Once or twice he looked down at the boy as though suddenly remembering his presence and inquired if he was "all right." But it was not until they had crossed the long, white-railed bridge, at the end of Sandyfield street —which spans not only the little, brown river overhung by black-stemmed alders, but a bit of marsh, reminiscent of the ancient ford, lush with water - grasses, beds of king-cups, and broad-leaved docks—not until then, did Colonel Ormiston make sustained effort at conversation. Beyond the bridge the road forks.

"Left to Newlands, isn't it?" he asked sharply.

Then, as the carriage swept round the turn, he woke up from his long reverie, waking Richard up also, from his long dream of mere seeing, to human drama but dimly apprehended close there at his side.

"Oh, well, well!" the man exclaimed, throwing back his head in sharp impatience, as a horse will against the restraint of the bearing-rein. He raised his eyebrows, while his lips set in a smile the reverse of gay. Then he looked down at Richard again, an unwonted softness in his expression.

"Been happy?" he said. "Enjoyed your drive? That's right. You understand the art of being really good company, Dick."

"What's that?"

"Allowing other people to be just as bad company as they like."

"I—I don't see how you could be bad company," Dickie said, flushing at the audacity of his little compliment.

"Don't you, dear old chap? Well, that's very nice of you. All the same I find, at times, I can be precious bad company to myself."

"Oh! but I don't see how," the boy argued, his enthusiasm protesting against all possibility of default in the object of it. Richard wanted to keep his hands down,—unconsciousness, if only assumed, told for personal dignity,—but, in the agitation of protest, spite of himself, he laid hold of the top edge of that same chastening strap. "It must be so awfully jolly to be like you—able to do everything and go everywhere. There must be such a lot to think about."

The softness was still upon Ormiston's face.—"Such a lot?" he said. "A jolly lot too much, believe me, very often, Dick."

He looked away up the copse-bordered road, over the ears of the trotting horses.

"You've read the story of Blue Beard and that unpleasant locked-up room of his, where the poor, little wives hung all of a row? Well, I'm sorry to say, Dick, most men when they come to my age have a room of that sort. It's an inhospitable place. One doesn't invite one's friends to dine and smoke there. At least no gentleman does. I've met one or two persons who set the door open and rather gloried in inviting inspection—but they were blackguards and cads. They don't count. Still each of us is obliged to go in there sometimes himself. I tell you it's anything but lively. I've been in there just now."

The dappled cloud creeping upward from the southern horizon veiled the sun, the light of which grew pale and thin. The scent of the larch wood, on the right, hung in the air. Richard's eyes were wide with inquiry. His mind suffered growing-pains, as young minds of any intellectual and poetic worth needs must. The possibility of moral experience, incalculable in extent as that golden-grey outspread of creeping, increasing vapour overhead, presented itself to him. The vastness of life touched him to fear. He struggled to find a limit, clothing his effort in childish realism of statement.

"But in that locked-up room, Uncle Roger, you can't have dead women—dead wives?"

Ormiston laughed quietly.

"You hit out pretty straight from the shoulder, Master Dick," he said. "Happily I can reassure you on one point. All manner of things are hung up in there—some ugly—almost all ugly now, to my eyes, though some of them had charming ways with them once upon a time. But, I give you my word, neither ugly nor charming, dead nor alive, are there any wives."

The boy considered a moment, then said stoutly:—"I wouldn't go in there again. I'd lock the door and throw away the key."

"Wait till your time comes! You'll find that is precisely what you can't do."

"Then I'd fetch them out, once and for all, and bury them."

The carriage had turned in at the lodge gate. Soon a long, low, white house and range of domed conservatories came into view.

"Heroic remedies!" Ormiston remarked, amused at the boy's vehemence. "But no doubt they do succeed now and then. To tell you the truth, Dick, I have been thinking of something of the kind myself. Only I'm afraid I shall need somebody to help me in carrying out so extensive a funeral."

"Anybody would be glad enough to help you," Richard declared, with a strong emphasis on the pronoun.

"Ah! but the bother is anybody can't help one. Only one person in all this great rough and tumble of a world can really help one. And often one finds out who that person is a little bit too late. However, here we are. Perhaps we shall know more about it all in the next half-hour, if these good people are at home."

In point of fact the good people in question were not at home. Ormiston, holding reins and whip in one hand, felt for his card-case.

"So we've had our journey for nothing you see, Dick," he said.

And to Richard the words sounded regretful. Moreover, the drama of this expedition seemed to him shorn of its climax. He knew there should be something more, and pushed for it.

"You haven't asked for Mary," he said. "And I thought we came on purpose to see Mary. She won't like us to go away like this. Do ask."

Colonel Ormiston's expression altered, hardened. And Richard, in his present hypersensitive state, remembered the cool scrutiny bestowed on the winged sea-gull of his dream last night.   This man had seemed so near him just now while they talked.   Suddenly he became remote again, all understanding of him shut away by that slight insolence of bearing.   Still he did as Richard prayed him.   Miss Cathcart was at home.   She had just come in from riding.

"Tell her Sir Richard Calmady is here, and would like, if he may, to see her."

Without waiting for a reply, Ormiston unbuckled that same chastening strap silently, quickly.   He got down and, coming round to the farther side of the carriage, lifted Richard out ; while Camp, who had jumped off the back seat, stood yawning, whining a little, shaking his heavy head and wagging his tail in welcome on the doorstep.   With the bull-dog close at his heels, Ormiston carried the boy into the house.

The inner doors were open, and, up the long, narrow, pleasantly fresh-tinted drawing-room, Mary Cathcart came to meet them.   The folds of her habit were gathered up in one hand.   In the other she carried a bunch of long-stalked, yellow and scarlet tulips.   Her strong, supple figure stood out against the young green of the lawns and shrubberies, seen through the French windows behind her.   She walked carefully, with a certain deliberation, thanks to her narrow habit and top-boots. The young lady carried her thirty-one years bravely.   Her irregular features and large mouth had always been open to criticism.   But her teeth, when her lips parted, were white and even, and her brown eyes frankly honest as ever.

"Why, Dickie dear, it is simply glorious to have you and Camp paying visits on your own account."—Her speech broke into a little cry, while her fingers closed so tightly on the tulips that the brittle stalks snapped, and the gay-coloured bells of them hung limply, some falling on to the carpet about her feet.   "Roger—Colonel Ormiston—I didn't know you were home — were here ! " — Her voice was uncontrollably glad.

Still carrying the boy, Ormiston stood before her, observing her keenly.   But he was no longer remote.   His insolence, which, after all, may have been chiefly self-protective, had vanished.

"I'm very sorry—I mean for those poor tulips.   I came to pay my respects to Mr. and Mrs. Cathcart, and not finding them was preparing to drive humbly home again.   But"— Certainly she carried her years well.   She looked absurdly young.   The brown and rose-red of her complexion was clear as that of the little maiden who had fought with, and over-

8

come, and kissed the rough, Welsh pony refusing the grip by the roadside long ago. The hint of a moustache emphasised the upturned corners of her mouth—but that was rather captivating. Her eyes danced, under eyelids which fluttered for the moment. She was not beautiful, not a woman to make men run mad. Yet the comeliness of her body, and the spirit to which that body served as index, was so unmistakably healthful, so sincere, that surely no sane man, once gathering her into his arms, need ask a better blessing.—"But," Ormiston went on, still watching her, "nothing would satisfy Dick but he must see you. With many injunctions regarding his safety, Katherine made him over to me for the afternoon. I'm on duty, you see. Where he goes, I'm bound to go also—even to the destruction of your poor tulips."

Miss Cathcart made no direct answer.

"Sit here, Dickie," she said, pointing to a sofa.

"But you don't really mind our coming in, do you?" he asked, rather anxiously.

The young lady placed herself beside him, drew his hand on to her knee, patted it gently.

"Mind? No; on the whole, I don't think I do mind very much. In fact, I think I should probably have minded very much more if you had gone away without asking for me."

"There, I told you so, Uncle Roger," the boy said triumphantly. Camp had jumped up on to the sofa too. He put his arm comfortably round the dog's neck. It was as well to acquire support on both sides, for the surface of the glazed chintz was slippery, inconveniently unsustaining to his equilibrium.—"It's an awfully long time since I've seen Mary," he continued, "more than three weeks."

"Yes, an awfully long time," Ormiston echoed, "more than six years."

"Dear Dickie," she said; "how pretty of you! Do you always keep count of my visits?"

"Of course I do. They were about the best things that ever happened, till Uncle Roger came home."

Forgetting herself, Mary Cathcart raised her eyes to Ormiston's in appeal. The boy's little declaration stirred all the latent motherhood in her. His fortunes at once passed so very far beyond, and fell so far short of, the ordinary lot. She wondered whether, and could not but trust that, this old friend and new-comer was not too self-centred, too hardened by ability and success, to appreciate the intimate pathos of the position. Ormiston read and answered her thought.

"Oh! we are going to do something to change all that," he said confidently. "We are going to enlarge our borders a bit, aren't we, Dick?   Only, I think, we should manage matters much better if Miss Cathcart would help us, don't you?"

Richard remembering the locked-up room of evil contents and that proposal of inclusive funeral rites, gave this utterance a wholly individual application.   His face grew bright with intelligence.   But, greatly restraining himself, he refrained from speech.   All that had been revealed to him in confidence, and so his honour was engaged to silence.

Ormiston pulled forward a chair and sat down by him, leaning forward, his hands clasped about one knee, while he gazed at the tulips scattered on the floor.

"So tell Miss Cathcart we all want her to come over to Brockhurst just as often as she can," he continued, "and help us to make the wheels go round a little faster.   Tell her we've grown very old, and discreet, and respectable, and that we are absolutely incapable of doing or saying anything foolish or naughty, which she would object to—and"—

But Richard could restrain himself no longer.—"Why don't you tell her yourself, Uncle Roger?"

"Because, my dear old chap, a burnt child fears the fire. I tried to tell Miss Cathcart something once, long ago.   She mayn't remember"—

"She does remember," Mary said quietly, looking down at Richard's hand and patting it as it lay on her lap.

"But she stopped me dead," Ormiston went on.   "It was quite right of her.   She gave the most admirable reasons for stopping me.   Would you care to hear them?"

"Oh! don't, pray don't," Mary murmured.   "It is not generous."

"Pardon me, your reasons were absolutely just—true in substance and in fact.   You said I was a selfish, good-for-nothing spendthrift, and so"—

"I was odious," she broke in.   "I was a self-righteous little Pharisee—forgive me"—

"Why—there's nothing to forgive.   You spoke the truth."

"I don't believe it," Richard cried, in vehement protest.

"Dickie, you're a darling," Mary Cathcart said.

Colonel Ormiston left off nursing his knee, and leaned a little farther forward.

"Well then, will you come over to Brockhurst very often, and help us to make the wheels go round, and cheer us all up, and do us no end of good, though—I am a selfish, good-for-nothing spendthrift? You see I run through the list of my titles again to make sure this transaction is fair and square and above-board."

A silence followed, which appeared to Richard protracted to the point of agitation. He became almost distressingly conscious of the man's still, bronzed, resolute face on the one hand, of the woman's mobile, vivid, yet equally resolute face on the other, divining far more to be at stake than he had clear knowledge of. Tired and excited, his impatience touched on anger.

"Say yes, Mary," he cried impulsively, "say yes. I don't see how anybody can want to refuse Uncle Roger anything."

Miss Cathcart's eyes grew moist. She turned and kissed the boy.

"I don't think—perhaps—Dickie, that I quite see either," she answered very gently.

"Mary, you know what you've just said?"—Ormiston's tone was stern. "You understand this little comedy? It means business. This time you've got to go the whole hog or none."

She looked straight at him, and drew her breath in a long half-laughing sigh.

"Oh, dear me! what a plague of a hurry you are in!" she said. "Well—then—then—I suppose I must—it is hardly a graceful expression, but it is of your choosing, not of mine—I suppose I must go the whole hog."

Roger Ormiston rose, treading the fallen tulips under foot. And Richard, watching him, beheld that which called to his remembrance, not the hopeless and impotent battle under the black, polished sky of his last night's dream, but the gallant stories he had heard, earlier last night, of the battles of Sobraon and Chillianwallah, of the swift dangers of sport, and large daring of travel. Here he beheld—so it seemed to his boyish thought—the aspect of a born conqueror, of the man who can serve and wait long for the good he desires, and who, winning it, lays hold of it with fearless might. And this, while causing Richard an exquisite delight of admiration, caused him also a longing to share those splendid powers so passionate that it amounted to actual pain.

Mary Cathcart's hand slid from under his hand. She too rose to her feet.

"Then you have actually cared for me all along, all these years?" Ormiston declared in fierce joy.

"Of course—who else could I care for? And—and—you've loved me, Roger, all the while?"

And Ormiston answered "Yes,"—speaking the truth, though

with a difference. There had been interludes that had contributed somewhat freely to the peopling of that same locked-up room. But it is possible for a man to love many times, yet always love one woman best.

All this, however, Dickie did not know. He only knew they dazzled him—the man triumphantly strong, the woman so bravely glad. He could not watch them any longer. He went hot all over, and his heart beat. He felt strangely desolate too. They were far away from him, in thought, though so close by. Dickie shut his eyes, put his arms round the bull-dog, pressed his face hard against the faithful beast's shoulder; while Camp, stretching his short neck to the uttermost, nuzzled against him and essayed to lick his cheek.

Thus did Richard Calmady gain yet further knowledge of things as they are.

CHAPTER IV

WHICH SMELLS VERY VILELY OF THE STABLE

APRIL softened into May, and the hawthorns were in blossom before Richard passed any other very noteworthy milestone on the road of personal development. Then, greatly tempted, he committed a venial sin; received prompt and coarse chastisement; and, by means of the said chastisement, as is the merciful way of the Eternal Justice, found unhoped of emancipation.

It happened thus. As the spring days grew warm Mademoiselle de Mirancourt failed somewhat. The darkness and penetrating chill of the English winter tried her, and this year her recuperative powers seemed sadly deficient. A fuller tide of life had pulsed through Brockhurst since Colonel Ormiston's arrival. The old stillness was departing, the old order changing. With that change Mademoiselle de Mirancourt had no quarrel, since, to her serene faith, all that came must, of necessity, come through a divine ordering and in conformity to a divine plan. Yet this more of activity and of movement strained her. The weekly drive over to Westchurch, to hear mass at the humble Catholic chapel tucked away in a side street, sorely taxed her strength. She returned fortified, her soul ravished by that heavenly love, which, in pure and innocent natures, bears such gracious kinship to earthly love. Yet in body she was outworn and weary. On such occasions she would rally Julius March, not without a touch of malice, saying :—

"Ah ! *très cher ami*, had you only followed the ever blessed footsteps of those dear Oxford friends of yours and entered the fold of the true Church, what fatigue might you not now spare me—let alone the incalculable advantages to your own poor, charming, fatally darkened soul ! "

While Julius—who, though no less devout than of yore, was happily less fastidiously sensitive—would reply :—

" But, dearest lady, had I followed the footsteps of my Oxford friends, remember I should not be at Brockhurst at all."

"Clearly, then, everything is well ordered," she would say, folding her fragile hands upon her embroidery frame, "since it is altogether impossible we could do without you. Yet I regret for your soul. It is so capable of receiving illumination. You English—even the most finished among you—remain really deplorably stubborn, and nevertheless it is my fate perpetually to set my affections upon one or other of you."

It followed that Katherine devoted much of her time to Mademoiselle de Mirancourt, walked slowly beside her up and down the sunny, garden paths sheltered by the high, red walls whereon the clematis and jasmine began to show for flower ; or took her for quiet, little drives within the precincts of the park. They spoke much of Lucia St. Quentin, of Katherine's girlhood, and of those pleasant days in Paris long ago. And this brought soothing and comfort, not only to the old lady, but to the young lady also—and of soothing and comfort the latter stood in need just now.

For it is harsh discipline even to a noble woman, whose life is still strong in her, to stand by and see another woman, but a few years her junior, entering on those joys which she has lost—marriage, probably motherhood as well. Roger Ormiston and Mary Cathcart's love-making was restrained and dignified. But the very calm of their attitude implied a security of happiness passing all need of advertisement. And Katherine was very far from grudging them this. She was not envious, still less jealous. She did not want to take anything of theirs ; but she wanted, she sorely wanted, her own again. A word, a look, a certain quickness of quiet laughter, would pierce her with recollection. Once for her too, below the commonplaces of daily detail, flowed that same magic river of delight. But the springs of it had gone dry. Therefore it was a relief to be alone with Mademoiselle de Mirancourt—virgin and saint—and to speak with her of the days before she, Katherine, had sounded the lovely depths of that same magic flood—days when she had known of its existence only by the mirage, born of the dazzle of its waters, which plays over the innocent, vacant spaces of a young girl's mind.

It was a relief even, though of sterner quality, to go into the red drawing-room on the ground floor and pace there, her hands clasped behind her, her proud head bowed, by the half-hour together. If personal joy is dead past resurrection, there is bitter satisfaction in realising to the full personal pain. The room was duly swept, dusted, casements set open to welcome breeze and sunshine, fires lighted in the grate. But no one ever sat there. It knew no cheerfulness of social intercourse. The crimson curtains and covers had become faded. They were not renewed. The furniture, save for the absence of the narrow bed, stood in precisely the same order as on the night when Sir Richard Calmady died. It was pushed back against the walls. And in the wide, empty way between the two doors, Katherine paced, saturating all her being with thoughts of that which was, and must remain, wholly and inalienably her own—namely her immense distress.

And in this she took the more comfort, because something else, until now appearing wholly her own, was slipping a little away from her. Dickie's health had improved notably in the last few weeks. His listlessness had vanished, while his cheeks showed a wholesome warmth of colour. But his cry was ever— "Mother, Uncle Roger's going to such a place. He says he'll take me. I can go, can't I?" Or—"Mother, Mary's going to do such a thing. She says she'll show me how. She may, mayn't she?" And Katherine's answer was always "Yes." She grudged the boy none of his new-found pleasures, rejoiced indeed to see him interested and gay. Yet to watch the new broom, which sweeps so clean, is rarely exhilarating to those that have swept diligently with the old one. The nest had held her precious fledgling so safely till now, and this fluttering of wings, eager for flight, troubled her somewhat. Not only was Dickie's readiness to be away from her a trifle hard to bear; but she knew that disappointment, of a certainty, lay in wait for him, and that each effort towards wider action would but reveal to him how circumscribed his powers actually were.

Meanwhile, however, Richard enjoyed himself recklessly, almost feverishly, in the attempt to disprove the teaching of that ugly dream, and keep truth at bay. There had been further drives, and the excitement of witnessing a forest fire—only too frequent in the Brockhurst country when the sap is up, and the easterly wind and May sun have scorched all moisture from the surface of the moorland. He and Mary had bumped over fir roots and scuttled down bridle-paths in the pony-carriage, to avoid the rush of flame and smoke; had skirmished round at a hand gallop, in search of recruits to reinforce Ormiston, and Iles, and a small army of beaters, battling against the blazing line that threatened destruction to the fir avenue. Now and again, with a mighty roar, which sent Dickie's heart into his mouth, great tongues of flame, clear as topaz and ruby in the steady sunshine, would leap upwards, converting a whole tall fir into a tree of fire, while the beaters running back, grimed with smoke and sweat, took a moment's breathing-space in the open.

There had been more peaceful pastimes as well—several days' fishing, enchanting beyond the power of language to describe. The clear trout-stream meandering through the rich water-meadows; the herds of cattle standing knee-deep in the grass, lazily chewing the cud and switching their tails at the cloud of flies; the birds and wild creatures haunting the streamside; the long dreamy hours of gentle sport, had opened up to Dickie a whole new world of romance. His donkey-chair had been left at the yellow-washed mill beneath the grove of silvery-leaved, ever-rustling, balsam poplars. And thence, while Ormiston and Mary sauntered slowly on ahead, the men — Winter in mufti, oblivious of plate-cleaning and cellarage, and the onerous duties of his high estate, Stamp, the water-bailiff, and Moorcock, one of the under-keepers—had carried him across the great, green levels. Winter was an old and tried friend, and it was somewhat diverting to behold him in this novel aspect, affable and chatty with inferiors, displaying, moreover, unexpected knowledge in the mysteries of the angler's craft. The other two men—sharp-featured, their faces ruddy as summer apples, merry-eyed, clad in velveteen coats, that bulged about the pockets, and wrinkled leather gaiters reaching half-way up the thigh—charmed Richard, when his first shyness was passed. They were eager to please him. Their talk was racy. Their laughter ready and sincere. Did not Stamp point out to him a water-ouzel, with impudently jerking tail, dipping and wading in the shallows of the stream? Did not Moorcock find him a water-rail's nest, hidden in a tuft of reeds and grass, with ten, yellowish, speckled eggs in it? And did not both men pluck him handfuls of cowslips, of tawny-pink avens, and of mottled, snake-headed fritillarias, and stow them away in the fishing-baskets above the load of silver-and-red spotted trout?

Mary had protested Dickie could throw a fly, if he had a light enough rod. And not only did he throw a fly, but at the

fourth or fifth cast a fish rose, and he played it—with skirling
reel and much advice and most complimentary excitement on
the part of the whole good company—and brought it skilfully
within range of Stamp's landing-net.   Never surely was trout
spawned that begot such bliss in the heart of an angler!   As,
with panting sides and open gills, this three - quarter - pound
treasure of treasures flopped about on the sunny stream bank all
the hereditary instinct of sport spoke up clearly in Dickie.   The
boy—such is youthful masculine human nature—believed he
understood at last why the world was made!   At dressing-time
he had his sacred fish carried on a plate up to his room to
show Clara; and, but for strong remonstrance on the part of
that devoted handmaiden, would have kept it by his bedside all
night, so as to assure himself at intervals, by sense of touch—let
alone that of smell—of the adorable fact of its veritable existence.

But all this, inspiring though it was, served but as prelude to
a more profoundly coveted acquaintance—that with the racing-
stable.   For it was after this last that Dickie still supremely
longed—the more so, it is to be feared, because it was, if not
explicitly, yet implicitly forbidden.   A spirit of defiance had
entered into him.   Being granted the inch, he was disposed to
take the ell.   And this, not in conscious opposition to his
mother's will; but in protest, not uncourageous, against the
limitations imposed on him by physical misfortune.   The boy's
blood was up, and consequently, with greater pluck than
discretion, he struggled against the intimate, inalienable enemy
that so marred his fate.   And it was this not ignoble effort
which culminated in disobedience.

For driving back one afternoon, later than usual,—Ormiston
had met them, and Mary and he had taken a by-path home
through the woods,—the pony-carriage, turned along the high
level road beside the lake, going eastward, just as the string of
racehorses, coming home from exercise, passed along it coming
west.   Richard was driving, Chaplin, the second coachman, sitting
in the dickey at the back of the low carriage.   He checked the
pony, and his eyes took in the whole scene — the blue-brown
expanse of the lake dotted with water-fowl, on the one hand,
the immense, blue-brown landscape on the other, ranging away to
the faint line of the chalk downs in the south; the downward
slope of the park, to the great square of red stable-buildings in
the hollow; the horses coming slowly towards him in single file.
Cawing rooks streamed back from the fallow-fields across the
valley.   Thrushes and blackbirds carolled.   A wren, in the
bramble-brake close by, broke into sharp, sweet song.   The

recurrent ring of an axe came from somewhere away in the fir plantations, and the strident rasping of a saw from the wood-yard in the beech grove near the house.

Richard stared at that oncoming procession.   Half-way between him and the foremost of the horses the tan ride branched off, and wound down the hillside to the stables.   The boy set his teeth.   He arrived at a desperate decision—touched up the pony and drove on.

Chaplin leaned forward, addressing him over the back of the seat.

"Better wait here, hadn't we, Sir Richard?   They'll turn off in a minute."

Richard did not look round.   He tried to answer coldly, but his voice shook.

"I know.   That's why I am going on."

There was a silence save for the cawing of the rooks, ring of the axe, and grinding of wheels on the gravel.   Chaplin, responsible, correct, over five-and-thirty, and fully intending to succeed old Mr. Wenham, the head coachman, on the latter's impending retirement from active service, went very red in the face.

"Excuse me, but I have my orders, Sir Richard," he said.

Dickie still looked straight ahead.

"Very well," he answered, "then perhaps you'd better get out and walk on home."

"You know I'm bound not to leave you, sir," the man said.

Dickie laughed a little in uncontrollable excitement.   He was close to them now.   The leading horse was just moving off the main road, its shadow lying long across the turf.   How was it possible to give way with the prize within reach?—"You can go or stay Chaplin, as you please.   I mean to speak to Chifney.   I—I mean to see the stables."

"It's as much as my place is worth, sir."

"Oh! bother your place!" the boy cried impetuously.— Dear heart alive, how fine they were as they filed by!   That chestnut filly, clean made as a deer, her ears laid back as she reached at the bit ; and the brown, just behind her— "I mean, I mean you needn't be afraid, Chaplin—I'll speak to her lady-ship.   I'll arrange all that.   Go to the pony's head."

At the end of the long string of horses came the trainer—a square-built, short-necked man, sanguine complexioned and clean shaven.   Of hair, indeed, Mr. Chifney could only boast a rim of carroty-grey stubble under the rim of the back of his

hard hat.   His right eye had suffered damage, and the pupil
of it was white and viscous.   His lips were straight and purplish
in colour.   He raised his hat and would have followed on down
the slope, but Dickie called to him.

As he rode up an unwonted expression came over Mr.
Chifney's shrewd, hard-favoured face.   He took off his hat and
sat there, bare-headed in the sunshine, looking down at the boy
his hand on his hip.

"Good-day, Sir Richard," he said.   "Anything I can do
for you?"

"Yes, yes," Dickie stammered, all his soul in his eyes, his
cheeks aflame, "you can do just what I want most.   Take me
down, Chifney, and show me the horses."

Here Chaplin coughed discreetly behind his hand.   But
that proved of small avail, save possibly in the way of provocation.   For, socially, between the racing and house stables was a
great gulf fixed ; and Mr. Chifney could hardly be expected to
recognise the existence of a man in livery standing at a pony's
head, still less to accept direction from such a person.   Servants
must be kept in their place—impudent, lazy enough lot anyhow,
bless you !   On his feet the trainer had been known to decline
to moments of weakness.   But in the saddle, a good horse under
him, he possessed unlimited belief in his own judgment, fearing
neither man, devil, nor even his own meek-faced wife with lilac
ribbons in her cap.   Moreover, he felt such heart as he had go
out strangely to the beautiful, eager boy gazing up at him.

"Nothing 'ud give me greater pleasure in life, Sir Richard,"
he said, "if you're free to come.   We've waited a long time, a
precious long time, sir, for you to come down and take a look
at your horses."

"I'd have been to see them sooner.   I'd have given anything
to see them.   I've never had the chance, somehow."

Chifney pursed up his lips, and surveyed the distant landscape with a very meaning glance.   "I daresay not, Sir Richard.
But better late than never, you know ; and so, if you are free to
come"—

Again Chaplin coughed.

"Free to come?   Of course I am free to come," Dickie
asserted, his pride touched to arrogance.   And Mr. Chifney
looked at him, an approving twinkle in his sound eye.

"I agree, Sir Richard.   Quite right, sir, you're free, of
course."

Stolen waters are sweet, says the proverb.   And to Richard
Calmady, his not wholly legitimate experience of the next hour

was sweet indeed. For there remains rich harvest of poetry in
all sport worth the name, let squeamish and sentimental persons
declaim against it as they may. Strength and endurance, disregard of suffering, have a permanent appeal and value, even in
their coarsest manifestations. No doubt the noble gentlemen
of the neighbourhood, who "lay at Brockhurst two nights" on
the occasion of Sir Denzil's historic house-warming, to witness
the mighty bear-baiting, were sensible of something more in that
somewhat disgusting exhibition, than the mere gratification of
brutal instincts, the mere savage relish for wounds and pain and
blood. And to Sir Denzil's latest descendant the first sight of
the training-stable—as the pony-carriage came to a standstill
alongside the grass plot in the centre of the great, gravelled
square—offered very definite and stirring poetry of a kind.

On three sides the quadrangle was shut in by one-storied,
brick buildings, the woodwork of doors and windows immaculate
with white paint. Behind, over the wide archway,—closed fortress-
like by heavy doors at night,—were the head-lad's and helpers'
quarters. On either side, forge and weighing-room, saddler's and
doctor's shop. To right and left a range of stable doors, with
round swing-lights between each; and, above these, the windows
of hay and straw lofts and of the boys' dormitories. In front
were the dining-rooms and kitchens, and the trainer's house—a
square clock tower, carrying an ornate gilt vane, rising from the
cluster of red roofs. Twenty years had weathered the raw of
brick walls, and painted the tiling with all manner of orange
and rusty-coloured lichens; yet the whole place was admirably
spick and span, free of litter. Many cats, as Dickie noted,
meditated in sunny corners, or prowled in the open with truly
official composure. Over all stretched a square of bluest sky,
crossed by a skein of homeward-wending rooks. While above
the roofs, on either side the archway, the high-lying lands of
the park showed up, broken here and there by clumps of
trees.

Mr. Chifney slipped out of the saddle.—"Here, boy, take
my horse," he shouted to a little fellow hurrying across the
yard. "I'm heartily glad to see you, Sir Richard," he went on.
"Now, if you care, as your father's son can't very well be off
caring, for horses"—

"If I care!" echoed Dickie, his eyes following the graceful,
chestnut filly as she was led in over the threshold of her stable.

"I like that. That'll do. Chip of the old block after all,"
the trainer said, with evident relish. "Well then, since you do
care for horses as you ought to, Sir Richard, we'll just make you

free of this establishment.   About the most first-class private
establishment in England, sir, though I say it that have run the
concern pretty well single-handed for the best part of the last
fifteen years—make you free of it right away, sir.   And, look you,
when you've got hold, don't you leave hold."

"No, I won't," Dickie said stoutly.

Mr. Chifney was in a condition of singular emotion, as he
wrapped Richard's rug about him and bore him away into the
stables.   He even went so far as to swear a little under his
breath; and Chifney was a very fairly clean-mouthed man,
unless members of his team of twenty and odd naughty boys
got up to some devilry with their charges.   He carried Richard
as tenderly as could any woman, while he tramped from stall to
stall, loose-box to loose-box, praising his racers, calling attention
to their points, recounting past prowess, or prophesying future
victories.

And the record was a fine one; for good luck had clung to
the masterless stable, as Lady Calmady's bank-books and ledgers
could testify.

"Vinedresser, by Red Burgundy out of Valeria—won two
races at the Newmarket Spring Meeting the year before last.
Lamed himself somehow in the horse-box coming back — did
nothing for eighteen months—hope to enter him for some of
the autumn events."—Then later :—" Sahara, by North African
out of Sally-in-our-Alley.   Beautiful mare?   I believe you, Sir
Richard.   Why she won the Oaks for you.   Jack White was up.
Pretty a race as ever I witnessed, and cleverly ridden.   Like to
go up to her in the stall?   She's as quiet as a lamb.   Catch
hold of her head, boy."

And so Dick found himself seated on the edge of the manger,
the trainer's arm round him, and the historic Sahara snuffing at
his jacket pockets.

Then they crossed the quadrangle to inspect the colts and
fillies, whose glories still lay ahead.

"Verdigris, by Copper King out of Valeria again.   And if he
doesn't make a name I'll never judge another horse, sir.   Strain
of the old Touchstone blood there.   Rather ugly?   Yes, they're
often a bit ugly that lot, but devilish good 'uns to go.   You ask
Miss Cathcart about them.   Never met a lady who'd as much
knowledge as she has of a horse.   The Baby, by Punch out of
Lady Bountiful.   Not much good, I'm afraid.   No grip, you see,
too contracted in the hoofs.   Chloroform, by Sawbones out of
sister to Castinette."

And so forth, an endless repetition of genealogies, comments, anecdotes to which Dickie lent most attentive ear. He was keen to learn, his attention was on the stretch. He was in process of initiation, and every moment of the sacred rites came to him with power and value. Yet it must be owned that he found the lessening of the strain on his memory and attention not wholly unwelcome when Mr. Chifney, sitting beside him on the big, white-painted corn-bin opposite Diplomacy's loose-box, began to tell him of the old times when he—a little fellow of eight to ten years of age—had been among the boys in his cousin, Sam Chifney's famous stable at Newmarket. Of the long, weary travelling, before the days of railways, when the horses were walked by highroad and country lane, ankle deep in mud, from Newmarket to Epsom; and after victory or defeat, walked by slow stages all the way home again. Of how, later, he had migrated to Doncaster; but, not liking the "Yorkshire tykes," had got taken on in some well-known stables upon the Berkshire downs.

"And it was there, Sir Richard," he said, "I met your father, and we fancied each other from the first. And he asked me to come to him. These stables were just building then. And here I've been ever since."

Mr. Chifney stared down at the clean, red quarries of the stable floor, and tapped his neat gaiters with the switch he held in his hand.

"Rum places, racing-stables," he went on, meditatively, "and a lot of rum things go on in 'em, one way and another, as you'll come to know. And it ain't the easiest thing going, I tell you, to keep your hands clean. Ungrateful business a trainer's, Sir Richard—wearing business—shortens a man's temper and makes him old before his time. Out by four o'clock on summer mornings, minding your cattle and keeping your eye on those shirking blackguards of boys. No real rest, sir, day or night. Wearing business—studying all the meetings and entering your horses where you've reason to reckon they've most chance. And if your horse wins, the jockey gets all the praise and the petting. And if it fails, the trainer gets all the blame. Yes, it's wearing work. But, confound it all, sir," he broke out hotly, "there's nothing like it on the face of God's earth. Horses—horses— horses—why the very smell of the bedding's sweeter than a bunch of roses. Love 'em? I believe you. And you'll love 'em too before you've done."

He turned and gripped Dickie hard by the shoulder.

"For we'll make a thorough-paced sportsman of you yet, Sir Richard," he said, "God bless you—danged if we don't."

Which assertion Mr. Chifney repeated at frequent intervals over his grog that evening, as he sat, not in the smart dining-room hung round with portraits of Vinedresser and Sahara and other equine notabilities, but in the snug, little, back parlour looking out on to the yard. Mrs. Chifney was a gentle, pious woman, with whom her husband's profession went somewhat against the grain. She would have preferred a nice grocery, or other respectable, uneventful business, in a country town, and dissipation in the form of prayer rather than of race-meetings. But as a slender, slightly self-righteous, young maiden she had fallen very honestly and completely in love with Tom Chifney. So there was nothing for it but to marry him and regard the horses as her appointed cross. She nursed the boys when they were sick or injured, intervened fairly successfully between their poor, little backs and her husband's all-too-ready ash stick; and assisted Julius March in promoting their spiritual welfare, even while deploring that the latter put his faith in forms and ceremonies rather than in saving grace. Upon the trainer himself she exercised a gently repressive influence.

"We won't swear, Mr. Chifney," she remarked mildly now.

"Swear! It's enough to make the whole bench of bishops swear to see that lad."

"I did see him," Mrs. Chifney observed.

"Yes, out of window. But you didn't carry him round, and hear him talk—knowledgeable talk as you could ask from one of his age. And watch his face—as like as two peas to his father's."

"But her ladyship's eyes," put in Mrs. Chifney.

"I don't know whose eyes they are, but I know he can use 'em. It was as pretty as a picture to see how he took it all."

Chifney tossed off the remainder of his tumbler of brandy and water at a gulp.

"Swear," he repeated, "I could find it in my heart to swear like hell. But I can find it in my heart to do more than that. I can forgive her ladyship. By all that's "—

"Thomas, forgiveness and oaths don't go suitably together."

"Well, but I can though, and I tell you, I do," he said solemnly. "I forgive her.—Shoot the Clown! by G—! I beg your pardon, Maria—but upon my soul, once or twice, when I had him in my arms to-day, I felt I could have understood it if she'd had every horse shot that stood in the stable."

He held the tumbler up against the lamp. But it was quite empty.

"Uncommon glad she didn't though, poor lady, all the

same," he added, parenthetically, as he set it down on the table
again.—"What do you say, Maria—about time we toddled off
to bed?"

CHAPTER V

IN WHICH DICKIE IS INTRODUCED TO A LITTLE DANCER WITH
BLUSH-ROSES IN HER HAT

"HER ladyship's inquired for you more than once, sir."—
This from Winter meeting the pony-carriage and the
returning prodigal at the bottom of the steps.

The sun was low.   Across the square lawn—whereon the
Clown had found death some thirteen years before—peacocks led
home their hens and chicks to roost within the two sexagonal,
pepper-pot summer-houses that fill in the angles of the red-walled
enclosure.   The pea-fowl stepped mincingly, high-shouldered,
their heads carried low, their long necks undulating with a self-
conscious grace.   Dickie's imagination was aglow like that
rose-red, sunset sky.   The virile sentiment of all just heard
and seen, and the exultation of admitted ownership were upon
him.   He felt older, stronger, more secure of himself, than ever
before.   He proposed to go straight to his mother and confess.
In his present mood he entertained no fear but that she would
understand.

"Is Lady Calmady alone?" he asked.

"Mr. and Mrs. Cathcart are with her, Sir Richard."—Winter
leant down, loosening the rug.   His usual undemonstrative
speech took on a loftiness of tone.   "Mrs. William Ormiston
and her daughter have driven over with Mrs. Cathcart."—
The butler was not without remembrance of that dinner on
the day following Dickie's birth.   Socially he had never considered Lady Calmady's sister-in-law quite up to the Brockhurst
level.

Richard leaned back, watching the mincing peacocks.   It
was so fair here out of doors.   The scent of the may hung in the
air.   The flame of the sunset bathed the façade of the stately
house.   No doubt it would be interesting to see new people,
new relations; but he really cared to see no one, just now,
except his mother.   From her he wanted to receive absolution,
so that, his conscience relieved of the burden of his disobedience,
he might revel to the full in the thought of the inheritance upon

which—so it seemed to him—he had to-day entered.   Still, in his present humour, Dickie's sense of *noblesse oblige* was strong.

"I suppose I've got to go in and help entertain everybody," he remarked.

"Her ladyship'll think something's wrong, Sir Richard, and be anxious if you stay away."

The boy held out his arms.   "All right then, Winter," he said.

Here Chaplin again gave that admonitory cough.   Richard, his face hardening to slight scorn, looked at him over the butler's shoulder.

"Oh ! You need not be uneasy, Chaplin.   When I say I'll do a thing, I don't forget."

Which brief speech caused the butler to reflect, as he bore the boy across the hall and upstairs, that Sir Richard was coming to have an uncommonly high manner about him, at times, considering his age.

An unwonted loudness of conversation filled the Chapel-Room.   It was filled also by the rose-red light of the sunset streaming in through the curve of the oriel-window.   This confused and dazzled Richard slightly, entering upon it from the silence and sober clearness of the stair-head.   A shrill note of laughter.—Mr. Cathcart's voice saying—"I felt it incumbent upon me to object, Lady Calmady.   I spoke very plainly to Fallowfeild."—Julius March's delicately refined tones—"I am afraid spirituality is somewhat deficient in that case."—Then the high, flute-like notes of a child, rising clearly above the general murmur—"*Ah ! enfin—le voilà, Maman.   C'est bien lui, n'est-ce pas ?*" And with that, Richard was aware of a sudden hush falling upon the assembled company.   He was sensible everyone watched him as Winter carried him across the room and set him down in the long, low arm-chair near the fireplace.   Poor Dickie's self-consciousness, which had been so agreeably in abeyance, returned upon him, and a red, not of the sunset, dyed his face. But he carried his head proudly.   He thought of Chifney and the horses.   He refused to be abashed.

And Ormiston, breaking the silence, called to him cheerily :—

"Hello, old chap, what have you been up to ?   You gave Mary and me the slip."

"I know I did," the boy answered bravely.   "How d'ye do, Mrs. Cathcart ?" as the latter nodded and smiled to him—a large, gentle, comfortable lady, uncertain in outline, thanks to voluminous draperies of black silk and black lace.   "How d'ye do, sir ?" this to Mr. Cathcart—a tall, neatly-made man, but for a

9

slight roundness of the shoulders. Seeing him, there remained no doubt as to whence Mary inherited her large mouth; but matter for thankfulness that she had avoided further inheritance. For Mr. Cathcart was notably plain. Small eyes and snub nose, long, lower jaw, and grey, forward-curled whiskers rendered his appearance unfortunately simian. He suggested a caricature; but one, let it be added, of a person undeniably well-bred.

"My darling, you are very late," Katherine said. Her back was towards her guests as she stooped down arranging the embroidered rug across Dickie's feet and legs. Laying his hand on her wrist he squeezed it closely for a moment.

"I—I'll tell you all about that presently, mummy, when they're gone. I've been enjoying myself awfully — you won't mind?"

Katherine smiled. But, looking up at her, it appeared to Richard that her face was very white, her eyes very large and dark, and that she was very tall and, somehow, very splendid just then. And this fed his fearlessness, fed his young pride, even as, though in a more subtle and exquisite manner, his late experience of the racing-stable had fed them. His mother moved away and took up her interrupted conversation with Mr. Cathcart regarding the delinquencies of Lord Fallowfeild. Richard looked coolly round the room.

Everyone was there—Julius, Mary, Mademoiselle de Miran-court, while away in the oriel-window Roger Ormiston stood talking to a pretty, plump, very much dressed lady, who chattered, laughed, stared, with surprising vivacity. As Dickie looked at her she stared back at him through a pair of gold eye-glasses. Against her knee, that rosy light bathing her graceful, little figure, leant a girl about Dickie's own age. She wore a pale pink and blue frock, short and outstanding in the skirts. She also wore a broad-brimmed, white hat, with a garland of blush-roses around the crown of it. The little girl did not stare. She contemplated Richard languidly, yet with sustained attention. Her attitude and bearing were attractive. Richard wanted to see her close, to talk to her. But to call and ask her to come to him was awkward. And to go to her—the boy grew a little hot again—was more awkward still.

Mrs. Ormiston dropped her gold eye-glasses into her lap.

"It really is ten thousand pities when these things happen in the wrong rank of life," she said. "Rightly placed they might be so profitable."

"For goodness sake, be careful, Charlotte," Ormiston put in quickly.

"Oh! my dear creature, don't be nervous. Everybody's attending to everybody else, and if they did hear they wouldn't understand. I'm one of the fortunate persons who are supposed never to talk sense and so I can say what I like." Mrs. Ormiston gave her shrill little laugh. "Oh! there are consolations, depend upon it, in a well-sustained reputation for folly!"

The laugh jarred on Richard. He decided that he did not quite like his aunt Charlotte Ormiston. All the same he wished the charming, little girl would come to him.

"But to return.—It's a waste. To some poor family it might have been a perfect fortune. And I hate waste. Perhaps you have never discovered that?"

Ormiston let his glance rest on the somewhat showy figure.

"I doubt if William has discovered it either," he remarked.

"Oh! as to your poor brother William, Heaven only knows what he has or has not discovered!—Now, Helen, this conversation becomes undesirable. You've asked innumerable questions about your cousin. Go and make acquaintance with him. I'm the best of mothers of course, but, at times, I really can do quite well without you."

Now surely this was a day of good fortune, for again Dickie had his desire. And a most surprisingly pretty, little desire it proved—seductive even, deliciously finished in person and in manner. The boy gazed at the girl's small hands and small, daintily shod feet, at the small, lovely, pink and white face set in a cloud of golden-brown hair, at the innocent, blue eyes, at the mouth with upturned corners to it. Richard was not of age to remark the eyes were rather light in colour, the lips rather thin. The exquisite refinement of the girl's whole person delighted him. She was delicate as a miniature, as a figure carved in ivory. She was like his uncle Roger, when she was silent and still. She was like—oh, poor Dick!—some bright glancing, small, saucy bird when she spoke and her voice had those clear, flute tones in it.

"Since you did not come to me, I had to come to you," she said. "I have wanted so much to see you. I had heard about you at home, in Paris."

"Heard about me?" Dickie repeated, flattered and surprised. "But won't you sit down? Look—that little chair. I can reach it."

And leaning sideways he stretched out his hand. But his finger-tips barely touched the top rail. Richard flushed.—"I'm awfully sorry," he said, "but I am afraid—it isn't heavy—I must let you get it yourself."

The girl, who had watched him intently, her hands clasped, gave a little sigh. Then the corners of her mouth turned up as she smiled. A delightful dimple showed in her right cheek.

"But, of course," she replied, "I will get it."

She settled herself beside him, folded her hands, crossed her feet, exposing a long length of fine, open-work, silk stocking.

"I desired enormously to see you," she continued. "But when you came in I grew shy. It is so with one sometimes."

"You should use your influence, Lady Calmady," Mr. Cathcart was saying. "Unquestionably the condition of the workhouse is far from satisfactory. And Fallowfeild is too lenient. That *laisser-aller* policy of his threatens to land us in serious difficulties. The place is insanitary, and the food is unnecessarily poor. I am not an advocate for extravagance, but I cannot bear to see discomfort which might be avoided. Fallowfeild is the most kind-hearted of men, but he has a fatal habit of believing what people tell him. And those workhouse officials have got round him. The whole matter ought to be subjected to the strictest investigation."

"It is very nice of you to have wanted so much to see me," Dickie said. His eyes were softly bright.

"Oh! but one always wants to see those who are talked about. It is a privilege to have them for one's relations."

"But—but—I'm not talked about?" the boy put in, somewhat startled.

"But certainly. You are so rich. You have this superb *château*. You are"—she put her head on one side with a pretty, saucy, birdlike movement — "*enfin*," she said, "I had the greatest curiosity to make your acquaintance. I shall tell all my young friends at the convent about this visit. I promised them that, as soon as mama said we should probably come here. The good sisters also are interested. I shall recount a whole history of this beautiful castle, and of you, and your"—

She paused, clasped her hands, looking away at her mother, then sideways at Richard, bowing her little person backwards and forwards, laughing softly all the while. And her laughing face was extraordinarily pretty under the shade of her broadbrimmed hat.

"It is a great misfortune we stay so short a time," she continued. "I shall not see the half of all that I wish to see."

Then an heroic plan of action occurred to Richard. The daring engendered by his recent act of disobedience was still active in him. He was in the humour to attempt the impossible. He longed, moreover, to give this delectable little person pleasure.

He was willing even to sacrifice a measure of personal dignity in her service.

"Oh! but if you care so much, I—I will show you the house," he said.

"Will you?" she cried, "You and I alone together? But that is precisely what I want. It would be ravishing."

Poor Dickie's heart misgave him slightly; but he summoned all his resolution. He threw off the concealing rug.

"I—I walk very slowly, I'm afraid," he said rather huskily, looking up at her, while in his expression appeal mingled pathetically with defiant pride.

"But, so much the better," she replied. "We shall be the longer together. I shall have the more to observe, to recount."

She was on her feet. She hovered round him, birdlike, intent on his every movement.

Meanwhile the sound of conversation rose continuous. Lady Calmady, calling to Julius, had moved away to the great writing-table in the farther window. Together they searched among a pile of papers for a letter of Dr. Knott's, embodying his scheme of the new hospital at Westchurch. Mr. Cathcart stood by, expounding his views on the subject.

"Of course a considerable income can be derived from letters of recommendation," he was saying, "in-patient and out-patient tickets. The clergy come in there. They cannot be expected to give large donations. It would be unreasonable to expect that of them."

Mademoiselle de Mirancourt, Mrs. Cathcart, and Mary, had drawn their chairs together. The two elder ladies spoke with a subdued enthusiasm, discussing pleasant details of the approaching wedding, which promised the younger lady so glad a future. Mrs. Ormiston chattered; while Ormiston, listening to her, gazed away down the green length of the elm avenue, beyond the square lawn and pepper-pot summer-houses, and pitied men who made such mistakes in the matter of matrimony as his brother William obviously had. The rose of the sunset faded in the west. Bats began to flit forth, hawking against the still-warm house-walls for flies.

And so, unobserved, Dickie slipped out of the security of his arm-chair, and rose to that sadly deficient full height of his. He was nervous, and this rendered his balance more than ever uncertain. He shuffled forward, steadying himself by a piece of furniture here and there in passing, until he reached the wide open space before the door on to the stair-head. And it required some fortitude to cross this space, for here was nothing to lay hold of for support.

Little Helen Ormiston had kept close beside him so far. Now she drew back, leaving him alone. Leaning against a table, she watched his laborious progress. Then a fit of uncontrollable laughter took her. She flew half-way across to the oriel-window, her voice ringing out clear and gay, though broken by bursts of irrepressible merriment.

"*Regardez, regardez donc, Maman! Ma bonne m'avait dit qu'il était un avorton, et que ce serait très amusant de le voir. Elle m'a conseiller de lui faire marcher.*"

She darted back, and clapping her hands upon the bosom of her charming frock, danced, literally danced and pirouetted around poor Dickie.

"*Moi, je ne comprenais pas ce que c'était qu'un avorton,*" she continued rapidly. "*Mais je comprends parfaitement maintenant. C'est un monstre, n'est-ce pas, Maman?*"

She threw back her head, her white throat convulsed by laughter.

"*Ah! mon Dieu, qu'il est drôle!*" she cried.

Silence fell on the whole room, for sight and words alike were paralysing in their grotesque cruelty. Ormiston was the first to speak. He laid his hand somewhat roughly on his sister-in-law's shoulder.

"For God's sake, stop this, Charlotte," he said. "Take the girl away. Little brute," he added, under his breath, as he went hastily across to poor Dick.

But Lady Calmady had been beforehand with him. She swept across the room, flinging aside the dainty, dancing figure as she passed. All the primitive fierceness, the savage tenderness, of her motherhood surged up within her. Katherine was in the humour to kill just then, had killing been possible. She was magnificently regardless of consequences, regardless of conventionalities, regardless of every obligation save that of sheltering her child. She cowered down over Richard, putting her arms about him, knew—without question or answer—that he had heard and understood. Then gathering him up against her, she stood upright, facing them all, brother, sister, old and tried friends, a terrible expression in her eyes, the boy's face pressed down upon her shoulder. For the moment she appeared alienated from, and at war with, even Julius, even Marie de Mirancourt. No love, however faithful, could reach her. She was alone, unapproachable, in her immense anger and immense sense of outrage.

"I will ask you to go," she said to her sister-in-law,—"to go and take your daughter with you, and to enter this house no more."

Mrs. Ormiston did not reply. Even her chatter was for the moment stilled. She pressed a handkerchief against the little dancer's forehead, and it was stained with blood.

"Ah! she is a wicked woman!" wailed the child. "She has hurt me. She threw me against the table. *Maman quel malheur ça se verra. Il y aura certainement une cicatrice!*"

"Nonsense," Ormiston said harshly. "It's nothing, Kitty, the merest scratch."

"Yes, my dear, we will have the carriage at once,"—this from Mr. Cathcart to his wife. The incident, from all points of view, shocked his sense of propriety. Immediate retirement became his sole object.

Lady Calmady moved away, carrying the boy. She trembled a little. He was heavy. Moreover, she sickened at the sight of blood. But little Helen Ormiston caught at her dress, and looked up at her.

"I hate you," she said, hissing the words out with concentrated passion between her pretty even teeth. "You have spoilt me. I will hate you always, when I grow up. I will never forget."

Alone in the great state-bedroom next door, a long time elapsed before either Richard or Katherine spoke. The boy leaned back against the sofa cushions, holding his mother's hand. The casements stood wide open, and little winds laden with the scent of the hawthorns in the park wandered in, gently stirring the curtains of the ebony bed, so that the Trees of the Forest of This Life, thereon embroidered, appeared somewhat mournfully to wave their branches, while the Hart fled forward and the Leopard, relentless in perpetual pursuit, followed close behind. There was a crunching of wheels on the gravel, a sound of hurried farewells. Then in a minute or two more the evening quiet held its own again.

Suddenly Dickie flung himself down across Katherine's lap, his poor body shaken by a tempest of weeping.

"Mother, I can't bear it—I can't bear it," he sobbed. "Tell me, does everybody do that?"

"Do what, my own precious?" she said, calm from very excess of sorrow. Later she would weep too, in the dark, lying lonely in the cold comfort of that stately bed.

"Laugh at me, mother, mock at me?" and his voice, for all that he tried to control it, tore at his throat and rose almost to a shriek.

CHAPTER VI

DEALING WITH A PHYSICIAN OF THE BODY AND A PHYSICIAN OF THE SOUL

HISTORY repeats itself, and to Katherine just now came most unwelcome example of such repetition. She had foreseen that some such crisis must arise as had arisen. Yet when it arose, the crisis proved none the less agonising because of that foreknowledge. Two strains of feeling struggled within her. A blinding sorrow for her child, a fear of and shame at her own violence of anger. Katherine's mind was of an uncompromising honesty. She knew that her instinct had, for a space at least, been murderous. She knew that, given equal provocation, it would be murderous again.

And this was, after all, but the active, objective aspect of the matter. The passive and subjective aspect showed danger also. In her extremity Katherine's soul cried out for God—for the sure resting-place only to be found by conscious union of the individual with the eternal will. But such repose was denied her. For her anger against God, even while thus earnestly desiring Him, was even more profound than her anger against man. The passion of those terrible early days when her child's evil fortune first became known to her—held in check all these years by constant employment and the many duties incident to her position—returned upon her in its first force. To believe God is not, leaves the poor human soul homeless, sadly desolate, barren in labour as is a slave. But the sorrow of such belief is but a trifle beside the hideous fear that God is careless and unjust, that virtue is but a fond imagination of all-too-noble human hearts, that the everlasting purpose is not good but evil continually. And, haunted by such fears, Katherine once again sat in outer darkness. All gracious things appeared to her as illusions ; all gentle delights but as passing anodynes with which, in his misery, man weakly tries to deaden the pain of existence. She suffered a profound discouragement.

And so it seemed to her but as part of the cruel whole when history repeated itself yet further, and Dr. Knott, pausing at the door of Richard's bedroom, turned and said to her :—

" It will be better, you know, Lady Calmady, to let him face it alone. He'll feel it less without you. Winter can give me all the assistance I want." Then he added, a queer smile playing about his loose lips :—"Don't be afraid.   I'll handle him very gently.   Probably I shan't hurt him at all—certainly not much."

"Ah !" Katherine said, under her breath.

"You see it is done by his own wish," John Knott went on.

"I know," she answered.

She respected and trusted this man, entertained for him, notwithstanding his harsh speech and uncouth exterior, some-thing akin to affection.   Yet remembering the part he had played in the fate of the father, it was very dreadful to her that he should touch the child.   And Dr. Knott read her thought. He did not resent it.   It was all natural enough !   From his heart he was sorry for her, and would have spared her had that been possible.   But he discriminated very clearly between primary and secondary issues, never sacrificing, as do feeble and sentimental persons, the former to the latter.   In this case the boy had a right to the stage, and so the mother must stand in the wings.   John Knott possessed a keen sense of values in the human drama which the exigencies of his profession so perpetually presented to him.   He waited quietly, his hand on the door-handle, looking at Katherine from under his shaggy eyebrows, silently opposing his will to hers.

Suddenly she turned away with an impatient gesture.

"I will not come with you," she said.

"You are right."

"But—but—do you think you can really do anything to help him, to make him happier?" Katherine asked, a desperation in the tones of her voice.

"Happier?   Yes, in the long-run, because certainty of whatever kind, even certainty of failure, makes eventually for peace of mind."

"That is a hard saying."

"This is a hard world."—Dr. Knott looked down at the floor, shrugging his unwieldy shoulders.   " The sooner we learn to accept that fact the better, Lady Calmady.   I know it is sharp discipline, but it saves time and money, let alone disappointment.—Now as to all these elaborate contrivances I've brought down from London, they're the very best of their kind.   But I am bound to own the most ingenious of such arrangements are but clumsy remedies for natural deficiency.   Man hasn't discovered how to make over his own body yet, and never will.   The Almighty will always have the whip-hand of us when it comes to dealing with flesh and blood.   All the same we've got to try these legs and things "—

Katherine winced, pressing her lips together.   It was brutal, surely, to speak so plainly? But John Knott went on quietly, commiserating her inwardly, yet unswerving in common sense.

"Try 'em every one, and so convince Sir Richard one way or the other. This is a turning-point. So far his general health has been remarkably good, and we've just got to set our minds to keeping it good. He must not fret if we can help it. If he frets, instead of developing into the sane, manly fellow he should, he may turn peevish, Lady Calmady, and grow up a morbid, neurotic lad, the victim of all manner of brain-sick fancies—become envious, spiteful, a misery to others and to himself."

"Is it necessary to say all this?" Katherine asked loftily.

Dr. Knott's eyes looked very straight into hers, and there were tears in them.

"Indeed, I believe it is," he replied, "or, trust me, I wouldn't say it. I take no pleasure in giving pain at this time of day, whether mental or physical. All I want is to spare pain. But one must sacrifice the present to the future, at times, you know—use the knife to save the limb. Now I must go to my patient. It isn't fair to keep him waiting any longer. I'll be as quick as I can. I suppose I shall find you here when I've finished?"

As he opened the door Dr. Knott's heavy person showed in all its ungainliness against the brightness of sunlight flooding Dickie's room. And to Katherine he seemed hideous just then —inexorable in his great common sense, in the dead weight of his personality and of his will, as some power of nature. He was to her the incarnation of things as they are—not things as they should be, not things as she so passionately desired they might be. He represented rationalism as against miracle, intellect as against imagination, the bitter philosophy of experience as against that for which all mortals so persistently cry out — namely the all-consoling promise of extravagant hope. As with chains he bound her down to fact. Right home on her he pressed the utter futility of juggling with the actual. From the harsh truth that, neither in matters practical nor spiritual, is any redemption without shedding of blood he permitted her no escape.

And all this Katherine's clear brain recognised and admitted, even while her poor heart only rebelled the more madly. To be convinced is not to be reconciled. And so she turned away from that closed door in a veritable tempest of feeling, and went out into the Chapel-Room. It was safer, her mind and heart thus working, to put a space between herself and that closed door.

Just then Julius March crossed the room, coming in from the stair-head. The austere lines of his cassock emphasised the height and emaciation of his figure. His appearance offered a marked contrast to that of the man with whom Katherine had just parted. His occupation offered a marked contrast also. He carried a gold chalice and paten, and his head was bowed reverentially above the sacred vessels. His eyes were downcast, and the dull pallor of his face and of his long, thin hands was very noticeable. He did not look round, but passed silently, still as a dream, into the chapel. Katherine paced the width of the great room, turned and paced back and forth again some half-dozen times, before he emerged from the chapel door. In her present humour she did not want him, yet she resented his abstraction. The physician of the soul, like the physician of the body, appeared to her lamentably devoid of power to sustain and give comfort at the present juncture.

This, it so happened, was one of those days when the mystic joy of his priestly office held Julius March forcibly. He had ministered to others, and his own soul was satisfied. His expression was exalted, his short-sighted eyes were alive with inward light. Tired and worn, there was still a remarkable suavity in his bearing. He had come forth from the holy of holies, and the vision beheld there dwelt with him yet.

Meanwhile, brooding storm sat on Katherine's brow, on her lips, dwelt in her every movement. And something of this Julius perceived, for his devotion to her was intact, as was his self-abnegation. Throughout all these years he had never sought to approach her more closely. His attitude had remained as delicately scrupulous, untouched by worldliness, or by the baser part of passion, as in the first hour of the discovery of his love. Her near presence gave him exquisite pleasure ; but, save when she needed his assistance in some practical matter, he refused to indulge himself by passing much time in her society. Abstinence still remained his rule of life. Just now, however, strong with the mystic strength of his late ministrations and perceiving her troubled state, he permitted himself to remain and pace beside her.

"You have been out all day ?" Katherine said.

"Yes, I stayed on to the end with Rebecca Light. They sent for me early this morning. She passed away very peacefully in that little attic at the new lodge looking out into the green heart of the woods."

"Ah! It's simple enough to die," Katherine said, "being old. The difficult thing is to live, being still young."

"Has my absence been inconvenient? Have you wanted me?" Julius asked.—Those quiet hours spent in the humble

death-chamber suddenly appeared to him as an act of possible
selfishness.

"Oh no!" she answered bitterly. "Why should I want
you? Have I not sent Roger and Mary away? Am I not
secretly glad dear Marie de Mirancourt is just sufficiently poorly
to remain in her room? When the real need comes—one
learns that among all the other merciless lessons—one is best
by oneself."

For a while, only the whisper of Lady Calmady's skirts, the
soft, even tread of feet upon the thick carpet. Then she said,
almost sharply :—

"Dr. Knott is with Richard."

"Ah! I understand," Julius murmured.

But Lady Calmady took up his words with a certain heat.

"No, you do not understand. You none of you understand,
and that is why I am better by myself. Mary and Roger in
their happiness, dear Marie in her saintly resignation, and
you"—Katherine turned her head, smiled at him in lovely scorn
—"you, my dear Julius, of all men, what should you know of
the bitter pains of motherhood, you who are too good to be
quite human, you who regard this world merely as the ante-
chamber of paradise, you, whose whole affection is set on your
Church—your God—how should you understand? Between
my experience and yours there is a very wide interval. How
can you know what I suffer—you who have never loved?"

Under the stress of her excitement Katherine's pace
quickened. The whisper of her skirts grew to a soft rush.
Julius kept beside her. His head was bent reverently, even as
over the sacred vessels he had so lately carried.

"I too have loved," he said at last.

Katherine stopped short, and looked at him incredulously.

"Really, Julius?" she said.

Raising his head, he looked back at her. This avowal gave
him a strange sense of completeness and mastery. So he allowed
his eyes to meet Katherine's, he allowed himself to reckon with
her grace and beauty.

"Very really," he answered.

"But when?"

"Long ago—and always."

"Ah!" she said. Her expression had changed. Brooding
storm no longer sat on her brow and lips. She was touched.
For the moment the weight of her personal distress was lifted.
Dickie and Dr. Knott together in that bed-chamber, experimenting with unlovely, mechanical devices for aiding locomotion

and concealing the humiliation of deformity, were almost forgotten. To those who have once loved, love must always supremely appeal. Julius appeared to her in a new aspect. She felt she had done him injustice. She placed her hand on his arm with a movement of apology and tenderness. And the man grew faint, trembled, feeling her hand, seeing it lie white and fair on the sleeve of his black cassock. Since childhood it was the first, the solitary, caress he had received.

"Pardon me, dear Julius," she said. "I must have pained you at times, but I did not know this. I always supposed you coldly indifferent to those histories of the heart which mean so much to some of us; supposed your religion held you wholly, and that you pitied us as the wise pity the foolish, standing above them, looking down. Richard told me many things about you, before he brought me home here, but he never told me this."

"Richard never knew it," he answered, smiling. Her perfect unconsciousness at once calmed and pained him. He had kept his secret, all these years, only too well.

Katherine turned and began to pace again, her hands clasped behind her back.

"But, tell me—tell me," she said. "You can trust me, you know. I will never speak of this unless you speak. But if I knew, it would bring us nearer together, and that would be comforting, perhaps, to us both. Tell me, what happened? Did she know, and did she love you? She must have loved you, I think. Then what separated you? Did she die?"

"No, thank God, she did not die," Julius said.—He paused. He longed to gain the relief of fuller confession, yet feared to betray himself. "I believe she loved me truly as a friend—and that was sufficient."

"Oh no, no!" Katherine cried. "Do not decline upon sophistries. That is never sufficient."

"In one sense, yes—in another sense, no," Julius said. "It was thus. I loved her exactly as she was. Had she loved me as I loved her she would have become other than she was."

"Ah! but surely you are too ingenious, too fastidious!" Katherine's voice took tones of delicate remonstrance and pleading. "That would be your danger, in such a case. Le mieux est l'ennemi du bien, and you would always risk sacrificing the real to the ideal. I am sorry. I would like you to have tasted the fulness of life. Even though the days of perfect joy are very few, it is well to have had them"—

She threw back her head, her eyebrows drew together, and her face darkened somewhat.

"Yes, it is well to have had them, though the memory of them cuts one to the very quick."—Then her manner changed again, gaining a touch of gaiety. "Really I am very unselfish in wishing all this otherwise," she said, "for it would have been a sore trial to part with you. I cannot imagine Brockhurst without you. I should have been in great straits deprived of my friend and counsellor. And yet, I would like you to have been very happy, dear Julius."

Their pacing had just brought them to the arched doorway of the chapel. Katherine stopped, and raising her arm leaned her hand against the stone jamb of it above her head.

"See," she went on, "I want to be truly unselfish. I know how generous you are. Perhaps you remain here out of all too great kindness towards my poor Dick and me. You mustn't do that, Julius. You say she is still living. Consider—is it too late?"

Was it indeed too late? All the frustrated manhood cried aloud in Julius March. He covered his face with his hands. His carefully restrained imagination ran riot, presenting enchantments.

And Katherine, watching him, found herself strangely moved. For it was very startling to see this so familiar figure under so unfamiliar an aspect — to see Julius March, her every-day companion and assistant, his reticence, his priestly aloofness, his mild and courtly calm, swept under by a tide of personal emotion. Lady Calmady was drawn to him by deepened sympathy. Yet regret arose in her that this man proved to be, after all, but as other men are. She was vaguely disappointed, having derived more security than she had quite realised from his apparent detachment and impassibility. And, as an indirect consequence, her revolt against God suffered access of bitterness. For not only was He—to her seeing—callous regarding the fate of the many, but He failed to support those few most devoted to His cause. In the hour of their trial He was careless even of His own elect.

"Ah! I think it is indeed by no means too late!" she exclaimed.

Julius March let his hands drop at his sides. He gazed at her, and her expression was of wistful mockery—compassionate rather than ironical. Then he looked away down the length of the chapel. In the warm afternoon light, the solid and rich brown of the arcaded stalls on either hand, emphasised the harmonious radiance of the great, east window, a radiance as of clear jewels.—Ranks of kneeling saints, the gold of whose orioles rose in an upward curve to the majestic image of the Christ in the central light—a Christ risen and glorified, enthroned, His feet shining forever upon heaven's sapphire floor. Before the altar hung three, silver-gilt lamps of Italian workmanship, in the crimson cup of each of which it had so long been Julius's pleasure to keep the tongue of flame constantly alive. The habits of a lifetime are not hastily set aside. Gazing on these things, his normal attitude returned to him. Not that which he essentially was but that which, by long and careful training of every thought, every faculty, he had become, authoritatively claimed him. His eyes fell from contemplation of the glories of the window to that of the long, straight folds of the cassock which clothed him. It was hardly the garb in which a man goes forth to woo! Then he looked at Lady Calmady—she altogether seductive in her innocence and in her wistful mockery as she leaned against the jamb of the door.

"You are mistaken, dear Katherine," he said. "It has always been too late."

"But why—why—if she is free to listen?"

"Because I am not free to speak."

Julius smiled at her. His suavity had returned, and along with it a dignity of bearing not observable before.

"Let us walk," he said. And then:—"After all I have given you a very mutilated account of this matter. Soon after I took orders, before I had ever seen the very noble, to me perfect, woman who unconsciously revealed to me the glory of human love, I had dedicated my life, and all my powers—poor enough, I fear—of mind and body to the service of the Church. I was ambitious in those days. Ambition is dead, killed by the knowledge of my own shortcomings. I have proved an unprofitable servant—for which may God in His great mercy forgive me. But, while my faith in myself has withered, my faith in Him has come to maturity. I have learned to think very differently on many subjects, and to perceive that our Heavenly Father's purposes regarding us are more generous, more far-reaching, more august, than in my youthful ignorance I had ever dreamed. All things are lawful in His sight. Nothing is common or unclean—if we have once rightly apprehended Him, and He dwells in us. And yet—yet, a vow once made is binding. We may not do evil to gain however great a good."

Katherine listened in silence. The words came with the power of immutable conviction. She could not believe, yet she was glad to have him believe.

"And that vow precludes marriage?" she said at last.

"It does," Julius answered.

For a time they paced again in silence. Then Lady Calmady spoke, a delicate intimacy and affection in her manner, while once more, for a moment, she let her hand rest on his arm.

"So Brockhurst keeps you—I keep you, dear Julius, to the last?"

"Yes, if you will, to the very last."

"I am thankful for that," she said. "You must forgive me if in the past I have been inconsiderate at times. I am afraid the constant struggle, which certain circumstances of necessity create, tends to make me harsh and imperious. I carry a trouble, which calls aloud for redress, forever in my arms. They ache with the burden of it. And there is no redress. And the trouble grows stronger, alas! Its voice — so dear, yet so dreaded—grows louder, till it deafens me to all other sounds. The music of this once beautiful world becomes faint. Only angry discord remains. And I become selfish. I am the victim of a fixed idea. I become heedless of the suffering of those about me. And you, my poor Julius, must have suffered very much!"

"Now, less than ever before," he answered.—But even as he spoke, Katherine was struck by his pallor, by the drawn look of his features and languor of his bearing.

"Ah, you have fasted all day!" she cried.

"What matter?" he said, smiling. "The body surely can sustain a trifle of hunger, if the soul and spirit are fed. I have feasted royally to-day in that respect. I am strangely at ease. As to baser sort of food, what wonder if I forgot?"

The door of Dickie's bed-chamber opened, letting in long shafts of sunlight, and Dr. Knott came slowly forward. His aspect was savage. Even his philosophy had been not wholly proof against the pathos of his patient's case. It irritated him to fall from his usual relentlessness of common sense into a melting mood. He took refuge in sarcasm, desirous to detect weakness in others, since he was, unwillingly, so disagreeably conscious of it in himself.

"Well, we're through with our business, Lady Calmady," he said.—"Eh! Mr. March, what's wrong with you? Putty-coloured skin and shortness of breath. A little less prayer and a little more physical exercise is what you want. Successful, Lady Calmady?—Umph—I'm afraid the less said about that the better. Sir Richard will talk it out with you himself. Upset? Yes, I don't deny he is a little upset—and, like a fool, I'm upset too. You can go to him now, Lady Calmady. Keep him cheerful, please, and give him his head as much as you can."

John Knott watched her as she moved away. He shrugged his shoulders and thrust his hands into his breeches pockets.

"She's going to hear what she won't much relish, poor thing," he said. "But I can't help that. One man's meat is another man's poison; and my affair is with the boy's meat, even if it should be of a kind to turn his mother's stomach. He shall have just all the chance I can get him, poor little chap.—And now, Mr. March, I propose to prescribe for you, for you look uncommonly like taking a short-cut to heaven, and, if I know anything about this house, you've got your work cut out for you here below for a long time to come. Through with this business? Pooh! we've only taken a preliminary canter as yet. That boy's out of the common in more ways than one, and, cripple or no cripple, he's bound to lead you all a pretty lively dance before he's done."

CHAPTER VII

AN ATTEMPT TO MAKE THE BEST OF IT

THE day had been hot, though the summer was but young. A wealth of steady sunlight bathed the western front of the house. All was notably still, save for a droning of bees, a sound of wood-chopping, voices now and again, and the squeak of a wheelbarrow away in the gardens.

Richard lay on his back upon the bed. He had drawn the blue embroidered coverlet up about his waist; but his silk shirt was thrown open, exposing his neck and chest. His arms were flung up and out across the pillow on either side his gold-brown, close-curled head. As his mother entered he turned his face towards the open window. There was vigour and distinction in the profile—in the straight nose, full chin, and strong line of the lower jaw, in the round, firm throat, and small ear set close against the head. The muscles of his neck and arms were well developed. Seen thus, lying in the quiet glow of the afternoon sunshine, all possibility of physical disgrace seemed far enough from Richard Calmady. He might indeed, not unfitly, have been compared to one of those nobly graceful lads, who, upon the frieze of some Greek temple, set forth forever the perfect pattern of temperance and high courage, of youth and health.

10

As Katherine sat down beside the bed, Richard thrust out his left hand. She took it in both hers, held and stroked the palm of it. But for a time she could not trust herself to speak. For she saw that, notwithstanding the resolute set of his lips, his breath caught in short quick sobs and that his eyelashes were glued in points by late shed tears. And, seeing this, Katherine's motherhood arose and confronted her with something of reproach. It seemed to her she had been guilty of disloyalty in permitting her thought to be beguiled even for the brief space of her conversation with Julius March. She felt humbled, a little in Dickie's debt, since she had not realised to the uttermost each separate moment of his trial as each of those moments passed.

"My darling, I am afraid Dr. Knott has hurt you very much?" she said at last.

"Oh! I don't know. I suppose he did hurt. He pulled me about awfully, but I didn't mind that. I told him to keep on till he made sure," Richard answered huskily, still turning his face from her. "But none of those beastly legs and things fitted. He could not fix them so that I could use them. It was horrid. They only made me more helpless than before. You see—my—my feet are in the way."

The last words came to Katherine as a shock. The boy had never spoken openly of his deformity, and in thus speaking he appeared to her to rend asunder the last of those veils with which she had earnestly striven to conceal the disgrace of it from him. She remained very still, bracing herself to bear—the while slowly stroking his hand. Suddenly the strong, young fingers closed hard on hers. Richard turned his head.

"Mother," he said, "the doctor can't do anything for me. It's no use. We've just got to let it be."

He set his teeth, choking a little, and drew the back of his right hand across his eyes.

"It's awfully stupid; but somehow I never knew I should mind so much. I—I never did mind much till just lately. It began—the minding, I mean—the day Uncle Roger came home. It was the way he looked at me, and hearing about things he'd done. And I had a beastly dream that night. And it's all grown worse since."

He paused a minute, making a strong effort to speak steadily.

"I suppose it's silly to mind. I ought to be accustomed to it by this time. I've never known anything else. But I never thought of all it meant and—and—how it looked to other people

till Helen was here and wanted me to show her the house.   I—
I supposed everyone would take it for granted, as you all do
here at home.   And then I'd a hope Dr. Knott might find a
way to hide it and so help me.   But—but he can't.   That
hope's quite gone."

"My own darling," Katherine murmured.

"Yes, please say that!" he cried, looking up eagerly.   "I
am your darling, mother, am I not, just the same?   Dr. Knott said
something about you just now.   He's an awfully fine old chap.
I like him.   He talked to me for a long time after we'd sent
Winter away, and he was ever so kind.   And he told me it
was bad for you too, you know—for both of us.   I'm afraid
I had not thought much about that before.   I've been thinking
about it since.   And I began to be afraid that—that I might
be a nuisance,—that you might be ashamed of me, later,
when I am grown up—since I've always got to be like this, you
see."

The boy's voice broke.

"Mother, mother, you'll never despise me, whoever does,
will you?" he sobbed.

And it seemed to Lady Calmady that now she must have
touched bottom in this tragedy.   There could surely be no
farther to go?   It was well that her mood was soft, that for a
little while she had ceased to be under the dominion of her so
sadly fixed idea.   In talking with Julius March she had been
reminded how constant a quantity is sorrow; how real, notwithstanding their silence, are many griefs; how strong is human
patience.   And this indirectly had fortified her.   Wrung with
anguish for the boy, she yet was calm.   She knelt down by the
bedside and put her arms round him.

"Most precious one—listen," she said.   "You must never
ask me such a question again.   I am your mother—you cannot
measure all that implies, and so you cannot measure the pain
your question causes me.   Only you must believe, because I tell
it you, that your mother's love will never grow old or wear thin.
It is always there, always fresh, always ready.   In utter security
you can come back to it again and again.   It is like one of those
clear springs in the secret places of the deep woods—you know
them—which bubble up forever.   Drink, often as you may,
however heavy the drought or shrunken the streams elsewhere,
those springs remain full to the very lip."—Her tone changed,
taking a tender playfulness.   "Why, my Dickie, you are the
light of my eyes, my darling, the one thing which makes me
still care to live.   You are your father's gift to me.   And so every

kiss you give me, every pretty word you say to me, is treasured up for his, as well as for your own, dear sake."

She leaned back, laid her head on the pillow beside his, cheek to cheek. Katherine was a young woman still—young enough to have moments of delicate shyness in the presence of her son. She could not look at him now as she spoke.

"You know, dearest, if I could take your bodily misfortune upon me, here, directly, and give you my wholeness, I would do it more readily, with greater thankfulness and delight than I have ever done anything in "—

But Richard raised his hand and laid it, almost violently, upon her mouth.

"Oh, stop, mother, stop!" he cried. "Don't—it's too dreadful to think of."

He flung away, and lay at as far a distance as the width of the bed would allow, gazing at her in angry protest.

"You can't do that. But you don't suppose I'd let you do it even if you could," he said fiercely. Then he turned his face to the sunny western window again.—"I like to know that you're beautiful anyhow, mother, all—all over," he said.

There followed a long silence between them. Lady Calmady still knelt by the bedside. But she drew herself up, rested her elbows on the bed and clasped her hands under her chin. And as she knelt there something of proud comfort came to her. For so long she had sickened, fearing the hour when Richard should begin clearly to gauge the extent of his own ill-luck; yet, now the first shock of plain speech over, she experienced relief. For the future they could be honest, she and he,—so she thought, —and speak heart to heart. Moreover, in his so bitter distress, it was to her—not to Mary, his good comrade, not to Roger Ormiston, the Ulysses of his fancy—that the boy had turned. He was given back to her, and she was greatly gladdened by that. She was gladdened too by Richard's last speech, by his angry and immediate repudiation of the bare mention of any personal gain which should touch her with loss. Katherine's eyes kindled as she knelt there watching her son. For it was very much to find him thus chivalrous, hotly sensitive of her beauty and the claims of her womanhood. In instinct, in thought, in word, he had shown himself a very gallant, high-bred gentleman—child though he was. And this gave Katherine not only proud comfort in the present, but cheered the future with hope.

"Look here, Dickie darling," she said softly at last, "tell me a little more about your talk with Dr. Knott."

"Oh! he was awfully kind," Richard answered, turning

towards her again, while his face brightened. "He said some awfully jolly things to me."

The boy put out his hand and began playing with the bracelets on Katherine's wrists. He kept his eyes fixed on them as he fingered them.

"He told me I was very strong and well made—except, of course, for it. And that I was not to imagine myself ill or invalidy, because I'm really less ill than most people, you know. And—and he said—you won't think me foolish, mother, if I tell you?—he said I was a very handsome fellow."

Richard glanced up quickly, while his colour deepened.

"Am I really handsome?" he asked.

Katherine smiled at him.

"Yes, you are very handsome, Dickie. You have always been that. You were a beautiful baby, a beautiful little child. And now, every day, you grow more like your father. I can't quite talk about him, my dear—but ask Uncle Roger—ask Marie de Mirancourt what he was when she knew him first."

The boy's face flashed back her smile, as the sea does the sunlight.

"Oh, I say, but that's good news!" he said. He lay quite still on his back for a little while, thinking about it.

"That seems to give one a shove, you know," he remarked presently. Then he fell to playing with her bracelets again. "After all, I've got a good many shoves to-day, mother. Dr. Knott's a regular champion shover. He told me about a number of people he'd known who had got smashed up somehow, or who'd always had something wrong, you know—and how they'd put a good face on it and hadn't let it interfere, but had done things just the same. And he told me I'd just got to be plucky—he knew I could if I tried—and not let it interfere either. He told me I mustn't be soft, or lazy, because doing things is more difficult for me than for other people. But that I'd just got to put my back into it, and go in and win. And I told him I would—and you'll help me, mummy, won't you?"

"Yes, darling, yes," Lady Calmady said.

"I want to begin at once," he went on hurriedly, looking hard at the bracelets. "I shouldn't like to be unkind to her, mother, but do you think Clara would give me up? I don't need a nurse now. It's rather silly. May one of the men-servants valet me? I should like Winter best, because he's been here always, and I shouldn't feel shy with him. Would it bore you awfully to speak about that now, so that he might begin to-night?"

Lady Calmady's brave smile grew a trifle sad.   The boy was less completely given back to her than she had fondly supposed. This day was after all to introduce a new order.   And the woman always pays.   She was to pay for that advance, so was the devoted handmaiden, Clara.   Still the boy must have his way— were it even towards a merely imagined good.

"Very well, dearest, I will settle it," she answered.

"You don't mind, though, mother?"

Katherine stroked the short, curly hair back from his forehead.

"I don't mind anything that promises to make you happier, Dickie," she said.   "What else did you and Dr. Knott settle— anything else?"

Richard waited, then he turned on his elbow and looked full and very earnestly at her.

"Yes, mother, we did settle something more.   And something that I'm afraid you won't like.   But it would make me happier than anything else—it would make all the difference that—that can be made, you know."

He paused, his expression very firm though his lips quivered.

"Dr. Knott wants me to ride."

Katherine drew back, stood up, threw out her hands as though to keep off some actual and tangible object of offence.

"Not that, Richard!" she cried.   "Anything in the world rather than that!"

He looked at her imploringly, yet with a certain determination, for the child was dying fast in him and the forceful desires and intentions of youth growing.

"Don't say I mustn't, mother.   Pray, pray don't, because"—

He left the sentence unfinished, overtaken by the old habit of obedience, yet he did not lower his eyes.

But Lady Calmady made no response.   For the moment she was outraged to the point of standing apart even from her child. For a moment, even motherhood went down before purely personal feeling—and this, by the irony of circumstance, immediately after motherhood had made supreme confession of immutability.   But remembering her husband's death, remembering the source of all her child's misfortune, it appeared to her indecent, a wanton insult to all her past suffering, that such a proposition should be made to her.   And, in a flash of cruelly vivid perception, she knew how the boy would look on a horse, the grotesque, to the vulgar wholly absurd, spectacle he must, notwithstanding his beauty, necessarily present.   For a moment the completeness of love failed before pride touched to the very quick.

"But, how can you ride?" she said. "My poor child, think —how is it possible?"

Richard sat upright, pressing his hands down on the bed-clothes on either side to steady himself. The colour rushed over his face and throat.

"It is possible, mother," he answered resolutely, "or Dr. Knott would never have talked about it. He couldn't have been so unkind. He drew me the plan of a saddle. He said I was to show it to Uncle Roger to-night. Of course it won't be easy at first, but I don't care about that. And Chifney would teach me. I know he would. He said the other day he'd make a sportsman of me yet."

"When did you talk with Chifney?"—Lady Calmady spoke very quietly, but there was that in her tone which came near frightening the boy. It required all his daring to answer honestly and at once.

"I talked to him the day Aunt Charlotte and Helen were here. I—I went down to the stables with him and saw all the horses."

"Then either you or he did very wrong," Lady Calmady remarked.

"It was my fault, mother, all my fault. Chifney would have ridden on, but I stopped him. Chaplin tried to prevent me. I —I told him to mind his own business. I meant to go. I—I saw all the horses, and they were splendid," he added, enthusiasm gaining over fear.—"I saw the stables, and the weighing-room, and everything. I never enjoyed myself so much before. I told Chaplin I would tell you, because he ought not to be blamed, you know. I did mean to tell you directly I came in. But all those people were here."—Richard's face darkened. "And you remember what happened? That put everything else out of my head."—A pause. Then he said :—" Are you very angry?"

Katherine made no reply. She moved away round the foot of the bed and stood at the sunny window in silence. Bitter-ness of hot humiliation possessed her. Heretofore, whatever her trial, she had been mistress of the situation; she had reigned a queen-mother, her authority undisputed. And now it appeared her kingdom was in revolt, conspiracy was rife. Richard's will and hers were in conflict; and Richard's will must eventu-ally obtain, since he would eventually be master. Already courtiers bowed to that will. All this was in her mind. And a wounding of feeling, far deeper and more intimate than this—since Katherine's nobility of character was great and the worldly aspect, the greed of personal power and undisputed rule, could not affect her for long. It wounded her, as a slight upon the memory of the man she had so wholly loved, that this first conflict between Richard and herself should turn on the question of horses and the racing-stable. The irony of the position appeared unpardonable. And then, the vision of poor Richard—her darling, whom she had striven so jealously to shield ever since the day, over thirteen years ago, when undressing her baby she had first looked upon its malformed limbs—Richard riding forth for all the staring, mocking world to see, again arose before her.

Thinking of all this, Katherine gazed out over the stately home scene—grass plot and gardens, woodland and distant landscape, rich in the golden splendour of steady sunshine—with smarting eyes and a sense of impotent misery that wrapped her about as a burning garment. The boy was beginning to go his own way. And his way was not hers. And those she had trusted were disloyal, helping him to go it. Alone, in retirement, she had borne her great trouble with tremendous courage. But how should she bear it under changed conditions, amid publicity, gossip, comment?

Dickie, meanwhile, had let himself drop back against the pillows. He set his teeth and waited. It was hard. An opportunity of escape from the galling restraints of his infirmity had been presented to him, and his mother—his mother after promise given, after the sympathy of a lifetime, his mother, in whom he trusted absolutely—was unwilling he should accept it! As he lay there all the desperate longing for freedom and activity that had developed in him of late—all the passion for sport, for that primitive, half-savage manner of life, that intimate, if somewhat brutal, relation to nature, to wild creatures and to the beasts whom man by centuries of usage has broken to his service, which is the special heritage of Englishmen of gentle blood—sprang up in Richard, strong, all-compelling. He must have his part in all this. He would not be denied. He cried out to her imperiously :—

"Mother, speak to me! I haven't done anything really wrong. I've a right to what any other boy has—as far as I can get it. Don't you see riding is just the one thing to—to make up—to make a man of me? Don't you see that?"

He sat bolt upright, stretching out his arms to her in fierce appeal, while the level sunshine touched his bright hair and wildly eager face.

"Mummy, mummy darling, don't you see? Try to see. You can't want to take away my one chance!"

Katherine turned at that reiterated cry, and her heart melted within her. The boy was her own, bone of her bone, flesh of her flesh. From her he had life. From her he had also lifelong disgrace and deprivation. Was there anything then, which, he asking, she could refuse to give? She cast herself on her knees beside the bed again and buried her face in the sheet.

" My precious one," she sobbed, "forgive me. I am ashamed, for I have been both harsh and weak. I said I would help you, and then directly I fail you. · Forgive me."

And the boy was amazed, speechless at first, seeing her broken thus ; shamed in his turn by the humility of her attitude. To his young chivalry it was an impiety to look upon her tears.

"Please don't cry, mother," he entreated tremulously, a childlike simplicity of manner taking him.—"Don't cry—it is dreadful. I never saw you cry before."—Then, after a pause, he added :—"And—never mind about my riding. I don't so very much care about it—really, I don't believe I do—after all."

At that dear lie Katherine raised her bowed head, a wonderful sweetness in her tear-stained face, tender laughter upon her lips. She drew the boy's hands on to her shoulders, clasped her hands across his extended arms, and kissed him upon the mouth.

"No, no, my beloved, you shall ride," she said. "You shall have your saddle—twenty thousand saddles if you want them ! We will talk to Uncle Roger and Chifney to-night. All shall be as you wish."

"But you're not angry, mother, any more ? " he asked, a little bewildered by her change of tone and by the passion of her lovely looks and speech.

Katherine shook her head, and still that tender laughter curved her lips.

"No, I am never going to be angry any more—with you at least, Dick. I must learn to be plucky too. A pair of us, Dickie, trying to keep up one another's pluck ! Only let us go forward hand in hand, you and I, and then, however desperate our doings, I at least shall be content."

CHAPTER VIII

TELLING, INCIDENTALLY, OF A BROKEN-DOWN POSTBOY AND A COUNTRY FAIR

THE Brockhurst mail-phaeton waited, in the shade of the three large sycamores, before Appleyard's shop at Farley Row. A groom stood stiff and straight at the horses' heads. While upon the high driving-seat, a trifle excited by the suddenness of his elevation, sat Richard. He held the reins in his right hand, and stretched his left to get the cramp out of his fingers. His arms ached—there was no question about it. He had never driven a pair before, and the horses needed a lot of driving. For the wind was gusty, piling up heavy masses of black-purple rain-cloud in the south-east. It made the horses skittish and unsteady, and Dickie found it was just all he could do to hold them, so that Chifney's reiterated admonition, "Keep 'em well in hand, Sir Richard," had been not wholly easy to obey.

From out the open shop-door came mingled odour of new leather and of horse clothing. Within Mr. Chifney delivered himself of certain orders; while Appleyard—a small, fair man, thin of nose, a spot of violent colour on either cheek-bone—skipped before him lamb-like, in a fury of complacent intelligence. For it was not every day so notable a personage as the Brockhurst trainer crossed his threshold. To Josiah Appleyard, indeed—not to mention his two apprentices stretching eyes and ears from the back-shop, to catch any chance word of Mr. Chifney's conversation—it appeared as though the gods very really condescended to visit the habitations of men. While Mrs. Appleyard, peeping from behind the wire blind of the parlour, had—as she afterwards repeatedly declared—"felt her insides turn right over," when she saw the carriage draw up. The conversation was prolonged and low-toned. For the order was of a peculiar and confidential character, demanding much explanation on the one part, much application on the other. It was an order, in short, wholly flattering to the self-esteem of the saddler, both as tribute to his social discretion and his technical skill. Thus did Josiah skip lamb-like, being glad.

Meanwhile, Richard Calmady waited without, resting his aching arms, gazing down the wide, dusty street, his senses lulled by the flutter of the sycamore leaves overhead. The said street

offered but small matter of interest.   For Farley Row is one of
those dead-alive, little towns on the borders of the forest land,
across which progress, even at the time in question, 1856, had
written Ichabod in capital letters.   During the early years of
the century some ninety odd coaches, plying upon the London
and Portsmouth road, would stop to change horses at the
White Lion in the course of each twenty-four hours.   That
was the golden age of the Row.   Horns twanged, heavy
wheels rumbled, steaming teams were led away, with drooping
heads, into the spacious inn yard, and fresh horses stepped
out cheerily to take their place between the traces.   The
next stage across Spendle Flats was known as a risky one.
Legends of Claude Duval and his fellow-highwaymen still haunt
the woods and moors that top the long hill going north-eastward.
And the passengers by those ninety coaches were wont to recover
themselves from terrors escaped, or fortify themselves against
terrors to come, by plentiful libations at the bar of the handsome
red-brick inn.   The house did a roaring trade.   But now the
traffic upon the great road had assumed a local and altogether
undemonstrative character.   The coaches had fallen into lumber,
the spanking teams had each and all made their squalid last
journey to the knacker's.   And the once famous Gentlemen of the
Road had long lain at rest in Mother Earth's lap—sleeping there
none the less peacefully because the necks of many of them had
suffered a nasty rick from the hangman's rope, and because the
hard-trodden pavement of the prison-yard covered them.
    The fine stables of the White Lion stood tenantless, now, from
year's end to year's end.   Rats scampered, and bats squeaked in
unlovely ardours of courtship, about the ranges of empty stalls
and cobweb-hung rafters.   Yet one ghost from out the golden
age haunted the place still—a lean, withered, bandy-legged, little
stick of a man, arrayed in frayed and tarnished splendour of sky-
blue waist-jacket, silver lace, and jackboots—of which the soles
and upper leathers threatened speedy and final divorce.   In all
weathers this bit of human wreckage—Jackie Deeds by name—
might be seen wandering aimlessly about the vacant yard, or
seated upon the bench beside the portico of the silent, bow-
windowed inn, pulling at a, too often empty, clay-pipe and
spitting automatically.
    Over Richard, tender-hearted as yet towards all creatures
whom nature or fortune had treated cavalierly, the decrepit
postboy exercised a fascination.   One day, when driving through
the Row with Mary Cathcart, he had succeeded in establishing
relations with Jackie Deeds through the medium of a half-crown.

And now, as he waited beneath the rustling sycamores, it was with a sensation of quick, yet half-shy, pleasure, that he saw the disreputable figure lurch out of the inn yard, stand for a minute shading eyes with hand while making observations, and then hobble across the street, touching the peak of a battered, black-velvet cap as it advanced.

" Be 'e come to zee the show, sir? " the old man coughed out, peering with dim, blear eyes up into the boy's fresh face.

" No, we've come about something from Appleyard's. I—I didn't know there was a show."

"Oh! bain't there though, Sir Richard! I tell 'e there be a prime sight of a show. There be monkeys down town, and dorgs what dances on their 'inder legs, and gurt iron cages chock-full er wild beastises, by what they tells me."

Dickie, feeling anxiously in his pockets for some coin of sufficient size to be worthy of Mr. Deeds' acceptance, ejaculated involuntarily :—" Oh! are there? I'd give anything to see them."

"Sixpence 'ud do most er they 'ere shows, I expect. The wild beastises 'ud run into a shilling may be."—The old postboy made a joyless, creaking sound, bearing but slightest affinity to laughter. "But you 'ud see your way round more'n a shilling, Sir Richard. A terrible, rich, young gentleman, by what they tells me."

Something a trifle malicious obtained in this attempt at jocosity, causing Dickie to bend down rather hastily over the wheel, and thrust his offering into the crumpled, shaky hands.

"There," he said. "Oh! it's nothing. I'm so pleased you —you don't mind. Where do you say this show is?"

"Gor a'mighty bless 'e, sir," the old man whimpered, with a change of tone. "Tain't every day poor old Jackie Deeds runs across a rich, young gentleman as 'll give him 'arf a crown. Times is bad, mortal bad—couldn't be much wuss."

"I'm so sorry," Richard answered. He felt apologetic, as though in some manner responsible for the decay of the coaching system and his companion's fallen estate.

"Mortal bad, couldn't be no wuss."

"I'm very sorry. But about the show—where is it, please?" the boy asked again, a little anxious to change the subject.

"Oh! that there show. Tain't much of a show neither, by what they tells me."

Mr. Deeds spoke with sudden irritability. Uplifted by the possession of half a crown, he became contemptuous of the present, jealous of the past when such coin was more plentiful with him.

"Not much of a show," he repeated. "The young 'uns 'll crack up most anything as comes along. But that's their stoopidness. Never zee'd nothing better. Law bless 'e, this ain't a patch on the shows I've a-zeen in my day. Cock-fightings, and fellows—wi' a lot er money laid on 'em by the gentry too—a-pounding of each other till there weren't an inch above the belt of 'em as weren't bloody. And the Irish giant, and dwarfs 'ad over from France. They tell me most Frencheys 's made that way. Ole Boney 'isself wasn't much of a one to look at. And I can mind a calf wi' two 'eads—'ud eat wi' both mouths at once, and all the food 'ud go down into the same belly. And a man wi' no arms, never 'ad none, by what they used to tell me "—

"Ah!" Richard exclaimed quickly.

"No, never 'ad none, and yet 'ud play the drum wi' 'is toes and fire off a horse pistol. Lor, you would er laughed to 'ave zeen 'im. 'E made fine sport for the folks 'e did."

Jackie Deeds had recovered his good-humour. He peered up into the boy's face again maliciously, and broke into cheerless, creaking merriment.

"Gor a'mighty 'as 'is jokes too," he said. "I'm thinking, by the curous-made creeturs 'e sends along sometimes."

"Chifney," Richard called imperatively. "Chifney, are you nearly ready? We ought to get home. There's a storm coming up."

"Well, we shall get that matter of the saddle done right enough, Sir Richard," the trainer remarked presently, as the carriage bowled up the street. "Don't be too free with the whip, sir.—Steady, steady there.—Mind the donkey-cart.—Bear away to the right. Don't let 'em get above themselves. Excuse me, Sir Richard."

He leaned forward and laid both hands quietly on the reins.

"Look here, sir," he said, "I think you'd better let Henry lead the horses past all this variety business."

The end of the street was reached. On either hand small red or white houses trend away in a broken line along the edge of a flat, grass common, backed by plantations of pollarded oak trees. In the foreground, fringing the broad roadway, were booths, tents, and vans. And the staring colours of these last, raw reds and yellows, the blue smoke beating down from their little stove-pipe chimneys, the dirty white of tent flaps and awnings, stood out harshly in a flare of stormy sunlight against the solid green of the oaks and uprolling masses of black-purple cloud.

Here indeed was the show. But to Richard Calmady's eyes it lacked disappointingly in attraction. His nerves were some-

what a-quiver. All the coarse detail, all the unlovely foundations, of the business of pleasure were rather distressingly
obvious to his sight. A merry-go-round was in full activity—
wooden horses and most unseaworthy boats describing a jerky
circle to the squeaking of tin whistles and purposeless thump-
ings of a drum. Close by a crop-eared lurcher, tied beneath one
of the vans, dragged choking at his chain and barked himself
frantic under the stones and teasing of a knot of idle boys. A
half-tipsy slut of a woman threatened a child, who, in soiled
tights and spangles, crouched against the muddy hind-wheel
of a waggon, tears dribbling down his cheeks, his arm raised
to ward off the impending blow. From the menagerie—an
amorphous huddle of grey tents, ranged behind a flight of
wooden steps leading up to an open gallery hung with advertise-
ments of the many attractions within—came the hideous laughter
of a hyena, and the sullen roar of a lion weary of the rows of
stolid English faces staring daily, hourly, between the bars of
his foul and narrow cage, heart-sick with longing for sight of
the open, starlit heaven and the white-domed, Moslem tombs
amid the prickly, desert thickets and plains of clean, hot sand.
On the edge of the encampment horses grazed—sorry beasts
for the most part, galled, broken-kneed and spavined, weary and
heart-sick as the captive lion. But weary not from idleness, as
he. Weary from heavy loads and hard travelling and scant
provender. Sick of collar and whip and reiterated curses.

About the tents and booths, across the grass, and along the
roadway, loitered a sad-coloured, country crowd. Even to the
children, it took its pleasure slowly and silently; save in the case
of a hulking, young carter in a smock-frock, who, being pretty
far gone in liquor, alternately shouted bawdy songs and offered
invitation to the company generally to come on and have its
head punched.

Such were the pictures that impressed themselves upon
Richard's brain, as Henry led the dancing carriage-horses up
the road. And it must be owned that from this first sight
of life, as the common populations live it, his soul revolted.
Delicately nurtured, finely bred, his sensibility accentuated by
the prickings of that thorn in the flesh which was so intimate
a part of his otherwise noble heritage, the grossness and brutality
of much which most boys of his age have already learned to take
for granted affected him to the point of loathing. And more
especially did he loathe the last picture presented to him on
the outskirts of the common. At the door of a gaudily-painted
van, somewhat apart from the rest, stood a strapping lass,

tambourine in one hand, tin mug for the holding of pennies in the other.   She wore a black, velvet bodice, rusty with age, and a blue, silk skirt of doubtful cleanliness, looped up over a widely distended scarlet petticoat.   Rows of amber beads encircled her brown throat.   She laughed and leered, bold-eyed and coarsely alluring, at a couple of sheepish country lads on the green below.   She called to them, pointing over her shoulder with the tin cup, to the sign-board of her show.   At the painting on that board Richard Calmady gave one glance.   His lips grew thin and his face white.   He jerked at the reins, causing the horses to start and swerve.   Was it possible that, as old Jackie Deeds said, God Almighty had His jokes too, jokes at the expense of His own creation?   That in cynical abuse of human impotence, as a wanton pastime, He sent human beings forth into the world thus ludicrously defective?   The thought was unformulated.   It amounted hardly to a thought indeed,— was but a blind terror of insecurity, which, coursing through the boy's mind, filled him with agonised and angry pity towards all disgraced fellow-beings, all enslaved and captive beasts.   Dimly he recognised his kinship to all such.

Meanwhile the carriage bowled along the smooth road and up the long hill, bordered by fir and beech plantations, which leads to Spendle Flats.   And there, in the open, the storm came down, in rolling thunder and lashing rain.   Tall, shifting, white columns chased each other madly across the bronze expanse of the moorland.   Chifney, mindful of his charge, hurried Dickie into a greatcoat, buttoned it carefully round him, offered to drive, almost insisted on doing so.   But the boy refused curtly. He welcomed the stinging rain, the swirling wind, the swift glare of lightning, the ache and strain of holding the pulling horses. The violence of it all heated his blood as with the stern passion of battle.   And under the influence of that passion his humour changed from agonised pity to a fierce determination of conquest.   He would fight, he would come through, he would win, he would slay dragons.   Prometheus-like he would defy the gods.   Again his thought was unformulated, little more than the push of young, untamed energy impatient of opposition. But that he could face this wild mood of nature and control and guide these high-mettled, headstrong horses gave him coolness and self-confidence.   It yielded him assurance that there was, after all, an immensity of distance between himself and all caged, outworn creatures, and that the horrible example of deformity upon the brazen-faced girl's show-board had really nothing to do with him.   Dickie's last humour was less noble

than his first, it is to be feared.   But in all healthy natures, in
all those in whom the love of beauty is keen, there must be in
youth strong repudiation of the brotherhood of suffering.   Time
will teach a finer and deeper lesson to those that have faith and
courage to receive it ; yet it is well the young should defy sorrow,
hate suffering, gallantly, however hopelessly, fight.

And the warlike instinct remained by Dickie all that evening.
He was determined to assert himself, to measure his power, to
obtain.   While Winter was helping him dress for dinner he
gave orders that his chair should be placed at the bottom of
the table.

" But the colonel sits there, Sir Richard."

Dickie's face did not give in the least.

" He has sat there," he answered rather shortly.   " But I
have spoken to her ladyship, and in future he will sit by her.
I'll go down early, Winter.   I prefer being in my place when
the others come in."

It must be added that Ormiston accepted his deposition in
the best possible spirit, patting the boy on the shoulder as he
passed him.

" Quite right, old chap.   I like to see you there.   Claim
your own, and keep it."

At which a lump rose in Dickie's throat, nearly causing him
to choke over his first spoonful of soup.   But Mary Cathcart,
whose kind eyes saw most things, smiled first upon her lover
and then upon him, and began talking to him of horses, as one
sportsman to another.   And so Dickie speedily recovered himself and grew eager, playing host very prettily at his own table.

He demanded to sit up to prayers, moreover, and took his
place in the dead Richard Calmady's stall nearest the altar rails
on the gospel side.   Next him was Dr. Knott, who had come in
unexpectedly just before dinner.   He had the boy a little on his
mind ; and, while contemptuous of his own solicitude in the
matter, wanted badly to know just how he was.   Lady Calmady
had begged him to stay.   He could be excellent company when
he pleased.   He had laid aside his roughness of manner and been
excellent company to-night.   Next him was Ormiston, while the
seats immediately below were occupied by the men-servants,
Winter at their head.

Opposite to Richard, across the chapel, sat Lady Calmady.
The fair, summer moonlight streaming in through the east
window spread a network of fairy jewels upon her stately, grey-
clad figure and beautiful head.   Beside her was Mary Cathcart,
and then came a range of dark, vacant stalls.   And below these

was a long line of women-servants, ranging from Denny, in rustling, black silk, and Clara,—alert and pretty, though a trifle tearful,—through many grades and orders, down to the little scullery-maid, fresh from the keeper's cottage on the Warren— home-sick, and half scared by the grand gentlemen and ladies in evening-dress, by the strange, lovely figures in the stained-glass windows, by the great, gold cross and flowers, and the rich altar-cloth and costly hangings but half seen in the conflicting light of the moonbeams and flickering candles.

John Knott was impressed by the scene too, though hardly on the same lines as the little scullery-maid. He had long ago passed the doors of orthodoxy and dogma. Christian church and heathen temple — could he have had the interesting experience of entering the latter—were alike to him. The attitude and office of the priest, the same in every age and under every form of religion, filled him with cynical scorn. Yet he had to own there was something inexpressibly touching in the nightly gathering together of this great household, gentle and simple; and in this bowing before the source of the impenetrable mystery which surrounds and encloses the so curiously urgent and vivid consciousness of the individual. He had to own, too, that there was something inexpressibly touching in the tones of Julius March's voice as he read of the young Galilean prophet "going about and doing good"—simple and gracious record of tenderness and pity, upon which, in the course of centuries, the colossal fabric of the modern Christianity, Catholic and Protestant, has been built up.

"'And great multitudes came to Him,'" read Julius, "'having with them those that were lame, blind, dumb, maimed, and many others, and cast them down at Jesus' feet, and He healed them; insomuch that the multitude marvelled when they saw the dumb to speak, and the maimed to be whole, and the lame to walk'"—

How simple it all sounded in that sweet, old-world story! And yet how lamentably, in striving to accomplish just these same things, his own far-reaching science failed!

"'The maimed to be whole, the lame to walk'"—involuntarily he looked round at the boy beside him.

Richard leaned back in his stall, tired with the long day and its varying emotions. His eyes were half closed, and his profile showed pale as wax against the background of dark woodwork. His eyebrows were drawn into a slight frown, and his face bore a peculiar expression of reticence. Once he glanced up at the reader, as though on a sudden a pleasant thought occurred to

11

him. But the movement was a passing one. He leaned back in his stall again and folded his arms, with a movement of quiet pride, almost of contempt.

Later that night, as her custom was, Katherine opened the door of Richard's room softly, and entering bent over his bed in the warm dimness to give him a last look before going to rest herself. To-night Dickie was awake. He put his arms round her coaxingly.

"Stay a little, mummy darling," he said. "I am not a bit sleepy. I want to talk."

Katherine sat down on the edge of the bed. All the mass of her hair was unbound, and fell in a cloud about her to the waist. Richard, leaning on one elbow, gathered it together, held and kissed it. He was possessed by the sense of his mother's great beauty. She seemed so magnificently far removed from all that is coarse, spoiled, or degraded. She seemed so superb, so exquisite a personage. So he gazed at her, kissed her hair, and gently touched her arms, where the open sleeves of her white dressing-gown left them bare, in reverential ecstasy.

Katherine became almost perplexed.

"My dearest, what is it?" she asked at last.

"Oh! it's only that you're so perfect, mother," he said. "You make me feel so safe somehow. I'm never afraid when you are there."

"Afraid of what?" she asked. A hope came upon her that he had grown nervous of riding, and wanted her to help him to retire gracefully from the matter. But his next words undeceived her. He threw himself back against the pillow and clasped his hands under his head.

"That's just it," he said. "I don't know exactly what I am afraid of, and yet I do get awfully scared at times. I suppose, mother, if one's in a good position—the position we're in, you know—nobody can ill-use one very much?"

Lady Calmady's eyes blazed with indignation.—"Ill-use you? Who has ever dared to hint at, to dream of, such a thing, dear Richard?"

"Oh, no one—no one! Only I can't help wondering about things, you know. And some—some people do get most awfully ill-used. I can't help seeing that."

Katherine paused before answering. The boy did not look at her. She spoke with quiet conviction, her eyes gazing out into the dimness of the room.

"I know," she said, almost reluctantly. "And perhaps it is as well you should know it too, though it is sad knowledge.

People are not always very considerate of one another.   But ill-usage cannot touch you, my dearest.   You are saved by love, by position, by wealth."

"You are sure of that, mother?"

"Sure?   Of course I am sure, darling," she answered.   Yet even while speaking her heart sank.

Richard remained silent for a space.   Then he said, with certain hesitancy:—"Mother, tell me, it is true then that I am rich?"

"Quite true, Dick."

"But sometimes people lose their money."

Katherine smiled.—"Your money is not kept in a stocking, dearest."

"I don't suppose it is," the boy said, turning towards her. "But don't banks break?"

"Yes, banks break.   But a good many broken banks would not affect you.   It is too long a story to tell you now, Dickie, but your income is very safe.   It would almost need a revolution to ruin you.   You are rich now ; and I am able to save consider-able sums for you yearly."

"It's—it's awfully good of you to take so much trouble for me, mother," he interrupted, stroking her bare arm again delicately.

To Katherine his half-shy endearments were the most delicious thing in life—so delicious that at moments she could hardly endure them.   They made her heart too full.

"Eight years hence, when you come of age and I give account of my stewardship, you will be very rich," she said.

Richard lay quite still, his eyes again fixed on the dim-ness.

"That—that's good news," he said at last, drawing a long breath.   "I saw things to-day, mother, while we were driving. It was nobody's fault.   There was a fair with a menagerie and shows at Farley Row.   I couldn't help seeing.   Don't ask me about it, mother.   I'd rather forget, if I can.   Only it made me understand that it is safer for anyone—well, anyone like—me—don't you know, to be rich."

Richard sat up, flung his arms round her and kissed her with sudden passion.

"Beautiful mother, honey-sweet mother," he cried, "you've told me just everything I wanted to know.   I won't be afraid any more."   Then he added, in a charming little tone of authority:—"Now you mustn't stay here any longer.   You must be tired.   You must go to bed and go to sleep."

BOOK III

LA BELLE DAME SANS MERCI

CHAPTER I

IN the autumn of 1862 Richard Calmady went up to Oxford.
Not through ostentation, but in obedience to the exigencies
of the case, his going was in a somewhat princely sort, so that the
venerable city, moved from the completeness of her scholarly
and historic calm, turned her eyes, in a flutter of quite mundane
excitement, upon the new-comer. Julius March accompanied
Richard. Time and thought had moved forward; but the
towers and spires of Oxford, her fair cloisters and enchanting
gardens, her green meadows and noble elms, her rivers, Isis
and Cherwell, remained as when Julius, too, had been among
the young and ardent of her sons. He was greatly touched by
this return to the Holy City of his early manhood. He renewed
old friendships. He reviewed the past, taking the measure
calmly of what life had promised, what it had given of good.
A pleasant house had been secured in St. Giles's; and a
contingent of the Brockhurst household, headed by Winter, went
with the two gentlemen, while Chaplin and a couple of grooms
preceded them, in charge of a goodly number of horse-boxes.

For that first saddle, fashioned now some six years ago by
Josiah Appleyard of Farley Row, had worked something as near a
miracle as ever yet was worked by pigskin. It was a singularly
ugly saddle, running up into a peak front and back, furnished
with a complicated system of straps and buckles and—in place of
stirrups and stirrup-leathers—with a pair of contrivances resembling old-fashioned holsters. Mary Cathcart's brown eyes had
grown moist on first beholding it. And Colonel Ormiston had
exclaimed:—"Good God! Oh, well, poor dear little chap, I

suppose it's the best we can do for him." An ugly saddle—yet had Josiah Appleyard ample reason to skip, lamb-like, being glad. For, ugly or not, it fulfilled its purpose, bringing custom to the maker, and happiness and health to the owner of it.

The boy rode fearlessly, while exercise and exertion begot in him a certain light-heartedness and audacity good to see. The window-seat of the Long Gallery, the bookshelves of the library, knew him but seldom now. He was no less courteous, no less devoted to his mother, no less in admiration of her beauty ; but the young barbarian was wide awake in Dickie, and drove him out of doors, on to the moorland or into the merry green-wood, with dog, and horse, and gun. On his well-broken pony he shot over the golden stubble fields in autumn ; brought down his pheasants, stationed at the edge of the great coverts ; went out for long afternoons, rabbiting in the warrens and field banks, escorted by spaniels and retrievers, and keepers carrying lithe, lemon-coloured ferrets tied up in a bag.

Later, when he was older,—but this tried Katherine some-what, reminding her too keenly of another Richard Calmady and days long dead,—Winter, a trifle reluctant at such shortening of his own virtuous slumbers, would call Dickie and help dress him, all in the grey of the summer morning ; while, at the little arched doorway in the west front, Chifney and a groom with a led horse would await his coming, and the boy would mount and ride away from the great, sleeping house. At such times a charm of dewy freshness lay on grass and woodland, on hill and vale. The morning star grew pale and vanished in the clear-flashing delight of sunrise, as Richard rode forth to meet the string of racers ; as he noted the varying form and fortune of Rattlepate or Sweet Rosemary, of Yellow Jacket, Morion or Light-o'-Love, over the short, fragrant turf of the gallop ; as he felt the virile joy which the strength of the horses, and the pounding rush of them as they swept past him, ever aroused in him. Then he would ride on, by a short-cut, to the old, red-brick rubbing-house, crowning the rising ground on the farther side of the lake, and wait there to see the finish, talking of professional matters with Chifney meanwhile ; or, turning his horse's head towards the wide, distant view, sit silent, drawing near to nature and worshipping—with the innocent gladness of a still virgin heart—in the Temple of the Dawn.

Life at Oxford was set in a different key. The university city was well disposed towards this young man of so great wealth and so strange fortunes ; and Richard was unsuspicious, and ready enough to meet friendliness half-way. Yet it must be owned he suffered many bad quarters of an hour. He was, at once, older in thought and younger in practical experience than his fellow-undergraduates. He was cut off, of necessity, from their sports. They would eat his breakfasts, drink his wine, and show no violent objection to riding his horses. They were considerate, almost anxiously careful of him, being generous and good-hearted lads. And yet poor Dick was perturbed by the fear that they were more at ease without him, that his presence acted as a slight check upon their genial spirits and their rattling talk. And so it came about that though his acquaintances were many, his friends were few. Chief among the latter was Ludovic Quayle, a younger son of Lord Fallowfeild—whom that kindly, if not very intelligent, nobleman had long ago proposed to export from the Whitney to the Brockhurst nursery with a view to the promotion of general cheerfulness. Mr. Ludovic Quayle was a rather superfine, young gentleman, possessed of an excellent opinion of himself, and a modest opinion of other persons—his father included. But under his somewhat supercilious demeanour there was a vein of true romance. He loved Richard Calmady. And neither time, nor opposing interests, nor certain black chapters which had later to be read in the history of life, destroyed or even weakened that love.

And so Dick, finding himself at sad disadvantage with most of the charming young fellows about him in matters of play, turned to matters of work, letting go the barbarian side of life for a while. In brain, if not in body, he believed himself the equal of the best of them. His ambition was fired by the desire of intellectual triumph. He would have the success of the schools, since the success of the river and the cricket-field were denied him. Not that Richard set any exaggerated value upon academic honours. Only two things are necessary—this at least was his code at that period—never to lapse from the instincts of high-breeding and honour, and to see just as much of life, of men and of affairs, as obedience to those instincts permits. Already the sense of proportion was strong in Richard, fed perhaps by the galling sense of personal deformity. Learning is but a part of the whole of man's equipment, and a paltry enough part unless wisdom go along with it. But the thirst of battle remained in him ; and in this matter of learning, at least, he could meet men of his own age and standing on equal terms and overcome them in fair fight.

And so, during the last two years of his university course, he did meet them and overcame, honours falling liberally to his share. Julius March looked on in pleased surprise at the

exploits of his former pupil.   While Ludovic Quayle, with
raised eyebrows and half - tender, half - ironical amusement
relaxing the corners of his remarkably beautiful mouth, would
say :—

"Calmady, you really are a shameless glutton!   How many
more immortal glories, any one of which would satisfy an
ordinary man, do you propose to swallow?"

"I suppose it's a bad year," Richard would answer.   "The
others can't amount to very much, or, needless to say, I shouldn't
walk over the course."

"A charming little touch of modesty as far as you yourself
are concerned," Ludovic answered.   "But not strikingly flattering to the others.   I would rather suppose you abnormally clever,
than all the rest abnormally stupid—for, after all, you know, am
not I, my great self, among the rest?"

At which Dickie would laugh rather shamefacedly, and
say :—"Oh you!— why you know well enough you could do
anything you liked if you weren't so confoundedly lazy !"

And meanwhile, at Brockhurst, as news arrived of these
successes, Lady Calmady's soul received comfort.   Her step
was light, her eyes full of clear shining as she moved to and
fro ordering the great house and great estate.   She felt repaid
for the bitter pain of parting with her darling, and sending him
forth to face the curious, possibly scornful, world of the university
city.   He had proved himself and won his spurs.   And this
solaced her in the solitude and loneliness of her present life.
For her dear friend and companion Marie de Mirancourt had
found the final repose, before seeking that of the convent.
Early one February morning, in the second year of Richard's
sojourn at Oxford, fortified by the rites of the Church, she had
passed the gates of death peacefully, blessing and blessed.
Katherine mourned for her, and would continue to mourn with
still and faithful sorrow, even while welcoming home her young
scholar, hearing the details of his past achievements and hopes
for the future, or entertaining — with all gracious hospitality—
such of his Oxford friends as he elected to invite to Brockhurst.

It was on one of these last occasions, the young men having
gone down to the Gun-Room to smoke and discuss the day's
pheasant - shooting, that Katherine had kept Julius March
standing before the Chapel-Room fire, and had looked at him, a
certain wistfulness in her face.

"He is happy—don't you think, Julius?" she said.   "He
seems to me really happier, more contented, than I have ever
seen him since his childhood."

"Yes, I also think that," Julius answered. "He has reason to be contented. He has measured himself against other men and is satisfied of his own powers."

"Everyone admires him at Oxford?"

"Yes, they admire and envy him. He has been brilliantly successful."

Katherine drew herself up, clasping her hands behind her, and smiling proudly as she mused, gazing into the crimson heart of the burning logs. Then, after a silence, she turned suddenly to her companion.

"It is very sweet to have you here at home again, Julius," she said gently. "I have missed you sorely since dearest Marie de Mirancourt died. Live a little longer than I do, please. Ah! I am afraid it is no small thing that I ask you to do for my sake, for I foresee that I shall survive to a lamentably old age. But sacrifice yourself, Julius, in the matter of living. Less than ever, when the shadows fall, shall I be able to spare you."

For which words of his dear lady's, though spoken lightly, half in jest, Julius March gave God great thanks that night.

It was about this period that two pieces of news, each proving eventually to have much personal significance, reached Lady Calmady from the outside world. The first took the form of a letter—a rather pensive and tired letter—from her brother, William Ormiston, telling her that his daughter Helen was about to marry the Comte de Vallorbes, a young gentleman very well known both to Parisian and Neapolitan society. The second took the form of an announcement in the *Morning Post*, to the effect that Lady Tobermory, whose lamented death that paper had already chronicled, had left the bulk of her not inconsiderable fortune to her god-daughter Honoria, eldest child of that distinguished officer General St. Quentin. In both cases Lady Calmady wrote letters of congratulation, in the latter with very sincere and lively pleasure. She held her cousin, General St. Quentin, in affection for old sake's sake. Honoria she remembered as a singularly graceful, high-bred, little maiden, fleet of foot as a hind—too fleet of foot indeed for little Dickie's comfort of mind, and therefore banished from the Brockhurst nursery. In the former case, her congratulations being somewhat conventional, she added—in her own name and that of Richard—a necklace of pearls, with a diamond clasp and bars to it, of no mean value.

In the spring of 1865 Richard left Oxford for good, and took up his residence once more at Brockhurst. But it was not until the autumn of the following year, when he had reached the age of three-and-twenty, and had already, for some six months, served his Queen and country in the capacity of Justice of the Peace for the county of Southampton, that any event occurred greatly affecting his fortunes, and therefore worthy to set forth at large in this history.

CHAPTER II

TELLING HOW DICKIE'S SOUL WAS SOMEWHAT SICK, AND HOW HE MET FAIR WOMEN ON THE CONFINES OF A WOOD

RICHARD CALMADY rode homeward through the autumn woods, and the aspect of them was very lovely. But their loveliness was hectic, a loveliness as it seemed, at all events at first sight, of death and burial, rather than of life and hope. The sky was overcast, and a chill clung to the stream-side and haunted the hollows. The young man's humour, unfortunately, was only too much in harmony with the more melancholy suggestions of the scene. For Richard was by nature something of a poet, though he but rarely wrote verses, and usually burned them as soon as written being scholar enough to know and feel impatient of the "second best." And this inherent strain of poetry in him tempered the active and practical side of his character, making wealth and position, and all those things which the worldly-minded seek, seem of slight value to him at times. It induced in him many and very varying moods. It carried him back often, even now in the strength of his young manhood, to the fine fancies and exquisite unreason of the fairy-world in which those so sadly ill-balanced footsteps of his had first been set. To-day had proved, so far, an unlucky one, prolific of warfare between his clear brain and all too sensitive heart. For it was the burden of Richard's temperament—the almost inevitable result of that ever-present thorn in the flesh—that he shrunk as a poet, even as a woman, while as a man, and a strong one, he reasoned and fought.

It fell out on this wise. He had attended the Quarter Sessions at Westchurch ; and a certain restlessness, born of the changing seasons, being upon him, he had ridden. His habit, when passing outside the limits of his own property, was to drive. He became aware—and angrily conscious his groom was aware also—that his appearance afforded a spectacle of the liveliest

interest to the passers-by; that persons of very various age
and class had stopped and turned to gaze at him; and that,
while crossing the bridge spanning the dark, oily waters of
the canal, in the industrial quarter of the pushing, wide-awake,
county town, he had been the subject of brutal comment,
followed by a hoarse laugh from the collarless throats of some
dozen operatives and bargees loitering thereupon.

The consequence was that the young man arrived in court,
his eyes rather hard and his jaw set.   Rich, well-born, not un-
distinguished too for his attainments, and only three-and-twenty,
Dickie had a fine fund of arrogance to draw upon yet.   He
drew upon it this morning, rather to the confusion of his
colleagues upon the bench.   Mr. Cathcart, the chairman, was
already present, and stood talking with Mr. Seymour, the rector
of Farley, a shrewd, able squarson of the old sporting type.
Captain Fawkes of Water End was there too; and so was
Lemuel Image, eldest son of the Mr. Image, sometime mayor
of Westchurch, who has been mentioned in the early pages of
this chronicle.

In the last twenty years, supported by ever-increasing piles
of barrels, the Image family had mounted triumphantly upward
in the social scale.   Lemuel, the man in question, married a
poor and distant relation of Lord Aldborough, the late lord
lieutenant of the county; and had by this, and by a rather
truculent profession of high Tory politics, secured himself a seat
on the bench.   He had given a fancy price, too, for that pretty,
little place, Frodsmill, the grounds of which form such an
exasperating Naboth's vineyard in the heart of the Newlands
property.   Neither his person, nor his politics, nor his absence of
culture, found favour in Richard Calmady's sight.   And to-day,
being somewhat on edge, the brewer's large, blustering presence
and manner—at once patronising and servile—struck him as
peculiarly odious.   Image betrayed an evil tendency to
emphasise his remarks by slapping his acquaintances upon the
back.   He was also guilty of supposing a defect of hearing in
all persons older than, or in any measure denied the absolute
plethora of physical vigour so conspicuous in, himself.   He
invariably raised his voice in addressing Richard.   In return for
which graceful attention Dickie most cordially detested him.

" Image is a bit of a cad, and certainly Calmady makes no
bones about letting him know it," Captain Fawkes remarked to
Mr. Seymour, as they drove back to Farley in the latter's dog-
cart.   " Fortunately he has a hide like a rhinoceros, or we
should have had a regular row between them more than once

this morning. Calmady's generally charming; but I must say, when he likes, he can be about the most insolent fellow I've ever met, in a gentleman-like way."

"A great deal of that is simply self-protective," the clergyman answered. "It is not difficult to see how it comes about, when you take his circumstances into account. If I was him, God forgive me, I know I shouldn't be half so sweet-tempered. He bears it wonderfully well, all things considered."

Nor did the disturbing incidents of the day end with the familiarities of the loud-voiced brewer. The principal case to be tried was a melancholy one enough—a miserable history of wayward desire, shame and suffering, followed by a despairing course of lies and petty thieving to help support the poor baby whose advent seemed so wholly a curse. The young mother—a pretty, desperate creature—made no attempt at denial. She owned she had robbed her mistress of a shilling here and sixpence there, that she had taken now a bit of table silver and then a garment to the pawn-shop. How could she help it? Her wages were a trifle, since her character was damaged. Wasn't it a charity to employ a girl like her at all? so her mistress said. And yet the child must live. And Richard Calmady, sitting in judgment there with those four other gentlemen of substantial means and excellent position, sickened as he listened to the sordid details, the relentless elementary arguments. For the girl, awed and frightened at first, grew eloquent in self-defence.—"She loved him"—he being a smart young fellow, who, with excellent recommendations from Chifney, had left the Brockhurst stables some two years before, to take service in Westchurch.—"And he always spoke her fair. Had told her he'd marry her right enough, after a bit—before God he would. But it would ruin his chance of first-class places if he married yet. The gentry wouldn't take any but single men of his age. A wife would stand in his way. And she didn't want to stand in his way—he knew her better than that. Not but that he reckoned her just as much his wife as any woman could be. Of course he did. What a silly she was to trouble about it. And then when there was no hiding any longer how it was with her, he up and awayed to London, saying he would make a home for her there. And he kept on writing for a bit, but he never told her where to write to him in return, so she couldn't answer. And then his letters came seldom, and then stopped altogether, and then—and then"—

The girl was rebuked for her much speaking, and so wasting the time of the Court. There were other cases. And Richard

Calmady sickened yet more, recognising in that a parable of perpetual application. For are there not always other cases? The tragedy of the individual life reaching its climax seems, to the chief actor, worthy to claim and hold universal attention. Yet the sun never stands still in heaven, nor do the footsteps of men tarry upon earth. No one person may take up too much space, too much time. The movement of things is not stayed. The single cry, however bitter, is drowned in the roar of the pushing crowd. The individual, however keen his griefs, however heinous the offence done him, must make way for those same other cases. This is the everlasting law.

And so pained, out of tune, troubled too by smouldering fires of anger, Richard left Westchurch and his fellow-magistrates as early as he decently could. Avoiding the highroad leading by Newlands and through Sandyfield village, he cut across country by field lanes and over waste-lands to Farley Row. The wide quiet of the autumn afternoon, the slight chill in the air, were grateful to him after the noise and close atmosphere of the court. Yet the young man strove vainly to think of pleasant things and to regain his serenity. The girl's tear-blotted face, the tones of her voice, haunted him. Six weeks' imprisonment. The sentence, after all, was a light one. Yet who was he, who were those four other well-to-do gentlemen, that they should judge her at all? How could they measure the strength of the temptation which had beset her? If temptation is strong enough, must not the tempted of necessity yield? If the tempted does not yield, is that not merely proof that the temptation was not strong enough? The whole thing appeared to him a matter of mathematics or mechanics. Given a greater weight than it can carry, the rope is bound to break. And then for those who have not felt the strain to blame the rope, punish the rope! It seemed to Richard, as he rode homeward, that human justice is too often a very comedy of injustice. It all appeared to him so exceedingly foolish. And yet society must be protected. Other pretty, weak, silly creatures must be warned, by such rather brutal object-lessons, not to bear bastards or pawn their mistresses' spoons.

"'*Je ne sais pas ce que c'est que la vie éternelle, mais celle çi est une mauvaise plaisanterie,*'" Dickie quoted to himself somewhat bitterly.

He turned aside at Farley Row, following the narrow road that runs behind the houses in the main street and the great, vacant stables and outbuildings of the White Lion Inn. And here, as though the immediate displeasures of this ill-starred day were insufficient, memory arose and recalled other displeasures of long ago.   Recalled old Jackie Deeds lurching out of that same inn yard, empty pipe in mouth, greedy of alms.   Recalled the old postboy's ugly morsel of profanity—"God Almighty had His jokes too."   And, at that, the laughter of those loafers upon the canal bridge saluted Richard's ears once more, as did the loud, familiar phrases of Mr. Lemuel Image, the Westchurch brewer.

Before him the flat expanse of Clerke's Green opened out ; and the turf of it—beaded with dew which the frail sunshine of the early morning had failed to burn up—was crossed by long tracks of darker green, where flocks of geese had wandered over its misty surface.   Here the travelling menagerie and all the booths of the fair had been stationed.   Memory rigged up the tents once more, painted the vans in crude, glaring colours, set drums beating and merry-go-rounds turning, pointed a malicious finger at the sign-board of a certain show.   How many times Richard had passed this way in the intervening years, and remembered in passing, yet thrown all hurt of remembrance from him directly and lightly !   To-day it gripped him.   He put his horse into a sharp trot.

Skirting the edge of the green, he rode down a rutted cart lane—farm buildings and well-filled rickyards on the left—and forded the shallow, brown stream which separates the parish of Farley from that of Sandyfield and the tithing of Brockhurst.

Ahead lay the wide, rough road, ending in a broken avenue of ancient oaks, and bordered on either hand by a strip of waste-land overgrown with coarse grasses and low thickets of maple—which leads up to the entrance of the Brockhurst woods.   Over these hung a soft, bluish haze, making them appear vast in extent, and upraising the dark ridge of the fir forest, which crowns them, to mountain height against the western sky.   A covey of partridges ran up the sandy road before Richard's horse ; and, rising at last with a long-drawn whir of wings, skimmed the top of the bank and dropped into the pale stubble field on the other side of it.   He paused at the head of the avenue while the keeper's wife—in lilac apron and sunbonnet—ran out to open the big, white gate ; the dogs meantime, from their kennels under the Spanish chestnuts upon the slope behind her gabled cottage, setting up a vociferous chorus.   Thus heralded, Richard passed into the whispering, mysterious still-ness of the autumn woods.

The summer had been dry and fine, the foliage unusually rich and heavy, all the young wood ripening well.   Consequently

the turn of the leaf was very brilliant that year.   The sweetly
sober English landscape seemed to have run mad and decked
itself, as for a masquerade, in extravagant splendours of colour.
The smooth-stemmed beeches had taken on every tint from
fiery brown, through orange and amber, to verdigris green
touching latest July shoots.   The round-headed oaks, practising
even in carnival time a measure of restraint, had arrayed themselves in a hundred rich, finely-gradated tones of russet and
umber.   While, here and there, a tall bird-cherry, waxing
wanton, had clothed itself like the Woman of Babylon in rose-
scarlet from crown to lowest black-barked twig.   Higher up,
the larch plantations rose in crowds of butter-coloured spires.
Amethystine, and blood-red, white-spotted toad-stools, in little
companies, pushed through the light soil on either side the road.
Trailing sprays of bramble glowed as flame.   Rowan berries
hung in heavy coral bunches, and the dogwood spread itself in
sparse, china-pink clusters.   Only the undergrowth of crooked
alders, in swampy, low-lying places, kept its dark, purplish
green ; and the light foliage of the ash waved in shadowy pallor
against its knobbed and knotted branches ; and the ranks of the
encircling firs retained their solemn habit, as though in protest
against the universal riot.

The stream hidden away in the hazel coppice gurgled and
murmured.   Beech-masts pattered down, startling the stillness
as with a sudden dropping of thunder rain.   Squirrels, disturbed
in the ingathering of their winter store, whisked up the boles of
the great trees and scolded merrily from the forks of the high
branches.   Shy, wild things rustled and scampered unseen
through the tangled undergrowth and beds of bracken.   While
that veil of bluish haze touched all the distance of the landscape
with a delicate mystery, and softly blotted the vista of each wide
shooting-drive, or winding pathway, to left and right.

And as Richard rode onward, leaves gay even in death
fluttering down around him, his mood began to suffer change.
He ceased to think and began to feel merely.   First came a
dreamy delight in the beauty of the scene about him.   Then the
sense of mystery grew upon him—of mystery, not merely hanging
in the delicate haze, but dwelling in the endless variety of form
and colour which met his eyes, of mystery inviting him in the
soft, multitudinous voices of the woodland.   And, as the minutes
passed, this sense grew increasingly provocative, became too
increasingly elusive.   The light leapt into Dickie's eyes.   He
smiled to himself.   He was filled with unreasoning expectation.
He seemed—it was absurd, yet very charming—to be playing

hide-and-seek with some glad secret which at any instant might
be revealed to him.   It murmured to him in the brook.   It
scolded at him merrily with the scolding squirrels.   It startled
the surrounding stillness, with the down-pattering beech-masts
and fluttering of leaves.   It eluded him deftly, rustling away
unseen through the green and gold of the bracken.   Lastly
when, reaching the summit of the ridge of hill, he entered upon
the levels of the great tableland, it hailed him in the long-drawn
sighing of the fir forest.   For a wind, suddenly awakened, swept
towards him from some far distance, neared, broke overhead,
as summer waves upon a shingly beach, died in delicious
whispers, only to sweep up and break and die again.   Meanwhile the grey pall of cloud parted in the west, disclosing spaces
of faint yet clearest blue, and the declining sun, from behind dim
islands of shifting vapour, sent forth immense rays of mild and
misty light.

Richard laughed involuntarily to himself.   For there was a
fantastic, curiously alluring influence in all this.   It spoke to
him as in delicate persuasion.   His sense of expectation intensified.   He would not ride homeward and shut himself within
four walls just yet; but yield himself to the wooing of these
fair sylvan divinities, to that of the spirit of the evening wind,
of the softly shrouding haze, and of the broadening sunlight, a
little longer.

A turf-ride branches away to the left, leading along a narrow
outstanding spur of tableland to a summer-house, the prospect
from which is among the noted beauties of Brockhurst.   This
summer-house or Temple, as it has come to be called, is an
octagonal structure.   Round-shafted pillars rise at each projecting angle.   In the recesses between them are low stone
benches, save in front where an open colonnade gives upon
the view.   The roof is leaded, and surmounted by a wooden
ball and tall, three-sided spike.   These last, as well as the
plastered, windowless walls, are painted white.   Within, the
hollow of the dome is decorated in fresco, with groups of gaily
clad ladies and their attendant cavaliers, with errant cupids,
garlands of flowers, trophies of rather impossible musical instruments, and cages full of imprisoned, and therefore doubtless
very naughty, loves.   The colours have grown faint by action of
insweeping wind and weather; but this lends a pathos to the
light-hearted, highly-artificial art, accentuating the contrast
between it and its immediate surroundings.

For the Temple stands on a platform of turf at the extreme
point of the spur of tableland.   The hillside, clothed with

heather and bracken, fringed lower down with a coppice of delicate birches, falls steeply away in front and on either hand. Outstretched below, besides the panorama of the great woods, lies all the country about Farley, on to Westchurch, and beyond again—pasture and cornlands, scattered hamlets and red-roofed farms half hidden among trees, the glint of streams set in the vivid green of water-meadows, and soft, blue range behind range of distance to that pale uprising of chalk down in the far south. Upon the right, some quarter of a mile away, blocking the end of an avenue of secular Scotch firs, the eastern façade of Brock-hurst House shows planted proudly upon the long grey and red lines of the terrace.

Richard checked his horse, pausing to look for a moment at that well-beloved home. Then musing, he let his horse go forward along the level turf-ride. The grey dome and white columns of the Temple standing out against the spacious pro-spect—the growing brightness of this last, still chastened by the delicious autumn haze—captivated his imagination. There was, seen thus, a simplicity and distinction altogether classic in the lonely building. To him it appeared not unfit shrine for the worship of that same all-pervasive spirit of mystery, not unfit spot for the revelation of that same glad, yet cunningly elusive secret, of which he suffered the so fond obsession.

And so it was that when, coming abreast of the building, the sound of young voices—women's voices—and finely modulated laughter saluted his ear, though startled, for no stranger had the right of entry to the park, he was by no means displeased. This seemed but part of the all-pervasive magic of this strange afternoon. Richard smiled at the phantasies of his own mood— Yet he forgot to be shy, forgot the distressing self-consciousness which made him shrink from the observation of strangers— specially those of the other sex. The adventure tempted his fancy. Even familiar things had put on a new and beguiling vesture in the last half-hour, so there were miracles abroad, perhaps. Anyhow he would satisfy himself as to the aspect of those sweet-voiced and, as yet, unseen trespassers. He let his horse go forward slowly across the platform of turf.

CHAPTER III

IN WHICH RICHARD CONFIRMS ONE JUDGMENT AND
REVERSES ANOTHER

"HOW magnificently your imagination gallops when it once
gets agoing! Here you are bearing away the spoils,
when the siege is not even yet begun—never will be, I venture
to hope, for I doubt if this would be a very honourable"—

The speaker broke off, abruptly, as the shadow of horse and
rider lengthened upon the turf. And, during the silence which
followed, Richard Calmady received an impression at once
arresting and subtly disquieting.

A young lady, of about his own age, leaned against one of
the white pillars of the colonnade. Her attitude and costume
were alike slightly unconventional. She was unusually tall, and
there was a lazy, almost boyish indifference and grace in the
pose of her supple figure and the gallant carriage of her small
head. She wore a straight, pale grey-green jacket, into the
pockets of which her hands were thrust. Her skirt, of the same
colour and material, hung in straight folds to her feet, being
innocent alike of trimming and the then prevailing fashion of
crinoline. Further, she wore a little, round matador's hat, three
black pompoms planted audaciously-upstanding above the left
ear. Her eyes, long in shape and set under straight, observant
brows, appeared at first sight of the same clear, light, warm
brown as her hair. Her nose was straight, rather short, and
delicately square at the tip. While her face, unlined, serenely,
indeed triumphantly, youthful, was quite colourless and sufficiently
thin to disclose fine values of bone in the broad forehead and
the cutting of jaw and cheek and chin.

In that silence, as she and Richard Calmady looked full at
one another, he apprehended in her a baffling element, a something untamed and remote, a freedom of soul, that declared
itself alike in the gallantries and severities of her dress, her
attitude, and all the lines of her person. She bore relation to
the glad mystery haunting the fair autumn evening. She also
bore relation to the chill haunting the stream-side and the deep
places of the woods. And her immediate action ratified
this last likeness in his mind. When he first beheld her she
was bright, with a certain teasing insouciance. Then, for a
minute, even more, she stood at gaze, as a hind does suddenly

12

startled on the edge of the covert—her head raised, her face keen with inquiry. Her expression changed, became serious, almost stern. She recoiled, as in pain, as in an approach to fear—this strong, nymphlike creature.

"Helen," she called aloud, in tones of mingled protest and warning. And thereupon, without more ado, she retired, nay, fled, into the sheltering, sun-warmed interior of the Temple.

At this summons her companion, who until now had stood contemplating the wide view from the extreme verge of the platform, wheeled round. For an appreciable time she, too, looked at Richard Calmady, and that haughtily enough, as though he, rather than she, was the intruder. Her glance travelled unflinchingly down from his bare head and broad shoulders to that pocket-like appendage—as of old-fashioned pistol holsters—on either side his saddle. Swiftly her bearing changed. She uttered an exclamation of unfeigned and un-alloyed satisfaction—a little, joyful outcry, such as a child will make on discovery of some lost treasure.

"Ah ! it is you—you !" she said, laughing softly, while she moved forward, both hands extended. Which hand, by the same token, she proposed to bestow on Dickie remained matter for conjecture, since in the one she carried a parasol with a staff-like gold and tortoiseshell handle to it, and in the other, between the first and second fingers, a cigarette, the blue smoke of which curled upward in transparent spirals upon the clear, still air.

As the lady of the grey-green gown retired precipitately within the Temple, a wave of hot blood passed over Richard's body. For notwithstanding his three-and-twenty years, his not contemptible mastery of many matters, and that same honour-able appointment of Justice of the Peace for the county of Southampton, he was but a lad yet, with all a lad's quick-ness of sensitive shame and burning resentment. The girl's repulsion had been obvious—that instinctive repulsion, as poor Dickie's too acute sympathies assured him, of the whole for the maimed, of the free for the bound, of the artist for some jarring colour or sound which mars an otherwise entrancing harmony. And the smart of all this was, to him, doubly salted by the fact that he, after all, was a man, his critic merely a woman. The bitter mood of the earlier hours of the day returned upon him. He cursed himself for a doting fool. Who was he, indeed, to seek revelation of glad secrets, cherish fair dreams and tempt adventures ?

Consequently it fell out when that other lady—she of the cigarette — advanced thus delightfully towards him. Richard's face was white with anger, and his lips rigid with pain—a rigidity begotten of the determination that they should not tremble in altogether too unmanly fashion.   Sometimes it is very sad to be young.   The flesh is still very tender, so that a scratch hurts more then than a sword-thrust later.   Only, let it be remembered, the scratch heals readily ; while of the sword-thrust we die, even though at the moment of receiving it we seem not so greatly to suffer.   And unquestionably as Dickie sat there, on his handsome horse, hat in hand, looking down at the lady of the cigarette, the hurt of that lately received scratch began quite sensibly to lessen. For her eyes, their first unsparing scrutiny accomplished, rested on his with a strangely flattering and engaging insistence.

"But this is the very prettiest piece of good fortune!" she exclaimed.   "Had I arranged the whole matter to suit my own fancy it could not have turned out more happily."

Her tone was that of convincing sincerity; while, as she spoke, the soft colour came and went in her cheeks, and her lips parting showed little, even teeth daintily precious as a row of pearls.   The outline of her face was remarkably pure—in shape an oval, a trifle wide in proportion to its length.   Her eyebrows were arched, the eyelids arched also—very thin, showing the movement of the eyeballs beneath them, drooping slightly, with a sweep of dark lashes at the outer corner.   It struck Richard that she bore a certain resemblance to his mother, though smaller and slighter in build.   Her mouth was less full, her hair fairer— soft, glistening hair of all the many shades of heather honey-comb, broken wax, and sweet, heady liquor, alike.   Her hands, he re-marked, were very finished—the fingers pointed, the palms rosy. The set of her black, velvet coat revealed the roundness of her bust. The broad brim of her large, black hat, slightly upturned at the sides, and with sweeping ostrich plumes as trimming to it, threw the upper part of her charming face into soft shadow.   Her heavy, dove-coloured, silk skirts stood out stiffly from her waist, declaring its slenderness.   The few jewels she wore were of notable value.   Her appearance, in fact, spoke the last word of contemporary fashion in its most refined application.   She was a great lady, who knew the world and the worth of it.   And she was absolute mistress both of that knowledge, and of herself— notwithstanding those outstretched hands, and outcry of child-like pleasure,—there, perhaps, lay the exquisite flattery of this last to her hearer !   She was all this, and something more than all this.   Something for which Dickie, his heart still virgin, had no name as yet.   It was new to his experience.   A something clear, simple, and natural, as the sunlight, yet infinitely subtle.

A something ravishing, so that you wanted to draw it very close, hold it, devour it. Yet something you so feared, you needs must put it from you, so that, faint with ecstasy, standing at a distance, you might bow yourself and humbly worship. But such extravagant exercises being, in the nature of his case, physically as well as socially inadmissible, the young man was constrained to remain seated squarely in the saddle—that singularly ungainly saddle, moreover, with holster-like appendages to it—while he watched her, wholly charmed, curious and shy, carried indeed a little out of himself, waiting for her to make further disclosures, since he felt absurdly slow and unready of speech.

Nor was he destined to wait in vain. The fair lady appeared agreeably ready to declare herself, and that with the finest turns of voice and manner, with the most coercive variety of appeal, pathos, caprice, and dignity.

"I know on the face of it I have not the smallest right to have taken possession in this way," she continued. "It is the frankest impertinence. But if you realised how extremely I am enjoying myself, you could not fail to forgive me. All this park of yours, all this nature," she turned sideways, sketching out the great view with a broad gesture of the cigarette and graceful hand that held it, "all this is divinely lovely. It is wiser to possess oneself of it in an illicit manner, to defy the minor social proprieties and unblushingly to steal, than not to possess oneself of it at all. If you are really hungry, you know, you learn not to be too nice as to the ways and means of acquiring sustenance."

"And you were really hungry?" Richard found himself saying, as he feared rather blunderingly. But he wanted, so anxiously, the present to remain present—wanted to continue to watch her, and to hear her. She turned his head. How then could he behave otherwise than with stupidity?

"La! la!" she replied, laughing indulgently, and thereby enchanting him still more, "what must your experience of life be if you suppose one gets a full meal of divine loveliness every day in the week? For my part, I am not troubled with any such celestial plethora, believe me. I was ravening, I tell you, positively ravening."

"And your hunger is satisfied?" he asked, still as he feared blunderingly, and with a queer inward movement of envy towards the wide view she looked upon, and the glory of the sunset which dared touch her hair.

"Satisfied?" she exclaimed. "Is one's hunger for the

divinely lovely ever satisfied? Just now I have stayed mine
with the merest mouthful — as one snatches a sandwich at a
railway *buffet*. And directly I must get into the train again, and
go on with my noisy, dusty, stifling journey. Ah! you are very
fortunate to live in this adorable and restful place; to see it in
all its fine drama of changing colour and season, year in and
year out."

She dropped the end of her cigarette into a little, sandy
depression in the turf, and drawing aside her silken skirts, trod
out the red heart of it neatly with her daintily shod foot. Just
then the other lady, she of the grey-green gown, came from
within the shelter of the Temple, and stood between the white
pillars of the colonnade. Dick's grasp tightened on the handle
of the hunting-crop lying across his thigh.

"Am I so very fortunate?" he said, almost involuntarily.

His companion looked up smiling, her eyes dwelling on his
with a strange effect of intimacy, wholly flattering, wholly, indeed,
distracting to common sense.

"Yes—you are fortunate," she answered, speaking slowly.
"And some day, Richard, I think you will come to know that."

Sudden comprehension, sudden recognition struck the young
man—very literally struck him a most unwelcome buffet.

"Oh! I see—I understand," he exclaimed, "you are my
cousin—you are Madame de Vallorbes."

For a moment his sense of disappointment was so keen, he
was minded to turn his horse and incontinently ride away. The
misery of that episode of his boyhood set its tooth very shrewdly
in him even yet. It seemed the most cruelly ironical turn of
fate that this entrancing, this altogether worshipful, stranger
should prove to be one and the same as the little dancer of long
ago with blush-roses in her hat.

But, though the colour deepened somewhat in the lady's
cheeks, she did not lower her eyes, nor did they lose their
smiling importunity. A little ardour, indeed, heightened the
charm of her manner—an ardour of delicate battle, as of one
whose honour has been ever so slightly touched.

"Certainly, I am your cousin, Helen de Vallorbes," she
replied. "You are not sorry for that, Richard, are you? At
this moment I am increasingly glad to be your cousin—though
not perhaps so very particularly glad to be Helen de Vallorbes."
Then she added, rapidly :—"We are here in England for a
few weeks, my father and I. Troublesome, distressing things
had happened, and he perceived I needed change. He brought
me away. London proved a desert and a dust-heap. There

was no solace, no distraction from unpleasant thoughts, to be found there. So we telegraphed and came down last night to the kind people at Newlands. Naturally my father wanted to see Aunt Katherine. I desired to see her also, well understood, for I have heard so much of her talent and her great beauty. But I knew they—the brother and sister—would wish to speak of the past and find their happiness in being very sad about it all. At our age—yours and mine—the sadness of any past one may possess is a good deal too present with one still to afford in the least consoling subject of conversation."—Madame de Vallorbes spoke with a certain vehemence. "Don't you think so, Richard?" she demanded.

And Richard could but answer, very much out of his heart, that he did indeed think so.

She observed him a moment, and then her tone softened. The colour deepened yet more in her cheeks. She became at once prettily embarrassed and prettily sincere.

"And then, to tell you quite the truth, I am a trifle afraid of Aunt Katherine. I have always wanted to come here and to see you, but—it is an absurd confession to make—I have been scared at the idea of meeting Aunt Katherine, and that is the real reason why I made Honoria take refuge with me in this lovely park of yours, instead of going on with my father to the house. There is a legend, a thrice accursed legend, in our family, —my mother employs it even yet when she proposes to reduce me to salutary depths of humility—that I came,—she brought me —here, once, long ago, when I was a child, and that I was fiendishly naughty, that I behaved odiously."

Madame de Vallorbes stretched out her hands, presenting the rosy palms of them in the most engaging manner.

"But it can't—it can't be true," she protested. "Why, in the name of all folly, let alone all common decency, should I behave odiously? It is not like me. I love to please, I love to have people care for me. And so I cannot but believe the legend is the malign invention of some nurse or governess, whom, poor woman, I probably plagued handsomely enough in her day, and who, in revenge, rigged up this detestable scarecrow with which to frighten me. Then, moreover, I have not the faintest recollection of the affair, and one generally has an only too vivid memory of one's own sins. Surely, *mon cher cousin*, surely I am innocent in your sight, as in my own? You do not remember the episode either?"

Whereupon Dickie, looking down at her,—and still enchanted notwithstanding his so sinister discovery, being first, and always a

gentleman, and secondly, though as yet unconsciously, a lover,—
proceeded to lie roundly.   Lied, too, with a notable cheerfulness
born, as cheerfulness needs must be, of every act of faith and
high generosity.

"I remember it? Of course not," he said.   "So let the
legend be abolished henceforth and for evermore.   Here, once
and for all, cousin Helen, we combine to pull down and bury
that scarecrow."

Madame de Vallorbes clapped her hands softly and laughed.
And her laughter, having the merit of being perfectly genuine—
for the young man very really pleased her fancy—was likewise
very infectious.   Richard found himself laughing too, he knew
not why, save that he was glad of heart.

"And now that matter being satisfactorily disposed of, you
will come to Brockhurst often," he said.   It seemed to him that
a certain joyous equality had been established between him and
his divinity, both by his repudiation of all former knowledge of
her, and by their moment of laughter.   He began fearlessly to
make her little offerings.—"Do you care about riding? I am
afraid there is not much to amuse you at Brockhurst; but there
are always plenty of horses."

"And I adore horses."

"Do you care about racing? We've some rather pretty
things in training this year.   I should like awfully to show them
to you."

But here the conversation, just setting forth in so agreeable a
fashion, suffered interruption.   For the other lady, she of the
grey-green gown, sauntered forward from the Temple.   The
carriage of her head was gallant, her air nonchalant as ever; but
her expression was grave, and the delicate thinness of her face
appeared a trifle accentuated.   She came up to Madame de
Vallorbes and passed her hand through the latter's arm caressingly.

"You know, really, Helen, we ought to go, if we are not to
keep your father and the carriage waiting."—Then she looked up
with a certain determined effort at Richard Calmady.   "We
promised to meet Mr. Ormiston at the first park gate," she
added in explanation.   "That is nearly a mile from here, isn't
it?"

"About three-quarters—hardly that," he answered.   Her
eyes were not brown, he perceived, but a clear, dim green, as the
soft gloom in the under-spaces of a grove of ilexes.   They
affected him as fearlessly observant—eyes that could judge both
men and things and could also keep their own counsel.

"Will you give your mother Honoria St. Quentin's love, please?" she went on. "I stayed here with her for a couple of days the year before last, while you were at Oxford. She was very good to me. Now, Helen, come "—

"I shall see you again," Richard cried to the lady of the cigarette. But his horse, which for some minutes had been increasingly fidgety, backed away down the hillside, and he could not catch the purport of her answer. To the lady of the grey-green gown and eyes he said nothing at all.

CHAPTER IV

JULIUS MARCH BEARS TESTIMONY

"SO you really wish me to ask them both to come, Richard?"

Lady Calmady stood on the tiger-skin before the Gun-Room hearth. Upon the said hearth a merry, little fire of pine logs clicked and chattered. Even here, on the dry upland, the night air had an edge to it; while in the valleys there would be frost before morning, ripening that same splendour of autumn foliage alike to greater glory and swifter fall. And the snap in the air, working along with other unwonted influences, made Katherine somewhat restless this evening. Her eyes were dark with unspoken thought. Her voice had a ring in it. The shimmering, black, satin dress and fine lace she wore gave a certain magnificence to her appearance. Her whole being was vibrant. She was rather dangerously alive. Her elder brother's unlooked-for advent had awakened her strangely from the reserve and stately monotony of her daily existence, had shaken even, for the moment, the completeness of the dominion of her fixed idea. She ceased, for the moment, to sink the whole of her personality in the maternal relationship. Memories of her youth, passed amid the varied interests of society and of the literary and political world of Paris and London, assailed her. All those other Katherines, in short, whom she might have been, and who had seemed to drop away from her, vanishing phantom-like before the uncompromising realities of her husband's death and her child's birth, crowded about her, importuning her with vague desires, vague regrets. The confines of Brockhurst grew narrow, while all that which lay beyond them called to her.

She craved, almost unconsciously, a wider sphere of action. She longed to obtain, and to lend a hand in the shaping of events and making of history.   Even the purest and most devoted among women—possessing the doubtful blessing of a measure of intellect—are subject to such vagrant heats, such uprisings of personal ambition, specially during the dangerous decade when the nine-and-thirtieth year is past.

Meanwhile Richard's answer to her question was unfortunately somewhat over-long in coming, for the young man was sunk in meditation and apparently oblivious of her presence.   He leaned back in the long, low arm-chair, his hands clasped behind his head, the embroidered rug drawn about his waist, a venerable, yellow-edged, calf-bound volume lying face downwards on his lap.   While young Camp—young no longer, full of years indeed beyond the allotted portion of his kind—reposed, outstretched and snoring, on the all-too-wide space of rug and chair-seat at his feet.   And this indifference, both of man and dog, grew irksome to Lady Calmady.   She moved across the shining yellow and black surface of the tiger-skin and straightened the bronzes of Vinedresser and Lazy Lad standing on the high chimneypiece.

"My dear, it grows late," she said.   "Let us settle this matter.   If your uncle and cousin are to come, I must send a note over to Newlands to-morrow before breakfast.   Remember I have no choice in the matter.   I leave it entirely to you.   Tell me seriously what you wish."

Richard stretched himself, turning his head in the hollow of his hands, and shrugged his shoulders slightly.

"That is exactly what I would thank you so heartily to tell me," he answered.   "Do I, or don't I seriously wish it?   I give you my word, mother, I don't know."

"Oh; but, my dearest, that is folly!   You must have inclination enough, one way or the other, to come to a decision. I was careful not to commit myself.   It is still easy not to ask them without being guilty of any discourtesy."

"It isn't that," Richard said.   "It is simply that being anything but heroic I am trying of two evils to choose the least. I should like to have my uncle—and Helen—here immensely. But if the visit wasn't a success I should be proportionately disappointed and vexed.   So is it worth the risk?   Disappointments are sufficiently abundant anyhow.   Isn't it slightly imbecile to run a wholly gratuitous risk of adding to their number?"

Then the fixed idea began stealthily, yet surely, to reassert

its dominion ; for there was a perceptible flavour of discouragement in the young man's speech.

"Dickie, there is nothing wrong, is there, — nothing the
matter, to-night?"

"Oh, dear no, of course not!" he answered, half closing his
eyes. "Nothing in the world's the matter."

He unclasped his hands, leaned forward and patted the bull-
dog lying across the rug at his feet.—"At least nothing more
than usual, nothing more than the abiding something which
always has been and always will be the matter."

'Ah, my dear!" Katherine cried softly.

"I've just been reading Burton's Anatomy here," he went on
bending down, so that his face was hidden, while he pulled the
dog's soft ears. "He assures all—whom it may concern—that
'bodily imperfections do not a whit blemish the soul or hinder
the operations of it, but rather help and much increase it.'
There, Camp, poor old man, don't start—it's nothing worse
than me. I wonder if the elaborate pains which have been
taken through generations of your ancestors to breed you into
your existing and very royal hideousness—your flattened nose
and perpetual grin, for instance—do help and much increase the
operations of your soul!"

He looked up suddenly.

"What do you think, mother?"

"I think — think, my darling," she said, "that perhaps
neither you nor I are quite ourselves to-night."

"Oh, well I've had rather a beastly day!"—Richard dropped
back against the chair cushions again, clasping his hands behind
his head. "Or I've seemed to have it, which comes practically
to much the same thing. I confess I have been rather hipped
lately. I suppose it's the weather. You're not really in a
hurry, mother, are you? Come and sit down."

And obediently Katherine drew forward a chair and sat beside
him. Those uprisings of vagrant desire still struggled, com-
bating the dominion of the fixed idea. But the struggle grew
faint and fainter. And then, for a measurable time, Richard
fell silent again while she waited. Verily there is no sharper
discipline for a woman's proud spirit, than that administered,
often quite unconsciously, by the man whom she loves.

"We gave a wretched girl six weeks to-day for robbing her
mistress," he remarked at last. "It was a flagrant case, so I
suppose we were justified. In fact I don't see how we could
have done otherwise. But it went against me awfully, all the
same. She has a child to support. Jim Gould got her into

trouble and deserted her, like a cowardly, young blackguard.
However, it's easy to be righteous at another person's expense.
Perhaps I should have done the same in his place.   I wonder if
I should?"—

"My dear, we need hardly discuss that point, I think,"
Lady Calmady said.

Richard turned his head and smiled at her.

"Poor dear mother, do I bore you?   But it is so comfortable to grumble.   I know it's selfish.   It's a horrid bad habit,
and you ought to blow me up for it.   But then, mother, take it
all round, really I don't grumble much, do I?"

"No, no!" Katherine said quickly.   "Indeed, Dickie, you
don't."

"I have been awfully afraid though, lately, that I do
grumble more than I imagine," he went on, straightening his
head, while his handsome profile showed clear cut against the
dancing brightness of the firelight.   "But it's almost impossible
always to carry something about with you which—which you
hate, and not let it infect your attitude of mind and, in a degree,
your speech.   Twenty or thirty years hence it may prove
altogether sufficient and satisfactory to know"—his lips worked,
obliging him to enunciate his words carefully—"that bodily
imperfections do not a whit blemish the soul or hinder its
operations—are, in short, an added means of grace.   Think
of it!   Isn't it a nice, neat, little arrangement, sort of spiritual
consolation stakes!   Only I'm afraid I'm some two or three
decades on the near side of that comfortable conclusion yet,
and I find"—

Richard shifted his position, letting his arms drop along the
chair arms with a little thud.   He smiled again, or at all events
essayed to do so.

"In fact, I find it's beastly difficult to care a hang about
your soul, one way or another, when you clearly perceive your
body's making you the laughing-stock of half the people—why,
mother, sweet dear mother,—what is it?"

For Lady Calmady's two hands had closed down on his
hand, and she bowed herself above them as though smitten
with sharp pain.

"Pray don't be distressed," he went on.   "I beg your
pardon.   I wasn't thinking what I was saying, I'm an ass.
It's nothing I tell you but the weather.   You're all a lot too
good to me and indulge me too much, and I grow soft, and
then every trifle rubs me the wrong way.   I'm a regular spoilt
child—I know it, and a jolly good spanking is what I deserve.

Burton, here, declares that the autumnal, like the vernal, equinox breeds hot humours and distempers in the blood. I believe we ought to be bled, spring and fall, like our forefathers. Look here, mother, don't take my grumbling to heart. I tell you I'm just a little hipped from the weather. Let's send for dear old Knott and get him to drive out the devil with his lancet! No, no, seriously, I tell you what we will do. It'll be good for us both. I have arrived at a decision. We'll have uncle William and—Helen "—

Richard had spoken very rapidly, half ashamed, trying to soothe her. He paused on the last word. He was conscious of a singular pleasure in pronouncing it. The perfectly finished figure of his cousin, outstanding against the wide, misty bright ness of the sunset, the scent of the wood and moorland, the haunting suggestion of glad secrets, even that upcurling of blue cigarette smoke, rising as the smoke of incense—with a difference —upon the clear, evening air, above all that silent flattery of intimate and fearless glances, those gay welcoming gestures, that merry calling, as of birds in the tree-tops, from the spirit of youth within him to the spirit of youth so visibly and radiantly resident in her—all this rose up before Richard. He grew reckless, though reckless of precisely what, innocent as he was in fact although mature in learning, he knew not as yet. Only he turned on his mother a face at once eager and shy, coaxing her as when in his long-ago baby-days he had implored some petty indulgence or the gift of some coveted toy on which his little heart was set.

"Yes, let us have them," he said. "You know Helen is very charming. You will admire her, mother. She is as clever as she can stick, one sees that at a glance. And she is very much *grande dame* too—and, oh, well, she is a whole lot of charming things! And her coming would be a wholesome breaking up of our ordinary ways of going on. We are usually very contented—at least, I think so—you, and dear Julius, and I, but perhaps we are getting into a bit of a rut. Helen's society might prove an even more efficacious method of driving out my blue-devils than Knott's lancet or a jolly good spanking."

He laughed quietly, patting Katherine's hand, but looking away.

"And there is no denying it would be a vastly more graceful one—don't you think so ? "

Thus were smouldering fires of personal ambition quenched in Lady Calmady, as so often before. Richard's tenderness brought her to her knees. She hugged, with an almost voluptuous movement of passion, that half-rejected burden of maternity, gathering it close against her heart once more. But, along with the rapture of self-surrender, came a thousand familiar fears and anxieties. For she had looked into Dickie's mind, as he spoke out his grumble, and had there perceived the existence of much which she had dreaded and to the existence of which she had striven to blind herself.

"My darling," she said, with a certain hesitation, "I will gladly have them if you wish it—only you remember what happened long ago, when Helen was here last?"

"Yes, I know. I was afraid you would think of that. But you can put that aside. Helen's not the smallest recollection of it. She told me so this afternoon."

"Told you so?" Katherine repeated.

"Yes," he said. "It was awfully sweet of her. Evidently she'd been bullied about her unseemly behaviour when she was small, till you, and I, and Brockhurst, had been made into a perfect bugbear. She's quite amusingly afraid of you still. But she's no notion what really happened. Of course she can't have, or she could not have mentioned the subject to me."—Richard shrugged his shoulders. "Obviously it would have been impossible."

There was a pause. Lady Calmady rose. The young man spoke with conviction, yet her anxiety was not altogether allayed.

"Impossible," he repeated. "Pretty mother, don't disquiet yourself. Trust me. To tell you the truth, I have felt to-day— is it very foolish?—that I should like someone of my own age for a little while, as—don't you know—a playfellow."

Katherine bent down and kissed him. But mother-love is not, even in its most self-sacrificing expression, without torments of jealousy.

"My dear, you shall have your playfellow," she said, though conscious of a tightening of the muscles of her beautiful throat. "Good-night. Sleep well."

She went out, closing the door behind her. The perspective of the dimly-lighted corridor, and the great hall beyond, struck her as rather sadly lifeless and silent. What wonder, indeed, that Richard should ask for a companion, for something young! Love made her selfish and cowardly she feared. She should have thought of this before. She turned back, again opening the Gun-Room door.

Richard had raised himself. He stood on the seat of the chair, steadying himself by one hand on the chair-back, while

with the other he pulled the rug from beneath the sleepy bull-
dog.

"Wake up, you lazy, old beggar," he was saying.   "Get down
can't you?   I want to go to bed, and you block the way, lying
there in gross comfort, snoring.   Make yourself scarce, old man!
If I'd your natural advantages in the way of locomotion, I
wouldn't be so slow in using them"—

He looked up, and slipped back into a sitting position
hastily.

"Oh, mother, I thought you had gone!" he exclaimed,
almost sharply.

And to Katherine, overstrung as she was, the words came
as a rebuke.

"My dearest, I won't keep you," she said.   "I only came
back to ask you about Honoria St. Quentin."

"What about her?"

"She is staying at Newlands—the two girls are friends, I
believe.   She seemed to me a fine creature when last I saw
her.   She knows the world, yet struck me curiously untouched
by it.   She is well read, she has ideas—some of them a little
extravagant, but time will modify that.   Only her head is awake
as yet, not her heart, I think.   Shall I ask her to come too?"

"So that we may wake up her heart?" Richard inquired
coldly.   "No thanks, dear mother, that's too serious an undertaking.   Have her another time, please.   I saw her to-day, and,
no doubt my taste is bad, but I must confess she did not
please me very much.   Nor—which is more to the point in this
connection perhaps—did I please her.—Would you ring the bell,
please, as you're there?   I want Powell.   Thanks so much.
Good-night."

Some ten minutes later Julius March, after kneeling in
prayer, as his custom was, before the divinely sorrowful and
compassionate image of the Virgin Mother and the Dead Christ,
looked forth through the many-paned study window into the
clair-obscure of the windless, autumn night.   He had been
sensible of an unusual element in the domestic atmosphere this
evening, and had been vaguely disquieted concerning both
Katherine and Richard.   It was impossible but that, as time
went on, life should become more complicated at Brockhurst,
and Julius feared his own inability to cope helpfully with such
complication.   He entertained a mean opinion of himself.   It
appeared to him he was but an unprofitable servant, unready,
tongue-tied, lacking in resource.   A depression possessed
him which he could not shake off.   What had he to show,

after all, for these fifty odd years of life granted to him? He feared his religion had walked in silver slippers, and would so walk to the end. Could it then, in any true and vital sense, be reckoned religion at all? Gross sins had never exercised any attraction over him. What virtue was there, then, in being innocent of gross sin? But to those other sins—sins of defective moral courage in speech and action, sins arising from over-fastidiousness—had he not yielded freely? Was he not a spiritual valetudinarian? He feared so. Offered, in the Eternal Mercy, endless precious opportunities of service, he had been too weak, too timorous, too slothful, to lay hold on them. And so, as it seemed to him very justly, to-night confession, prayer, worship, left him unconsoled.

Then, looking out of the many‑paned window while the shame of his barrenness clothed him even as a garment, he beheld Lady Calmady pacing slowly over the grey quarries of the terrace pavement. A dark, fur-bordered mantle shrouded her tall figure from head to foot. Only her face showed, and her hands folded stiffly high upon her bosom, strangely pale against the blackness of her cloak. Ordinarily Julius would have scrupled to intrude upon her lonely walk. But just now the cry within him for human sympathy was urgent. Her near neighbourhood in itself was very dear to him, and she might let fall some gracious word testifying that, in her opinion at least, his life had not been wholly vain. For very surely that which survives when all other passions are uprooted and cast forth— survives even in the case of the true ascetic and saint—is the unquenchable yearning for the spoken approval of those whom we love and have loved.

And so, pushed by his poverty of self-esteem, Julius March, throwing a plaid on over his cassock, went out and paced the grey quarries beside Katherine Calmady.

On one hand rose the dark, rectangular masses of the house, crowned by its stacks of slender, twisted chimneys. On the other lay the indefinite and dusky expanse of the park and forest. The night was very clear. The stars were innumerable —fierce, cold points of pulsing light.—Orion's jewelled belt and sword flung wide against the blue‑black vault. Cassiopeia seated majestic in her golden chair. Northward, above the walled gardens, the Bear pointing to the diamond flashing of the Pole star. While across all high heaven, dusty with incalculable myriads of worlds, stretched the awful and mysterious highroad of the Milky-Way. The air was keen and tonic though so still. An immense and fearless quiet seemed to hold all things—a quiet not of sleep, but of conscious and perfect equilibrium, a harmony so sustained and absolute that to human ears it issued, of necessity, in silence.

And that silence Lady Calmady was in no haste to break. Twice she and her companion walked the length of the terrace, and back, before she spoke. She paused, at length, just short of the arcade of the farther garden-hall.

"This great peace of the night puts all violence of feeling to the blush," she said.   "One perceives that a thousand years are very really as one day.   That calms one—with a vengeance."

Katherine waited, looking out over the vague landscape, clasping the fur-bordered edges of her cloak with either hand. It appeared to Julius that both her voice and the expression of her face were touched with irony.

"There is nothing new under the sun," she went on, "nor under the 'visiting moon,' nor under those somewhat heartless stars.   Does it occur to you, Julius, how hopelessly unoriginal we are, how we all follow in the same beaten track?   What thousands of men and women have stood, as you and I stand now, at once calmed—as I admit that I am—and rendered not a little homeless by the realisation of their own insignificance in face of the sleeping earth and this brooding immensity of space ! *A quoi bon, à quoi bon ?* Why can't one learn to harden one's poor silly heart, and just move round, stone-like, with the great movement of things, accepting fate and ceasing to struggle or to care ?"

"Just because, I think," he answered, "the converse of that same saying is equally true.   If, in material things, a thousand years are as one day, in the things of the spirit one day is as a thousand years.   Remember the Christ crying upon the cross, 'My God, my God, why hast thou forsaken me?' and suffering, during that brief utterance, the sum of all the agony of sensible insignificance and sensible homelessness human nature ever has borne or will bear."

"Ah, the Christ ! the Christ !" Lady Calmady exclaimed, half wistfully as it seemed to Julius March, and half impatiently. She turned and paced the pale pavement again.

"You are too courteous, my dear friend, and cite an example august out of all proportion to my little lament."—She looked round at him as she spoke, smiling; and in the uncertain light her smile showed tremulous, suggestive of a nearness to tears. "Instinctively you scale Olympus,—Calvary?—yes, but I am afraid both those heights take on an equally and tragically mythological character to me—and would bring me consolation from the dwelling-places of the gods. And my feet, all the while, are very much upon the floor, alas! That is happening to me which never yet happened to the gods, according to the orthodox authorities. Just this—a commonplace—dear Julius, I am growing old."

Katherine drew her cloak more severely about her and moved on hastily, her head a little bent.

"No, no, don't deny it," she added, as he attempted to speak. "We can be honest and dispense with conventional phrases, here, alone, under the stars. I am growing old, Julius—and being, I suppose, but a vain, doting woman, I have only discovered what that really means to-day! But there is this excuse for me. My youth was so blessed, so — so glorious, that it was natural I should strive to delude myself regarding its passing away. I perceive that for years I have continued to call that a bride-bed which was, in truth, a bier. I have struggled to keep my youth in fancy, as I have kept the red drawing-room in fact, unaltered. Is not all this pitifully vain and self-indulgent? I have solaced myself with the phantom of youth. And I am old—old."

"But you are yourself, Katherine, yourself. Nothing that has been, has ceased to be," Julius broke in, unable in the fulness of his reverent honour for his dear lady to comprehend the meaning of her present bitterness. "Surely the mere adding of year to year can make no so vital difference?"

"Ah! you dear stupid creature," she cried, — "stupid, because, manlike, you are so hopelessly sensible—it makes just all the difference in the world. I shall grow less alert, less pliable of mind, less quick of sympathy, less capable of adjusting myself to altered conditions, and to the entertaining of new views. And, all the while, the demand upon me will not lessen."

Katherine stopped suddenly in her swift walk. The two stood facing one another.

"The demand will increase," she declared. "Richard is not happy."

And thereupon—since, even in the most devout and holy, the old Adam dies extremely hard—Julius March fell a prey to very lively irritation. While she talked of herself, bestowing unreserved confidence upon him, he could listen gladly forever. But if that most welcome subject of conversation should be dropped, let her give him that which he craved to-night, so specially—a word for himself. Let her deal, for a little space, with his own private needs, his own private joys and sorrows.

"Ah! Richard is not happy!" he exclaimed, his irritation

13

finding voice. "We reach the root of the matter. Richard is
not happy. Alas, then, for Richard's mother!"

"Are you so much surprised?" Katherine asked hotly.
"Do you venture to blame him? If so, I am afraid religion has
made you rather cruel, Julius. But that is not a new thing
under the sun either. Those who possess high spiritual consolations—unknown to the rank and file of us—have generally
displayed an inclination to take the misfortunes of others with
admirable resignation. Dearest Marie de Mirancourt was an
exception to that rule. You might do worse perhaps than learn
to follow her example."

As she finished speaking Lady Calmady turned from him
rather loftily, and prepared to move away. But even in so
doing she received an impression which tended to modify her
resentful humour.

For an instant Julius March stood, a tall, thin, black figure,
rigid and shadowless upon the pallor of the grey pavement, his
arms extended wide, as one crucified, while he looked, not at
her, not out into the repose of the night-swathed landscape, but
up at the silent dance of the eternal stars in the limitless fields
of space. As Katherine, earlier in the evening, had taken up
the momentarily rejected burden of her motherhood, so Julius
now, with a movement of supreme self-surrender, took up the
momentarily rejected burden of the isolation of the religious
life. Self-wounded by self-love, he had sought comfort in the
creature rather than the Creator. And the creature turned and
rebuked him. It was just. Now Julius gave himself back,
bowed himself again under the dominion of his fixed idea; and,
so doing, gained, unconsciously, precisely that which he had
gone forth to seek. For Katherine, struck alike by the strange
vigour, and strange resignation, of his attitude, suffered quick
fear, not only for, but of him. His aloofness alarmed her.

"Julius! dear Julius!" she cried. "Come, let us walk. It
grows cold. I enjoy that, but it is not very safe for you. And,
pardon me, dear friend, if I spoke harshly just now. I told you
I was getting old. Put my words down to the peevishness of old
age then."

Katherine smiled at him with a sweet, half-playful humility.
Her face was very wan. And speech not coming immediately
to him, she spoke again.

"You have always been very patient with me. You must go
on being so."

"I ask nothing better," Julius said.

Lady Calmady stopped, drew herself up, shook back her head.

"Ah! what sorry creatures we all are," she cried, rather bitterly. "Discontented, unstable, forever kicking against the pricks, and fighting against the inevitable. Always crying to one another, 'See how hard this is, know how it hurts, feel the weight!' My poor darling cries to me—that is natural enough"—Katherine paused—"and as it should be. But I must needs run out and cry to you. In this we are like links of an endless chain. What is the next link, Julius? To whom will you cry in your turn?"

"The chain is not endless," he replied. "The last link of it is riveted to the steps of the throne of God. I will make my cry there—my threefold cry—for you, for Richard, and for myself, Katherine."

Lady Calmady had reached the arched side-door leading from the terrace into the house. She paused, with her hand on the latch.

"Your God and I quarrelled nearly four-and-twenty years ago—not when Richard, my joy, died, but when Richard, my sorrow, was born," she said. "I own I see no way, short of miracle, of that quarrel being made up."

"Then a miracle will be worked," he answered.

"Ah! you forget I grow old," Katherine retorted, smiling; "so that for miracles the time is at once too long and too short."

CHAPTER V

TELLING HOW QUEEN MARY'S CRYSTAL BALL CAME TO FALL ON THE GALLERY FLOOR

THIS world is unquestionably a vastly stimulating and entertaining place if you take it aright—namely if you recognise that it is the creation of a profound humorist, is designed for wholly practical and personal uses, and proceed to adapt your conduct to that knowledge in all light-heartedness and good faith. Thus, though in less trenchant phrase since she was still happily very young, meditated Madame de Vallorbes, while standing in the pensive October sunshine upon the wide flight of steps which leads down from the main entrance of Brockhurst House. Tall, stone pinnacles alternating with seated griffins—long of tail, fierce of beak and sharp of claw—fill in each of the many angles of the descending stone balustrade on either hand. Behind her, the florid, though rectangular, decoration of the house-front ranged up, storey above storey, in arcade and pilaster, heavily-mullioned window, carven plaque and string course, to pairs of matching pinnacles and griffins — these last rampant, supporting the Calmady shield and coat-of-arms—the quaint forms of which break the long line of the pierced, stone parapet in the centre of the façade, and rise above the rusty red of the low-pitched roofs, until the spires of the one and crested heads of the other are outlined against the sky.   About her feet the pea-fowl stepped in mincing and self-conscious elegance—the cocks with rustlings of heavy-trailing quills, the hens and half-grown chicks with squeakings and whifflings—subdued, conversational—accompanied by the dry tap of many bills picking up the glossy grains of Indian-corn which she let dribble slowly down upon the shallow steps from between her pretty fingers.   She had huddled a soft sable tippet about her throat and shoulders.   The skirt of her indigo-coloured, poplin dress, turning upon the step immediately above that on which she stood, showed some inches of rose-scarlet, silken frill lining the hem of it.

Helen de Vallorbes had a lively consciousness of her surroundings.   She enjoyed every detail of them.   Enjoyed the gentle, south-westerly wind which touched her face and stirred her bright hair, enjoyed the plaintive, autumn song of a robin perched on a rose-grown wall, enjoyed the impotent ferocity of the guardian griffins, enjoyed the small sounds made by the feeding pea-fowl, the modest quaker greys and the imperial splendours of their plumage.   She enjoyed the turn of her own wrist, its gold chain-bracelet and the handsome lace falling away from and displaying it, as she held out the handfuls of corn. She enjoyed even that space of rose-scarlet declaring itself between the dull blue of her dress and the grey, weathered surface of the stone.

But all these formed only the accompaniment, the ground-tone, to more reasoned, more vital, enjoyments.   Before her, beyond the carriage sweep, lay the square lawn enclosed by red walls and by octagonal, pepper-pot summer-houses, whereon— unwillingly, yet in obedience to the wild justice of revenge— Roger Ormiston had shot the Clown, half-brother to Touchstone, racehorse of mournful memory.   As a child Helen had heard that story.   Now her somewhat light, blue-grey eyes, their beautiful lids raised wide for once, looked out curiously upon the space of dew-powdered turf; while the corners of her mouth —a mouth a trifle thin lipped, yet soft and dangerously sweet for kissing—turned upward in a reflective smile.   She, too, knew what it was to be angry, to the point of revenge; had indeed come to Brockhurst not without purpose of that last tucked away in some naughty convolution of her active brain.   But Brockhurst and its inhabitants had proved altogether more interesting than she had anticipated.   This was the fourth day of her visit, and each day had proved more to her taste than the preceding one. So she concluded this matter of revenge might very well stand over for the moment, possibly stand over altogether.   The present was too excellent, of its kind, to risk spoiling.   Helen de Vallorbes valued the purple and fine linen of a high civilisation ; nor did she disdain, within graceful limits, to fare sumptuously every day.   She valued all that is beautiful and costly in art, of high merit and distinction in literature.   Her taste was sure and just, if a little more disposed towards that which is sensuous than towards that which is spiritual.   And in all its many forms she appreciated luxury, even entertaining a kindness for that necessary handmaid of luxury—waste.   Appreciated these the more ardently, that, with birth-pangs at the beginning of each human life, death-pangs and the corruption of the inevitable grave at the close of each, all this lapping, meanwhile, of the doomed flesh in exaggerations of ease and splendour seemed to her among the very finest ironies of the great comedy of existence.   It heightened, it accentuated the drama.   And among the many good things of life, drama, come how and where and when it might, seemed to her supremely the best.   She desired it as a lover his mistress.   To detect it, to observe it, gave her the keenest pleasure.   To take a leading part in and shape it to the turn of her own heart, her own purpose, her own wit, was, so far, her ruling passion.

And of potential drama, of the raw material of it, as the days passed, she found increasingly generous store at Brockhurst.   It invaded and held her imagination, as the initial conception of his poem will that of the poet, or of his picture that of the painter. She brooded over it, increasingly convinced that it might be a masterpiece.   For the drama—as she apprehended it—contained not only elements of virility and strength, but an element, and that a persistent one, of the grotesque.   This put the gilded dome to her silent, and perhaps slightly unscrupulous, satisfaction.   How could it be otherwise, since the presence of the grotesque is, after all, the main justification of the theory on which her philosophy of life was based—namely the belief that above all eloquence of human speech, behind all enthusiasm of human action or emotion, the ear which hears aright can always detect the echo of eternal laughter?   And this grim echo did not affect the charming young lady to sadness as yet.   Still less

did it make her mad, as the mere suspicion of it has made so
many, and those by no means unworthy or illiterate persons.
For the laugh, so far, had appeared to be on her side, never at
her expense—which makes a difference.   And the chambers of
her House of Life were too crowded by health and agreeable
sensations, mental activities and sparkling audacities to leave any
one of them vacant for reception, more than momentary, of that
thrice-blessed guest, pity.

And so it followed that, as she fed the mincing pea-fowl,
Madame de Vallorbes' smile changed in character from reflection to impatience.   A certain heat running through her,
she set her pretty teeth and fell to pelting the pea-hens and
chicks mischievously, breaking up all their aristocratic reserve
and making them jump and squeak to some purpose.   For this
precious, this very masterpiece of a drama was not only here
potentially, but actually.   It was alive.   She had felt it move
under her hand—or under her heart, which was it?—yesterday
evening.   Again this morning, just now, she had noted signs of
its vitality, wholly convincing to one skilled in such matters.
Impatience, then, became very excusable.

"For my time is short and the action disengages itself so
deplorably slowly!" she exclaimed.—"Pah! you greedy, conceited birds, which do you hold dearest after all, the filling of
your little stomachs, or the supporting of your little dignities?
Be advised by a higher intelligence.   Revenge yourselves on the
grains that hit and sting you by gobbling them up.   It is a
venerable custom that of feasting upon one's enemies.   And
has been practised, in various forms, both by nations and
individuals.   There, I give you another chance of displaying
wisdom — there — there! — La! la! what an absurd com-
motion!   You little idiots, don't flutter.   Agitation is a waste of
energy, and advances nothing.   I declare peace.   I want to
consider."

And so, letting the remaining handfuls of corn dribble down
very slowly, while the sunshine grew warmer and the shadows of
the guardian griffins more distinct upon the lichen-encrusted
stones, Helen de Vallorbes sank back into meditation.—Yes,
unquestionably the drama was alive.   But it seemed so difficult
to bring it to the birth.   And she wanted, very badly, to hear its
first half-articulate cries and watch its first staggering footsteps.
All that is so entertaining, you yourself safely grown-up, standing
very firm on your feet, looking down!—And it would be a lusty
child, this drama, very soon reaching man's estate and man's
inspiring violence of action, striking out like some blind, giant

Samson, blundering headlong in its unseeing, uncalculating strength.—Helen laid her hands upon her bosom, and threw back her head, while her throat bubbled with suppressed laughter. Ah! it promised to be a drama of ten thousand, if she knew her power, and knew her world—and she possessed considerable confidence in her knowledge of both. Only, how on earth to set the crystal free of the matrix, how to engage battle, how to get this thing fairly and squarely born? For, as she acknowledged, in the flotation of all such merry schemes as her present one, chance encounters, interludes, neatly planned evasions and resultant pursuits, play so large and important a part. But at Brockhurst this whole chapter of accidents was barred, and received rules of strategy almost annihilated, by the fact of Richard Calmady's infirmity and the hard-and-fast order of domestic procedure, the elaborate system of etiquette, which that infirmity had gradually produced. At Brockhurst there were no haphazard exits and entrances. These were either hopelessly official and public, or guarded to an equally hopeless point of secrecy. A contingent of tall, civil men-servants was always on duty. Richard was invariably in his place at table when the rest of the company came down. The ladies took their after-dinner coffee in the drawing-room, and joined the gentlemen in the Chapel-Room, library, or gallery, as the case might be. If they rode, Richard was at the door ready mounted, along with the grooms and led-horses. If they drove, he was already seated in the carriage.

"And how, how in the name of common sense," Madame de Vallorbes exclaimed, stamping her foot, and thereby throwing the now thoroughly nervous pea-fowl into renewed agitation, "are you to establish any relation worth mentioning with a man who is perpetually being carried in procession like a Hindu idol? My good birds, one's never alone with him—whether by design and arrangement, I know not. But, so far, never, never, picture that! And yet, don't tell me, matchless mixture of pride and innocence though he is, he wouldn't like it!"

However, she checked her irritation by contemplation of yesterday.—Ah! that had been very prettily done assuredly. For riding in the forenoon along the road skirting the palings of the inner park, while they walked their horses over the soft, brown bed of fallen fir-needles,—she, her father, and Dick,—the conversation dealt with certain first editions and their bindings, certain treasures, unique in historic worth, locked in the glass tables and fine Florentine and *piétra dura* cabinets of the Long Gallery. Mr. Ormiston was a connoisseur and talked well. And

Helen had sufficient acquaintance with such matters both to appreciate, and to add telling words to the talk.

"Ah! but I cannot go without seeing those delectable things, Richard," she said. "Would it be giving you altogether too much trouble to have them out for me?"

"Why, of course not. You shall see them whenever you like," he answered. "Julius knows all about them. He'll be only too delighted to act showman."

Just here the road narrowed a little, and Mr. Ormiston let his horse drop a few lengths behind, so that she, Helen, and her cousin rode forward side by side. The tones of the low sky, of the ranks of firs and stretches of heather formed a rich, though sombre, harmony of colour. Scents, pungent and singularly exhilarating, were given off by the damp mosses and the peaty moorland soil. The freedom of the forest, the feeling of the noble horse under her, stirred Helen as with the excitement of a mighty hunting, a positively royal sport. While the close presence of the young man riding beside her sharpened the edge of that excitement to a perfect keenness of pleasure.

"Ah, how glorious it all is!" she cried. "How glad I am that you asked me to come here."

And she turned to Richard, looking at him as, since the first day of their meeting, she had not, somehow, quite ventured to look.

"But, oh! dear me! please," she went on, "I know Mr. March is an angel, a saint—but—but—*mea culpa, mea maxima culpa*, I don't want him to show me those special treasures of yours. He'll take the life out of them. I know it. And make them seem like things read of merely in a learned book. Be very charming to me, Richard. Waste half an hour upon me. Show me those moving relics yourself."

As she spoke, momentary suspicion rose in Dickie's eyes. But she gazed back unflinchingly, with the uttermost frankness, so that suspicion died, giving place to the shy, yet triumphant, gladness of youth which seeks and finds youth.

"Do, Richard, pray do," she repeated.

The young man had averted his face rather sharply, and both horses, somehow, broke into a hand gallop.

"All right," he answered. "I'll arrange it. This evening, about six, after tea? Will that suit you? I'll send you word."

Then the road had widened, permitting Mr. Ormiston to draw up to them again. The remainder of the ride had been a little silent.

Yes, all that had been prettily done. Nor had the piece that followed proved unworthy of the prelude. She ran over the scene in her mind now, as she stood among the pecketing peafowl, and it caused her both mirth and delightful little heats, in which the heart has a word to say.—Madame de Vallorbes was ravished to feel her heart, just now and again. For, contradictory as it may seem, no game is perfect that has not moments of seriousness.—She recalled the aspect of the Long Gallery, as one of those civil, ever-present men-servants had opened the door for her, and she waited a moment on the threshold. The true artist is never in a hurry. The breadth of the great room immediately before her showed very bright with candle-light and lamp-light. But that died away, through gradations of augmenting obscurity, until the extreme end, towards the western bay, melted out into complete darkness. This produced an effect of almost limitless length which moved her to a childish, and at first pleasing, fancy of vague danger—an effect heightened by the ranges of curious and costly objects standing against, or decorating, the walls in a perspective of deepening gloom. Turquoise-coloured, satin curtains, faded to intimate accord with the silvered surface of the panelling, were drawn across the wide windows. They reached to the lower edge of the stonework merely, leaving blottings of impenetrable shadow below. While, as culmination of interest, as living centre to this rich and varied setting, was the figure of Richard Calmady—seen, as his custom was, only to the waist—seated in a high-backed chair drawn close against an antique, oak table, upon which a small *piètra dura* cabinet had been placed. The doors of the cabinet stood open, displaying slender columns of jasper and porphyry, and little drawers encrusted with raised work in marble and precious stones. The young man sat stiffly upright, as one who listens, expectant. His expression was almost painfully serious. In one hand he held a string of pearls, attached to which, and enclosed by intersecting hoops of gold, was a crystal ball that shone with the mild effulgence of a mimic moon. And the great room was so very quiet, that Helen, in her pause upon the threshold, had remarked the sound of raindrops tapping upon the many window - panes as with impatiently nervous fingers.

And this bred in her a corresponding nervousness—sensation to her, heretofore, almost unknown. The darkness yonder began to provoke a disagreeable impression, queerly challenging both her eyesight and her courage. Old convent teachings, regarding the Prince of Darkness and his emissaries, returned upon her. What if diabolic shapes lurked there, ready to become stealthily emergent? She had scoffed at such archaic fancies in the convent, yet, in lonely hours, had suffered panic fear of them, as will the hardiest sceptic. A certain little scar, moreover, carefully hidden under the soft hair arranged low on her right temple, smarted and pricked. In short, her habitual self-confidence suffered partial eclipse. She was visited by the disintegrating suspicion, for once, that the eternal laughter might, possibly, be at her expense, rather than on her side.

But she conquered such suspicion as contemptible, and cast out the passing weakness.—The bare memory of it angered her now, causing her to fire a volley of yellow corn at a lordly peacock, which sent him scuttling down the steps on to the gravel in most plebeian haste. Yes, she had speedily cast out her weakness, thank Heaven! What was all the pother about after all? This was not the first time she had played merry games with the affairs and affections of men. Madame de Vallorbes smiled to herself, recalling certain episodes, and shook her charming shoulders gleefully, as she looked out into the sunny morning. And then, was there not ample excuse? This man moved her more than most—more than any. She swore he did. Her attitude towards him was something new, something quite different, thereby justifying her campaign. And therefore, all the bolder for her brief self-distrust and hesitation, she had swept across the great room, light of foot, and almost impertinently graceful of carriage.

"Here you are at last!" Dickie had exclaimed, with a sigh as of relief. "I shan't want anything more, Powell. You can come back when the dressing-bell rings."— Then, as the valet closed the door behind him, he continued rapidly :—"Not that I propose to victimise you till then, Helen. You mustn't stay a moment longer than you like. I confess I'm awfully fond of this room. I'm almost ashamed to think how much time I waste in it. Doing what? Oh, well, just dreaming! You see it contains samples of the doings of all my father's people, and I return to primitive faiths here and perform acts of ancestor worship."

"Ah! I like that!" Helen said. And she did. Picture this man, long of arm, unnaturally low of stature, and astonishingly—yes, quite astonishingly—good-looking, moving about among these books and pictures, these trophies of war and of sport, these oriental jars, tall almost as himself, and all the other strange furnishings from out distant years and distant lands! Picture him emerging from that wall of soft darkness yonder, for instance! Helen's eyes danced under their arched and drooping lids, and she registered the fact that, though still frightened, her fright had changed in character.   It was grateful to her palate.   She relished it as the bouquet of a wine of finest quality.   Meanwhile her companion talked on.

"The ancestor worship?   Oh yes!   I daresay you might like it for a change.   Getting it as I do, as habitual diet, it is not remarkably stimulating.   The natural man prefers to find occasion for worshipping himself rather than his ancestors, after all, you know.   But a little turn of it will serve to fill in a gap and lessen the monotony of your visit.   I am afraid you must be a good deal bored, Helen.   It must seem rather terribly hum-drum here after Paris and Naples, and—well—most places, at that rate, as you know them."

Richard shifted his position.   And the crystal moon encom-passed by golden bands, crossing and intersecting one another like those of a sidereal sphere, gleamed as with an inward and unearthly light, swinging slowly upon the movement of his hand.

"You must feel here as though the clock had been put back two or three centuries.   I know we move slowly, and conduct ourselves with tedious deliberation.   And so, you understand, you mustn't let me keep you.   Just look at what you like of these odds and ends, and then depart without scruple. It's rather a fraud, in any case, my showing them to you.   Julius March, as I told you, is much better qualified to."

"Julius March, Julius March!" Madame de Vallorbes broke in.   "Do, I beseech you, dear cousin Richard, leave him to the pious retirement of his study.   Is he not middle-aged, and a priest into the bargain?"

"Unquestionably," Dickie said.   "But, pardon me, I don't quite see what that has to do with it,"

Thereupon Madame de Vallorbes made a very naughty, little grimace and drummed with her finger-tips upon the table.

"La! la!" she cried, "you're no better than all the rest. Commend me to a clever man for incapacity to apprehend what is patent to the intelligence of the most ordinary woman.   Look about you."—Helen sketched in their surroundings with a quick descriptive gesture.   "Observe the lights and shadows.   The ghostly wavings of those pale curtains.   Smell the pot-pourri and spices.   Think of the ancestor worship.   Listen to the lamenting wind and rain.   See the mysterious treasure you hold in your hand.   And then ask me what middle-age and the clerical profession have to do with all this!   Why, nothing, just precisely nothing, nothing in the whole world.   That's the point of my argument. They'd ruin the sentiment, blight the romance, hopelessly blight it—for me at least."

The conversation was slightly embarrassed, both Helen and Richard talking at length, yet at random. But she knew that it was thus, and not otherwise, that it behoved them to talk. For that which they said mattered not in the least. The thing said served as a veil, as a cloak, merely, wherewith to disguise those much greater things which, perforce, remained unsaid.—To cover his and her lively consciousness of their present isolation, desired these many days and now obtained. To conceal the swift, silent approaches of spirit to spirit, so full of inquiry and self-revelation, fugitive reserves and fugitive distrusts. To hide, as far as might be, the existence of the hungry, all-compelling *joie de vivre* which is begotten whensoever youth thus seeks and finds youth.—These unspoken and, as yet, unspeakable things were alone of real moment, making eyes lustrous and lips quick with tremulous, uncalled-for smiles irrespective of the purport of their speech.

" Ah! but that's rather rough on poor dear Julius, you know," Dickie said. " I suppose you wanted to learn all "—

" Learn ? " she interrupted. " I wanted to feel. Don't you know there is only one way any woman worth the name ever really learns—through her emotions? Only the living feel. Such men as he, if they are sincere, are already dead. He would have made feeling impossible."

A perceptible hush descended upon the room. Richard Calmady's hand usually was steady enough, but, in the silence, the pearls chattered against the table. He went rather pale and his face hardened.

" And are you getting anything of that which you wanted, Helen ? " he asked. " For sometimes in the last few days— since you have been here—I—I have wondered if perhaps we were not all like that—all dead "—

" You mean do I get emotion, am I feeling? " she said. " Rest contented. Much is happening. Indeed I have doubted, during the last few days, since I have been here, whether I have ever known what it is to feel actually and seriously before."

She sat down at right angles to him, resting her elbows upon the table, her chin upon her folded hands, leaning a little towards him. One of those pleasant heats swept over her, flushing her delicate skin, lending a certain effulgence to her beauty. The scent of roses long faded hung in the air. But here was a rose sweeter far than they. No white rose of paradise, it must be confessed. Rather, like her immortal namesake, that classic Helen, was she *rosa mundi,* glowing with warmth and colour, rose-red rose altogether of this dear, naughty, lower world!

"Richard," she said impulsively, "why don't you understand? Why do you underrate your own power? Don't you know that you are quite the most moving, the most attractive—well—cousin, a woman ever had?"

She looked closely at him, her lips a little parted, her head thrown back.

"Life is sweet, dear cousin. Reckon with yourself and with it, and live—live."—Then she put out her hand and held up the crystal between her face and his. "There," she went on, "tell me about this. I become indiscreet, thanks I suppose to your Brockhurst habit of putting back the clock, and speak with truly Elizabethan frankness. It belongs to semi-barbaric ages, doesn't it, thus, to tell the true truth? Show me this. It seems rather fascinating."

And Richard obeyed mechanically, pointing out to her the signs of the Zodiac, those of the planets, and other figures of occult significance engraved on the encircling, golden bands. Showed her how those same bands, turning on a pivot, formed a golden cradle, in which the crystal sphere reposed. He lifted it out from that cradle, moreover, and laid it in the softer cradle of her palm. And of necessity, in the doing of all this, their heads—his and hers—were very near together, and their hands met. But they were very solemn all the while, solemn, eager, busy, as two babies revealing to each other the mysteries of a newly acquired toy. And it seemed to Madame de Vallorbes that all this was as pretty a bit of business as ever served to help forward such gay purposes as hers. She was pleased with herself too—for did she not feel very gentle, very sincere, really very innocent and good?

"No, hold it so," Richard said, rounding her fingers carefully, that the tips of them might alone touch the surface of the crystal. "Now gaze into the heart of it steadily, fixing your will to see. Pictures will come presently, dimly at first, as in a mist. Then the mist will lift and you will read your own fortune and—perhaps—some other person's fate."

"Have you ever read yours?"

"Oh! mine's of a sort that needs no crystal to reveal it," he answered, with a queer drop in his voice. "It's written in rather indecently big letters and plain type. Always has been."

Helen glanced at him. His words whipped up her sense of drama, fed her excitement. But she bent her eyes upon the crystal again, and the hush descended once more, disturbed only by that nervous tapping of rain.

"I see nothing,—nothing," she said presently. "And there is much I would give very much to see."

"You must gaze with a simple intention."—The young man's voice came curiously hoarse and broken. "Purify your mind of all desire."

Helen did not raise her head.

"Alas! if those are the conditions of revelation my chances of seeing are extremely limited. To purify one's mind of all desire is to commit emotional suicide. Of course I desire, all the while I desire. And equally, of course, you desire. Every one who is human and in their sober senses must do that. Absence of desire means idiotcy, or "—

"Or what?"

For an instant she looked up at him, a very devil of dainty malice in her expression, in the shrug of her shoulders too, beneath their fine laces and the affected sobriety of that same dull-blue, poplin gown.

"Or priestly, saintly middle-age—from which may Heaven in its mercy ever deliver us," she said.

Richard shifted his position a little, gathering himself back from her so near neighbourhood—a fact of which the young lady was not unaware.

"I'm not quite sure whether I echo your prayer," he said slowly. "I doubt whether that attitude, or one approximate to it, is not the safest and best for some of us."

"Safest, no doubt."—Madame de Vallorbes' eyes were bent on the crystal sphere again. "As it is safer to decline a duel, than go out and meet your man. Best? On that point you must permit me to hold my own opinion. The word 'best' has many readings according to the connection in which it is employed. Personally I should always fight."

"Whatever the odds?"

"Whatever the odds."—And almost immediately Madame de Vallorbes uttered a little cry, curiously at variance with her bold words. "Something is moving inside the crystal, something is coming. I don't half like it, Richard. Perhaps we are tempting Providence. Yes, it moves, it moves, like mist rising off a river. It is poisonous. Some woman has looked into this before—a woman of my temperament—and read an evil fortune. I know it. Tell me, quick, how did the crystal come here, to whom did it belong?"

"To Mary Stuart—Mary, Queen of Scots," Dickie said.

"Ah! unhappy woman, ill-omened woman! You should have told me that before and I would never have looked. Here take it, take it. Lock it up, hide it. Let no woman ever look in it again!"

As she spoke Helen crossed herself hastily, pushing the magic ball towards him. But, as though endowed with life and volition of its own—or was it merely that Dick's hand was even yet not quite of the steadiest?—it evaded his grasp, fell off the table edge and rolled, gleaming moonlike, far across the floor, away behind the pedestal of the bronze Pompeian Antinous, into the dusky shadow of those ghostly - waving, turquoise, satin curtains.

With a sense of catastrophe upon her Helen had sprung to her feet.—Even now, standing in the peaceful warmth of the autumn sunshine, among the feeding pea-fowl, the remembrance of it caused her a little shiver. For at sight of that gleaming ball hurrying across the carpet, all the nervousness, the distrust of herself, and the vague spiritual alarms, which had beset her on first entering the room, returned on her with tenfold force. The superstitious terrors of the convent-bred girl mastered the light-hearted scepticism of the woman of the world, and regions of sinister possibility seemed disclosing themselves around her.

"Oh! how horrible! What does it mean?" she cried.

And Richard answered cheerily, somewhat astonished at her agitation, trying to reassure her.

"Mean? Nothing, except that I was abominably awkward and the crystal abominably slippery. What does it matter? We can find it again directly."

Then, self-forgetful in the fulness of his longing to pacify her, Richard had pushed his chair back from the table, intending to go in search of the vagrant jewel. But the chair was high, and its make not of the most solid sort; and so he paused, instinctively calculating the amount of support it could be trusted to render him in his descent. And during that pause Helen had felt her heart stand still.—She set her little teeth now, recalling it. For the extent of his deformity was fully apparent for once. And, apprehending that which he proposed to do, she was smitten by immense curiosity to realise the ultimate of the grotesque in respect of his appearance as he should move, walk, grope in the dimness over there after the lost crystal. But there are some indulgences which can be bought at too high a price, and along with the temptation to gratify her curiosity came an intensification of superstitious alarm. What if she had sinned, and trafficked with diabolic agencies in trying to read the future? Payment of an actively disagreeable character might be exacted for that, and would not such payment risk disastrous augmentation if she gratified her curiosity thus further? Helen de Vallorbes became quite wonderfully prudent and humane.

"No, no, don't bother about it, don't move, dear Richard," she cried. "Let me find it, please. I saw exactly the direction in which it went."

And to enforce her speech, and keep the young man in his place, she laid her hands persuasively upon his shoulders. This brought her charming face, so pure in outline, set in its aureole of honey-coloured hair, very near to his, she looking down, he up. And in this position the two remained longer than was absolutely necessary, silent, quite still, while the air grew thick with the push of unspoken and as yet unspeakable matters, and Helen's hands resting upon his shoulders grew heavy, as the seconds passed, with languorous weight.

"There are better things than crystals to read in, after all, Richard," she said at last. Then she lifted her hands almost brusquely and stepped back.—"All the same it is stupid I should have to go away," she continued, speaking more to herself than to him. "I am happy here. And when I am happy it's easy to be good—and I like to be good."

She crossed the room and passed behind the bronze Pompeian Antinous. Under the shadow of the curtains, in the angle of the bay, against the wainscot, Queen Mary's magic ball glowed softly luminous. Helen could have believed that it watched her. She hesitated before stooping to pick it up and looked over her shoulder at Richard Calmady. His back was towards her, his chair close against the table again. He leaned forward on his elbows, his face buried in his hands. Something in the bowed head, in the set of the almost crouching figure reassured Madame de Vallorbes. She picked up the crystal without more ado, with, indeed, a certain flippancy of gesture. For she had received pleasing assurance that she had been frightened in the wrong place, and that the eternal laughter was very completely on her side after all.

And just then a bell had rung in some distant quarter of the great house. Powell, incarnation of decent punctualities, had appeared. Whereupon the temperature fell to below normal from fever-heat. Drama, accentuations of sensibility, in short all the unspoken and unspeakable, withered as tropic foliage at a touch of frost. No doubt it was as well, Madame de Vallorbes reflected philosophically, since the really psychological moment was passed. There had been a dinner party last night, and—

But here the young lady's reminiscences broke off short. She gathered up her blue, poplin, scarlet-lined skirts, ran down the steps, scattering the pea-fowl to right and left, and hastened across the gravel.

"Wait half a minute for me, dear Aunt Katherine," she cried. "Are you going to the conservatories? I would so like to see them. May I go too?"

Lady Calmady stood by the door in the high, red-brick wall. She wore a white, lace scarf over her hair—turned up and back, dressed high, as of old, though now somewhat grey upon the temples. The lace was tied under her chin, framing her face. In her grey dress she looked as some stately, yet gracious, lady abbess might—a lady abbess who had known love in all fulness, yet in all honour—a lady abbess painted, if such happy chance could be, by the debonair and clean-hearted Reynolds. She stood smiling, charmed—though a trifle unwillingly—by the brilliant vision of the younger woman.

"Assuredly you may come with me, if it would amuse you," she said.

"I may? Then let me open that door for you. La! la! how it sticks. Last night's rain must have swelled it"—and she wrestled unsuccessfully with the lock.

"My dear, don't try any more," Katherine said. "You will tire yourself. The exertion is too great for you. I will go back and call one of the servants."

"No, no"—and regardless of her fine laces, and trinkets, and sables Madame de Vallorbes put her shoulder against the resisting door and fairly burst it open.

"See," she cried, breathless but triumphant, "I am very strong."

"You are very pretty," Katherine said, almost involuntarily.

The steeply-terraced kitchen-gardens, neat box edgings, wide flower borders in which a few clumps of chrysanthemum and Michaelmas daisy still resisted the frost, ranged down to greenish brown ponds in the valley bottom spotted with busy, quacking companies of white ducks. Beyond was an ascending slope of thick wood, the topmost trees of which showed bare against the sky line. All this was framed by the arch of the door. Madame de Vallorbes glanced at it, while she pulled down the soft waves of hair, which her late exertions had slightly disarranged, over her right temple. Then she turned impulsively to Lady Calmady.

14

"Thank you, dear Aunt Katherine," she said. "I would so like you to like me, you know."

"I should be rather unpardonably difficult to please, if I did not like you, my dear," Lady Calmady answered. But she sighed as she spoke.

The two women moved away, side by side, down the path to the glistering greenhouses. But Camp, who, missing Richard, had followed his mistress out of the house for a leisurely morning potter, turned back sulkily across the gravel homewards, his tail limp, his heavy head carried low. His instincts were conservative, as has been already mentioned. He was suspicious of new-comers. And, whoever liked this particular new-comer, Madame de Vallorbes, he was sorry to say — and on more than one occasion he said it with quite inconvenient distinctness—he did not.

CHAPTER VI

IN WHICH DICKIE TRIES TO RIDE AWAY FROM HIS OWN
SHADOW, WITH SUCH SUCCESS AS MIGHT HAVE BEEN
ANTICIPATED

THAT same morning Richard was up and out early. Fog had followed on the evening's rain, and at sunrise still shrouded all the landscape.

"Let her ladyship know I breakfast at the stables and shan't be in before luncheon," he had said to Powell while settling himself in the saddle. Then, followed by a groom, he fared forth. The house vanished phantom-like behind him, and the clang of the iron gates as they swung to was muffled by the heavy atmosphere, while he rode on by invisible ways across an invisible land, hemmed in, close-encompassed, pressed upon, by the chill, ashen whiteness of the fog.

And for the cold silence and blankness surrounding him Richard was grateful. It was restful—after a grim fashion—and he welcomed rest, having passed a but restless night. For Dickie had been the victim of much travail of spirit. His imagination vexed him, pricking up slumbering lusts of the flesh. His conscience vexed him likewise, suggesting that his attitude had not been pure cousinly; and this shamed him, since he was still singularly unspotted from the world, noble modesties and decencies still paramount in him. He was keenly, some might say mawkishly, sensible of the stain and dishonour of casting, even involuntarily and passingly, covetous glances upon another man's goods.   In sensation and apprehension he had lived at racing pace during the last few days.   That hour in the Long Gallery last night had been the climax.   The gates of paradise had opened before him.   And, since opposites of necessity imply their opposites, the gates of hell had opened likewise.   It appeared to Dickie that the great poets, and painters, and musicians, the great lovers even, had nothing left to tell him—for he knew.   Knew, moreover, that his Eden had come to him with the angel of the fiery sword that "turneth every way" standing at the threshold of it—knew, yet further, as he had never known before, the immensity of the difficulties, disabilities, humiliations, imposed on him by his deformity. Bitterly, nakedly, he called his trouble by that offensive name. Then he straightened himself in the saddle.   Yes, welcome the cold weight against his chest, welcome the silence, the blankness, the dead, ashen pallor of the fog !

But just where the tan ride, leading down across the road to the left, diverges from the main road, this source of negative consolation began to fail him.   For a draw of fresher air came from westward, causing the blurred, wet branches to quiver and the pall of mist to gather, and then break and melt under its wholesome breath, while the rays of the laggard sun, clearing the edge of the fir forest, eastward, pierced it, hastening its dissolution.   Therefore it followed that by the time Richard rode in under the stable archway, he found the great yard full of noise and confused movement.   The stable doors stood wide along one side of the quadrangle.   Stunted, boyish figures shambled hither and thither, unwillingly deserting the remnants of half-eaten breakfasts, among the iron mugs and platters of the long, deal tables of the refectory.   Chifney and Preiston —the head-lad—hurried them, shouting orders, admonishing, inciting to greater rapidity of action.   And the boys were sulky. The thick morning had promoted hopes of an hour or two of unwonted idleness.   Now those poor, little hopes were summarily blighted.   Lazy, pinched with cold by the raw morning air, still a bit hungry, sick even, or downright frightened, they must mount and away—the long line of racehorses streaming, in single file, up the hillside to the exercising ground—with as short delay as possible, or Mr. Chifney and his ash stick would know the reason why.

There were elements of brutality in the scene from which Richard would, oftentimes, have recoiled.   To-day he was selfish, absorbed to the point of callousness. If he remarked them at all, it was in bitter welcome, as he had welcomed the chill and staring blankness of the fog. He was indifferent to the fact that Chifney was harsh, the horses testy or wicked, that the boys' noses were red, and that they blew their purple fingers before laying hold of the reins in a vain attempt to promote circulation. Dickie sat still as a statue in the midst of all the turmoil, the handle of his crop resting on his thigh, his eyes hot from sleeplessness and wild thoughts, his face hard as marble.—Unhappy? Wasn't he unhappy too? Suffer? Well, let them suffer—within reasonable limits. Suffering was the fundamental law of existence. They must bow to the workings of it along with the rest.

But one wretched, little chap fairly blubbered. He had been kicked in the stomach some three weeks earlier, and had been in hospital. This was his first morning out. He had grown soft, and was light-headed, his knees all of a shake. By means of voluminous threats Preiston got him up. But he sat his horse all of a huddle, as limp as a half-empty sack of chaff. Richard looked on feeling, not pity, but only irritation, finally amounting to anger. The child's whole aspect and the snivelling sounds he made were so hatefully ugly. It disgusted him.

"Here, Chifney, leave that fellow at home," he said. "He's no good."

"He's malingering, Sir Richard. I know his sort. Give in to him now and we shall have the same game, and worse, over again to-morrow."

"Very probably," Richard answered. "Only it is evident he has no more hand and no more grip than a sick cat to-day. We shall have some mess with him, and I'm not in the humour for a mess, so just leave him. There, boy, stop crying. Do you hear?" he added, wheeling round on the small unfortunate. "Mr. Chifney'll give you another day off and the doctor will see you. Only if he reports you fit and you give the very least trouble to-morrow, you'll be turned out of the stables there and then. We've no use for shirkers. Do you understand?"

In spite of his irritation, the hardness of Richard's expression relaxed as he finished speaking. The poor, little beggar was so abject — too abject indeed for common decency, since he too, after all, was human. Richard's own self-respect made it incumbent upon him to lift the creature out of the pit of so absolutely unseemly a degradation. He looked kindly at him, smiled, and promptly forgot all about him. While to the boy it seemed that the gods had verily descended in the likeness of men, and he would have bartered his little, dirty, blear-eyed rudiment of a soul thenceforward for another such a look from Richard Calmady.

Dickie promptly forgot the boy, yet some virtue must have been in the episode for he began to feel better in himself.   As the horses filed away through the misty sunshine—Preiston riding beside the fourth or fifth of the string, while Richard and Chifney brought up the rear, his chestnut suiting its paces to the shorter stride of the trainer's cob—the fever of the night cooled down in him.   Half thankfully, half amusedly, he perceived things begin to assume their normal relations.   He filled his lungs with the pure air, felt the sun-dazzle pleasant in his eyes. He had run somewhat mad in the last twenty-four hours surely? He was not such a fatuous ass as to have mistaken Helen's frank *camaraderie*, her bright interest in things, her charming little ways of showing cousinly regard, for some deeper, more personal feeling?   She had been divinely kind, but that was just her—just the outcome of her delightful nature.   She would go away on Friday—Saturday perhaps—he rather hoped Saturday —and be just as divinely kind to other people.   And then he shook himself, feeling the languid weight of her hands on his shoulders again.   Would she—would—?   For an instant he wanted to get at, and incontinently brain, those other people. After which, Richard mentally took himself by the throat and proceeded to choke the folly out of himself.—Yes, she would go back to all those other people, back moreover to the Vicomte de Vallorbes—whom, by the way, it occurred to him she so seldom mentioned.   Well, we don't continually talk about the people we love best, do we, to comparative strangers?   She would go back to her husband—her husband.—Richard repeated the words over to himself sternly, trying to drive them home, to burn them into his consciousness past all possibility of forgetting.

Anyhow she had been wonderfully sweet and charming to him.   She had shown him—quite unconsciously, of course—what life might be for—for somebody else.   She had revealed to him— what indeed had she not revealed!   He remembered the spirit of expectation that possessed him riding back through the autumn woods the day he first met her.   The expectation had been more than justified by the sequel.   Only — only — and then Dick became stern with himself again.   For, she having, unconsciously, done so much for him, was it not his first duty never to distress her?—never to let her know how much deeper it had all gone with him than with her?—never to insult her beautiful innocence by a word or look suggesting an affection less frank and cousinly than her own?

Only, since even our strongest purposes have moments of lapse and weakness in execution, it would be safer, perhaps, not to be much alone with her—since she didn't know—how should she? Yes, Richard agreed with himself not to loaf, to allow no idle hours. He would ride, he would see to business. There were a whole heap of estate matters claiming attention. He had neglected them shamefully of late. Unquestionably Helen counted for very much, would continue to do so. He supposed he would carry the ache of certain memories about with him henceforth and forever. She had become part of the very fibre of his life. He never doubted that. And yet, he told himself,—assuming a second-hand garment of slightly cynical philosophy which suited singularly ill with the love-light in his eyes, there radiantly apparent for all the world to see,—that woman, even the one who first shows you you have a heart, and a body too, worse luck, even she is but a drop in the vast ocean of things. There remains all The Rest. And with praiseworthy diligence Dickie set himself to reckon how immensely much all The Rest amounts to. There is plenty, exclusive of her, to think about. More than enough, indeed, to keep one hard at work all day, and send one to bed honestly tired, to sleeping-point, at night. Politics for instance, science, literature, entertaining little controversial rows of sorts — the simple, almost patriarchal, duties of a great land-owner; pleasant hobbies such as the collection of first editions, or a pretty taste in the binding of favourite books — the observation of this mysterious, ever young, ever fertile nature around him now, immutable order underlaying ceaseless change, the ever new wonder and beauty of all that, and : — "I say, Chifney, isn't the brown Lady-Love filly going rather short on the off foreleg? Anything wrong with her shoulder?" — and sport. Yes, thank God, in the name of everything healthy and virile, sport and, above all, horses—yes, horses.

Thus did Richard Calmady reason with, and essay to solace, himself for the fact that some fruits are forbidden to him who holds honour dear. Reasoned with and solaced himself to such good purpose, as he fondly imagined, that when, an hour and a half later, he established himself in the trainer's dining-room, a mighty breakfast outspread before him, he felt quite another man. Racing cups adorned the chimneypiece and sideboard, portraits of racehorses and jockeys adorned the walls. The sun streamed in between the red rep curtains, causing the pot-plants in the window to give off a pleasant scent, and the canary, in his swinging, blue and white painted, cage above them, to sing. Mrs. Chifney, her cheeks pink, her manner slightly fluttered,—as were her lilac cap strings,—presided over the silver tea and coffee service, admonished the staid and bulky tom-cat who, jumping on the arm of Dickie's chair, extended a scooping tentative paw towards his plate, and issued gentle though peremptory orders to her husband regarding the material needs of her guest.   To Mrs. Chifney such entertainings as the present marked the red-letter days of her calendar.   Temporarily she forgave Chifney the doubtful nature of his calling, and his occasional outbreaks of profane swearing likewise.   She ceased to regret that snug, might-have-been, little, grocery business in a country town.   She forgot even to hanker after prayer-meetings, anniversary teas, and other mild, soul-saving dissipations un-authorised by the Church of England.   She ruffled her feathers, so to speak, and cooed to the young man half in feudal, half in unsatisfied maternal affection—for Mrs. Chifney was childless. And it followed that as he teased her a little, going back banter-ingly on certain accepted subjects of difference between them, praised, and made a hole in, her fresh-baked rolls, her nicely browned, fried potatoes, her clear, crinkled rashers, assuring her it gave one an appetite merely to sit down in a room so shiningly clean and spick and span, she was supremely happy. And Dickie was happy too, and blessed the exercise, the food, and the society of these simple persons, which, after his evil night, seemed to have restored to him his wiser and better self.

"He always was the noblest looking young gentleman I ever saw," Mrs. Chifney remarked subsequently to her husband. "But here at breakfast this morning, when he said, 'If you won't be shocked, Mrs. Chifney, I believe I could manage a second helping of that game pie,' his face was like a very angel's from heaven.   Unearthly beautiful, Thomas, and yet a sort of pain at the back of it.   It gave me a regular turn. I had to shed a few tears afterwards when I got alone by myself."

"You're one of those that see more than's there, half your time, Maria," the trainer answered, with an unusual effort at sarcasm, for he was not wholly easy about the young man himself.—"There's something up with him, and danged if I know what it is."   But these reflections he kept to himself.

Dr. Knott, later that same day, made reflections of a similar nature.   For though Dickie adhered valiantly to his good resolutions—going out with the second lot of horses between ten and eleven o'clock, riding on to Banister's farm to inspect the new barn and cowsheds in course of erection, then hurrying down to Sandyfield Street and listening to long and heated arguments regarding a right-of-way reported to exist across the meadows skirting the river just above the bridge, a right strongly denied by the present occupier, — notwithstanding these improving and public-spirited employments, the love-light grew in his eyes all through the long morning, causing his appearance to have something, if not actually angelic, yet singularly engaging, about it.   For, unquestionably, next to a fortunate attachment, an unfortunate one, if honest, is among the most inspiring and grace-begetting of possessions granted to mortals.—Helen must never know—that was well understood. Yet the more Dickie thought the whole affair over, the more he recognised the fine romance of thus cherishing a silent and secret devotion.   He was very young in this line as yet, it may be observed.   Meanwhile it was nearly two o'clock.   He would need to ride home sharply if he was to be in time for luncheon. And at luncheon he would meet her.   And remembering that, his heart—traitorous heart—beat quick, and his lips—traitorous lips—began to repeat her name.   Thus do the gods of life and death love to play chuck-farthing with the wise purposes of men, the theory of the eternal laughter having a root of truth in it, as it would seem, after all!   And there ahead of him, under the shifting, dappled shadow of the over-arching firs, Dr. Knott's broad, cumbersome back, and high, two-wheeled trap, blocked the road, while Timothy, the old groom,—stiff-kneed now and none too active,—slowly pushed open the heavy, white gate of the inner park.

As Richard rode up, the doctor turned in his seat and looked at him from under his rough eyebrows, while his loose lips worked into a half-ironical smile.   He loved this lad of great fortune, and great misfortune, more tenderly than he quite cared to own.   Then, as Dick checked his horse beside the cart, he growled out :—

"No need to make anxious inquiries regarding your health, young sir.   What have you been doing with yourself, eh?   You look as fit as a fiddle and as fresh as paint."

"If I look as I feel I must look ravenously hungry," Richard answered, flushing up a little.   "I've been out since six."

"Had some breakfast?"

"Oh dear, yes!   Enough to teach one to know what

a jolly thing a good meal is, and make one wish for another."

"Hum!" Dr. Knott said. "That's a healthy state of affairs, anyhow. Young horses going well?"

"Famously."

"Bless me, everything's beer and skittles with you just at present then!"

Richard looked away down the smooth yellow road whereon the dappled shadows kissed and mingled, mingled and kissed, and his heart cried "Helen, Helen," once again.

"Oh! I don't know about that," he said. "I get my share as well as the rest I suppose — at least — anyway the horses are doing capitally this season."

"I should like to have a look at them."

"Oh, well you've only got to say when, you know. I shall be only too delighted to show them you."

As he walked the trap through the gateway, Dr. Knott watched Richard riding alongside. — "What's up with the boy," he thought. "His face is as keen as a knife, and as soft as—God help us, I hope there's no sweethearting on hand! It's bound to come sooner or later, but the later the better, for it'll be a risky enough set out, come when it may.—Ah, look out there now, you old fool,"—this to Timothy,—"don't go missing the step and laying yourself up with broken ribs for another three months, just when my work's at its heaviest. Be careful, can't you?"

"But why not come in to luncheon now?" Richard said, wisdom whipping up good resolutions once more, and bidding him check the gladness that gained on him at thought of that approaching meeting. Oh yes! he would be discreet, he would erect barriers, he would flee temptation. Knott's presence offered a finely rugged barrier, surely. Therefore, he repeated :— "Come in now. My mother will be delighted to see you, and we can have a look round the stables afterwards."

"I'll come fast enough if Lady Calmady will take me as I am. Work-a-day clothes, and second best lot at that. You're alone, I suppose?"

He watched the young man as he spoke. Noted the lift of his chin, and the slightly studied indifference of his manner.

"No, for once we're not. But that doesn't matter. My uncle William Ormiston is with us. You remember him?"

"I remember his wife."

"Oh! she's not here," Dickie said. "Only he and his daughter, Madame de Vallorbes. You'll come?"

" Oh dear, yes, I'll come, if you'll be good enough to prepare
your ladies for a rough-looking customer.   Don't let me keep you.
Wonder what the daughter's like ? " he added to himself.   " The
mother was a bit of a baggage."

CHAPTER VII

WHEREIN THE READER IS COURTEOUSLY INVITED TO IMPROVE
HIS ACQUAINTANCE WITH CERTAIN PERSONS OF QUALITY

B
UT Richard might have spared himself the trouble of
erecting barriers against too intimate intercourse with
his cousin.   Providence, awaking suddenly, as it would seem, to
the perils of his position, had already seen to all that.   For since
he went forth, hot-eyed and hot-headed, into the blank chill of the
fog, the company at Brockhurst—as Powell announced to him—
had suffered large and unlooked-for increase.   Ludovic Quayle
was the first of the self-invited guests to appear when Richard
was settled in the dining-room.   He sauntered up to the head of
the table with his accustomed air of slightly supercilious inquiry,
as of one who expects to meet little save fools and foolishness,
yet suffers these gladly, being quite secure of his own wisdom.

"How are you, Dickie ? " he said.   "Fairly robust I hope,
for the Philistines are upon you.   Still it might have been worse.
I have done what I could.   My father, who has never grasped
that there is an element of comedy in the numerical strength of
his family, wished to bring us over a party of eight.   But I
stopped that.   Four, as I tried to make him comprehend,
touched the limits of social decency.   He didn't comprehend.
He rarely does.   But he yielded, which was more to the point
perhaps.   Understand though, we didn't propose to add surprise
to the other doubtful blessings of our descent on you.   I wrote
to you yesterday, but it appears you went out at some unearthly
hour this morning superior alike to the state of the weather and
arrival of your letters."

" Fine thing going out early—excellent thing going out early.
Very glad to see you, Calmady, and very kind indeed of you and
Lady Calmady to take us in in this friendly way and show us
hospitality at such short notice "—

This from Lord Fallowfeild — a remarkably tall, large, and
handsome person.   He affected a slightly antiquated style of
dress, with a sporting turn to it,—coats of dust colour or grey,

notably long as to the skirts, well fitted at the waist, the surface
of them traversed by heavy seams. His double chin rested
within the points of a high, white collar, and was further
supported by a voluminous, black, satin stock. His face, set
in soft, grey hair and grey whisker, brushed well forward, suggested that of a benign and healthy infant—an infant, it may
be added, possessed of a small and particularly pretty mouth.
Save in actual stature, indeed, his lordship had never quite
succeeded in growing up. Very full of the milk of human kindness, he earnestly wished his fellow-creatures—gentle and simple
alike—to be as contented and happy as he, almost invariably,
himself was. When he had reason to believe them otherwise, it
perplexed and worried him greatly. It followed that he was
embarrassed, apologetic even, in Richard Calmady's presence.
He felt vaguely responsible as for some neglected duty, as though
there was something somehow which he ought to set right. And
this feeling harassed him, increasing the natural discursiveness
and inconsequence of his speech. He was so terribly nervous
of forgetting and of hurting the young man's feelings by saying
the wrong thing, that all possible wrong things got upon his
brain, with the disastrous result that of course he ended by saying
them. In face of a person so sadly stationary as poor Dick,
moreover, his own perfect ability to move freely about appeared
to him as little short of discourteous, not to say coarse. He,
therefore, tried to keep very still, with the consequence that he
developed an inordinate tendency to fidget. Altogether Lord
Fallowfeild did not show to advantage in Richard Calmady's
company.

"Ah yes ! fine thing going out early," he repeated. "Always
made a practice of it myself at your age, Calmady. Can't stand
doctor's stuff, don't believe in it, never did. Though I like
Knott, good fellow Knott—always have liked Knott. But never
was a believer in drugs. Nothing better than a good sharp walk,
now, early, really early before the frost's out of the grass. Excellent for the liver walking "—

Here, perceiving that his son Ludovic looked very hard at
him, eyebrows raised to most admonitory height, he added
hastily :—

"Eh?—yes, of course, or riding. Riding, nothing like that
for health—better exercise still "—

"Is it ?" Richard put in. He was too busy with his own
thoughts to be greatly affected by Lord Fallowfeild's blunders
just then.—"I'm glad to know you think so. You see it's a
matter in which I'm not very much of a judge."

"No—no—of course not.—Queer fellow Calmady," Lord Fallowfeild added to himself. "Uncommonly sharp way he has of setting you down."

But just then, to his relief, Lady Calmady, Lady Louisa Barking, and pretty, little Lady Constance Quayle entered the room together. Mr. Ormiston and John Knott followed engaged in close conversation, the rugged, rough-hewn aspect of the latter presenting a strong contrast to the thin, tall figure and face, white and refined to the point of emaciation, of the diplomatist. Julius March, accompanied by Camp—still carrying his tail limp and his great head rather sulkily—brought up the rear. And Dickie, while greeting his guests, disposing their places at table, making civil speeches to his immediate neighbour on the left,— Lady Louisa,—smiling a good-morning to his mother down the length of the table, felt a wave of childish disappointment sweep over him. For Helen came not, and with a great desiring he desired her. Poor Dickie, so wise, so philosophic in fancy, so enviably, disastrously young in fact !

"Oh ! thanks, Lady Louisa—it's so extremely kind of you to care to come. The fog was rather beastly this morning wasn't it ? And I shouldn't be surprised if it came down on us again about sunset. But it's a charming day meanwhile.—There, Ludovic, please—next Dr. Knott. We'll leave this chair for Madame de Vallorbes. She's coming, I suppose ? "

And Richard glanced towards the door again, and, so doing, became aware that little Lady Constance, sitting between Lord Fallowfeild and Julius March, was staring at him. She had an innocent face, a small, feminine copy of her father's save that her eyes were set noticeably far apart. This gave her a slow, ruminant look, distinctly attractive. She reminded Richard of a gentle, well-conditioned, sweet-breathed calf staring over a bank among ox-eyed daisies and wild roses. As soon as she perceived— but Lady Constance did not perceive anything very rapidly—that he observed her, she gave her whole attention to the contents of her plate and her colour deepened perceptibly.

"Pretty country about you here, uncommonly pretty," Lord Fallowfeild was saying in response to some remark of Lady Calmady's. "Always did admire it. Always liked a meet on this side of the county when I had the hounds. Very pleasant friendly spirit on this side too. Now Cathcart, for instance— sensible fellow Cathcart, always have liked Cathcart, remarkably sensible fellow. Plain man though—quite astonishingly plain. Daughter very much like him, I remember. Misfortune for a girl that. Always feel very much for a plain woman. She married well though—can't recall who just now, but somebody we all know. Who was it now, Lady Calmady?"

Between that haunting sense of embarrassment, and the kindly wish to carry things off well, and promote geniality, Lord Fallowfeild spoke loud. At this juncture Mr. Quayle folded his hands and raised his eyes devoutly to heaven.

"Oh, my father! oh, my father!" he murmured. Then he leant a little forward watching Lady Calmady.

"But, as you may remember, Mary Cathcart had a charming figure," she was saying, very sweetly, essaying to soften the coming blow.

"Ah! had she though? Great thing a good figure. I knew she married well."

"Naturally I agree with you there. I suppose one always thinks one's own people the most delightful in the world. She married my brother."

"Did she though!" Lord Fallowfeild exclaimed, with much interest. Then suddenly his tumbler stopped half-way to his mouth, while he gazed horror-stricken across the table at Mr. Ormiston.

"Oh no, no! not that brother," Katherine added quickly. "The younger one, the soldier. You wouldn't remember him. He's been on foreign service almost ever since his marriage. They are at the Cape now."

"Oh! ah! yes—indeed, are they?" he exclaimed. He breathed more easily. Those few thousand miles to the Cape were a great comfort to him. A man could not overhear your strictures on his wife's personal appearance at that distance anyhow.—"Very charming woman, uncommonly tactful woman, Lady Calmady," he said to himself gratefully.

Meanwhile Lady Louisa Barking, at the other end of the table, addressed her discourse to Richard and Julius, on either side of her, in the high, penetrating key affected by certain ladies of distinguished social pretensions. Whether this manner of speech implies a fine conviction of superiority on the part of the speaker, or a conviction that all her utterances are replete with intrinsic interest, it is difficult to determine. Certain it is that Lady Louisa practically addressed the table, the attendant men-servants, all creation in point of fact, as well as her two immediate neighbours. Like her father she was large and handsome. But her expression lacked his amiability, her attitude his pleasing self-distrust. In age she was about six-and-thirty and decidedly mature for that. She possessed a remarkable power of concentrating her mind upon her own affairs. She also laboured under the impression that she was truly religious, listening weekly to the sermons of fashionable preachers on the convenient text that "worldliness is next to godliness" and entertaining prejudices, finely unqualified by accurate knowledge, against the abominable errors of Rome.

"I was getting so terribly fagged with canvassing that my doctor told me I really must go to Whitney and recruit. Of course Mr. Barking is perfectly secure of his seat. I am in no real anxiety, I am thankful to say. He does not speak much in the House. But I always feel speaking is quite a minor matter, don't you?"

"Doubtless," Julius said, the remark appearing to be delivered at him in particular.

"The great point is that your party should be able to depend absolutely upon your loyalty. Being rather behind the scenes, as I can't help being, you know, I do feel that more and more. And the party depends absolutely upon Mr. Barking. He has so much moral stamina, you know. That is what they all feel. He is ready at any moment to sacrifice his private convictions to party interests. And so few members of any real position are willing to do that. And so, of course, the leaders do depend on him. All the members of the Government consult him in private."

"That is very flattering," Richard remarked.—Still Helen tarried; while again, glancing in the direction of the door, he encountered Lady Constance's mild, ruminant stare.

"Can one pronounce anything flattering when one sees it to be so completely deserved?" Ludovic Quayle inquired in his most urbane manner. "Prompt and perpetual sacrifice of private conviction to party interest, for example—how can such devotion receive recognition beyond its deserts?"

"Do have some more partridge, Lady Louisa," Richard put in hastily.

"In any case such recognition is very satisfactory.—No more, thank you, Sir Richard," the lady replied, not without a touch of acerbity. Ludovic was very clever no doubt; but his comments often struck her as being in equivocal taste. He gave a turn to your words you did not expect and so broke the thread of your conversation in a rather exasperating fashion.—"Very satisfactory," she repeated. "And, of course, the constituency is fully informed of the attitude of the Government towards Mr. Barking, so that serious opposition is out of the question."

"Oh! of course," Richard echoed.

"Still I feel it a duty to canvass. One can point out many things to the constituents in their own homes which might not come quite so well, don't you know, from the platform.   And of course they enjoy seeing one so much."

"Of course, it makes a great change for them," Richard echoed dutifully.

"Exactly, and so on their account, quite putting aside the chance of securing a stray vote here or there, I feel it a duty not to spare myself, but to go through with it just for their sakes, don't you know."

"My sister is nothing if not altruistic, you'll find, Calmady," Mr. Quayle here put in in his most exquisitely amiable manner.

But now encouraged thereto by Lady Calmady, Lord Fallowfeild had recovered his accustomed serenity and dis coursed with renewed cheerfulness.

"Great loss to this side of the county, my poor friend Denier," he remarked.   "Good fellow Denier—always liked Denier.   Stood by him from the first—so did your son.—No, no, pardon me—yes, to be sure—excellent claret this—never tasted a better luncheon claret.—But there was a little prejudice, little narrowness of feeling about Denier, when he first bought Grimshott and settled down here.   Self-made man, you see, Denier.   Entirely self-made.   Father was a clergyman, I believe, and I'm told his grandfather kept an umbrella shop in the Strand.   But a very able, right-minded man Denier, and wonderfully good-natured fellow, always willing to give you an opinion on a point of law.   Great advantage to have a first-rate authority like that to turn to in a legal difficulty.   Very useful in county business Denier, and laid hold of country life wonder-fully, understood the obligations of a land-owner.   Always found a fox in that Grimshott gorse of his, eh, Knott?"

"Fox that sometimes wasn't very certain of his country," the doctor rejoined.   "Hailed from the neighbourhood of the umbrella shop perhaps, and wanted to get home to it."

Lord Fallowfeild chuckled.

"Capital," he said, "very good—capital!   Still, it's a great relief to know of a sure find like that.   Keeps the field in a good temper.   Yes, few men whose death I've regretted more than poor Denier's.   I miss Denier.   Not an old man either.   Shouldn't have let him slip through your fingers so early, Knott, eh?"

"Oh! that's a question of forestry," John Knott answered grimly.   "If one kept the old wood standing, where would the saplings' chances come in?"

"Oh! ah! yes—never thought of that before,"—and thinking of it now the noble lord became slightly pensive.   "Wonder if it's unfair my keeping Shotover so long out of the property?" he said to himself. "Amusing fellow Shotover, very fond of Shotover—but extravagant fellow, monstrously extravagant."

"Lord Denier's death gave our host here a seat on the local bench just at the right moment," the doctor went on. "One man's loss is another man's opportunity. Rather rough, perhaps, on the outgoing man, but then things usually are pretty rough on the outgoing man in my experience."

"I suppose they are," Lord Fallowfeild said, rather ruefully, his face becoming preternaturally solemn.

"Not a doubt of it. The individual may get justice. I hope he does. But mercy is kept for special occasions—few and far between. One must take things on the large scale. Then you find they dovetail very neatly," Knott continued, with a somewhat sardonic mirthfulness. The simplicity and perplexity of this handsome, kindly gentleman amused him hugely. "But to return to Lord Denier—let alone my skill, that of the whole medical faculty put together couldn't have saved him."

"Couldn't it though?" said Lord Fallowfeild.

"That's just the bother with your self-made man. He makes himself—true. But he spends himself, physically, in the making. All his vitality goes in climbing the ladder, and he's none left over by the time he reaches the top. Lord Denier had worked too hard as a youngster to make old bones. It's a long journey from the shop in the Strand to the woolsack you see, and he took silk at two-and-thirty I believe. Oh yes! early death, or premature decay, is the price most outsiders pay for a great professional success. Isn't that so, Mr. Ormiston?"

But at this juncture the conversation suffered interruption by the throwing open of the door and the entrance of Madame de Vallorbes.

"Pray let no one move," she said, rather as issuing an order than preferring a request—for her father, Lord Fallowfeild, all the gentlemen, had risen on her appearance—save Richard.— Richard, his blue eyes ablaze, the corners of his mouth a-tremble, his heart going forth tumultuously to meet her, yet he alone of all present denied the little obvious act of outward courtesy from man to woman.

"Pinned to his chair, like a specimen beetle to a collector's card," John Knott said to himself. "Poor dear lad — and with that face on him too. I hoped he might have been spared taking fire a little longer. However, here's the conflagration. No question about that. Now let's have a look at the lady."

And the lady, it must be conceded, manifested herself under

a new and somewhat agitating aspect, as she swept up the room and into the vacant place at Richard's right hand with a rush of silken skirts.   She produced a singular effect at once of energy and self-concentration—her lips thin and unsmiling, an ominous vertical furrow between the spring of her arched eyebrows, her eyes narrow, unresponsive, severe with thought under their delicate lids.

"I am sorry to be late, but it was unavoidable.   I was kept by some letters forwarded from Newlands," she said, without giving herself the trouble of looking at Richard as she spoke.

"What does it matter?   Luncheon's admittedly a moveable feast, isn't it?"

Madame de Vallorbes made no response.   A noticeable hush had descended upon the whole company, while the men-servants moved to and fro serving the new-comer.   Even Lady Louisa Barking ceased to hold high discourse, political or other, and looked disapprovingly across the table.   An hour earlier she had resented the younger woman's merry wit, now she resented her sublime indifference.   Both then and now she found her perfect finish of appearance unpardonable.   Lord Fallowfeild's disjointed conversation also suffered check.   He fidgeted, vaguely conscious that the atmosphere had become somewhat electric.—"Monstrously pretty woman—effective woman—very effective — rather dangerous though.   Changeable too.   Made me laugh a little too much before luncheon.   Louisa didn't like it.   Very correct views, my daughter Louisa.   Now seems in a very odd temper.   Quite the grand air, but reminds me of somebody I've seen on the stage somehow.   Suppose all that comes of living so much in France," he said to himself.   But, for the life of him, he could not think of anything to say aloud, though he felt it would be eminently tactful to throw in a casual remark at this juncture.   Little Lady Constance was disquieted likewise.   For she, girl-like, had fallen dumbly and adoringly in love with this beautiful stranger but a few years her senior.   And now the stranger appeared as an embodiment of unknown emotions and energies altogether beyond the scope of her small imagination.   Her innocent stare lost its ruminant quality, became alarmed, tearful even, while she instinctively edged her chair closer to her father's.   There was a great bond of sympathy between the simple-hearted gentleman and his youngest child.   Mr. Quayle looked on with lifted eyebrows and his air of amused forbearance.   And Dr. Knott looked on also, but that which he saw pleased him but moderately.   The grace of every movement,

15

the distinction of face and figure, the charm of that finely-poised, honey-coloured head showing up against the background of grey-blue, tapestried wall, were enough—he owned,—having a very pretty taste in women as well as in horses—to drive many a man crazy.—" But if the mother's a baggage, the daughter's a vixen," he said to himself. " And, upon my soul if I had to choose between 'em—which God Almighty forbid—I'd take my chance with the baggage." As climax Lady Calmady's expression was severe. She sat very upright, and made no effort at conversation. Her nerves were a little on edge. There had been awkward moments during this meal, and now her niece's entrance struck her as unfortunately accentuated, while there was that in Richard's aspect which startled the quick fears and jealousies of her motherhood.

And to Richard himself, it must be owned, this meeting so hotly desired, and against the dangers of which he had so wisely guarded, came in fashion altogether different to that which he had pictured. Helen's manner was cold to a point far from flattering to his self-esteem. The subtle intimacies of the scene in the Long Gallery became as though they had never been. Dickie thinking over his restless night, his fierce efforts at self-conquest, those long hours in the saddle designed for the reduction of a perfervid imagination, wrote himself down an ass indeed. And yet—yet—the charm of Helen's presence was great ! And surely she wasn't quite herself just now, there was something wrong with her ? Anybody could see that. Everybody did see it in fact, he feared, and commented upon it in no charitable spirit. Hostility towards her declared itself on every side. He detected that—or imagined he did so —in Lady Louisa's expression, in Ludovic Quayle's extra-superfine smile, in the doctor's close and rather cynical attitude of observation, and last but not least, in the reserve of his mother's bearing and manner. And this hostility, real or imagined, begot in Richard a new sensation—one of tenderness, wholly unselfish and protective, while the fighting blood stirred in him. He grew slightly reckless.

" What has happened ? We appear to have fallen most un-accountably silent," he said, looking round the table, with an air of gallant challenge good to see.

"So we have, though," exclaimed Lord Fallowfeild, half in relief, half in apology. " Very true—was just thinking the same thing myself."

While Mr. Quayle, leaning forward, inquired with much sweetness :—" To whom shall I talk ? Madame de Vallorbes is far more profitably engaged in discussing her luncheon, than she could be in discussing any conceivable topic of conversation with such as I. And Dr. Knott is so evidently diagnosing an interesting case that I have not the effrontery to interrupt him."

Disregarding these comments Richard turned to his neighbour on the left.

"I beg your pardon, Lady Louisa," he said, "but before this singular dumbness overtook us all, you were saying?"—

The lady addressed, electing to accept this as a tribute to the knowledge, the weight, and distinction, of her discourse, thawed, became condescending and gracious again.

"I believe we were discussing the prospects of the party," she replied. "I was saying that, you know, of course there must be a large Liberal majority."

"Yes, of course."

"You consider that assured?" Julius put in civilly.

"It is not a matter of personal opinion, I am thankful to say —because of course everyone must feel it is just everything for the country. There is no doubt at all about the majority among those who really know—Mr. Barking, for instance. Nobody can be in a better position to judge than he is. And then I was speaking the other night to Augustus Tremiloe at Lord Combmartin's—not William, you know, but Augustus Tremiloe, the man in the Treasury, and he"—

"Uncommonly fine chrysanthemums those," Lord Fallowfeild had broken forth cheerfully, finding sufficient, if tardy, inspiration in the table decorations. "Remarkably perfect blossoms and charming colour. Nothing nearly so good at Whitney this autumn. Excellent fellow my head-gardener, but rather past his work—no enterprise, can't make him go in for new ideas."

Mr. Ormiston, leaning across Dr. Knott, addressed himself to Ludovic, while casting occasional and rather anxious glances upon his daughter. Thus did voices rise, mingle, and the talk get fairly upon its legs again. Then Richard permitted himself to say quietly :—

"You had no bad news, I hope, in those letters, Helen?"

"Why should you suppose I have had bad news?" she demanded, her teeth meeting viciously in the morsel of kissing-crust she held in her rosy-tipped fingers.

It was as pretty as a game to see her eat. Dickie laughed a little, charmed even with her naughtiness, embarrassed too by the directness of her question.

"Oh! I don't exactly know why—I thought perhaps you seemed "—

"You do know quite exactly why," the young lady asserted, looking full at him. "You saw that I was in a detestable, a diabolic temper."

"Well, perhaps I did think I saw something of the sort," Richard answered audaciously, yet very gently.

Helen continued to look at him, and as she did so her cheek rounded, her mouth grew soft, the vertical line faded out from her forehead.—"You are very assuaging, cousin Richard," she said, and she too laughed softly.

"Understands the vineries very well though," Lord Fallow-feild was saying, "and doesn't grow bad peaches, not at all bad peaches, but is stupid about flowers. He ought to retire. Never shall have really satisfactory gardens till he does retire. And yet I haven't the heart to tell him to go. Good fellow, you know, good, honest, hard-working fellow, and had a lot of trouble. Wife ailing for years, always ailing, and youngest child got hip disease—nasty thing hip disease, very nasty—quite a cripple, poor little creature, I am afraid a hopeless cripple. Terrible anxiety and burden for parents in that rank of life, you know."

"It can hardly be otherwise in any rank of life," Lady Calmady said slowly, bitterly. An immense weariness was upon her — weariness of the actual and present, weariness of the possible and the future. Her courage ebbed. She longed to go away, to be alone for a while, to shut eyes and ears, to deaden alike perception and memory, to have it all cease. Then it was as though those two beautiful, and now laughing, faces of man and woman in the glory of their youth, seen over the perspective of fair, white damask, glittering glass and silver, rich dishes, graceful profusion of flowers and fruit, at the far end of the avenue of guests, mocked at her. Did they not mock at the essential conditions of their own lives too? Katherine feared, consciously or unconsciously they did that. Her weariness dragged upon her with almost despairing weight.

"Do you get your papers the same day here, Sir Richard?" Lady Louisa asked imperatively.

"Yes, they come with the second post letters, about five o'clock," Julius March answered.

But Lady Louisa Barking intended to be attended to by her host.

"Sir Richard," she paused, "I am asking whether your papers reach you the same day?"

And Dickie replied he knew not what, for he had just registered the discovery that barriers are quite useless against a certain sort of intimacy.   Be the crowd never so thick about you, in a sense at least, you are always alone, exquisitely, delicately alone with the person you love.

CHAPTER VIII

RICHARD PUTS HIS HAND TO A PLOUGH FROM WHICH THERE IS NO TURNING BACK

"DEAREST mother, you look most deplorably tired."
Richard sat before the large study table, piled up with letters, papers, county histories, racing calendars, in the Gun-Room, amid a haze of cigar smoke.—"I don't wonder," he went on, "we've had a regular field-day, haven't we?   And I'm afraid Lord Fallowfeild bored you atrociously at luncheon.   He does talk most admired foolishness half his time, poor old boy.   All the same Ludovic shouldn't show him up as he does. It's not good form.   I'm afraid Ludovic's getting rather spoilt by London.   He's growing altogether too finicking and elaborate. It's a pity.   Lady Louisa Barking is a rather exterminating person.   Her conversation is magnificently deficient in humour. It is to be hoped Barking is not troubled by lively perceptions, or he must suffer at times.   Lady Constance is a pretty little girl, don't you think so?   Not oppressed with brains, I daresay, but a good little sort."

"You liked her?" Katherine said.   She stood beside him, that mortal weariness upon her yet.

"Oh yes!—well enough—liked her in passing, as one likes the wild roses in the hedge.   But you look regularly played out, mother, and I don't like that in the least."

Richard twisted the revolving-chair half round, and held out his arms in invitation.   As his mother leaned over him, he stretched upward and clasped his hands lightly about her neck.— "Poor dear," he said coaxingly, "worn to fiddle-strings with all this wild dissipation!   I declare it's quite pathetic."—He let her go, shrugging his shoulders with a sigh and a half laugh. "Well, the dissipation will soon enough be over now, and we shall resume the even tenor of our way, I suppose.   You'll be glad of that, mother?"

The caress had been grateful to Katherine, the cool cheek

dear to her lips, the clasp of the strong arms reassuring. Yet, in her present state of depression, she was inclined to distrust even that which consoled, and there seemed a lack in the fervour of this embrace. Was it not just a trifle perfunctory, as of one who pays toll, rather than of one who claims a privilege?

"You'll be glad too, my dearest, I trust?" she said, craving further encouragement.

Richard twisted the chair back into place again, leaned forward to note the hour of the clock set in the centre of the gold and enamel inkstand.

"Oh! I'm not prophetic. I don't pretend to go before the event and register my sensations until both they and I have fairly arrived. It's awfully bad economy to get ahead of yourself and live in the day after to-morrow. To-day's enough—more than enough for you, I'm afraid, when you've had a large contin.ent of the Whitney people to luncheon. Do go and rest, mother. Uncle William is disposed of. I've started him out for a tramp with Julius, so you need not have him on your mind."

But neither in Richard's words nor in his manner did Lady Calmady find the fulness of assurance she craved.

"Thanks, dearest," she said. "That is very thoughtful of you. I will see Helen and find out"—

"Oh! don't trouble about her either," Richard put in. Again he studied the jewel-rimmed dial of the little clock. "I found she wanted to go to Newlands to bid Mrs. Cathcart good-bye. It seems Miss St. Quentin is back there for a day or two. So I promised to drive her over as soon as we were quit of the Fallowfeild party."

"It is late for so long a drive."

Richard looked up quickly and his face wore that expression of challenge once again.

"I know it is—and so I am afraid we ought to start at once. I expect the carriage round immediately."—Then repenting:—"You'll take care of yourself, won't you, mother, and rest?'

"Oh yes! I will take care of myself," Katherine said. "Indeed, I appear to be the only person I have left to take care of, thanks to your forethought. All good go with you, Dick."

It followed—perhaps unreasonably enough—that Richard, some five minutes later, drove round the angle of the house and drew the mail-phaeton up at the foot of the grey, griffin-guarded flight of steps — whereon Madame de Vallorbes, wrapped in furs, the cavalier hat and its trailing plumes shadowing the upper part of her face and her bright hair, awaited his coming—in a rather defiant humour. His cousin was troubled, worried, and she met with scant sympathy. This aroused all his chivalry. Whatever she wished for, that he could give her, she should very certainly have. Of after consequences to himself he was contemptuous. The course of action which had shown as wisdom a couple of hours ago, showed now as selfishness and pusillanimity. If she wanted him, he was there joyfully to do her bidding, at whatever cost to himself in subsequent unrest of mind seemed but a small thing. If heartache and insidious provocations of the flesh came later, let them come. He was strong enough to bear the one and crush out the other, he hoped. It would give him something to do—he told himself, a little bitterly— and he had been idle of late!

And so it came about that Richard Calmady held out his hand, to help his cousin into her place at his side, with more of meaning and welcome in the gesture than he was quite aware. He forgot the humiliation of the broad strap about his waist, of the high, ingeniously contrived driving-iron against which his feet rested, steadying him upon the sharply sloping seat. These were details, objectionable ones it was true, but, to-day, of very second- ary importance. In the main he was master of the situation. For once it was his to render, rather than receive, assistance. Helen was under his care, in a measure dependent on him, and this gratified his young, masculine pride, doomed too often to suffer sharp mortification. A fierce pleasure possessed him. It was fine to bear her thus away, behind the fast trotting horses, through the pensive, autumn brightness. Boyish self-conscious- ness and self-distrust died down in Richard, and the man's self-reliance, instinct of possession and of authority, grew in him. His tone was that of command, for all its solicitude, as he said : —

"Look here, are you sure you've got enough on? Don't go and catch cold, under the impression that there's any meaning in this sunshine. It is sure to be chilly driving home, and it's easy to take more wraps."

Helen shook her head, unsmiling, serious.

"I could face polar snows."

Richard let the horses spring forward, while little pebbles rattled against the body of the phaeton, and the groom, running a few steps, swung himself up on to the back seat, immediately becoming immoveable as a wooden image, with rigidly folded arms.

"Oh! the cold won't quite amount to that," Richard said. "But I observe women rarely reckon with the probabilities of the return journey."

"The return journey is invariably too hot, or too cold, too soon, or too late—for a woman. So it is better not to remember its existence until you are compelled to do so. For myself, I confess to the strongest prejudice against the return journey."

Madame de Vallorbes' speech was calm and measured, yet there was a conviction in it suggestive of considerable emotion. She sat well back in the carriage, her head turned slightly to the left, so that Richard, looking down at her, saw little but the pure, firm line of her jaw, the contour of her cheek, and her ear—small, lovely, the soft hair curling away from above and behind it in the most enticing fashion. Physical perfection, of necessity, provoked in him a peculiar envy and delight. And nature appeared to have taken ingenious pleasure, not only in conferring an unusual degree of beauty upon his companion, but in finishing each detail of her person with unstinted grace. For a while the young man lost himself in contemplation of that charming ear and partially averted face. Then resolutely he bestowed his attention upon the horses again, finding such contemplation slightly enervating to his moral sense.

"Yes, return journeys are generally rather a nuisance, I suppose," he said, "though my experience of that particular form of nuisance is limited. I have not been outward-bound often enough to know much of the regret of being homeward-bound. And yet, I own, I should not much mind driving on and on everlastingly on a dreamy afternoon like this, and—and as I find myself just now—driving on and seeking some El Dorado—of the spirit, I mean, not of the pocket—seeking the Fortunate Isles that lie beyond the sunset. For it would be not a little fascinating to give one's accustomed self, and all that goes to make up one's accepted identity, the slip—to drive clean out of one's old circumstances and find new heavens, a new earth, and a new personality elsewhere. What do you say, Helen, shall we try it?"

But Helen sat immobile, her face averted, listening intently, revolving many things in her mind, meditating how and when most advantageously to speak.

"It would be such an amiable and graceful experiment to try on my own people, too, wouldn't it?" the young man con-

tinued, with a sudden change of tone.   "And I am so eminently
fitted to lose myself in a crowd without fear of recognition, just
the person for a case of mistaken identity !"

"Do not say such things, Richard, please.   They distress
me," Madame de Vallorbes put in quickly.   "And, believe me,
I have no quarrel with the return journey in this case.   At
Brockhurst I could fancy myself to have found the Fortunate
Isles 'of which you spoke just now.   I have been very happy
there—too happy, perhaps, and therefore, to-day, the whip has
come down across my back, just to remind me."

"Ah ! now you say the painful things," Dick interrupted.
"Pray don't—I—I don't like them."

Madame de Vallorbes turned her head and looked at him
with the strangest expression.

"My metaphor was not out of place.   Do you imagine
horses are the only animals a man drives, *mon beau cousin* ?
Some men drive the woman who belongs to them, and that
not with the lightest bit, I promise you.   Nor do they
forget to tie blood-knots in the whip-lash when it suits them to
do so."

"What do you mean ?" he asked abruptly.

"Merely that the letters, which so stupidly endangered my self-
control at luncheon, contained examples of that kind of driving."

"How—how damnable," the young man said between his
teeth.

The red and purple trunks of the great fir trees reeled
away to right and left as the carriage swept forward down the
long avenue.   To Richard's seeing they reeled away in disgust,
even as did his thought from the images which his companion's
words suggested.   While, to her seeing, they reeled, smitten by
the eternal laughter, the echoes of which it stimulated her to
hear. — "The drama develops," she said to herself, half
triumphant, half abashed.   "And yet I am telling the truth, it
is all so—I hardly even doctor it."—For she had been angered,
genuinely and miserably angered, and had found that odious to
the point of letting feeling override diplomacy.   There was
subtle pleasure in now turning her very lapse of self-control to
her own advantage.   And then, this young man's heart was the
finest, purest-toned instrument upon which she had ever had the
chance to play as yet.   She was ravished by the quality and
range of the music it gave forth.   Madame de Vallorbes pressed
her hands together within the warm comfort of her sable muff,
averted her face again, lest it should betray the eager excitement
that gained on her, and continued : —

"Yes, whip and rein and bit are hardly pretty in that connection, are they? If you would willingly give your identity the
slip at times, dear cousin, I have considerably deeper cause to
wish to part company with mine! You, in any case, are morally
and materially free. A whole class of particularly irritating and
base ca es can never approach you. And it was in connection
with just such cares that I spoke of the hatefulness of return
journeys."

Helen paused, as one making an effort to maintain her
equanimity.

"My letters recall me to Paris," she said, "where detestable
scenes and most ignoble anxieties await me."

"How soon must you go?"

"That is what I ask myself," she said, in the same quiet, even
voice. "I have not yet arrived at a decision, and so I asked
you to bring me out, Dickie, this afternoon."—She looked up at
him, smiling, lovely and with a certain wistful dignity, wholly
coercive. "Can you understand that the orderly serenity of
your splendid house became a little oppressive? It offered
too glaring a contrast to my own state of mind and outlook. I fancied my brain would be clearer, my conclusions
more just, here out of doors, face to face with this half-savage
nature."

"Ah, I know all that," Richard said. Had not the blankness
of the fog brought him help this very morning?—"I know it,
but I wish you did not know it too."

"I know many things better not known," Helen replied.
Her conscience pricked her. She thanked her stars confession
had ceased with enlargement from the convent-school, and was a
thing of the past.—"You see, I want to decide just how long I
dare stay—if you will keep me?"

"We will keep you," Richard said.

"You are very charming to me, Dick," she exclaimed impulsively, sincerely, again slightly abashed. "How long can I
dare stay, I wonder, without making matters worse in the end,
both for my father and for myself? I am young, after all, and I
suppose I am tough. The cuticle of the soul—if souls can have
a cuticle—like that of the body, thickens under repeated blows.
But my father is no longer young. He is terribly sensitive where
I am concerned. And he is inevitably drawn into the whirlpool
of my wretched affairs sooner or later. On his account I should
be glad to defer the return journey as long"—

"But—but—I don't understand," Richard broke out, pity and
deep concern for her, a blind fury against a person, or persons

unknown, getting the better of him.   "Who on earth has the power to plague you and make you miserable, or your father either ? "

The young man's face was white, his eyes, full of pain, full of a great love, burning down on her.   As once long ago, Helen de Vallorbes could have danced and clapped her hands in naughty glee.   For her hunting had prospered above her fondest hopes. She had much ado to stifle the laughter which bubbled up in her pretty throat.   She was in the humour to pelt peacocks royally, had such pastime been possible.   As it was, she closed her eyes for a little minute and waited, biting the inside of her lip.   At last, she said slowly, almost solemnly : —

" Don't you know that for certain mistakes, and those usually the most generous, there is no redress ? "

" What do you mean ? " he demanded.

" Mean ?—the veriest commonplace in my own case," she answered.   " Merely an unhappy marriage.   There are thousands such."

They had left the shadow of the fir woods now.   The carriage crossed the white-railed culvert—bridging the little stream that taking its rise amid the pink and emerald mosses of the peat-bog, meanders down the valley—and entered the oak plantation just inside the park gate.   Russet leaves in rustling, hurrying companies, fled up and away from the rapidly turning wheels and quick horse hoofs.   The sunshine was wan and chill as the smile on a dead face.   Lines of pale, lilac cloud—shaped like those flights of cranes which decorate the oriental cabinets of the Long Gallery—crossed the western sky above the bare, balsam poplars, the cluster of ancient, half-timbered cottages at the entrance to Sandyfield church lane, and the rise of the grey-brown fallow beyond, where sheep moved, bleating plaintively, within a wattled fold.

The scene, altogether familiar though it was, impressed itself on Richard's mind just now, as one of paralysing melancholy. God help us, what a stricken, famished world it is !   Will you not always find sorrow and misfortune seated at the root of things if, disregarding overlaying prettiness of summer days, of green leaf and gay blossom, you dare draw near, dig deep, look close? And can nothing, no one, escape the blighting touch of that canker stationed at the very foundations of being?   Certainly it would seem not—Richard reasoned—listening to the words of the radiant woman beside him, ordained, in right of her talent and puissant grace, to be a queen and idol of men.   For sadder than the thin sunshine, bare trees and complaint of the hungry sheep, was that assured declaration that loveless and unlovely marriages—of which her own was one—exist by the thousand, are, indeed, the veriest commonplace !

These reflections held Richard, since he had been thinker and poet—in his degree—since childhood ; lover only during the brief space of these last ten surprising days. Thus the general application claimed his attention first. But hard on the heels of this followed the personal application. For, as is the way of all true lovers, the universality of the law under which it takes its rise mitigates, by most uncommonly little, either the joy or sorrow of the particular case. Poignant regret that she suffered, strong admiration that she bore suffering so adherent with such lightness of demeanour—then, more dangerous than these, a sense of added unlooked-for nearness to her, and a resultant calling not merely of the spirit of youth in him to that same spirit resident in her, but the deeper, more compelling, more sonorous call from the knowledge of tragedy in him to that same terrible knowledge now first made evident in her.—And here Richard's heart—in spite of pity, in spite of tenderness which would have borne a hundred miseries to save her five minutes' discomfort—sang *Te Deum*, and that lustily enough ! For by this revelation of the in-felicity of her state, his whole relation to, and duty towards her changed and took on a greater freedom. To pour forth worship and offers of service at the feet of a happy woman is at once an impertinence to her and a shame to yourself. But to pour forth such worship, such offers of service, at the feet of an unhappy woman — age-old sophistry, so often ruling the speech and actions of men to their fatal undoing ! —this is praiseworthy and legitimate, a matter not of privilege merely, but of obligation to whoso would claim to be truly chivalrous.

The perception of his larger liberty, and the consequences following thereon, kept Richard silent till Sandyfield rectory, the squat-towered, Georgian church and the black-headed, yew trees in the close-packed churchyard adjoining, the neighbouring farm and its goodly show of golden-grey wheat-ricks were left behind, and the carriage entered on the flat, furze-dotted expanse of Sandyfield common. Flocks of geese, arising from damp repose upon the ragged, autumn turf, hissed forth futile declarations of war. A gipsy caravan painted in staring colours, and hung all over with heath-brooms and basket-chairs, caused the horses to swerve. Parties of home-going school-children backed on to the loose gravel at the roadside, bobbing curtsies or pulling forelocks, staring at the young man and his companion, curious and half afraid. For, in the youthful, bucolic mind, a mystery surrounded

Richard Calmady and his goings and comings, causing him to rank with crowned heads, ghosts, the Book of Daniel, funerals, the Northern Lights, and kindred matters of dread fascination. So wondering eyes pursued him down the road.

And wondering eyes, as the minutes passed, glanced up at him from beneath the sweeping plumes and becoming shadow of the cavalier's hat. For his prolonged silence rendered Madame de Vallorbes anxious. Had she spoken unadvisedly with her tongue? Had her words sounded crude and of questionable delicacy? Given his antecedents and upbringing, Richard was bound to hold the marriage tie in rather superstitious reverence, and was likely to entertain slightly superannuated views regarding the obligation of reticence in the discussion of family matters. She feared she had reckoned insufficiently with all this, in her eagerness, forgetting subtle diplomacies. Her approach had lacked tact and *finesse*. In dealing with an adversary of coarser fibre her attack would have succeeded to admiration. But this man was refined and sensitive to a fault, easily disgusted, narrowly critical in questions of taste.

Therefore she glanced up at him again, trying to divine his thought, her own mind in a tumult of opposing purposes and desires. And just as the contemplation of her beauty had so deeply stirred him earlier this same afternoon, so did the contemplation of his beauty now stir her. It satisfied her artistic sense. Save that the nose was straighter and shorter, the young man reminded her notably of a certain antique, terra-cotta head of the young Alexander which she had once seen in a museum at Munich, and which had left an ineffaceable impression upon her memory. But, the face of the young Alexander beside her was of nobler moral quality than that other—undebauched by feasts and licentious pleasures as yet, masculine yet temperate, the sanctuary of generous ambitions. Merciless it might be, she fancied, but never base, never weak. Thus was her artistic sense satisfied, morally as well as physically. Her social sense was satisfied also. For the young man's high-breeding could not be called in question. He held himself remarkably well. She approved the cut of his clothes moreover, his sure and easy handling of the spirited horses.

And then her eyes, following down the lines of the fur rug, received renewed assurance of the fact of his deformity—hidden as far as might be, with decent pride, yet there, permanent and unalterable. This worked upon her strongly. For, to her peculiar temperament, the indissoluble union in one body of elements so noble and so monstrous, of youthful vigour and abject helplessness, the grotesque in short, supplied the last word of sensuous and dramatic attraction. As last evening, in the Long Gallery, so now, she hugged herself, at once frightened and fascinated, wrought upon by excitement as in the presence of something akin to the supernatural, and altogether beyond the confines of ordinary experience.

And to think that she had come so near holding this inimitable creature in her hand, and by overhaste, or clumsiness of statement should lose it! Madame de Vallorbes was wild with irritation, racked her brain for means to recover her—as she feared—forfeited position. It would be maddening did her mighty hunting prove but a barren pastime in the end. And thereupon the little scar on her temple, deftly concealed under the soft, bright hair, began to smart and throb. Ah! well, the hunting should not prove quite barren anyhow, of that she was determined, for, failing her late gay purpose, that small matter of long-deferred revenge still remained in reserve. If she could not gratify one passion, she would gratify quite another. For in this fair lady's mind it was—perhaps unfortunately—but one step from the Eden bowers of love to the waste places of vindictive hate.—"Yet I would rather be good to him, far rather," she said to herself, with a movement of quite pathetic sincerity.

But here, just at the entrance to the village street, an altogether unconscious *deus ex machinâ*—destined at once to relieve Helen of further anxiety, and commit poor Dickie to a course of action affecting the whole of his subsequent career—presented itself in the shape of a white-tented miller's waggon, which, with somnolent jingle of harness bells and most admired deliberation, moved down the centre of the road. A yellow-washed garden-wall on one side, the brook on the other, there was not room for the phaeton to pass.

"Whistle," Richard commanded over his shoulder. And the wooden image, thereby galvanised into immediate activity, whistled shrilly, but without result as far as the waggon was concerned.

"The fellow's asleep. Go and tell him to pull out of the way."

Then, while the groom ran neatly forward in twinkling, white breeches and flesh-coloured tops, Richard, bending towards her, as far as that controlling strap about his waist permitted, shifted the reins into his right hand and laid his left upon Madame de Vallorbes' sable muff.

"Look here, Helen," he said, rather hoarsely, "I am inde-

scribably shocked at what you have just told me.   I supposed it
was all so different with you.   I'd no suspicion of this.   And—
and—if I may say so, you've taught me a lesson which has gone
home—steady there—steady, good lass "—for the horses danced
and snorted.—"I don't think I shall ever grumble much in
future about troubles of my own, having seen how splendidly
you bear yours.   Only I can't agree with you no remedy is
possible for generous mistakes.   The world isn't quite so badly
made as all that.   There is a remedy for every mistake except—
a few physical ones, which we euphuistically describe as visitations
of God.—Steady, steady there—wait a bit.—And I—I tell you
I can't sit down under this unhappiness of yours and just put
up with it.   Don't think me a meddling fool, please.   Something's got to be done.   I know I probably appear to you the
last person in the world to be of use.   And yet I'm not sure
about that.   I have time—too much of it—a..d I'm not quite
an ass.   And you—you must know, I think, there's nothing in
heaven or earth I would not do for you that I could "—

The miller hauled his slow-moving team aside, with beery-
thick objurgations and apologies.   The groom swung himself up
at the back of the carriage again.   The impatient horses, getting
their heads, swung away down Sandyfield Street—scattering a
litter of merry, little, black pigs and many remonstrant fowls to
right and left—past modest village shop, and yellow-washed tavern,
and red, lichen-stained cottage, beneath the row of tall Lombardy
poplars that raised their brown-grey spires to the blue-grey of the
autumn sky.   Richard's left hand held the reins again.

"Half confidences are no good," he said.   "So, as you've
trusted me thus far, Helen, don't you think you will trust somewhat further?   Be explicit.   Tell me the rest."

And hearing him, seeing him, just then, Madame de Vallorbes'
heart melted within her, and, to her own prodigious surprise, she
had much ado not to weep.

CHAPTER IX

WHICH TOUCHES INCIDENTALLY ON MATTERS OF FINANCE

AS Richard had predicted the fog reappeared towards sunset.
At first, as a frail mist, through which the landscape
looked colourless and blurred.   Later it rose, growing in density,
until all objects beyond a radius of some twenty paces were

engulfed in its nothingness and lost. Later still—while Helen
de Vallorbes paid her visit at Newlands—it grew denser yet,
heavy, torpid, close yet cold, penetrated by earthy odours as
the atmosphere of a vault, oppressive to the senses, baffling to
sight and hearing alike. From out it, half-leafless branches,
like gaunt arms in tattered draperies, seemed to claw and
beckon at the passing carriage and its occupants. The silver
mountings of the harness showed in points and splashes of hard,
shining white as against the shifting, universal dead-whiteness of
it, while the breath from the horses' nostrils rose into it as
defiant jets of steam, that struggled momentarily with the opaque,
all-enveloping vapour, only to be absorbed and obliterated as
light by darkness, or life by death.

     The aspect presented by nature was sinister, had Richard
Calmady been sufficiently at leisure to observe it in detail. But,
as he slowly walked the horses up and down the quarter of a mile
of woodland drive, leading from the thatched lodge on the right
of the Westchurch road to the house, he was not at leisure. He
had received enlightenment on many subjects. He had acquired
startling impressions, and he needed to place these, to bring
them into line with the general habit of his thought. The
majority of educated persons—so-called—think in words, words
often arbitrary and inaccurate enough, prolific mothers of mental
confusion. The minority, and those of by no means contemptible intellectual calibre,—since the symbol must count for
more than the mere label,—think in images and pictures. Dickie
belonged to the minority. And it must be conceded that his
mind now projected against that shifting, impalpable background
of fog, a series of pictures which in their cynical pathos, their
suggestions at once voluptuous and degraded, were hardly
unworthy of the great master, William Hogarth, himself.

     For Helen, in the reaction and relief caused by finding her
relation to Richard unimpaired, caused too by that joyous
devilry resident in her and constantly demanding an object on
which to wreak its derision, had by no means spared her lord
and master, Angelo Luigi Francesco, Vicomte de Vallorbes.
And this only son of a thrifty, hard-bitten, Savoyard banker-
noble and a Neapolitan princess of easy morals and ancient
lineage, this Parisian *viveur*, his intrigues, his jealousies, his
practical ungodliness and underlying superstition, his outbursts
of temper, his shrewd economy in respect of others, and extensive
personal extravagance, offered fit theme, with aid of little romancing, for such a discourse as it just now suited his very brilliant,
young wife to pronounce.

The said discourse opened in a low key, broken by pauses, by tactful self-accusations, by questionings as to whether it were not more merciful, more loyal, to leave this or that untold.   But as she proceeded, not only did Helen suffer the seductions of the fine art of lying, but she really began to have some ado to keep her exuberant sense of fun within due limits.   For it proved so excessively exhilarating to deal thus with Angelo Luigi Francesco! She had old scores to settle.   And had she not this very day received an odiously disquieting letter from him, in which he not only made renewed complaint of her poor, little miseries of debts and flirtations, but once more threatened retaliation by a cutting-off of supplies?   In common justice did he not deserve vilifica-tion?   Therefore, partly out of revenge, partly in self-justification, she proceeded with increasing enthusiasm to show that to know M. de Vallorbes was a lamentably liberal education in all civilised iniquities.   With a hand, sure as it was light, she dissected out the unhappy gentleman, and offered up his mangled and bleeding reputation as tribute to her own so-perpetually-outraged moral sense and feminine delicacy, not to mention her so-repeatedly and vilely wounded heart.   And there really was truth—as at each fresh flight of her imagination she did not fail to remind herself—in all that which she said.   Truth?—yes, just that misleading sufficiency of it in which a lie thrives.   For, as every artist "in this kind" is aware, precisely as you would have the overgrowth of your improvisation richly phenomenal and preposterous, must you be careful to set the root of it in the honest soil of fact.   To omit this precaution is to court eventual detection and consequent confusion of face.

As it was, Helen entered the house at Newlands, a house singularly unused to psychological aberrations, in buoyant spirits, mischief sitting in her discreetly downcast eyes, laughter perplexing her lips.   She had placed her cargo of provocation, of resentment, to such excellent advantage!   She was, moreover, slightly intoxicated by her own eloquence.   She was at peace with herself and all mankind, with de Vallorbes even since his sins had afforded her so rare an opportunity.   And this occasioned her to congratulate herself on her own conspicuous magnanimity.   It is so exceedingly pleasing not only to know yourself clever, but to believe yourself good!   She would be charming to these dear, kind, rather dull people.   Not that Honoria was dull, but she had inconveniently austere notions of honour and loyalty at moments.   And then the solitary drive home with Richard Calmady lay ahead, full of possible drama, full of, well, Heaven knew what!   Oh! how entrancing a pastime is life!

But to Richard, walking the snorting and impatient horses slowly up and down the woodland drive in the blear and sightless fog, life appeared quite other than an entrancing pastime. The pictures projected by his thought, and forming the medium of it, caused him black indignation and revolt, desolated him, too, with a paralysing disgust of his own disabilities. For poor Dick had declined somewhat in the last few hours, it must be owned, from the celestial altitudes he had reached before luncheon. Some part of his cousin's discourse had been dangerously intimate in character, suggesting situations quite other than platonic. To him there appeared a noble innocence in her treatment of matters not usually spoken of. He had listened with a certain reverent amazement. Only out of purity of mind could such speech come. And yet an undeniable effect remained, and it was not altogether elevating. Richard was no longer the young Sir Galahad of the noontide of this eventful day. He was just simply a man—in a sensible degree the animal man—loving a woman, hating that other man to whom she was legally bound. Hating that other man, not only because he was unworthy and failed to make her happy, but because he stood in his—Richard's—way. Hating the man all the more fiercely because, whatever the uncomeliness of his moral constitution, he was physically very far from uncomely. And so, along with nobler incitements to hatred, went the fiend envy, which just now plucked at poor Dickie's vitals as the vulture at those of the chained Titan of old. Whereupon he fell into a meditation somewhat morbid. For, contemplating in pictured thought that other man's bodily perfection, contemplating his property and victim,—the fair modern Helen, who by her courage and her trials exercised so potent a spell over his imagination,—Richard loathed his own maimed body, maimed chances and opportunities, as he had never loathed them before. How often since his childhood had some casual circumstance or trivial accident brought the fact of his misfortune home to him, causing him—as he at the moment supposed—to reckon, once and for all, with the sum total of it! But, as years passed and experience widened, below each depth of this adhering misery another deep disclosed itself. Would he never reach bottom? Would this inalienable disgrace continue to show itself more restricting and impeding to his action, more repulsive and contemptible to his fellow-men, through all the succeeding stages and vicissitudes of his career, right to the very close?

To her hosts Madame de Vallorbes appeared in her gayest and most engaging humour.—"It was only a flying visit, she mustn't stay, Richard was waiting for her.   Only she felt she must just have two words with Honoria.   And say good-bye ? Yes, ten thousand sorrows, it was good-bye.   She was recalled to Paris, home, and duty "—She made an expressive little grimace at Miss St. Quentin.

"Your husband will be "— began Mrs. Cathcart, in her large, gently authoritative manner.

"Enchanted to see me, of course, dear cousin Selina, or he would not have required my return thus urgently.   We may take that for said.   Meanwhile what strange sprigs of nobility flourish in the local soil here."

And she proceeded to give an account of the Fallowfeild party at luncheon, more witty, perhaps, than veracious.   Helen could be extremely entertaining on occasion.   She gave reins to her tongue, and it galloped away with her in most surprising fashion.

"My dear, my dear," interrupted her hostess, "you are a little unkind surely !   My dear, you are a little flippant ! "

But Madame de Vallorbes enveloped her in the most assuaging embrace.

"Let me laugh while I can, dearest cousin Selina," she pleaded.   "I have had a delightful, little holiday.   Everyone has been charming to me.   You, of course—but then you always are that.   Your presence breathes consolation.   But Aunt Katherine has been charming too, and that, quite between ourselves, was a little more than I anticipated.   Now the holiday draws to a close and pay-day looms large ahead.   You know nothing about such pay-days thank Heaven, dear cousin Selina.   They are far from joyous inventions ; and so "—the young lady spread abroad her hands, palms upward, and shrugged her shoulders under their weight of costly furs—"and so I laugh, don't you understand, I laugh ! "

Miss St. Quentin's delicate, square-cut face wore an air of solicitude as she followed her friend out of the room.   There was a trace of indolence in her slow, reflective speech, as in her long, swinging stride—the indolence bred of unconscious strength rather than of weakness, the leisureliness which goes with staying power both in the moral and the physical domain.

"See here, Nellie," she said, "forgive brutal frankness, but which is the real thing to-day—they're each delightful in their own way—the tears or the laughter ? "

"Both ! oh, well-beloved seeker after truth ! " Madame de Vallorbes answered.   "There lies the value of the situation."

"Fresh worries ? "

"No, no, the old, the accustomed, the well-accredited, the normal, the stock ones—a husband and a financial crisis."

As she spoke Madame de Vallorbes fastened the buttons of her long driving-coat. Miss St. Quentin knelt down and busied herself with the lowest of these. Her tall, slender figure was doubled together. She kept her head bent.

"I happen to have a pretty tidy balance just now," she remarked parenthetically, and as though with a certain diffidence. "So you know, if you are a bit hard up—why—it's all perfectly simple, Nellie, don't you know."

For a perceptible space of time Madame de Vallorbes did not answer. A grating of wheels on the gravel arrested her attention. She looked down the long vista of ruddily lighted hall, with its glowing fire and cheerful lamps to the open door, where, against the blear whiteness of the fog, the mail-phaeton and its occupant showed vague in outline and in proportions almost gigantic against the thick, shifting atmosphere. Miss St. Quentin raised her head, surprised at her companion's silence. Helen de Vallorbes bent down, took the upturned face in both hands and kissed the soft cheeks with effusion.

"You are adorable," she said. "But you are too generous. You shall lend me nothing more. I believe I see my way. I can scrape through this crisis."

Miss St. Quentin rose to her feet.

"All right," she said, smiling upon her friend from her superior height with a delightful air of affection and apology. "I only wanted you just to know, in case—don't you see. And—and—for the rest, how goes it, Helen? Are you turning all their poor heads at Brockhurst? You're rather an upsetting being to let loose in an ordinary, respectable, English country-house. A sort of *Mousquetaire au couvent* the other way about, don't you know. Are you making things fly generally?"

"I am making nothing fly," the other lady rejoined gaily. "I am as inoffensive as a stained-glass saint in a chapel window. I am absolutely angelic."

"That's worst of all," Honoria exclaimed, still smiling. "When you're angelic you are most particularly deadly. For the preservation of local innocents, somebody ought to go and hoist danger signals."

Miss St. Quentin, after just a moment's hesitation, followed her friend through the warm, bright hall to the door. Then Helen de Vallorbes turned to her.

"*Au revoir*, dearest Honoria," she said, "and the sooner the better. Leave your shopgirls and distressed needlewomen,

and all your other good works, for a still better one—namely
for me.   Come and reclaim, and comfort, and support me for
a while in Paris."

Again she kissed the soft cheek.

"I am as good as gold.   I am just now actually mawkish
with virtue," she murmured, between the kisses.

Richard witnessed this exceedingly pretty leave-taking not
without a movement of impatience.   The fog was thickening
once more.   It grew late.   He wished his cousin would get
through with these amenities.   Then, moreover, he did not
covet intercourse with Miss St. Quentin.   He pulled the fur
rug aside with his left hand, holding reins and whip in his
right.

"I say, are you nearly ready?" he asked.   "I don't want to
bother you ; but really it's about time we were moving."

"I come, I come," Madame de Vallorbes cried, in answer.
She put one neatly-shod foot on the axle, and stepped up—
Richard holding out his hand to steady her.   A sense, at once
pleasurable and defiant, of something akin to ownership, came
over him as he did so.   Just then his attention was claimed by
a voice addressing him from the farther side of the carriage.
Honoria St. Quentin stood on the gravel close beside him,
bare-headed, in the clinging damp and chill of the fog.

"Give my love to Lady Calmady," she said.   "I hope I
shall see her again some day.   But, even if I never have the luck
to do that, in a way it'll make no real difference.   I've written
her name in my private calendar, and shall always remember
it."—She paused a moment.   "We got rather near each other
somehow, I think.   We didn't dawdle or beat about the bush,
but went straight along, passed the initial stages of acquaintance
in a few hours, and reached that point of friendship where
forgetting becomes impossible."

"My mother never forgets," Richard asserted, and there was,
perhaps, a slight edge to his tone.   Looking down into the girl's
pale, finely-moulded face, meeting the glance of those steady,
strangely clear and observant eyes, he received an impression of
something uncompromisingly sincere and in a measure protective.
This, for cause unknown, he resented.   Notwithstanding her
high-breeding, Miss St. Quentin's attitude appeared to him a
trifle intrusive just then.

"I am very sure of that—that your mother never forgets, I
mean.   One knows, at once, one can trust her down to the
ground and on to the end of the ages."—Again she paused,
as though rallying herself against a disinclination for further

speech. "All captivating women aren't made on that pattern,
unfortunately, you know, Sir Richard. A good many of them
it's wisest not to trust anything like down to the ground, or
longer than—well—the day before yesterday."

And without waiting for any reply to this cryptic utterance,
she stepped swiftly round behind the carriage again, waved her
hand from the door-step and then swung away, with lazy, long-
limbed grace, past the waiting men-servants and through the
ruddy brightness of the hall.

Madame de Vallorbes settled herself back rather languidly
in her place. She was pricked by a sharp point of curiosity,
regarding the tenor of Miss St. Quentin's mysterious colloquy
with Richard Calmady. She had been able to catch but a
word here and there, and these had been provokingly suggestive.
Had the well-beloved Honoria, in a moment of over-scrupulous
conscientiousness permitted herself to hoist danger signals?
She wanted to know, for it was her business to haul such down
again with all possible despatch. She intended the barometer
to register "set fair" whatever the weather actually impending.
Yet to institute direct inquiries might be to invite suspicion.
Helen, therefore, declined upon diplomacy, upon the inverted
sweetnesses calculated nicely to mask an intention quite other
than sweet. She really held her friend in very warm affection
But Madame de Vallorbes never confused secondary and
primary issues. When you have a really big deal on hand—
and of the bigness of her present deal the last quarter of
an hour had brought her notably increased assurance—even
the dearest friend must stand clear and get very decidedly out
of the way. So, while the muffled thud of the horses' hoofs
echoed up from the hard gravel of the carriage drive through
the thick atmosphere, and the bare limbs of the trees clawed,
as with lean arms clothed in tattered draperies, at the passing carriage and its occupants, she contented herself by
observing :—

"I am grateful to you for driving me over, Richard.
Honoria is very perfect in her own way. It always does me
good to see her. She's quite unlike anybody else, isn't
she?"

But Richard's eyes were fixed upon the blank wall of fog
just ahead, which, though always stable, always receded before
the advancing carriage. The effect of it was unpleasant somehow, holding, as it did to his mind, suggestion of other things
still more baffling and impending, from which—though you
might keep them at arm's length—there was no permanent

or actual escape. The question of Miss St. Quentin's characteristics did not consequently greatly interest him. He had arrived at conclusions. There was a matter of vital importance on which he desired to speak to his cousin. But how to do that? Richard was young and excellently modest. His whole purpose was rather fiercely focused on speech. But he was diffident, fearing to approach the subject which he had so much at heart clumsily and in a tactless, tasteless manner.

"Miss St. Quentin? Oh yes!" he replied, rather absently. "I really know next to nothing about her. And she seems merely to regard me as a vehicle of communication between herself and my mother. She sent her messages just now—I hope to goodness I shan't forget to deliver them! She and my mother appear to have fallen pretty considerably in love with one another."

"Probably," Madame de Vallorbes said softly. An agreeable glow of relief passed over her. She looked up at Richard with a delightful effect of pensiveness from beneath the sweeping brim of her cavalier hat.—"I can well believe Aunt Katherine would be attracted by her," she continued. "Honoria is quite a woman's woman. Men do not care very much about her as a rule. There is a good deal of latent vanity resident in the members of your sex, you know, Richard; and men are usually conscious that Honoria does not care so very much about them. They are quite right, she does not. I really believe when poor, dreadful, old Lady Tobermory left her all that money Honoria's first thought was that now she might embrace celibacy with a good conscience. The St. Quentins are not precisely millionaires, you know. Her wealth left her free to espouse the cause of womanhood at large. She is a little bit Quixotic, dear thing, and given to tilting at windmills. She wants to secure to working women a fair business basis—that is the technical expression, I believe. And so she starts clubs, and forms circles. She says women must be encouraged to combine and to agitate. Whether they are capable of combining I do not pretend to say. These high matters transcend my small wit. But, as I have often pointed out to her, agitation is the natural attitude of every woman. It would seem superfluous to encourage or inculcate that, for surely wherever two or three petticoats are gathered together, there, as far as my experience goes, is agitation of necessity in the midst of them."

Madame de Vallorbes leaned back with a little sigh and air of exquisite resignation.

" All the same, the majority of women are unhappy enough, Heaven knows ! If Honoria, or any other sweet, feminine Quixote, can find means to lighten the burden of our lives, she has my very sincere thanks, well understood."

Richard drew his whip across the backs of the trotting horses, making them plunge forward against that blank, impalpable wall of all-encircling, ever-receding, ever-present fog. The carriage had just crossed the long, white-railed bridge, spanning the little river and space of marsh on either side, and now entered Sandy-field Street. The tops of the tall Lombardy poplars were lost in gloom. Now and again the redness of a lighted cottage window, blurred and contorted in shape, showed through the grey pall. Slow-moving, country figures, passing vehicles, a herd of some eight or ten cows—preceded by a diabolic looking billy-goat, and followed by a lad astride the hind-quarters of a bare-backed donkey—grew out of pallid nothingness as the carriage came abreast of them, and receded with mysterious rapidity into nothingness again. The effect was curiously fantastic and unreal. And, as the minutes passed, that effect of unreality gained upon Richard's imagination, until now—as last evening in the stately solitude of the Long Gallery—he became increasingly aware of the personality of his companion, increasingly penetrated by the feeling of being alone with that personality, as though the world, so strangely blotted out by these dim, obliterating vapours, were indeed vacant of all human interest, human purpose, human history, save that incarnate in this fair woman and in his own relation to her. She alone existed, concrete, exquisite, sentient, amid the vague, shifting immensities of fog. She alone mattered. Her near neighbourhood worked upon him strongly, causing an excitement in him which at once hindered and demanded speech.

Night began to close in in good earnest. Passing the broad, yellowish glare streaming out from the rounded tap-room window of the Calmady Arms, and passing from the end of the village street on to the open common, the light had become so uncertain that Richard could no longer see his companion's face clearly. This was almost a relief to him, so that, mastering at once his diffidence and his excitement, he spoke.

" Look here, Helen," he said, " I have been thinking over all that you told me. I don't want to dwell on subjects that must be very painful to you, but I can't help thinking about them. It's not that I won't leave them alone, but that they won't leave me. I don't want to presume upon your confidence, or take too much upon myself. Only, don't you see, now that I do know it's impossible to sit down under it all and let things go on just the same.—You're not angry with me?"

The young man spoke very carefully and calmly, yet the tones of his voice were heavily charged with feeling.

Madame de Vallorbes clasped her hands rather tightly within her sable muff. Unconsciously she began to sway a little, just a very little, as a person will sway in time to strains of stirring music. An excitement, not mental merely but physical, invaded her. For she recognised that she stood on the threshold of developments in this very notable drama. Still she answered quietly, with a touch even of weariness.

"Ah! dear Richard, it is so friendly and charming of you to take my infelicities thus to heart! But to what end, to what end, I ask you? The conditions are fixed. Escape from them is impossible. I have made my bed—made it most abominably uncomfortably, I admit, but that is not to the point—and I must lie on it. There is no redress. There is nothing to be done."

"Yes, there is this," he replied. "I know it is wretchedly inadequate, it doesn't touch the root of the matter. Oh! it's miserably inadequate — I should think I did know that! Only it might smooth the surface a bit, perhaps, and put a stop to one source of annoyance. Forgive me if I say what seems coarse or clumsy—but would not your position be easier if, in regard to— to money, you were quite independent of that—of your husband, I mean,—M. de Vallorbes?"

For a moment the young lady remained very still, and stared very hard at the fog. The most surprising visions arose before her. She had a difficulty in repressing an exclamation.

"Ah! there now, I have blundered. I've hurt you. I've made you angry," Dickie cried impulsively.

"No, no, dear Richard," she answered, with admirable gentleness, "I am not angry. Only what is the use of romancing?"

"I am not romancing. It is the simplest thing out, if you will but have it so."

He hesitated a little. The horses were pulling, the fog was in his throat thick and choking—or was it, perhaps, something more unsubstantial and intangible even than fog? The spacious barns and rickyards of the Church Farm were just visible on the right. In less than five minutes more, at their present pace, the horses would reach the first park gate. The young man felt he must give himself time. He quieted the horses down into a walk.

"If I were your brother, Helen, I should save you all these sordid money worries as a matter of course. You have no brother—so, don't you see, I come next.   It's a perfectly obvious arrangement.   Just let me be your banker," he said.

Madame de Vallorbes shut her pretty teeth together.   She could have danced, she could have sung aloud for very gaiety of heart.   She had not anticipated this turn to the situation ; but it was a delicious one.   It had great practical merits.   Her brain worked rapidly.   Immediately those practical merits ranged themselves before her in detail.   But she would play with it a little—both diplomacy and good taste, in which last she was by no means deficient, required that.

" Ah ! you forget, dear Richard," she said, "in your friendly zeal you forget that, in our rank of life, there is one thing a woman cannot accept from a man.   To take money is to lay yourself open to slanderous tongues, is to court scandal.   Sooner or later it is known, the fact leaks out.   And however innocent the intention, however noble and honest the giving, however grateful and honest the receiving, the world puts but one construction upon such a transaction."

" The world's beastly evil-minded then," Richard said.

"So it is.   But that is no news, Dickie dear," Madame de Vallorbes answered.   " Nor is it exactly to the point."

Inwardly she trembled a little.   What if she had headed him off too cleverly, and he should regard her argument as convincing, her refusal as final ?   Her fears were by no means lessened by the young man's protracted silence.

"No, I don't agree," he said at last.   " I suppose there are always risks to be run in securing anything at all worth securing, and it seems to me, if you look at it all round, the risks in this case are very slight.   Only you—and M. de Vallorbes need know.   I suppose he must.   But then, if you will pardon my saying so, after what you have told me I can't imagine he is the sort of person who is likely to object very much to an arrangement by which he would benefit, at least indirectly.   As for the world,"—Richard ceased to contemplate his horses.   He tried to speak lightly, while his eyes sought that dimly seen face at his elbow.—"Oh, well, hang the world, Helen !   It's easy enough for me to say so, I daresay, being but so slightly acquainted with it and the ways of it.   But the world can't be so wholly hide-bound and idiotic that it denies the existence of exceptional cases.   And this case, in some of its bearings at all events, is wholly exceptional, I am—happy to think."

"You are a very convincing special pleader, Richard," Madame de Vallorbes said softly.

"Then you accept?" he rejoined exultantly. "You accept?"

The young lady could not quite control herself.

"Ah! if you only knew the prodigious relief it would be," she exclaimed, with an outbreak of impatience. "It would make an incalculable difference. And yet I do not see my way. I am in a cleft stick. I dare not say Yes. And to say No"— Her sincerity was unimpeachable at that moment. Her eyes actually filled with tears. "Pah! I am ashamed of myself," she cried, "but, to refuse is distracting."

The gate of the outer park had been reached. The groom swung himself down and ran forward, but confused by the growing darkness and the thick atmosphere he fumbled for a time before finding the heavy latch. The horses became some-what restive, snorting and fidgeting.

"Steady there, steady, good lass," Richard said soothingly. Then he turned again to his companion. "Believe me it's the very easiest thing out to accept, if you'll only look at it all from the right point of view, Helen."

Madame de Vallorbes withdrew her right hand from her muff and laid it, almost timidly, upon the young man's arm.

"Do you know, you are wonderfully dear to me, Dick?" she said, and her voice shook slightly. She was genuinely touched and moved.—"No one has ever been quite so dear to me before. It is a new experience. It takes my breath away a little. It makes me regret some things I have done. But it is a mistake to go back on what is past, don't you think so? Therefore we will go forward. Tell me, expound. What is this so agreeably reconciling point of view?"

But along with the touch of her hand, a great wave of emotion swept over poor Richard, making his grasp on the reins very unsteady. The sensations he had suffered last evening in the Long Gallery again assailed him. The flesh had its word to say. Speech became difficult. Meanwhile his agitation communicated itself strangely to the horses. They sprang forward against that all-encircling, ever-present, yet ever-receding, blank wall of fog, to which the over-arching trees lent an added gloom and mystery, as though some incarnate terror pursued them. The gate clanged-to behind the carriage. The groom scrambled breathlessly into his place. Sir Richard's driving was rather reckless, he ventured to think, on such a nasty, dark night, and with a lady along of him too. He was not sorry when the pace slowed down to a walk. That was a long sight safer, to his thinking.

"The right point of view is this," Richard said at last; "that in accepting you would be doing that which, in some ways, would make just all the difference to my life."

He held himself very upright on the sloping driving-seat, rather cruelly conscious of the broad strap about his waist, and the high, unsightly driving-iron against which, concealed by the heavy, fur rug, his feet pushed as he balanced himself. He paused, gazing away into the silent desolation of the now invisible woods, and when he spoke again his voice had deepened in tone.

"It must be patent to you—it is rather detestably patent to everyone, I suppose, if it comes to that—that I am condemned to be of precious little use to myself or anyone else. I share the fate of the immortal Sancho Panza in his island of Barataria. A very fine feast is spread before me, while I find myself authoritatively forbidden to eat first of this dish and then of that, until I end by being every bit as hungry as though the table was bare. It becomes rather a nuisance at times, you know, and taxes one's temper and one's philosophy. It seems a little rough to possess all that so many men of my age would give just everything to have, and yet be unable to get anything but unsatisfied hunger, and—in plain English—humiliation, out of it."

Madame de Vallorbes sat very still. Her charming face had grown keen. She listened, drawing in her breath with a little sobbing sound—but that was only the result of accentuated dramatic satisfaction.

"You see I have no special object or ambition. I can't have one. I just pass the time. I don't see any prospect of my ever being able to do more than that. There's my mother, of course. I need not tell you she and I love one another. And there are the horses. But I don't care to bet, and I never attend a race-meeting. I—I do not choose to make an exhibition of myself."

Again Helen drew her hand out of her muff, but this time quickly, impulsively, and laid it on Richard's left hand which held the reins. The young man's breath caught in his throat, he leaned sideways towards her, her shoulder touching his elbow, the trailing plumes of her hat—now limp from the clinging moisture of the fog—for a moment brushing his cheek.

"Helen," he said rapidly, "don't you understand it's in your power to alter all this? By accepting you would do infinitely more for me than I could ever dream of doing for you. You'd give me something to think of and plan about.

If you'll only have whatever wretched money you need now, and have more whenever you want it—if you'll let me feel, however rarely we meet, that you depend on me and trust me and let me make things a trifle easier and smoother for you, you will be doing such an act of charity as few women have ever done. Don't refuse, for pity's sake don't! I don't want to whine, but things were not precisely gay before your coming, you know. Need it be added they promise to be less so than ever after you are gone? So listen to reason. Do as I ask you. Let me be of use in the only way I can."

"Do you consider what you propose?" Madame de Vallorbes asked, slowly. "It is a good deal. It is dangerous. With most men such a compact would be wholly inadmissible."

Then poor Dickie lost himself. The strain of the last week, the young, headlong passion aroused in him, the misery of his deformity, the accumulated bitterness and rebellion of years arose and overflowed as a great flood. Pride went down before it, and reticence, and decencies of self-respect. Richard turned and rent himself, without mercy and, for the moment, without shame. He pelted himself with cruel words, with scorn and self-contempt, while he laughed, and the sound of that laughter wandered away weirdly through the chill density of the fog, under the tall, shadowy firs of the great avenue, over the sombre heather, out into the veiled, crowded darkness of the wide woods.

"But I am not as other men are," he answered. "I am a creature by myself, a unique development as much outside the normal social, as I am outside the normal physical law. I— alone by myself—think of it!—abnormal, extraordinary.—You are safe enough with me, Helen. Safe to indulge and humour me as you might a monkey or a parrot. All the world will understand that! Only my mother, and a few old friends and old servants take me seriously. To everyone else I am an embarrassment, a more or less distressing curiosity."—He met little Lady Constance Quayle's ruminant stare again in imagination, heard Lord Fallowfeild's blundering speech.—"Remember our luncheon to-day. It was flattering, at moments, wasn't it? And so if I do queer things, things off the conventional lines, who will be surprised? No one, I tell you, not even the most strait-laced or censorious. Allow me at least the privileges of my disabilities. I am a dwarf—a cripple. I shall never be otherwise. Had I lived a century or two ago I should have made sport for you, and such as you, as some rich man's professional fool. And so, if I overstep the usual limits, who will comment on that? Queer things, crazy things, are in the part. What do I matter?"

Richard laughed aloud.

"At least I have this advantage, that in my case you can do what you can do in the case of no other man. With me you needn't be afraid. No one will think evil. With me—yes, after all, there is a drop of comfort in it—with me, Helen, you're safe enough."

CHAPTER X

MR. LUDOVIC QUAYLE AMONG THE PROPHETS

THAT same luncheon party at Brockhurst, if not notably satisfactory to the hosts, afforded much subsequent food for meditation to one at least of the guests. During the evening immediately following it, and even in the watches of the night, Lady Louisa Barking's thought was persistently engaged with the subject of Richard Calmady, his looks, his character, his temper, his rent-roll, the acreage of his estates, and his prospects generally. Nor did her interest remain hidden and inarticulate. For, finding that in various particulars her knowledge was superficial and clearly insufficient, on her journey from Westchurch up to town next day, in company with her brother Ludovic, she put so many questions to that accomplished, young gentleman that he shortly divined some serious purpose in her inquiry.

"We all recognise, my dear Louisa," he remarked presently, laying aside the day's *Times*, of which he had vainly essayed the study, with an air of gentle resignation, crossing his long legs and leaning back in his corner of the railway carriage,—"that you are the possessor of an eminently practical mind. You have run the family for some years now, not without numerous successes, among which may be reckoned your running of yourself into the arms—if you will pardon my mentioning them—of my estimable brother-in-law, Barking."

"Really, Ludovic!" his sister protested.

"Let me entreat you not to turn restive, Louisa," Mr. Quayle rejoined with the utmost suavity. "I am paying a high compliment to your intelligence. To have run into the arms of Mr. Barking, or indeed of anybody else, casually and involuntarily, to have blundered into them—if I may so express myself—would have been a stupidity. But to run into them intentionally and voluntarily argues considerable powers of strategy, an intelligent direction of movement which I respect and admire."

"You are really exceedingly provoking, Ludovic!"

Lady Louisa pushed the square, leather-covered dressing-case, on which her feet had been resting, impatiently aside.

"Far from it," the young man answered. "Can I put that box anywhere else for you? You like it just where it is?—Yes? But I assure you I am not provoking. I am merely complimentary. Conversation is an art, Louisa. None of my sisters ever can be got to understand that. It is dreadfully crude to rush in waist-deep at once. There should be feints and approaches. You should nibble at your sugar with a graceful coyness. You should cut a few frills and skirmish a little before setting the battle actively in array. And it is just this that I have been striving to do during the last five minutes. But you do not appear to appreciate the commendable style of my preliminaries. You want to engage immediately. There is usually a first-rate underlying reason for your interest in anybody"—

Again the lady shifted the position of the dressing-case.

"To the right?" inquired Mr. Quayle extending his hand, his head a little on one side, his long neck directed forward, while he regarded first his sister and then the dressing-case with infuriating urbanity. "No? Let us come to Hecuba, then. Let us dissemble no longer, but put it plainly. What, oh, Louisa! what are you driving at in respect of my very dear friend, Dickie Calmady?"

Now it was unquestionably most desirable for her to keep on the fair-weather side of Mr. Quayle just then. Yet the flesh is weak. Lady Louisa Barking could not control a movement of self-justification. She spoke with dignity, severely.

"It is all very well for you to say those sorts of things, Ludovic"—

"What sorts of things?" he inquired mildly.

"But I should be glad to know what would have become of the family by now, unless someone had come forward and taken matters in hand? Of course one gets no thanks for it. One never does get any thanks for doing one's duty, however wearing it is to oneself and however much others profit. But somebody had to sacrifice themselves. Mama is unequal to any exertion. You know what papa is"—

"I do, I do," murmured Mr. Quayle, raising his gaze piously to the roof of the railway carriage.

"If he has one of the boys to tramp over the country with

him at Whitney, and one of the girls to ride with him in London, he is perfectly happy and content. He is alarmingly improvident. He would prefer keeping the whole family at home doing nothing "—

"Save laughing at his jokes. My father craves the support of a sympathetic audience."

"Shotover is worse than useless."

"Except to the guileless Israelite he is. Absolutely true, Louisa."

"Guy would never have gone into the army when he left Eton unless I had insisted upon it. And it was entirely through the Barkings' influence—at my representation of course—that Eddie got a berth in that Liverpool cotton-broker's business. I am sure Alicia is very comfortably married. I know George Winterbotham is not the least interesting, but he is perfectly gentlemanlike and presentable, and so on, and he makes her a most devoted husband. And from what Mr. Barking heard the other day at the Club from somebody or other, I forget who, but someone connected with the Government, you know, there is every probability of George getting that permanent under-secretaryship."

"Did I not start by declaring you had achieved numerous successes?" Ludovic inquired. "Yet we stray from the point, Louisa. For do I not still remain ignorant of the root of your sudden interest in my friend Dickie Calmady? And I thirst to learn how you propose to work him into the triumphant development of our family fortunes."

The proportions of Lady Louisa's small mouth contracted still further into an expression of great decision, while she glanced at the landscape reeling away from the window of the railway carriage. In the past twelve hours autumn had given place to winter. The bare hedges showed black, while the fallen leaves of the hedgerow trees formed unsightly blotches of sodden brown and purple upon the dirty green of the pastures. Over all brooded an opaque, grey-brown sky, sullen and impenetrable. Lady Louisa saw all this. But she was one of those persons happily, for themselves, unaffected by such abstractions as the aspects of nature. Her purposes were immediate and practical. She followed them with praiseworthy persistence. The landscape merely engaged her eyes because she, just now, preferred looking out of the window to looking her brother in the face.

"Something must be done for the younger girls," she announced. "I feel pretty confident about Emily's future. We need not go into that. Maggie, if she marries at all—and she really is very useful at home, in looking after the servants and entertaining, and so on—if she marries at all, will marry late. She has no particular attractions as girls go. Her figure is too solid, and she talks too much. But she will make a very present-able middle-aged woman — sensible, dependable, an excellent *ménagère*. Certainly she had better marry late."

"A mature clergyman when she is rising forty—a widowed bishop, for instance. Yes, I approve that," Mr. Quayle rejoined reflectively. "It is well conceived, Louisa. We must keep an eye on the Bench and carefully note any episcopal matrimonial vacancy. Bishops have a little turn, I observe, for marrying somebody who *is* somebody—specially *en secondes ·noces*, good men. Yes, it is well thought of. With careful steering we may bring Maggie to anchor in a palace yet. Maggie is rather dogmatic, she would make not half a bad Mrs. Proudie. So she is disposed of, and then?"

For a few seconds the lady held silent converse with herself. At last she addressed her companion in tones of unwonted cordiality.

"You are by far the most sensible of the family, Ludovic," she began.

"And in a family so renowned for intellect, so conspicuous for 'parts and learning,' as Macaulay puts it, that is indeed a distinction!"—Mr. Quayle bowed slightly in his comfortable corner. "A thousand thanks, Louisa," he murmured.

"I would not breathe a syllable of this to any of the others," she continued. "You know how the girls chatter. Alicia, I am sorry to say, is as bad as any of them. They would discuss the question without intermission—simply, you know, talk the whole thing to death."

"Poor thing!— Yet, after all, what thing?" the young man inquired urbanely.

Lady Louisa bit her lip. He was very irritating, while she was very much in earnest. It was her misfortune usually to be a good deal in earnest.

"There is Constance," she remarked, somewhat abruptly.

"Precisely—there is poor, dear, innocent, rather foolish, little Connie. It occurred to me we might be coming to that."

In his turn Mr. Quayle fell silent, and contemplated the reeling landscape. Pasture had given place to wide stretches of dark moorland on either side the railway line, with a pallor of sour bog grasses in the hollows. The outlook was uncheerful. Per-haps it was that which caused the young man to shake his head.

"I recognise the brilliancy of the conception, Louisa. It

17

reflects credit upon your imagination and—your daring," he said presently. "But you won't be able to work it."

"Pray why not?" almost snapped Lady Louisa.

Mr. Quayle settled himself back in his corner again. His handsome face was all sweetness, indulgent though argumentative. He was nothing, clearly, unless reasonable.

"Personally, I am extremely fond of Dickie Calmady," he began. "I permit myself — honestly I do — moments of enthusiasm regarding him. I should esteem the woman lucky who married him. Yet I could imagine a prejudice might exist in some minds—minds of a less emancipated and finely comprehensive order than yours and my own of course—against such an alliance. Take my father's mind, for instance — and unhappily my father dotes on Connie. And he is more obstinate than nineteen dozen——well, I leave you to fill in the comparison mentally, Louisa. It might be slightly wanting in filial respect to put it into words."

Again he shook his head in pensive solemnity.

"I give you credit for prodigious push and tenacity, for a remarkable capacity of generalship, in short. Yet I cannot disguise from myself the certainty that you would never square my father."

"But suppose she wishes it herself? Papa would deny Connie nothing," the other objected. She was obliged to raise her voice to a point of shrillness, hardly compatible with the dignity of the noble house of Fallowfeild, *double* with all the gold of all the Barkings, for the train was banging over the points and roaring between the platforms of a local junction. Mr. Quayle made a deprecating gesture, put his hands over his ears, and again gently shook his head, intimating that no person possessed either of nerves or self-respect could be expected to carry on a conversation under existing conditions. Lady Louisa desisted. But, as soon as the train passed into the comparative quiet of the open country, she took up her parable again, and took it up in a tone of authority.

"Of course I admit there is something to get over. It would be ridiculous not to admit that. And I am always determined to be perfectly straightforward. I detest humbug of any kind. So I do not deny for a moment that there is something. Still it would be a very good marriage for Constance, a very good marriage, indeed. Even papa must acknowledge that. Money, position, age, everything of that kind, in its favour. One could not expect to have all that without some make-weight. I should not regret it, for I feel it might really be bad for Connie to have so much without some make-weight. And I remarked yesterday—I could not help remarking it—that she was very much occupied about Sir Richard Calmady."

"Connie is a little goose," Mr. Quayle permitted himself to remark, and for once there was quite a sour edge to his sweetness.

"Connie is not quick, she is not sensitive," his sister continued. "And, really, under all the circumstances, that perhaps is just as well. But she is a good child, and would believe almost anything you told her. She has an affectionate and obedient disposition, and she never attempts to think for herself. I don't believe it would ever occur to her to object to his—his peculiarities, unless some mischievous person suggested it to her. And then, as I tell you, I remarked she was very much occupied about him."

Once again Mr. Quayle sought counsel of the landscape which once again had changed in character. For here civilisation began to trail her skirts very visibly, and the edges of those skirts were torn and frayed, notably unhandsome. The open moorland had given place to flat market-gardens and leafless orchards sloppy with wet. Innumerable cabbages, innumerable stunted, black-branched apple and pear trees, avenues of dilapidated pea and bean sticks, reeled away to right and left. The semi-suburban towns stretched forth long, rawly-red arms of ugly, little, jerry-built streets and terraces. Tall chimneys and unlovely gasometers — these last showing as collections of some monstrous spawn — rose against the opaque sky, a sky rendered momentarily more opaque, dirtier and more dingy, by the masses of London smoke hanging along the eastern horizon.

Usually Ludovic knew his own mind clearly enough. The atmosphere of it was very far from being hazy. Now that atmosphere bore annoying resemblance to the opacity obtaining overhead and along the eastern horizon. The young man's sympathies — or were they his prejudices? — had a convenient habit of ranging themselves immediately on one side or other of any question presenting itself to him. But in the present case they were mixed. They pulled both ways, and this vexed him. For he liked to suppose himself very ripe, cynical, and disillusioned, while, in good truth, sentiment had more than a word to say in most of his opinions and decisions. Now sentiment ruled him strongly and pushed him—but, unfortunately, in diametrically opposite directions. The sentiment of friendship compelled him hitherward. While another sentiment, which he refused to define—he recognised it as wholesome, yet he was a trifle ashamed of it—compelled him quite other-where. He took refuge in an adroit begging of the question.

"After all are you not committing the fundamental error of reckoning without your host, Louisa?" he inquired. "Connie may be a good deal occupied about Calmady, but thereby may only give further proof of her own silliness. I certainly discovered no particular sign of Calmady being occupied about Connie. He was very much more occupied about the fair cousin, Helen de Vallorbes, than about any one of us, my illustrious self included, as far as I could see."

In her secret soul his hearer had to own this statement just. But she kept the owning to herself, and, with a rapidity upon which she could not help congratulating herself, instituted a flanking movement.

"You hear all the gossip, Ludovic," she said. "Of course it is no good my asking Mr. Barking about that sort of thing. Even if he heard it he would not remember it. His mind is too much engaged. If a woman marries a man with large political interests she must just give herself to them generously. It is very interesting, and one feels, of course, one is helping to make history. But still one has to sacrifice something. I hear next to nothing of what is going on—the gossip, I mean. And so tell me, what do you hear about her, about Madame de Vallorbes?"

"At first hand only that which you must know perfectly well yourself, my dear Louisa.—Didn't you sit opposite to her at luncheon, yesterday?—That she is a vastly good-looking and attractive woman."

"At second hand, then?"

"At second hand? Oh! at second hand I know various amiable little odds and ends such as are commonly reported by the uncharitable and censorious," Ludovic answered mildly. "Probably more than half of those little treasures are pure fiction, generated by envy, conceived by malice."

"Pray, Ludovic!" his sister exclaimed. But she recovered herself,—and added :—"You may as well tell me all the same. I think, under the circumstances, it would be better for me to hear."

"You really wish to hear? Well, I give it you for what it is worth. I don't vouch for the truth of a single item. For all we can tell, nice, kind friends may be recounting kindred anecdotes of Alicia and the blameless Winterbotham, or even of you, Louisa, and Mr. Barking."

Mr. Quayle fixed a glance of surpassing graciousness upon his sister as he uttered these agreeable suggestions, and fervid curiosity alone enabled her to resist a rejoinder and to maintain a dignified silence.

"It is said—and this probably is true—that she never cared two straws for de Vallorbes, but was jockeyed into the marriage—just as you might jockey Constance, you know, Louisa—by her mother, who has the reputation of being a somewhat frisky matron with a keen eye to the main chance. She is not quite all, I understand, a tender heart could desire in the way of a female parent. It is further said that *la belle Helène* makes the dollars fly even more freely than did de Vallorbes in his best days, and he has the credit of having been something of a *viveur*. He knew not only his Paris, but his Baden-Baden, and his Naples, and various other warm corners where great and good men do commonly congregate. It is added that *la belle Helène* already gives promise of being playful in other ways besides that of expenditure. And that de Vallorbes has been heard to lament, openly, that he is not a native of some enlightened country in which the divorce court charitably intervenes to sever over-hard connubial knots. In short, it is rumoured that de Vallorbes is not a conspicuous example of the wildly happy husband."

"In short, she is not respec "—

But the young man held up his hands and cried out feelingly:—

"Don't, pray don't, my dear Louisa. Let us walk delicately as Agag—my father's morning ministrations to the maids again! For how, as I pointed out just now, do we know what insidious little tales may not be in circulation regarding yourself and those nearest and dearest to you?"

Ludovic Quayle turned his head and once more looked out of the window, his beautiful mouth visited by a slightly malicious smile. The train was sliding onward above crowded, sordid courts and narrow alleys, festering, as it seemed, with a very plague of poverty-stricken and unwholesome humanity. Here the line runs parallel to the river—sullen to-day, blotted with black floats and lines of grimy barges, which straining, smoke-vomiting steam-tugs towed slowly against a strong flowing tide. On the opposite bank the heavy masses of the Abbey, the long decorated façade and towers of the Houses of Parliament, stood out ghostly and livid in a gleam of frail, unrelated sunshine against the murk of the smoky sky.

"I should have supposed Sir Richard Calmady was steady," Lady Louisa remarked, inconsequently and rather stiffly.— Ludovic really was exasperating.

"Steady? Oh! perfectly. Poor, dear chap, he hasn't had much chance of being anything else as yet."

"Still, of course, Lady Calmady would prefer his being settled. Clearly it would be much better in every way. All things considered, he is certainly one of the people who should marry young.   And Connie would be an excellent marriage for him, excellent—thoroughly suitable, better, really, than on the face of it he could hope for.—Ludovic, just look out please and see if the carriage is here.   Pocock always loses her head at a terminus, and misses the men-servants.   Yes, there is Frederic—with his back to the train, looking the wrong way, of course.   He really is too stupid."

Mr. Quayle, however, succeeded in attracting the footman's attention, and, assisted by that functionary and the lean and anxious Pocock—her arms full of bags and umbrellas—conveyed his sister out of the railway carriage and into the waiting brougham.   She graciously offered to put him down at his rooms, in St. James's Place, on her way to the Barking mansion in Albert Gate, but the young man declined that honour.

"Good-bye, Louisa," he said, leaning his elbows on the open window of the brougham and thereby presenting the back view of an irreproachably cut overcoat and trousers to the passers-by. "I have to thank you for a most interesting and instructive journey.   Your efforts to secure the prosperity of the family are wholly praiseworthy.   I commend them.   I have a profound respect for your generalship.   Still, pauper though I am, I am willing to lay you a hundred to one in golden guineas that you will never square papa."

Subsequently the young man bestowed himself in a hansom, and rattled away in the wake of the Barking equipage down the objectionably steep hill which leads from the roar and turmoil of the station into the Waterloo Bridge road.

"I might have offered heavier odds," he said to himself, "for never, never will she square papa !"

And, not without a slight sense of shame, he was conscious that he made this reflection with a measure of relief.

CHAPTER XI

CONTAINING SAMPLES BOTH OF EARTHLY AND HEAVENLY LOVE

KATHERINE stood in the central space of the great, state bedroom.   It was just upon midnight, yet she still wore her jewels and her handsome, trailing, black, velvet dress.   She was very tired.   But that tiredness proceeded less from physical than mental weariness.   This she recognised, and foresaw that weariness of this character was not likely to find relief and extinction within the shelter of the curtains of the stately bed, whereon the ancient Persian legend of the flight of the Hart through the tangled Forest of This Life was so deftly and quaintly embroidered. For, unhappily to-night, the leopard, Care, followed very close behind. And Katherine, taking the ancient legend as very literally descriptive of her existing state of mind, feared that, should she undress and seek the shelter of the rose-lined curtains the leopard would seek it also; and, crouching at her feet, his evil, yellow eyes would gaze into her own, wide open, all through that which remained of the night. The night, more-over, was very wild. A westerly gale, with now and again tumultuous violence of rain, rattled the many panes of the windows, wailed in every crevice of door and casement, roared through the mile-long elm avenue below, and roared in the chimneys above. The Prince of the Powers of the Air was let loose, and announced his presence as with the shout of battle. Sleep was out of the question under present conditions and in her present humour. Therefore Lady Calmady had dismissed Clara,—now promoted to the dignified office of lady's-maid,—and that bright-eyed and devoted waiting-woman had departed reluctant, almost in tears, protesting that:—"It was quite too bad, for her ladyship was being regularly worn out with all the talking and company. And she, for her part, should be heartily glad when the entertaining was over and they were all comfort-ably to themselves again."

Nor could Katherine honestly assert that she would be altogether sorry when the hour struck, to-morrow, for the departure of her guests. For it appeared to her that, notwith-standing the courtesy and affection of her brother and the triumphant charm of her niece, a spirit of unrest had entered Brockhurst along with their entry. Would that same spirit depart along with their departing? She questioned it. She was oppressed by a fear that spirit of unrest had come to stay. And so it was that as she walked the length and breadth of the lofty, white-panelled room, for all the rage and fury of the storm without, she still heard the soft padding of Care, the leopard, close behind.

Then a singular desolation and sense of homelessness came upon Katherine. Turn where she would there seemed no com-fort, no escape, no sure promise of eventual rest. Things human and material were emptied not of joy only, but of invitation to effort. For something had happened from which there was no going back. A fair woman from a far country had come and looked upon her son, with the inevitable result, that youth had

called to youth. And though the fair woman in question, being
already wedded wife,—Katherine was rather pathetically pure-
minded,—could not in any dangerously practical manner steal
away her son's heart, yet she would, only too probably, prepare
that heart and awaken in it desires of subsequent stealing away
on the part of some other fair woman, as yet unknown, whose
heart Dickie would do his utmost to steal in exchange. And
this filled her with anxiety and far-reaching fears, not only
because it was bitter to have some woman other than herself
hold the chief place in her son's affections, but because she—as
John Knott, even as Ludovic Quayle, though from quite other
causes—could not but apprehend possibilities of danger, even of
disaster, surrounding all question of love and marriage in the
strange and unusual case of Richard Calmady.

    And thinking of these things, her sensibilities heightened and
intensified by fatigue and circumstances of time and place, a
certain feverishness possessed her. That bed-chamber of many
memories — exquisite and tragic — became intolerable to her.
She opened the double doors and passed into the Chapel-Room
beyond, the light, thrown by the tall wax-candles set in silver
branches upon her toilet-table, passing with her through the
widely open doors and faintly illuminating the near end of the
great room. There was other subdued light in the room as well.
For a glowing mass of coal and wood still remained in the
brass basket upon the hearth; and the ruddy brightness of
it touched the mouldings of the ceiling, glowed on the polished
corners and carvings of tables, what-nots, and upon the mahogany
frames of solid, Georgian sofas and chairs.

    At first sight, notwithstanding the roaring of wind and
ripping of rain without, there seemed offer of comfort in this
calm and spacious place, the atmosphere of it sweet with bowls
of autumn violets and greenhouse-grown roses. Katherine sat
down in Richard's low arm-chair and gazed into the crimson
heart of the fire. She made a valiant effort to put away haunting fears, to resume her accustomed attitude of stoicism, of
tranquil, if slightly defiant, courage. But Care, the leopard,
refused to be driven away. Surely, stealthily, he had followed
her out of her bed-chamber and now crouched at her side,
making his presence felt so that all illusion of comfort speedily
fled. She knew that she was alone, consciously and bitterly
alone, waking in the midst of the sleeping house. No footstep
would echo up the stairs, hot to find her. No voice would call
her name, in anxiety for her well-being or in desire. It seemed
to Katherine that a desert lay outstretched about her on every

hand, while she sat desolate with Care for her sole companion. She recognised that her existing isolation was, in a measure at all events, the natural consequence of her own fortitude and ability. She had ruled with so strong and discreet a hand that the order she had established, the machinery she had set agoing, could now keep going without her. Hence her loneliness. And that loneliness as she sat by the dying fire, while the wind raved without, was dreadful to her, peopled with phantoms she dared not look upon. For, not only the accustomed burden of her motherhood was upon her, but that other unaccustomed burden of admitted middle-age. And this other burden, which it is appointed a woman shall bear while her heart often is still all too sadly young, dragged her down. The conviction pressed home on her that for her the splendid game was indeed over, and that, for very pride's sake, she must voluntarily stand aside and submit to rank herself with things grown obsolete, with fashions past and out of date.

Katherine rose to her feet, filled, for the moment, by an immense compassion for her own womanhood, by an overmastering longing for sympathy. She was so tired of the long struggle with sorrow, so tired of her own attitude of sustained courage. And now, when surely a little respite and repose might have been granted her, it seemed that a new order of courage was demanded of her—a courage passive rather than active, a courage of relinquishment and self-effacement. That was a little too much. For all her valiant spirit, she shrank away. She grew weak. She could not face it.

And so it happened that to-night—as once long ago, when poor Richard suffered his hour of mental and physical torment at the skilful, yet relentless, hands of Dr. Knott, in the bed-chamber near by—Katherine's anguish and revolt found expression in restless pacings, and those pacings brought her to the chapel door. It stood ajar. Before the altar the three hanging lamps showed each its tongue of crimson flame. A whiteness of flowers, set in golden vases upon the re-table, was just distinguishable. But the delicately carved spires and canopies of stalls, the fair pictured saints, and figure of the risen Christ—His wounded feet shining like pearls upon the azure floor of heaven—in the east window, were lost in soft, thick, all-pervading gloom. The place was curiously still, as though waiting silently, in solemn and strained expectation for the accomplishment of some mysterious visitation. And, all the while without, the gale flung itself wailing against the angles of the masonry, and the rain beat upon the glass of the high, narrow windows as with a passion of despairing tears.

For some time Katherine waited in the doorway, a sombre figure in her trailing, velvet dress. The hushed stillness of the chapel, the confusion and clamour of the tempest, taken thus in connection, were very telling. They exercised a strong influence over her already somewhat exalted imagination. Could it be, she asked herself, that these typified the rest of the religious, and the unrest of the secular life? Julius March would interpret the contrast they afforded in some such manner no doubt. And what if Julius, after all, were right? What if, shutting God out of the heart, you also shut that heart out from all peaceful dwelling places, leaving it homeless, at the mercy of every passing storm? Katherine was bruised in spirit. The longing for some sure refuge, some abiding city was dominant in her. The needs of her soul, so long ignored and repudiated, asserted themselves. Yes, what if Julius were right, and if content and happiness—the only happiness which has in it the grace of continuance—consisted in submission to, and glad acquiescence in, the will of God?

Thus did she muse, gazing questioningly at the whiteness of the altar flowers and those steady tongues of flame, hearing the silence, as of reverent waiting, which dwelt in the place. But, on the other hand, to give, in this her hour of weakness, that which she had refused in the hours of clear-seeing strength,—to let go, because she was alone and the unloveliness of age claimed her, that sense of bitter injury and injustice which she had hugged to her breast when young and still aware of her empire,—would not such action be contemptibly poor spirited? She was no child to be humbled into confession by the rod, frightened into submission by the dark. To abase herself, in the hope of receiving spiritual consolation, appeared to her as an act of disloyalty to her dead love and her maimed and crippled son. She turned away with a rather superb lift of her beautiful head, and went back to her own bed-chamber again. She hardened herself in opposition, putting the invitations of grace from her as she might have put those of temptation. She would yield to weakness, to feverish agitations and aimless longings, no more. Whether sleep elected to visit her or not, she would undress and seek her bed.

But hardly had she closed the door and, standing before her toilet-table, begun to unclasp the pearls from her throat and bracelets from her wrists, than a sound, quite other than agreeable or reassuring, saluted her ears from close by. It proceeded from the room next door, now unoccupied, since Richard, some five or six years ago, jealous of the dignity of his youth, had petitioned to be permitted to remove himself and his possessions to the suite of rooms immediately below. This comprised the

Gun-Room, a bed and dressing room, and a fourth room, connecting with the offices, which came in handy for his valet.   Since his decline upon this more commodious apartment, the old nursery had stood vacant.   Katherine could not find it in her heart to touch it.   It was furnished now as in Dickie's childish days, when, night and morning, she had visited it to make sure of her darling's health and safety.

And it was in this shrine of tender recollections that disquieting sounds now arose.   Hard claws rattled upon the boarded spaces of the floor.   Some creature snored and panted against the bottom of the door, pushed it with so heavy a weight that the panels creaked, flung itself down uneasily, then moved to and fro again, with that harsh rattling of claws.   The image of Care, the leopard, as embroidered upon the curtains of her bed, was so present to Katherine's imagination to-night that, for a moment, she lost her hold on probability and common sense.   It appeared to her that the anxieties and perturbations which oppressed her had taken on bodily form, and, in the shape of a devouring beast, besieged her chamber door.   The conception was grisly.   Both mind and body being rather overstrained, it filled her with something approaching panic.   No one was within call.   To rouse her brother, or Julius, she must make a tour of half the house.   Again the creature pushed against the creaking panels, and, then, panting and snoring, began ripping away the matting from the door-sill.

The terror of the unknown is, after all, greater than that of the known.   It was improbable, though the hour was late and the night wild, that savage beasts or cares incarnate should actually be in possession of Dickie's disused nursery.   Katherine braced herself and turned the handle.   Still the vision disclosed by the opening door was at first sight monstrous enough.   A moving mass of dirty white, low down against the encircling darkness, bandy legs, and great grinning mouth.   The bull-dog stood up, whining, fawning upon her, thrusting his heavy head into her hand.

"Why, Camp, good old friend, what brings you here?   Are you, too, homeless to-night?   But why have you deserted your master?"

And then Lady Calmady's panic fears took on another aspect.   Far from being allayed they were increased.   An apprehension of something actively evil abroad in the great, sleeping house assailed her.   She trembled from head to foot.   And yet, even while she shrank and trembled, her courage reawoke.   For she perceived that as yet she need not rank herself wholly among fashions passed and things grown obsolete.   She had her place and value still.   She was wanted, she was called for—that she knew—though by whom wanted and for what purpose she, as yet, knew not.

The bull-dog, meanwhile, his heavy head carried low, his crooked tail drooping, trotted slowly away into the darkness and then trotted back. He squatted upon his haunches, looking up with anxious, bloodshot eyes.   He trotted away again, and again returned and stood waiting, his whole aspect eloquent in its dumb appeal.   He implored her to follow, and Katherine, fetching one of the silver candlesticks from her dressing-table, obeyed.

She followed her ugly, faithful guide across the vacant dis-used nursery, and on down the uncarpeted turning staircase which opens into the square lobby outside the Gun-Room.   The diamond panes of the staircase windows chattered in their leaded frames, and the wind shrieked in the spouts, and angles, and carved stonework, of the inner courtyard as she passed.   The gale was at its height, loud and insistent.   Yet the many-toned violence of it seemed to bear strange and intimate relation—as that of a great orchestra to a single dominant human voice—to the subtle, evil influence which she felt to be at large within the sleeping house.   And so, without pausing to consider the wisdom of her action, pushed by the conviction that something of profound import was taking place, and that someone, or something, must be saved by her from threatening danger, Katherine threw open the Gun-Room door.

The shout of the storm seemed far away.   This place was quick with stillness too, with the hush of waiting for the accom-plishment of some mysterious event or visitation, even as the dark chapel upstairs had been.   Only here moving effect of soft, brilliant light, of caressing warmth, of vague, insidious fragrance met her.   Katherine Calmady had only known passion in its purest and most legitimate form.   It had been for her, innocent of all grossness, or suggestion of degradation, fair and lovely and natural, revelation of highest and most enchanting secrets.   But having once known it in its fulness, she could not fail to recognise its presence, even though it wore a diabolic, rather than angelic face.   That passion met her now, exultant, effulgent, along with that light and heat and fragrance, she did not for an instant doubt.   And the splendour of its near neighbourhood turned her faint with dread and with poignant memories.   She paused upon the threshold, supporting herself with one hand against the cold, stone jamb of the arched doorway, while in the other she held the massive candlestick and its flickering, draught-driven lights.

A mist was before her eyes, a singing in her ears, so that she had much ado to see clearly and reckon justly with that which she did see.   Helen de Vallorbes, clothed in a flowing, yet clinging, silken garment of turquoise, shot with blue purple and shimmering glaucous green—a garment in colour such as that with which the waves of Adriatic might have clothed the rosy limbs of new-born Aphrodite, as she rose from the cool, translucent sea-deeps—knelt upon the tiger-skin before the dancing fire.   Her hands grasped the two arms of Richard's chair.   She leaned down right across it, the lines and curves of her beautiful body discernible under her delicate draperies.   The long, open sleeves of her dress fell away from her outstretched arms, showing them in their completeness from wrist to shoulder.   Her head was thrown back, so that her rounded throat stood out, and the pure line of her lower jaw was salient.   Her eyes were half closed, while all the mass of her honey-coloured hair was gathered low down on the nape of her neck into a net of golden thread.   A golden, netted girdle was knotted loosely about her loins, the tasselled ends of it dragging upon the floor.   She wore no jewels, nor were they needed, for the loveliness of her person, discovered rather than concealed by those changeful sea-blue draperies, was already dangerously potent.

All this Katherine saw—a radiant vision of youth, an incarnation, not of care and haunting fears, but of pleasure and haunting delights.   And she saw more than this.   For in the depths of that long, low arm-chair Richard sat, stiffly erect, his face dead white, thin, and strained—Richard, as she had never beheld him before, though she knew the face well enough.   It was his father's face as she had seen it on her marriage night, and on his death night too, when his fingers had been clasped about her throat to the point of strangulation.   Katherine dared look no longer.   Her heart stood still.   Shame and anger took her, and along with these an immense nostalgia for that which had once been and was not.   Her instinct was of flight.   But Camp trotted forward, growling, and squatted between the pedestals of the library table, his red eyes blinking sullenly in the square shadow. Involuntarily Katherine followed him part way across the room.

Richard looked full at his cousin, absorbed, rigid, an amazement of question in his eyes.   Not a muscle of his face moved. But Madame de Vallorbes' absorption was less complete.   She started slightly and half turned her head.

"Ah! there is that dog again," she said.   "What has brought him back?   He hates me."

"Damn the dog!" Richard exclaimed, hoarsely under his breath.   Then he said :—" Helen, Helen, you know "—

But Madame de Vallorbes had turned her head yet farther,

and her arched eyelids opened quite wide for once, while she smiled a little, her lips parting and revealing her pretty teeth tightly set.

"Ah! the advent of the bull-dog explains itself," she exclaimed. "Here is Aunt Katherine herself!"

Slowly, and with an inimitable grace, she rose to her feet. Her long, winged sleeves floated back into place, covering her bare arms. Her composure was astonishing, even to herself. Yet her breath came a trifle quick as she contemplated Lady Calmady with the same enigmatic smile, her chin carried high—the finest suggestion of challenge and insolence in it—her eyes still unusually wide open and startlingly bright.

"Richard holds a little court to-night," she continued airily, "thanks to the storm. You also have come to seek the protection of his presence it appears, Aunt Katherine. Indeed, I am not surprised, for you certainly brew very wild weather at Brockhurst, at times."

Something in the young lady's bearing had restored Katherine's self-control.

"The wind is going down," she replied calmly. "The storm need not alarm you, or keep you watching any longer, Helen."

"Ah! pardon me—you know you are accustomed to these tempests," the younger woman rejoined. "To me it still sounds more than sufficiently violent."

"Yes, but merely on this side of the house, where Richard's and my rooms are situated. The wind has shifted, and I believe on your side you will suffer no further disturbance. You will find it quite quiet. Then, moreover, you have to rise early to-morrow—or rather to-day. You have a long journey before you and should secure all the rest you can."

Madame de Vallorbes gathered her silken draperies about her absently. For a moment she looked down at the tiger-skin, then back at Lady Calmady.

"Ah yes!" she said, "it is thoughtful of you to remind me of that. To-day I start on my homeward journey. It should give me very much pleasure, should it not? But—do not be shocked, Aunt Katherine—I confess I am not altogether enraptured at the prospect. I have been too happy, too kindly treated, here at Brockhurst, for it to be other than a sorrow to me to depart."

She turned to Richard, her expression serious, intimate, appealing. Then she shook back her fair head, and as though in obedience to an irresistible movement of tenderness, stooped down swiftly over him—seeming to drown him in the shimmering waves of some azure, and thin, clear green, and royal, blue-purple sea—while she kissed him full and daringly upon the mouth.

"Good-night, good-bye, dear Dickie," she said. "Yes, good-bye—for I almost hope I may not see you in the morning. It would be a little chilly and inadequate, any other farewell after this. I am grateful to you.—And remember, I too am among those who, to their sorrow, never forget."

She approached Lady Calmady, her manner natural, un-abashed, playful even, and gay.

"See, I am ready to go to bed like a good child, Aunt Katherine," she said, " supported by your assurance that my side of the house is no longer rendered terrific by wind and rain. But — I am so distressed to trouble you—but all the lamps are out, and I am none too sure of my way. It would be a rather tragic ending to my happy visit if I incontinently lost myself and wandered till dawn, disconsolate, up and down the passages and stairways of Richard's magnificent house. I might even wander in here by mistake again, and that would be unpardonably indis-creet, wouldn't it? So, will you light me to my own quarters, Aunt Katherine? Thank you—how charmingly kind and sweet you are ! "

As she spoke Madame de Vallorbes moved lightly away and passed on to the lobby, the heels of her pretty, cloth-of-gold slippers ringing quite sharply on the grey, stone quarries without. And, even as a little while back she had followed the heavy-headed and ungainly bull-dog, so now Lady Calmady, in her trailing, black, velvet dress, silver candlestick in hand, followed this radiant, fleet-footed creature, whose every movement was eloquent of youth and health and an almost prodigal joy of living. Neither woman spoke as they crossed the lobby, and passed the pierced and arcaded stone screen which divides the outer from the inner hall. Now and again the flickering candle-light glinted on the younger woman's girdle or the net which controlled the soft masses of her honey-coloured hair. Now and again a draught taking the folds of her silken raiment blew it hither and thither, disclosing her beautiful arms or quick-moving slippered feet. She was clothed with splendour of the sea, crowned, and shod, and girt about the loins, with gold. And she fled on silently, till the wide, shallow-stepped stairway, leading up to the rooms she occupied, was reached. There, for a moment, she paused.

"Pray come no farther," she said, and went on rapidly up the flight. On the landing she stopped, a dimly discerned figure, blue and gold against the dim whiteness of high panelled walls, moulded ceiling, stairway, and long descending balustrade.

"I have arrived!" she cried, and her clear voice took strange inflections of mockery and laughter. "I have arrived! I am perfectly secure now and safe. Let us hope all other inmates of Brockhurst are equally so this stormy night. A thousand thanks, dear Aunt Katherine, for your guidance, and a thousand apologies for bringing you so far. Now let me trouble you no longer."

The Gun-Room Katherine found just as she had left it, save that Camp stood on the tiger-skin before the fire, his fore-paws and his great, grinning muzzle resting on the arm of Richard's chair. Camp whined a little. Mechanically the young man raised his hand and pulled the dog's long, drooping ears. His face was still dead white, and there were lines under his eyes and about the corners of his mouth, as of one who tries to subdue expression of physical pain. He looked straight at Lady Calmady.

"Ah!" he said, "so you have come back! You observe I have changed partners!"

And again he pulled the dog's ears, while it appeared to the listener that his voice curiously echoed that other voice which had so lately addressed and dismissed her, taking on inflections of mockery. But as she nerved herself to answer, he continued, hastily :—

"I want nothing, dear mother, nothing in the world. Pray don't concern yourself any more about me to-night. Haven't I Camp for company? Lamps? Oh! I can put them out perfectly well myself. You were right, of course, perfectly right, to come if you were anxious about me. But now surely you are satisfied?"

Suddenly Richard bowed his head, putting both hands over his eyes.

"Only now, mother, if you love me, go," he said, with a great sob in his voice. "For God's sake go, and leave me to myself."

But after sleepless hours, in the melancholy, blear dawn of the November day, Katherine lying, face downwards, within the shelter of the embroidered curtains of the state bed, made her submission at last and prayed.

"I am helpless, O Father Almighty! I have neither wit nor understanding, nor strength. Have mercy, lest my reason depart from me. I have sinned, for years I have sinned, setting my will, my judgment, my righteousness, against Thine. Take me, forgive me, teach me. I bring nothing. I ask everything. I am empty. Fill me with Thyself, even as with water one fills an empty cup. Give me the courage of patience instead of the courage of battle. Give me the courage of meekness in place of the courage of pride."

BOOK IV

A SLIP BETWIXT CUP AND LIP

CHAPTER I

THE spirit of unrest, which had entered Brockhurst in the dim October weather, along with certain guests, did not—Lady Calmady had foreseen as much—leave with their leaving. It remained a constant quantity. Further, it engendered events very far away from and, at first sight, wholly at variance with those which had accompanied its advent.

For example, Lady Louisa Barking, passing through Lowndes Square one bleak, March morning on her way from Albert Gate to do a little, quiet shopping in Sloane Street, observed that the Calmadys' house—situated at the corner of the square and of —— Street—was given over to a small army of work-people. During Richard's minority it had been let for a term of years to Sir Reginald Aldham, of Aldham Revel in Midlandshire. Since Dickie's coming of age it had stood empty, pending a migration of the Brockhurst establishment, which migration had, in point of fact, never yet taken place. But now, as Lady Louisa, walking with a firm and distinguished tread along the grey, wind-swept pavements, remarked, the house was in process of redecoration, of painting within and without. And, looking on these things, Lady Louisa's soul received very sensible comfort. She was extremely tenacious of purpose. And, in respect of one purpose at least, Heaven had not seen fit, during the last four or five months, to smile upon her. Superstitious persons might have regarded this fact as a warning. Lady Louisa, however, merely regarded it as an oversight. Now at last, so it appeared to her, Heaven had awakened to a consciousness of its delinquencies, with the satisfactory

18

result that her own commendable patience touched on reasonable hope of reward. And this was the more agreeable and comforting to her because the Quayle family affairs were not, it must be owned, at their brightest and best just at present. Clouds lowered on the family horizon. For some weeks she had felt the situation called for effective action on her part. But then, how to act most effectively she knew not. Now the needed opportunity stared her in the face, along with those high ladders and scaffolding poles surrounding the Calmady mansion. She decided, there and then, to take the field; but to take it discreetly, to effect a turning movement, not attempt a front attack.

So, on her return to Albert Gate, after the completion of her morning shopping, she employed the half-hour before luncheon in writing an affectionate, sisterly letter to Ludovic Quayle. That accomplished, young gentleman happened, as she was aware, to be staying at Brockhurst. She asked his opinion—in confidence —on the present very uncomfortable condition of the family fortunes, declaring how implicitly she trusted his good sense and respected his judgment. Then, passing adroitly to less burning questions, she ended thus—

"Pray let Lady Calmady know how really *delighted everybody* is to hear she and Sir Richard will be up this season. I do trust, as I am such a near neighbour, that if there is *anything* I can do for her, either now, or later when they are settling, she will not hesitate to let me know. It would be such a *sincere* pleasure to me. Mr. Barking is too busy with tiresome, parliamentary committees to be able to allow himself more than a week at Easter. I should be *thankful* for a longer rest, for I am feeling dreadfully fagged. But you know how conscientious he always is; and of course one *must* pay a certain price for the confidence the leaders of one's party repose in one. So do tell Lady Calmady we are *quite sure* to be back immediately after Easter."

Reading which sentences Mr. Quayle permitted himself a fine smile on more than one count.

"Louisa reminds me of the sweet little poem of 'Bruce and the Spider,'" he said to himself. "She displays heroic persistence. Her methods are a trifle crude though. To provoke statements by making them is but a primitive form of diplomacy. Yet why be hard upon Louisa? Like my poor, dear father, she, more often than not, means well."

It followed that some few days later, on his return to Whitney, Ludovic indited a voluminous letter to his sister, in his very best style.—"It is rather a waste," he reflected regretfully. "She will miss the neatest points. The happiest turns of phrase will be lost upon Louisa!" To recoup himself for which subjective loss the young man amused himself by giving a very alarmist account of certain matters, though he was constrained to admit the pleasing fact that Sir Richard and Lady Calmady really had it in contemplation to go up to town somewhere about Easter.

And, truth to tell, the main subject of Mr. Quayle's letter could hardly be otherwise than disquieting, for it was undeniable that Lord Shotover's debts were causing both himself and others serious embarrassment at this period. There was nothing new in this, that young nobleman's indebtedness being a permanent factor in his family's financial situation. This spring his indebtedness had passed from the chronic to the acute stage, that was all; with the consequence that it became evident Lord Shotover's debts must be paid, or his relations must submit to the annoyance of seeing him pass through the Bankruptcy Court. Which of these objectionable alternatives was least objectionable Lord Fallowfeild still stood in doubt, when, in obedience to the parental summons, the young man reached Whitney. Lord Fallowfeild had whipped himself up into a laudable heat of righteous indignation before the arrival of the prodigal. Yet he contrived to be out when the dog-cart conveying the said prodigal, and Mr. Decies, of the 101st Lancers—a friend of Guy Quayle, home on leave from India, whence he brought news of his fellow-subaltern—actually drove up to the door. When, pushed thereto by an accusing conscience, he did at last come in, Lord Fallowfeild easily persuaded himself that there really was not time before dinner for the momentous conversation. Moreover, being very full of the milk of human kindness, he found it infinitely more agreeable to hear the praises of the absent son, Guy, than to fall foul of the present son, Shotover. So that it was not till quite late that night, by which time he was slightly sleepy, while his anger had sensibly evaporated, that the interview did actually take place.

"Now then, Shotover, march off to the place of execution," Ludovic Quayle said sweetly, as he picked up his bedroom candlestick. "It was a deep and subtle thought that of bringing down Decies. Only, query, did you think of it, or was it just a bit of your usual luck?"

Lord Shotover smiled rather ruefully upon his prosperous, and, it may be added, slightly parsimonious, younger brother.

"Well, I don't deny it did occur to me it might work," he

admitted. "And after all, you know, one mercy is there's no real vice about his dear old lordship."

Lord Fallowfeild fidgeted about the library, his expression that of a well-nourished and healthy, but rather fretful infant.

"Oh! ah!—well—so here you are, Shotover," he said. "Unpleasant business this of yours—uncommonly disagreeable business for both of us."

"Deucèd unpleasant business," the younger man echoed heartily. He closely resembled his father in looks, save that he was clean shaven and of a lighter build. Both father and son had the same slight lisp in speaking.—"Deucèd unpleasant," he repeated. "Nobody can feel that more than I do."

"Can't they though?" said Lord Fallowfeild, with a charmingly innocent air of surprise. "There, sit down, Shotover, won't you? It's a painful thing to do, but we've got to talk it over, I suppose."

"Well, of course, if you're kind enough to give me the time, you know,—that's rather what I came down here for."

"So you did though," the elder man returned, brightening as though making an illuminating discovery. Then, fearing he was forgetting his part and becoming amiable too rapidly, he made a gallant effort to whip up his somnolent indignation. "It's very distressing to me to put it so plainly, but in my opinion it's a disgraceful business."

"Oh! I give you my word I know it," Lord Shotover replied, with most disarming candour. His father affected, with difficulty, not to hear the remark.

"It doesn't do for a man in your position to be owing money all over the country. It brings the aristocracy into contempt with the shop-keeping class. They're always on the lookout for the shortcomings of their superiors, those people. And they do pay their debts, you see."

"They've always got such a thundering lot of money," Lord Shotover put in. "Don't know how they'd contrive to spend it unless they did pay their debts."

"Oh! ah!—yes"— His father hesitated. It struck him Shotover was a reasonable fellow, very reasonable, and he took the whole matter in a very proper spirit. In short, it was not easy to blow up Shotover. Lord Fallowfeild thrust his hands far down into his trouser pockets and turned sideways in the great, leather-covered chair.

"I'm not narrow-minded or prejudiced," he began. "I always have kept on civil terms with those sort of people and always will. Courtesy is an obligation on the part of a gentleman and a Christian. I'd as soon be rude to my tailor as eat with my knife. But a man must respect his own rank or others won't respect it, especially in these nasty, radical, levelling times. You must stand by your class. There's a vulgar proverb about the bird that fouls its own nest, you know. Well, I never did that. I've always stood by my own class. Helped my poor brother Archibald—you can't remember him—weren't born at the time —to run away with Lady Jane Bateman. Low, common fellow Bateman. I never liked Bateman. She left Ludovic all that money, you know "—

"Wish to goodness she'd left it to me," murmured Lord Shotover.

"Eh?" inquired his father. Then he fell into a moralising vein. "Nasty, disreputable things elopements. I never did approve of elopements. Leave other men's wives alone, Shotover."

The younger man's mouth worked a little.

"The nuisance is sometimes they won't leave you alone."

Lord Fallowfeild gazed at him a moment, very genially.

"Oh! ah!—well—I suppose they won't," he said, and he chuckled. "Anyhow I stood by your poor uncle Archibald. He was my brother of course, and she was a second cousin of your mother's, so I felt bound to. And I saw them across the Channel and into the Paris train. Dreadfully bad crossing that night I remember, no private cabins to be had, and Lady Jane was dreadfully ill. Never take your wife to sea on your honey moon, Shotover. It's too great a risk. That business cost me a lot of money one way and another, and let me in for a most painful scene with Bateman afterwards. But, as I say, you're bound to stand by your own class. That'll be my only reason for helping you, you understand, Shotover, if I do help you."

"And I am sure I hope you will."—The young man rose and stood with his back to the fire and his hands under his coat-tails. He stooped a little, looking down pensively at the hearth-rug between his feet. His clothes—not yet paid for, or likely to be— claimed admiration, so did the length of his legs and the neatness of his narrow hips.

"I can only assure you I shall be most awfully grateful if you do help me," he said quietly. "I don't pretend to deserve it— but that doesn't lessen gratitude—rather the other way, don't you know. I shall never forget it."

"Won't you though?"

And for the life of him Lord Fallowfeild could not help beaming upon this handsome prodigal.—"Uncommonly high-bred looking fellow, Shotover," he said to himself. "Don't wonder women run after him. Uncommonly high-bred, and shows very nice feeling too."

And then the kindly and simple gentleman drew himself up with a mental jerk, remembering that he was there to curse rather than to bless. He fidgeted violently.

"Not that I have actually made up my mind to help you yet," he went on. "I am very much inclined to cast you adrift. It distresses me to put it to you so plainly, but you are disgracefully extravagant, you know, Shotover."

"Oh! I know," the young man admitted.

"You're a selfish fellow."—Lord Fallowfeild became relentless. "Yes, it's extremely painful to me to say it to you, but you are downright selfish. And that, in the long-run, comes uncommonly hard on your sisters. Good girls, your sisters. Never given your mother or me any trouble, your sisters. But money has to come from somewhere, and each time I pay your debts I have to cut down your sisters' portions."

"Yes, I know, and that's what's made me so infernally unwilling to come to you about my affairs," Lord Shotover said, in tones of perfectly genuine regret.

"Is it though?" his father commented.—"Good fellow at heart," he added to himself. "Displays very proper feeling. Always was a good-hearted fellow."

"I can only tell you I've been awfully wretched about it for the last three months."

"Have you though?" said Lord Fallowfeild, with sympathy.

"I got just about as low as I well could. I felt I was nothing but a nuisance and encumbrance. It was beastly to think of fleecing the girls, don't you know. I came precious near cutting my throat—only that seemed rather a dirty way of getting out of it all."

"So it is — poor boy — quite right. Nasty mean way of shirking your responsibilities. Quite agree with you. I have never had any opinion of a man who cut his throat. Never mention such a thing, Shotover." He blew his nose resonantly.—"Never talk of such a thing," he repeated. "And —poor boy—I—I'll pay your debts. Only I tell you this really is the last time. There must be no misunderstanding about that. You must reform, Shotover, if it's only on account of your sisters. I don't want to take an unfair advantage of you in alluding to your sisters. Only you must understand clearly this is the last time. You see it's becoming too frequent. I don't want to press the case unduly against you, but you recollect—I'm sure you do—

I paid your debts in fifty-eight, and again in sixty-two, or sixty-three, was it? Yes, it must have been sixty-three, because that was the year my poor friend Tom Henniker died. Good fellow Henniker—I missed Henniker. And they wanted me to take over the hounds. Nice fellow in the hunting-field, Henniker. Never saw him lose his temper but once, and that was when Image rode over the hounds on the edge of Talepenny Wood."

"Rather coarse sort of brute, Image," put in Lord Shotover.

"And Henniker had such an excellent manner with the farmers, genial and cheery, very cheery at times and yet without any loss of dignity. Great test of a man's breeding that, being cheery without loss of dignity. Now my poor friend, Henniker —oh! ah! yes, where was I though? Your debts now, Shotover. Yes, it must have been sixty-three, because they all wanted me to succeed him as master, and I had to tell them I could not afford it, so it must have been just after I cleared you."

He looked at his erring son with the most engaging air of appeal and remonstrance.

"Really it won't do, Shotover," he repeated. "You must reform. It's becoming too frequent. You'd better travel for a time. That's the proper thing for a man in your position to do when he's in low water. Not scuttle, of course. I wouldn't on any account have you scuttle. But, three weeks or a month hence when things are getting into shape, just travel for a time. I'll arrange it all for you. Only never talk of cutting your throat again. And you quite understand this is positively the last time. I am very much in earnest, my dear boy, nothing will move me. This settlement is final. And we'll just run up quietly to town to-morrow and have a talk with my lawyers, Fox and Goteway. Very civil and accommodating fellow, Goteway—he may be able to make some suggestions. Very nice, confidential-mannered person, Goteway. Knows how to hold his tongue and doesn't ask unnecessary questions—useful man, Goteway"—

Which things coming to the knowledge of Lady Louisa Barking moved her at once to wrath, and to deepened conviction that the moment for decisive action had arrived. It appeared to her that her father had put himself out of court. His weakness regarding his eldest son had practically delivered him into her hand. She congratulated herself upon the good which is thus beneficently permitted to spring out of evil. Yet while recognising that a just Providence sometimes, at all events, over-rules human folly to the production of happy results, she was by no means disposed to spare the mortal whose individual

foolishness had given the divine wisdom its opportunity. Therefore when, some few days later, Lord Fallowfeild called on her,
after a third or fourth interview with Messrs. Fox and Goteway—
beaming, expansive, from the sense of a merciful action accomplished—she received him in a distinctly repressive manner. The
great, white and gold drawing-rooms in Albert Gate were not more
frigid or unbending than the bearing of their mistress as she
suffered her father's embrace. And that amiable nobleman,
notwithstanding his large frame and exalted social position, felt
himself shiver inwardly in the presence of his daughter, even as
he could remember shivering when, as a small schoolboy, he had
been summoned to the dread presence of the headmaster.

"Very good rooms these of yours, Louisa," he began hastily.
"Always have admired these rooms. Capital space for entertaining. Barking was quite right to secure the house as soon as
it was in the market. I told him at the time he would never
regret it."

Lady Louisa did not answer, but called after the retreating
footman, who had just brought in a stately and limited tea-tray,
much silver and little food :—"I am not at home, William."

Then, as she put small and accurate measures of tea into a
massive teapot, she added severely :—"What is all this I hear
about Shotover, papa?"

"Oh! ah! yes—poor Shotover. Came up to town together
again to-day. Good-hearted fellow, your brother Shotover, but
thoughtless. However, I have had a most satisfactory talk with
my men of business, Fox and Goteway. I know Barking does
not think much of Fox and Goteway. Wanted me to go to his
own lawyers, Hodges and Banquet. But if anyone serves you
conscientiously you should not leave them. It's against my
principles to turn off those who serve me conscientiously. I told
Barking so at the time, I remember. It came out of the
business about your settlements, wasn't it—or the last time I
paid Shotover's"— He cleared his throat hurriedly. "I see the
Calmadys' house is being done up," he continued. "Nice
young fellow, Calmady. But I never can help feeling a certain
awkwardness with him. Takes you up rather short in conversation too sometimes. Terribly distressing thing his deformity
and all that, both for himself and Lady Calmady. Hope, perhaps,
she doesn't feel it as some women would though—tactful woman,
Lady Calmady, and very good woman of business. Still, never
feel quite at my ease with Lady Calmady. Can't help wondering
how they'll do in London, you know. Rather difficult thing his
going about much with that "—

Lady Louisa held out a small teacup. Her high penetrating voice asserted itself resolutely against her father's kindly, stumbling chatter, as she asked :—

"Is it true you are not coming up from Whitney this season?"

"Oh!—tea—yes, thank you very much, my dear. No—well, I think possibly we may not come up this year. Goteway believes he has heard of a very eligible tenant for the Belgrave Square house, very eligible. And so, nothing actually decided yet, but I think very possibly we may not come up."

He spoke apologetically, regarding his daughter, over the small teacup, with an expression of entreaty. Every feature of his handsome, innocent countenance begged her not to deal harshly with him. But Lady Louisa remained obdurate.

"Shotover's conduct is becoming a positive scandal," she said.

"Not conduct, my dear—no, not conduct, only money," protested Lord Fallowfeild.

"If money is not conduct I really don't know what is," retorted his daughter. "I do not pretend to go in for such fine distinctions. In any case Mr. Barking heard the most shocking rumours at his club the other day."

"Did he though?" ejaculated Lord Fallowfeild.

"He was too considerate to tell me anything very definite, but he felt that, going out and seeing everybody as of course I have to, it was only right I should have some hint of what was being said. Everyone is talking about Shotover. You can imagine how perfectly intolerable it is for me to feel that my brother's debts are being canvassed in this sort of way."

"I am very sorry there should be any gossip," Lord Fallowfeild said humbly. "Nasty thing gossip—lies, too, mostly, all of it. Nasty, low, unprofitable thing gossip."

"And, of course, your all not coming up will give colour to it."

"Will it though? I never thought of that. You always see straight through things, Louisa. You have by far the best head in the family, except Ludovic — uncommonly clever fellow, Ludovic. Wonder if I had better talk it all over with Ludovic? If you and he agree in thinking our not coming up will make more talk, why, if only on Shotover's account, I "—

But this was not in the least the turn which his daughter desired the conversation to take.

"Pray remember you have other children besides Shotover, papa!" she said hastily. "And for everyone's sake run no further risk of impoverishing yourself. It is obvious that you must save where you can. If there is the chance of a good let for the Belgrave Square house, it would be madness to refuse it. And, after all, you do not really care about London. If there are any important debates in the Lords, you can always come up for a night or so. It does not matter about you."

"Oh! doesn't it though?" Lord Fallowfeild put in quite humbly and gently.

"And mama would always rather stay on at Whitney. Only it must not appear as if we were the least uncomfortable at meeting people. I shall make it a point to go everywhere. I shall be dreadfully fagged, of course, but I feel it a duty to all of you to do so. And I should like the girls to go out too. People must not suppose they have no gowns to their backs. Maggie and Emily have had several seasons. I am less worried about them. But Connie must be seen. She is looking extremely pretty."

"Isn't she though?" Lord Fallowfeild chimed in, brightening. The picture of those reportedly gownless backs had depressed him abominably.

"Yes, and she must have every advantage. I have quite decided that. She must come up to me at once. I shall write to mama and point out to her how necessary it is that one of the girls, at least, should be very much *en evidence* this year. And I am most anxious it should be Connie. As I undertake all the fatigue and responsibility I feel I have a right of choice. I will see that she is properly dressed. I undertake everything. Now, papa, if you are going down by the 6.10 train you ought to start. Will you have a hansom?"

Then, as she shook hands with him, and presented an unresponsive cheek to the paternal lips, Lady Louisa clinched the matter.

"I may consider it quite settled, then, about Constance?" she said. "I mentioned it to Mr. Barking yesterday, and we agreed it ought to be done even if it entailed a little inconvenience and expense. It is not right to be indifferent to appearances. The other two girls can come up for a little while later. Alicia must help. Of course there is not much room in that wretched, little Chelsea house of hers, but George Winterbotham can turn out of his dressing-room. Alicia must exert herself for once. And, papa, Connie need not bring a maid. Those country girls from Whitney don't always fit in quite well with the upper servants, and yet there is a difficulty about keeping them out of the housekeeper's room. I will provide a maid for her. I'll write to mama about everything to-morrow.   And, papa, I do beg you will discourage Shotover from coming here, for really I would much rather not see him at present.   Good-bye.   Pray start at once.   You have barely time to get to Waterloo."

And so Lord Fallowfeild started, a little flustered, a little crestfallen, on his homeward journey.

"Able woman, Louisa," he said to himself.   "Uncommonly clear-sighted woman, Louisa.   But a trifle hard.   Wonder if Barking ever feels that, now?   Not very sensitive man, Barking, though.   Suppose that hardness in Louisa comes of her having no children.   Always plenty of children in our family—except my poor brother Archibald and Lady Jane, they had no children. Yet somebody told me she'd had one by Bateman, which died. Never understood about that.   Capital thing for Ludovic she never did have any by Archibald.   But it's always curious to me Louisa should have no children.   Shouldn't have expected that somehow of Barking and Louisa.   Sets her more free, of course, in regard to her sisters.   Very thoughtful for her sisters, Louisa. I suppose she must have Connie.   Nuisance all this gossip about Shotover.   Pretty child, Connie—best looking of the lot.   People say she's like me.—Wonderfully pretty child, Connie.   That young fellow Decies thinks so too, or I'm very much mistaken. Very much attracted by Connie.   Fine young fellow, Decies— comfort to hear of Guy from him.   Suppose she must go up to Louisa?   Gentleman-like fellow, Decies.   I shouldn't care to part with Connie "—

And then, his reflections becoming increasingly interjectional as the train trundled away south-westward, Lord Fallowfeild leaned back in the corner of the railway carriage and fell very fast asleep.

CHAPTER II

TELLING HOW VANITY FAIR MADE ACQUAINTANCE WITH
RICHARD CALMADY

THERE was no refusing belief to the fact.   The old, cloistered life at Brockhurst, for good or evil, was broken up. Katherine Calmady recognised that another stage had been reached on the relentless journey, that new prospects opened, new horizons invited her anxious gaze.   She recognised also that all which had been was dead, according to its existing form, and should receive burial, silent, somewhat sorrowful, yet not without hope of eventual resurrection in regard to the nobler part of it.   The fair coloured petals of the flower fall away from the maturing fruit, the fruit rots to set free the seed.   Yet the vital principle remains, life lives on, though the material clothing of it change.   And, therefore, Katherine—an upspringing of patience and chastened fortitude within her, the result of her reconciliation to the Divine Light and resignation of herself to its indwelling—set herself, not to arrest the falling of the flower, but to help the ripening of the seed.   If the old garments were out of date, too strait and narrow for her child's growth, then let others be found him.   She did not wait to have him ask, she offered, and that without hint of reproach or of unwillingness.

Yet so to offer cost her not a little.   For it was by no means easy to sink her natural pride, and go forth smiling with this son of hers, at once beautiful and hideous in person, for all the world to see.   Something of personal heroism is demanded of whoso prescribes heroic remedies, if those remedies are to succeed.   At night, alone in the darkness, Katherine, suddenly awaking, would be haunted by perception of the curious glances, and curious comments, which must of necessity attend Richard through all the brilliant pageant of the London season.   How would he bear it?   And then—self-distrust laying fearful hands upon her—how would she bear it, also?   Would her late acquired serenity of soul depart, her faith in the gracious purposes of Almighty God suffer eclipse?   Would she fall back into her former condition of black anger and revolt?   She prayed not.   So long as these evils did not descend upon her, she could bear the rest well enough.   For, could she but keep her faith, Katherine was beginning to regard all other suffering which might be in store for her as a negligible quantity.   With her healthy body, and wholesome memories of a great and perfect human love, it was almost impossible that she should adopt a morbid and self-torturing attitude.   Yet any religious ideal, worth the name, will always have in it an ascetic element.   And that element was so far present with her that personal suffering had come to bear a not wholly unlovely aspect.   She had ceased to gird against it.   So long as Richard was amused and fairly content, so long as the evil which had been abroad in Brockhurst House, that stormy autumn night, could be frustrated, and the estrangement between herself and Richard,—unacknowledged, yet sensibly present,—which that evil had begotten, might be lessened, she cared little what sacrifices she made, what fatigue, exertion, even pain, she might be called on to endure.   An enthusiasm of self-surrender animated her.

During the last five months, slowly and with stumbling feet, yet very surely, she had carried her life and the burden of it up to a higher plane. And, from that more elevated standpoint, she saw both past events and existing relationships in perspective, according to their just and permanent values. Only one object, one person, refused to range itself, and stood out from the otherwise calm, if pensive, landscape as a threatening danger, a monument of things wicked and fearful. Katherine tried to turn her eyes from that object, for it provoked in her a great hatred, a burning indignation, sadly at variance with the saintly ideals which had so captivated her mind and heart. Katherine remained—always would remain, happily for others—very much a woman. And, as woman and mother, she could not but hate that other woman who had, as she feared, come very near seducing her son.

Therefore very various causes combined to reconcile her to the coming adventure. Indeed she set forth on it with so cheerful a countenance, that Richard, while charmed, was also a trifle surprised by the alacrity with which she embraced it. He regarded her somewhat critically, questioning whether his mother was of a more worldly and light-minded disposition than he had heretofore supposed.

There had been some talk of Julius March joining the contemplated exodus. But he had declined, smiling rather sadly.

"No, no," he said. "To go would be a mistake and a weakly selfish one on my part. I have long ceased to be a man of cities, and am best employed, and indeed am most at my ease, herding my few sheep here in the wilderness. I am part and parcel of just all that, which we have agreed it is wise you shall leave behind you for a while. My presence would lessen the thoroughness of the change of scene and of thought. You take up a way of life which was familiar to you years ago. The habits of it will soon come back. I have never known them. I should be a hindrance, rather than a help. No, I will wait and keep the lamps burning before the altar, and the fire burning upon the hearth until—and, please God, it may be in peace, crowned with good fortune—you both come back."

But the adventure, fairly embarked on, displayed quite other characteristics—as is the way with such skittish folk—than Katherine had anticipated. Against possibilities of mortification, against possibilities of covert laughter and the pointing fingers of the crowd, she had steeled herself. But it had not occurred to her that both Richard's trial and her own might take the form of an exuberant and slightly vulgar popularity ; and that, far from being shoved aside into the gutter, the young man might be hoisted, with general acclamation, on to the very throne of Vanity Fair.

The Brockhurst establishment moved up to town at the beginning of April. And by the end of the month, Sir Richard Calmady, his wealth, his house, his horses, his dinners, his mother's gracious beauty, and a certain mystery which surrounded him, came to be in everyone's mouth. A new star had arisen in the social firmament, and all and sundry gathered to observe the reported brightness of its shining. Rich, young, good-looking, well-connected, and strangely unfortunate, here indeed was a novel and telling attraction among the somewhat fly-blown shows of Vanity Fair! Many-tongued rumour was busy with Dickie's name, his possessions and personality. The legend of the man— a thing often so very other than the man himself—grew, Jonah's gourd-like, in wild luxuriance. All those many persons who had known Lady Calmady before her retirement from the world, hastened to renew acquaintance with her. While a larger, and it may be added less distinguished, section of society, greedy of intimacy with whoso or whatsoever might represent the fashion of the hour, crowded upon their heels. Invitations showered down thick as snowflakes in January. To *get* Sir Richard and Lady Calmady was to secure the success of your entertainment, whatever that entertainment might be—to secure it the more certainly because the two persons in question exercised a rather severe process of selection, and were by no means to be had for the asking.

All these things Ludovic Quayle noted, in a spirit which he flattered himself was cynical, but which was, in point of fact, rather anxiously affectionate. It had occurred to him that this sudden and unlooked-for popularity might turn Richard's head a little, and develop in him a morbid self-love, that *vanité de monstre* not uncommon to persons disgraced by nature. He had feared Richard might begin to plume himself—as is the way of such persons—less upon the charming qualities and gifts which he possessed in common with many other charming persons, than upon those deplorable peculiarities which differentiated him from them. And it was with a sincerity of relief, of which he felt a trifle ashamed, that, as time went on, Mr. Quayle found himself unable to trace any such tendency, that he observed his friend's wholesome pride and carefulness to avoid all exposure of his deformity. Richard would drive anywhere, and to any festivity, where driving was possible. He would go to the theatre and opera. He would dine at a few houses, and entertain largely at

his own house.   But he would not put foot to ground in
the presence of the many women who courted him, or in that of
the many men who treated him with rather embarrassed kindness
and civility to his face and spoke of him with pitying reserve
behind his back.

Other persons, besides Mr. Quayle, watched Richard Calmady's
social successes with interest.   Among them was Honoria St.
Quentin.   That young lady had been spending some weeks with
Sir Reginald and Lady Aldham in Midlandshire, and had now
accompanied them up to town.   Lady Aldham's health was
indifferent, confining her often for days together to the sofa and
a darkened room.   Her husband, meanwhile, possessed a craving
for agreeable feminine society, liable to be gratified in a somewhat
errant manner abroad, unless gratified in a discreet manner at
home.   So Honoria had taken over the duty, for friendship's
sake, of keeping the well-favoured, middle-aged gentleman
innocently amused.   To Honoria, at this period, no experience came amiss.   For the past three years, since the death of
her god-mother, Lady Tobermory, and her resultant access of
fortune, she had wandered from place to place, seeing life, now
in stately English country-houses, now among the overtaxed,
under-fed women-workers of Whitechapel and Soho, now in
some obscure Italian village among the folds of the purple
Apennines.   Now she would patronise a middle-class British
lodging-house, along with some girl friend richer in talent than
in pence, in some seaside town.   Now she would fancy the
stringent etiquette of a British embassy at foreign court or
capital.   Honoria was nothing if not various.   But, amid all
mutations of occupation and of place, her fearlessness, her lazy
grace, her serious soul, her gallant bearing, her loyalty to the
oppressed, remained the same.   "Chaste and fair" as Artemis,
experimental as the Comte de St. Simon himself, Honoria
roamed the world — fascinating yet never quite fascinated,
enthusiastic yet evasive, seeking earnestly to live, yet too self-
centred as yet to be able to recognise in what, after all, consists
the heart of living.

She and Mr. Quayle had met at Aldham Revel during the
past winter.   She attracted, while slightly confusing, that accomplished young gentleman—confusing his judgment, well understood, since Mr. Quayle himself was incapable of confusion.
Her views of men and things struck him as distinctly original.
Her attitude of mind appeared unconventional, yet deeply rooted
prejudices declared themselves where he would least have anticipated their existence.   And so it became a favourite pastime of

Mr. Quayle's to present to her cases of conscience, of conduct, of manners or morals—usually those of a common acquaintance—for discussion, that he might observe her verdict. He imagined this a scientific, psychologic exercise. He desired, so he supposed, to gratify his own superior, masculine intelligence, by noting the aberrations, and arriving at the rationale, of her thought. From which it may be suspected that even Ludovic Quayle had his hours of innocent self-deception. Be that, however, as it may, certain it is that in pursuit of this pastime he one day presented to her the peculiar case of Richard Calmady for discussion, and that, not without momentous, though indirect, result.

It happened thus. One noon in May, Ludovic had the happiness of finding himself seated beside Miss St. Quentin in the Park, watching the endless string of passing carriages and the brilliant crowd on foot. Sir Reginald Aldham had left his green chair—placed on the far side of the young lady's—and leaned on the railings talking to some acquaintance.

"A gay maturity," Ludovic remarked with his air of patronage, indicating the elder gentleman's shapely back. "The term 'old boy' has, alas, declined upon the vernacular and been put to base uses of jocosity, so it is a forbidden one. Else, in the present instance, how applicable, how descriptive a term! Should we, I wonder, give thanks for it, Miss St. Quentin, that the men of my generation will mature according to a quite other pattern?"

"Will not ripen, but sour?" Honoria asked maliciously. Her companion's invincible self-complacency frequently amused her. Then she added :—"But, you know, I'm very fond of him. It isn't altogether easy to keep straight as a young boy, is it? Depend upon it, it is ten times more difficult to keep straight as an old one. For a man of that temperament it can't be very plain sailing between fifty and sixty."

Mr. Quayle looked at her in gentle inquiry, his long neck directed forward, his chin slightly raised.

"Sailing? The yacht is?"—

"The yacht is laid up at Cowes. And you understand perfectly well what I mean," Honoria replied, somewhat loftily. Her delicate face straightened with an expression of sensitive pride. But her anger was shortlived. She speedily forgave him. The sunshine and fresh air, the radiant green of the young leaves, the rather superb spectacle of wealth, vigour, beauty, presented to her by the brilliant London world in the brilliant summer noon, was exhilarating, tending to lightness of heart. There was poetry of an opulent, resonant sort in the brave show. Just then a company of Life Guards clattered by, in splendour of white and scarlet and shining helmets. The rattle of accoutrements, and thud of the hoofs of their trotting horses, detached itself arrestingly from the surrounding murmur of many voices and ceaseless roar of the traffic at Hyde Park Corner. A light came into Honoria's eyes. It was good to be alive on such a day! Moreover, in her own purely platonic fashion, she really entertained a very great liking for the young man seated at her side.

"You have missed your vocation," she said, while her eyes narrowed and her upper lip shortened into a delightful smile. "You were born to be a schoolmaster, a veritable pedagogue and terror of illiterate youth. You love to correct. And my rather sketchy English gives you an opportunity of which I observe you are by no means slow to take advantage. You care infinitely more for the manner of saying, than for the thing said. Whereas I"— she broke off abruptly, and her face straightened, became serious, almost severe, again. "Do you see who Sir Reginald is speaking to?" she added. "There are the Calmadys."

A break had come in the loitering procession of correctly clothed men and gaily clothed women, of tall hats and many coloured parasols; and, in the space thus afforded, the Brock-hurst mail-phaeton became apparent drawn up against the railings. The horses, a noticeably fine and well-matched pair of browns, were restless, notwithstanding the groom at their heads. Foam whitened the rings of their bits, and falling flakes of it dabbled their chests. Lady Calmady leaned sideways over the leather folds of the hood, answering some inquiry of Sir Reginald, who, hat in hand, looked up at her. She wore a close-fitting, grey, velvet coat, which revealed the proportions of her full, but still youthful figure. The air and sunshine had given her an unusual brightness of complexion, so that in face as well as in figure, youth still, in a sensible measure, claimed her. She turned her head, appealing, as it seemed, to Richard, and the nimble breeze playing caressingly with the soft white laces and grey plumes of her bonnet added thereby somehow to the effect of glad and gracious content pervading her aspect. Richard looked round and down at her, half laughing. Unquestionably he was victoriously handsome, seen thus, uplifted above the throng, handling his fine horses, all trace of bodily disfigure-ment concealed, a touch of old-world courtliness and tender respect in his manner as he addressed his mother.

19

Ludovic Quayle watched the little scene with close attention. Then, as the ranks of the smart procession closed up again, hiding the carriage and its occupants from sight, he leaned back with a movement of quiet satisfaction and turned to his companion. Miss St. Quentin sat round in her chair, presenting her slender, dust-coloured, lace-and-silk-clad person in profile to the passers-by, and so tilting her parasol as to defy recognition. The expression of her pale face and singular eyes was far from encouraging.

"Indeed—and why?" Ludovic permitted himself to remark, in tones of polite inquiry. "I had been led to believe that you and Lady Calmady were on terms of rather warm friendship."

"We are," Honoria answered, "that is, at Brockhurst."

"Forgive my indiscretion—but why not in London?"

The young lady looked full at him.

"Mr. Quayle," she asked, "is it true that you are responsible for this new departure of theirs, for their coming up, I mean?"

"Responsible? You do me too great an honour. Who am I that I should direct the action of my brother man? But Lady Calmady is good enough to trust me a little, and I own that I advocated a modification of the existing *régime*." — Ludovic crossed his long legs and fell to nursing one knee. "It is no breach of confidence to tell you — since you know the fact already — that fate decreed an alien element should obtrude itself into the situation at Brockhurst last autumn. I need name no names, I think?"

Honoria's head was raised. She regarded him steadfastly, but made no sign.

"Ah! I need not name names," he repeated; "I thought not. Well, after the alien element removed itself—the two facts may have no connection—Lady Calmady very certainly never implied that they had—but, as I remarked, after the alien element removed itself, it was observable that our poor, dear Dickie Calmady became a trifle difficult, a trifle distrait, in plain English most remarkably grumpy and far from delightful to live with. And his mother"—

"It's too bad, altogether too bad!" broke out Honoria hotly.

"Too bad of whom?" Mr. Quayle asked, with the utmost suavity. "Of the nameless, obtrusive, alien element, or of poor, dear Dick?"

The young lady closed her parasol slowly, and, turning, faced the sauntering crowd again.

"Of Sir Richard Calmady, of course," she said.

Her companion did not answer immediately. His eyes

pursued a receding carriage far down the string, amid the gaily shifting sunshine and shadow, and the fluttering lace and grey feathers of a woman's bonnet. When he spoke, at last, it was with an unusual trace of feeling.

"After all, you know, there are a good many excuses for Richard Calmady."

"If it comes to that there are a good many excuses for Helen de Vallorbes," Honoria put in quickly.

"For? For?" the young man repeated, relaxing into the blandest of smiles. "Yes, thanks—I see I was right. It was unnecessary to name names.—Oh! undoubtedly, innumerable excuses, and of the most valid description, were they needed— were they not swallowed up in the single, self-evident excuse that the lady you mention is a supremely clever and captivating person."

"You think so?" said Honoria.

"Think so? Show me the man so indifferent to his reputation for taste that he could venture to think otherwise!"

"Still she should have left him alone."—Honoria's indolent, reflective speech took on a peculiar intonation, and she pressed her long-fingered hands together, as though controlling a shudder. "I—I'm ashamed to confess it, I do not like him. But, as I told you, just on that account"—

"Pardon me, on what account?"

Miss St. Quentin was quick to resent impertinence, and now momentarily anger struggled with her natural sincerity. But the latter conquered. Again she forgave Mr. Quayle. Yet a dull flush spread itself over her pale skin, and he perceived that she was distinctly moved. This piqued his curiosity.

"I know I'm awfully foolish about some things," she said. "I can't bear to speak of them. I dread seeing them. The sight of them takes the warmth out of the sunshine."

Again Ludovic fell to nursing his knee.—What an amazing invention is the feminine mind! What endless entertainment is derivable from striving to follow its tergiversations!

"And you saw that which takes the warmth out of the sunshine just now?" he said. "Ah! well — alas, for Dickie Calmady!"

"Still I can't bear anyone not to play fair. You should only hit a man your own size. I told Helen de Vallorbes so. I'm very, very fond of her, but she ought to have spared him."—She paused a moment. "All the same if I had not promised Lady Aldham to stay on—as she's so poorly—I should have gone out of town when I found the Calmadys had come up."

"Oh! it goes as far as that, does it?" Ludovic murmured.

"I don't like to see them with all these people. The extent to which he is petted and fooled becomes rather horrible."

"Are you not slightly—I ask it with all due deference and humility—just slightly merciless?"

"No, no," the girl answered earnestly. "I don't think I'm that. The women who run after him, and flatter him so outrageously, are really more merciless than I am. I do not pretend to like him—I can't like him, somehow. But I'm growing most tremendously sorry for him. And still more sorry for his mother. She was very grand—a person altogether satisfying to one's imagination and sense of fitness, at home, with that noble house and park and racing-stable for setting. But here, she is shorn of her glory somehow."

The girl rose to her feet with lazy grace.

"She is cheapened. And that's a pity. There are more than enough pretty cheap people among us already.—I must go. There's Sir Reginald looking for me.—If I could be sure Lady Calmady hated it all I should be more reconciled."

"Possibly she does hate it all, only that it presents itself as the least of two evils."

"There is a touch of dancing dogs about it, and that distresses me," Miss St. Quentin continued. "It is Lady Calmady's *rôle* to be apart, separate from and superior to the rest."

"The thing's being done as well as it can be," Mr. Quayle put in mildly.

"It shouldn't be done at all," the girl declared.—"Here I am, Sir Reginald. You want to go on? I'm quite ready."

CHAPTER III

IN WHICH KATHERINE TRIES TO NAIL UP THE WEATHER-GLASS TO "SET FAIR"

IT is to be feared that intimate acquaintance with Lady Calmady's present attitude of mind would not have proved altogether satisfactory to that ardent idealist Honoria St. Quentin. For, unquestionably, as the busy weeks of the London season went forward, Katherine grew increasingly far from "hating it all." At first she had found the varied interests and persons presented to her, the rapid interchange of thought, the constant movement of society, slightly bewildering. But, as Julius March had foretold, old habits reasserted themselves. The great world, and the ways of it, had been familiar to her in her youth. She soon found herself walking in its ways again with ease, and speaking its language with fluency. And this, though in itself of but small moment to her, procured her, indirectly, a happiness as greatly desired as it had been little anticipated.

For to Richard the great world was, as yet, something of an undiscovered country. Going forth into it he felt shy and diffident, though a lively curiosity possessed him. The gentler and more modest elements of his nature came into play. He was sensible of his own inexperience, and turned with instinctive trust and tender respect to her in whom experience was not lacking. He had never, so he told himself, quite understood how fine a lady his mother was, how conspicuous was her charm and distinguished her intelligence. And he clung to her, grown man though he was, even as a child, entering a bright room full of guests, clings to its mother's hand, finding therein much comfort of encouragement and support. He desired she should share all his interests, reckoning nothing worth the doing in which she had not a part. He consulted her before each undertaking, talked and laughed over it with her in private afterwards, thereby unconsciously securing to her halcyon days, a honeymoon of the heart of infinite sweetness, so that she, on her part, thanked God and took courage.

And, indeed, it might very well appear to Katherine that her heroic remedy was on the road to work an effectual cure. The terror of lawless passion and of evil, provoked by that fair woman clothed as with the sea-waves, crowned and shod with gold, whom she had withstood so manfully in spirit in the wild autumn night, departed from her. She began to fear no more. For surely her son was wholly given back to her—his heart still free, his life still innocent? And, not only did this terror depart, but her anguish at his deformity was strangely lessened, the pain of it lulled as by the action of an anodyne. For, witnessing the young man's popularity, seeing him so universally courted and welcomed, observing his manifest power of attraction, she began to ask herself whether she had not exaggerated the misfortune of that same deformity and the impediment that it offered to his career and chances of personal happiness. She had been morbid, hypersensitive. The world evidently saw in his disfigurement no such horror and hopeless bar to success as she had seen. It was therefore a dear world, a world rich in consolation and promise. It smiled upon Richard, and so she smiled upon it, gratefully, trustfully, finding in the plenitude of her thankfulness no wares save honest ones set out for sale in the booths of Vanity Fair. A large hopefulness arose in her. She began to form projects calculated, as she believed, to perpetuate the gladness of the present.

Among other tender customs of Richard's boyhood into which Katherine, at this happy period, drifted back was that of going, now and again, to his room at night, and gossiping with him, for a merry yet somewhat pathetic half-hour, before herself retiring to rest. It fell out that, towards the middle of June, there had been a dinner-party at the Barkings, on a scale of magnificence unusual even in that opulent house. It was not the second, or even the third, time Richard and his mother had dined in Albert Gate. For Lady Louisa had proved the most assiduously attentive of neighbours. Little Lady Constance Quayle was with her. The young girl had brightened notably of late. Her prettiness was enhanced by a timid and appealing playfulness. She had been seized, moreover, with one of those innocent and absorbing devotions towards Lady Calmady that young girls often entertain towards an elder woman, following her about with a sort of dog-like fidelity, and watching her with eyes full of wistful admiration. On the present occasion the guests at the Barking dinner had been politicians of distinction — members of the then existing Government. A contingent of foreign diplomatists from the various embassies had been present, together with various notably smart women. Later there had been a reception, largely attended, and music, the finest that Europe could produce and money could buy.

"Louisa climbs giddy heights," Mr. Quayle had said to himself, with an attempt at irony. But, in point of fact, he was far from displeased, for it appeared to him the house of Barking showed to uncommon advantage to-night.—"Louisa has no staying power in conversation, and her voice is too loud, but in snippets she is rather impressive," he added. "And, oh! how very diligent is Louisa!"

Driving home, Richard kept silence until just as the brougham drew up, then he said abruptly :—

"Tired? No—that's right. Then come and sit with me. I want to talk. I haven't an ounce of sleep in me somehow to-night."

It was hot, and when, some three-quarters of an hour later, Katherine entered the big bedroom on the ground floor the upper sashes of the window were drawn low behind the blinds, letting in the muffled roar of the great city as an undertone to the intermittent sound of footsteps, or the occasional passing of

a belated carriage or cab. It formed an undertone, also, to
Richard's memory of the music to which he had lately listened,
and the delight of which was still in his ears and pulsing in his
blood, making his blue eyes bright and dark and curving his
handsome lips into a very eloquent smile as he lay back against
the piled-up pillows of the bed.

"Good heavens, how divinely Morabita sang," he said,
looking up at his mother as she stood looking down on him,
"better even than in *Faust* last night! I want to hear her
again just as often as I can. Her voice carries one right away,
out of oneself, into regions of pure and unmitigated romance.
All things are possible for the moment. One becomes as the
gods, omnipotent. We've got the box as usual on Saturday,
mother, haven't we? Do you remember if she sings?"

Katherine replied that the great soprano did sing.

"I'm glad," Richard said. "And yet I don't know that it's
particularly wholesome to hear her. After being as the gods,
one descends with rather too much of a run to the level of the
ordinary mortal."—He turned on his elbow restlessly, and the
movement altered the lie of the bedclothes, thereby disclosing the
unsightly disproportion of his person through the light blanket
and sheet.—"And if one's own level happens unfortunately to
be below that of even the ordinary mortal—well—well—don't
you know "—

"My dear!" Katherine put in softly.

Richard lay straight on his back again, and held out his
hand to her.

"Sit down, do," he said. "Turn the big chair round so
that I may see you. I like you in that frilly, white, dressing-
gown thing. Don't be afraid, I'm not going to be a brute and
grumble. You're much too good to me, and I know I am
disgustingly selfish at times. I was this winter, but "—

"The past is past," Katherine put in again very softly.

"Yes, please God, it is," he said,—"in some ways."—He
paused, and then spoke as though with an effort, returning from
some far distance of thought :—"Yes, I like you in that white,
frilly thing. But I liked that new, black gown of yours to-night
too. You looked glorious, do you mind my saying so?
And no woman walks as well as you do. I compared, I
watched. There's nothing more beautiful than seeing a woman
walk really well—or a man either, for that matter."

Then he caught at her hand again, laughing a little.—"No,
I'm not going to grumble," he said. "Upon my word, mother,
I swear I'm not. Here let's talk about your gowns. I should

like to know, shall you never wear anything but grey or black?"

"Never, not even to please you, Dickie."

"Ah, that's so delicious with you!" he exclaimed. "Every now and then you bring one up short, one knocks one's head against a stone wall! There is an indomitable strain in you. I only hope you've transmitted it to me. I'm afraid I need stiffening.—I beg your pardon," he added quickly and courteously, "it strikes me I am becoming slightly impertinent. But that woman's voice has turned my brain and loosed the string of my tongue so that I speak words of unwisdom. You enjoyed her singing too, though, didn't you? I thought so, catching sight of you while it was going on, attended by the faithful Ludovic and little Lady Constance. It's quite touching to see how she worships you. And wasn't Miss St. Quentin with you too? Yes, I thought so. I can't quite make up my mind about Honoria St. Quentin. Sometimes she strikes me as one of the loveliest women here—and she can walk, if you like, it's a joy to see her. And then again, she seems to me altogether too long, and off-hand somehow, and boyish! And then, too,"— Richard moved his head against the white pillows, and stared up at the window, where the blind sucked, with small creaking noises, against the top edge of the open sash, — "she fights shy of me, and personal feeling militates against admiration, you know. I am sorry, for I rather want to talk to her about— oh, well, a whole lot of things. But she avoids me. I never get the opportunity."

"My darling, don't you think that is partly imagination?"

"Perhaps it is," he answered. "I daresay I do indulge in unnecessary fancies about people's manner and so on. I can't very well be off it, you know. And everyone is really very kind to me. Morabita was perfectly charming when I thanked her in very floundering Italian. It's a pity she's so fat. But, never mind, the fat vanishes, to all intents and purposes, when she begins to sing.—And old Barking is as kind as he can be. I feel awfully obliged to him, though his ministrations to-night amounted to being slightly embarrassing. He brought me cabinet ministers and under-secretaries, and gorgeous Germans and Turks, in batches—and even a real live Chinaman with a pig-tail. Mother, do you remember the cabinets at home in the Long Gallery? I used to dream about them. And that Chinaman gave me the queerest feeling to-night. It was idiotic, but—did I ever tell you?—when I was a little chap, I was always dreaming about war or something, from

which I couldn't get away.   Others could, but for me—from
circumstances, don't you know—there was no possibility of
scuttling.   And the little Chinese figures on the black, lacquer
cabinets were mixed up with it.   As I say, it gripped me to-
night in the midst of all those people and— Oh yes ! old Barking
is very kind," he went on, with a change of tone.   "Only I wish
Lady Louisa would warn him he need not trouble himself to
be amusing.   He came and sat by me, towards the end of the
evening, and told me the most inane stories in that inflated
manner of his.   Verily, they were ancient as the hills, and a
weariness to the spirit.   But that good-looking, young fellow,
Decies, swallowed them all down with the devoutest attention
and laughed aloud in all that he conceived to be the right places."

A pause came in Richard's flow of words.   He moved again
restlessly and clasped his hands under his head.   Katherine had
seldom seen him thus excited and feverish.   A sense of alarm
grew on her lest her heroic remedy was, after all, not working
a wholly satisfactory cure.   For there was a violence in his
utterance and in his face, a certain recklessness of speech and
of demeanour, very agitating to her.

"Oh, everyone's kind, awfully kind," he repeated, looking
away at the sucking blind again, "and I'm awfully grateful to
them, but— Oh ! I tell you, that woman's voice has got me and
made me drunk, made me mad drunk.   I almost wish I had
never heard her.   I think I won't go to the opera again.   Emotion
that finds no outlet in action only demoralises one and breaks
up one's philosophy, and she makes me know all that might be,
and is not, and never, never can be.   Good God ! what a
glorious, what an amazing, business I could have made of life
if"— He slipped a little on the pillows, had to unclasp his hands
hastily and press them down on either side him to keep his
body fairly upright in the bed.   His features contracted with
a spasm of anger.—"If I had only had the average chance," he
added harshly.   "If I had only started with the normal equipment."

And, as she listened, the old anguish, lately lulled to rest
in Katherine's heart, arose and cried aloud.   But she sought
resolutely to stifle its crying, strong in faith and hope.

"I know, my dearest, I know," she said pleadingly.   "And
yet, since we have been here, I have thought perhaps we had
a little underrated both your happy gift of pleasing and the
readiness of others to be pleased.   It seems to me, Dickie, all
doors open if you stretch out your hand.   Well, my dear, I
would have you go forward fearlessly.   I would have you more

ambitious, more self-confident. I see and deplore my own cowardly mistake. Instead of hiding you away at home, and keeping you to myself, I ought to have encouraged you to mix in the world and fill the position to which both your powers and your birth entitle you. I was wrong—I lament my folly. But there is ample time in which to rectify my mistake."

Richard's face relaxed.

"I wonder—I wonder," he said.

"I am sure," she replied.

"You are too sanguine," he said. "Your love for me blinds you to fact."

"No, no," she replied again. "Love is the only medium in which vision gains perfect clearness, becomes trustworthy and undistorted."—Instinctively Katherine folded her hands as in prayer, while the brightness of a pure enthusiasm shone in her sweet eyes. "That I have learned beyond all possibility of dispute. It has been given me, through much tribulation, to arrive at that."

Richard smiled upon her tenderly, then, turning his head, remained silent for a while. The sullen roar of the great city invaded the quiet room through the open windows, the heavy regular tread of a policeman on his beat, a shrill whistle hailing a hansom from a house some few doors distant up the square, and then an answering rumble of wheels and clatter of hoofs. Richard's face had grown fierce again, and his breath came quick. He turned on his side, and once more the dwarfed proportions of his person became perceptible. Lady Calmady averted her eyes, fixing them upon his. But even there she found sad lack of comfort, for in them she read the inalienable distress and desolation of one unhandsomely treated by Nature, maimed and incomplete. Even the Divine Light, resident within her, failed to reconcile her to that reading. She shrank back in protest, once again, against the dealing of Almighty God with this only child of hers. And yet—such is the adorable paradox of a living faith—even while shrinking, while protesting, she flung herself for support, for help, upon the very Being who had permitted, in a sense caused, her misery.

"Mother, can I say something to you?" Richard asked, rather hoarsely, at last.

"Anything—in heaven or earth."

"But it is a thing not usually spoken of as I want to speak of it. It may seem indecent. You won't be disgusted, or think me wanting in respect or in modesty?"

"Surely not," Lady Calmady answered quietly, yet a certain

trembling took her, a nervousness as in face of the unknown. This strong, young creature developed forces, presented aspects, in his present feverish mood, with which she felt hardly equal to cope.

"Mother, I—I want to marry."

"I, too, have thought of that," she said.

"You don't consider that I am debarred from marriage?"

"Oh no, no!" Katherine cried, a little sob in her voice.

He looked at her steadily, with those profoundly desolate eyes.

"It would not be wrong? It would not be otherwise than honourable?" he asked.

If doubts arose within Katherine of the answer to that question, she crushed them down passionately.

"No, my dearest, no," she declared. "It would not be wrong—it could not, could not be so—if she loved you, and you loved whomsoever you married."

"But I'm not in love—at least not in love with any person who can become my wife. Yet that does not seem to me to matter very much. I should be faithful, no fear, to anyone who was good enough to marry me. Enough of love would come, if only out of gratitude, towards the woman who would accept me as—as I am—and forgive that—that which cannot be helped."

Again trembling shook Katherine. So terribly much seemed to her at stake just then! Silently she implored that wisdom and clear-seeing might be accorded her. She leaned a little forward and taking his left hand held it closely in both hers.

"Dearest, that is not all. Tell me all," she said, "or I cannot quite follow your thought."

Richard flung his body sideways across the bed, and kissed her hands as they held his. The hot colour rushed over his face and neck, up to the roots of his close-cropped, curly hair. He spoke, lying thus upon his chest, his face half buried in the sheet.

"I want to marry because—because I want a child—I want a son," he said.

No words came to Katherine just then. But she disengaged one hand and laid it upon the dear brown head, and waited in silence until the violence of the young man's emotion had spent itself, until the broad, muscular shoulders had ceased to heave and the strong, young hands to grasp her wrist. Suddenly Richard recovered himself, sat up, rubbing his hands across his eyes, laughing, but with a queer catch in his voice.

"I beg your pardon," he said. "I'm a fool, an awful fool.

Hang Morabita and her voice and the golden houses of the gods, and beastly, showy omnipotence, to which her voice carries one away! To talk sense—mother—just brutal common sense. My fate is fixed, you know. There's no earthly use in wriggling. I am condemned to live a cow's life and die a cow's death.—The pride of life may call, but I can't answer. The great prizes are not for me. I'm too heavily handicapped. I was looking at that young fellow, Decies, to-night, and considering his chances as against my own— Oh! I know there's wealth in plenty. The pasture's green enough to make many a man covet it, and the stall's well bedded-down. I don't complain. Only, mother, you know—I know. Where's the use of denying that which we neither of us ever really forget?—And then sometimes my blood takes fire. It did to-night. And the splendour of living being denied me, I—I—am tempted to say a Black Mass. One must take it out somehow. And I know I could go to the devil as few men have ever gone, magnificently, detestably, with subtleties and refinements of iniquity."

He laughed again a little. And, hearing him, his mother's heart stood still.

"Verily, I have advantages!" he continued. "There should be a picturesqueness in my descent to hell which would go far to place my name at the head of the list of those sinners who have achieved immortality"—

"Richard! Richard!" Lady Calmady cried, "do you want to break my heart quite?"

"No," he answered, simply. "I'd infinitely rather not break your heart. I have no ambition to see my name in that devil's list except as an uncommonly ironical sort of second best. But then we must make some change, some radical change. At times, lately, I've felt as if I was a caged wild beast—blinded, its claws cut, the bars of its cage soldered and riveted, no hope of escape, and yet the vigour, the immense longing for freedom and activity, there all the while."

Richard stretched himself.

"Poor beast, poor beast, poor beast!" he said, shaking his head and smiling. "I tell you I get absurdly sentimental over it at times."

And then, happily, there came a momentary lapse in the entirety of his egoism. He turned on his side, took Lady Calmady's hand again, and fell to playing absently with her bracelets.

"You poor darling, how I torture you!" he said. "And yet, now we've once broken the ice and begun talking of all this, we're bound to talk on to the finish—if finish there is.   You see these few weeks in London—I've enjoyed them—but still they've made me understand, more than ever, all I've missed.   Life calls, mother, do you see?   And though the beast is blind, and his claws are cut, and his cage bolted, yet, when life calls, he must answer—must—or run mad—or die—do you see?"

"And you shall answer, my beloved.   Never fear, you will answer," Katherine replied proudly.

Richard's hand closed hard upon hers.

"Thank you," he said.   "You were made to be a mother of heroes, not of a useless log like me.—And that's just why I want to be good.   And to be good I want a wife, that I may have that boy.   I could keep straight for him, mother, though I'm afraid I can't keep straight for myself, and simply because it's right, much longer.   I want him to have just all that I am denied. I want him to restore the balance, both for you and for me.   I may have something of a career myself, perhaps, in politics or something.   It's possible ; but that will come later, if it comes at all.   And then it would be for his sake.   What I want first is the boy, to give me an object and keep up my pluck, and keep me steady.   I, giving him life, shall find my life in him, be paid for my wretched circumscribed existence by his goodly and complete one.   He may be clever or not—I'd rather, of course, he was not quite a dunce—but I really don't very much mind, so long as he isn't an outrageous fool, if he's only an entirely sound and healthy human animal."

Richard stretched himself upon the bed, straightened the sheet across his chest, and clasped his hands under his head again.   The desolation had gone out of his eyes.   He seemed to look afar into the future, and therein see manly satisfaction and content.   His voice was vibrant, rising to a kind of chant.

"He shall run, and he shall swim, he shall fence, and he shall row," he said.   "He shall learn all gallant sports, as becomes an English gentleman.   And he shall ride,—not as I ride, God forbid ! like a monkey strapped on a dog at a fair, but as a centaur, as a young demi-god.   We will set him, stark naked, on a bare-backed horse, and see that he's clean-limbed, perfect, without spot or blemish, from head to heel."

And once more Katherine Calmady held her peace, some-what amazed, somewhat tremulous, since it seemed to her the young man was drawing a cheque upon the future which might, only too probably, be dishonoured and returned marked "no account."   For who dare say that this child would ever come to the birth, or, coming, what form it would bear?   Yet, even so, she rejoiced in her son and the high spirit he displayed, while the instinct of romance which inspired his speech touched an answering chord in, and uplifted, her.

By now the brief June night was nearly spent. The blind still creaked against the open window sash, but the thud of horse-hoofs and beat of passing footsteps had become infrequent, while the roar of the mighty city had dwindled to a murmur, as of an ebbing tide upon a shallow, sand-strewn beach. The after-light of the sunset, walking the horizon, beneath the Pole star from west to east, broadened upward now towards the zenith. Even here, in the heart of London, the day broke with a spacious solemnity. Richard raised himself, and, sitting up, blew out the candles placed on the table at the bedside.

"Mother," he said, "will you let in the morning?"

Lady Calmady was pale from her long vigil, and her unspoken, yet searching, emotion. She appeared very tall, ghostlike even, in her soft, white raiment, as she moved across and drew up the sucking blind. Above the grey parapets of the houses, and the ranks of contorted chimney-pots, the loveliness of the summer dawn grew wide. Warm amber shaded through gradations of exquisite and nameless colour into blue. While, across this last, lay horizontal lines of fringed, semi-transparent, opalescent cloud. To Katherine those heavenly blue interspaces spoke of peace, of the stilling of all strife, when the tragic, yet superb, human story should at last be fully told and God be all in all. She was very tired. The struggle was so prolonged. Her soul cried out for rest. And then she reminded herself, almost sternly, that the Kingdom of God and the peace of it is no matter of time or of place; but is within the devout believer, ever present, immediate, possessing his or her soul, and by that soul in turn possessed. Just then the sparrows, roosting in the garden of the square, awoke with manifold and vociferous chirping and chattering. The voice from the bed called to her.

"Mother," it said imperatively, "come to me. You are not angry at what I have told you? You understand? You will find her for me?"

Lady Calmady turned away from the open window and the loveliness of the summer dawn. She was less tired somehow. God was with her, so she could not be otherwise than hopeful. Moreover, the world had proved itself very kind towards her son. It would not deny him this last request, surely?

"My dearest, I think I have found her already," Lady Calmady answered.

Yet, even as she spoke, she faltered a little, recognising the energy and strength manifest in the young man's countenance, remembering his late discourse, and the pent-up fires of his nature to which that discourse had borne only too eloquent testimony. For who was a young girl, but just out of the school-room, a girl in pretty, fresh frocks—the last word of contemporary fashion,—whose baby face and slow, wide-eyed gaze bore witness to her entire innocence of the great primitive necessities, the rather brutal joys, the intimate vices, the far-ranging intellectual questionings, which rule and mould the action of mankind,—who was she, indeed, to cope with a nature such as Richard's?

"Mother, tell me, who is it?"

And instinctively Katherine fell to pleading. She sat down beside the bed again and smoothed the sheet.

"You will be tender and loving to her, Dickie?" she said. "For she is young and very gentle, and might easily be made afraid. You will not forget what is due to your wife, to your bride, in your longing for a child?"

"Who is it?" Richard demanded again.

"Ludovic's sister—little Lady Constance Quayle."

He drew in his breath sharply.

"Would she—would her people consent?" he said.

"I think so. Judging by appearances, I am almost sure they would consent."

A long silence followed. Richard lay still, looking at the rosy flush that broadened in the morning sky and touched the bosoms of those delicate clouds with living, pulsating colour. And he flushed too, all his being softened into a great tenderness, a great shyness, a quick yet noble shame. For his whole attitude towards this question of marriage changed strangely as it passed from the abstract, from regions of vague purpose and desire, to the concrete, to the thought of a maiden with name and local habitation, a maiden actual and accessible, whose image he could recall, whose pretty looks and guileless speech he knew.

"I almost wish she was not Ludovic's sister, though," he remarked presently. "It is a great deal to ask."

"You have a great deal to offer," Katherine said, adding:— "You can care for her, Dickie?"

He turned his head, his lips working a little, his flushed face very young and bright.

"Oh yes! I can care fast enough," he said. "And I think —I think I could make her happy. And, you see, already she worships you. We would pet her, mother, and give her all manner of pretty things, and make a little queen of her—and she would be pleased—she's a child, such a child."

Richard remained awake far into the morning, till the rose had died out of the sky, and the ascending smoke of many kitchen-chimneys began to stain the expanse of heavenly blue. The thought of his possible bride was very sweet to him. But when at last sleep came, dreams came likewise. Helen de Vallorbes' perfect face arose, in reproach, before him, and her azure and purple draperies swept over him, stifling and choking him as the salt waves of an angry sea. Then someone—it was the comely, long-limbed, young soldier, Mr. Decies—whom he had seen last night at the Barkings' great party when Morabita sang—and the soprano's matchless voice was mixed up, in the strangest fashion, with all these transactions — lifted Helen and all her magic sea-waves from off him, setting him free. But, even as he did so, Dickie perceived that it was not Helen, after all, whom the young soldier carried in his arms, but little Lady Constance Quayle. Whereupon, waking with a start, Dickie conceived a wholly unreasoning detestation of Mr. Decies ; while, along with that, his purpose of marrying Lady Constance increased notably, waxed strong and grew, putting forth all manner of fair flowers of promise and of hope.

CHAPTER IV

A LESSON UPON THE ELEVENTH COMMANDMENT—" PARENTS OBEY YOUR CHILDREN "

A FAMILY council was in course of holding in the lofty white-and-gold boudoir, overlooking the Park, in Albert Gate. Lady Louisa Barking had summoned it. She had also exercised a measure of selection among intending members. For instance Lady Margaret and Lady Emily—the former having a disposition, in the opinion of her elder sister, to put herself forward and support the good cause with more zeal than discretion, the latter being but a weak-kneed supporter of the cause at best—were summarily dismissed.

"It was really perfectly unnecessary to discuss this sort of thing before the younger girls," she said. "It put them out of their place and rather rubbed the freshness off their minds. And then they would chatter among themselves. And it all became a little foolish and missy. They never knew when to stop."

One member of the Quayle family, and that a leading one, had taken his dismissal before it was given and, with a nice mixture of defective moral-courage and good common-sense, had removed himself bodily from the neighbourhood of the scene of action. Lord Shotover was still in London. Along with the payment of his debts had come a remarkable increase of cheerfulness. He made no more allusions to the unpleasant subject of cutting his throat, while the proposed foreign tour had been relegated to a vague future. It seemed a pity not to see the season out. It would be little short of a crime to miss Goodwood. He might go out with Decies to India in the autumn, when that young soldier's leave had expired, and look Guy up a bit. He would rather like a turn at pig-sticking—and there were plenty of pig, he understood, in the neighbourhood of Agra, where his brother was now stationed. On the morning in question, Lord Shotover, in excellent spirits, had walked down Piccadilly with his father, from his rooms in Jermyn Street to Albert Gate. The elder gentleman, arriving from Westchurch by an early train, had solaced himself with a share of the by no means ascetic breakfast of which his eldest son was partaking at a little after half-past ten. It was very much too good a breakfast for a person in Lord Shotover's existing financial position—so indeed were the rooms—so, in respect of locality, was Jermyn Street itself. Lord Fallowfeild knew this, no man better. Yet he was genuinely pleased, impressed even, by the luxury with which his erring son was surrounded, and proceeded to praise his cook, praise his valet's waiting at table, praise some fine, old, sporting prints upon the wall. He went so far, indeed, as to chuckle discreetly—immaculately faithful husband though he was — over certain photographs of ladies, more fair and kind than wise, which were stuck in the frame of the looking-glass over the chimney-piece. In return for which acts of good-fellowship Lord Shotover accompanied him as far as the steps of the mansion in Albert Gate. There he paused, remarking with the most disarming frankness :—

"I would come in. I want to awfully, I assure you. I quite agree with you about all this affair, you know, and I should uncommonly like to let the others know it. But, between ourselves, Louisa's been so short with me lately, so infernally short—if you'll pardon my saying so—that it's become downright disagreeable to me to run across her. So I'm afraid I might only make matters worse all round, don't you know, if I put in an appearance this morning."

"Has she, though ?" ejaculated Lord Fallowfeild, in reference

presumably to his eldest daughter's reported shortness.   "My
dear boy, don't think of it.   I wouldn't have you exposed to
unnecessary unpleasantness on any account."

Then, as he followed the groom-of-the-chambers up the bare,
white, marble staircase—which struck almost vault-like in its chill
and silence, after the heat and glare and turmoil of the great
thoroughfare without—he added to himself:—

"Good fellow, Shotover.   Has his faults, but upon my word,
when you come to think of it, so have all of us.   Very good-
hearted, sensible fellow at bottom, Shotover.   Always responds
when you talk rationally to him.   No nonsense about him."—
His lordship sighed as he climbed the marble stair.   "Great
comfort to me at times Shotover.   Shows very proper feeling
on the present occasion, but naturally feels a diffidence about
expressing it."

Thus, in the end, it happened that the family council consisted only of the lady of the house, her sister Lady Alicia
Winterbotham, Mr. Ludovic Quayle, and the parent whom all
three of them were, each in their several ways, so perfectly
willing to instruct in his duty towards his children.

Ludovic, perhaps, displayed less alacrity than usual in offering good advice to his father.   His policy was rather that of
masterly inactivity.   Indeed, as the discussion waxed hot—his
sisters' voices rising slightly in tone, while Lord Fallowfeild's
replies disclosed a vein of dogged obstinacy—he withdrew from
the field of battle and moved slowly round the room staring
abstractedly at the pictures.   There was a seductive, female head
by Greuze, a couple of reposeful landscapes by Morland, a little
Constable — waterways, trees, and distant woodland, swept by
wind and weather.   But upon these the young man bestowed
scant attention.   That which fascinated his gaze was a series of
half-length portraits, in oval frames, representing his parents,
himself, his sisters, and brothers.   These portraits were the work
of a lady whose artistic gifts, and whose prices, were alike modest.
They were in coloured chalks, and had, after adorning her own
sitting-room for a number of years, been given, as a wedding
present, by Lady Fallowfeild to her eldest daughter.   Mr. Quayle
reviewed them leisurely now, looking over his shoulder now and
again to note how the tide of battle rolled, and raising his eyebrows in mute protest when the voices of the two ladies became
more than usually elevated.

"You see, papa, you have not been here"— Lady Louisa was
saying.

"No, I haven't," interrupted Lord Fallowfeild.   "And very

much I regret that I haven't. Should have done my best to put a stop to this engagement at the outset—before there was any engagement at all, in fact."

"And so you cannot possibly know how the whole thing—any breaking off I mean—would be regarded."

"Can't I, though?" said Lord Fallowfeild. "I know perfectly well how I should regard it myself."

"You do not take the advantages sufficiently into consideration, papa. Of course with their enormous wealth they can afford to do anything."—Mr. Winterbotham's income was far from princely at this period, and Lady Alicia was liable to be at once envious of, and injured by, the riches of others. Her wardrobe was limited. She was, this morning, vexatiously conscious of a warmer hue in the back pleats than in the front breadth of her mauve, cashmere dress, sparsely decorated with bows of but indifferently white ribbon.—"It has enabled them to make an immense success. One really gets rather tired of hearing about them. But everybody goes to their house, you know, and says that he is perfectly charming."

"Half the parents in London would jump at the chance of one of their girls making such a marriage,"—this from Lady Louisa.

Mr. Quayle looked over his shoulder and registered a conviction that his father did not belong to that active, parental moiety. He sat stubbornly on a straight-backed, white-and-gold chair, his hands clasped on the top of his favourite, gold-headed walking-stick. He had refused to part with this weapon on entering the house. It gave him a sense of authority, of security. Meanwhile his habitually placid and infantile countenance wore an expression of the acutest worry.

"Would they, though?" he said, in response to his daughter's information regarding the jumping moiety.—"Well, I shouldn't. In point of fact, I don't. All that you and Alicia tell me may be perfectly true, my dear Louisa. I would not, for a moment, attempt to discredit your statements. And I don't wish to be intemperate.—Stupid thing intemperance, sign of weakness, intemperance.—Still I must repeat, and I do repeat, I repeat clearly, that I do not approve of this engagement."

"Did I not prophesy long, long ago what my father's attitude would be, Louisa?" Mr. Quayle murmured gently, over his shoulder.

Then he fell to contemplating the portrait of his brother Guy, aged seven, who was represented arrayed in a brown-holland blouse of singular formlessness confined at the waist by

a black leather belt, and carrying, cupid-like, in his hands a bow
and arrows decorated with sky-blue ribbons.—"Were my brothers
and I actually such appallingly insipid-looking little idiots?" he
asked himself. "In that case the years do bring compensations.
We really bear fewer outward traces of utter imbecility now."

"I don't wish to be harsh with you, my dears—never have
been harsh, to my knowledge, with any one of my children.
Believe in kindness. Always have been lenient with my
children"—

"And, as indirect consequence thereof, note my eldest
brother's frequent epistles to the Hebrews!" commented Mr.
Quayle softly. "The sweet simplicity of this counterfeit presentment of him, armed with a pea-green bait-tin and jointless
fishing-rod, hardly shadows forth the copious insolvencies of
recent times!"

"Never have approved of harshness," continued Lord Fallowfeild. "Still I do feel I should have been given an opportunity
of speaking my mind sooner. I ought to have been referred to
in the first place. It was my right. It was due to me. I don't
wish to assert my authority in a tyrannical manner. Hate
tyranny, always have hated parental tyranny. Still I feel that it
was due to me. And Shotover quite agrees with me. Talked
in a very nice, gentlemanly, high-minded way about it all this
morning, did Shotover."

The two ladies exchanged glances, drawing themselves up
with an assumption of reticence and severity.

"Really!" exclaimed Lady Alicia. "It seems a pity, papa,
that Shotover's actions are not a little more in keeping with his
conversation, then."

But Lord Fallowfeild only grasped the head of his walking-
stick the tighter, congratulating himself the while on the un-
shakable firmness both of his mental and physical attitude.

"Oh! ah! yes," he said, rising to heights of quite reckless
defiance. "I know there is a great deal of prejudice against
Shotover, just now, among you. He alluded to it this morning
with a great deal of feeling. He was not bitter, but he is very
much hurt, is Shotover. You are hard on him, Alicia. It is a
painful thing to observe upon, but you are hard, and so is Winterbotham. I regret to be obliged to put it so plainly, but I was
displeased by Winterbotham's tone about your brother, last time
you and he were down at Whitney from Saturday to Monday."

"At all events, papa, George has never cost his parents a
single penny since he left Balliol," Lady Alicia replied, with some
spirit and a very high colour.

But Lord Fallowfeild was not to be beguiled into discussion of side issues, though his amiable face was crumpled and puckered by the effort to present an uncompromising front to the enemy.

"Some of you ought to have written and informed me as soon as you had any suspicion of what was likely to happen. Not to do so was underhand. I do not wish to employ strong language, but I do consider it underhand. Shotover tells me he would have written if he had only known. But, of course, in the present state of feeling, he was shut out from it all. Ludovic did know, I presume. And, I am sorry to say it, but I consider it very unhandsome of Ludovic not to have communicated with me."

At this juncture Mr. Quayle desisted from contemplation of the family portraits and approached the belligerents, threading his way carefully between the many tables and chairs. There was much furniture, yet but few ornaments, in Lady Louisa's boudoir. The young man's long neck was directed slightly forward and his expression was one of polite inquiry.

"It is very warm this morning," he remarked parenthetically, "and, as a family, we appear to feel it. You did me the honour to refer to me just now, I believe, my dear father? Since my two younger sisters have been banished, it has happily become possible to hear both you, and myself, speak. You were saying?"

"That you might very properly have written and told me about this business, and given me an opportunity of expressing my opinion before things reached a head."

Mr. Quayle drew forward a chair and seated himself with mild deliberation. Lord Fallowfeild began to fidget.—"Very clever fellow, Ludovic," he said to himself. "Wonderfully cool head"— and he became suspicious of his own wisdom in having made direct appeal to a person thus distinguished.

"I might have written, my dear father. I admit that I might. But there were difficulties. To begin with, I—in this particular—shared Shotover's position. Louisa had not seen fit to honour me with her confidence.—I beg your pardon, Louisa, you were saying?—And so, you see, I really hadn't anything to write about."

"But—but—this young man"—Lord Fallowfeild was sensible of a singular reluctance to mention the name of his proposed son-in-law—"this young Calmady, you know, he's an intimate friend of yours"—

"Difficulty number two. For I doubted how you would take the matter"—

"Did you, though?" said Lord Fallowfeild, with an appreciable smoothing of crumples and puckers.

"I'm extremely attached to Dickie Calmady. And I did not want to put a spoke in his wheel."

"Of course not, my dear boy, of course not. Nasty unpleasant business putting spokes in other men's wheels, specially when they're your friends. I acknowledge that."

"I am sure you do," Mr. Quayle replied, indulgently. "You are always on the side of doing the generous thing, my dear father,—when you see it."

Here his lordship's grasp upon the head of his walking-stick relaxed sensibly.

"Thank you, Ludovic. Very pleasant thing to have one's son say to one, I must say, uncommonly pleasant."—Alas! he felt himself to be slipping, slipping. "Deucèd shrewd, diplomatic fellow, Ludovic," he remarked to himself somewhat ruefully. All the same, the little compliment warmed him through. He knew it made for defeat, yet for the life of him he could not but relish it.—"Very pleasant," he repeated. "But that's not the point, my dear boy. Now, about this young fellow Calmady's proposal for your sister Constance?"

Mr. Quayle looked full at the speaker, and for once his expression held no hint of impertinence or raillery.

"Dickie Calmady is as fine a fellow as ever fought, or won, an almost hopeless battle," he said. "He is somewhat heroic, in my opinion. And he is very lovable."

"Is he, though?" Lord Fallowfeild commented, quite gently.

"A woman who understood him, and had some idea of all he must have gone through, could not well help being very proud of him."

Yet, even while speaking, the young man knew his advocacy to be but half-hearted. He praised his friend rather than his friend's contemplated marriage.—"But his dear, old lordship's not very quick. He'll never spot that," he added mentally. And then he reflected that little Lady Constance was not very quick either. She might marry obediently, even gladly. But was it probable she would develop sufficient imagination ever to understand, and therefore be proud of, Richard Calmady?

"He is brilliant too," Ludovic continued. "He is as well read as any man of his standing whom I know, and he can think for himself. And, when he is in the vein, he is unusually good company."

"Everybody says he is extraordinarily agreeable," broke in

Lady Alicia.   "Old Lady Combmartin was saying only yesterday—George and I met her at the Aldhams', Louisa, you know, at dinner—that she had not heard better conversation for years.   And she was brought up among Macaulay, and Rogers, and all the Holland House set, so her opinion really is worth having."

But Lord Fallowfeild's grasp had tightened again upon his walking-stick.

" Was she, though?" he said rather incoherently.

"Pray, from all this, don't run away with the notion Calmady is a prig," Ludovic interposed.   "He is as keen a sportsman as you are—in as far, of course, as sport is possible for him."

Here Lord Fallowfeild, finding himself somewhat hard pressed, sought relief in movement.   He turned sideways, throwing one shapely leg across the other, grasping the supporting walking-stick in his right hand, while with the left he laid hold of the back of the white-and-gold chair.

"Oh! ah! yes," he said valiantly, directing his gaze upon the tree-tops in the Park.   "I quite accept all you tell me. I don't want to detract from your friend's merits—poor, mean sort of thing to detract from any man's friend's merits.   Gentlemanlike young fellow Calmady, the little I have seen of him— reminds me of my poor friend his father.   I liked his father. But, you see, my dear boy, there is—well, there's no denying it, there is—and Shotover quite "—

"Of course, papa, we all know what you mean," Lady Louisa interposed, with a certain loftiness and, it must be owned, asperity.   "I have never pretended there was not something one had to get accustomed to.   But really you forget all about it almost immediately—everyone does—one can see that —don't they, Alicia?   If you had met Sir Richard everywhere, as we have, this season, you would realise how very very soon that is quite forgotten."

" Is it, though?" said Lord Fallowfeild somewhat incredulously.   His face had returned to a sadly puckered condition.

"Yes, I assure you, nobody thinks of it, after just the first little shock, don't you know,"—this from Lady Louisa.

" I think one feels it is not quite nice to dwell on a thing of that kind," her sister chimed in, reddening again.   "It ought to be ignored."—From a girl, the speaker had enjoyed a reputation for great refinement of mind.

"I think it amounts to being more than not nice," echoed Lady Louisa.   "I think it is positively wrong, for nobody can tell what accident may not happen to any of us at any moment. And so I am not at all sure that it is not actually unchristian to make a thing like that into a serious objection."

"You know, papa, there must be deformed people in some families, just as there is consumption or insanity."

"Or under-breeding, or attenuated salaries," Mr. Quayle softly murmured. "It becomes evident, my dear father, you must not expect too much of sons, or I of brothers, in-law."

"Think of old Lord Sokeington—I mean the great uncle of the present man, of course—of his temper," Lady Louisa proceeded, regardless of ironical comment. "It amounted almost to mania. And yet Lady Dorothy Hellard would certainly have married him. There never was any question about it."

"Would she, though? Bad, old man, Sokeington. Never did approve of Sokeington."

"Of course she would. Mrs. Crookenden, who always has been devoted to her, told me so."

"Did she, though?" said Lord Fallowfeild. "But the marriage was broken off, my dear."

He made this remark triumphantly, feeling it showed great acuteness.

"Oh, dear no! indeed it wasn't," his daughter replied. "Lord Sokeington behaved in the most outrageous manner. At the last moment he never proposed to her at all. And then it came out that for years he had been living with one of the still-room maids."

"Louisa!" cried Lady Alicia, turning scarlet.

"Had he, though? The old scoundrel!"

"Papa," cried Lady Alicia.

"So he was, my dear. Very bad old man, Sokeington. Very amusing old man too, though."

And, overcome by certain reminiscences, Lord Fallowfeild chuckled a little, shamefacedly. His second daughter thereupon arranged the folds of her mauve cashmere, with bent head.—"It is very clear papa and Shotover have been together to-day," she thought. "Shotover's influence over papa is always demoralising. It's too extraordinary the subjects men joke about and call amusing when they get together."

A pause followed, a brief cessation of hostilities, during which Mr. Quayle looked inquiringly at his three companions.

"Alicia fancies herself shocked," he said to himself, "and my father fancies himself wicked, and Louisa fancies herself a chosen vessel. Strong delusion is upon them all. The only

question is whose delusion is the strongest, and who, consequently, will first renew the fray? Ah! the chosen vessel!
I thought as much."

"You see, papa, one really must be practical," Lady Louisa
began in clear, emphatic tones. "We all know how you have
spoiled Constance. She and Shotover have always been your
favourites. But even you must admit that Shotover's wretched
extravagance has impoverished you, and helped to impoverish
all your other children. And you must also admit, notwithstanding your partiality for Constance, that "—

"I want to see Connie. I want to hear from herself that
she "— broke out Lord Fallowfeild. His kindly heart yearned
over this ewe-lamb of his large flock. But the eldest of the
said flock interposed sternly.

"No, no," she cried, "pray, papa, not yet. Connie is quite
contented and reasonable—I believe she is out shopping just
now, too. And while you are in this state of indecision yourself,
it would be the greatest mistake for you to see her. It would
only disturb and upset her—wouldn't it, Alicia?"

And the lady thus appealed to assented. It is true that
when she arrived at the great house in Albert Gate that
morning she had found little Lady Constance with her pretty,
baby face sadly marred by tears. But she had put that down
to the exigencies of the situation. All young ladies of refined
mind cried under kindred circumstances. Had she not herself
wept copiously, for the better part of a week, before finally
deciding to accept George Winterbotham? Moreover, a point
of jealousy undoubtedly pricked Lady Alicia in this connection.
She was far from being a cruel woman, but, comparing her own
modest material advantages in marriage with the surprisingly
handsome ones offered to her little sister, she could not be
wholly sorry that the latter's rose was not entirely without thorns.
That the flower in question should have been thornless, as well
as so very fine and large, would surely have trenched on injustice
to herself. This thought had, perhaps unconsciously, influenced
her when enlarging on the becomingness of a refined indifference
to Sir Richard Calmady's deformity. In her heart of hearts she
was disposed, perhaps unconsciously, to hail rather than deplore
the fact of that same deformity. For did it not tend sub-
jectively to equalise her lot and that of her little sister, and
modify the otherwise humiliating disparity of their respective
fortunes? Therefore she capped Lady Louisa's speech, by
saying immediately:—

"Yes, indeed, papa, it would only be an unkindness to run

any risk of upsetting Connie.   No really nice girl ever really
quite likes the idea of marriage "—

"Doesn't she, though?" commented Lord Fallowfeild, with
an air of receiving curious, scientific information.

"Oh, of course not! How could she? And then, papa, you
know how you have always indulged Connie "—Lady Alicia's
voice was slightly peevish in tone. She was not in very good
health at the present time, with the consequence that her face
showed thin and bird-like. While, notwithstanding the genial
heat of the summer's day, she presented a starved and chilly
appearance.—"Always indulged Connie," she repeated, "and
that has inclined her to be rather selfish and fanciful."

The above statements, both regarding his own conduct and
the effect of that conduct upon his little ewe-lamb, nettled the
amiable nobleman considerably.   He faced round upon the
speaker with an intention of reprimand, but in so doing his eyes
were arrested by his daughter's faded dress and disorganised
complexion.   He relented.—"Poor thing looks ill," he thought.
"A man's an unworthy brute who ever says a sharp word to a
woman in her condition."—And, before he had time to find a
word other than sharp, Lady Louisa Barking returned to the
charge.

"Exactly," she asserted.   "Alicia is perfectly right.   At
present Connie is quite reasonable.   And all we entreat, papa,
is that you will let her remain so, until you have made up your
own mind.   Do pray let us be dignified.   One knows how the
servants get hold of anything of this kind and discuss it, if there
is any want of dignity or any indecision.   That is too odious.
And I must really think just a little of Mr. Barking and myself
in the matter.   It has all gone on in our house, you see.   One
must consider appearances, and with all the recent gossip about
Shotover, we do not want another *esclandre*—the servants knowing all about it too.   And then, with all your partiality for
Constance, you cannot suppose she will have many opportunities
of marrying men with forty or fifty thousand a year."

"No, papa, as Louisa says, in your partiality for Connie you
must not entirely forget the claims of your other children.   She
must not be encouraged to think exclusively of herself, and it is
not fair that you should think exclusively of her.   I know that
George and I are poor, but it is through no fault of our own.   He
most honourably refuses to take anything from his mother, and
you know how small my private income is.   Yet no one can
accuse George of lack of generosity.   When any of my family
want to come to us he always makes them welcome.   Maggie

only left us last Thursday, and Emily comes to-morrow.   I know
we can't do much.   It is not possible with our small means and
establishment.   But what little we can do, George is most willing
should be done."

"Excellent fellow Winterbotham," Lord Fallowfeild put in
soothingly.   "Very steady, painstaking man Winterbotham."

His second daughter looked at him reproachfully.

"Thank you, papa," she said.   "I own I was a little hurt
just now by the tone in which you alluded to George."

"Were you, though?   I'm sure I'm very sorry, my dear
Alicia.   Hate to hurt anybody, specially one of my own children.
Unnatural thing to hurt one of your own children.   But you see
this feeling of all of you about Shotover has been very painful
to me.   I never have liked divisions in families.   Never know
where they may lead to.   Nasty, uncomfortable things divisions
in families."

"Well, papa, I can only say that divisions are almost invariably caused by a want of the sense of duty."—Lady Louisa's
voice was stern.   "And if people are over-indulged they become
selfish, and then, of course, they lose their sense of duty."

"My sister is a notable logician," Mr. Quayle murmured,
under his breath.   "If logic ruled life, how clear, how simple our
course!   But then, unfortunately, it doesn't."

"Shotover has really no one but himself to thank for any
bitterness that his brothers and sisters may feel towards him.
He has thrown away his chances, has got the whole family talked
about in a most objectionable manner, and has been a serious
encumbrance to you, and indirectly to all of us.   We have all
suffered quite enough trouble and annoyance already.   And so
I must protest, papa, I must very strongly and definitely protest,
against Connie being permitted, still more encouraged, to do
exactly the same thing."

Lord Fallowfeild, still grasping his walking-stick,—though he
could not but fear that trusted weapon had proved faithless and
sadly failed in its duty of support,—gazed distractedly at the
speaker.   Visions of Jewish money-lenders, of ladies more fair
and kind than wise, of guinea points at whist, of the prize ring,
of Baden-Baden, of Newmarket and Doncaster, arose con-
fusedly before him.   What the deuce,—he did not like bad
language, but really,—what the dickens, had all these to do with
his ewe-lamb, innocent, little Constance, her virgin-white body
and soul, and her sweet, wide-eyed prettiness?

"My dear Louisa, no doubt you know what you mean, but I
give you my word I don't," he began.

"Hear, hear, my dear father," put in Mr. Quayle. "There I am with you. Louisa's wing is strong, her range is great. I myself, on this occasion, find it not a little difficult to follow her."

"Nonsense, Ludovic," almost snapped the lady. "You follow me perfectly, or can do so if you use your common sense. Papa must face the fact, that Constance cannot afford—that I cannot afford to have her—throw away her chances, as Shotover has thrown away his. We all have a duty, not only to ourselves, but to each other. Inclination must give way to duty—though I do not say Constance exhibits any real disinclination to this marriage. She is a little flurried. As Alicia said just now, every really nice-minded girl is flurried at the idea of marriage. She ought to be. I consider it only delicate that she should be. But she understands—I have pointed it out to her—that her money, her position, and those two big houses—Brockhurst and the one in Lowndes Square—will be of the greatest advantage to the girls and to her brothers. It is not as if she was nobody. The scullery-maid can marry whom she likes, of course. But in our rank of life it is different. A girl is bound to think of her family, as well as of herself. She is bound to consider"—

The groom-of-the-chambers opened the door and advanced solemnly across the boudoir to Lord Fallowfeild.

"Sir Richard Calmady is in the smoking-room, my lord," he said, "to see you."

CHAPTER V

IPHIGENIA

CHASTENED in spirit, verbally acquiescent, yet unconvinced, a somewhat pitiable sense of inadequacy upon him, Lord Fallowfeild travelled back to Westchurch that night. Two days later the morning papers announced to all whom it might concern, —and that far larger all, whom it did not really concern in the least—in the conventional phrases common to such announcements, that Sir Richard Calmady and Lady Constance Quayle had agreed shortly to become man and wife. Thus did Katherine Calmady, in all trustfulness, strive to give her son his desire, while the great and little world looked on, and made comments various as the natures and circumstances of the units composing them.

Lady Louisa was filled with the pride of victory.   Her
venture had not miscarried.   At church on Sunday—she was
really too busy socially, just now, to attend what it was her
habit to describe as "odds and ends of week-day services," and
therefore worshipped on the Sabbath only, and then by no means
in secret or with shut door—she repeated the General Thanksgiving
with much unction and in an aggressively audible voice.   And
Lady Alicia Winterbotham expressed a peevish hope that—"such
great wealth might not turn Constance's head and make her just
a little vulgar.   It was all rather dangerous for a girl of her age,
and she"—the speaker—"trusted *somebody* would point out to
Connie the heavy responsibilities towards others such a position
brought with it."   And Lord Shotover delivered it as his opinion
that—"It might be all right.   He hoped to goodness it was, for
he'd always been uncommonly fond of the young 'un.   But it
seemed to him rather a put-up job all round, and so he meant
just to keep his eye on Con, he swore he did."   In furtherance of
which laudable determination he braved his eldest sister's frowns
with heroic intrepidity, calling to see the young girl whenever
all other sources of amusement failed him, and paying her the
compliment—as is the habit of the natural man, when unselfishly
desirous of giving pleasure to the women of his family—of talking
continuously and exclusively about his own affairs, his gains at
cards, his losses on horses, even recounting, in moments of more
than ordinarily expansive affection, the less wholly disreputable
episodes of his many adventures of the heart.   And Honoria St.
Quentin's sensitive face straightened and her lips closed rather
tight whenever the marriage was mentioned before her.   She
refused to express any view on the subject, and to that end
took rather elaborate pains to avoid the society of Mr. Quayle.
And Lady Dorothy Hellard—whose unhappy disappointment
in respect of the late Lord Sokeington and other nonsuccessful
excursions in the direction of wedlock, had not cured her of
sentimental leanings—asserted that—"It was quite the most
romantic and touching engagement she had ever heard of."
To which speech her mother, the Dowager Lady Combmartin,
replied, with the directness of statement which made her acquaintance so cautious of differing from her : — "Touching?
Romantic? Fiddle-de-dee ! You ought to be ashamed of yourself
for thinking so at your age, Dorothy.   A bargain's a bargain, and
in my opinion the bride has got much the best of it.   For she's
a mawkish, milk-and-water, little schoolgirl, while he is charming
—all there is of him.   If there'd been a little more I declare I'd
have married him myself."   And good-looking Mr. Decies, of the

101st Lancers, got into very hot water with the mounted con-
stables, and with the livery-stable keeper from whom he hired
his hacks, for "furious riding" in the Park.   And Julius March
walked the paved ways and fragrant alleys of the red-walled
gardens at Brockhurst, somewhat sadly, in the glowing June
twilights, meditating upon the pitiless power of change which
infects all things human, and of his own lifelong love doomed to
"find no earthly close."   And Mrs. Chifney, down at the racing-
stables, rejoiced to the point of tears, being possessed by the
persistent instinct of matrimony common to the British, lower
middle-class.   And Sandyfield parish rejoiced likewise, and pealed
its church-bells in token thereof, foreseeing much carnal gratification in the matter of cakes and ale.   And Madame de Vallorbes,
whose letters to Richard had come to be pretty frequent during
the last eight months, was overtaken by silence and did not write
at all.

But this omission on the part of his cousin was grateful, rather
than distressing, to the young man.   It appeared to him very
sympathetic of Helen not to write.   It showed a finely, imaginative sensibility and considerateness on her part, which made
Dickie sigh, thinking of it, and then, so to speak, turn away his
head.   And to do this last was the less difficult that his days
were very full just now.   And his mind was very full, likewise,
of gentle thoughts of, and many provisions for, the happiness of
his promised bride.

The young girl was timid in his presence, it is true.   Yet she
was transparently, appealingly, anxious to please.   Her conversation was neither ready nor brilliant, but she was very fair to look
upon in her childlike freshness and innocence.   A protective
element, a tender and chivalrous loyalty, entered into Richard's
every thought of her.   A great passion and a happy marriage
were two quite separate matters—so he argued in his inexperience.   And this was surely the wife a man should desire, modest,
guileless, dutiful, pure in heart as in person?   The gentle
dumbness which often held her did not trouble him.   It was a
pretty pastime to try to win her confidence and open the doors of
her artless speech.

And then, to Richard, tempted it is true, but as yet himself
unsullied, it was so sacred and wonderful a thing that this
spotless woman-creature in all the fragrance of her youth
belonged to him in a measure already, and would belong to him,
before many weeks were out, wholly and of inalienable right.
And so it happened that the very limitations of the young girl's
nature came to enhance her attractions.   Dickie could not get

very near to her mind, but that merely piqued his curiosity and provoked his desire of discovery. She was to him as a book written in strange character, difficult to decipher. With the result that he accredited her with subtleties and many fine feelings she did not really possess, while he failed to divine—not from defective sympathy so much as from absorption in his self-created idea of her—the very simple feelings which actually animated her. His masculine pride was satisfied, in that so eligible a maiden consented to become his wife. His moral sense was satisfied also, since he had—as he supposed—put temptation from him and chosen the better part. Very certainly he was not violently in love. That he supposed to be a thing of the past. But he was quietly happy. While ahead lay the mysterious enchantments of marriage. Dickie's heart was very tender, just then. Life had never turned on him a more gracious face.

Nevertheless, once or twice, a breath of distrust dimmed the bright surface of his existing complacency. One day, for instance, he had taken his *fiancée* for a morning drive and brought her home to luncheon. After that meal she should sit for a while with Lady Calmady, and then join him in the library downstairs, for he had that which he coveted to show to her.—But it appeared to him that she tarried unduly with his mother, and he grew impatient waiting through the long minutes of the summer afternoon. A barrel-organ droned slumberously from the other side of the square, while to his ears, so long attuned to country silences or the quick, intermittent music of nature, the ceaseless roar of London became burdensome. Ever after, thinking of this first wooing of his, he recalled—as slightly sinister—that ever-present murmur of traffic,—bearing testimony, as it seemed later, to the many activities in which he could play, after all, but so paltry and circumscribed a part.

And, listening to that same murmur now, something of rebellion against circumstance arose in Dickie for all that the present was very good. For, as he considered, any lover other than himself would not sit pinned to an arm-chair awaiting his mistress' coming, but, did she delay, would go to seek her, claim her, and bear her merrily away. The organ-grinder, meanwhile, cheered by a copper shower from some adjacent balcony, turned the handle of his instrument more vigorously, letting loose stirring valse-tune and march upon the sultry air. Such music was, of necessity, somewhat comfortless hearing to Richard, debarred alike from deeds of arms or joy of dancing. His impatience increased. It was a little inconsiderate of his mother surely to detain Constance for so long! But just then the sound of women's voices reached him through the half-open door. The two ladies were leisurely descending the stairs. There was a little pause, then he heard Lady Calmady say, as though in gentle rebuke :—

"No, no, dear child, I will not come with you. Richard would like better to see you alone. Too, I have a number of letters to write. I am at home to no one this afternoon. You will find me in the sitting-room here. You can come and bid me good-bye—now, dear child, go."

Thus admonished, Lady Constance moved forward. Yet, to Dickie's listening ears, it appeared that it took her an inordinate length of time to traverse the length of the hall from the foot of the stairs to the library door. And there again she paused — the organ, now nearer, rattling out the tramp of a popular military march. But the throb and beat of the quick-step failed to hasten Lady Constance's lagging feet, so that further rebellion against his own infirmity assaulted poor Dick.

At length the girl entered with a little rush, her soft cheeks flushed, her rounded bosom heaving, as though she arrived from a long and arduous walk, rather than from that particularly deliberate traversing of the cool hall and descent of the airy stairway.

"Ah! here you are at last, then!" Richard exclaimed. "I began to wonder if you had forgotten all about me."

The young girl did not attempt to sit down, but stood directly in front of him, her hands clasped loosely, yet somewhat nervously, almost in the attitude of a child about to recite a lesson. Her still, heifer's eyes were situate so far apart that Dickie, looking up at her, found it difficult to focus them both at the same glance. And this produced an effect of slight uncertainty, even of a defect of vision, at once pathetic and quaintly attractive. Her face was heart-shaped, narrowing from the wide, low brow to the small, rounded chin set below a round, babyish mouth of slight mobility but much innocent sweetness. Her light, brown hair, rising in an upward curve on either side the straight parting, was swept back softly, yet smoothly, behind her small ears. The neck of her white, alpaca dress, cut square according to the then prevailing fashion, was outlined with flat bands of pale, blue ribbon, and filled up with lace to the base of the round column of her throat. Blue ribbons adorned the hem of her simple skirt, and a band of the same colour encircled her shapely, though not noticeably slender, waist. Her bosom was rather full for so young a woman ; so that, notwithstanding her perfect freshness and air of almost childlike simplicity, there was a certain statuesque quality in the effect of her white-clad figure seen thus in the shaded library, with its russet-red walls and ranges of dark bookshelves.

"I am so sorry," she said breathlessly. "I should have come sooner, but I was talking to Lady Calmady, and I did not know it was so late. I am not afraid of talking to Lady Calmady, she is so very kind to me, and there are many questions I wanted to ask her. She promises to help and tell me what I ought to do. And I am very glad of that. It will prevent my making mistakes."

Her attitude and the earnestness of her artless speech were to Richard almost pathetically engaging. His irritation vanished. He smiled, looked up at her, his own face flushing a little.

"I don't fancy you will ever make any very dangerous mistakes !" he said.

"Ah! but I might," the girl insisted. "You see I have always been told what to do."

"Always?" Dickie asked, more for the pleasure of watching her stand thus than for any great importance he attached to her answer.

"Oh yes !" she said. "First by our nurses, and then by our governesses. They were not always very kind. They called me obstinate. But I did not mean to be obstinate. Only they spoke in French or German, and I could not always understand. And since I have grown up my elder sisters have told me what I ought to do."

It seemed to Richard that the girl's small, round chin trembled a little, and that a look of vague distress invaded her soft, ruminant, wide-set eyes.

"And so I should have been very frightened, now, unless I had had Lady Calmady to tell me."

"Well, I think there's only one thing my mother will need to tell you, and it won't run into either French or German. It can be stated in very plain English. Just to do whatever you like, and—and be happy."

Lady Constance stared at the speaker with her air of gentle perplexity. As she did so undoubtedly her pretty chin did tremble a little.

"Ah! but to do what you like can never really make you happy," she said.

"Can't it? I'm not altogether so sure of that. I had ventured to suppose there were a number of things you and I

21

would do in the future, which will be most uncommonly pleasant without being conspicuously harmful."

He leaned sideways, stretching out to a neighbouring chair with his right hand, keeping the light, silk-woven, red blanket up across his thighs with his left.

"Do sit down, Constance, and we will talk of things we both like to do, at greater length— Ah! bother—forgive me—I can't reach it."

"Oh! please don't trouble. It doesn't matter. I can get it quite well myself," Lady Constance said, quite quickly for once. She drew up the chair and sat down near him, folding her hands again nervously in her lap. All the colour had died out of her cheeks. They were as white as her rounded throat. She kept her eyes fixed on Richard's face, and her bosom rose and fell, while her words came somewhat gaspingly. Still she talked on with a touching little effect of determined civility.

"Lady Calmady was very kind in telling me I might sometimes go over to Whitney," she said. "I should like that. I am afraid papa will miss me. Of course there will be all the others just the same. But I go out so much with him. Of course I would not ask to go over very often, because I know it might be inconvenient for me to have the horses."

"But you will have your own horses," Richard answered. "I wrote to Chifney to look out for a pair of cobs for you last week—browns — you said you liked that colour I remember. And I told him they were to be broken until big guns, going off under their very noses, wouldn't make them so much as wince."

"Are you buying them just for me?" the girl said.

"Just for you?" Dickie laughed. "Why, who on earth should I buy anything for but just you, I should like to know?"

"But"— she began.

"But—but"— he echoed, resting his hands on the two arms of his chair, leaning forward and still laughing, though somewhat shyly. "Don't you see the whole and sole programme is that you should do all you like, and have all you like, and—and be happy."—Richard straightened himself up, still looking full at her, trying to focus both these quaintly-engaging, far-apart eyes. "Constance, do you never play?" he asked her suddenly.

"I did practise every morning at home, but lately"—

"Oh! I don't mean that," the young man said. "I mean quite another sort of playing."

"Games?" Lady Constance inquired. "I am afraid I am

rather stupid about games. I find it so difficult to remember numbers and words, and I never can make a ball go where I want it to, somehow."

"I was not thinking of games either, exactly," Richard said, smiling.

The girl stared at him in some perplexity. Then she spoke again, with the same little effect of determined civility.

"I am very fond of dancing and of skating. The ice was very good on the lake at Whitney this winter. Rupert and Gerry were home from Eton, and Eddy had brought a young man down with him—Mr. Hubbard—who is in his business in Liverpool, and a friend of my brother Guy's was staying in the house too, from India. I think you have met him—Mr. Decies. We skated till past twelve one night—a Wednesday, I think. There was a moon, and a great many stars. The thermometer registered fifteen degrees of frost Mr. Decies told me. But I was not cold. It was very beautiful."

Richard shifted his position. The organ had moved farther away. Uncheered by further copper showers it droned again slumberously, while the murmur sent forth by the thousand activities of the great city waxed loud, for the moment, and hoarsely insistent.

"I do not bore you?" Lady Constance asked, in sudden anxiety.

"Oh no, no!" Richard answered. "I am glad to have you tell me about yourself, if you will; and all that you care for."

Thus encouraged, the girl took up her little parable again, her sweet, rather vacant, face growing almost animated as she spoke.

"We did something else I liked very much, but from what Alicia said afterwards I am afraid I ought not to have liked it. One day it snowed, and we all played hide-and-seek. There are a number of attics in the roof of the bachelor's wing at Whitney, and there are long up-and-down passages leading round to the old nurseries. Mama did not mind, but Alicia was very displeased. She said it was a mere excuse for romping. But that was not true. Of course we never thought of romping. We did make a great noise," she added conscientiously, "but that was Rupert and Gerry's fault. They would jump out after promising not to, and of course it was impossible to help screaming. Eddy's Liverpool friend tried to jump out too, but Maggie snubbed him. I think he deserved it. You ought to play fair; don't you think so? After promising, you would never jump out, would you?"

And there Lady Constance stopped, with a little gasp.

"Oh! I beg your pardon. I am so sorry. I forgot," she added breathlessly.

Richard's face had become thin and keen.

"Forget just as often as you can, please," he answered huskily. "I would infinitely rather have you—have everybody —forget altogether—if possible."

"Oh! but I think that would be wrong of me," she rejoined, with gentle dogmatism. "It is selfish to forget anything that is very sad."

"And is this so very sad?" Richard asked, almost harshly.

The girl stared at him with parted lips.

"Oh yes!" she said slowly. "Of course,—don't you think so? It is dreadfully sad."—And then, her attitude still unchanged and her pretty, plump hands still folded on her lap, she went on, in her touching determination to sustain the conversation with due readiness and civility. "Brockhurst is a much larger house than Whitney, isn't it? I thought so the day we drove over to luncheon—when that beautiful, French cousin of yours was staying with you, you remember?"

"Yes, I remember," Richard said.

And as he spoke Madame de Vallorbes, clothed in the seawaves, crowned and shod with gold, seemed to stand for a moment beside his innocent, little *fiancée*. How long it was since he had heard from her! Did she want money, he wondered? It would be intolerable if, because of his marriage, she never let him help her again. And all the while Lady Constance's unemotional, careful, little voice continued, as did the ceaseless murmur of London.

"I remember," she was saying, "because your cousin is quite the most beautiful person I have ever seen. Papa admired her very much too. We spoke of that as soon as Louisa had left us, when we were alone. But there seemed to me so many staircases at Brockhurst, and rooms opening one out of the other. I have been wondering—since—lately—whether I shall ever be able to find my way about the house."

"I will show you your way," Dickie said gently, banishing the vision of Helen de Vallorbes.

"You will show it me?" the girl asked, in evident surprise.

Then a companion picture to that of Madame de Vallorbes arose before Dickie's mental vision—namely the good-looking, long-legged, young, Irish soldier, Mr. Decies, of the 101st Lancers, flying along the attic passages of the Whitney bachelor's wing, in company with this immediately-so-demure and dutiful maiden and all the rest of that admittedly rather uproarious, holiday throng.   Thereat a foolish lump rose in poor Richard's throat, for he too was, after all, but young.   He choked the foolish lump down again.   Yet it left his voice a trifle husky.

"Yes, I will show you your way," he said.   "I can manage that much, you know, at home, in private, among my own people. Only you mustn't be in a hurry.   I have to take my time.   You must not mind that.   I—I go slowly."

"But that will be much better for me," she answered, with rather humble courtesy, "because then I am more likely to remember my way.   I have so much difficulty in knowing my way.   I still lose myself sometimes in the park at Whitney.   I did once this winter with—my brother Guy's friend, Mr. Decies. The boys always tease me about losing my way.   Even papa says I have no bump of locality.   I am afraid I am stupid about that.   My governesses always complained that I was a very thoughtless child."

Lady Constance unfolded her hands.   Her timid, engagingly vague gaze dwelt appealingly upon Richard's handsome face.

"I think, perhaps, if you do not mind, I will go now," she said.   "I must bid Lady Calmady good-bye.   We dine at Lady Combmartin's to-night.   You dine there too, don't you?   And my sister Louisa may want me to drive with her, or write some notes, before I dress."

"Wait half a minute," Dickie said.   "I've got something for you.   Let's see—   Oh! there it is!"

Raising himself he stood, for a moment, on the seat of the chair, steadying himself with one hand on the back of it, and reached a little, silver-paper covered parcel from the neighbouring table.   Then he slipped back into a sitting position, drew the silken blanket up across his thighs, and tossed the little parcel gently into Lady Constance Quayle's lap.

"I as near as possible let you go without it," he said.   "Not that it's anything very wonderful.   It's nothing—only I saw it in a shop in Bond Street yesterday, and it struck me as rather quaint. I thought you might like it.   Why—but—Constance, what's the matter?"

For the girl's pretty, heart-shaped face had blanched to the whiteness of her white dress.   Her eyes were strained, as those of one who beholds an object of terror.   Not only her chin but her round, baby mouth trembled.   Richard looked at her, amazed at these evidences of distressing emotion.   Then suddenly he understood.

"I frighten you.   How horrible!" he said.

But little Lady Constance had not suffered persistent training at the hands of nurses, and governesses, and elder sisters, during all her eighteen years of innocent living for nothing. She had her own small code of manners and morals, of honour and duty, and to the requirements of that code, as she apprehended them, she yielded unqualified obedience, not unheroic in its own meagre and rather puzzle-headed fashion. So that now, notwithstanding trembling lips, she retained her intention of civility and entered immediate apology for her own weakness.

"No, no, indeed you do not," she replied. "Please forgive me. I know I was very foolish. I am so sorry. You are so kind to me, you are always giving me beautiful presents, and indeed I am not ungrateful. Only I had never seen—seen—you like that before. And, please forgive me—I will never be foolish again—indeed, I will not. But I was taken by surprise. I beg your pardon. I shall be so dreadfully unhappy if you do not forgive me."

And all the while her shaking hands fumbled helplessly with the narrow ribbon tying the dainty parcel, and big tears rolled down slowly out of her great, soft, wide-set, heifer's eyes. Never was there more moving or guileless a spectacle ! Witnessing which, Richard Calmady was taken somewhat out of himself, his personal misfortune seeming matter inconsiderable, while his childlike *fiancée* had never appeared more engaging. All the sweetest of his nature responded to her artless appeal in very tender pity.

"Why, my dear Constance," he said, "there's nothing to forgive. I was foolish, not you. I ought to have known better. Never mind. I don't. Only wipe your pretty eyes, please. Yes —that's better. Now let me break that tiresome ribbon for you."

"You are very kind to me," the girl murmured. Then, as the ribbon broke under Richard's strong fingers, and the delicate necklace of many, roughly-cut, precious stones—topaz, amethyst, sapphire, ruby, chrysolite, and beryl, joined together, three rows deep, by slender, golden chains — slipped from the enclosing paper wrapping into her open hands, Constance Quayle added, rather tearfully :—"Oh ! you are much too kind ! You give me too many things. No one I know ever had such beautiful presents. The cobs you told me of, and now this, and the pearls, and the tiara you gave me last week. I—I don't deserve it. You give me too much, and I give nothing in return."

"Oh yes, you do !" Richard said, flushing. "You—you give me yourself."

Lady Constance's tears ceased.   Again she stared at him in gentle perplexity.

"You promise to marry me"—

"Yes, of course, I have promised that," she said slowly.

"And isn't that about the greatest giving there can be?   A few horses, and jewels, and such rubbish of sorts, weigh pretty light in the balance against that—I being I"—Richard paused a moment—"and you—you."

But a certain ardour which had come into his speech, for all that he sat very still, and that his expression was wholly gentle and indulgent, and that she felt a comfortable assurance that he was not angry with her, rather troubled little Lady Constance Quayle.   She rose to her feet, and stood before him again, as a child about to recite a lesson.

"I think," she said, "I must go.   Louisa may want me. Thank you so much.   This necklace is quite lovely.   I never saw one like it.   I like so many colours.   They remind me of flowers, or of the colours at sunset in the sky.   I shall like to wear this very much.   You—you will forgive me for having been foolish—or if I have bored you?"

Her bosom rose and fell, and the words came breathlessly.

"I shall see you at Lady Combmartin's?   So—so now I will go."

And with that she departed, leaving Richard more in love with her, somehow, than he had ever been before or had ever thought to be.

CHAPTER VI

IN WHICH HONORIA ST. QUENTIN TAKES THE FIELD

IT had been agreed that the marriage should take place, in the country, one day in the first week of August.   This at Richard's request.   Then the young man asked a further favour, namely that the ceremony might be performed in the private chapel at Brockhurst, rather than in the Whitney parish church.   This last proposal, it must be owned, when made to him by Lady Calmady caused Lord Fallowfeild great searchings of heart.

"I give you my word, my dear boy, I never felt more awkward in my life," he said, subsequently, to his chosen confidant, Shotover.   "Can quite understand Calmady doesn't care to court publicity.   Told his mother I quite understood.

Shouldn't care to court it myself if I had the misfortune to share his—well, personal peculiarities, don't you know, poor young fellow. Still this seems to me an uncomfortable, hole and corner sort of way of behaving to one's daughter—marrying her at his house instead of from my own. I don't half approve of it. Looks a little as if we were rather ashamed of the whole business."

" Well, perhaps we are," Lord Shotover remarked.

"For God's sake, then, don't mention it!" the elder man broke out, with unprecedented asperity. "Don't approve of strong language," he added hastily. "Never did approve of it, and very rarely employ it myself. An educated man ought to be able to express himself quite sufficiently clearly without having recourse to it. Still, I must own this engagement of Constance's has upset me more than almost any event of my life. Nasty, anxious work marrying your daughters. Heavy responsibility marrying your daughters. And, as to this particular marriage, there's so very much to be said on both sides. And I admit to you, Shotover, if there's anything I hate it's a case where there's very much to be said on both sides. It trips you up, you see, at every turn. Then I feel I was not fairly treated. I don't wish to be hard on your brother Ludovic and your sisters, but they sprung it upon me, and I am not quick in argument, never was quick, if I am hurried. Never can be certain of my own mind when I am hurried—was not certain of it when Lady Calmady proposed that the marriage should be at Brockhurst. And so I gave way. Must be accommodating to a woman, you know. Always have been accommodating to women—got myself into uncommonly tight places by being so more than once when I was younger "—

Here the speaker cheered up visibly, contemplating his favourite son with an air at once humorous and contrite.

"You're well out of it, you know, Shotover, with no ties," he continued, "at least, I mean, with no wife and family. Not that I don't consider every man owning property should marry sooner or later. More respectable if you've got property to marry, roots you in the soil, gives you a stake, you know, in the future of the country. But I'd let it be later—yes, thinking of marriageable daughters, certainly I'd let it be later."

From which it may be gathered that Richard's demands were conceded at all points. And this last concession involved many preparations at Brockhurst, to effect which Lady Calmady left London with the bulk of the household about the middle of July, while Richard remained in Lowndes Square and the neighbourhood of his little *fiancée*—in company with a few servants and many brown holland covers—till such time as that young lady should also depart to the country. It was just now that Lady Louisa Barking gave her annual ball, always one of the latest, and this year one of the smartest, festivities of the season.

"I mean it to be exceedingly well done," she said to her sister Alicia. "And Mr. Barking entirely agrees with me. I feel I owe it not only to myself, but to the rest of the family to show that none of us see anything extraordinary in Connie's marriage, and that whatever Shotover's debts may have been, or may be, they are really no concern at all of ours."

In obedience to which laudable determination the handsome mansion in Albert Gate opened wide its portals, and all London —a far from despicable company in numbers, since Parliament was still sitting and the session promised to be rather indefinitely prolonged—crowded its fine stairways and suites of lofty rooms, resplendent in silks and satins, jewels and laces, in orders and titles, and manifold personal distinctions of wealth, or office, or beauty, while strains of music and scent of flowers pervaded the length and breadth of it, and the feet of the dancers sped over its shining floors.

It chanced that Honoria St. Quentin found herself, on this occasion, in a meditative, rather than an active, mood. True, the scene was remarkably brilliant. But she had witnessed too many parallel scenes to be very much affected by that. So it pleased her fancy to moralise, to discriminate—not without a delicate sarcasm—between actualities and appearances, between the sentiments which might be divined really to animate many of the guests, and those conventional presentments of sentiment which the manner and bearing of the said guests indicated. She assured Lord Shotover she would rather not dance, that she preferred the attitude of spectator, whereupon that gentleman proposed to her to take sanctuary in a certain ante-chamber, opening off Lady Louisa Barking's boudoir, which was cool, dimly lighted, and agreeably remote from the turmoil of the entertainment now at its height.

The acquaintance of these two persons was, in as far as time and the number of their meetings went, but slight, and, at first sight, their tastes and temperaments would seem wide asunder as the poles. But contrast can form a strong bond of union. And the young man, when his fancy was engaged, was among those who do not waste time over preliminaries. If pleased, he bundled, neck and crop, into intimacy. And Miss St. Quentin, her fearless speech, her amusingly detached attitude of mind, and her gallant bearing, pleased him mightily from a certain point of view. He pronounced her to be a "first-rate sort," and entertained a shrewd suspicion that, as he put it, Ludovic "was after her." He commended his brother's good taste. He considered she would make a tip-top sister-in-law. While the young lady, on her part, accepted his advances in a friendly spirit. His fraternal attitude and unfailing good-temper diverted her. His rather doubtful reputation piqued her curiosity. She accepted the general verdict, declaring him to be good-for-nothing, while she enjoyed the conviction that, rake or no rake, he was incapable of causing her the smallest annoyance, or being guilty—as far as she herself was concerned—of the smallest indiscretion.

"You know, Miss St. Quentin," he remarked, as he established himself comfortably, not to say cosily, on a sofa beside her,—"over and above the pleasure of a peaceful little talk with you, I am not altogether sorry to seek retirement. You see, between ourselves, I'm not, unfortunately, in exactly good odour with some members of the family just now. I don't think I'm shy"—

Honoria smiled at him through the dimness.

"I don't think you're shy," she said.

"Well, you know, when you come to consider it from an unprejudiced standpoint, what the dickens is the use of being shy? It's only an inverted kind of conceit at best, and half the time it makes you stand in your own light."

"Clearly it's a mistake every way," the young lady asserted. "And, happily, it's one of which I can entirely acquit you of being guilty."

Lord Shotover threw back his head and looked sideways at his companion.—Wonderfully graceful woman she was certainly! Gave you the feeling she'd all the time there was or ever would be. Delightful thing to see a woman who was never in a hurry.

"No, honestly I don't believe I'm weak in the way of shyness," he continued. "If I had been, I shouldn't be here tonight. My sister Louisa didn't press me to come. Strange as it may appear to you, Miss St. Quentin, I give you my word she didn't. Nor has she regarded me with an exactly favourable eye since my arrival. I am not abashed, not a bit. But I can't disguise from myself that again I have gone, and been, and jolly well put my foot in it."

He whistled very softly under his breath.—"Oh! I have, I promise you, even on the most modest computation, very extensively and comprehensively put my foot in it!"

"How?" inquired Honoria.

Lord Shotover's confidences invariably amused her, and just now she welcomed amusement. For, crossing her hostess' boudoir, she had momentarily caught sight of that which changed the speculative sarcasm of her meditations to something approaching pain—namely a pretty, wide-eyed, childish face rising from out a cloud of white tulle, white roses, and diamonds, the expression of which had seemed to her distressingly remote from all the surrounding gaiety and splendour. Actualities and appearances here were surely radically at variance? And, now, she smilingly turned on her elbow and made brief inquiry of her companion, promising herself good measure of superficial entertainment which should serve to banish that pathetic countenance, and allay her suspicion of a sorrowful happening which she was powerless alike to hinder or to help.

Lord Shotover pushed his hands into his trousers pockets, leaned far back on the sofa, turning his head so that he could look at her comfortably without exertion and chuckling, a little, as he spoke.

"Well, you see," he said, "I brought Decies. No, you're right, I'm not shy, for to do that was a bit of the most barefaced cheek. My sister Louisa hadn't asked him. Of course she hadn't. At bottom she's awfully afraid he may still upset the apple-cart. But I told her I knew, of course, she had intended to ask him, and that the letter must have got lost somehow in the post, and that I knew how glad she'd be to have me rectify the little mistake. My manner was not jaunty, Miss St. Quentin, or defiant—not a bit of it. It was frank, manly, I should call it manly and pleasing. But Louisa didn't seem to see it that way somehow. She withered me, she scorched me, reduced me to a cinder, though she never uttered one blessed syllable. The hottest corner of the infernal regions resided in my sister's eye at that moment, and I resided in that hottest corner, I tell you. Of course I knew I risked losing the last rag of her regard when I brought Decies. But you see, poor chap, it is awfully rough on him. He was making the running all through the winter. I could not help feeling for him, so I chucked discretion"—

"For the first and only time in your life," put in Honoria gently. "And pray who and what is this disturber of domestic peace, Decies?"

"Oh! you know the whole affair grows out of this engagement of my little sister Connie's. By the way, though, the Calmadys are great friends of yours, aren't they, Miss St. Quentin?"

The young man regarded her anxiously, fearful lest he should have endangered the agreeable intimacy of their present relation by the introduction of an unpalatable subject of conversation. Even in this semi-obscurity he perceived that her fine smile had vanished, while the lines of her sensitive face took on a certain rigidity and effect of sternness. Lord Shotover regretted that. For some reason, he knew not what, she was displeased. He, like an ass, evidently had blundered.

"I'm awfully sorry," he began, "perhaps—perhaps"—

"Perhaps it is very impertinent for a mere looker-on like myself to have any views at all about this marriage," Honoria put in quickly.

"Bless you, no, it's not," he answered. "I don't see how anybody can very well be off having views about it—that's just the nuisance. The whole thing shouts, confound it. So you might just as well let me hear your views, Miss St. Quentin. I should be awfully interested. They might help to straighten my own out a bit."

Honoria paused a moment, doubting how much of her thought it would be justifiable to confide to her companion. A certain vein of knight-errantry in her character inclined her to set lance in rest and ride forth, rather recklessly, to redress human wrongs. But in redressing one wrong it too often happens that another wrong—or something perilously approaching one—must be inflicted. To save pain in one direction is, unhappily, to inflict pain in the opposite one. Honoria was aware how warmly Lady Calmady desired this marriage. She loved Lady Calmady. Therefore her loyalty was engaged, and yet—

"I am no match-maker," she said at last, "and so probably my view is unnecessarily pessimistic. But I happened to see Lady Constance just now, and I cannot pretend that she struck me as looking conspicuously happy."

Lord Shotover flattened his shoulders against the back of the sofa, expanding his chest and thrusting his hands still farther into his pockets with a movement at once of anxiety and satisfaction.

"I don't believe she is," he asserted. "Upon my word you're right. I don't believe she is. I doubted it from the first, and now I'm pretty certain. Of course I know I'm a bad lot, Miss St. Quentin. I've been very little but a confounded nuisance to my people ever since I was born. They're all ten thousand times better than I am, and they're doing what they honestly think right. All the same I believe they're making a ghastly mistake. They're selling the poor, little girl against her will, that's about the long and short of it."

He bowed himself together, looking at his companion from

under his eyebrows, and speaking with more seriousness than she had ever heard him yet speak.

"I tell you it makes me a little sick sometimes to see what excellent, well-meaning people will do with girls in respect of marriage. Oh, good Lord! it just does! But then a high moral tone doesn't come quite gracefully from me. I know that. I'm jolly well out of it. It's not for me to preach. And so I thought for once I'd act—defy authority, risk landing myself in a worse mess than ever, and give Decies his chance. And I tell you he really is a charming chap, a gentleman, you know, and a nice, clean-minded, decent fellow—not like me, not a bit. He's awfully hard hit too, and would be as steady as old time for poor, little Con's sake if"—

"Ah! now I begin to comprehend," Honoria said.

"Yes, don't you see, it's a perfectly genuine, for-ever-and-ever-amen sort of business."

Lord Shotover leaned back once more, and turned a wonderfully pleasant, if not pre-eminently responsible, countenance upon his companion.

"I never went in for that kind of racket myself, Miss St. Quentin," he continued. "Not being conspicuously faithful, I should only have made a *fiasco* of it. But I give you my word it touches me all the same when I do run across it. I think it's awfully lucky for a man to be made that way. And Decies is. So there seemed no help for it. I had to chuck discretion, as I told you, and give him his chance."

He paused, and then asked with a somewhat humorous air of self-depreciation:—"What do you think now, have I done more harm than good, made confusion worse confounded, and played the fool generally?"

But again Honoria vouchsafed him no immediate reply. The meditative mood still held her, and the present conversation offered much food for meditation. Her companion's confession of faith in true love, if you had the good fortune to be born that way, had startled her. That the speaker enjoyed the reputation of being something of a profligate lent singular point to that confession. She had not expected it from Lord Shotover, of all men. And, as coming from him, the sentiment was in a high degree arresting and interesting. Her own ideals, so far, had a decidedly anti-matrimonial tendency; while being in love appeared to her a much overrated, if not actively objectionable, condition. Personally she hoped to escape all experience of it. Then her thought travelled back to Lady Calmady—the charm of her personality, her sorrows, her splendid self-devotion, and to the object of that devotion—namely Richard Calmady, a being of strange contrasts, at once maimed and beautiful, a being from whom she—Honoria—shrank in instinctive repulsion while unwillingly acknowledging that he exercised a permanent and intimate fascination over her imagination. She dwelt, in quick pity, too, upon the frightened, wide-eyed, childish face recently seen rising from out its diaphanous cloud of tulle, the prettiness of it heightened by fair wealth of summer roses and flash of costly diamonds, and upon Mr. Decies, the whole-hearted, young, soldier lover, whose existence threatened such dangerous complications in respect of the rest of this strangely assorted company. Finally her meditative survey returned to its point of departure. In thought she surveyed her present companion—his undeniable excellence of sentiment and clear-seeing, his admittedly defective conduct in matters ethical and financial. Never before had she been at such close quarters with living and immediate human drama, and, notwithstanding her detachment, her lofty indifference and high-spirited theories, she found it profoundly agitating. She was sensible of being in collision with unknown and incalculable forces. Instinctively she rose from her place on the sofa, and, moving to the open window, looked out into the night.

Below, the Park, now silent and deserted, slept peacefully, as any expanse of remote country pasture and woodland, in the mildly radiant moonlight. Here and there were blottings of dark shadow cast by the clumps or avenues of trees. Here and there the timid, yellow flame of gas lamps struggled to assert itself against the all-embracing silver brightness. Here and there windows glowed warm, set in the pale, glistering façades of the adjacent houses. A cool, light wind, hailing from the direction of the unseen Serpentine, stirred the hanging clusters of the pink geraniums that fell over the curved lip of the stone vases, standing along the broad coping of the balcony, and gently caressed the girl's bare arms and shoulders.

Seen under these unaccustomed conditions familiar objects assumed a fantastic aspect. For the night is a mighty magician, with power to render even the weighty brick and stone, even the hard, uncompromising outlines, of a monster, modern city, delicately elusive, mockingly tentative and unsubstantial. Meanwhile, within, from all along the vista of crowded and brilliantly illuminated rooms, came the subdued, yet confused and insistent, sound of musical instruments, of many voices, many footsteps, the hush of women's trailing garments, the rise and fall of unceasing conversation. And to Honoria, standing in this quiet, dimly-seen place, the sense of that moonlit world without, and this gas and candle-lit world within, increased the nameless agitation which infected her. A haunting persuasion of the phantasmagoric character of all sounds that saluted her ears, all sights that met her eyes, possessed her. A vast uncertainty surrounded and pressed in on her; while those questionings of appearances and actualities, of truth and falsehood, right and wrong, justice and injustice, with which she had played idly earlier in the evening, took on new and almost terrible proportions, causing her intelligence, nay, her heart itself, to reach out, as never before, in search of some sure rock and house of defence against the disintegrating apprehension of universal instability and illusion.

"Ah! it is all very difficult, difficult to the point of alarm!" she exclaimed suddenly, turning to Lord Shotover and looking him straight in the face, with an unself-consciousness and desire of support so transparent that that gentleman found himself at once delighted and slightly abashed.

"Bless my soul, but Ludovic is a lucky devil!" he said to himself.—"What's—what's so beastly difficult, Miss St. Quentin?" he asked aloud. And the sound of his cheery voice recalled Honoria to the normal aspects of existence with almost humorous velocity. She smiled upon him.

"I really believe I don't quite know," she said. "Perhaps that the two people, of whom we were speaking, really care for each other, and that this engagement has come between them, and that you have chucked discretion and given him his chance. Tell me, what sort of man is he—strong enough to make the most of his chance when he's got it?"

But at that moment Lord Shotover stepped forward, adroitly planting himself right in front of her and thus screening her from observation.

"By George!" he said under his breath, in tones of mingled amusement and consternation, "he's making the most of his chance now, Miss St. Quentin, and that most uncommonly comprehensively, unless I'm very much mistaken."

Her companion's tall person and the folds of a heavy curtain, while screening Honoria from observation, also, in great measure, obscured her view of the room. Yet not so completely but that she saw two figures cross it, one black, one white, those of a man and a girl. They were both speaking, the man apparently pleading, the girl protesting and moving hurriedly the while, as though in actual flight. She must have been moving blindly, at random, for she stumbled against the outstanding, gilded leg of a consol table, set against the farther wall causing the ornaments on it to rattle. And so doing, she gave a plaintive exclamation of alarm, perhaps even of physical pain. Hearing which, that nameless agitation, that sense of collision with unknown and incalculable forces, seized hold on Honoria again, while Lord Shotover's features contracted and he turned his head sharply.

"By George!" he repeated under his breath.

But the girl recovered herself, and, followed by her companion,—he still pleading, she still protesting,—passed by the farther window on to the balcony and out of sight. There followed a period of embarrassed silence on the part of the usually voluble Shotover, while his pleasant countenance expressed a certain half-humorous concern.

"Really, I'm awfully sorry," he said. "I'd not the slightest intention of landing you in the thick of the brown like this."

"Or yourself either," she replied, smiling; though, with that sense of nameless agitation still upon her, her heart beat rather quick.

"Well, perhaps not. Between ourselves, moral courage isn't my strong point. There's nothing I funk like a row. I say, what shall we do? Don't you think we'd better quietly clear out?"

But, just then, a sound caught Honoria's ear before which all vague questions of ultimate truth and falsehood, right and wrong fled away. Whatever might savour of illusion, here was something real and actual, something pitiful, moreover, arousing the spirit of knight-errantry in her, pushing her to lay lance in rest and go forth, reckless of conventionalities, reckless even of considerations of justice, to the succour of oppressed womanhood. What words the man on the balcony, without, was saying, she could not distinguish — whether cruel or kind; but that the young girl was weeping, with the abandonment of long-resisted tears, she could not doubt.

"No, no, listen, Lord Shotover," she exclaimed authoritatively. "Don't you hear? She is crying as if her poor heart would break. You must stay. If I understand you rightly your sister has only got you to depend on. Whatever happens you must stand by her and see her through."

"Oh! but, my dear Miss St. Quentin"— The young man's aspect was entertaining. He looked at the floor, he looked at Honoria, he rubbed the back of his neck with one hand as though there might be placed the seat of fortitude. "You're inviting me to put my head into the liveliest hornet's nest. What the deuce—excuse me—am I to say to her and all the rest of them? Decies, even, mayn't quite understand my interference and may resent it. I think it is very much safer, all round, to let them—him and her—thrash it out between them, don't you know. I say though, what a beastly thing it is to hear a woman cry! I wish to goodness we'd never come into this confounded place and let ourselves in for it."

As he spoke, Lord Shotover turned towards the door, meditating escape in the direction of that brilliant vista of crowded rooms. But Honoria St. Quentin, her enthusiasm once aroused, became inexorable. With her long, swinging stride she outdistanced his hesitating steps, and stood, in the doorway, her arms extended—as to stop a runaway horse—her clear eyes aglow as though a lamp burned behind them, her pale, delicately cut face eloquent of very militant charity. A spice of contempt, moreover, for his display of pusillanimity was quite perceptible to Shotover in the expression of this charming, modern angel, clad in a ball-dress, bearing a fan instead of the traditional fiery-sword, who, so determinedly, barred the entrance of that comfortably conventional, worldly paradise to which he, just now, so warmly desired to regain admittance.

"No, no," she said, with a certain vibration in her quiet voice, "you are not to go! You are not to desert her. It would be unworthy, Lord Shotover. You brought Mr. Decies here and so you are mainly responsible for the present situation. And think, just think what it means. All the course of her life will be affected by that which takes place in the next half-hour. You would never cease to reproach yourself if things went wrong."

"Shouldn't I?" the young man said dubiously.

"Of course you wouldn't," Honoria asserted, "having it in your power to help, and then shirking the responsibility! I won't believe that of you. You are better than that. For think how young she is, and pretty and dependent. She may be driven to do some fatally, foolish thing if she's left unsupported. You must at least know what is going on. You are bound to do so. Moreover, as a mere matter of courtesy, you can't desert me and I intend to stay."

"Do you, though?" faltered Lord Shotover, in tones curiously resembling his father's.

Honoria drew herself up proudly, almost scornfully.

"Yes, I shall stay," she continued. "I am no match-maker. I have no particular faith in or admiration for marriage"—

"Haven't you, though?" said Lord Shotover. He was slightly surprised, slightly amused, but to his credit be it stated

22

that he put no equivocal construction upon the young lady's frank avowal. He felt a little sorry for Ludovic, that was all, fearing the latter's good fortune was less fully established than he had supposed.

"No, I don't believe very much in marriage — modern, upper-class marriage," she repeated. "And, just precisely on that account, it seems to me all the more degrading and shameful that a girl should risk marrying the wrong man. People talk about a broken engagement as though it was a disgrace. I can't see that. An unwilling, a—a—loveless marriage is the disgrace. And so at the very church door I would urge and encourage a woman to turn back, if she doubted, and have done with the whole thing."

"Upon my word!" murmured Lord Shotover.—The infinite variety of the feminine outlook, the unqualified audacity of feminine action, struck him as bewildering. Talk of women's want of logic! It was their relentless application of logic—as they apprehended it—which staggered him.

Honoria had come close to him. In her excitement she laid her fan on his arm.

"Listen," she said, "listen how Lady Constance is crying. Come—you must know what is happening. You must comfort her."

The young man thrust his hands into his pockets with an air of good-humoured and despairing resignation.

"All right," he replied, "only I tell you what it is, Miss St. Quentin, you've got to come too. I refuse to be deserted."

"I have not the smallest intention of deserting you," Honoria said. "Even yet discretion, though so lately chucked, might return to you. And then you might cut and run, don't you know."

CHAPTER VII

RECORDING THE ASTONISHING VALOUR DISPLAYED BY A CERTAIN SMALL MOUSE IN A CORNER

AS Honoria St. Quentin and the reluctant Shotover stepped, side by side, from the warmth and dimness obtaining in the anteroom, into the pleasant coolness of the moonlit balcony, Lady Constance Quayle, altogether forgetful of her usual careful civility and pretty correctness of demeanour, uttered an inarticulate cry—a cry, indeed, hardly human in its abandon and unreasoning anguish, resembling rather the shriek of the doubling hare as the pursuing greyhound nips it across the loins. Regardless of all her dainty finery of tulle, and roses, and flashing diamonds, she flung herself forward, face downwards, across the coping of the balustrade, her bare arms outstretched, her hands clasped above her head. Mr. Decies, blue-eyed, black-haired, smooth of skin, looking noticeably long and lithe in his close-fitting, dress clothes, made a rapid movement as though to lay hold on her and bear her bodily away. Then, recognising the futility of any such attempt, he turned upon the intruders, his high-spirited, Celtic face drawn with emotion, his attitude rather dangerously warlike.

"What do you want?" he demanded hotly.

"My dear good fellow," Lord Shotover began, with the most assuaging air of apology, "I assure you the very last thing I— we—I mean I—want is to be a nuisance. Only Miss St. Quentin thought—in fact, Decies, don't you see—dash it all, you know, there seemed to be some sort of worry going on out here and so "—

But Honoria did not wait for the conclusion of elaborate explanations, for that cry and the unrestraint of the girl's attitude not only roused, but shocked her. It was not fitting that any man, however kindly or even devoted, should behold this well-bred, modest and gentle, young maiden in her present extremity. So she swept past Mr. Decies and bent over Lady Constance Quayle, raised her, strove to soothe her agitation, speaking in tones of somewhat indignant tenderness.

But, though deriving a measure of comfort from the steady arm about her waist, from the strong, protective presence, from the rather stern beauty of the face looking down into hers, Lady Constance could not master her agitation. The train had left the metals, so to speak, and the result was confusion dire. A great shame held her, a dislocation of mind. She suffered that loneliness of soul which forms so integral a part of the misery of all apparently irretrievable disaster, whether moral or physical, and places the victim of it, in imagination at all events, rather terribly beyond the pale.

"Oh!" she sobbed, "you ought not to be so kind to me. I am very wicked. I never supposed I could be so wicked. What shall I do? I am so frightened at myself and at everything. I did not recognise you. I didn't see it was only Shotover."

"Well, but now you do see, my dear Con, it's only me," that gentleman remarked, with a cheerful disregard of grammar.

"And so you mustn't upset yourself any more.   It's awfully bad for you, and uncomfortable for everybody else, don't you know. You must try to pull yourself together a bit and we'll help you —of course, I'll help you.   We'll all help you, of course we will, and pull you through somehow."

But the girl only lamented herself the more piteously.

"Oh no, Shotover, you must not be so kind to me!   You couldn't, if you knew how wicked I have been."

"Couldn't I?" Lord Shotover remarked, not without a touch of humorous pathos.   "Poor little Con!"

"Only, only please do not tell Louisa.   It would be too dreadful if she knew—she, and Alicia, and the others.   Don't tell her, and I will be good.   I will be quite good, indeed I will."

"Bless me, my dear child, I won't tell anybody anything. To begin with I don't know anything to tell."

The girl's voice had sunk away into a sob.   She shuddered, letting her pretty, brown head fall back against Honoria St. Quentin's bare shoulder,—while the moonlight glinted on her jewels and the night wind swayed the hanging clusters of the pink geraniums.   Along with the warmth and scent of flowers, streaming outward through the open windows, came a confused sound of many voices, of discreet laughter, mingled with the wailing sweetness of violins.   Then the pleading, broken, childish voice took up its tale again :—

"I will be good.   I know I have promised, and I have let him give me a number of beautiful things.   He has been very kind to me, because he is clever, and of course I am stupid. But he has never been impatient with me.   And I am not ungrateful, indeed, Shotover, I am not.   It was only for a minute I was wicked enough to think of doing it.   But Mr. Decies told me he—asked me—and—and we were so happy at Whitney in the winter.   And it seemed too hard to give it all up, as he said it was true.   But I will be good, indeed I will.   Really it was only for a minute I thought of it.   I know I have promised. Indeed, I will make no fuss.   I will be good.   I will marry Richard Calmady."

"But this is simply intolerable!" Honoria said in a low voice.

She held herself tall and straight, looking gallant yet pure, austere even, as some pictured Jeanne d'Arc, a great singleness of purpose, a high courage of protest, an effect at once of fearless challenge and of command in her bearing.—"Is it not a scandal," she went on, "that in a civilised country, at this time of day, a woman should be allowed, actually forced, to suffer so much?

You must not permit this martyrdom to be completed—you can't!"

As she spoke Decies watched her keenly. Who this stately, young lady—so remarkably unlike the majority of Lord Shotover's intimate, feminine acquaintance—might be, he did not know. But he discerned in her an ally and a powerful one.

"Yes," he said impulsively, "you are right. It is a martyrdom and a scandalous one. It's worse than murder, it's sacrilege. It's not like any ordinary marriage. I don't want to be brutal, but it isn't. There's something repulsive in it, something unnatural."

The young man looked at Honoria, and read in her expression a certain agreement and encouragement.

"You know it, Shotover — you know it just as well as I do. And that justified me in attempting what I suppose I would not otherwise have felt it honourable to attempt.—Look here, Shotover, I will tell you what has just happened. I would have had to tell you to-morrow, in any case, if we had carried the plan out. But I suppose I have no alternative but to tell you now, since you've come."

He ranged himself in line with Miss St. Quentin, his back against one of the big, stone vases. He struggled honestly to keep both temper and emotion under control, but a rather volcanic energy was perceptible in him.

"I love Lady Constance," he said. "I have told her so, and—and she cares for me. I am not a Crœsus like Calmady. But I am not a pauper. I have enough to keep a wife in a manner suitable to her position and my own. When my uncle, Ulick Decies, dies—which I hope he'll not hurry to do, since I am very fond of him—there'll be the Somersetshire property in addition to my own dear, old place in County Cork. And your sister simply hates this marriage "—

"Lord bless me, my dear fellow, so do I!" Lord Shotover put in with evident sincerity.

"And so, when at last I had spoken freely, I asked her to "—

But the young girl cowered down, hiding her face in Honoria St. Quentin's bosom.

"Oh! don't say it again—don't say it," she implored. "It was wicked of me to listen to you even for a minute. I ought to have stopped you at once and sent you away. It was very wrong of me to listen, and talk to you, and tell you all that I did. But everything is so strange, and I have been so miserable. I never supposed anybody could ever be so miserable. And I knew it was ungrateful of me, and so I dared not tell anybody.

I would have told papa, but Louisa never let me be alone with him. She said papa indulged me, and made me selfish and fanciful, and so I have never seen him for more than a little while. And I have been so frightened."—She raised her head, gazing wide-eyed first at Miss St. Quentin and then at her brother. "I have thought such dreadful things. I must be very bad. I wanted to run away. I wanted to die"—

"There, you hear, you hear," Decies cried hoarsely, spreading abroad his hands, in sudden violence of appeal to Honoria. "For God's sake help us! I am not aware whether you are a relation, or a friend, or what. But I am convinced you can help, if only you choose to do so. And I tell you she is just killing herself over this accursed marriage. Someone's got at her and talked her into some wild notion of doing her duty, and marrying money for the sake of her family"—

"Oh, I say, damn it all!" Lord Shotover exclaimed, smitten with genuine remorse.

"And so she believes she's committing the seven deadly sins, and I don't know what besides, because she rebels against this marriage and is unhappy. Tell her it's absurd, it's horrible, that she should do what she loathes and detests. Tell her this talk about duty is a blind, and a fiction. Tell her she isn't wicked. Why, God in heaven, if we were none of us more wicked than she is, this poor old world would be so clean a place that the holy angels might walk barefoot along the Piccadilly pavement there, outside, without risking to soil so much as the hem of their garments! Make her understand that the only sin for her is to do violence to her nature by marrying a man she's afraid of, and for whom she does not care. I don't want to play a low game on Sir Richard Calmady and steal that which belongs to him. But she doesn't belong to him—she is mine, just my own. I knew that from the first day I came to Whitney, and looked her in the face, Shotover. And she knows it too, only she's been terrorised with all this devil's talk of duty."

So far the words had poured forth volubly, as in a torrent. Now the speaker's voice dropped, and they came slowly, defiantly, yet without hesitation.

"And so I asked her to go away with me, now, to-night, and marry me to-morrow. I can make her happy—oh, no fear about that! And she would have consented and gone. We'd have been away by now—if you and this lady had not come just when you did, Shotover."

The gentleman addressed whistled very softly.

"Would you, though?" he said, adding meditatively :—

"By George now, who'd have thought of Connie going the pace like that !"

"Oh, Shotover, never tell, promise me you will never tell them !" the poor child cried again. "I know it was wicked, but"—

"No, no, you are mistaken there," Honoria put in, holding her still closer. "You were tempted to take a rather desperate way out of your difficulties. It would have been unwise, but there was nothing wicked in it. The wrong thing is—as Mr. Decies tells you—to marry without love, and so make all your life a lie, by pretending to give Richard Calmady that which you do not, and cannot, give him."

Then the young soldier broke in resolutely again.

"I tell you I asked her to go away, and I ask her again now"—

"The deuce you do !" Lord Shotover exclaimed, his sense of amusement getting the better alike of astonishment and of personal regrets.

"Only now I ask you to sanction her going, Shotover. And I ask you"—he turned to Miss St. Quentin—"to come with her. I am not even sure of your name, but I know, by all that you've said and done in the last half-hour, I can be very sure of you. And, I perceive, that if you come nobody will dare to say anything unpleasant—there'll be nothing, indeed, to be said."

Honoria smiled. The magnificent egoism of mankind in love struck her as distinctly diverting. Yet she had a very kindly feeling towards this black-haired, bright-eyed, energetic, young lover. He was in deadly earnest—to the removing even of mountains. And he had need to be so, for that mountains immediately blocked the road to his desires was evident even to her enthusiastic mind. She looked across compellingly at Lord Shotover. Let him speak first. She needed time, at this juncture, in which to arrange her ideas and to think.

"My dear good fellow," that gentleman began obediently, patting Decies on the shoulder, "I'm all on your side. I give you my word I am, and I've reason to believe my father will be so too. But you see, an elopement—specially in our sort of highly respectable, hum-drum family—is rather a strong order. Upon my honour it is, you know, Decies. And, even though kindly countenanced by Miss St. Quentin, and sanctioned by me, it would make a precious undesirable lot of talk. It really is a rather irregular fashion of conducting the business you see. And then—advice I always give others and only wish I could always remember to take myself—it's very much best to be off with the old love before you're on with the new."

"Yes, yes," Miss St. Quentin put in with quick decision. "Lord Shotover has laid his finger on the heart of the matter. It is just that. — Lady Constance's engagement to Richard Calmady must be cancelled before her engagement to you, Mr. Decies, is announced. For her to go away with you would be to invite criticism, and put herself hopelessly in the wrong. She must not put herself in the wrong. Let me think! There must be some way by which we can avoid that."

An exultation, hitherto unexperienced by her, inspired Honoria St. Quentin. Her attitude was slightly unconventional. She sat on the stone balustrade, with long-limbed, lazy grace, holding the girl's hand, forgetful of herself, forgetful, in a degree, of appearances, concerned only with the problem of rescue presented to her. The young man's honest, whole-hearted devotion, the young girl's struggle after duty and her piteous despair, nay, the close contact of that soft, maidenly body that she had so lately held against her in closer, more intimate, embrace than she had ever held anything human before, aroused a new class of sentiment, a new order of emotion, within her. She realised, for the first time, the magnetism, the penetrating and poetic splendour of human love. To witness the spectacle of it, to be thus in touch with it, excited her almost as sailing a boat in a heavy sea, or riding to hounds in a stiff country, excited her. And it followed that now, while she perched aloft boylike, on the balustrade, her delicate beauty took on a strange effulgence, a something spiritual, mysterious, elusive, and yet dazzling as the moonlight which bathed her charming figure. Seeing which, it must be owned that Lord Shotover's attitude towards her ceased to be strictly fraternal, while the attractions of ladies more fair and kind than wise paled very sensibly.

"I wish I hadn't been such a fool in my day, and run amuck with my chances," he thought.

But Miss St. Quentin was altogether innocent of his observation or any such thinkings. She looked up suddenly, her face irradiated by an exquisite smile.

"Yes, I have it," she cried. "I see the way clear."

"But I can't tell them," broke in Lady Constance.

Honoria's hand closed down on hers reassuringly.

"No," she said, "you shall not tell them. And Lord Shotover shall not tell them. Sir Richard Calmady shall tell Lord

Fallowfeild that he wishes to be released from his engagement, as he believes both you and he will be happier apart.   Only you must be brave, both for your own sake, and for Mr. Decies', and for Richard Calmady's sake also.—Lady Constance," she went on, with a certain gentle authority, "do you want to go back to Whitney to-morrow, or next day, all this nightmare of an unhappy marriage done away with and gone?   Well, then, you must come and see Sir Richard Calmady to-night, and, like an honourable woman, tell him the whole truth.   It must be done at once, or your courage may fail.   We will come with you— Lord Shotover and I"—

"Good Lord, will we though!" the young man ejaculated, while the girl's great, heifer's eyes grew strained with wonder at this astounding announcement.

"I know it will be rather terrible," Honoria continued calmly. "But it is a matter of a quarter of an hour, as against a lifetime, and of honour as against a lie.   So it's worth while, don't you think so, when your whole future, and Mr. Decies'"—she pressed the soft hand again steadily—"is at stake?   You must be brave now, and tell him the truth—just simply that you do not love him enough—that you have tried,—you have, I know you have done that,—but that you have failed, that you love someone else, and that therefore you beg him, in mercy, before it is too late, to set you free."

Fascinated both by her appearance and by the simplicity of her trenchant solution of the difficulty, Lord Shotover stared at the speaker.   Her faith was infectious.   Yet it occurred to him that all women, good and bad, are at least alike in this—that their methods become radically unscrupulous when they find themselves in a tight place.

"It is a fine plan.   It ought to work, for—cripple or not— poor Calmady's a gentleman," he said, slowly.   "But doesn't it seem just a trifle rough, Miss St. Quentin, to ask him to be his own executioner?"

Honoria had slipped down from the balustrade, and stood erect in the moonlight.

"I think not," she replied.   "The woman pays, as a rule. Lady Constance has paid already quite heavily enough, don't you think so?   Now we will have the exception that proves the rule.   The man shall pay whatever remains of the debt.   But we must not waste time.   It is not late yet, we shall still find him up, and my brougham is here.   I told Lady Aldham I should be home fairly early.   Get a cloak, Lady Constance, and meet us in the hall.   I suppose you can go down by some back way so as to avoid meeting people. Lord Shotover, will you take me to say good-night to your sister, Lady Louisa?"

The young man fairly chuckled.

"And you, Mr. Decies, must stay and dance."—She smiled upon him very sweetly. "I promise you it will come through all right, for, as Lord Shotover says, whatever his misfortunes may be, Richard Calmady is a gentleman.—Ah! I hope you are going to be very happy. Good-bye."

Decies' black head went down over her hand, and he kissed it impulsively.

"Good-bye," he said, the words catching a little in his throat. "When the time comes, may you find the man to love you as you deserve—though I doubt if there's such a man living, or dead either, for that matter! God bless you."

Some half-hour later Honoria stood among the holland-shrouded furniture in Lady Calmady's sitting-room in Lowndes Square. The period of exalted feeling, of the conviction of successful attainment, was over, and her heart beat somewhat painfully. For she had had time, by now, to realise the surprising audacity of her own proceedings. Lord Shotover's parley with Richard Calmady's man-servant, on the doorstep, had brought that home to her, placing what had seemed obvious, as a course of action to her fervid imagination, in quite a new light.— Sir Richard Calmady was at home? He was still up?—To that, yes. Would he see Lady Constance Quayle upon urgent business?—To that again, yes—after a rather lengthy delay, while the valet, inscrutable, yet evidently highly critical, made inquiries.—The trees in the square had whispered together uncomfortably, while the two young ladies waited in the carriage. And Lord Shotover's shadow, which had usually, very surely, nothing in the least portentous about it, lay queerly, three ways at once, in varying degrees of density, across the grey pavement in the conflicting gas and moon-light.

And now, as she stood among the shrouded furniture, which appeared oddly improbable in shape seen in the flickering of two hastily-lighted candles, Honoria could hear Shotover walking back and forth, patiently, on that same grey pavement outside. She was overstrained by the emotions and events of the past hours. Small matters compelled her attention. The creaking of a board, the rustle of a curtain, the silence even of this large, but half-inhabited, house, were to her big with suggestion, disquietingly replete with possible meaning, of exaggerated importance to her anxiously listening ears.

Lord Shotover had stopped walking. He was talking to the

coachman.   Honoria entertained a conviction that, in the overflowing of his good-nature, he talked—sooner or later—to every
soul whom he met.   She derived almost childish comfort from
the knowledge of the near neighbourhood of that eminently good-
natured presence.   Lord Shotover's very obvious faults faded
from her remembrance.   She estimated him only by his size,
his physical strength, his large indulgence of all weaknesses
—including his own.   He constituted a link between her and
things ordinary and average, for which she was rather absurdly
thankful at this juncture.   For the minutes passed slowly, very
slowly.   It must be getting on for half an hour since little Lady
Constance, trembling and visibly affrighted, had passed out of
sight, and the door of the smoking-room had closed behind her.
The nameless agitation which possessed her earlier that same
evening returned upon Honoria St. Quentin.   But its character
had suffered change.   The questioning of the actual, the
suspicion of universal illusion, had departed; and in its place
she suffered alarm of the concrete, of the incalculable force of
human passion, and of a manifestation of tragedy in some active
and violent form.   She did not define her own fears, but they
surrounded her nevertheless, so that the slightest sound made
her start.

For, indeed, how slowly the minutes did pass !   Lord Shotover
was walking again.   The horse rattled its bit, and pawed the
ground impatient of delay.   Though lofty, the room appeared
close and hot, with drawn blinds and shut windows.   Honoria
began to move about restlessly, threading her way between
the pieces of shrouded furniture.   A chalk drawing of Lady
Calmady stood on an easel in the far corner.   The portrait
emphasised the sweetness and abiding pathos, rather than the
strength, of the original; and Honoria, standing before it, put
her hands over her eyes.   For the pictured face seemed to plead
with and reproach her.   Then a swift fear took her of disloyalty,
of hastiness, of self-confidence trenching on cruelty.   She had
announced, rather arrogantly, that whatever balance remained
to be paid, in respect of Sir Richard and Lady Constance Quayle's
proposed marriage, should be paid by the man.   But would the
man, in point of fact, pay it ?   Would it not, must it not, be
paid, eventually, by this other noble and much enduring woman—
whom she had called her friend, and towards whom she played
the part, as she feared, of betrayer ?   In her hot espousal of Lady
Constance's cause she had only saved one woman at the expense
of another— Oh ! how hot the room grew !   Suffocating— Lord
Shotover's steps died away in the distance.   She could look

Lady Calmady in the face no more. Secure in her own self-conceit and vanity, she had betrayed her friend.

Suddenly the sharp peal of a bell, the opening of a door, the dragging of silken skirts, and the hurrying of footsteps.— Honoria gathered up her somewhat scattered courage and swung out into the hall. Lady Constance Quayle came towards her, groping, staggering, breathless, her face convulsed with weeping. But to this, for the moment, Miss St. Quentin paid small heed. For, at the far end of the hall, a bright light streamed out from the open doorway. And in the full glare of it stood a young man—his head, with its cap of close-cropped curls, proudly distinguished as that of some classic hero, his features the beautiful features of Katherine Calmady, his height but two-thirds the height a man of his make should be, his face drawn and livid as that of a corpse, his arms hanging down straight at his sides, his hands only just not touching the marble quarries of the floor on either side of him.

Honoria uttered an exclamation of uncontrollable pity and horror, caught Constance Quayle by the arm, and hurried out into the moonlit square to the waiting carriage. Lord Shotover flung away the end of his cigar and strolled towards them.

"Got through, fixed it all right—eh, Connie? Bravo—that's grand!—Oh, you needn't tell me! I can imagine it's been a beastly piece of work, but anyway it's over now. You must go home and go to bed, and I'll account for you somehow to Louisa. My mind's becoming quite inventive to-night, I promise you.—There, get in—try to pull yourself together. Miss St. Quentin, upon my word I don't know how to thank you. You've been magnificent, and put us under an everlasting obligation, Con and Decies, and my father and me.—Nice night isn't it? You'll put us down in Albert Gate? All right. A thousand thanks.—Yes, I'll go on the box again. You haven't much room for my legs among all those flounces. Bless me, it occurs to me I'm getting confoundedly hungry. I shall be awfully glad of some supper."

CHAPTER VIII

A MANIFESTATION OF THE SPIRIT

BROCKHURST HOUSE had slumbered all day long in the steady warmth of the July sun. The last three weeks had been rainless, so that the short turf of the uplands began to grow crisp and discoloured, while the resinous scent of the fir forest, at once stimulating and soothing, was carried afar out over the sloping cornfields and low-lying pastures. Above the stretches of purple-budding heather and waste sandy places, upon the moors, the heat-haze danced and quivered as do vapours arising from a furnace. Along the under side of the great woods, and in the turn of the valleys, shadows lingered, which were less actual shadows than blottings of blue light. The birds, busy feeding wide-mouthed, hungry fledgelings, had mostly ceased from song. But the drowsy hum of bees and chirrup of grasshoppers was continuous, and told, very pleasantly, of the sunshine and large plenty reigning out of doors.

For Katherine the day in question had passed in Martha-like occupations.—A day of organising, of ordering and counter-manding, a day of much detail, much interviewing of heads of departments, a day of meeting respectful objections, enlightening thick understandings, gently reducing decorously opposing wills. Commissariat, transport, housing of guests, and the servants of guests—all these entered into the matter of the coming wedding. To compass the doing of all things, not only decently and in order, but handsomely, and with a becoming dignity, this required time and thought. And so, it was not until after dinner that Katherine found herself at leisure to cease taking thought for the morrow. Too tired to rest herself by reading, she wandered out on the troco-ground followed by Camp.

London had not altogether suited the bull-dog as the summer wore on. Now, in his old age, so considerable a change of sur-roundings put him about both in body and mind. Seeing which, Richard had begged his mother to take the dog with her on leaving town. Camp benefited, unquestionably, by his return to country air. His coat stared less. He carried his ears and tail with more sprightliness and conviction. Still he fretted after his absent master, and followed Katherine's footsteps very closely, his forehead more than ever wrinkled and his unsightly mouth pensive notwithstanding its perpetual grin. He attended

her now, squatting beside her when she paused, trotting slowly
beside her when she moved, a silent, persistent, and, as it might
seem, somewhat fatefully faithful companion.

Yet the occasion was to all appearances far from fateful, the
night and the scene, alike, being very fair. The moon had not
yet risen, but a brightness behind the sawlike edge of the fir
woods eastward heralded its coming, while sufficient light yet
remained in the western and northern sky for the mass of the
house, its ruddy walls and ranges of mullioned windows, its
pierced, stone parapet and stacks of slender, twisted chimneys,
to be seen with a low-toned distinctness of form and colour
infinitely charming.   Soft and rich as velvet, it rose, with a certain
noble serenity, above its terraces and fragrant, red-walled gardens,
under the enormous dome of the tranquil, far-off, evening sky.

Every aspect of this place, in rain and shine, summer and
winter, from dawn to dark and round to dawn again, was
familiar to Katherine Calmady.   Coming here first, as a bride,
the homely splendour of the house, and the gladness of its
situation crowning the ridge of hill, appealed strongly to her
imagination.   Later it sheltered her long sorrow, following so
hard on the heels of her brief joy.   But, in both alike, during all
the vicissitudes of her thought and of her career, the face of
Brockhurst remained as that of a friend, kindly, beneficent, increasingly trusted and beloved.   And so she had come to know
every stick and stone of it, from spacious, vaulted cellar to equally
spacious, low-roofed, sun-dried attic—the outlook from each
window, the character of each room, the turn of each stairway,
the ample proportions of each lobby and stair-head, all the
pleasant scents, and sounds, and colours, that haunted it both
within and without.   It might have been supposed that after
so many years of affectionate observation and commerce,
Brockhurst could have no new word in its tongue, could hold no
further self-revelation, for Lady Calmady.   Yet, as she passed
now from the arcaded garden-hall, supporting the eastern bay of
the Long Gallery, on to the level, green square of the troco-ground,
and stood gazing out over the downward sloping park—the
rough, short turf of it dotted with ancient thorn trees and broken
by beds of bracken and dog-roses—to the Long Water, glistening like some giant mirror some quarter-mile distant in the
valley, she became sensible of a novel element in her present
relation to this place.

For the first time, in all her long experience, she was at
Brockhurst quite alone.   The house was vacant even of a friend.
For Julius March had, rather to Katherine's surprise, selected just

this moment for the paying of his yearly visit to a certain college friend, a scholarly and godly person, now rector of a sleepy, country parish away in the heart of the great Midlandshire grasslands. Katherine experienced a momentary sense of injury at his going. Yet perhaps it was as well. Between the turmoil of the past London season, the coming turmoil of the wedding and the large and serious issues which that wedding involved, this time of solitude might be salutary. To Katherine, just now, it seemed as a bridge carrying her over from one way of life to another. A but slightly known country lay ahead. Solitude and self-recollection are good for the soul if it would possess itself in peace. The fair brightness of the Indwelling Light had not been obscured in her during these months devoted to the world and to society. But it was inevitable that her consciousness of it, and consequently its clear-shining, should have suffered diminution at times. The eager pressure of things to be done, things to be seen, of much conversation, the varied pageant of modern life perpetually presented to her eyes and her intelligence, could not but crowd out the spiritual order somewhat. Of late she had had only time to smile upon her God in passing, instead of spending long hours within the courts of His temple. This she knew. It troubled her a little. She desired to return to a condition of more complete self-collectedness. And so, the first movement of surprise past, she hailed her solitude as a means of grace, and strove, in sweet sincerity, to make good use of it.

And yet—since the human heart, if sound and wholesome, hungers, even when penetrated by godward devotion, for some fellow-creature on whom to expend its tenderness—Katherine, just now, regretted to be alone. The scene was so beautiful, she would gladly have had someone look on it beside herself, and share its charm. Then thoughts of the future obtruded themselves. How would little Constance Quayle view Brockhurst? Would it claim her love? Would she embrace the spirit of it, and make it not only the home of her fair, young body, but the home of her guileless heart? Katherine yearned in spirit over this girl standing on the threshold of all the deeper experiences of a woman's life, of those amazing revelations which marriage holds for an innocent and modest maiden.—But oh! how lovely are such revelations when the lover is also the beloved!

Katherine moved on a few paces. The thought of all that, even now at forty-eight, cut her a little too sharply. It is not wise to call up visions of joys that are dead. She would think of something else, so she told herself, as she paused in her rustling grey dress upon the dry, gravel path, the surface of which still sensibly held the warmth of the sun, while Camp squatted soberly on his haunches beside her. But, at first, only worrying thoughts responded to her call.—It was not quite kind, surely, of Julius to have left home just now. It was a little inconsiderate of him. If she dwelt on the thought of that, clearly it would vex her—so it must be banished. Reynolds, the housekeeper, had really been very perverse about the turning of the two larger china-closets into extra dressing-rooms for the week of the wedding, and Clara showed an inclination to back her up in opposition. Of course the maids would give in—they always did, and that without any subsequent attempt at small reprisals. Still the thought of that, too, was annoying and must be banished.—At dinner she had received a singular letter from Honoria St. Quentin. It contained what appeared to Katherine as rather over-urgent protestations of affection and offers of service, if at any future time she—the writer—could be of use. The letter was charming in its slight extravagance. But it struck Katherine as incomprehensibly penitent in tone—the letter of one who has not treated a friend quite loyally and is hot with anxiety to atone. It was dated this morning too, and must have been posted at some surprisingly early hour to have thus reached Brockhurst by the day mail. Lady Calmady did not quite relish the missive, somehow, notwithstanding its affection. It lacked the perfection of personal dignity which had pleased her heretofore in Honoria St. Quentin. She felt vaguely disappointed. And it followed that this thought, therefore, must go along with the rest. For she refused to be disquieted. She would compel herself to be at peace.

So, putting these small sources of discomfort from her, as unworthy both of her better understanding and of this fair hour and fair place, Katherine yielded herself wholly to the influences of her surroundings. The dew was rising—promise of another hot, clear day to-morrow—and along with it rose a fragrance of wild thyme from the grass slopes immediately below. That fragrance mingled with the richer scents of jasmine, full-cupped, July roses, scarlet, trumpet-flowered honeysuckle, tall lilies, and great wealth of heavy-headed, clove carnations, veiling the red walls or set in the trim borders of the gardens behind. A strangely belated nightingale still sang in the big, Portugal laurel beside the quaint, pepper-pot summer-house in the far corner of the troco-ground, where the twenty-foot, brick wall dips, in steps of well-set masonry, to the grey, three-foot balustrade. She never remembered to have heard one sing so late in the summer. The bird was answered, moreover, by another singer from the coppice, bordering the trout-stream which feeds the Long Water, away across the valley.   In each case the song was, note for note, the same.   But the chant of the near bird was hotly urgent in its passion of "wooing and winning;" while the song of the answerer came chastened and etherealised by distance.   A fox barked sharply on the left, out in the Warren.   And the churring of the night-hawks, as they flitted hither and thither over the beds of bracken and dog-roses, like gigantic moths, on swift, silent wings, formed a continuous accompaniment, as of a spinning-wheel, to the other sounds.

Never, as she watched and listened, had the genius of Brockhurst appeared more potent or more enthralling.   For a space she rested in it, asking nothing beyond that which sight and hearing could give.   It was very good to breathe the scented air and be lulled by the inarticulate music of nature.   It was good to cease from self and from all individual striving, to become a part merely of the universal movement of things, a link merely in the mighty chain of universal being.   But such an impersonal attitude of mind cannot last long, least of all in the case of a woman !   Katherine's heart awoke and cried again for some human object on which to expend itself, some kindred intelligence to meet and reflect her own.   Ah, were she but better, more holy and more wise, these cravings would doubtless not assail her !   The worship of the Indwelling Light would suffice, and she would cease from desire of the love of any creature. But she had not journeyed so far upon the road of perfection yet, as she sadly told herself.   Far from it.   The nightingale sang on, sang of love, not far hence, not far above, not within the spirit only, but here, warm, immediate, and individual.   And, do what she would, the song brought to her mind such love, as she herself had known it during the few golden months of her marriage—of meetings at night, sweet and sacred ; of partings, sweet and sacred too, at morning ; of secret delights ; of moments, at once pure and voluptuous, known only to virtuous lovers.   It was not often that remembrance of all this came back to her, save as a faint echo of a once clear-sounding voice.   Indeed she had supposed it all laid away forever, done with, even as the bright colours it had once so pleased her to wear were laid away in high, mahogany presses that lined one side of the lofty state-bedroom upstairs.   But now remembrance laid violent hands on her, shaking both mind and body from their calm.   The passion of the bird's song, the caressing suavity of the summer night, the knowledge, too, that so soon another bride and bridegroom would dwell here at Brockhurst, worked upon her strangely.   She struggled with herself, surprised and half angered by the force of her own

23

emotion, and pleaded at once against, and for, the satisfaction of the immense nostalgia which possessed her.

"Ah! it is bitter, very bitter, to have had at once so much and so little. Bow my proud neck, O Lord, to Thy yoke.—If my beloved had but been spared to me I had never walked in darkness, far from the way of faith, and my child had never suffered bodily disfigurement. Perfect me, O God, even at the cost of further suffering. It is sad to be shut away from the joys of my womanhood, while my life is still strong in me. Break me, O Lord, even as the ploughshare breaks the reluctant clod. Hold not Thy hand till the work be fully accomplished, and the earth be ready for the sowing which makes for harvest.—Give me back the beloved of my youth, the beloved of my life, if only for an hour. Teach me to submit.—Show me, beyond all dread of contradiction that vows, truly made, hold good even in that mysterious world beyond the grave. Show me that though the body—dear home and vehicle of love—may die, yet love in its essence remains everlastingly conscious, faithful and complete. Bend my will to harmony with Thine, O Lord, and cleanse me of self-seeking.—Ah! but still let me see his face once again, once again, oh, my God—and I will rebel no more. Let me look on him, once again, if only for a moment, and I shall be content. Hear me, I am greatly troubled, I am athirst—I faint"—

Katherine's prayer, which had risen into audible speech, sank away into silence. The near nightingale had fallen silent also. But from across the valley, chastened and etherealised by distance, still came the song of the answering bird. To Katherine those fine and delicate notes were full of promise. They bore testimony to the soul which dwells forever behind the outward aspect and sense. Whether she fainted in good truth, or whether she passed, for a while, into that sublimated state of consciousness wherein the veils of habit cease to blind and something of the eternal essence and values of things is revealed— perception overstepping, for once, the limits of ordinary, earthbound apprehension and transcending ordinary circumscription of time and place—she could not tell. Nor did she greatly care. For a great peace descended upon her, accompanied by a gentle, yet penetrating expectancy. She stood very still, her feet set on the warm gravel, the night air wrapping her about as with a fragrant garment, the ghostly sweetness of that far-away bird-song in her ears, while momentarily the conviction of the near presence of the man who had so loved her, and whom she had so loved, deepened within her. And therefore it was without alarm, without any shock of amazement, that gradually she found her awareness of that presence change from something felt, to something actually seen.

He came towards her—that first Richard Calmady, her husband and lover — across the smooth, green levels of the troco-ground which lay dusky in the mingling half-lights of the nearly departed sunset and the rising moon—as he had come to her a hundred times in life, back from the farms or the moorlands, from sport or from business, or from those early morning rides, the clean freshness of the morning upon him, after seeing his racehorses galloped. He came bareheaded, in easy workmanlike garments, short coat, breeches, long boots and spurs. He came with the repose of movement which is born of a wellknit frame, and a temperate life, and the grace of gentle blood. He came with the half smile on his lips, and the gladness in his eyes when they first met hers, which had always been there however brief the parting. And Katherine perceived it was just thus our beloved dead must needs return to us—should they return at all—laying aside the splendours of the spirit in tenderness for mortal weakness. Even as the Christ laid aside the visible glory of the Godhead, and came a babe among men, so must they come in humble, every-day fashion, graciously taking on the manner and habit common to them during earthly life. Therefore she suffered no shrinking, but turned instinctively, as she had turned a hundred times, laughing very softly in the fulness of content, raising her hands, throwing back her head, knowing that he would come behind her and take her hands in his, and kiss her, so, bending down over her shoulder. And, when he came, she did not need to speak, but only to gaze into the wellbeloved face, familiar, yet touched—as it seemed to her—with a mysterious and awful beauty, beholding which she divined the answer to many questions.

For she perceived, as one waking from an uneasy dream perceives the comfortable truth of day, that her love was not given back to her, for the dear reason that her love had never been taken away. The fiction of Time ceased to rule in her, so that the joy of bride and new-wed wife, the strange, sweet perplexities of dawning motherhood were with her now, not as memories merely, but as actual, ever-present, deathless facts—the culminating, and therefore permanent, revelation of her individual experience. She perceived this continued and must continue, since it was the fine flower of her nature, the unit of her personal equation, the realisation of the eternal purpose concerning her of Almighty God. The fiction of old age was discredited, so was the bitterness of deposition, the mournful fiction of being passed

by and relegated to the second place. Her place was her own.
Her standing ground in the universal order, a freehold, absolute
and inalienable.   She could not abdicate her throne, neither
could any wrest it away from her.   She perceived that not self-
effacement, but self-development, not dissolution, but evolution,
was the service required of her.   And, as divinely designed
contribution to that end was every joy, every sorrow, laid
upon her ; since by these was she differentiated from all others,
by these was she built up into a separate existence, sane,
harmonious, well-proportioned, a fair lamp lighted with a
burning coal from off the altar of that God of whom it is written,
not only that He is a consuming fire, but that He is Love.

All this, and more, did Katherine apprehend, beholding the
familiar, yet mysterious countenance of her well-beloved.   And
the tendency of that apprehension made for tranquillity of
spirit, for a sure and certain hope.   The faculty which reasons,
demands explanation and proof, might not be satisfied ; but that
higher faculty which divines, accepts, believes, assuredly was so.
Nor could it be otherwise, since it is the spirit, the idea, not the
letter, which giveth life.

How long she stood thus, in tender and illuminating, though
wordless, communion with the dead, Katherine did not know.
The deepest spiritual experiences, like the most exquisite
physical ones, are to be measured by intensity rather than
duration.   For a space the vision sensibly held her, the so
ardently desired presence there incontestibly beside her, a
personality vivid and distinct, yet in a way remote, serene as the
immense dome of the cloudless sky, chastened and etherealised
as the song of the answering nightingale ; and in this differing
from any bodily presence, as the song in question differed from
that of the bird in the laurel close at hand.

Gradually, and with such sense of refreshment as one enjoys
who, bathing in some clear stream at evening, washes away
all soil and sweat of a weary journey, Katherine awoke to
more ordinary observation of her material surroundings.   She
became aware that the dog, Camp, had turned singularly
restless.   He slunk away as though wishing to avoid her near
neighbourhood, crawled back to her, with dragging hind-
quarters, cringing and whining as though in acute distress.   And,
by degrees, another sound obtruded itself, speaking of haste and
effort, notably at variance with the delicate and gracious stillness.
It came from the highroad crossing the open moor, which
loomed up a dark, straight ridge against the southern horizon.
It came in rising and falling cadence, but ever nearer and

nearer, increasingly distinct, increasingly urgent—the fast, steady trot of a horse. The moon, meanwhile, had swept clear of the sawlike edge of the fir forest; and, while the thin, white light of it broadened upon the dewy grass and the beat of the horse-hoofs rang out clearer and clearer, Katherine was aware that the dear vision faded and grew faint. As it had come, softly, without amazement or fear, so it departed, without agitation or sadness of farewell, leaving Katherine profoundly consoled, the glory of her womanhood restored to her in the indubitable assurance that what had been of necessity continued, and forever was.

And, therefore, she still listened but idly to the approaching sound, not reckoning with it as yet, though the roll of wheels was now added to the rapid beat of the hoofs of a trotting horse. It had turned down over the hillside by the cross road leading to the upper lodge. Suddenly it ceased. The shout of a man's voice, loud and imperative, a momentary pause, then the clang of heavy, iron gates swinging back into place; and once again the roll of wheels and that steady, urgent, determined trot, coming nearer and nearer down the elm avenue, whose stately rows of trees looked as though made of ebony and burnished silver in the slanting moonlight. On it came across the bridge spanning the glistering whiteness of the Long Water. And on again, steadily and no less rapidly, as though pressed by the hand of a somewhat merciless driver, hot to arrive, bearer of stirring tidings, up the steeply ascending hill to the house.

Lady Calmady listened, beginning to question whom this nocturnal disturber of the peace of Brockhurst might be. But only vaguely as yet, since that which she had recently experienced was so great, so wide-reaching in its meaning and promise, that, for the moment, it dwarfed all other possible, all other imaginable, events. The gracious tranquillity which enveloped her could not be penetrated by any anxiety or premonition of momentous happenings as yet. It was not so, however, with Camp. For a spirit of extravagant and unreasoning excitement appeared to seize on the dog. Forgetful of age, of stiff limbs and short-coming breath, he gambolled round Lady Calmady, describing crazy circles upon the grass, and barking until the unseemly din echoed back harshly from against the great red and grey façade. He fawned upon her, abject, yet compelling; and, at last, as though exasperated by her absence of response, turned tail and bounded away through the garden-hall and along the terrace, disappearing through the small, arched side-door into the house. And there, within, stir and movement became momentarily more apparent. Shifting lights flashed out through the many-paned windows, as though in quick search of some eagerly desired presence.

Nevertheless, for a little space, Katherine lingered, the fragrance of the wild thyme and of the fair gardens still about her, the somnolent churring of the night-hawks and faint notes of the nightingale's song still saluting her ears. It was so difficult to return to and cope with the demands of ordinary life. For had she not been caught up into the third heaven and heard words unspeakable, unlawful, in their entirety, for living man to utter?

But things terrestrial, in this case as in so many other cases, refused to make large room for, or brook delay from, things celestial. Two servants came out, hurriedly, from that same arched side-door. Then Clara, that devoted handmaiden, called from the window of the red drawing-room.

"Her ladyship's there, on the troco-ground. Don't you see, Mr. Winter?"

The butler hurried along the terrace. Katherine met him on the steps of the garden-hall.

"Is anything wrong, Winter?" she asked kindly, for the trusted servant betrayed unusual signs of emotion. "Am I wanted?"

"Sir Richard has returned, my lady," he said, and his voice shook. "Sir Richard is in the Gun-Room. He gave orders that your ladyship should be told that he would be glad to speak to you immediately."

CHAPTER IX

IN WHICH DICKIE SHAKES HANDS WITH THE DEVIL

"MY dear, this is quite unexpected."

Lady Calmady's tone was one of quiet, innate joyousness. A gentle brightness pervaded her whole aspect and manner. She looked wonderfully young, as though the hands of the clock had been put back by some twenty and odd years. Every line had disappeared from her face, and in her eyes was a clear shining very lovely to behold. Richard glanced at her as she came swiftly towards him across the room. Then he looked down again, and answered deliberately :—

"Yes, it is, as you say, quite unexpected. This time last night I as little anticipated being back here as you anticipated my coming. But one's plans change rapidly and radically at times. Mine have done so."

He sat at the large, library writing-table, a pile of letters, papers, circulars, before him, judged unworthy of forwarding, which had accumulated during his absence. He tore off wrappers, tore open envelopes, quickly yet methodically, as though bending his mind with conscious determination to the performance of a self-inflicted task. Looking at the contents of each in turn, with an odd mixture of indifference and close attention, he flung the major part into the waste-paper basket set beside his revolving-chair. A tall, green-shaded lamp shed a circle of vivid light upon the silver and maroon leather furnishings of the writing-table, upon the young man's bent head, and upon his restless hands as they grasped, and straightened, and then tore, with measured if impatient precision, the letters and papers lying before him.

Lady Calmady stood resting the tips of her fingers on the corner of the table, looking down at him with those clear shining eyes. His reception of her had not been demonstrative, but of that she was hardly sensible. The reconciling assurances of faith, the glories of the third heaven, still dazzled her somewhat. Her feet hardly touched earth yet, so that her mother-love, and all its sensitive watchfulness was, as yet, somewhat in abeyance. She spoke again with the same quiet joyousness of tone.

"You should have telegraphed to me, dearest, and then all would have been ready to welcome you. As it is, I fear, you must feel yourself a trifle neglected. I have been, or have fancied myself, mightily busy all day—foolishly cumbered about much serving—and had gone out to forget maids, and food, and domesticities generally, into the dear garden."—She paused, smiling. "Ah! it is a gracious night," she said, "full of inspiration. You must have enjoyed the drive home. The household refuses to take this marriage of yours philosophically, Dickie. It demands great magnificence, quite as much, be sure, for its own glorification as for yours. It also multiplies small difficulties, after the manner of well-conducted households, as I imagine, since the world began."

Richard tore the prospectus of a mining company, offering wealth beyond the dreams of avarice, right across with a certain violence.

"Oh, well, the household may forego its magnificence and cease from the multiplication of small difficulties alike, as far as any marriage of mine is concerned. You can tell the household so to-morrow, mother, or I can. Perhaps the irony of the position would be more nicely pointed by the announcement coming directly from myself. That would heighten the drama."

"But, Dickie, my dearest?" Katherine said, greatly perplexed.

"The whole affair is at an end.   Lady Constance Quayle is not going to marry me, and I am not going to marry Lady Constance Quayle.—On that point at least she and I are entirely at one.   All London will know this to-morrow.   Perhaps Brockhurst, in the interests of its endangered philosophy, had better know it to-night."

Richard leaned forward, opening, tearing, sorting the papers again.   A rasping quality was in his voice and speech, hitherto unknown to his mother; a cold, imperious quality in his manner, also, new to her.   And these brought her down to earth, setting her feet thereon uncompromisingly.   And the earth on which they were thus set was, it must be owned, rather ugly. A woman made of weaker stuff would have cried out against such sudden and painful declension.   But Katherine, happily both for herself and for those about her, waking even from dreams of noble and far-reaching attainment, waked with not only her wits, but her heart, in steady action.   Yet she in nowise went back on the revelation that had been vouchsafed to her.   It was in nowise disqualified or rendered suspect, because the gamut of human emotion proved to have more extended range and more jarring discords than she had yet reckoned with.   Her mind was large enough to make room for novel experience in sorrow, as well as in joy, retaining the while its poise and sanity.   Therefore, recognising a new phase in the development of her child, she, without hesitation or regret of self-love for the disturbance of her own gladness, braced herself to meet it.   His pride had been wounded—somehow, she knew not how—to the very quick.   And the smart of that wound was too shrewd, as yet, for any precious balms of articulate tenderness to soothe it.   She must give it time to heal a little, meanwhile setting herself scrupulously to respect his dark humour, meet his pride with pride, his calm with at least equal calmness.

She drew a chair up to the end of the table, and settled herself to listen quite composedly.

"It will be well, dearest," she said, "that you should explain to me clearly what has happened.   To do so may avert possible complications."

Richard's hands paused among the papers.   He regarded Lady Calmady reflectively, not without a grudging admiration. But an evil spirit possessed him, a necessity of mastery—inevitable reaction from recently endured humiliation — which provoked him to measure his strength against hers. He needed a sacrifice to propitiate his anger. That sacrifice must be in some sort a human one. So he deliberately pulled the tall lamp nearer, and swung his chair round sideways, leaning his elbow on the table, with the result that the light rested on his face. It did more. It rested upon his body, upon his legs and feet, disclosing the extent of their deformity.

Involuntarily Katherine shrank back. It was as though he had struck her. Morally, indeed, he had struck her, for there was a cynical callousness in this disclosure, in this departure from his practice of careful and self-respecting concealment. Meanwhile Richard watched her, as, shrinking, her eyelids drooped and quivered.

"Mother," he said, quietly and imperatively.—And when, not without perceptible effort, she again raised her eyes to his, he went on :—" I quite agree with you that it will be well for me to explain with a view to averting possible complications. It has become necessary that we should clearly understand one another—at least that you, my dear mother, should understand my position fully and finally. We have been too nice, you and I, heretofore, and, the truth being very far from nice, have expended much trouble and ingenuity in our efforts to ignore it. We went up to London in the fond hope that the world at large would support us in our self-deception. So it did, for a time. But, being in the main composed of very fairly honest and sensible persons, it has grown tired of sentimental lying, of helping us to bury our heads ostrich-like in the sand. It has gone over to the side of truth—that very far from flattering or pretty truth to which I have just alluded—with this result, among others, that my engagement has come to an abrupt and really rather melodramatic conclusion."

He paused.

"Go on, Richard," Lady Calmady said, " I am listening."

He drew himself up, sitting very erect, keeping his eyes steadily fixed on her, speaking steadily and coldly, though his lips twitched a little.

"Lady Constance did me the honour to call on me last night, rather later than this, absenting herself in the very thick of Lady Louisa Barking's ball for that purpose."

Katherine moved slightly, her dress rustled.

"Yes—considering her character and her training it was a rather surprising *démarche* on her part, and bore convincing testimony to her agitation of mind."

"Did she come alone ? "

Richard lapsed into an easier position.

"Oh, dear no!" he said. "Allowing for the desperation which dictated her proceedings, they were carried out in a very regular manner, with a praiseworthy regard for appearances. Lady Constance is, in my opinion, a very sweet person. She is perfectly modest and has an unusual regard—as women go—for honour and duty—as women understand them."—Again his voice took on that rasping quality. "She brought a friend, a young lady, with her. Fortunately there was no occasion for me to speak to her—she had the good taste to efface herself during our interview. But I saw her in the hall afterwards. I shall always remember that very distinctly. So, I imagine, will she. Then Lord Shotover waited outside with the carriage. Oh! believe me, admitting its inherent originality, the affair was conducted with an admirable regard for appearances."

Again the regular flow of Richard's speech was broken. His throat had gone very dry.

"Lady Constance appealed to me in extremely moving terms, articulate and otherwise, to set her free."

"To set her free—and upon what grounds?"

"Upon the rather crude, but pre-eminently sensible grounds, my dear mother, that after full consideration, she found the bid was not high enough."

"Indeed," Katherine said.

"Yes, indeed, my dear mother," Richard repeated. "Does that surprise you? It quite ceased to surprise me, when she pointed out the facts of the case. For she was touchingly sincere. I respected her for that. The position was an ungracious one for her. She has a charming nature, and really wanted to spare me just as much as was possible along with the gaining of her cause. Her gift of speech is limited, you know; but then no degree of eloquence or diplomacy could have rendered that which she had to say agreeable to my self-esteem. Oh! on the whole she did it very well, very conclusively."

Richard raised his head, pausing a moment. Again that dryness of the throat checked his utterance. And then, recalling the scene of the past night, a great wave of unhappiness, pure and simple, of immense disappointment, immense self-disgust broke over him. His anger, his outraged pride, came near being swamped by it. He came near losing his bitter self-control and crying aloud for help. But he mastered the inclination, perhaps unfortunately, and continued speaking.

"Yes, decidedly, with the exception of Ludovic, that family do not possess ready tongues, yet they contrive to make their meaning pretty plain in the end.   I have just driven over from Whitney, and am fresh from a fine example of eventual plain speaking from that excellent father of the family, Lord Fallow-feild.   It was instructive.   For the main thing, after all, as we must both agree, mother, is to understand oneself clearly and to make oneself clearly understood.   And in this respect you and I, I'm afraid, have failed a good deal.   Blinded by our own fine egoism we have even failed altogether to understand others. Lady Constance, for instance, possesses very much more character than it suited us to credit her with."

"You are harsh, dearest," Katherine murmured, and her lips trembled.

"Not at all," he answered.   "I have only said good-bye to lying.   Can you honestly deny, my dear mother, that the whole affair was just one of convenience?   I told you—it strikes me now as a rather brutally primitive announcement—that I wanted a wife because I wanted a son—a son to prove to me the entirety of my own manhood, a son to give me at second hand certain obvious pleasures and satisfactions which I am debarred, as you know, from obtaining at first hand.   You engaged to find me a bride.   Poor, little Lady Constance Quayle, unluckily for her, appeared to meet our requirements, being pretty and healthy, and too innocent and undeveloped to suspect the rather mean advantage we proposed to take of her.—What?   I know it sounds rather gross stated thus plainly.   But, the day of lies being over, dare you deny it?—Well then, we proceeded to traffic for this desirable bit of young womanhood, of pro-spective maternity,—to buy her from such of her relations as were perverted enough to countenance the transaction, just as shamelessly as though we had gone into the common bazaar, after the manner of the cynical East, and bargained for her, poor child, in fat-tailed sheep or cowries.   Doesn't it appear to you almost incredible, almost infamous that we—you and I, mother —should have done this thing?   The price we offered seemed sufficient to some of her people—not to all, I have learned that past forgetting to-day, thanks to Lord Fallowfeild's thick-headed, blundering veracity.   But, thank Heaven, she had more heart, more sensibility, more self-respect, more decency, than we allowed for.   She plucked up spirit enough to refuse to be bought and sold like a pedigree filly or heifer.   I think that was rather heroic, considering her traditions and the pressure which had been brought to bear to keep her silent.   I can only honour and reverence her for coming to tell me frankly, though at the eleventh hour, that she preferred a man of no particular position or fortune, but with the ordinary complement of limbs, to Brockhurst, and the house in London, and my forty to forty-five thousand a year, plus "—

Richard laughed savagely, leaning forward, spreading out his arms.

"Well, my dear mother,—since, as I say, the day of lies is over,—plus the remnant of a human being you may see here, at this moment, if you will only have the kindness to look!"

At first Katherine had listened in mute surprise, bringing her mind, not without difficulty, into relation to the immediate and the present. Then watchful sympathy had been aroused, then anxiety, then tenderness, denying itself expression since the time for it was not yet ripe. But as the minutes lengthened and the flow of Richard's speech not only continued, but gained in volume and in force, sympathy, anxiety, tenderness, were merged in an emotion of ever-deepening anguish, so that she sat as one who contemplates, spell-bound, a scene of veritable horror. From regions celestial to regions terrestrial she had been hurried with rather dislocating suddenness. But her sorry journey did not end there. For hardly were her feet planted on solid earth again, than the demand came that she should descend still further—to regions sub-terrestrial, regions frankly infernal. And this descent to hell, though rapid to the point of astonishment, was by no means easy. Rather was it violent and remorseless—a driving as by reiterated blows, a rude, merciless dragging onward and downward. Yet, even so, for all the anguish and shame—as of unseemly exposure—the perversion of her intention and action, the scorn so ruthlessly poured upon her, it was less of herself, the compelled, than of Richard, the compelling, that she thought. For even while his anger thus drove and dragged her, he himself was tortured in the flame far below—so it seemed, and that constituted the finest sting of her agony—beyond her power to reach or help. She, after all, but stood on the edge of the crater, watching. He fought, right down in the molten waves of it—fought with himself, too, more fiercely even than he fought with her. So that now, as years ago waiting outside the red drawing-room hearing the stern, peremptory tones of the surgeons, the moan of unspeakable physical pain, the grating of a saw, picturing the dismemberment of the living body she so loved, Katherine was tempted to run a little mad and beat her beautiful head against the wall. But age, while taking no jot or tittle from the capacity of suffering, still, in sane and healthy natures, brings a certain steadiness to the brain and coolness to the blood. Therefore Katherine sat very still and silent, her sweet eyes half closed, her spirit bowed in unspoken prayer. Surely the all-loving God, who, but a brief hour ago, had vouchsafed her the fair vision of the delight of her youth, would ease his torment and spare her son?

And, all the while, outward nature remained reposeful and gracious in aspect as ever. The churring of the night-hawks, the occasional bark of the fox in the Warren, the song of the answering nightingales, wandered in at the open casements. And, along with these, came the sweetness of the beds of wild thyme from the grass slopes, and the rich, languid scent of the blossom of the little, round-headed, orange trees set, in green tubs, below the carven guardian griffins on the flight of steps leading up to the main entrance. That which had been lovely, continued lovely still. And, therefore perhaps,—she could hope it even amid the fulness of her anguish,—the gates of hell might stand open to ascending as well as descending feet ; and so that awful road might at last—at last—be retraced by this tormented child of hers, whom, though he railed against her, she still supremely loved.

But Richard, whether actually or intentionally it would be difficult to say, misinterpreted and resented her silence and apparent calm. He waited for a time, his eyes fastened upon her half-averted face. Then he picked up one of the remaining packets from the table, tore off the wrapper, glanced at the contents, stretched out his left arm holding the said contents suspended over the waste-paper basket.

"Yes, it is evident," he declared, "even you do not care to look! Well, then, must you not admit that you and I have been guilty of an extravagance of fatuous folly, and worse, in seriously proposing that a well-born, sensitive girl should not only look at, habitually and closely, but take for all her chance in life a crippled dwarf like me—an anomaly, a human curiosity, a creature so unsightly that it must be carried about like any baby-in-arms lest its repulsive ungainliness should sicken the bystanders if, leaving the shelter of a railway-rug and an arm-chair, it tries—unhappy brute—to walk?—Oh! I'm not angry with her. I don't blame her. I'm not surprised. I agree with her down to the ground. I sympathise and comprehend—no man more. I told her so last night—only amazed at the insane egoism that could ever have induced me to view the matter in any other light. Women are generally disposed to be hard on one another. But if you, my dear mother, should be in any degree tempted to be hard on Constance Quayle, I beg you to consider your own engagement, your own marriage, my father's"—

Here Katherine interrupted him, rising in sudden revolt.

"No, no, Richard," she said, "that is more, my dear, than I can either permit or can bear. If you have any sort of mercy left in you, do not bring your father's name, and that which lies between him and me, into this hideous conversation."

The young man looked hard at her, and then opening his hand, let the pieces of torn paper flutter down into the basket. It was done with a singularly measured action, symbolic of casting off some last tie, severing some last link, which bound his life and his allegiance to his companion.

"Yes, exactly," he said. "As I expected, the day of lying being over, you as good as own it an outrage to your taste, and your affections, that so frightful a thing, as I am, should venture to range itself alongside your memories of your husband. Out of your own mouth are you judged, my dear mother. And, if I am thus to you, upon whom, after all, I have some natural claim, what must I be to others? Think of it! What indeed!"

Katherine made no attempt to answer. Perception of the grain of truth which seasoned the vast, the glaring, injustice of his accusations unnerved her. His speech was ingeniously cruel. His humour such, that it was vain to protest. And the hopelessness of it all affected her to the point of physical weakness. She moved across the room, intending to gain the door and go, for it seemed to her the limit of her powers of endurance had been reached. But her strength would not carry her so far. She stumbled on the upturned corner of the shining, tiger-skin rug, recovered herself trembling, and laid hold of the high, narrow, marble shelf of the chimney-piece for support. She must rest a little lest her strength should wholly desert her, and she should fall before reaching the door.

Behind her, within the circle of lamplight, Richard remained, still sorting, tearing, flinging away that which remained of the pile of papers. This deft, persistent activity of his, in its mixture of purpose and abstraction, was agitating—seeming, to Katherine's listening ears, as though it might go on endlessly, until not only these waste papers, but all and everything within his reach, things spiritual, things of the heart, duties, obligations, gracious and tender courtesies, as well as things merely material, might be thus relentlessly scrutinised, judged worthless, rent asunder and cast forth. What would be spared she wondered, what left? And, when the work of destruction was completed, what would follow next?—Bracing herself, she turned, purposing to close the interview by some brief pleading of indisposition and to escape. But, as she did so, the sound of tearing ceased. Richard slipped down from his place at the writing-table, and shuffling across the room, flung himself into the long, low arm-chair on the opposite side of the fireplace.

"I don't want to detain you for an unreasonable length of time, mother," he said. "We understand each other in the main, I think, and that without subterfuge or self-deception at last. But there are details to be considered; and, as I leave here early to-morrow morning, I think you'll feel with me it's desirable we should have our talk out. There are a good many eventualities for which it's only reasonable and prudent to make provision on the eve of an indefinitely long absence. Practically a good many people are dependent on me, one way and another, and I don't consider it honourable to leave their affairs at loose ends, however uncertain my own future may be."

Richard's voice had still that rasping quality, while his bearing was instinct with a coldly dominating, and almost aggressive, force. Katherine, though little addicted to fear, felt strangely shaken, strangely alienated by the dead weight of the personality, by perception of the innate and tremendous vigour, of this being to whom she had given birth. She had imagined, specially during the last few months of happy and intimate companionship, that if ever mother knew her child, she knew Richard—through and through. But it appeared she had been mistaken. For here was a new Richard, at once terrible and magnificent, regarding whom she could predicate nothing with certainty. He defied her tenderness, he outpaced her imagination, he paralysed her will. Between his thoughts, desires, intentions, and hers, a blind blank space had suddenly intruded itself, impenetrable to her thought. In person he was here close beside her, in mind he was despairingly far away. And to this last, not only his words, but his manner, his expression, his singular, yet sombre beauty, bore convincing testimony. He had matured with an almost unnatural rapidity, leaving her far behind. In his presence she felt diffident, mentally insecure, even as a child.

She remained standing, holding tightly to the narrow ledge of the mantelpiece. She felt dazed and giddy as in face of some upheaval, some cataclysm, of nature. In relation to her son she was conscious, in truth, that her whole world had suffered shipwreck.

"Where are you going, Dickie?" she asked at last very simply.

"Anywhere and everywhere where amusement, or even the semblance of it, is to be had," he answered.—"Do you wish to know how long I shall be away? Just precisely as long as amusement in any form offers itself, and as my power of being amused remains to me.   This strikes you as slightly ignoble ?   I am afraid that's a point, my dear mother, upon which I am supremely indifferent.   You and I have posed rather extensively on the exalted side of things so far, have strained at gnats and finished up by swallowing a remarkably full-grown camel.   This whole business of my proposed marriage has been anything but graceful, when looked at in the common-sense way in which most people, of necessity, look at it.   Lord Fallowfeild appealed to me against myself—which appeared to me slightly humorous—as one man of the world to another.   That was an eye-opener.   It was likewise a profitable lesson.   I promptly laid it to heart. And it is exclusively from the point of view of the man of the world that I propose to regard myself, and my circumstances, and my personal peculiarities, in future.   So, to begin with, if you please, from this time forth, we put aside all question of marriage in my case.   We don't make any more attempts to buy innocent and well-bred, young girls, inviting them to condone my obvious disabilities in consideration of my little title and my money."

Richard ceased to look at Lady Calmady.   He looked away through the open window into the serene sky of the summer night, a certain hunger in his expression not altogether pleasant to witness.

"Fortunately," he continued, with something between a laugh and a sneer, "there is a mighty army of women—always has been—who don't come under the head of innocent, young girls, though some of them have plenty of breeding of a kind.   They attach no superstitious importance to the marriage ceremony. My position and money may obtain me consolations in their direction."

Lady Calmady ceased to require the cold support of the marble mantelshelf.

"It is unnecessary for us to discuss that subject, at least, Richard," she said.

The young man turned his head again, looking full at her. And again the distance that divided her from him became, to her, cruelly apparent, while his strength begot in her a shrinking of fear.

"I am sorry," he replied, "but I can't agree with you there. It is inevitable that we should differ in the future, and that you should frequently disapprove.   I can't expect you to emancipate yourself from prejudice, as I am already emancipated.   I am not sure I even wish that.   Still, whatever the future may bring forth, of this, my dear mother, I am determined to make a clean breast to-night, so that you shall never have cause to charge me with lack of frankness or of attempt to deceive you."

Yet, at the moment, the poor mother's heart cried out to be deceived, if thereby it might be eased a little of suffering. Then, a nobler spirit prevailing within her, Katherine rallied her fortitude. Better he should be bound to her even by cynical avowal of projected vice, than not bound at all. Listening now, she gained the right—a bitter enough right—to command a measure of his confidence in those still darker days which, as she apprehended, only too certainly lay ahead. So she answered, calmly :—

"Go on, Richard. As you say we may differ in the future. I may disapprove, but I can be silent. You are right. It is better for us both that I should hear."

And once more the young man was compelled to yield her a grudging admiration. His tone softened somewhat.

"I don't like to see you stand, mother," he said. "Our conversation may be prolonged. One never quite knows what may crop up. You will be overtired. And to-morrow, when I am gone, there will be things to do."

Lady Calmady drew forward the chair from the end of the writing-table. Her back was towards the lamp, her face in shadow. Of this she was glad. In a degree it lessened the strain. The sweet, night air, coming in at the open casements, fluttered the lace on her bodice, as with the touch of a light, cool hand. Of this she was glad too. It was refreshing, and she grew increasingly exhausted and physically weak. Richard observed her, not without solicitude.

"I am afraid you are not well, mother," he said.

But Katherine shook her head, smiling upon him with misty eyes and lips somewhat tremulous.

"I am always well," she replied. "Only to-night it has been given me to scale heights and sound opposing depths, and I am a little overcome by perplexity and by surprise. But what does that signify? I shall have plenty of time—too much probably—in which to rest and range my ideas when—you are gone, my dearest."

"You must not be here alone."

"Oh no! People will visit me, no doubt, animated by kindly wishes to lessen my solitude," she answered, still smiling. Remembrance of Honoria St. Quentin's letter came to her mind. Could it be that the girl had some inkling of what was in store for her, and that this had inspired the slight over-warmth of her protestations of affection?—"Honoria would always be ready to come, should I ask her," she said.

24

All solicitude passed from Richard's expression, all softening from his tone.

"By all means ask her. That would cap the climax, and round the irony of the situation to admiration!"

"Indeed? Why?" Katherine inquired, painfully impressed by the renewed bitterness of his manner.

"If you're fond of her that is convincingly sufficient. She and I have never been very sympathetic, but that's a detail. I shall be gone. Therefore pray have her, or anybody else you happen to fancy, so long as you do have someone. You mustn't be here alone."

"Julius remains faithful through all chances and changes."

"But I imagine even Julius has sufficient social sense to perceive that faithfulness may be a little out of place at this juncture. At least I sincerely hope he'll perceive it, for otherwise he will have to be made to do so—and that will be a nuisance."

"Dickie, Dickie, what are you implying?" Lady Calmady exclaimed. "By what strange and unlovely thoughts are you possessed to-night?"

"I am learning to look at things as the average man of the world looks at them, that's all," he said. "We have been too refined, you and I, to be self-critical, with the consequence that we have allowed ourselves a considerable degree of latitude in many directions. Julius' permanent residence here ranks among the fine-fanciful disregardings of accepted proprieties with which we have indulged ourselves. But spades are to be called spades in future—at least by me. So, for the very same reason that I go forth, like the average man of the world, to enjoy the pleasures of sin for a season, do I object to Julius, or any other man, being your guest during my absence, unless you have some woman of your own position in life living here with you. The levels in social matters have changed, once and for all. I have come to a sane mind and renounced the eccentric subterfuges and paltry hypocrisies, by means of which we have attempted, you and I, to keep disagreeable facts at bay. Truth, bare and unabashable, is the only goddess I worship henceforth."

He leaned forward, laying his hands upon the arms of his chair. His manner was harsh still. But all coldness had departed from it, rather did a white heat of passion consume him dreadful to witness.

"Yes, it is wisest to repeat that, so that, on your part, there may be no excuse for any shadow of misapprehension. The levels have altered. The old ones can never be restored. I

want to have you grasp this, mother—swallow it, digest it, so that
it passes into fibre and tissue of your every thought about me.
For an acutely unscientific, an ingeniously unreasonable, idea
obtains widely among respectable, sentimental, so-called religious
persons, regarding those who are the victims of disfiguring
accident, or, like myself, are physically disgraced from birth.
Because we have been deprived of our natural rights, because
we have so abominably little, we are expected to be slavishly
grateful for the contemptible pittance that we have.   Because,
slothfully, by His neglect, or, wantonly, for His amusement, the
Creator has tortured us, maiming, distorting us, setting us up as
a laughing-stock before all man and womankind—because He
has played a ghastly and brutal practical joke on us, fixing the
marks of low comedy in our living flesh and bone—therefore we,
forsooth, are to be more pious, more clean-living, temperate, and
discreet than the rest—to bow amiably beneath the cross, gratefully to kiss the rod !   Those irregularities of conduct which are
smiled at, and taken for granted, in a man made after the normal,
comely fashion, become a scandal in the case of a poor, unhappy
devil like me, at which good people hold up their hands in
horror.   Faugh !—I tell you I'm sick of such cowardly cant.   A
pretty example the Almighty's set me of justice and mercy !
Handsome encouragement He has given me to be virtuous and
sober !   Much I have for which to praise His holy name !
Arbitrarily, without excuse, or faintest show of antecedent reason,
He has elected to curse.   And the curse will cling forever and
ever, till they lay me in a coffin nearly half as short again as that
of any other man, and leave the hideousness of my deformity to
be obliterated and purged at last—eaten away by the worms in
the dark."

Richard stretched out his hands, palms upward.

"And in return for all this shall I bless? No, indeed—no,
thank you.   Not even towards God Almighty Himself will I
play the part of lick-spittle and sycophant.   I have fine enough
stuff in me, let alone the energy begotten by the flagrance of
His injustice, to take higher grounds with Him than that.   I
will break what men hold to be His laws, wherever and whenever
I can—I will make hay of His so-called natural and moral order,
just as often as I get the chance.   I will curse, and again curse,
back."

The speaker's voice was deep and resonant, filling the whole
room.   His utterance deliberate and unshaken.   His face dark
with the malign beauty of implacable hatred.   Hearing him,
seeing him thus, Katherine Calmady's fortitude forsook her.   She

ceased to distinguish or discriminate.   Nature gave way.   She
knelt upon the floor before him, her hands clasped, tears
coursing down her cheeks.   But of her attitude and aspect she
was unconscious.

"Oh, Richard, Richard," she cried, "forgive me!   Curse me,
my dearest, throw all the blame on me, my dearest—I accept
it—not on God.   Only try, try to forgive!   Forgive me for
being your mother.   Forgive me that I ever loved and married.
Forgive me the intolerable wrong which, all unknowingly, I did
you before your birth.   I humble myself before you, and with
reason.   For I am the cause; I, who would give my life for your
happiness, my blood for your healing, a thousand times.   But
through all these years I have done my poor best to serve you
and to make up.   The hypocrisies and subterfuges which you
lash so scornfully—and rightly perhaps—were the fruit of my
overcare for you.   Rail at me.   I deserve it.   Perhaps I have
been faithless, but only once or twice, and for a moment.   I was
faithless towards you here, in the garden to-night.   But then I
supposed you content.   Ah! I hardly know what I say!—Only
rail at me, my beloved, not at God.   And then try—try not to
leave me in anger.   Try, before you go, to forgive!"

Richard had sunk back in his chair, his hands clasped behind
his head, watching her.   It gave him the strangest sensation to
see his mother kneeling before him thus.   At first it shocked
him almost to the point of heated protest, as against a thing
unpermissible and indecorous.   Then, the devils of wounded pride,
of anarchy, and of revolt asserting themselves, he began to relish,
to be appeased by, the unseemly sight.   Little Lady Constance
Quayle, and all that of which she was the symbol, had disappointed and escaped him.   But here was a woman, worth a
dozen Constance Quayles, in beauty, in intellect, and in heart,
prostrate before him, imploring his clemency as the penitent
implores the absolution of the priest!   An evil gladness took
him that he had power thus to subjugate so regal a creature.
His gluttony of inflicting pain—since he himself suffered—his
gluttony of exercising dominion—since he himself had been
defied and defrauded—was in a degree satisfied.   His arrogance
was at once reinforced and assuaged.

"It is absurd to speak of forgiveness," he said presently, and
slowly, "as it is absurd to speak of restitution.   These are mere
words, having no real tally in fact.   We appear to have volition,
but actually and essentially we are as leaves driven by the wind.
Where it blindly drives, there we blindly go.   So it has been
from the beginning.   So it always will be.   In the last twenty-

four hours there are many things I have ceased to believe in, and among them, my dear mother, is human responsibility."

He paused, and motioned Lady Calmady towards her chair with a certain authority.

"Therefore calm yourself," he said. "Grieve as little as may be about all this matter, and let us talk it over without further emotion."

He waited a brief space, giving her time to recover her composure, and then continued coldly, with a careful abstention from any show of feeling.

"Let us clear our minds of cant, and go forward knowing that there is really neither good nor evil. For these—even as God Himself, whose existence I treated from the anthropomorphic standpoint just now, so as to supply myself with a target to shoot at, a windmill at which to tilt, a row of ninepins set up for the mere satisfaction of knocking them down again— these are plausible delusions invented by man, in the vain effort to protect himself and his fellows from the profound sense of loneliness, and impotence, which seizes on him if he catches so much as a passing glimpse of the gross comedy of human aspiration, human affection, briefly human existence."

But, strive as he might, excitement gained on Richard once more, for young blood is hot and gallops masterfully along the veins, specially under the whip of real or imagined disgrace. He sat upright, grasping the arms of his chair, and looking, not at his mother, but away into the deep of the summer night.

"Perhaps my personal peculiarities confer on me unusually acute perception of the inherent grossness of the human comedy. I propose to take the lesson to heart. They teach me not to sacrifice the present to the future; but to fling away ideals like so much waste paper, and just take that which I can immediately get. They tell me to limit my horizon, and go the common way of common, coarse-grained, sensual man—in as far as that way is possible to me—and be of this world worldly. And so, mother, I want you to understand that from this day forth I turn over a new leaf, not only in thought, but in conduct. I am going to have just all that my money and position, and even this vile deformity—for, by God, I'll use that too—what people won't give for love they'll give for curiosity—can bring me of pleasure and notoriety. I am going to lay hold of life with these rather horribly strong arms of mine"— he looked across at Lady Calmady with a sneering smile.—"Strong?" he repeated, "strong as a young bull-ape's. I mean to tear the very vitals out of living; to tear knowledge, excitement, intoxication, out of it, making them, by right of conquest, my own. I will compel existence to yield me all that it yields other men, and more—because my senses are finer, my acquaintance with sorrow more intimate, my quarrel with fortune more vital and more just. As I cannot have a wife, I'll have mistresses. As I cannot have honest love, I'll have gratified lust. I am not stupid. I shall not follow the beaten track. My imagination has been stimulated into rather dangerous activity by the pre-natal insult put upon me. And now that I have emancipated myself, I propose to apply my imagination practically."

The young man flung himself back in his chair again.

"There ought to be startling results," he said, with gloomy exultation. "Don't you think so, mother? There should be startling results."

Lady Calmady bowed herself together, putting her hands over her eyes. Then raising her head, she managed to smile at him, though very sadly, her sweet face drawn by exhaustion and marred by lately shed tears.

"Ah yes, my dearest," she answered, "no doubt the results will be startling; but whether any sensible increase of happiness, either to yourself or others, will be counted among them is open to question."

Richard laughed bitterly.—"I shall have lived, anyhow," he rejoined. "Worn out, not rusted and rotted out—which, according to our former fine-fanciful programme, seemed the only probable consummation of my unlucky existence."

His tone changed, becoming quietly businesslike and indifferent.

"I am entering horses for some of the French events, and I go through to Paris to-morrow to see various men there and make the necessary arrangements. I shall take Chifney with me for a few days. But the stables will not give you any trouble. He will have given all the orders."

"Very well," Katherine said mechanically.

"Later I shall go on to Baden-Baden."

Katherine rallied somewhat.

"Helen de Vallorbes is there," she said, not without a trace of her former pride.

"Certainly Helen de Vallorbes is there," he answered. "That is why I go. I want to see her. It is inconsistent, I admit, for Helen remains the one person gloriously untouched by the wreck of the former order of things. Pray let there be no misconception on that point. She belonged to the ideal order, she belongs to it still."

"Ah, my dear, my dear!" Katherine almost cried.   His per-
versity hurt her a little too much so that the small, upspringing
flame of decent pride was quenched.

"Yes," he went on, "there was my initial, my cardinal,
mistake.   For I was a traitor to all that was noblest and best in
me, when I persuaded myself, and weakly permitted you to
persuade me, that a loveless marriage is better than a love in
which marriage is impossible,—that Lady Constance Quayle,
poor little soul, bought, paid for, and my admitted property,
could fill Helen's place,—though Helen was—and I intend her
to remain so, for I care for her enough to hold her honour as
sacred as I do your own—for ever inaccessible."

Lady Calmady staggered to her feet.

"That is enough, Richard," she said.   "That is enough.   If
you have more to say, in pity leave it until to-morrow."

The young man looked at her strangely.

"You are ill, mother," he said.

"No, no, I am only broken-hearted," she replied.   "And a
broken heart, alas! never killed so healthy a body as mine.   I
shall survive this—and more perhaps.   God knows.   Do not vex
yourself about me, Dickie.—Go, live your life as it seems fit to
you.   I have not the will, even had I the right, to restrain you.
And meanwhile I will be the steward of your goods, as, long
ago, when you were a child and belonged to me wholly.   You
can trust me to be faithful and discreet, at least in financial and
practical matters.   If you ever need me, I will come even to the
ends of the earth.   And should the desire take you to return,
here you will find me.—And so, good-bye, my darling.   I am
foolishly tired.   I grow light-headed, and dare not linger, lest in
my weakness I say that which I afterwards regret."

She passed to the door and went out, without looking back.

Left to himself Richard Calmady crossed to the writing-table,
swung himself up into the revolving-chair, and remained there
sorting and docketing papers far into the night.   But once,
stooping, with long-armed adroitness, to unlock the lowest drawer
of the table, a madness of disgust towards the unsightliness of
his own person seized on and tore him.

"O God, God, God!" he cried aloud, in the extremity of
his passion, "why hast Thou made me thus?"

And to that question, as yet, there was no answer, though it
rang afar over the sleeping park, and up to the clear shining stars
of the profound and peaceful summer night.

BOOK V

RAKE'S PROGRESS

CHAPTER I

IN WHICH THE READER IS COURTEOUSLY ENTREATED TO GROW
OLDER BY THE SPACE OF SOME FOUR YEARS, AND TO
SAIL SOUTHWARD HO! AWAY

THE south-easterly wind came fresh across the bay from the
crested range of the Monte Sant' Angelo. The blossoms
of the Judas-trees, breaking from the smooth grey stems and
branches—on which they perch so quaintly—fell in a red-mauve
shower upon the slabs of the marble pavement, upon the mimic
waves of the fountain basin, and upon the clustering curls, and
truncated shoulders, of the bust of Homer standing in the shade
of the grove of cypress and ilex which sheltered the square, high-
lying hill-garden, at this hour of the morning, from the fierceness
of the sun. They floated as far even as the semicircular steps
of the pavilion on the extreme right—the leaded dome of which
showed dark and livid on the one side, white and glistering
on the other, against the immense and radiant panorama of
mountain, sea, and sky.

The garden, its fountains, neatly clipped shrubs, and formal
paved alleys, was backed by a large villa of the square, flat-roofed
order common to southern Italy. The record of its age had
recently suffered modification by application of a coat of stucco,
of a colour intermediate between faint lemon-yellow and pearl-
grey, and by the renovation of the fine arabesques—Pompeian in
character—decorating the narrow interspaces between its treble
range of Venetian shutters. Otherwise the aspect of the Villa
Vallorbes showed but small alteration since the year when, for
a few socially historic weeks, the "glorious Lady Blessington,"
and her strangely assorted train, condescended to occupy it prior

to taking up their residence at the Palazzo Belvedere near by. The walls were sufficiently massive to withstand a siege. The windows of the ground floor, set in deeply-hewn ashlar work, were cross-barred as those of a prison. Above, the central windows and door of the entresol opened on to a terrace of black and white marble, from which, at either end, a wide, shallow-stepped, curved stairway led down into the garden. The first floor consisted of a suite of noble rooms, each of whose lofty windows gave on to a balcony of wrought ironwork, very ornate in design. The topmost storey, immediately below the painted frieze of the parapet, coincided in height and in detail with the entresol.

The villa was superbly situated upon an advancing spur of hill; so that, looking down from its balconies, looking out from between the pale and slender columns of the pavilion, the whole city of Naples lay revealed below.—Naples, that bewildering union of modern commerce and classic association—its domes, its palms, its palaces, its crowded, hoarse-shouting quays, its theatres and giant churches, its steep and filthy lanes black with shadow, its reeking markets, its broad, sun-scorched piazzas, its glittering, blue waters, its fringing forest of tall masts, and innumerable, close-packed hulls of ocean-going ships! Naples, city of glaring contrasts—heaven of rascality, hell of horses, unrivalled all the western world over for natural beauty, for spiritual and moral grossness! Naples, breeding, teeming, laughing, fighting, festering, city of music, city of fever and death! Naples, at once abominable and enchanting — city to which, spite of noise, stenches, cruelty and squalor, those will return, of necessity, and return again, whose imagination has once been taken captive in the meshes of her many-coloured net.

And among the captives of Naples, on the brilliant morning in question in the early spring of the year 1871, open-eared and open-eyed to its manifest and manifold incongruities, relishing alike the superficial beauty and underlying bestiality of it, was very certainly Helen de Vallorbes. Several years had elapsed since she had visited this fascinating locality; and she could congratulate herself upon conditions adapted to a more intimate and comprehensive acquaintance with its very various humours than she had ever enjoyed before. She had spent more than one winter here, it is true, immediately subsequent to her marriage. But she had then been required to associate exclusively with the members of her husband's family, and to fill a definite position in the aristocratic society of the place. The tone of that society was not a little lax. Yet, being notably defective in the saving grace of humour—as to the feminine portion of it, at all events—its laxity proved sadly deficient in vital interest. The fair Neapolitans displayed as small intelligence in their intrigues as in their piety. In respect of both they remained ignorant, prejudiced, hopelessly conventional. Their noble ancestresses of the Renaissance understood and did these things better—so Helen reflected. She found herself both bored and irritated. She feared she had taken up her residence in southern Italy quite three centuries too late.

But all that was in the past—heaven be praised for it! Just now she was her own mistress, at liberty—thanks to the fortunes of war—to comport herself as she pleased and obey any caprice that took her. The position was ideal in its freedom, while the intrinsic value of it was enhanced by contrast with recent disagreeable experiences. For the alarms and deprivations of the siege of Paris were but lately over. She had come through them unscathed in health and fortune. Yet they had left their mark. During those months of all-encompassing disappointment and disaster the eternal laughter—in which she trusted—had rung harshly sardonic, to the breaking down of self-confidence, and light-hearted, cynic philosophy. It scared her somewhat. It made her feel old. It chilled her with suspicion of the actuality of The Four Last Things—death and judgment, heaven and hell. The power of a merry scepticism waxed faint amid the scream of shells and long-drawn, murderous crackle of the *mitrailleuse.* Helen, indeed, became actively superstitious, thereby falling low in her own self-esteem. She took to frequenting churches, and spending long, still days with the nuns, her former teachers, within the convent of the Sacré Cœur. Circumstances so worked upon her that she made her submission, and was solemnly and duly received back into the fold of the Church. She confessed ardently, yet with certain politic reservations. The priest, after all, is but human. It is only charitable to be considerate of his feelings— so she argued—and avoid overburdening his conscience, poor dear man, by blackening your own reputation too violently! The practice of religion was a help—truly it was, since it served to pass the time. And then, who could tell but that it might not prove really useful hereafter, as, when all is said and done, those dread Four Last Things will present themselves to the mind in hours of depression with haunting pertinacity. It is clearly wise, then, to be on the safe side of Holy Church in these matters, accepting her own assertion that she is very certainly on the safe side of the Deity.

Yet, notwithstanding her pious exercises, Helen de Vallorbes

found existing circumstances excessively disturbing and disquieting. She was filled with an immense self-pity. She feared her
health was failing. She became nervously sensible of her eight-
and-twenty years, telling herself that her youth and the glory of it
had departed. She wore black dresses, rolled bandages, pulled
lint. Selecting Mary Magdalene as her special intercessor, she
made a careful study of the life and legends of that saint. This
proved stimulating to her imagination. She proceeded to write
a little one-act drama concerning the holy woman's dealings,
subsequent to her conversion, quite late in life in fact, with
such as survived of her former lovers. The dialogue was very
moving in parts. Helen read it aloud one bleak January evening, by the light of a single candle, to her friend M. Paul
Destournelle, poet and novelist—with whom just then, by her
own desire, her relations were severely platonic—and they both
wept. The application, though delicate, was obvious. And
those tears appeared to lay the dust of so many pleasant sins,
and promise fertilisation of so heavy a crop of virtue, that—by
inevitable action of the law of contraries—the two friends found
it more than ever difficult to say farewell and part that night.

Now looking back on all that, viewing it calmly in perspective,
her action and attitude struck Helen as somewhat imbecile.
Prayer and penitence have too often a tendency to kick the beam
when fear ceases to weight the balance. And so it followed that
the lust of the flesh, the lust of the eye, and the pride of life,
presented themselves to her as powers by no means contemptible,
or unworthy of invocation, this morning, while she sat at the
luxuriously furnished breakfast-table beneath the glistering dome
of the airy pavilion and gazed out between its slender columns,
over the curving lines of the painted city and glittering waters of
the bay, to the cone of Vesuvius rising, in imperial purple, against
the azure sky. To-day, sign, as she noted, of fine weather, omen,
as she trusted, of good fortune, the smoke of its everlasting burnings towered up and up into the translucent atmosphere, and
then drifted away—a gigantic, wedge-shaped pennon—toward
Capri and the open sea. And, beholding these things, out of
simple, physical well-being, fulness of bread, conviction of her
own undiminished beauty, and the merry devilry begotten of
these, she fell to projecting a second, a companion, one-act
drama founded upon the life of the Magdalene, but, this time,
before the saint's conversion, at an altogether earlier stage of her
very instructive history. And this drama she would not read to
M. Destournelle—not a bit of it. In it he should have neither
part nor lot. Registering which determination, she shook her

charming, honey-coloured head, holding up both hands with a gesture of humorous and well-defined repudiation.

For, in truth, the day of M. Destournelle appeared, just now, to be very effectually over. It had been reasonable enough to urge her natural fears in journeying through a war-distracted land—although guarded by Charles, most discreet and resourceful of English men-servants, and Zélie Forestier, most capable of French lady's-maids—as excuse for Paul Destournelle joining her at a wayside station a short distance out of Paris and accompanying her south. *À la guerre comme à la guerre.* A beautiful woman can hardly be too careful of her person amid the many and primitive dangers which battle and invasion let loose. De Vallorbes himself—detestably jealous though he was—could hardly have objected to her thus securing effective protection, had he been acquainted with the fact. That he was not so acquainted was, of course, the veriest oversight. But, the frontier once reached—the better part of three weeks had elapsed in the reaching of it—and all danger of war and tumult past, both the necessity and, to be frank, the entertainment of M. Destournelle's presence became less convincing. Helen grew a trifle weary of his transports, his suspicions, his *bel tête de Jesu souffrant,* his insatiable literary and personal vanity. The charm, the excitement, of the situation, began to wear rather threadbare, while the practical inconveniences and restrictions it imposed increasingly disclosed themselves. A lover, as Helen reflected, provided you see enough of him, offers but small improvement upon a husband. He is liable to become possessive and didactic, after the manner of the natural man. He is liable to forget that the relation is permitted, not legalised; that it exists on sufferance merely, and is therefore terminable at the will of either party. The last days of that same southern journey had been marked by misunderstandings and subsequent reconciliations, in an ascending scale of acrimony and fervour on the part of her companion. In Helen's case familiarity tended very rapidly to breed contempt. She ceased to be in the least amused by these recurring agitations. At Pisa, after a scene of a particularly excited nature, she lost all patience, frankly told her admirer that she found him not a little ridiculous, and requested him to remove himself, his grievances, and his *bel tête de Jesu* elsewhere. M. Destournelle took refuge in nerves, threats of morphia, and his bed-chamber,—in the chaste seclusion of which apartment Helen left him, unvisited and unconsoled, while, attended by her servants, she gaily resumed her journey.

An adorable sense of independence possessed her, of the charm of her own society, of the absence of all external compelling or directing of her movements—no circumscription of her liberty possible—the world before her where to choose ! Not only were privations, dismal hauntings of siege and slaughter, left behind, and M. Destournelle, just now most wearisome of lovers, left behind also, but de Vallorbes himself had, for the time being, become a permissibly negligible quantity. The news of more fighting, more bloodshed, had just reached her, though the German armies were marching back to the now wholly German Rhine. For upon unhappy Paris had come an hour of deeper humiliation than any which could be procured by the action of foreign foes. She was a kingdom divided against herself, a mother scandalously torn by her own children. News had reached Helen too, news special and highly commendatory, of her husband, Angelo Luigi Francesco. Early in that eventful struggle he had enlisted in the Garde Mobile, all the manhood and honest sentiment resident in him stirred into fruitful activity by the shame and peril of his adopted country. Now Helen learned he had distinguished himself in the holding of Chatillon against the insurgents, had been complimented by MacMahon upon his endurance and resource, had been offered, and had accepted, a commission in the regular army. Promotion was rapid during the later months of the war, and probability pointed to the young man having started on a serious military career.

"Well, let him both start and continue," Helen commented. "I am the last person to be otherwise than delighted thereat. Just in proportion as he is occupied he ceases to be inconvenient. If he succeeds—good. If he is shot—good likewise. For him laurels and a hero's tomb. For me crape and permanent emancipation. An agreeably romantic conclusion to a profoundly unromantic marriage—fresh proof, were such needed, of the truth of the immortal Dr. Pangloss saying, that ' all is for the best in this best of all possible worlds ! ' "

In such happy frame of mind did Madame de Vallorbes continue during her visit to Florence and upon her onward way to Perugia. But there self-admiration ceased to be all-sufficient for her. She needed to read confirmation of that admiration in other eyes. And the grey Etruscan city, uplifted on its star-shaped hill, offered her a somewhat grim reception. Piercing winds swept across the Tiber valley from the still snow-clad Apennines above Assisi. The austere, dark-walled, lombard-gothic churches and palaces showed forbidding, merciless almost, through the driving wet. Even in fair summer weather suspicion of ancient and implacable terror lurks in the shadow of those cyclopean gateways, and stalks over the unyielding, rock-hewn pavements of those solemn, mediæval streets. There was an incalculable element in Perugia which raised a certain anger in Helen. The place seemed to defy her and make light of her pretensions. As during the siege of Paris, so now, echoes of the eternal laughter saluted her ears, ironic in tone.

Nor was the society offered by the residents in the hotel, weather-bound like herself, of a specially enlivening description. It was composed almost exclusively of middle-aged English and American ladies — widows and spinsters—of blameless morals and anxiously active intelligence. They wrapped their lean forms in woollen shawls and ill-cut jackets. They pervaded salon and corridors guide-book in hand. They discoursed of Umbrian antiquities, Etruscan tombs, frescoes and architecture. Having but little life in themselves, they tried, rather vainly, to warm both hands at the fire of the life of the past. Among them, Helen, in her vigorous and self-secure, though fine-drawn, beauty, was about as much at home as a young panther in a hen-roost. They admired, they vaguely feared, they greatly wondered at her. Had one of those glorious young gallants, Baglioni or Oddi, clothed in scarlet, winged, helmeted, sword on thigh, as Perugino has painted them on the walls of the Sala del Cambio—very strangest union of sensuous worldliness and radiant, arch-angelic grace—had one of these magnificent gentlemen ruffled into the hotel parlour, he could hardly have startled the eyes, and perplexed the understanding, of the virtuous and learned Anglo-Saxon and Transatlantic feminine beings there assembled more than did Madame de Vallorbes.

For all such sexless creatures, for the great company of women in whose outlook man plays no immediate or active part, Helen had, in truth, small respect. They appeared to her so absurdly inadequate, so contemptibly divorced from the primary interests of existence. More than once, in a spirit of mischievous malice, she was tempted to bid the good ladies lay aside their Baedekers and Murrays, and increase their knowledge of the Italian character and language by study of the *Novelle* of Bandello, or of certain merry tales to be found in the pages of the Decameron. She had copies of both works in her travelling-bag. She was prepared, moreover, to illustrate such ancient saws by modern instances, for the truth of which last she could quite honestly vouch. But on second thoughts she spared her victims. The quarry was not worth the chase. What self-

respecting panther can, after all, go a-hunting in a hen-roost?
So from the neighbourhood of their unlovely clothes, questioning
glances, and under-vitalised pursuit of art and literature, she
removed herself to her sitting-room upstairs. Charles should
serve her meals there in future; for to sit at table with these
neuters, clothed in amorphous garments, came near upsetting
her digestion.

Meanwhile, as she watched the rain streaming down the panes
of the big windows, watched thin-legged, heavily-cloaked figures
tacking, wind-buffeted, across the grey-black street into the
shelter of some cavernous *port cochère*, it must be owned her
spirits went very sensibly down into her boots. Even the
presence of the despised and repudiated Destournelle would
have been grateful to her. Remembrance of all the less
successful episodes of her career assaulted her. And in that
connection, of necessity, the thought of Brockhurst returned
upon her. For neither the affair of her childhood—that of the
little dancer with blush-roses in her hat—or the other affair—
of now nearly four years back—the intimate drama frustrated,
within sight of its climax, by intervention of Lady Calmady—
could be counted otherwise than as failures. It was strange
how deep-seated was her discontent under this head. As on
Queen Mary's heart the word Calais, so on hers Brockhurst, she
sometimes thought, might be found written when she was dead.
In the last four years Richard had given her princely gifts. He
had treated her with a fine, old-world chivalry, as something
sacred and apart. But he rarely sought her society. He seemed,
rather carefully, to elude her pursuit. His name was not exactly
a patent of discretion and rectitude in these days unfortunately.
Still Helen found his care of her reputation—as far as association
of her name with his own went—somewhat exaggerated. She
could hardly believe him to be indifferent to her, and yet— Oh!
the whole matter was unsatisfactory, abominably unsatisfactory—
of a piece with the disquieting influences of this grim and fateful
city, with the detestable weather evident there without!

And then, suddenly, an idea came to Helen de Vallorbes,
causing the delicate colour to spring into her cheeks, and the light
into her eyes, veiled by those fringed, semitransparent lids.
For, some two years earlier, Richard Calmady had taken her
husband's villa at Naples on lease, it offering, as he said, a
convenient *pied à terre* to him while yachting along the adjacent
coasts, up the Black Sea to Odessa, and eastward as far as
Aden, and the Persian Gulf. The house, save for the actual
fabric of it, had become rather dilapidated and ruinate. To

de Vallorbes it appeared clearly advantageous to get the property off his hands, and touch a considerable yearly sum, rather than have his pocket drained by outgoings on a place in which he no longer cared to live. So the Villa Vallorbes passed for the time being into Richard Calmady's possession. It pleased his fancy. Helen heard he had restored and refurnished it at great expenditure of money and of taste.

These facts she recalled. And, recalling them, found both the actuality of rain-blurred, wind-scourged town without, and anger-begetting memories of Brockhurst within, fade before a seductive vision of sun-bathed Naples and of that nobly placed and painted villa, in which—as it seemed to her—was just now resident promise of high entertainment, the objective delight of abnormal circumstance, the subjective delight of long-cherished revenge. All the rapture of her existing freedom came back on her; while her brain, fertile in forecast of adventure, projected scenes and situations not unworthy of the pen of Boccaccio himself. Fired by such thoughts, she moved from the window, stood before a tall glass at right angles to it and contemplated her own fair reflection long and intimately. An absorbing interest in the general effect, and in the details, of her person possessed her. She moved to and fro observing the grace of her carriage, the set of her hips, the slenderness of her waist. She unfastened her soft, trailing tea-gown, throwing the loose bodice of it back, critically examining her bare neck, the swell of her beautiful bosom, the firm contours of her arms from shoulder to elbow. Her skin was of a clear, golden whiteness, smooth, fine in texture, as that of a child. Placing her hands on the gilded frame of the mirror, high up on either side, she observed her face, exquisitely healthful in colour, even as seen in this mournful, afternoon light. She leaned forward, gazing intently into her own eyes—meeting in them, as Narcissus in the surface of the fatal pool, the radiant image of herself. And this filled her with a certain intoxication, a voluptuous self-love, a profound persuasion of the power and completeness of her own beauty. She caressed her own neck, her own lips, with lingering finger-tips. She bent her bright head and kissed the swell of her cuplike breasts. Never had she received so entire assurance of the magic of her own personality.

"It is all—all, as perfect as ever!" she exclaimed exultantly. "And while it remains perfect, it should be made use of."

Helen waved her hand, smiling, to the smiling image in the mirror.

"You and I together—your beauty and my brains—I pit

the pair of us against all mankind! Together we have worked pretty little miracles before now, causing the proud to lay aside their pride and the godly their virtue. A man of strange passions shall hardly escape us—nor shall the mother that bare him escape either."

Her face hardened, her laughing eyes paled to the colour of fine steel. She lifted the soft-curling hair from off her right temple, disclosing a small, crescent-shaped scar.

"That is the one blemish, and we will exact the price of it—you and I—to the ultimate *sous*."

Then she moved away, smitten by sudden amusement at her own attitude, which she perceived risked being slightly ridiculous. Heroics were, to her thinking, unsuitable articles for home consumption. Yet her purpose held none the less strongly and steadily because excitement lessened. She refastened her tea-gown, tied the streaming azure ribbons of it, patted bows and laces into place, walked the length of the room a time or two to recover her composure, then rang the bell. And, on the arrival of Charles,—irreproachably correct in dress and demeanour, his clean-shaven, sharp-featured, rakish countenance controlled to praiseworthy nullity of expression,—she said :—

"The weather is abominable."

The man-servant set down the tray on a little table before her, turned out the corners of the napkin, deftly arranged the tea-things.

"It is a little dull, my lady."

"How is the glass ?"

"Falling steadily, my lady."

"I cannot remain here."

"No, my lady ?"

"Find out about the trains south—to Naples."

"Yes, my lady. We can join the Roman express at Chiusi. When does your ladyship wish to start ?"

"I must telegraph first."

"Certainly, my lady."

Charles produced telegraph forms. It was Helen's boast that, upon request, the man could produce any known object from a packet of pins to a white elephant, or fully manned battleship. She had a lively regard for her servant's ability. So had he, it may be added, for that of his mistress. The telegram was written and despatched. But the reply took four days in reaching Madame de Vallorbes, and during those days it rained incessantly. The said reply came in the form of a letter. Sir Richard Calmady was at Constantinople, so the writer

25

—Bates, his steward—had reason to believe. But it was probable
he would return to Naples shortly. Meanwhile he—the steward
—had permanent orders to the effect that the villa was at
Madame de Vallorbes' disposition should she at any time
express the wish to visit it. She would find everything prepared
for her reception. This information caused Helen singular
satisfaction. It was very charming, very courteous, of Richard
thus to remember her. She set forth from Perugia full of
ingenious purpose, deliciously light of heart.

Thus did it come about that, on the afore-mentioned gay,
spring morning, Madame de Vallorbes breakfasted beneath the
glistering dome of the airy pavilion, all Naples outstretched
before her, while the blossoms of the Judas-trees fell in a red-
mauve shower upon the slabs of the marble pavement, and the
mimic waves of the fountain basin, and upon the clustered curls
and truncated shoulders of the bust of Homer stationed within
the soft gloom of the ilex and cypress grove. She had arrived
the previous evening, and had met with a dignified welcome from
the numerous household. Her manner was gracious, kindly,
captivating—she intended it to be all that. She slept well, rose
in buoyant health and spirits, partook of a meal offering example
of the most finished Italian cooking. Finish, in any department,
appealed to Helen's artistic sense. Life was sweet—moreover
it was supremely interesting! Her breakfast ended, rising
from her place at table, she looked away to the purple cone
of the great volcano and the uprising of the smoke of its everlasting burnings. The sight of this, magnificent, menacing,
evidence of the anarchic might of the powers of nature,
quickened the pagan instinct within her. She wanted to
worship. And even in so doing, she became aware of a kindred
something in herself—of an answering and anarchic energy, a
certain menace to the conventional works and ways, and
fancied security, of groping, purblind man. The insolence
of a great lady, the dangerously primitive instincts of a great
courtesan, filled her with an enormous pride, a reckless self-
confidence.

Turning, she glanced back across the formal garden, bright
with waxen camellias set in glossy foliage, with early roses, with
hyacinths, lemon and orange blossom, towards the villa. Upon
the black-and-white marble balustrade a man leaned his elbows.
She could see his broad shoulders, his bare head. From his
height she took him, at first, to be kneeling, as, motionless, he
looked towards her and towards the splendid view. Then she
perceived that he was not kneeling, but standing upright. She

understood, and a very vital sensation ran right through her, causing the queerest turn in her blood.

"Mercy of heaven!" she said to herself, "is it conceivable that now, at this time of day, I am capable of the egregious folly of losing my head?"

CHAPTER II

WHEREIN TIME IS DISCOVERED TO HAVE WORKED CHANGES

HELEN, however, did not stay to debate as to the state of her emotions. She had had more than enough of reflection of late. Now action invited her. She responded. The sweep of her turquoise-blue, cloth skirts sent the fallen Judas-blossoms dancing, to left and right, in crazy whirling companies. She did not wait even to put on her broad-brimmed, garden hat, —the crown of it encircled, as luck would have it, by a garland of pale, pink tulle and pale, pink roses,—but braved the sunshine with no stouter head-covering than the coils of her honey-coloured hair. Rapidly she passed up the central alley between the double row of glossy leaved camellia bushes, laughter in her downcast eyes and a delicious thrill of excitement at her heart. She felt strong and light, her being vibrant, penetrated and sustained throughout by the bracing air, the sparkling, crystal-clear atmosphere. Yet for all her eagerness Helen remained an artist. She would not forestall effects. Thriftily she husbanded sensations. Thus, reaching the base of the black-and-white marble wall supporting the terrace, where, midway in its long length, it was broken by an arched grotto of rough-hewn stonework, in which maiden-hair fern rooted,—the delicate fronds of it caressing the shoulders of an undraped nymph, with ever-dripping water-pitcher upon her rounded hip,—Helen turned sharp to the left, and arrived at the bottom of the descending flight of steps without once looking up. That Richard Calmady still leaned on the bulustrade, some twelve to fourteen feet above that same cool, green grotto, she knew well enough. But she did not choose to anticipate either sight or greeting of him. Both should come to her as a whole. She would receive a single and unqualified impression.

So, silently, without apparent haste, she passed up the flight of shallow steps on to the edge of the wide, black-and-white, chequer-board platform. It was sun-bathed, suspended, as it seemed, between that glorious prospect of city, mountain, sea, and the unsullied purity of the southern heavens. It was vacant, save for the solitary figure and the sharp-edged, yet amorphous, shadow cast by that same figure. For the young man had moved as she came up from the garden below. He stood clear of the balustrade, only the fingers of his left hand resting upon the handrail of it. Seeing him thus, the strangeness, the grotesque incompleteness, of his person struck her as never before. But this, though it did not move her to mirth, as in her childhood, moved her to pity no more now than it then had. That which it did was to deepen, to stimulate, her excitement, to provoke and to satisfy the instinct of cruelty latent in every pagan nature such as hers. Could Helen have chosen the moment of her birth she would have been a great lady of Imperial Rome, holding power of life and death over her slaves, and the mutes and eunuchs with which the East should have furnished her palace in the eternal city, and her dainty villa away there on the purple flanks of Vesuvius at Herculaneum or Pompeii. The delight of her own loveliness, of her own triumphant health and activity, would have been increased tenfold by the sight of, by power over, such stultified and hopelessly disfranchised human creatures. And the first sight of Richard Calmady now, though she did not stop very certainly to analyse the exact how and why of her increasing satisfaction, took its root in this same craving for ascendency by means of the suffering and loss of others. While, unconsciously, the fine flavour of her satisfaction was heightened by the fact that the victim, now before her, was her equal in birth, her superior in wealth, in intelligence and worldly station.

But, as she drew nearer, Richard the while making no effort to go forward and receive her, buoyant self-complacency and self-congratulation suffered diminution. For, rehearsing this same meeting during those rain-blotted days of waiting at Perugia, imagination had presented Dickie as the inexperienced, tender-hearted, sweet-natured lad she had known and beguiled at Brockhurst four years earlier. As has already been stated her meetings with him, since then, had been brief and infrequent. Now she perceived that imagination had played a silly trick upon her. The boy she had left, the man who stood awaiting her so calmly were, save in one distressing peculiarity, two widely different persons. For, in the interval, Richard Calmady had eaten very freely of the fruit of the Tree of the Knowledge of Good and Evil, and that diet had left its mark not only on his character, but on his appearance. He had matured notably, all trace of ingenuous, boyish charm having vanished. His skin, though darkened by recent sea-faring, was colourless.   His features were at once finer and more pronounced than of old— the bone of the face giving it a noticeable rigidity of outline, index at once of indomitable will and irreproachable breeding. The powerful jaw and strong muscular neck might have argued a measure of brutality.   But happily the young man's mouth had not coarsened.   His lips were compressed, relaxing rarely into the curves which, as a lad, had rendered his smile so peculiarly engaging.   Still there was no trace of grossness in their form or expression.   Hard living had, indeed, in Richard's case, been matter of research rather than of appetite.   The intellectual part of him had never fallen wholly into bondage to the animal.   He explored the borders of the Forbidden hoping to find some anodyne with which to assuage the ache of a vital discontent, rather than by any compulsion of natural lewdness.

Much of this quick-witted Helen quickly apprehended.   He was cleverer, more serious, and mentally more distinguished, than she had supposed him.   And this, while opening up new sources of interest and pricking her ambition of conquest, disclosed unforeseen difficulties in the way of such conquest. Moreover, she was slightly staggered by the strength and inscrutability of his countenance, the repose of his bearing and manner.   His eyes affected her oddly.   They were cold and clear as some frosty, winter's night, the pupils of them very small.   They seemed to see all things, yet tell nothing.   They were as windows opening onto endless perspectives of empty space.   They at once challenged curiosity and baffled inquiry. Helen's excitement deepened, and she was sensible it needed all the subjective support, all the indirect flattery, with which the fact of his deformity supplied her self-love to prevent her standing in awe of him.   As consequence her address was impulsive rather than studied.

"Richard, I have had a detestable winter," she said.   "It wore upon me.   It demoralised me.   I was growing dull, superstitious even.   I wanted to get away, to put a long distance between myself and certain experiences, certain memories.   I wanted to hear another language.   You have always been sympathetic to me.   It was natural, if a little unconventional, to take refuge with you."

Madame de Vallorbes spoke with an unaccustomed and very seductive air of apology, her face slightly flushed, her arms hanging straight at her sides, the long, pink, tulle strings of the hat she carried in her left hand trailing upon the black-and-white squares of the pavement.

"To do so seemed obvious in contemplation. I did not stop to consider possible objections. But, in execution, the objections become hourly more glaringly apparent. I want you to reassure me. Tell me I have not dared too greatly in coming thus uninvited?"

"Of course not," he answered. "I hope you found the house comfortable and everything prepared for you? The servants had their orders."

"I know, I know. That you should have provided against the possibility of my coming some day moved me a little more than I care to tell you."—Helen paused, looking upon him, and that look had in it a delicate affinity to a caress. But the young man's manner, though faultlessly courteous, was lacking in any hint of enthusiasm. Helen could have imagined, and that angered her, something of irony in his tone.

"Oh, there's no matter for thanks," he said. "The house was yours, will be yours again. The least I can do, since you and de Vallorbes are good enough to let me live in it meanwhile, is to beg you to make any use you please of it. Indeed it is I, rather than you, who come uninvited just now. I had not intended being back here for another month. But there was a case of something suspiciously like cholera on board my yacht at Constantinople, and it seemed wisest to get away to sea as soon as possible. One of the firemen—oh, he's all right now.—Still I shall send him home to England. He's a married man—the only one I have on board. A useful fellow, but he must go. I don't choose to take the responsibility of creating the widow and the fatherless whenever one of my crew chances to fall sick and depart into the unknown."

Richard talked on, very evidently for the mere sake of passing the time. And all the while those eyes, which told nothing, dwelt quietly upon Helen de Vallorbes until she became nervously impatient of their scrutiny. For it was not at all thus that she had pictured and rehearsed this meeting during those days of waiting at Perugia!

"We got in last night," he continued. "But I slept on board. I heard you had just arrived, and I did not care to run the risk of disturbing you after your journey."

"You are very considerate," Helen remarked.

She was surprised out of all readiness of speech. This new Richard impressed her, but she resented his manner. He took her so very much for granted. Admiration and homage were to her as her daily bread, and that any man should fail to offer them caused her frank amazement. It did more. It raised in her a longing to inflict pain. He might not admire, but at least he should not remain indifferent. Therefore she backed a couple of steps, so as to get a good view of Richard Calmady. And, without any disguise of her purpose, took a comprehensive and leisurely survey of his dwarfed and mutilated figure. While so doing she pinned on her rose-trimmed hat, and twisted the long, tulle strings of it about her throat.

"You have altered a good deal, Richard," she said reflectively.

"Probably," he answered. "I had a good deal to learn, being a very thin-skinned, young simpleton. In part, anyhow, I have learned it. And I do my best practically to apply my knowledge. But if I have altered, so, happily, have not you."

"I remain a simpleton?" she inquired, her irritation finding voice.

"You cannot very well remain that which you never have been. What you do remain is—if I may say so—victoriously yourself, unspoiled, unmodified by contact with that singularly stupid invention, society, true to my earliest recollections of you even "— Richard shuffled closer to the balustrade, threw his left arm across it, grasping the outer edge of the broad coping,— "even in small details of dress."

He looked away over the immense and radiant prospect, and then up at the radiant woman in her vesture of turquoise, pink, and gold.

And, so doing, for the first time his face relaxed, being lighted up by a flickering, mocking smile. And something in his shuffling movements, in the fine irony of his expression, pierced Helen with a sensation hitherto unknown, broke up the absoluteness of her egotism, stirred her blood. She forgot resentment in an absorbed and absorbing interest. The ordinary man of the world she knew as thoroughly as her old shoe. Such an one presented small field of discovery to her. But this man was unique in person, and promised to be so in character also. Her curiosity regarding him was profound. For the moment it sunk all personal considerations, all humorous or angry criticism, either of her own attitude towards him or of his attitude towards her. Silently she came forward, sat down on the marble bench, close to where he stood, and, turning sideways, leaned her elbows upon the top of the balustrade beside him. She looked up now, rather than down at him; and it went home to her, had nature spared him infliction of that hideous deformity, what a superb creature physically he would have been! There was a silence,

Helen remaining intent, quiet, apprehension and imagination sensibly upon the stretch.

At last Richard spoke abruptly.

"By the way, did you happen to observe the decorations of your room ?   Do you like them ? "

"Yes and no," she answered.   "They struck me as rather wonderful, but liable to induce dreams of Scylla and Charybdis, of the Fata Morgana, and other inconvenient accidents of the deep.   Fortunately I was too tired last night to be excursive in fancy, or I might have slept badly.   You have gathered all the colours of the ocean and fixed them, somehow, on those carpets and hangings and strangely frescoed walls."

"You saw that ? "

"How could I fail to see it, since you kindly excuse me of being, or ever having been, a simpleton ? "—Helen spoke lightly, tenderly almost.   An overmastering desire to please had taken her.   "You have employed a certain wizardry in the furnishing of that room," she continued.   "It lays subtle influences upon one.   What made you think of it ? "

"A dream, an idea, which has stuck by me queerly, though all other fond things of the sort were pitched overboard long ago. I suppose one is bound to be illogical on one point, if only to prove to oneself the absolutism of one's logic on all others. Thus do I, otherwise sane and consistent realist, materialist, pessimist, cling to my one dream and ideal—take it out, dandle it, nourish and cherish it, with weakly sentimental faithfulness. To do so is ludicrous.   But then my being here at all, calmly considered, is ludicrous.   And it, too, is among the results of the one idea."

He paused, and Helen, leaning beside him, waited.   The sunshine covered them both.   The sea wind was fresh in their faces.   While the many voices of Naples came up to them confused, strident, continuous, with sometimes a bugle-call, sometimes a clang of hammers, or quick pulse of stringed instruments, or jangle o' church-bells, or long-drawn bellow of a steamship clearing for sea, detaching itself from the universal chorus.   Capri, Ischia, Procida, floated, islands of amethyst, upon the sapphire of the bay, and the smoke of Vesuvius rolled ceaselessly upward.

"You see and hear and feel all this ? " Richard continued presently.   "Well, when I saw it for the first time I was pretty thoroughly out of conceit with myself and all creation.   I had been experimenting freely in things not usually talked of in polite society.   And I was abominably sold, for I found the enjoyment

such things procure is decidedly overrated.   Unmentionable
matters, once fully explored, are just as tedious and inadequate as
those which supply the most unexceptionable subjects of conversation.   Moreover, in the process of exploration I had
touched a good deal of pitch, and, the simpleton being still
superfluously to the fore in me, I was squeamishly sensible of
defilement."

The young man shifted his position slightly, resting his chin
in the hollow of his hands, speaking quietly and indifferently,
as of some matter foreign to himself and his personal interests.

"I have reason to believe I was as fairly and squarely
wretched as it is possible for an intelligent being to be.   I had
convinced myself, experimentally, that human existence, human
nature, was a bottomless pit and an uncommonly filthy one at
that.   Reaction was inevitable.   Then I understood why men
have invented gods, subscribed to irrational systems of theology,
hailed and accredited transparently ridiculous miracles.   Such
lies are necessary to certain stages of development simply for the
preservation of sanity, just as, at another stage, sanity, for its own
preservation, is necessarily driven to declare their falsehood.
And so I, after the manner of my kind, was driven to take refuge
in a dream.   The subjective, in some form or other, alone makes
life continuously possible.   And all this we now look at
determined the special nature of my attempt at subjective
support and consolation."

Richard paused again, contemplating the view.

"All this—its splendour, its diversity, its caprices and seductions, its suggestion of underlying danger—presented itself to me
as the embodiment of a personality that has had remarkable
influence in the shaping of my life."

So far Helen had listened intently and silently.   Now she
moved a little, straightening up her charming figure, pulling down
the wide brim of her hat to shelter her eyes from the heat and
brightness of the sun.

"A woman?" she asked briefly.

Richard turned to her, that same flickering of mockery in his
still face.

"Oh! you mustn't require too much of me!" he said.   "Remember the simpleton was not wholly eradicated then.—Yes, very
much a woman.   Of course.   How should it be otherwise?   It
gave me great pleasure to look at that which looked like her.   It
gives me pleasure even yet.   So I wrote and asked de Vallorbes
to be kind enough to let me rent the villa.   You remember it
was not particularly well cared for.   There was an air of fallen

greatness about the poor place. Inside it was something of a barrack."

"I remember," Helen said.

"Well, I restored and refurnished it—specially the rooms you now occupy—in accordance with what I imagined to be her taste. The whole proceeding was not a little feeble-minded, since the probability of her ever inhabiting those rooms was more than remote. But it amused, it pacified me, as prayer to their self-invented deities pacifies the devout. I never stay here for long together. If I did the spell might be broken. I go away, I travel. I even experiment in things not usually spoken of; but with a cooler judgment and less morbidly sensitive conscience than of old. I amuse myself after more active and practical fashions in other places. Here I amuse myself only with my idea."

The even flow of his speech ceased.—"What do you think of it, Helen?" he demanded, almost harshly.

"I think it can't last. It is too intangible, too fantastic."

"I admit that to keep it intact needs an infinity of precautions. For instance, I can make no near acquaintance with Naples. I cannot permit myself to see the town at close quarters. I only look at it from here. If I want to go to or from the yacht, I do so at night and in a closed carriage. I took on de Vallorbes' box at the San Carlo. If any good opera is given I go and hear it. Otherwise I remain exclusively in the house and garden. I am not acquainted with a single soul in the place."

"And the woman?" Helen exclaimed, a singular emotion at once of envy and protest upon her. "Do you treat her with the same cold-blooded calculation?"

"Of the woman I know just as much and just as little as I know of Naples. It is conceivable there may be unlovely elements in her character, as well as unlovely quarters of this beautiful city. I have avoided knowledge of both. You see the whole arrangement is designed not for her benefit, but for my own. It's an elaborate piece of self-seeking on my part; but, so far, it has really worked rather successfully."

"It is preposterous. It cannot in the nature of things continue successful," Helen declared.

"I am not so sure of that," he replied calmly. "Even the most preposterous of religious systems proves to have a remarkable power of survival. Why not this one? In any case, neither the success nor the failure depends on me. I shall be true, on my part. The rest depends on her."

As Richard spoke he turned, leaning his back against the

balustrade, his face away from the sunlight and the wide view. Again the extent of his deformity became arrestingly apparent to Madame de Vallorbes.

"Has this woman ever been here?" she asked.

"Yes—she has been here."

"And then? And then?" Helen cried.

The young man looked up at her, his face keen yet impassive, his eyes—as windows opening onto endless perspectives of empty space—telling nothing. She recognised, once again, that he was very strong. She also recognised that, notwithstanding his strength, he was horribly sad.

"Ah! then," he said, "the last of the poor, little, subjective supports and consolations seemed in danger of going overboard and joining their fellows in the uneasy deeps of the sea.—But the history of that will keep till a more convenient season, Cousin Helen. You have stood in the mid-day sun, and I have talked about myself, quite long enough. However, it was only fair to acquaint you with the limited resources in the way of society and amusement offered by your present dwelling. There are horses and carriages of course. Give what orders you please. Only remember both the town and the surrounding country are pretty rough. It is not fit for a lady to drive by herself. Always take your own man, or one of mine, with you if you go out. I hope you won't be quite intolerably bored. Ask for whatever you want.—You let me dine with you? Thanks."

CHAPTER III

HELEN DE VALLORBES APPREHENDS VEXATIOUS COMPLICATIONS

FOUR gowns lay outspread upon the indigo-purple, embroidered coverlet of the bed. The after-glow of an orange and crimson sunset touched the folds of them, ranged upward to the vaultings of the frescoed ceiling, and stained the lofty walls as with the glare of a furnace. Sea-greens, sea-blues, died in the heat of it, abashed and vanquished. But so did not Madame de Vallorbes' white lawn and lace *peignoir*, or her abundant hair, which Zélie Forestier—trim of figure, and sour of countenance— was in the act of dressing. These caught the fiery light and held it, so that from head to foot Helen appeared as an image of living gold. Sitting before the toilet-table, her reflection in the great, oval mirror pleased her.

"Which shall I wear?"

"That depends upon the length of time madame proposes to stay here. The black dress might be worn on several occasions with impunity. The peacock brocade, the *eau de Nil*, the crocus yellow, but once—twice at the uttermost. They are ravishing costumes, but wanting in repose. They are unsuited for frequent repetition."

Zélie's lean fingers twisted, puffed, pinned, the shining hair very skilfully.

"I will put on the black dress."

"Relieved by madame's *parure* of pink topaz?"

"Yes, I will wear the pink topazes."

"Then it will be necessary to modify the style of madame's *coiffure*."

"There is plenty of time."

Helen took a hand-glass from the table and leaned forward in the low, round-backed chair—faithful copy of a fine classic model. She wanted to see the full glory of the after-glow upon her profile, upon her neck and bosom. Thus might Cassiopeia, glass in hand, in her golden chair sit in high heaven!—Helen smiled at the pretty conceit. But the glory was already departing. Sea-blues, sea-greens, sad by contrast, began to reassert their presence on walls and carpet and hangings."

"The black dress? Madame decides to remain then?"

As she spoke the lady's-maid laid out the jewels,—chains, bracelets, brooches,—each stone set in a rim of tiny rose-knots of delicate workmanship. As she fingered them little, yellow-pink flames seemed to dance in their many facets. Then the after-glow died suddenly. The flames ceased to dance. Helen's white garments turned livid, her neck and bosom grey—and that, somehow, was extremely unpleasing to Madame de Vallorbes.

"Light the candles," she said, almost sharply. "Yes, I remain. Do hurry, Zélie. It is impossible to see. I detest darkness. Hurry. Do you suppose I want to stay here all night? And look—you must bring that chain farther forward. It is not graceful. Make it droop. Let it follow the line of my hair so that the pendant may fall there, in the centre. You have it too much to the right. The centre—the centre—I tell you. There, let the drop just clear my forehead."

Thus admonished the Frenchwoman wound the jewels in her mistress' hair. But Madame de Vallorbes remained dissatisfied. The day had been one of uncertainty, of conflicting emotions; and Helen's love of unqualified purposes was

great. Confusion in others was highly diverting. But in herself
—no thank you ! She hated it. It touched her self-confidence.
It endangered the absoluteness of her self-belief and self-
worship. And these once shaken, small superstitions assaulted
her. In trivial happenings she detected indication of ill-luck.
Now Zélie's long, narrow face, divided into two unequal portions
by a straight bar of black eyebrow, and her lean hands as
reflected in the mirror, awoke unreasoning distrust. They
appeared to be detached from the woman's dark-clothed person,
the outlines of which were absorbed in the increasing dimness of
the room. The sallow face moved, peered, the hands clutched
and hovered, independent and unrelated, about Helen's graceful
head.

" For pity's sake, more candles, Zélie ! " she repeated. " You
look absolutely diabolic in this uncertain light."

" In an instant, madame. I am compelled first to fix this
curl in place."

She accomplished the operation with most admired deliberation, and moved away more than once, to observe the effect,
before finally adjusting the hair-pin.

" I cannot but regret that madame is unable to wear her hair
turned back from the face. Such an arrangement confers height
and an air of spirituality, which, in madame's case, would be not
only becoming but advantageous."

Helen skidded the hand-glass down upon the dressing-table,
causing confusion amid silver-topped pots and bottles, en-
dangering a jar of hyacinths, upsetting a tray of hair-pins.

" Have I not repeatedly given you orders never to allude to
that subject ? " she cried.

The maid was on her knees calmly collecting the scattered
contents of the tray.

" A thousand pardons, madame," she said, with a certain sour
impudence. " Still, it must ever be a matter of regret to anyone
truly appreciating madame's style of beauty, that she should be
always constrained to wear her hair shading her forehead."

Modern civilisation imposes restrictions even upon the most
high-spirited. At that moment Madame de Vallorbes was ripe
for the commission of atrocities. Had she been—as she coveted
to be—a lady of the Roman decadence it would have gone
hard with her waiting-woman, who might have found herself
ordered for instant execution or summarily deprived of the
organs of speech. But, latter-day sentiment happily forbidding
such active expressions of ill-feeling on the part of the employer
towards the employed, Helen was forced to swallow her wrath,

reminding herself, meanwhile, that a confidential servant is either most invaluable of friends or most dangerous of enemies. There is no *viâ media* in the relation. And Zélie as an enemy was not to be thought of. She could not—displeasing reflection —afford to quarrel with Zélie. The woman knew too much. Therefore Madame de Vallorbes took refuge in lofty abstraction; while the tiresome uncertainties, the conflicting inclinations of the past day, quick to seize their opportunity,—as is the habit of such discourteous gentry,—returned upon her with redoubled importunity and force.

She had not seen Richard since parting with him at noon, the enigmatic suggestions of his conversation still unresolved, the alternate resentment at his apparent indifference and attraction of his strong and somewhat mysterious personality still vitally present to her. Later, she had driven out to Pozzuoli. But neither stone-throwing urchins, foul and disease-stricken beggars, the pale sulphur plains and subterranean rumblings of the Solfaterra, nor stirring of nether fires therein resident by a lanky, wild-eyed lad—clothed in leathern jerkin and hairy, goat-skin leggings—with the help of a birch broom and a few local newspapers, served effectually to rouse her from inward debate and questioning. The comfortable, cee-spring carriage might swing and sway over the rough, deep-rutted roads behind the handsome, black, long-tailed horses, the melodramatic-looking coachman might lash stone-throwing urchins and anathematise them, their ancestors and descendants, alike, to the third and fourth generation in the vilest, Neapolitan argot, Charles might resort to physical force in the removal of wailing, alms-demanding, vermin-eaten wrecks of humanity, but still Helen asked herself only—should she go? Should she stay? Was the game worth the candle? Was the risk, not only of social scandal, but of possible *ennui*, worth the projected act of revenge? And worth something more than that. For revenge, it must be owned, already took a second place in her calculations. Worth, namely, the enjoyment of possible conquest, the humiliation of possible defeat and rejection, by that strangely coercive, strangely in-scrutable being, her cousin, Dickie Calmady?

No man had ever impressed her thus. And she returned on her thought, when first seeing him upon the terrace that morning, that she might lose her head. Helen laughed a little bitterly. She, of all women, to lose her head, to long and languish, to entreat affection, and to be faithful—heaven help us! faithful, could it ever come to that?—like any sentimental schoolgirl, like —and the thought turned her not a little wicked—like Katherine

Calmady herself! And then, that other woman of whom Richard had told her with a cynical disregard of her own claims to admiration, who on earth could she be? She reviewed those ladies with whom gossip had coupled Richard's name. Morabita, the famous *prima donna*, for instance. But surely, it was inconceivable that mountain of fat and good-nature, with the voice of a seraph, granted, but also with the intellect of a frog, could ever inspire so fantastic and sublimated a passion! And passing from these less legitimate affairs of the heart—in which rumour accredited Richard with being very much of a pluralist—her mind travelled back to the young man's projected marriage with Lady Constance Decies, sometime Lady Constance Quayle. Remembering the slow, sweet baby-face and gentle, heifer's eyes, as she had seen them that day at luncheon at Brockhurst, nearly five years ago, she again laughed.—No, very certainly there was no affinity between the glorious and naughty city of Naples and that mild-natured, well-drilled, little, English girl! Who was it then—who? But, whoever the fair unknown rival might be, Helen hated her increasingly as the hours passed, regarding her as an enemy, a creature to be exterminated, and swept off the board. Jealousy pricked her desire of conquest. An intrigue with Richard Calmady offered singular, unique, attractions. But the force of such attractions was immensely enhanced by the excitement of wresting his affections away from another woman.

Suddenly, in the full swing of these meditations, as she reviewed them for the hundredth time, Zélie's voice claimed her attention.

"I made the inquiries madame commanded."

"Well?" Helen said. She was standing fastening clusters of topaz in the bosom of her dress.

"The servants in this house are very reserved. They are unwilling to give information regarding their master's habits. I could only learn that Sir Richard occupies the entresol. Communicating as it does with the garden, no doubt it is convenient to a gentleman so afflicted as himself."

Helen bowed herself together, while the black lace and China-crape skirt slipped over her head. Emerging from which temporary eclipse, she said :—

"But do people stay here much? Does my cousin entertain? That is what I told you to find out."

"As I tell madame, the servants are difficult of approach. They are very discreet. They fear their master, but they also adore him. Charles can obtain little more information than myself. But he infers that Sir Richard, when at the villa, lives in retirement—that he is subject to fits of melancholy. There will be little diversion for madame it is to be feared! But what would you have? Even though one should be young and rich *ce ne serait que peu amusant d'être estropié, d'être monstre enfin* ! "

Helen drew in her breath with a little sigh of content when taking a final look at herself in the oval glass. The soft, floating draperies, the many jewels, each with its heart of quick, yellow-pink light, produced a combination at once sombre and vivid. It satisfied her sense of artistic fitness. Decidedly she did well to begin with the black dress, since it had in it a quality rather of romance than of worldliness! Meanwhile Zélie, kneeling, straightened out the folds of the long train.

"Ah!" she exclaimed. "I had forgotten also to inform madame that M. Destournelle has arrived in Naples. Charles, thinking of nothing less than such an encounter, met him this morning on the quay of the Santa Lucia."

Helen wheeled round violently, much to the discomfiture of those carefully adjusted folds.

"Intolerable man!" she cried. "What on earth is he doing here?"

"That, Charles naturally could not inquire.—Will madame kindly remain tranquil for a moment? She has torn a small piece of lace which must be controlled by a pin. Probably *monsieur* is still *en voyage*, is visiting friends as is madame herself."

A sudden distrust ¦that the black dress was too mature, that it constituted an admission of departing youth, invaded Helen. The reflection in the oval mirror once more caused her discomfort.

"Tell Charles that I am no longer acquainted with M. Destournelle. If he presumes to call he is to be refused."

Helen set her teeth. But whether in anger towards her discarded lover, or the black dress, she would have found it difficult to declare. Again uncertainty held her, suspicion of circumstance, and, in a degree, of herself. The lady's-maid, imperturbable, just conceivably impertinent in manner, had risen to her feet.

"There," she said, "it will be secure for to-night, if madame will exercise a moderate degree of caution and avoid abrupt movements. Charles says that *monsieur* inquired very urgently after madame. He appeared dejected and in weak health. He was agitated on meeting Charles. He trembled. A little more and he would have wept. It would be well, perhaps, that madame should give Charles her orders regarding *monsieur* herself."

"You should not have made me wear this gown," Helen broke out inconsequently. "It is depressing, it is hideous. I want to change it."

"Impossible. Madame is already a little late, and there is nothing wrong with the costume. Madame looks magnificent. Also her wardrobe is, at present, limited. The evening dresses will barely suffice for a stay of a week, and it is not possible for me to construct a new one under ten days."

Thereupon an opening of doors and voice from the ante-room, announcing :—

"Dinner is served, my lady. Sir Richard is in the dining-room."

And Helen swept forward, somewhat stormy and Cassandra-like in her dusky garments. Passing out through the high narrow doorway, she turned her head.

"Charles, under no circumstance—none, understand—am I at home to Monsieur Destournelle."

"Very good, my lady," and, as he closed the double-doors, the man-servant looked at the lady's-maid his tongue in his cheek.

But, on the journey through the noble suite of rooms, Helen's spirits revived somewhat. Her fair head, her warm glancing jewels, her graceful and measured movements, as given back by many tall mirrors, renewed her self-confidence. She too must be fond of her own image, by the way, that unknown rival to the dream of whose approval Richard Calmady had consecrated these splendid furnishings—witness the multiplicity of looking-glasses !— And then the prospect of this *tête-à-tête* dinner, the interest of her host's powerful and enigmatic personality, provoked her interest to the point not only of obliterating remembrance of the ill-timed advent of her ex-lover, but of inducing something as closely akin to self-forgetfulness as was possible to her self-centred nature. She grew hotly anxious to obtain, to charm—if it might be to usurp the whole field of Richard's attention and imagination.

A small round table showed as an island of tender light in the dimness of the vast room. And Richard, sitting at it awaiting her coming, appeared more nearly related to the Richard of Brockhurst and of five years ago than he had done during the interview of the morning. In any case, she took him more for granted. While he, if still inscrutable and unsmiling, proved an eminently agreeable companion, ready of conversation, very much at his ease, very much a cultivated man of the world, studious—a little excessively so, she thought—in his avoidance of the personal note. And this at once piqued

26

Helen, and incited her to intellectual effort. If this was what he wanted, well, he should have it ! If he elected to talk of travel, of ancient and alien religions, of modern literature and art, she could meet him more than half way. Her intelligence ran nimbly from subject to subject, from point to point. She struck out daring hypotheses, indulged in ingenious paradox, her mind charmed by her own eloquence, her body comforted by costly wines and delicate meats. Nor did she fail to listen also, knowing how very dear to every man is the sound of his own voice, or omit to offer refined flattery of quick agreement and seasonable laughter. It was late when she rose from the table at last.

"I have had a delightful dinner," she said. "Absolutely delightful. And now I will encroach no longer on your time or good-nature, Richard. You have your own occupations, no doubt. So, with thanks for shelter and generous entertainment, we part for to-night."

She held out her hand smiling, but with an admirable effect of discretion, all ardour, all intimacy, kept in check by self-respect and well-bred dignity. Madame de Vallorbes was enchanted with the reserve of her own demeanour. Let it be understood that she was the least importunate, the least exacting, the most adaptable, of guests !

Richard took her outstretched hand for the briefest period compatible with courtesy. And a momentary spasm—so she fancied—contracted his face.

"You are very welcome, Helen," he said. "If it is warm let us breakfast in the pavilion to-morrow. Twelve—does that suit you ? Good-night."

Upon the inlaid writing-table in the anteroom, Helen found a long and impassioned epistle from Paul Destournelle. Perusal of it did not minister to peaceful sleep. In the small hours she left her bed, threw a silk dressing-gown about her, drew aside the heavy, blue-purple window curtain and looked out. The sky was clear and starlit. Naples, and its curving lines of innumerable lights, lay outstretched below. In the south-east, midway between the two, a blood-red fire marked the summit of Vesuvius. While in the dimly seen garden immediately beneath — the paved alleys of which showed curiously pale, asserting themselves against the darkness of the flower borders, and otherwise impenetrable shadows of the ilex and cypress grove—a living creature moved, black, slow of pace, strange of shape. At first Helen took it for some strayed animal. It alarmed her, exciting her to wildest conjectures as to its nature and purpose, wandering in the grounds of the villa thus. Then, as it passed beyond the dusky shade of the trees, she recognised it. Richard Calmady shuffled forward, haltingly, to the terminal wall of the garden, leaned his arms on it, looking down at the beautiful and vicious city and out into the night.

Helen de Vallorbes shivered—the marble floor striking up chill, for all the thickness of the carpet, to her bare feet. Her eyes were hard with excitement and her breath came very quick. Suddenly, yielding to an impulse of superstitious terror, she dragged the curtains together, shutting out that very pitiful sight, and, turning, fled across the room and buried herself, breathless and trembling, between the sheets of the soft, warm, faintly fragrant bed.

"He is horrible," she said aloud, "horrible! And it has come to me at last. It has come—I love—I love!"

CHAPTER IV

"MATER ADMIRABILIS"

"THERE, there, my good soul, don't blubber! Hysterics won't restore Lady Calmady to health, or bring Sir Richard back to England, home, and duty, or be a ha'porth of profit to yourself or any other created being. Keep your tears for the first funeral. For I tell you plainly I shan't be surprised out of seven days' sleep if this business involves a visit to the churchyard before we get to the other side of it."

John Knott stood with his back to the Chapel-Room fire, his shoulders up to his ears, his hands forced down into the pockets of his riding-breeches. Without, black-thorn winter held the land in its cheerless grasp. The spring was late. Night frosts obtained, followed by pallid, half-hearted sunshine in the early mornings, too soon obliterated by dreary, easterly blight. This afternoon offered exception to the rule only in the additional discomfort of small, sleeting rain and a harsh skirling of wind in the eastward-facing casements.—"Livery weather," the doctor called it, putting down his existing lapse from philosophic tolerance to insufficient secretions of the biliary duct.

Before him stood Clara—sometime Dickie Calmady's devoted nurse and playfellow—her eyes very bright and moist, the reds and whites of her fresh complexion in lamentable disarray.

"I'd never have believed it of Sir Richard," she asserted chokingly. "It isn't like him, so pretty as he was in all his little ways, and loving to her ladyship, and civilly behaved to everybody, and careful of hurting anybody's feelings—more so than you'd expect in a young gentleman like him. No! it isn't like him. In my opinion he's been got hold of by some designing person, who's worked on him to keep him away to serve their own ends. There, I'd never have believed it of him, that I wouldn't!"

The doctor's massive head sank lower, his massive shoulders rose higher, his loose lips twisted into a snarling smile.

"Lord bless you, that's nothing new! We none of us ever do believe it of them when the little beggars are in long clothes, or first breeched for that matter. It's a trick of Mother Nature's—one-idead old lady, who cares not a pin for morality, but only for increase. She knows well enough if we did believe it of them we should clear them off wholesale, along with the blind kittens and puppies. A bucket full of water, and broom to keep them under, would make for a mighty lessening of subsequent violations of the Decalogue! Don't tell me King Herod was not something of a philanthropist when he got to work on the infant population of Bethlehem. One woman wept for each of the little brats then; but his Satanic Majesty only knows how many women wouldn't have had cause to weep for each one of them later, if they'd been spared to grow up."

While speaking, Dr. Knott kept his gaze fixed upon his companion. His humour was none of the gentlest truly, yet he did not let that obscure the main issue. He had business with Clara, and merely waited till the reds and whites of her comely face should have resumed their more normal relations before pursuing it. He talked, as much to afford her opportunity to overcome her emotion, as to give relief to his own. Though now well on the wrong side of sixty, John Knott was hale and vigorous as ever. His rough-hewn countenance bore even closer resemblance, perhaps, to that of some stone gargoyle carved on cathedral buttress or spout. But his hand was no less skilful, his tongue no less ready in denunciation of all he reckoned humbug, his heart no less deeply touched, for all his superficial irascibility, by the pains, and sins, and grinding miseries, of poor humanity, than of old.

"That's right now," he said approvingly, as the heaving of Clara's bosom became less pronounced. "Wipe your eyes, and keep your nerves steady. You've got a head on your shoulders —always had. Well, keep it screwed on the right way; for you'll need all the common sense that is in it if we are to pull Lady Calmady through. Do?—To begin with this, give her food every two hours or so. Coax her, scold her, reason with her, cry even.—After all, I give you leave to, just a little, if that will serve your purpose and not make your hand shake—only make her take nourishment. If you don't wind up the clock regularly, some fine morning you'll find the wheels have run down."

"But her ladyship won't have anyone sit up with her."

"Very well, then sleep next door. Only go in at twelve and two, and again between five and six.

"But she won't have anybody occupy the dressing-room. It used to be the night nursery you remember, sir, and not a thing in it has been touched since Sir Richard moved down to the Gun-Room wing."

"Oh, fiddle-de-dee! It's just got to be touched now, then. I can't be bothered with sentiment when it's ten to one whether I save my patient."

Again sobs rose in Clara's throat. The poor woman was hard pressed. But that fixed gaze from beneath the shaggy eyebrows was upon her, and, with quaint gurglings, she fought down the sobs.

"My lady's as gentle as a lamb," she said, "and I'd give the last drop of my blood for her. But talk of managing her, of making her do anything, as well try to manage the wind, she's that set in her ways and obstinate!"

"If you can't manage her, who can?—Mr. March?"

Clara shook her head. Then reluctantly, for though honestly ready to lay down her life for her mistress, she found it far from easy to invite supersession in respect of her, she said:—"Miss St. Quentin's more likely to get round my lady than anyone else."

"Well, then, I'll talk to her. Where is Miss St. Quentin?"

"Here, Dr. Knott. Do you want me?"

Honoria had strolled into the room from the stairhead, her attention arrested by the all-too-familiar sound—since sorrowful happenings often of late had brought him to Brockhurst—of the doctor's voice. The skirt of the young lady's habit, gathered up in her left hand, displayed a slightly unconventional length of muddy riding-boot. The said skirt, her tan, covert coat, and slouched, felt hat, were furred with wet. Her garments, indeed, showed evident traces of hard service, and, though notably well cut, were far from new or smart. They were sad-coloured, moreover, as is the fashion of garments designed for work. And this weather-stained, mud-bespattered costume, taken in connection with her pale, sensitive face, her gallant bearing, and the luminous smile with which she greeted not only Dr. Knott but the slightly flustered Clara, offered a picture pensive in tone, but very harmonious, and of a singularly sincere and restful quality.   To all, indeed, save those troubled by an accusing conscience and fear of detection, Honoria St. Quentin's presence brought a sense of security and reassurance at this period of her development.   Her enthusiasms remained to her ; but they were tempered by a wider experience and a larger charity—at least in the majority of cases.

"I'm in a beastly mess," she observed casually.

"So are we," Knott answered.—He had a great liking for this young lady, finding in her a certain stoicism along with a quickness of practical help.   "But our mess is worse than yours, in that it is internal rather than external.   Yours 'll brush off. Not so ours—eh, Clara ?   There, you can go.   I'll talk things over with Miss St. Quentin, and she'll talk 'em over with you later."

Honoria's expression had grown anxious.   She spoke in a lower tone of voice.

" Is Lady Calmady worse ? "

"In a sense, yes—simply because she is no better.   And she's ill, I tell you, just as dangerously ill as any woman can be who has nothing whatever actually the matter with her."

"Except an only son," put in Honoria.   "I am beginning to suspect that is about the most deadly disease going.   The only thing to be said in its favour is that it is not infectious."

John Knott could not quite keep admiration from his eyes, or provocation from his tongue.   He richly enjoyed getting a rise out of Miss St. Quentin.

"I am not so sure of that," he said.   "In the case of beautiful women, judging by history, it has shown a tendency to be recurrently sporadic in any case."

"Recommend all such to spend a few months at Brockhurst then, under existing circumstances !" Honoria answered.   "There will be very little fear for them after that ; they will have received such a warning, swallowed such an antidote !—It is like assisting at the infliction of slow torture.   It almost gets on one's brain at times."

"Why do you stay on then ? "

Honoria looked down at her muddy boots and then across at the doctor.   She was slightly the taller of the two, for in these days his figure had fallen together and he had taken to stooping.   Her expression had a delightful touch of self-depreciation.

"Why does anyone stay by a sinking ship, or volunteer for

a forlorn hope? Why do you sit up all night with a case of confluent smallpox, or suck away the poisonous membrane from a diphtheritic throat, as I hear you did only last week? I don't know. Just because, if we are made on certain lines, we have to, I suppose. One would be a trifle too much ashamed to be seen in one's own company, afterwards, if one deserted. It really requires less pluck to stick than to run—that's the reason probably.—But about dear Lady Calmady. The excellent Clara was in tears. Is there any fresh mischief over and above the only son?"

"Not at present. But it's an open question how soon there may be.—Good-day, Mr. March. Been riding? Ought to be a bit careful of that cranky chest of yours in this confounded weather.—Lady Calmady?—Yes, as I was telling Miss St. Quentin, her strength is so reduced that complications may arise any day. A chill, and her lungs may go, a shock, and her heart. It comes to a mere question of the point of least resistance. I won't guarantee the continued soundness of any one organ unless we get changed conditions, a let up of some sort."

The doctor looked up from under his eyebrows, first at Honoria and then at Julius. He spoke bitterly, defiant of his inclination towards tenderness.

"She's just worn herself out," he said, "that's the fact, in the service of others, loving, giving, attempting the impossible in the way of goodness all round. 'Be not righteous over much'—there's a text to that effect in the Scriptures, Mr. March, isn't there? Preach a good, rattling sermon on it next Sunday to Lady Calmady, if you want to keep her here a bit longer. Nature abhors a vacuum. Granted. But nature abhors excess, even of virtue. And punishes it just as harshly as excess of vice.—Yes, I tell you, she's worn herself out."

Miss St. Quentin dropped into a chair and sat bowed together, her hands on her knees, her feet rather far apart. The brim of her hat, pulled down in front to let the rain run off, partially concealed her face. She was not sorry, for a movement of defective courage was upon her, evidence of which she preferred to keep to herself. Julius March remained silent. And this she resented slightly, for she badly wanted somebody to say something, either vindictive or consolatory. Then, indignation getting the better alike of reticence and charity, she exclaimed :—

"It is unpardonable. It ought to be impossible one person should have power to kill another by inches, like this, with impunity."

Ludovic Quayle had sauntered into the room behind Julius

March. He too was wet and dirty, but such trifles in no wise affected the completeness of his urbanity. His long neck directed forward, as in polite inquiry, he advanced to the little group by the fire, and took up his station beside Honoria's chair.

"Pardon me, my dear Miss St. Quentin," he asked sweetly, "but why the allusions to murder? What is unpardonable?"

"Sir Richard Calmady's conduct," she answered shortly. She threw back her head and addressed Dr. Knott. "It is so detestably unjust. What possible quarrel has he with her, after all?"

"Ah! that—that—lies very deep. A thing, perhaps, only a man, or a mother, can quite comprehend," the doctor answered slowly.

Honoria's straight eyebrows drew together. She objected to extenuating circumstances in this connection, yet, as she admitted, reason usually underlay all Dr. Knott's statements. She divined, moreover, that reason just now touched upon matters inconveniently intimate. She abstained, therefore, from protest or comment. But, since feminine emotion, even in the least weakly of the sex, is bound to find an outlet, she turned upon poor Mr. Quayle.

"He is your friend," she said. "The rest of us are helpless. You ought to take measures. You ought to suggest a remedy."

"With all the pleasure in life," the young man answered. "But you may remember that you delivered yourself of precisely the same sentiments a year and a half ago. And that, fired with the ardour of a chivalrous obedience, I fled over the face of the European continent in hot pursuit of poor, dear Dickie Calmady."

"Poor, dear!" ejaculated Honoria.

"Yes, very much poor, dear, through it all," the young man affirmed. "Breathless, but still obedient, I came up with him at Odessa."

"What was he doing there?" put in the doctor.

Mr. Quayle regarded him not without humour.

"Really, I am not my friend's keeper, though Miss St. Quentin is pleased to make me a handsome present of that enviable office. And so—well—I didn't inquire what he was doing. To tell the truth, I had not much opportunity, for though I found him charming,—yes, charming, Miss St. Quentin, —I also found him wholly unapproachable regarding family affairs. When, with a diplomatic ingenuity upon which I cannot but congratulate myself, I suggested the advisability of a return to Brockhurst, in the civilest way in the world he showed me the door. Impertinence is not my *forte*. I am by nature humble-minded. But, I give you my word, that was a little episode of which I do not crave the repetition."

Growling to himself, clasping his hands behind his back, John Knott shifted his position. Then, taken with that desire of clergy-baiting, which would seem to be inherent in members of the Faculty, he addressed Julius March.

"Come now," he said, "your pupil doesn't do you an over-whelming amount of credit it must be admitted, still you ought to be able to give an expert's opinion upon the tendencies of his character. How much longer do you allow him before he grows tired of filling his belly with the husks the swine eat?"

"God knows, not I," Julius answered sadly, but without rancour. "I confess to the faithlessness of despair at times. And yet, being his mother's son, he cannot but tire of it eventually, and when he does so the revulsion will be final, the restoration complete"—

"He'll die the death of the righteous? Oh yes! I agree there, for there's fine stuff in him, never doubt that. He'll end well enough. Only the beginning of that righteous ending, if delayed much longer, may come a bit too late for the saving of my patient's life and—reason."

"Do you mean it is as serious as all that?" Ludovic asked with sudden anxiety.

"Every bit as serious!— Oh! you should have let your sister marry him, Mr. Quayle. Then he would have settled down, come into line with the average, and been delivered from the morbid sense of outlawry which had been growing on him—it couldn't be helped, on the whole he's kept very creditably sane in my opinion—from the time he began to mix freely in general society. I'm not very soft or sickly sentimental at my time of day, but I tell you it turns my stomach to think of all he must have gone through, poor chap. It's a merciless world, Miss St. Quentin, and no one knows that better than we case-hardened old sinners of doctors.—Yes, your sister should have married him, and we might have been saved all this. I doubted the wisdom of the step at the time. But I was a fool. I see now his mother's instinct was right."

Mr. Quayle pursed up his small mouth and gently shrugged his shoulders.

"It is a delicate subject on which to offer an opinion," he said. "I debated it freely in the privacy of my inner consciousness at the time, I assure you. If Lady Calmady had lighted upon the right, the uniquely right, woman—perhaps—yes. But to shore up a twenty-foot, stone wall with a wisp of straw,—my dear doctor, does that proceeding approve itself to your common sense? And, as is a wisp of straw to such a wall, so was my poor, little sister,—it's hardly flattering to my family pride to admit it,—but thus indeed was she, and no otherwise, to Dickie Calmady."

Whereupon Honoria glanced up gratefully at the speaker, for even yet her conscience pricked her concerning the part she had played in respect of that broken engagement. While John Knott, observant of that upward glance, was once again struck by her manifest sincerity, and the gallant grace of her, heightened by those workmanlike and mud-bespattered garments. And, being so struck, he was once again tempted by, and once again yielded himself to, the pleasures of provocation.

"Marry him yourself, Miss St. Quentin," he growled, a touch of earnest behind his raillery, "marry him yourself and so set the rest of us free of the whole pother. I'd back you to handle him, or any fellow living, with mighty great success if you'd the mind to!"

For a moment it seemed open to question whether that very fair fish might not make short work of angler as well as of bait. But Honoria relented, refusing provocation. And this not wholly in mercy to the speaker, but because it offered her an opportunity of reading Mr. Quayle a, perhaps useful, lesson. Her serious eyes narrowed, and her upper lip shortened into a delightful smile.

"Hopeless, Dr. Knott!" she answered. "To begin with he'll never ask me, since we like each other very royally ill. And to end with"—she carefully avoided sight of Mr. Quayle—"I—you see—I'm not what you call a marrying man."

CHAPTER V

EXIT CAMP

ABOUT twenty minutes later the young lady, still booted and spurred, opened the door which leads from the Chapel-Room into Lady Calmady's bed-chamber. As she did so a gentle warmth met her, along with a sweetness of flowers. Within, the melancholy of the bleak twilight was mitigated by the soft brightness of a pink-shaded lamp, and a fitful flickering of firelight. This last, playing upon the blue-and-white, Dutch tiling of the hearth and chimney-space, conferred a quaint effect of activity upon the actors in the biblical scenes thereon depicted. The patriarch Abraham visibly flourished his two-inch sword above the prostrate form of hapless Isaac. The elders pranced, unblushingly, in pursuit of the chaste Susanna. While poor little Tobit, fish in hand, clung anxiously to the flying draperies of his long-legged, and all-too-peripatetic, guardian angel. Such profane vivacity, on the part of persons usually accounted sacred, offered marked and almost cynical contrast to the extreme quiet otherwise obtaining, accentuated the absoluteness, deepened the depth, of it. For nothing stirred within the length and breadth of the room, nor did any smallest sound disturb the prevailing silence. At these southward-facing casements no harsh wind shrilled. The embroidered curtains of the state-bed hung in stiff, straight folds. The many-coloured leaves and branches of the trees of the Forest of This Life were motionless. Care, the leopard, crouched, unobservant, forgetful to spring ; while the Hart was fixed spell-bound in the midst of its headlong flight. A spell seemed, indeed, to rest on all things, which had in it more than the watchful hush of the ordinary sick-room. It suggested a certain moral attitude—a quiet, not acquiesced in merely, but promoted.

Upon Honoria—her circulation quickened by recent exercise, her cheeks still tingling from the stinging sleet, her retina still retaining impressions of the stern grandeur of the wide-ranging fir woods and grey-brown desolation of the moors—this extreme quiet produced an extremely disquieting effect. Passing from the Chapel-Room and the society of her late companions—all three persons of distinct individuality, all three possessing, though from very differing standpoints, a definitely masculine outlook on life—into this silent bed-chamber, she seemed to pass with startling abruptness from the active to the passive, from the objective to the subjective side of things, from the world that creates to that which obeys, merely, and waits. The present and masculine, with its clear practical reason, its vigorous purposes, was exchanged for a place peopled by memories only, dedicated wholly to submissive and patient endurance. And this fell in extremely ill with Honoria's present humour ; while the somewhat unseemly antics of the small, scriptural personages, pictured upon the chimney-space and hearth, troubled her imagination, in that they added a point of irony to this apparent triumph of the remote over the immediate, of tradition over fact.

Nor as, stung by unspoken remonstrance, she approached Lady Calmady was this sense of intrusion into an alien region lessened ; or her appreciation of the difficulties of the mission she had been deputed by doctor, priest, and amiable, young fine-gentleman — her late companions — to fulfil, by any means lightened.

For Katherine lay back in the great rose-silk and muslin-covered arm-chair, at right angles to the fireplace, motionless, not a participant merely, so it seemed to the intruder, in that all-embracing quiet, but the very source and centre of it, its nucleus and heart. The lines of her figure were shrouded in a loose, wadded gown of dove-coloured silk, bordered with swans-down. A coif of rare, white lace covered her upturned hair. Her eyes were closed, the rim of the eye-socket being very evident. While her face, though smooth and still graciously young, was so emaciated as to appear almost transparent. Now, as often before, it struck Honoria that a very exquisite spiritual quality was present in her aspect—her whole bearing and expression betraying, less the languor and defeat of physical illness, than the exhaustion of long sustained moral effort, followed by the calm of entire self-dedication and renunciation of will.

On the table at her elbow were a bowl of fresh-picked violets and greenhouse-grown tea-roses, some books of the hour, both English and French, a miniature of Dickie at the age of thirteen —the proud, little head and its cap of close-cropped curls show-ing up against a background of thick-set foliage. On the table, too, lay a well-worn, vellum-bound copy of that holiest of books ever, probably, conceived by the heart and written by the hand of man—Thomas à Kempis' Imitation of Christ. It was open at the chapter which is thus entitled—" Of the Zealous Amendment of our Whole Life." While close against it was a packet of Richard's letters — those curt, businesslike communications, faultlessly punctual in their weekly arrival, which, while they relieved her anxiety as to his material well-being, stabbed his mother's heart only less by the little they said, than by all they left unsaid.

And looking upon that mother now, taking cognisance of her surroundings, Honoria St. Quentin's young indignation, once again, waxed hot. While, since it was the tendency of her mind to run eagerly towards theory, to pass from the particular to the general, and instinctively to apprehend the relation of the individual to the mass, looking thus upon Katherine, she rebelled, not only against the doom of this one woman, but against that doom of universal womanhood of which she offered,

just now, only too eloquent an example. And a burning compassion animated Honoria for all feminine as against all masculine
creatures; for the bitter patience demanded of the passive, as
against the large latitude permitted the active principle; for the
perpetual humiliation of the subjective and spiritual under the
heavy yoke of the objective and practical; for the brief joy and
long barrenness of all those who are condemned to obey and to
wait, merely, as against those who are born to command and
to create.

From a child she had been aware of the element of tragedy
inherent in the fact of womanhood. It had quickened exaggerations of sentiment in her at times, and pushed her into not a
little knight-errantry,—witness the affair of Lady Constance
Quayle's engagement. But, though more sober in judgment
than of old and less ready to set her lance in rest, the existence
of that tragic element had never disclosed itself more convincingly to her than at the present moment, nor had the necessity
to attempt the assuaging of the smart of it called upon her with
more urgent voice. Yet she recognised that such attempt taxed
all her circumspection, all her imaginative sympathy and tact.
Very free criticism of the master of the house, of his sins of
omission and commission alike, were permissible in the Chapel-
Room and in the presence of her late companions. The subject,
unhappily, had called for too frequent mention, by now, for any
circumlocution to be incumbent in the discussion of it. But
here, in the brooding quiet of this bed-chamber, and in Lady
Calmady's presence, all that was changed. Trenchant statements of opinion, words of blame, were proscribed. The sinner,
if spoken of at all, must be spoken of with due reticence and
respect, his wilfulness ignored, the unloveliness of his conduct
gently, even eagerly, explained away.

And, therefore, it came about that this fair champion of much-
wronged womanhood, though fired with the zeal of righteous
anger, had to go very softly and set a watch before her lips.
But as she paused, fearful to break in too abruptly upon Lady
Calmady's repose, she began to question fearfully whether speech
was, in truth, still available as a means of communication between
herself and the object of her solicitude. For Lady Calmady lay
so very still, her sweet face showed so transparent against the
rose-silk, muslin-covered pillows, that the younger woman was
shaken by a swift dread that Dr. Knott's melancholy predictions
had already found fulfilment, and that the lovely, labour-wasted
body had already let the valiant, love-wasted soul depart.

"Cousin Katherine, dear Cousin Katherine," she called very

gently, under her breath; and then waited almost awestricken, sensible, to the point of distress, alike of the profound quiet, which it seemed as an act of profanity to have even assayed to break, and of the malign activity of those little, scriptural figures anticking so wildly in the chimney-space and on the hearth.

Seconds, to Honoria of measureless duration, elapsed before Lady Calmady gave sign of life. At length she moved her hands, as though gathering, with infinite tenderness, some small and helpless creature close and warm against her bosom. Honoria's vision grew somewhat blurred and misty. Then, with a long-drawn, fluttering sigh, Katherine looked up at the tall, straight figure.

"Dick—ah, you've come in! My beloved—have you had good sport?" she said.

Honoria sat down on the end of the sofa, bowing her head.

"Alas, alas, it is only me, Cousin Katherine. Nothing better than me, Honoria St. Quentin. Would that it were someone better," and her voice broke.

But Lady Calmady had come into full possession of herself.

"My dear, I must have been dozing, and my thoughts had wandered far on the backward road, as is the foolish habit of thoughts when one grows old and is not altogether well and strong."—Katherine spoke faintly, yet with an air of sweetly playful apology. "One is liable to be confused, under such circumstances, when one first wakes—and—you have the smell of the sleet and the freshness of the moors upon you." She paused, and then added:—"But, indeed, the confusion of sleep once past, I could hardly have anything dearer for my eyes first to light on than your very dear self."

Hearing which gracious words, indignation in the cause of this woman, burning compassion for the wrongs and sorrows of universal womanhood, both of which must be denied utterance, worked very forcibly in Honoria. She bent down and taking Lady Calmady's hand kissed it. And, as she did this, her eyes were those of an ardent, yet very reverent lover, and so, when next she spoke, were the tones of her voice.

But Katherine, still anxious to repair any defect in her recognition and greeting, and still with that same effect of playful self-depreciation, spoke first.

"I had been reviewing many things, with the help of blessèd Thomas à Kempis here, before I became so drowsy. The dear man lays his finger smartly upon all the weak places in one's fancied armour of righteousness. It is sometimes not quite easy to be altogether grateful to him. For instance, he has pointed out to me conclusively that I grow reprehensibly selfish."

"Oh, come, come!" Honoria answered, in loving raillery. "Thomas is acute to the point of lying if he has convinced you of that!"

"Unhappily, no," Katherine returned. "I know it, I fear, without any pointing of Thomas's finger. But I rather shirked admission of my knowledge—well, for the very bad reason that I wanted very badly to put off the day of amendment. Now the holy man has touched my witness and"— she turned her head against the pillows and looked full at the younger woman, while her under-lip quivered a little. "My dear, I have come to be very greedy of the comfort of your companionship. I have been tempted to consider not your advantage, but solely my own. The pointing finger of Thomas has brought it home to me that Brockhurst and I are feeding upon your generosity of time, and helpfulness, to an unconscionable extent. We are devouring the best days of your life, and hindering you alike from work and from pleasure. It must not be. And so, my dear, I beg you go forth, once more, to all your many friends and to society. You are too young, and too gifted, to remain here in this sluggish back-water, alongside a derelict like me. It is not right. You must make for the open stream again and let the free wind and the strong current bear you gladly on your appointed course. And my gratitude and my blessing will go with you always. But you must delay no longer. For me you have done enough."

For a little space Honoria held her friend's hand in silence.

"Are—are—you tired of me then?" she said.

"Ah, my dear!" Katherine exclaimed. And the exclamation was more reassuring, somehow, than any denial could have been.

"After all," Honoria went on, "I really don't see why you're to have a monopoly of faithfulness. There's selfishness now, if you like—to appropriate a virtue *en bloc*, not leaving a rag, not the veriest scrappit of it for anybody else! And then, has it never occurred to you, that I may be just every bit as greedy of your companionship as you of mine—more so, I fancy, because —because"—

Honoria bowed her head and kissed the hand she held, once again.

"You see—I know it sounds as if I was rather a beast— perhaps I am—but I never cared for anyone—really to care, I mean—till I cared for you."

"My dear!"—Katherine said again, wondering, shrinking somewhat, at once touched and almost repulsed. The younger woman's attitude was so far removed from her own experience.

"Does it displease you? Does it seem to you unnatural?" Honoria asked quickly.

"A little," Lady Calmady answered, smiling, yet very tenderly.

"All the same it's quite true. You opened a door, somehow, that had always been shut. I hardly believed in its existence. Of course I had read plenty about the—affections, shall we call them? And had heard women and girls, and men, too, for that matter, talk about them pretty freely. But it bored me a good deal. I thought it all rather silly, and rather nasty perhaps."—Honoria shook her head. "It didn't appeal to me in the least. But when you opened the door"— she paused, her face very grave, yet with a smile on it, as she looked away at the little figures anticking upon the hearth. "Oh, dear me, I own I was half scared," she said, "it let in such a lot of light!"

But, for this speech, Lady Calmady had no immediate answer. And so the quiet came back, settling down sensibly on the room again — even as, when at dawn the camp is struck, the secular quiet of the desert comes back and possesses its own again. And, in obedience to that quiet, Katherine's hand rested passively in the hand of her companion, while she gazed wonderingly at the delicate, half-averted face, serious, lit up by the eagerness of a vital enthusiasm. And, having a somewhat sorrowful fund of learning to draw upon in respect of the dangers which all eccentricity, either of character or development, inevitably brings along with it, she trembled, divining that noble and strong and pure though it was, that face, and the temperament disclosed by it, might work sorrow, both to its possessor and to others, unless the enthusiasm animating it should find some issue at once large and simple enough to engage its whole aspiration and power of work.

But abruptly Honoria broke up the brooding quiet, laughing gently, yet with a catch in her throat.

"And when you had let in the light, Cousin Katherine, good heavens, how thankful I was I had never married. Picture finding out all that after one had bound oneself, after one had given oneself! What an awful prostitution."—Her tone changed and she stroked the elder woman's hand softly. "So you see you can't very well order me off, the pointing finger of Thomas notwithstanding. You have taught me"—

"Only half the lesson as yet," Katherine said. "The other

half, and the doxology which closes it, neither I, nor any other woman, can teach you."

"You really believe that?"

"Ah! my dear," Katherine said, "I do more than believe. I know it."

The younger woman regarded her searchingly. Then she shook her charming head.

"It's no good to arrive at a place before you've got to it," she declared. "And I very certainly haven't got to the second half of the lesson, let alone the doxology, yet. And then I'm so blissfully content with the first half, that I've no disposition to hurry. No, dear Cousin Katherine, I am afraid you must resign yourself to put up with me for a little while longer. Your foes, unfortunately, are of your own household in this affair. Dr. Knott has just been holding forth to us—Julius March, and Mr. Quayle, and me—and swearing me over not only to stay, but to make you eat and drink and come out of doors, and even to go away with me. Because—yes, in a sense your Thomas is right with his pointing finger, though he got a bit muddled, good man, not being quite up-to-date, and pointed to the wrong place"—

Honoria left her sentence unfinished. She knelt down—her tall, slender figure, angular, more like that of a youth than like that of a maid, in her spare, mud-stained habit and coat. Impulsively she put her hands on Lady Calmady's hips, laid her head in her lap.

"Have you but one blessing, oh! my more than mother?" she cried. "Do we count for nothing, all the rest of us—your household, and tenants rich and poor, and Julius the faithful, and Ludovic the bland, and that queer lump of sagacity and ugliness, John Knott? Why will you kill yourself? Why will you die and leave us all, just because one person is perverse? That's hardly the way to make us—who love you—bear with and pity him and welcome him home.—Oh! I know I am treading on dangerous ground and venturing to approach very close. But I don't care—not a hang! We're at the end of our patience. We want you, and we mean to have you back."

Honoria raised herself, knelt bolt upright, her hands on the arms of Lady Calmady's chair, her expression full of appeal.

"Be kind to us, be kind," she said. "We only ask you, after all, to eat and drink—to let Clara take care of you at night, and let me do so by day.—And then, when you are stronger, you must come away with me, up north, to Ormiston. You have not

27

been there for years, and its grey towers are rather splendid over-looking that strong, uneasy, northern sea. It stirs the Viking blood in one, and makes that which was hard seem of less moment. Roger and Mary are there, too—will be all this summer. And you know it refreshed you to see them last year. And if we go pretty soon the boys will be at school, so they won't tire you with their racketing. They're jolly monkeys, though, in my opinion, Godfrey wants smacking. He comes the elder-brother a lot too much over poor, little Dick.—But that's neither here nor there. Oh! it's for you to get out of the backwater into the stream, ten times more than for me. Dearest physician, heal thyself!"

But Katherine, though deeply touched by the loving ardour of the younger woman's appeal, and the revelation of tenderness and watchful care, constantly surrounding her, which that appeal brought along with it, could not rouse herself to any immediate response. Sternly, unremittingly, since the fair July night when Richard had left her nearly five years earlier, she had schooled herself into unmurmuring resignation and calm. In the prosecution of such a process there must be loss as well as gain. And Katherine had, in great measure, atrophied impulse; and, in eradicating personal desire, had come near destroying all spontaneity of emotion. She could still give, but the power of receiving was deadened in her. And she had come to be jealous of the quiet which surrounded her. It was her support and solace. She asked little more than not to have it broken up. She dreaded even affection, should that strive to draw her from the cloistered way of life. The world, and its many interests, had ceased to be of any moment to her. She asked to be left to contemplation of things eternal and to the tragedy of her own heart. And so, though it was beautiful to know herself to be thus cherished and held in high esteem, that beauty came to her as something unrelated, as sweet words good to hear, yet spoken of some person other than herself, or of a self she had ceased to be. All privilege implies a corresponding obligation, and to the meeting of fresh obligations Katherine felt herself not only unequal, but indisposed. And so, she smiled now upon Honoria St. Quentin, leaning back against the rose-silk and muslin-covered pillows, with a lovely indulgence, yet rather hopelessly unmoved and remote.

"Ah! my dear, I am beyond all wish to be healed after the fashion you, in your urgent loving-kindness, would have me," she said. "I look forward to the final healing, when my many mistakes and shortcomings shall be forgiven and the smart of them removed. And I am very tired. I do not think it can be required of me to go back."

"I know, I know," Honoria replied.—She rose to her feet and moved across to the fireplace, her straight eyebrows drawn together, her expression one of perplexity. "I must seem a brute for trying to drag you back. When Dr. Knott, and the other two men, asked me to come and reason with you, I was on the edge of refusing. I hardly had the heart to worry you. And yet," she added wistfully, "after all, in a way, it is just simply your own dear fault. For if you will be a sort of little kingdom of heaven to us, you see, it's inevitable that, when you threaten to slip away from us, we should play the part of the violent and do our best to take our kingdom by force and keep it in spite of itself."

"You overrate the heavenliness of the poor little kingdom," Katherine said. "Its soil has become barren, its proud cities are laid waste. It's an unprofitable place, believe me, dearest child. Let it be. Seek your fortune in some kingdom from which the glory has not departed and whose motto is not *Ichabod*."

"Unfortunately, I can't do that," the younger woman answered. "I've explained why already. Where my heart is, there, you see, my kingdom is also."

"Ah! my dear, my dear," Katherine said, touched, yet somewhat weary.

"And after all it is not wholly for our own sakes we make this fight to keep you."—Miss St. Quentin's voice sank. She spoke slowly and as though with reluctance. "We do it for the sake of the person you love best in the world. I don't say we love him very much, but that is beside the mark. We owe him a certain duty—I, because I am living in his house, the others because they are his friends. When he comes home— as come he surely will—they all say that, even while they blame him—would it not be an almost too cruel punishment if he found Brockhurst empty of your presence? You would not wish that. It's not a question of me, of course. I don't count. But you gone, no one—not even the old servants, I believe— would stay. Blame would be turned into something awkwardly near to hatred."

Lady Calmady's serenity did not desert her, but a touch of her old loftiness of manner was apparent. And Miss St. Quentin was very glad. Anything, even anger, would be welcome if it dissipated that unnatural, paralysing calm.

"You forget Julius, I think," she said. "He will be faithful

to the very end, faithful unto death.   And so will another friend
of happier days, poor, blind, old Camp."

A sudden inspiration came to Honoria St. Quentin.

"You must only count on Julius, I am afraid, Cousin
Katherine—not on Camp."

And to her immense relief she perceived Lady Calmady's
serenity give a little.   It was as though she came nearer.   Her
sweet face was troubled, her eyes full of questioning.

"Camp grew a little too tired of waiting about three weeks
ago.   You did not ask for him"—

"Didn't I?" Katherine said, smitten by self-reproach.

"Never once—and so we did not tell you, fearing to distress
you."

Miss St. Quentin came over and sat down on the end of the
sofa again.   She rested her hands on her knees.   Her feet were
rather far apart.   She fixed her eyes upon the small prophets
and patriarchs anticking upon the hearth.

"But it wasn't really so very bad," she said reflectively.
"And we did all we could to smooth his passage, poor, dear
beast, to the place where all good dogs go.   We had the vet
out from Westchurch two or three times, but there was nothing
much he could do.   And I thought him a bit rough.   Nervousness,
I fancy.   You see the dog did not like being handled by a
stranger, and made it rather hot for him once or twice.   I could
not let him be worried, poor old man, and so Julius March,
and Winter, and I, took turn and turn about with him."

"Where did he die?"

"In the Gun-Room, on the tiger-skin."—Honoria did not
look round.   Her voice grew perceptibly husky.   "Chifney and
I sat up with him that last night."

"You and Chifney?" Lady Calmady exclaimed, almost in
protest.

"Yes.   Of course the men would have been as kind as kind
could be.   Only I had a feeling you would be glad to know
I was there, later, when we told you.   You see Chifney's as
good as any vet, and I had to have somebody.   The dog was
rather queer.   I did not quite know how to manage him alone."

Lady Calmady put out her hand.   Honoria took it silently,
and fell to stroking it once more.   It was a declaration of peace,
she felt, on the part of the obstinate well-beloved—possibly a
declaration of something over and above peace.

"Winter saw to our creature comforts," the young lady
continued.   "Oh, we weren't starved, I promise you!   And
Chifney was excellent company."

She hesitated a moment.

"He told me endless yarns about horses—about Doncaster, and Newmarket, and Goodwood. I was greatly flattered at being regarded as sufficiently of the equestrian order to hear all that.—And he told me stories about Richard, when he was quite a little boy—and about his father also."

Honoria had a conviction the tears were running down Lady Calmady's cheeks, but she would not look round. She only stroked the hand she held softly, and talked on.

"They were fine," she said, "some of those stories. I am glad to have heard them. They went home to me. When all is said and done, there is nothing like breeding and pluck, and the courtesy which goes along with them. But after midnight Camp grew very restless. He had his blanket in the big arm-chair—you know the one I mean—as usual. But he wouldn't stay there. We had to lift him down. You see his hindquarters were paralysed, and he couldn't help himself much. It was pathetic. I can't forget the asking look in his half-blind eyes. But we couldn't make out what he wanted. At last he dragged himself as far as the door, and we set it open and watched him, poor, dear beast. He got across the lobby to the bottom of the little staircase"—

The speaker's breath caught.

"Then we made out what it was. He wanted to get up here, to come to you.—Well, I could understand that! I should want just that myself, shall want it, when it comes to the last. He whimpered when Chifney carried him back into the Gun-Room."

Honoria turned her head and looked Lady Calmady in the face. Her own was more than commonly white and very gentle in expression.

"He died in the grey of the morning, with his great head on my lap. I fancy it eased him to have something human, and—rather pitiful—close against him. Julius had just come in to see how we were getting on. I won't declare he did not say a prayer—I think he did. But I wasn't quite as steady as I might have been just then."

She turned her head, looking back at the figures upon the hearth. She was satisfied. Lady Calmady's long-sustained calm had given way, and she wept.

"We buried him, in his blanket, under the big Portugal-laurel, where the nightingale sings, at the corner of the troco-ground, close to Camp the First and Old Camp. The upper servants came, and Chaplin and Hariburt from the house-stables, and Chifney and the head-lad—and some of the gardeners.

Poor, old Wenham drove up in his donkey-chair from the west lodge. Julius was there, of course. We did all things decently and in order."

Honoria's voice ceased. She sat stroking the dear hand she held and smiling to herself, notwithstanding a chokiness in her throat, for she had a comfortable belief the situation was saved.

Then Clara entered, prepared to encounter remonstrance, bearing a tray.

"It's all right, Clara," Miss St. Quentin said. "Lady Calmady is quite ready for something to eat. I've been telling her about Camp."

And Katherine, sitting upright, with great docility and a certain gentle shame, accepted food and drink.

"Since you wish it, dearest," she said, "and since Julius must not be left alone in a quite empty house."

"Our kingdom of heaven stays with us then?" Honoria exclaimed joyously.

"Such as it is—poor thing—it will do its best to stay. I thought I had cried my eyes dry forever, long ago. But it seems not. You and Camp have broken up the drought."

"I have not hurt you?" Honoria said, in sudden penitence.

"No, no—you have given me relief. I was ceasing to be human. The blessèd Thomas was right—I grew very selfish."

"But you're not displeased with me?" Honoria insisted. Lady Calmady's playfulness had returned, but with a new complexion.

"Ah! it is a little soon to ask that!" she said. "Still I will go north with you a fortnight hence—go to Ormiston. And by then, perhaps, you may be forgiven. Open the casement, dearest, and let in the wind. The air of this room is curiously dead. Give my love to Julius and Ludovic. Tell them I will come into the Chapel-Room after dinner to-night.—What—my child, are you so very glad?—Kiss me.—God keep you.—Now I will rest."

CHAPTER VI

IN WHICH M. PAUL DESTOURNELLE HAS THE BAD TASTE TO THREATEN TO UPSET THE APPLE-CART

HELEN DE VALLORBES rose from her knees and slipped out from under the greasy and frayed half-curtain of the confessional box. The atmosphere of that penitential spot had been such as to make her feel faint and dizzy. She needed to recover herself. And so she stood, for a minute or more, in the clear, cool brightness of the nave of the great basilica, her highly-civilised figure covered by a chequer-work of morning sunshine streaming down through the round-headed windows of the lofty clere-storey. As the sense of physical discomfort left her she instinctively arranged her veil, and adjusted her bracelets over the wrists of her long gloves. Yet, notwithstanding this trivial and mundane occupation, her countenance retained an expression of devout circumspection, of the relief of one who has accomplished a serious and somewhat distasteful duty. Her sensations were increasingly agreeable. She had rid herself of an oppressive burden. She was at peace with herself and with—almost—all man and womankind.

Yet, it must be admitted, the measure had been mainly pre-cautionary. Helen had gone to confession, on the present occasion, in much the same spirit as an experienced traveller visits his dentist before starting on a protracted journey. She regarded it as a disagreeable, but politic, insurance against possible accident. Her distaste had been increased by the fact that there really were some rather risky matters to be confessed. She had even feared a course of penance might have been enforced before the granting of absolution—this certainly would have been the case had she been dealing with that firm disciplinarian, and very astute man of the world, the Jesuit father who acted as her spiritual adviser in Paris. But here in Naples, happily, it was different. The fat, sleepy, easy-going, old canon—whose person exuded so strong an odour of snuff that, at the solemnest moment of the *confiteor*, she had been unable to suppress a convulsive sneeze —asked her but few inconvenient questions. Pretty fine-ladies will get into little difficulties of this nature. He had listened to very much the same story not infrequently before, and took the position amiably, almost humorously, for granted. It was very wicked, a deadly sin, but the flesh—specially such delicately bred, delicately fed, feminine flesh—is admittedly weak, and the wiles of Satan are many. Is it not an historic fact that our first mother did not escape?—Was Helen's repentance sincere, that was the point? And of that Helen could honestly assure him there was no smallest doubt. Indeed, at this moment, she abhorred, not only her sin, but her co-sinner, in the liveliest and most compre-hensive manner. Return to him? Sooner the dog return to its vomit! She recognised the iniquity, the shame, the detestable folly, of her late proceedings far too clearly. Temptation in that direction had ceased to be possible.

Then followed the mysterious and merciful words of absolu-

tion.   And. Helen rose from her knees and slipped out from
beneath the frayed and greasy curtain a free woman, the guilt of
her adultery wiped off by those awful words, as, with a wet cloth,
one would wipe writing off a slate leaving the surface of it clean
in every part.   Precisely how far she literally believed in the
efficacy of that most solemn rite she would not have found it
easy to declare.   Scepticism warred with expediency.   But that
appeared to her beside the mark.   It was really none of her
business.   Let her teachers look to all that.   To her it was
sufficient that she could regard it from the practical standpoint
of an insurance against possible accident—the accident of sin
proving actually sinful and actually punishable by a narrow-
minded deity; the accident of the veritable existence of heaven
and hell, and of Holy Church veritably having the keys of both
these in her keeping; the accident—more immediately probable
and consequently worth guarding against—that, during wakeful
hours, some night, the half-forgotten lessons of the convent school
would come back on her, and, as did sometimes happen, would
prove too much for her usually victorious audacity.

But, it should be added that another and more creditable
instinct did much to dictate Madame de Vallorbes' action at this
juncture.   As the days went by the attraction exercised over her
by Richard Calmady suffered increase rather than diminution.
And this attraction affected her morally, producing in her
modesties, reticencies of speech, even of thought, and prickings
of unflattering self-criticism unknown to her heretofore.   Her
ultimate purpose might not be virtuous.   But undeniably, such is
the complexity—not to say hypocrisy—of the human heart, the
prosecution of that purpose developed in her a surprising sensibility of conscience.   Many episodes in her career, hitherto
regarded as entertaining, she ceased to view with toleration,
let alone complacency.   The remembrance of them made her
nervous.   What if Richard came to hear of them?   The effect
might be disastrous.   Not that he was any saint; but she
perceived that, with the fine inconsistency common to most well-
bred Englishmen, he demanded from the women of his family
quite other standards of conduct to those which he himself
obeyed.   Other women might do as they pleased.   Their lapses
from the stricter social code were no concern of his.   He might,
indeed, be not wholly averse to profiting by such lapses.   But in
respect of the women of his own rank and blood the case was
quite otherwise.   He was alarmingly capable of disgust.   And, not
a little to her own surprise, fear of provoking, however slightly,
that disgust had become a reigning power with her.   Never had

she felt as she now felt. Her own sensations at once captivated and astonished her. This had ceased to be an adventure dictated by merry devilry, undertaken out of lightness of heart, inspired by a mischievous desire to see dust whirl and straws fly; or undertaken even out of necessity to support self-satisfaction by ranging herself with cynical audacity on the side of the eternal laughter. This was serious. It was desperate—the crisis, as she told herself, of her life and fate. The result was singular. Never had she been more vividly, more electrically, alive. Never had she been more diffident and self-distrustful.

And this complexity of sensation served to press home on her the high desirability of insurance against accident, of washing clean, as far as might be possible, the surface of the slate. So it followed that now, standing in the chequer-work of sunshine within the great basilica, self-congratulation awoke in her. The lately concluded ceremony, some of the details of which had really been most distasteful, might or might not be of vital efficacy, but, in any case, she had courageously done her part. Therefore, if Holy Church spoke truly, her first innocence was restored. Helen hugged the idea with almost childish satisfaction. Now she could go back to the Villa Vallorbes in peace, and take what measures—

She left the sentence unfinished. Even in thought it is often an error to define. Let the future and her intentions regarding it remain in the vague! She signed to Zélie Forestier—seated on the steps of a side-chapel, yellow-paper-covered novel in hand—to follow her. And, after making a genuflexion before the altar of Our Lady of the Immaculate Conception, gathered up her turquoise-coloured skirts—the yellow-tufa quarries were not superabundantly clean—and pursued her way towards the great main door. The benevolent priest, charmed by her grace of movement, watched her from his place in the confessional, although another penitent now kneeled within the greasy curtain.—Verily the delinquencies of so delectable a piece of womanhood were easily comprehensible! Neither God nor man, in such a case, would be extreme to mark what was done amiss. Moreover, had she not promised generous gifts alike to church and poor? The sin which in an ugly woman is clearly mortal, in a pretty one becomes little more than venial. Making which reflection a kindly, fat chuckle shook his big paunch, and, crossing himself, he turned his attention to the voice murmuring from behind the wooden lattice at his side.

Yet it would appear that abstract justice judged less leniently of the position. For, passing out on to the portico—about the base of whose enormous columns half-naked beggars clustered, exposing sores and mutilations, shrilly clamouring for alms—the dazzling glare of the empty, sun-scorched piazza behind him, Helen came face to face with no less a personage than M. Paul Destournelle.

It was as though someone had struck her. The scene reeled before her eyes. Then her temper rose as in resentment of insult. To avoid all chance of such a meeting she had selected this church in an unfashionable quarter of the town. Here, at least, she had reckoned herself safe from molestation. And, that precisely in the hour of peace, the hour of politic insurance against accident, this accident of all others should befall her, was maddening! But anger did not lessen her perspicacity. How to inflict the maximum of discomfort upon M. Destournelle with the minimum of risk to herself was the question. An interview was inevitable. She wanted, very certainly, to get her claws into him; but, for safety's sake, that should be done not in attack, but in defence. Therefore he should speak first, and in his words, whatever those words might be, she promised herself to discover legitimate cause of offence. So, leisurely, and with studied ignorance of his presence, she flung largesse of *centissimi* to right and left, and, while the chorus of blessing and entreaty was yet loud, walked calmly past M. Destournelle down the wide, shallow steps, from the solid shadow of the portico to the burning sun-glare of the piazza.

The young man's countenance went livid.

" Do you dare to pretend not to recognise me?" he literally gasped.

" On the contrary I recognise you perfectly."

" I have written to you repeatedly."

" You have—written to me with a ridiculous and odious persistence."

Madame de Vallorbes picked her steps. The pavement was uneven, the heat great. Destournelle's hands twitched with agitation, yet he contrived not only to replace his Panama hat, but opened his white umbrella as a precaution against sunstroke. And this diverted, even while exasperating, Helen. Measures to ensure personal safety were so characteristic of Destournelle!

" And with what fault, I ask you, can you reproach me, save that of a too absorbing, a too generous, adoration?"

" That fault in itself is very sufficient."

" Do you not reckon, then, in any degree, with the crime you are in process of committing? Have you no sense of gratitude, of obligation? Have you no regret for your own loss in leaving me?"

Helen drew aside to let a herd of goats pass. They jostled one another impudently, carrying their inquisitive heads and short tails erect, at right angles to the horizontal line of their narrow backs. They bleated, as in impish mischief. Their little beards wagged. Their little hoofs pattered on the stone, and the musky odour of them hung in the burning air. Madame de Vallorbes put her handkerchief up to her face, and over the edge of it she contemplated Paul Destournelle. Every detail of his appearance was not only familiar, but associated in her mind with some incident of his and her common past. Now the said details asserted themselves, so it seemed to her, with an impertinence of premeditated provocation.—The high, domed skull, the smooth, prematurely-thin hair parted in the middle and waved over the ears. The slightly raised eyebrows, and fatigued, red-lidded, and vain, though handsome eyes. The straight, thin nose, and winged, open nostrils, so perpetually a-quiver. The soft, sparse, forked beard which closely followed the line of the lower jaw and pointed chin. The moustache, lightly shading the upper lip, while wholly exposing the fretful and rather sensuous mouth. The long, effeminate, and restless hands. The tall, slight figure. The clothes, of a material and pattern fondly supposed by their wearer to present the last word of English fashion in relation to foreign travel, the colour of them accurately matched to the pale, brown hair and beard.—So much for the detail of the young man's appearance. As a whole, that appearance was elegant as only French youth ventures to be elegant. Refinement enveloped Paul Destournelle—refinement, over-sensitised and under-vitalised, as that of a rare exotic forced into precocious blossoming by application of some artificial horticultural process. And all this—elaborately effective and seductive as long as one should happen to think so, elaborately nauseous when one had ceased so to think—had long been familiar to Helen to the point of satiety. She turned wicked, satiety transmuting itself into active vindictiveness. How gladly would she have torn this emasculated creature limb from limb, and flung the lot of it among the refuse of the Neapolitan gutter!

But, from beneath the shade of his umbrella, the young man recommenced his plaint.

"It is inconceivable that, knowing my cruel capacity for suffering, you should be indifferent to my present situation," he asserted, half violently, half fretfully. "The whole range of history would fail to offer a case of parallel callousness. You, whose personality has penetrated the recesses of my being ! You, who are acquainted with the infinite intricacy of my mental and emotional organisation ! A touch will endanger the harmony of that exquisite mechanism. The interpenetration of the component parts of my being is too entire. I exist, I receive sensations, I suffer, I rejoice, as a whole. And this lays me open to universal, to incalculable, pain. Now my nerves are shattered — intellectual, moral, physical anguish permeates in every part. I rally my self-reverence, my nobility of soul. I make efforts. By day I visit spots of natural beauty and objects of art. But these refuse to gratify me. My thought is too turgid to receive the impress of them. Concentration is impossible to me. Feverish agitation perverts my imagination. My ideas are fugitive. I endure a chronic delirium. This by day," he extended one hand with a despairing gesture, "but by night"—

"Oh, I implore you," Helen interrupted, "spare me the description of your nights ! The subject is a hardly modest one. And then, at various times, I have already heard so very much about them, those nights ! "

Calmly she resumed her walk. The amazing vanity of the young man's speech appeased her in a measure, since it fed her contempt. Let him sink himself beyond all hope of recovery, that was best. Let him go down, down, in exposition of fatuous self-conceit. When he was low enough, then she would kick him ! Meanwhile her eyes, ever greedy of incident and colour, registered the scene immediately submitted to them. In the centre of the piazza, women—saffron and poppy-coloured handkerchiefs tied round their dark heads—washed, with a fine impartiality, soiled linen and vegetables in an iron trough, grated for a third of its length, before a fountain of debased and flamboyant design. Their voices were alternately shrill and guttural. It was perhaps as well not to understand too clearly all which they said. On the left came a break in the high, painted house-fronts, off which in places the plaster scaled, and from the windows of which protruded miscellaneous samples of wearing apparel and bedding soliciting much-needed purification by means of air and light. In the said break was a low wall where coarse plants rooted, and atop of which lay some half-dozen ragged youths, outstretched upon their stomachs, playing cards. The least decrepit of the beggars, armed with Helen's largesse of copper coin, had joined them from beneath the portico. Gambling, seasoned by shouts, imprecations, blows,

grew fast and furious.   In the steep roadway on the right a dray,
loaded with barrels, creaked and jolted upward.   The wheels
of it were solid discs of wood.   The great, mild-eyed, cream-
coloured oxen strained, with slowly swinging heads, under the
heavy yoke.   Scarlet, woollen bands and tassels adorned their
broad foreheads and wide-sweeping, black-tipped horns, and
here and there a scarlet drop their flanks, where the goad had
pricked them too shrewdly.   And upon it all the unrelenting
southern sun looked down, and Helen de Vallorbes' unrelenting
eyes looked forth.   One of those quick realisations of the inexhaustible excitement of living came to her.   She looked at
the elegant young man walking beside her, appraised, measured
him.   She thought of Richard Calmady, self-imprisoned in the
luxurious villa, and of the possibilities of her, so far platonic,
relation to him.   She glanced down at her own rustling skirts
and daintily-shod feet travelling over the hot stones ; then at the
noisy gamblers, then at the women washing, with that consummate disregard of sanitation, food and raiment together in
the rusty iron trough by the fountain.   The violent contrasts,
the violent lights and shadows, the violent diversities of purpose
and emotion, of rank, of health, of fortune and misfortune, went
to her head.   Whatever the risks or dangers, that excitement
remained inexhaustible.   Nay, those very dangers and risks
ministered to its perpetual upflowing.   It struck her she had
been over - scrupulous, weakly conscientious, in making confession and seeking absolution.   Such timid moralities do
not really shape destiny, control or determine human fate.
The shouting, fighting youths there, with their filthy pack
of cards and few *centissimi*, sprawling in the unstinted sunshine,
were nearer the essential truth.   They were the profound,
because the practical philosophers.   Therefore let us gamble,
gamble, gamble, be the stake small or great, as long as the
merest flicker of life, or fraction of uttermost farthing, is left !
And so, when Destournelle took up his lament again, she
listened to him, for the moment, with remarkable lightness of
heart.

   " I appeal to you in the name of my as yet unwritten poems,
my masterpieces, for which France, for which the whole brotherhood of letters, so anxiously waits, to put a term to this appalling
chastisement ! "

   " Delicious ! " said Helen, under her breath.

   " Your classicism is the natural complement of my
mediævalism.   The elasticity, the concreteness, of your temperament fertilised the too-brooding introspectiveness of my

own. It lightened the reverence which I experience in the contemplation of my own nature. It induced in me the hint of frivolity which is necessary to procure action. Our union was as that of high-noon and impenetrable night. I anticipated extraordinary consequences."

"Marriage of a butterfly and a bat? Yes, the progeny should be surprising little animals certainly," commented Madame de Vallorbes.

"In deserting me you have rendered me impotent. That is a crime. It is an atrocity. You assassinate my genius."

"Then, indeed, I have reason to congratulate myself on my ingenuity," she returned, "since I succeed in the assassination of the non-existent!"

"You, who have praised it a thousand times—you deny the existence of my genius?" almost shrieked M. Destournelle. He was very much in earnest, and in a very sorry case. His limbs twitched. He appeared on the verge of an hysteric seizure. To plague him thus was a charmingly pretty sport, but one safest carried on with closed doors—not in so public a spot.

"I do not deny the existence of anything, save your right to make a scene and render me ridiculous as you repeatedly did at Pisa."

"Then you must return to me."

"Oh! la, la!" cried Helen.

"That you should leave me and live in your cousin's house constitutes an intolerable insult."

"And where, pray, would you have me live?" she retorted, her temper rising, to the detriment of diplomacy. "In the street?"

"It appears to me the two localities are synonymous—morally."

Madame de Vallorbes drew up. Rage almost choked her. M. Destournelle's words stung the more fiercely because the in-sinuation they contained was not justified by fact. They brought home to her her non-success in a certain direction. They called up visions of that unknown rival, to whom—ah, how she hated the woman!—Richard Calmady's affections were, as she feared, still wholly given. That her own relation to him was innocent, filled her with humiliation. First she turned to Zélie Forestier, who had followed at a discreet distance across the piazza.

"Go on," she said, "down the street. Find a cab, a clean one. Wait in it for me at the bottom of the hill."

Then she turned upon M. Destournelle.

"Your mind is so corrupt that you cannot conceive of an honest friendship, even between near relations. You fill me with repulsion—I measured the depth of your degeneracy at Pisa. That is why I left you. I wanted to breathe an uninfected atmosphere. My cousin is a person of remarkable intellectual powers, of chivalrous ideals, and of superior character. He has had great troubles. He is far from well. I am watching over and nursing him."

The last statement trenched boldly on fiction. As she made it Madame de Vallorbes moved forward, intending to follow the retreating Zélie down the steep, narrow street. For a minute M. Destournelle paused to recollect his ideas. Then he went quickly after her.

"Stay, I implore you," he said. "Yes, I own at Pisa I lost myself. The agitation of composition was too much for me. My mind seethed with ideas. I became irritable. I comprehend I was in fault. But it is so easy to recommence, and to range oneself. I accept your assurances regarding your cousin. It is all so simple. You shall not return to me. You shall continue your admirable work. But I will return to you. I will join you at the villa. My society cannot fail to be of pleasure to your cousin, if he is such a person as you describe. In a *milieu* removed from care and trivialities I will continue my poem. I may even dedicate it to your cousin. I may make his name immortal. If he is a person of taste and ideals, he cannot fail to appreciate so magnificent a compliment. You will place this before him. You will explain to him how necessary to me is your presence. He will be glad to co-operate in procuring it for me. He will understand that in making these propositions I offer him a unique opportunity, I behave towards him with signal generosity. And if, at first, the intrusion of a stranger into his household should appear inconvenient, let him but pause a little. He will find his reward in the development of my genius and in the spectacle of our mutual felicity."

Destournelle spoke with great rapidity. The street which they had now entered, from the far end of the piazza, was narrow. It was encumbered by a string of laden mules, by a stream of foot passengers. Interruption of his monologue, short of raising her voice to screaming pitch, was impossible to Madame de Vallorbes. But when he ceased she addressed him, and her lips were drawn away from her pretty teeth viciously.

"Oh! you unspeakable idiot!" she said. "Have you no remnant of shame?"

"Do you mean to imply that Sir Richard Calmady would

have the insolence, is so much the victim of insular prejudice as, to object to our intimacy?"

Madame de Vallorbes clapped her hands together in a sort of frenzy.

"Idiot, idiot," she repeated.   "I wish I could kill you."

Suddenly M. Paul Destournelle had all his wits about him.

"Ah!" he said, with a short laugh, curiously resembling in its malice the bleating of the little goats, "I perceive that which constitutes the obstacle to our reunion.   It shall be removed."

He lifted his Panama hat with studied elegance, and turning down a break-neck, side alley, called, over his shoulder:—

"*À bientôt très chère madame.*"

CHAPTER VII

SPLENDIDE MENDAX

UNPUNCTUALITY could not be cited as among Madame de Vallorbes' offences.   Yet, on the morning in question, she was certainly very late for the twelve o'clock breakfast. Richard Calmady—awaiting her coming beneath the glistering dome of the airy pavilion, set in the angle of the terminal wall of the high-lying garden—had time to become conscious of slight irritation.   It was not merely that he was constitutionally impatient of delay, but that his nerves were tiresomely on edge just now.   Trifles had power to endanger his somewhat stoic equanimity.   But, when at length Helen emerged from the house, irritation was forgotten.   Moving through the vivid lights and shadows of the ilex and cypress grove, her appearance had a charm of unwonted simplicity.   At first sight her graceful person had the effect of being clothed in a religious habit.   Richard's youthful delight in seeing a woman walk beautifully remained to him.   It received a satisfaction now. Helen advanced without haste, a certain grandeur in her demeanour, a certain gloom, even as one who takes serious counsel of himself, indifferent to external things, at once actor in, and spectator of, some drama playing itself out in the theatre of his own soul.   And this effect of dignity, of self-recollection, was curiously heightened by her dress — of a very soft and fine woollen material, of spotless white, the lines of it at once flowing and statuesque.   While as head-gear, in place of some startling construction of contemporary, Parisian millinery, she wore, after the modest Italian fashion, a black lace mantilla over her bright hair.

Arrived, she greeted Richard curtly; and, without apology for delay, accepted the contents of the first dish offered to her by the waiting men-servants, ate as though determinedly and putting a force upon herself, and—that which was unusual with her before sundown—drank wine. And, watching her, involuntarily Richard's thought travelled back to a certain luncheon party at Brockhurst, graced by the presence of genial, puzzle-headed Lord Fallowfeild and members of his numerous family, when Helen had swept in, even as now, had been self-absorbed, even as now. Of the drive to Newlands, all in the sad November afternoon, following on that luncheon, he also thought, of communications made by Helen during that drive, and of the long course of event and action directly or indirectly consequent on those communications. He thought of the fog, too, enveloping and almost choking him, when in the early morning driven by furies, still virgin in body as in heart, he had ridden out into a blank and sightless world hoping the chill of it would allay the fever in his blood; and of the fog again, in the afternoon, from out which the branches of the great trees, like famine-stricken arms in tattered draperies, seemed to pluck evilly at the carriage, as he walked the smoking horses up and down the Newlands drive, waiting for Helen to rejoin him. And now, somehow, that fog seemed to come up between him and the well-covered breakfast-table, between him and the radiant expanse of the vivacious, capricious, half-classic, half-modern, mercantile city outstretched there, teeming, breeding, fermenting, in the fecundating heat of the noonday sun. The chill of the fog struck cold into his vitals, giving him the strangest physical sensation. Richard straightened himself in his chair, passed his hands across his eyes impatiently. Brockhurst, and all the old life of it, was a subject of which he forbade himself remembrance. He had divorced himself from all that, cut himself adrift from it long ago. By an act of will, he tried to put it out of his mind now. But the fog remained—an actual clouding of his physical vision, blurring all he looked upon. It was horribly uncomfortable. He wished he was alone. Then he might have slipped down from his chair and, according to his poor capacity of locomotion, sought relief in movement.

Meanwhile, silently, mechanically, Helen de Vallorbes continued her breakfast. And as she so continued, in addition to his singular physical sensations of blurred vision and clinging chill, he became aware of a growing embarrassment and constraint

28

between himself and his companion.   So far, his and her intercourse had been easy and spontaneous, because superficial. Since that first interview on the terrace a tacit agreement had existed to avoid the personal note.   Now, for cause unknown, that intercourse threatened entering upon a new phase.   It was as though the concentration, the tension, which he observed in her, and of which he was sensible in himself, must of necessity, eventuate in some unbosoming, some act—almost involuntary— of self-revelation.   This unaccustomed silence and restraint seemed to Richard charged with consequences, which, in his present condition of defective volition, he was powerless to prevent.   And this displeased him, mastery of surrounding influences being very dear to him.

At last, coffee having been served, the men-servants withdrew to the house; but the constraint was not thereby lessened.   Helen sat upright, her chin resting upon the back of her left hand, her eyes, under their drooping lids, looking out with a veiled fierceness upon the fair and glittering prospect.   Richard saw her face in profile.   The black mantilla draped her shoulders and bust with a certain austerity of effect.   It was evident that—by something—she had been stirred to the extinction of her habitual vivacity and desire to shine.   And Richard, for all his coolness of head and rather cynical maturity of outlook, had a restless suspicion of going forth—even as on that foggy morning at Brockhurst—into a blank and sightless world, full of hazardous possibility, where the safe way was difficult of discovery and where masked dangers might lurk.   Solicitous to dissipate his discomfort he spoke a little at random.

"You must forgive me for being such an abominably bad host," he said courteously.   "I am not quite the thing this morning, somehow.   I had a little go of fever last night.   My brain is like so much pulp."

Helen dropped her hand upon the table as though putting a term to an importunate train of thought.

"I have always understood the villa to be remarkably free from malaria," she remarked abstractedly.

"So it is.   I quite believe that.   The servants certainly keep well enough.   But so, unfortunately, is not the port."

Helen turned her head.   A vertical line was observable between her arched eyebrows.

"The port?" she repeated.

Richard swallowed his black coffee.   Perhaps it might steady him and clear his head.   The numbness of his faculties and senses alike exasperated him, filling him with a persuasion he would say precisely those things wisdom would counsel to leave unsaid.

"Yes—you know I generally go down and sleep on board the yacht."

There was a momentary pause. Madame de Vallorbes' lips parted in a soundless exclamation. Then she pushed back the modest folds of the mantilla, leaving her neck free. The action of her hands was very graceful as she did this, and she looked fixedly at Richard Calmady.

"I did not know that," she said slowly. Then added, as though reasoning out her own thought :—"And Naples harbour is admittedly one of the most pestilential holes on the face of the earth. Are you not tempting providence in the matter of disease, Richard? Are you not rather wantonly indiscreet?"

"On the contrary," he answered, and something of mockery touched his expression, "I see it quite otherwise. I have been congratulating myself on the praiseworthy abundance of my discretion."

And the words were no sooner out of his mouth than Richard cursed himself for a bungler, and a slightly vulgar one at that. But upon his hearer those same words worked a remarkable change. Her gloom, her abstraction, departed, leaving only a pretty pensiveness. She smiled with chastened sweetness upon Richard Calmady—a smile nicely attuned to the semi-religious simplicity of her dress.

"Ah! perhaps we are both a trifle out of sorts this morning!" she said. "I, too, have had my little turn of sickness—sickness of heart. And that seems unfair, since I rose in the best disposition of spirit. Quite early I went to confession."

"Confession?" Richard repeated. "I did not know your reconciliation with the Church carried you to such practical lengths."

"Evidently we are each fated to make small discoveries regarding the habits of the other, to-day," she rejoined. "Possibly confession is to me just what those nights spent on board the yacht, lying in that malodorous harbour, are to you!"

Helen's smile broadened to a dainty naughtiness, infinitely provoking. But pensiveness speedily supervened. She folded her hands upon the edge of the table and looked down at them meditatively.

"I relieved my conscience. Not that there was much to relieve it of, thank Heaven! We have lived austerely enough most of us, this winter in France. Only it becomes a matter of moral, personal cleanliness, after a time, all that—exaggerated, but very comfortable. Just as one takes one's bath twice daily, not that it is necessary but that it is a luxury of physical purity and self-respect, so one comes to go to confession. That is a luxury of moral purification. It is as a bath to the soul, ministering to the perfection of its cleanliness and health."

She looked up at Richard smiling, that same dainty naughtiness very present.

"You observe I am eminently candid. I tell you exactly how my religion affects me. I can only reach high-thinking through acts which are external and concrete. In short, I am a born sacramentalist."

And Richard listened, interested and entertained. Yet, since that strange blurring of fog still confused his vision and his judgment, vaguely suspicious that he missed the main intent of her speech. Suspicious as one who, listening to the clever patter of a conjurer, detects in it the effort to distract attention from some difficult feat of legerdemain, until that feat has past from attempt merely into accomplished fact.

"And, indirectly, that is where my heart-sickness comes in," she continued, with a return to something of her former abstraction and gloom. "I was coming away, coming back here—and I was very happy. It is not often one can say that. And then—*pouf*—like that," she brought her hands smartly together, "the charming bubble burst! For, upon the very church steps, I met a man whom I have every cause to hate."

As she spoke, the fog seemed to draw away, burnt up by the great, flaming sun-god there. Richard's brain grew clear—clearer, indeed, than in perfect health—and his still face grew more still than was, even to it, quite natural.

"Well?" he asked, almost harshly.

And Helen, whose faith in her own diplomacy had momentarily suffered eclipse, rejoiced. For the tone of his voice betrayed, not disgust, but anxiety. It stirred her as a foretaste of victory. And victory had become a maddening necessity to her. Destournelle had forced her hand. His natural infirmity of purpose relieved her of the fear he could work her any great mischief. Yet his ingenuity, inspired by wounded vanity, might prove beyond her calculations. It is not always safe to forecast the future by experience of the past in relation to such a being as Destournelle! Therefore it became of supreme importance, before that gentleman had time further to obtrude himself, to bind Richard Calmady by some speech, some act, from which there was no going back. And more than just that. The sight of her ex-lover, though she now loathed him—

possibly just because she so loathed him—provoked passion in her. It was as though only in a new intrigue could she rid herself of the remembrance of the old intrigue which was now so detestable to her. She craved to do him that deepest, most ultimate, despite. And passion cried out in her. The sight of him, though she loathed him, had made her utterly weary of chastity. All of which emotions—but held as hounds in a leash, ready to be slipped when the psychological moment arrived, and by no means to be slipped until the arrival of it—dictated the tenor of her next speech.

"Well," she answered, with an air of half-angry sincerity altogether convincing, "I really don't know that I am particularly proud of the episode. I know I was careless, that I laid myself open to the invidious comment, which is usually the reward of all disinterested action. One learns to accept it as a matter of course. And you see Paul Destournelle"—

"Oh, Destournelle!" Richard exclaimed.

"You have read him?"

"Everyone has read him."

"And what do you think of him?"

"That his technique is as amazingly clever as his thought is amazingly rotten."

"I know—I know," she said eagerly. "And that is just what induced me to do all I could for him. If one could cut the canker away, give him backbone and decency, while retaining that wonderful technique, one would have a second and a greater Théophile Gautier."

Richard was looking full at her. His face had more colour, more animation, than usual.

"If—yes—if," he returned. "But that same *if* bulks mighty big to my mind."

"I know," she repeated. "Yet it seemed to me worth the attempt. And then, you understand,—who better?—that if one's own affairs are not conspicuously happy, one has all the more longing the affairs of others should be crowned with success. And this winter specially, among the sordid miseries, disgraces, deprivations, of the siege, one was liable to take refuge in an over-exalted altruism. It was difficult in so mad a world not to indulge in personal eccentricity—to the neglect of due worship of the great goddess Conventionality. With death in visible form at every street corner, one's sense of humour, let alone one's higher faculties, rebelled against the futility of such worship. So many detestable sights and sounds were perpetually presented to one—not to mention broth of abominable things daily for dinner

—that one turned, with thanksgiving, to beautiful form in art, to perfectly felicitous words and phrases. The meaning of them mattered but little just then. They freed one from the tyranny of more or less disgusting fact. They satisfied eye and ear. One asked nothing more just then—luckily, you will say, since the animal Destournelle has very surely nothing more to give."

In speaking, Helen pushed her chair back, turning it sideways to the table. Her speech was alive with varied and telling inflections. Her smallest gesture had in it something descriptive and eloquent.

"And so I fell to encouraging the animal," she continued, almost plaintively, yet with a note of veiled laughter in her voice. "Reversing the order of Circe—Naples inclines one to classic illustration, sometimes a little hackneyed—by the way, speaking of Naples, look at the glory of it all just now, Richard!—I tried to turn, not men to swine, but swine to men. And I failed, of course. The gods know best. They never attempt metamorphosis on the ascending scale ! I let Destournelle come to see me frequently. The world advised itself to talk. But, being rather bitterly secure of myself, I disregarded that. If one is aware that one's heart was finally and long ago disposed of, one ceases to think seriously of that side of things. You must know all that well enough—witness the sea-born furnishings of my bedroom upstairs ! "

For half a minute she paused. Richard made no comment.

"Hard words break no bones," she added lightly. "And so, to show how much I despised all such censorious cackle, I allowed Destournelle to travel south with me when I left Paris."

"You pushed neglect of the worship of conventionality rather far," Richard said.

Helen rose to her feet. Excitement gained on her, as always during one of her delightful improvisations, her talented *vivâ voce* improvements on dry-as-dust fact. She laughed softly, biting her lip. More than one hound had been slipped by now. They made good running. She stood by Richard Calmady, looking down at him, covering him, so to speak, with her eyes. The black mantilla no longer veiled her bright head. It had fallen to the ground, and lay a dark blot upon the mellow fairness of the tesselated pavement. White-robed, statuesque—yet not with the severe grace of marble, but with that softer, more humanly seductive grace of some figure of cunningly tinted ivory—she appeared, just then, to gather up in herself all the poetry, the intense and vivid light, the victorious vitality, of the clear, burning, southern noon.

"Ah, well, conventionality proved perfectly competent to avenge herself!" she exclaimed. "The animal Destournelle took the average, the banal view, as might have been anticipated. He had the insane presumption to suppose it was himself, not his art, in which I was interested. I explained his error, and departed. I recovered my equanimity. That took time. I felt soiled, degraded. And then to-day I meet him again, unashamed, actually claiming recognition. I repeated my explanation with uncompromising lucidity "—

Richard moved restlessly in his chair, looking up almost sharply at her.

"Waste of breath," he said. "No explanation is lucid if the hearer is unwilling to accept it."

And then the two cousins, as though they had reached unexpectedly some parting of the ways, calling for instant decision in respect of the future direction of their journey, gazed upon one another strangely—each half defiant of the other, each diligent to hide his own and read the other's thought, each sensible of a crisis, each at once hurried and arrested by suspicion of impending catastrophe, unless this way be chosen that declined—though it seemed, in good truth, not in their keeping, but in that of blind chance only that both selection and rejection actually resided. And, in this strait, neither habit of society, fine sword-play of diplomacy and tact, availed to help them. For suddenly they had outpaced all that, and brought up amongst ancient and secular springs of action and emotion before which civilisation is powerless and the ready tongue of fashion dumb.

But even while he so gazed, in fateful suspense and indecision, the fog came up again, chilling Richard Calmady's blood, oppressing his brain as with an uprising of foul miasma, blurring his vision, so that Helen's fair, downward-gazing face was distorted, rendered illusive and vague. And, along with this, distressing restlessness took him, compelling him to seek relief in change of posture and of place. He could not stop to reckon with how that which he proposed to do might strike an onlooker. His immediate sensations filled his whole horizon. Silently he slipped down from his chair, stood a moment, supporting himself with one hand on the edge of the table, and then moved forward to that side of the pavilion which gave upon the garden. Here the sunshine was hot upon the pavement, and upon the outer half of each pale, slender column. Richard leant his shoulder against one of these, grateful for the genial heat.

Since her first and somewhat inauspicious meeting with him in childhood, Helen had never, close at hand, seen Richard

Calmady walk thus far.   She stared, fascinated by that cruel
spectacle.   For the instant transformation of the apparently tall,
and conspicuously well-favoured, courtly gentleman, just now
sitting at table with her, into this shuffling, long-armed,
crippled dwarf was, at first utterly incredible, then portentous,
then, by virtue of its very monstrosity, absorbing and, to her,
adorable, whetting appetite as veritable famine might.   Chastity
became to her more than ever absurd, a culpable waste of her
own loveliness, of sensation, of emotion, a sin against those
vernal influences working in this generous nature surrounding
her and working in her own blood.   All the primitive instinct
of her womanhood called aloud in her that she must wed—
must wed.   And the strident voice of the great, painted city
coming up to her, urgent, incessant, carried the same message ;
as did the radiant sea, whose white lips kissed the indented
coast-line as though pale and hungry with love.   While the man
before her, by his very abnormality and a certain secretness
inevitable in that, heightened her passion.   He was to her of
all living men most desirable, so that she must win him and
hold him, must see and know.

In a few steps, light as those of the little, rose-crowned
dancer of long ago, she followed him across the shining floor.
There was a point of north in the wind, adding exhilaration to
the firm sunshine as ice to rare wine.   The scent of narcissus,
magnolia, and lemon blossom was everywhere.   The cypresses
yielded an aromatic, myrrh-like sweetness.   The uprising waters
of the fountain, set in the central alley, swerved southward,
falling in a jewelled rain.   Helen, in her spotless raiment, came
close and Richard Calmady turned to her.   But his eyes no
longer questioned hers.   They were as windows opening on
to empty space, seeing all, yet telling nothing.   His face had
become still again and inscrutable, lightened only by that
flickering, mocking smile.   It seemed as though the psychological moment were passed ; and social sense, ordinary fashions of
civilised intercourse, had not only come back but come to stay.

"I think we will omit Destournelle from our talk in
future," he said.   "As a subject of conversation I find he
disagrees with me, notwithstanding his felicity of style and his
admirable technique.   I will give orders which, I hope, may help
to protect you from annoyance in future.   In this delightful
land, by wise exercise of just a little bribery and corruption, it is
still possible to make the unwelcome alien prefer to seek health
and entertainment elsewhere.   Now, will you like to go back to
the house ?"

The approach to the pavilion from the lower level of the garden was by a carefully graded slope of Roman brick, set edgewise. At regular intervals of about eighteen inches this was crossed—on the principle of a gang-plank—by raised marble treads. Without waiting for his cousin's reply, Richard started slowly down the slope. At the best of times this descent for him demanded caution. Now his vision was again so queerly blurred that he miscalculated the distance between the two lowest treads, slipped and stumbled, lunging forward. Quick as a cat, Madame de Vallorbes was behind him, her right hand grasping his right elbow, her left hand under his left armpit.

"Ah! Dickie, Dickie, don't fall!" she cried, a sudden terror in her voice.

Her muscles hardened like steel. It needed all her strength to support him, for he was heavy, his body inert as that of one fainting. For a moment his head rested against her bosom; and her breath came short, sighing against his neck and cheek.

By sheer force of will Richard recovered his footing, disengaging himself from her support, shuffling aside from her.

"A thousand thanks, Helen," he said.

Then he looked full at her, and she—untender though she was—perceived that the perspective of space on which, as windows might, his eyes seemed to open, was not empty. It was peopled, crowded—even as those steep teeming byways of Naples —by undying, unforgetable misery, by humiliation, by revolt.

"Yes, it is rather unpardonable to be—as I am—isn't it?" he said. Adding hastily, yet with a certain courteous dignity:— "I am ashamed to trouble you, to ask you—of all people—to run messages for me—but would you go on to the house"—

"Dickie, why may not I help you?" she interrupted.

"Ah!" he said, "the answer to that lies away back in the beginning of things. Even unlucky devils, such as myself, are not without a certain respect for that which is fitting, for seemliness and etiquette. Send one of my men please. I shall be very grateful to you—thanks."

And Helen de Vallorbes, her passion baulked and therefore more than ever at white heat, swept up the paved alley, amid the sweet scents of the garden, beneath the jewelled rain of the fountain, that point of north in the wind dallying with her as in laughing challenge, making her the more mad to have her way with Richard Calmady, yet knowing that of the two—he and she—he was the stronger as yet.

CHAPTER VIII

" I HEAR Morabita sings, in *Ernani*, at the San Carlo on
Friday night. Do you care to go, Helen ? "
The question, though asked casually, had, to the listener,
the effect of falling with a splash, as of a stone into a well,
awakening unexpected echoes, disturbing, rather harshly, the
constrained silence which had reigned during the earlier part
of dinner.

All the long, hot afternoon, Madame de Vallorbes had been
alone—Richard invisible, shut persistently away in those rooms
of the entresol into which, as yet, she had never succeeded in
penetrating. Richard had not proposed to her to do so. And
it was part of that praiseworthy discretion which she had
agreed with herself to practise—in her character of scrupulously
unexacting guest—only to accept invitations, never to issue them.
How her cousin might occupy himself, whom even he might
receive, during the time spent in those rooms, she did not know.
And it was idle to inquire. Neither of her servants, though
skilful enough, as a rule, in the acquisition of information, could,
in this case, acquire any. And so it came about that during
those many still bright hours, following on her rather agitated
parting with Richard at midday, while she paced the noble
rooms of the first floor—once more taking note of their costly
furnishings and fine pictures, meeting her own restless image
again and again in their many mirrors—and later, near sundown,
when she walked the dry, brown pathways of the ilex and cypress
grove, the wildest suspicions of his possible doings assailed her.
For she was constrained to admit that, though she had spent
a full week now under his roof, it was but the veriest fringe,
after all, of the young man's habits and thought with which she
was actually acquainted. And this not only desperately
intrigued her curiosity, but the apartness, behind which he
entrenched himself and his doings, was as a slight put upon
her and consequent source of sharp mortification. So to-day
she ranged all permitted spaces of the villa and its grounds
softly, yet lithe, watchful, fierce as a she-panther—her ears
strained to hear, her eyes to see, driven the while by jealousy
of that nameless rival, to remembrance of whom all the whole
place was dedicated, and by baffled passion, as with whips.

Nor did superstition fail to add its word of ill-omen at this juncture. A carrion crow, long-legged, heavy of beak, alighting on the clustered curls of the marble bust of Homer, startled her with vociferous croakings. A long, narrow, many-jointed, blue-black, evil-looking beetle crawled from among the rusty, fibrous, cypress roots across her path. A funeral procession, priest and acolytes, with lighted tapers, sitting within the glass-sided hearse at head and foot of the flower-strewn coffin, wound slowly along the dusty, white road—bordered by queer growth of prickly-pear and ragged, stunted palm-trees—far below. She crossed herself, turning hurriedly away. Yet, for an instant, Death, triumphant, hideous, inevitable, and all the spiritual terror and physical disgust of it, grinned at her, its fleshless face, as it seemed, close against her own. And alongside Death—by some malign association of ideas and ugly antic of profanity—she saw the *bel tête de Jésu* of M. Paul Destournelle as she had seen it this morning, he looking back, hat in hand, while he plunged down the break-neck, Neapolitan side-street, with that impish, bleating, goatlike laugh.

By the time the dinner-hour drew near she found her outlook in radical need of reconstruction, and to that end bade Zélie dress her in the crocus-yellow brocade, reserved for some emergency such as the present. It was a gown, surely, to restore self-confidence and induce self-respect! Fashioned fancifully, according to a picturesque, seventeenth-century, Venetian model, the full sleeves and the long-waisted bodice of it—this cut low, generously displaying her shoulders and swell of her bosom—were draped with superb *guipure de Flandres à brides frisées* and strings of seed pearls. All trace of ascetic simplicity had very certainly departed. Helen was resplendent —strings of seed pearls twisted in her honey-coloured hair, a clear red in her cheeks and hard brilliance in her eyes, bred of eager, jealous excitement. She had, indeed, reached a stage of feeling in which the sight of Richard Calmady, the fact of his presence, worked upon her to the extent of dangerous emotion. And now this statement of his, and the question following it, caused the flame of the inward fires tormenting her to leap high.

"Ah! Morabita!" she exclaimed. "What an age it is since I have heard her sing, or thought about her! How is her voice lasting, Richard?"

"I really don't know," he answered, "and that is why I am rather curious to hear her. There was literally nothing but a voice in her case—no dramatic sense, nothing in the way of intelligence to fall back on.   On that account it interested me to watch her.   She and her voice had no essential relation to one another.   Her talent was stuck into her, as you might stick a pin into a cushion.   She produced glorious effects without a notion how she produced them, and gave expression —and perfectly just expression—to emotions she had never dreamed of.   At the best of times singers are a feeble folk intellectually, but, of all singers I have known, she was mentally the very feeblest."

"No, perhaps she was not very wise," Helen put in, but quite mildly, quite kindly.

"And so if the voice went, everything went.   And that made one reflect agreeably upon the remarkably haphazard methods employed by that which we politely call Almighty God in His construction of our unhappy selves.   Design?—There's not a trace of design in the whole show.   Bodies, souls, gifts, superfluities, deficiencies, just pitched together anyhow.   The most bungling of human artists would blush to turn out such work."

Richard spoke rapidly.   He had refused course after course. And now the food on his plate remained untasted.   Seen in the soft light of the shaded candles his face had a strange look of distraction upon it, as though he too was restless with an intimate, deep-seated restlessness.   His skin was less colourless than usual, his manner less colourless also.   And this conferred a certain youthfulness on him, making him seem nearer—so Helen thought—to the boy she had known at Brockhurst, than to the man, whom lately she had been so signally conscious that she failed to know.

"No, I hope Morabita's voice remains to her," he continued. "Her absolute nullity minus it is disagreeable to think of.   And much as I relish collecting telling examples of the fatuity of the Creator—she, voiceless, would offer a supreme one—I would spare her that, poor dear.   For she was really rather charming to me at one time."

"So it was commonly reported," Helen remarked.

"Was it?" Richard said absently.

Though as a rule conspicuously abstemious, he had drunk rather freely to-night, and that with an odd haste of thirst. Now he touched his champagne tumbler, intimating to Bates, the house-steward—sometime the Brockhurst under butler—that it should be refilled.

"I can't have seen Morabita for nearly three years," he went on.   "And my last recollections of her are unfortunate.

She had sent me a box, in Vienna it was I think, for the *Traviata*. She was fat then, or rather, fatter. Stage furniture leaves something to desire in the way of solidity. In the death scene the middle of the bed collapsed. Her swan-song ceased abruptly. Her head and heels were in the air, and the very large rest of her upon the floor, bed and bedclothes standing out in a frill all round. It was a sight discouraging to sentiment. I judged it kinder not to go to supper with her after the performance that night."

Richard paused, again drained his glass.

"I beg your pardon," he said, "what atrocious nonsense I am talking!"

"I think I rather enjoy it," Madame de Vallorbes answered. She looked sideways at the young man, from under her delicate eyelids. He was perfectly sober—of that there was no question. Yet he was less inaccessible, somehow, than usual. She inclined to experiment.—"Only I am sorry for Morabita in more ways than one, poor wretch. But then perhaps I am just a little sorry for all those women whom you reject, Richard."

"The women whom I reject?" he said harshly.

"Yes, whom you reject," Helen repeated.—Then she busied herself with a small black fig, splitting it deftly open, disclosing the purple, and rose, and clear living greens of the flesh and innumerable seeds of it, colours rich as those of a tropic sky at sunset.—"And there are so many of those women it seems to me! I am coming to have a quite pathetic fellowship for them." She buried her white teeth in the softness of the fig.—"Not without reason, perhaps. It is idle to deny that you are a past-master in the ungentle art of rejection. What have you to say in self-defence, Dickie?"

"That talking nonsense appears to be highly infectious—and that it is a disagreeably oppressive evening."

Helen de Vallorbes smiled upon him, glanced quickly over her shoulder to assure herself the servants were no longer present—then spoke, leaning across the corner of the table towards him, while her eyes searched his with a certain daring provocation.

"Yes, I admit I have finished my fig. Dinner is over. And it is my place to disappear according to custom."—She laid her rosy finger-tips together, her elbows resting on the table. "But I am disinclined to disappear. I have a number of things to say. Take that question of going to the opera, for instance. Half Naples will be there, and I know more than half Naples, and more than half Naples knows me. I do not crave to run incontinently into the arms of any of de Vallorbes' many relations.

They were not conspicuously kind to me when I was here as a girl and stood very much in need of kindness. So the question of going to the San Carlo, you see, requires reflection. And then,"—her tone softened to a most persuasive gentleness,—"then, the evenings are a trifle long when one is alone and has nothing very satisfactory to think about. And I have been worried to-day, detestably worried."—She looked down at her finger-tips. Her expression became almost sombre. "In any case I shall not plague you very much longer, Richard," she said rather grandly. "I have determined to remove myself bag and baggage. It is best, more dignified to do so. Reluctantly I own that. Here have I no abiding city. I wish I had, perhaps, but I haven't. Therefore it is useless, and worse than useless, to play at having one. One must just face the truth."

She looked full at the young man, smiling at him, as though somehow forgiving him a slight, an unkindness, a neglect.

"And so, just because to you it all matters so uncommonly little, let us talk rather later this evening."

She rose.

"I'll go on into the long drawing-room," she said. "The windows were still open there when I came in to dinner. The room will be pleasantly cool. You will come?"

And she moved away quietly, thoughtfully, opened the high double-doors, left them open, and that without once looking back. Yet her hearing was strained to catch the smallest sound above that which accompanied her, namely the rustling of her dress. Then a queer shiver ran all down her spine and she set her teeth, for she perceived that halting, shuffling footsteps had begun to follow those light and graceful footsteps of her own.

"*Ce n'est que le premier pas qui coute,*" she said to herself. "I have no fear for the rest."

Yet, crossing the near half of the great room, she sank down on a sofa, thankful there was no farther to go. In the last few minutes she had put forth more will-power, felt more deeply, than she had supposed. Her knees gave under her. It was a relief to sit down.

The many candles, in the cut-glass chandeliers hanging from along the centre of the painted ceiling, were lighted, filling the length and breadth of the room with a bland, diffused radiance. It touched picture and statue, tall mirror, rich curtain, polished woodwork of chair and table, gleaming ebony and ivory cabinet. It touched Helen de Vallorbes' bright head and the strings of pearls twisted in her hair, her white neck, the swell of her bosom, and all that delicate wonder of needlework—the Flanders lace—

trimming her bodice. It lay on her lap, too, as she leaned back in the corner of the sofa, her hands pressed down on either side her thighs—lay there bringing the pattern of her brocaded dress into high relief. This was a design of pomegranates—leaves, flowers, and fruit—and of trailing, peacock feathers, a couple of shades lighter than the crocus-yellow ground. The light took the over-threads and stayed in them.

The window stood wide open on to the balcony, the elaborately wrought-ironwork of which—scroll and vase, plunging dolphin and rampant sea-horse—detached itself from the opaque background of the night. And in at the window came luscious scents from the garden below, a chime of falling water, the music, faint and distant, in rising and falling cadence of a marching military band. In at it also, and rising superior to all these in imperativeness and purpose, came the voice of Naples itself—no longer that of a city of toil and commerce, but that of a city of pleasure, a city of licence, until such time as the dawn should once again break, and the sun arise, driving back man and beast alike to labour, the one from merry sinning, the other from hard-earned sleep. And once again, but in clearer, more urgent, accents, the voice of the city repeated its message to Helen de Vallorbes, calling aloud to her to do even as it was doing, namely to wed—to wed. And, hearing it, understanding that message, for a little space shame took her, in face both of its and her own shamelessness; so that she closed her eyes, unable for the moment to look at Richard Calmady as he crossed the great room in that bland and yet generous light. But, almost immediately, his voice, cold and measured in tone, there close beside her, claimed her attention.

"That which you said at dinner rather distresses me, Helen."

Then shame, or no shame, Madame de Vallorbes, of necessity, opened her eyes. And, so doing, it needed all her self-control to repress a cry. She forced her open hands down very hard on the mattress of the sofa. For Richard leaned his back against the jamb of the open window, and she saw his face and all his poor figure in profile. His left hand hung straight at his side, the tips of his fingers only just not touching the floor. And again, as at midday, the spectacle of his deformity worked upon her strangely.

"What of all that which I said at dinner distresses you?" she asked gently, with sudden solicitude.

"You showed me that I have been a wretchedly negligent host."—In speaking, the young man turned his head and looked at her, paused a moment, almost startled by her resplendent aspect. Then he looked down at his own stunted and defective limbs. His expression became very grim. He raised his shoulders just perceptibly. "I reproach myself with having allowed you to be so much alone. It must have been awfully dull for you."

"It was a little dull," Helen said, still gently.

"I ought to have begged you to ask some of the people you know in Naples to come here. It was stupid of me not to think of it. I need not have seen them, neither need they have seen me."

He looked at her steadily again, as though trying to fix her image in his memory.

"Yes, it was stupid of me," he repeated absently. "But I have got into churlish, bachelor habits—that can hardly be helped, living alone, or on board ship, as I do—and I have pretty well forgotten how to provide adequately for the entertainment of a guest."

"Oh! I have had that which I wanted, that which I came for," Helen answered, very charmingly,—"had it in part, at all events. Though I could have put up with just a little more of it, Dickie, perhaps."

"I warned you, if you remember, that opportunities of amusement—as that word is generally understood—would be limited."

"Amusement?" she exclaimed, with an almost tragic inflection of contempt.

"Oh yes!" he said, "amusement is not to be despised. I'd give all I am worth, half my time, to be amused—but that again, like hospitality, is rather a lost art with me. You remember, I warned you life at the villa in these days was not precisely hilarious."

Helen clapped her hands together.

"Ah! you are wilfully obtuse, you are wilfully, cruelly pig-headed!" she cried. "Pardon me, dear Richard, but your attitude is enough to exasperate a saint. And I am no saint as yet. I am still human—radically, for my own peace of mind lamentably, human. I am only too capable of being grieved, humiliated, hurt. But there, it is folly to say such things to you! You are hopelessly insensible to all that. So I take refuge in quoting your own words of this morning against you—that no explanation is lucid if the hearer refuses to accept it."

"I am dull, no doubt, but honestly I fail to see how that remark of mine can be held to apply in the present case."

"It applies quite desolatingly well!" Helen declared, with spirit. Then her manner softened into a seductiveness of forgiveness once again.—"And so, dear Richard, I am glad that I had already determined to leave here to-morrow. It would have been a little too wretched to arrive at that determination after this conversation. You must go alone to hear your old flame, Morabita, sing. Only, if her voice is still as sympathetic as of old, if it moves you from your present insensibility, you may read remembrance of some aspects of my visit into the witchery of it if you like. It may occur to you what those aspects really meant."

Helen smiled upon him, leaning a little forward. Her eyes shone, as though looking out through unshed tears.

"It's not exactly flattering to one's vanity to be compelled to depute to another woman the making of such things clear. But it is too evident I waste my time in attempting to make them clear myself. No explanation is lucid, *et cætera* "—

Helen shook back her head with an extraordinary charm of half-defiant, half-tearful laughter. She was playing a game, her whole intelligence bent on the playing of it skilfully. Yet she was genuinely touched. She was swayed by her very real emotion. She spoke from her heart, though every word, every passing action, subserved her ultimate purpose in regard to Richard Calmady.

"And, after all, one must retain some remnant of self-respect with which to cover the nakedness of one's— Oh yes! decidedly, Morabita's voice had best do the rest!"

Richard had moved from his station in the window. He stood at the far end of the sofa, resting his hands on the gilded and carven arm of it. Now the ungainliness of his deformity was hidden, and his height was greater than that of his companion, obliging her to look up at him.

"I give you my word, Helen," he said, "I have no notion what you are driving at."

"Driving at, driving at?" she cried. "Why, the self-evident truth that you are forcing me rather brutally to pay the full price of my weakness in coming here, in permitting myself the indulgence of seeing you again. You told me directly I arrived, with rather cynical frankness, that I had not changed. That is quite true. What I was at Brockhurst, four years ago, what I then felt, that I am and that I feel still. Oh! you have nothing to reproach yourself with in defect of plain speaking, or excess of amiable subterfuge! You hit out very straight from the shoulder! Directly I arrived you also told me how you had devoted this place—with which, after all, I am not wholly unconnected—to the cult, to the ideal worship, of a woman whom you loved."

29

" So I have devoted it," Richard said.

" And yet I was weak enough to remain ! "

The young man's face relaxed, but its expression remained enigmatic.

" And why not ? " he asked.

" Because, in remaining, I have laid myself open to misconstruction, to all manner of pains and penalties, not easy to be endured, to the odious certainty of appearing contemptible in your estimation as well as in my own."

Helen patted her pretty foot upon the floor in a small frenzy of irritation.

" How can I hope to escape, since even the precious being whom you affect to worship you keep sternly at arm's length— hat is among the other pleasing things you confided to me immediately on my arrival—lest, seen at close quarters, she should fall below your requirements and so you should suffer disillusion ? Ah ! you are frightfully cold-blooded, repulsively inhuman ! Whether you judge others by yourself, reckoning them equally devoid of natural feeling, or whether you find a vindictive relish in rejecting the friendship and affection so lavishly offered you "—

" Is it offered lavishly ? That comes as news to me," he put in.

" Ah ! but it is. And I leave you to picture the pleasing entertainment afforded the offerer in seeing you ignore the offering, or, worse still, take it, examine it, and throw it aside like a dirty rag ! In one case you underline your rejection almost to the point of insult."

" This is very instructive. I am learning a whole lot about myself," Richard said coolly.

" But look," Madame de Vallorbes cried, " do you not prefer exposing yourself to the probability of serious illness rather than remain under the same roof with me ? The inference hits one in the face. To you the pestilential exhalations, the unspeakable abominations, of Naples harbour appear less dangerous than my near neighbourhood."

" You put it more strongly than I should," he answered, smiling. " Yet, from a certain standpoint, that may very well be true."

For an instant Helen hesitated. Her intelligence, for all its alertness, was strained exactly to appraise the value of his words, neither over, nor under, rating it. And her eyes searched his with a certain boldness and imperiousness of gaze. Richard, meanwhile, folding his arms upon the carven and gilt frame of the sofa, looked back at her, smiling still, at once ironically and very sadly. Then swift assurance came to her of the brazen card she had best play. But, playing it, she was constrained to avert her eyes and set her glance pensively upon the light-visited surface of her crocus-yellow, silken lap.

"I will do my possible to accept your nightly journeys as a compliment in disguise, then," she said, quite softly. "For truly, when I come to think of it, were she, herself, here—she, the woman you so religiously admire that you take an infinitude of pains to avoid having anything on earth to do with her—were she herself here, you could hardly take more extensive measures to secure yourself against risk of disappointment, hardly exercise a greater range of caution!"

"Perhaps that's just it. Perhaps you have arrived at it all at last. Perhaps she is here," he said.

And he turned away, steadying himself with one hand against the jamb of the window, and shuffled out slowly, laboriously, on to the balcony into the night.

For a quite perceptible length of time Helen de Vallorbes continued to contemplate the light-visited surface of her crocus-yellow, silken lap. She followed the lines of the rich pattern—pomegranate, fruit and blossom, trailing peacock's feather. For by such mechanical employment alone could she keep the immensity of her excitement and of her triumph in check. To shout aloud, to dance, to run wildly to and fro, would have been only too possible to her just then. All that for which she had schemed, had ruled herself discreetly, had ridden a waiting race, had been hers, in fact, from the first—the prize adjudged before ever she left the starting-post. She held this man in the hollow of her hand; and that by no result of cunning artifice, but by right divine of beauty and wit and the manifold seductions of her richly-endowed personality. And, thinking of that, she clenched her dainty fists, opened them again, and again clenched them, upon the yielding mattress of the sofa, given over to an ecstasy of physical enjoyment, weaving, even as, with clawed and padded paws, her prototype the she-panther might. Slowly she raised her downcast eyes and looked after Richard Calmady, his figure a blackness, as of vacancy, against the elaborate wrought-iron-work of the balcony. And so doing, an adorable sensation moved her, at once of hungry tenderness and of fear—fear of something unknown, in a way fundamental, incalculable, the like of which she had never experienced before. Ah! indeed, of all her many loves, here was the crown and climax! Yet, in the midst of her very vital rapture, she could still find time for remembrance of the little, crescent-shaped scar upon her temple, and for remembrance of Katherine Calmady, who had, unwittingly, fixed that blemish upon her and had also more than once frustrated her designs.   This time frustration was not possible.   She was about to revenge the infliction of that little scar!   And, all the while, the intellectual part of her was agreeably intrigued, trying to disentangle the why and wherefore of Richard's late action and utterances.   And self-love was gratified to the highest height of its ambition by the knowledge that not only in his heart had she long reigned, but that he had dedicated time and wealth and refined ingenuity to the idea of her, to her worship, to the making of this, her former dwelling-place, into a temple for her honour, a splendid witness to her victorious charm, a shrine not unfitting to contain the idol of his imagination.

For a little space she rested in all this, savouring the sweetness of it as some odour of costly sacrifice.   For, whatever her sins and lapses, Helen de Vallorbes had the fine æsthetic appreciations, as well as the inevitable animality, of the great courtesan.   The artist was at least as present in her as the whore.   And it was not, therefore, until realisation of her present felicity was complete, until it had soaked into her, so to speak, to the extent of a delicious familiarity, that she was disposed to seek change of posture or of place.   Then, at last, softly, languidly, for indeed she was somewhat spent by the manifold emotions of the day, she rose and followed Richard into the starless, low-lying night.   Her first words were very simple, yet to herself charged with far-reaching meaning—as a little key may give access to a treasure-chest containing riches of fabulous worth.

"Richard, is it really true, that which you have told me?"

"What conceivable object could I have in lying?"

"Then why have you delayed?—why wasted the precious days—the precious months and years, if it comes to that?"

"How in honour and decency could I do otherwise—circumstances being such as they are, I being that which I am?"

The two voices were in notable contrast.   Both were low, both were penetrated by feeling.   But the man's was hoarse and rasping, the woman's smooth and soft as milk.

"Ah! it is the old story!" she said.   "Will you never comprehend, Dickie, that what is to you hateful in yourself, may to someone else be the last word of attraction, of seduction, even?"

"God forbid I should ever comprehend that!" he answered. "When I take to glorying in my shame, pluming myself upon my abnormality, then, indeed, I become beyond all example loathsome. The most deplorable moment of my very inglorious career will be precisely that in which I cease to look at myself with dispassionate contempt."

Helen knelt down, resting her beautiful arms upon the dark handrail of the balcony, letting her wrists droop over it into the outer dimness. The bland light from the open window dwelt on her kneeling figure and bowed head. But it was as well, perhaps, that the night dropped a veil upon her face.

"And yet so it is," she said. "You may repudiate the idea, but the fact remains. I do not say it would affect all women alike—affect those, for instance, whose conception of love, and of the relation between man and woman, is dependent upon the slightly improper and very tedious marriage service as authorised by the English Church. Let the conventional be conventional still! So much the better if you don't appeal to them—meagre, timid, inadequate, respectable—a generation of fashion-plates with a sixpenny book of etiquette, moral and social, stuck inside them to serve for a soul."

Helen's voice broke in a little spasm of laughter; and her hands began, unconsciously, to open and close, open and close, weaving in soft, outer darkness.

"We may leave them out of the argument.—But there remain the elect, Richard, among whom I dare count myself. And over them, never doubt it, just that which you hate and which appears at first sight to separate you so cruelly from other men, gives you a strange empire. You stimulate, you arrest, you satisfy one's imagination, as does the spectacle of some great drama. You are at once enslaved and emancipated by this thing—to you hateful, to me adorable—beyond all measure of bondage or freedom inflicted upon, or enjoyed by, other men. And in this, just this, lies magnificent compensation if you would but see it. I have always known that—known that if you would put aside your arrogance and pride, and yield yourself a little, it was possible to love you, and give you such joy in loving, as one could give to no one else on earth."

Her voice sweetened yet more. She leaned forward, pressing her bosom against the rough ironwork of the balcony.

"I knew that from the first hour we met in the variegated, autumn sunshine, upon the green-sward, before the white summer-house overlooking that noble, English, woodland view. I saw you, and so doing I saw mysteries of joy in myself unimagined by me before. It went very hard with me then, Richard. It has gone very hard with me ever since."

Madame de Vallorbes' words died away in a grave and delicate whisper. But she did not turn her head, nor did Richard speak. Only, close there beside her, she heard him breathe, panting short and quick even as a dog pants, while a certain vibration seemed to run along the rough ironwork against which she leaned. And by these signs Helen judged her speech, though unanswered, had not been wholly in vain. From below, the luscious fragrance of the garden, the chime of falling water, and the urgent voice of the painted pleasure-city came up about her. Night had veiled the face of Naples, even as Helen's own. Yet lines of innumerable lights described the suave curve of the bay, climbed the heights of Posilipo, were doubled in the oily waters of the harbour, spread abroad alluring gaiety in the wide piazzas, and shone like watchful and soliciting eyes from out the darkness of narrow street, steep lane, and cut-throat alley. While, above all that, high uplifted against the opacity of the starless sky, a blood-red beacon burned on the summit of Vesuvius, the sombre glow of it reflected upon the under side of the masses of downward-rolling smoke as upon the belly of some slow-crawling, monstrous serpent.

Suddenly Helen spoke once again, and with apparent inconsequence.

" Richard, you must have known she could never satisfy you —why did you try to marry Constance Quayle? "

" To escape. "

" From whom—from me? "

" From myself, which is much the same thing as saying from you, I suppose. "

" And you could not escape? "

" So it seems. "

" But—but, dear Richard, " she said plaintively, yet with very winning sweetness, " why, after all, should you want so desperately to escape? "

Richard moved a little farther from her.

" I have already explained that to you, to the point of insult so you tell me, " he said. " Surely it is unnecessary to go over the ground again? "

" You carry your idealism to the verge of slight absurdity, " she answered. " Oh! you of altogether too little faith, how should you gauge the full flavour of the fruit till you have set your teeth in it? Better, far better, be a sacramentalist like me and embrace the idea through the act, than refuse the act in dread of imperilling the dominion of the idea. You put the cart before the horse with a vengeance, Dickie! There's such a thing as being so reverently-minded towards your god that he ceases to be the very least profit or use to you."

And again she heard that panting breath beside her. Again laughter bubbled up in her fair throat, and her hands fell to weaving the soft, outer darkness.

"You must perceive that it cannot end here and thus," she said presently.

"Of course not," he answered.—Then, after a moment's pause, he added, coldly enough :—"I foresaw that, so I gave orders yesterday that the yacht was not to be laid up, but only to coal and provision, and undergo some imperatively necessary repairs. She should be ready for sea by the end of the week."

Helen turned sideways, and the bland light, from the room within, touched her face now as well as her kneeling figure.

"And then, and then?" she demanded, almost violently.

"Then I shall go," Richard replied. "Where, I do not yet know, but as far, anyhow, as the coal in the yacht's bunkers will drive her. Distance is more important than locality just now. And I leave you here at the villa, Helen. Do not regret that you came. I don't."

He too had turned to the light, which revealed his face ravaged and aged by stress of emotion, revealed too the homelessness, as of empty space, resident in his eyes.

"I shall be glad to remember the place pleases and speaks to you. It has been rather a haven of rest to me during these last two years. You would have had it at my death, in any case. You have it a little sooner—that's all."

But Helen held out her arms.

"The villa, the villa," she cried, "what do I want with that! God in heaven, are you utterly devoid of all sensibility, all heart? Or are you afraid — afraid even yet, oh, very chicken-livered lover—that behind the beauty of Naples you may find the filth? It is not so, Dickie. It is not so, I tell you.—Look at me. What would you have more? Surely, for any man, my love is good enough!"

And then hurriedly, with a rustling of silken skirts, hot with anger from head to heel, she sprang to her feet.

Across the room one of the men-servants advanced.

"The carriage is at the door, sir," he said.

And Madame de Vallorbes' voice broke in with a singular lightness and nonchalance :—

"Surely it is rather imprudent to go out again to-night? You told me, at dinner, you were not well, that you had had a touch of fever."

She held out her hand, smiling serenely.

"Be advised," she said, "avoid malaria.—I shall see you before I go to-morrow? Yes—an afternoon train, I think. Good-night, we meet at breakfast as usual."

She stepped in at the window, gathered up certain small properties—a gold scent-bottle, one or two books, a blotting-case, as with a view to final packing and departure. Just as she reached the door she heard Richard say curtly :—

"Send the carriage round. I shall not want it to-night."

But even so Helen did not turn back. On the contrary, she ran, light of foot as the little dancer, of long ago, with blush-roses in her hat, through all the suite of lofty rooms to her own sea-blue, sea-green bed-chamber, and there, sitting down before the toilet-table, greeted her own radiant image in the glass. Her lips were very red. Her eyes shone like pale stars on a windy night.

"Quick, quick, undress me, Zélie! Put me to bed. I am simply expiring of fatigue," she said.

CHAPTER IX

CONCERNING THAT DAUGHTER OF CUPID AND PSYCHE WHOM MEN CALL VOLUPTAS

THE furniture, though otherwise of the customary proportions, had all been dwarfed. This had been achieved in some cases by ingenious design in its construction, in others by the simple process of cutting down, thus reducing table and chair, couch and bureau, in itself of whatever grace of style, dignity of age, or fineness of workmanship, to an equality of uncomely degradation in respect of height. The resultant effect was of false perspective. Nor was this unpleasing effect lessened by the proportions of the room itself. In common with all those of the entresol, it was noticeably low in relation to its length and width, while the stunted vaultings of its darkly-frescoed ceiling produced an impression of heaviness rather than of space. Bookcases, dwarfed as were all the other furnishings, lined the walls to within about two feet of the spring of the said vaulting. Made of red cedar and unpolished, the cornices and uprights of them were carved with arabesques in high relief. An antique, Persian carpet, sombre in colouring and of great value, covered the greater portion of the pale, pink and grey, mosaic pavement of the floor. Thick, rusty-red, Genoa-velvet curtains were drawn

over each low, square window.   A fire of logs burned on the
open hearth.   And this, notwithstanding the unaccustomed
warmth of the outside air, did but temper the chill atmosphere
of the room and serve to draw a faint aroma from the carven
cedar wood.

It was here, to his library,—carried downstairs by his men-
servants as a helpless baby-child might be,—that Richard
Calmady had come when Helen de Vallorbes departed so
blithely to her bed-chamber.   And it was here he remained,
though nearly two hours had elapsed since then, finding sleep
impossible.

For the wakefulness and unrest of rapidly breeding illness
were upon him.   His senses and his will had been in very active
conflict.   Desire had licked him, as with fiery tongues, driving
him onward.   Honour, self-contempt in face of temptation
to sensual indulgence, an aspiration after somewhat stoic
asceticism which had come to influence his action of late, held
him back.   But now, here and alone, the immediately provoking
cause of passion removed, reaction against the strain of all that
had very sensibly set in.   He felt strangely astray, as though
drifting at hazard upon the waters of an unquiet, mist-blinded
sea.   He was conscious of a deep-seated preoccupation regarding
some matter, which he was alike unable to forget or to define.
Formless images perplexed his vision.   Formless thoughts
pursued one another, as with the hurry of rumoured calamity,
through his mind.   A desolating apprehension of things insufficiently developed, of the inconclusive, the immature, the
unattained, of things mutilated, things unfinished, born out of
due time and incomplete, oppressed his fancy.   Even the events
of the last few hours, in which he had played so considerable a
part, took on a shadowy semblance, ceased to appeal to him as
realities, began to merge themselves in that all-pervading apprehension of defectiveness, of that which is wanting, lopped off, so
to speak, and docked.   It was to him as though all natural,
common-sense relations were in abeyance, as though his own,
usually precise, mental processes were divorced from reason and
experience, had got out of perspective, in short—even as this low,
wide, cedar-scented library, of which the vaulted ceiling seemed
to approach unduly close to the marble floor, and all its
dwarfed furnishings, its squat tables and almost legless chairs,
had got out of perspective.

The alternate purposeless energy and weariful weakness of
fever, just as the alternate dry flush and trembling chill of it,
distressed him.   He had slipped on a smoking-coat, but even

the weight of this thin, silk garment seemed oppressive, although, now and again, he felt as though around his middle he wore a belt of ice.   Not without considerable exertion he rolled forward a couch—wide, high-backed, legless, mounted upon little wheels —to the vicinity of the fire.   He drew himself up on to it and rested among the piled-up cushions.   Perhaps, if he waited, exercising patience, sleep might mercifully visit him and deliver him from this intolerable confusion of mind.   Deliver him, too, from that hideous apprehension of universal mutilation, of maimed purposes, maimed happenings, of a world peopled by beings maimed as he was himself, but after a more subtle and intimate fashion—a fashion intellectual or moral rather than merely physical—so that they had to him, just now, an added hatefulness of specious lying, since to ordinary seeing they appeared whole, while whole they truly and actually were not.

Sternly he tried to shake himself free of these morbid fancies, to bring his imagination under control and force himself once again to join hands with reality and common sense.   And, to this end, he turned his attention to the consideration of practical matters.   He dwelt on the details of the coaling and revictualling of his yacht, upon the objective of the voyage upon which he proposed to start a few days hence.   He reviewed the letters which must be written and the arrangements which must be made with a view to putting his cousin legally in possession of the villa, the rent of which he proposed still to pay to her husband.   This suite of rooms he would retain for his own use.   That was necessary, obligatory.   Yet, why must he retain it? He did not propose to return and live here at any future time. This episode was over—or rather, had it not simply failed of completion?   Was it not, like all the rest, maimed, lopped off, ungainly docked?   Then, where came in the obligation to reserve these rooms?   He could not remember.   Yet he knew that he was compelled to do so, because—because—

And, once again, Richard's power of concentration broke down.   Once again his thought eluded him, becoming tangled, fugitive, not to be grasped.   While, like swarms of shrill squeaking bats disturbed in the recesses of some age-old cavern by sudden intrusion of voices and of lights, half-formed visions, half-formed ideas, once again flapped duskily about him, torturing in their multiplicity alike to his senses and his brain. He fought with them, striving to beat them off in a madness of disgust, half suffocated by the fanning of their foul and stifling wings.   Then, exhausted by the conflict, he stumbled and fell, while they closed down on him. And he, losing consciousness, slept.

That unconsciousness lasted in point of fact but for a few minutes. Yet to Richard those minutes were as years, as centuries. At length, still heavy with dreamless slumber, he was aware of the stealthy turning of a key in a lock. Little padding foot-falls, soft as those of some strong, yet dainty, cat-creature crossed the carpet. A whisper of silk came along with them, like the murmur of the breeze in an oak grove on a clear, hot, summer noon, or the sibilant ripple of the sea upon spaces of fine-ribbed, yellow sand. And the impression produced upon Richard was delicious, as of one passing from a close room into the open air. Confusion and exhaustion left him. Energy returned. The energy of breeding fever merely; yet to him it appeared that of refreshment, of renewed and abounding health. He was conscious, too, of a will outside himself, acting upon his will—a will self-secure, impregnable, working with triumphant daring toward a single end. It certainly was unmaimed—in its present manifestation in any case. It told, and with assurance, of completion, of attainment. Yielding himself to it, with something of the recklessness a man yields himself to the poison which yet promises relief, Richard opened his eyes.

Before him stood Helen de Vallorbes. In one hand she carried a little lamp. In the other her high-heeled, cloth-of-gold slippers. Her feet were bare. In the haste of the journey, from her bed-chamber upstairs through the great rooms and down the marble stairs, the fronts of the sea-blue, sea-green dressing-gown she wore had flown apart, thus disclosing not only her delicate night-dress, but—since this last was fine to the point of transparency—all the secret loveliness of her body and her limbs. Her shining hair curled low upon her forehead, half concealed her pretty ears, and lay upon her shoulders like a little, golden cape. And, from out this brightness of her hair, the exultant laughter bubbling in her throat, the small lamp carried high in one hand, she looked down at Richard Calmady.

" I waited till the hours grew old and you did not come to me, so I have come to you, Dickie," she said. " Let what will happen to-morrow, this very certainly shall happen to-night— that with you and me Love shall have his own way, speak his own language, be worshipped with the rites, be found in the sacraments, ordained by himself, and to which all nature is, and has been, obedient since life on earth first began ! "

Helen set down her lamp, let drop her slippers upon the floor, sprang across the intervening space, fierce, yet graceful, as some lithe and amorous beast, flung herself down beside Richard Calmady upon the couch, and caressed him with quick, lascivious fingers, while her lips fastened on his lips.

Not till the grey of a rain-washed, windy morning had come, and Naples had put off its merry sinning, changing from a city of pleasure to a city of labour and, too often, of callously inflicted pain, did Helen de Vallorbes leave the cedar-scented library. The fire of logs had burnt itself out upon the hearth, and other fires, perhaps, had pretty thoroughly burnt themselves out like-wise. Then, with the extinguished lamp in one hand and her high-heeled, cloth-of-gold slippers in the other, she had run swiftly, barefoot, up the cold, marble stairs, through the suite of lofty rooms, her image, in the bleak dimness of the wet morning, given back by their tall mirrors as that of no mortal woman but some fear-driven, hurrying ghost. Carefully closing the door of the bed-chamber behind her, she threw her dressing-gown aside and buried herself in the luxurious softness of the unslept-in bed. And she was only just in time. Servants began to move to and fro. The house was awake.

CHAPTER X

THE ABOMINATION OF DESOLATION

SULLENLY, persistently, the rain came down. In the harbour the wash was just sufficient to make the ravelled fruit-baskets, the shredded vegetables, the crusts and offal thrown out from the galleys, heave and sway upon the oily surface of the water, while screaming gulls dropped greedily upon the floating refuse, and rising, circled over the black, liquid lanes and open spaces between the hulls of the many ships. But it was insufficient to lift the yacht, tied up to the southern quay of the Porto Grande. She lay there inert and in somewhat sorry plight under the steady downpour. For the moment all the winsome devilry of a smart, sea-going craft was dead in her; and she sulked, ashamed through all her eight hundred tons of wood and iron, copper, brass, and steel. For she was coaling over-deck, and was grimy from stem to stern. While, arrayed in the cast clothes of all Europe, tattered, undersized, gesticulating, the human scum of Naples swarmed up the steep, narrow planks from the inky lighters and in over her side.

"Beastly dirty job this. Shan't get her paint clean under a

week!" the first mate grumbled to his companion, the second mate—a dark-haired, dreamy-eyed, West-country lad, but just out of his teens.

The two officers, in dripping oilskins, stood at the gangway checking the tally of coal-baskets as they came on board. Just now there was a pause in the black procession, as an empty lighter sheered off, making room for a full one to come alongside, thus rendering conversation momentarily possible.

"Pity the Boss couldn't have stayed on shore till we were through with it and cleaned up a bit," the speaker continued. "Makes the old man no end waxy to have anyone on board when the yacht's like she is. I don't blame him. She's as neat and pretty as a white daisy in a green pasture when she's away to sea. And now, poor little soul, she's a regular slut."

"I know I'd 'ave stayed ashore fast enough if I was the Boss," the boy said, half wistfully. "That villa of his is like a piece of poetry. I keep on saying over to myself how it looks."

"Oh! it's not so bad for foreign parts," the senior officer replied. "And you're young yet and soft, Penberthy. You'll come off that presently. England's best for houses, town and country; and most other things—women, and fights, and even sunshine, for when you do get sunshine at home there's no spite in it.—Hi! there, you, ganger," he shouted suddenly, and resentfully, leaning out over the bulwarks, "hurry 'em up a bit, can't you? You don't suppose I mean to stand here till the second anniversary of the Day of Judgment, watching your blithering, chicken-shanked macaronies suck rotten oranges, do you? Start 'em up again. Whatever are you waiting for, man? Start 'em up, I say."

The boy's dreamy eyes, full of unwritten verse, dwelt with a curious indifference upon the broken procession of ascending, black figures. He had but lately joined, and to him both the fine vessel and her owner were invested with a certain romance.

"What was the fancy for calling the yacht the *Reprieve*?" he asked presently.

"Wait till you've had the chance to take a good look at Sir Richard, and you'll answer your question yourself," the other man answered oracularly. Then he broke out again into sustained invective:—"Hold up there, you little fool of a tight-rope-dancing, *bella Napoli* gorilla, and don't go dropping good, honest, Welsh steam-coal overboard into your confounded, stinking, local sewer! I don't care to see any of your blamed posturings, don't flatter yourself. Hold up your grimacing, great-grandson of a lousy she-ape, can't you, and walk straight.—Take him all round Sir Richard Calmady's the best Boss I ever sailed with—one of the sternest, but the civilest too.—Shove 'em along, ganger, will you? Shove 'em along, I say.—He's one of the few men I've loved, I'm not ashamed to say it, Mr. Penberthy, and about the only one I ever remember to have feared, in all my life."

Meanwhile, if the scene to seaward was cheerless, that to landward offered but small improvement. For the murk of low-brooding cloud and falling rain blotted out the Castel S. Elmo, and the Capo di Monte and Pizzafalcone heights. Even the Castello del'Ovo down on the shore line, comparatively near at hand, loomed up but a denser mass of indigo-grey amid the all obtaining greyness. The tall multi-coloured, many-shuttered houses fronting the quays—restaurants, *cafés*, money-changers' bureaux, ships' chandlers, and slop-shops—looked tawdry and degraded as a clown's painted face seen by daylight. Thick, malodorous vapours arose from the squalid streets, lying back on the level, and from the crowded shipping of the port. These hung in the stagnant air, about the forest of masts and the funnels of steamers. And the noise of the place was as that of Bedlam let loose.—The long-drawn, chattering rush of the coal pitched from the baskets down the echoing, iron shoots. The grate and scream of saws cutting through blocks of stone and marble. The grind of heavy wheels upon the broken, irregular flags. The struggling clatter of hoofs, lashing of whips, squeal of mules, savage voices raised in cries and imprecations. The clank and roar of machinery. The repeated bellowing of a great liner, blowing off steam as she took up her berth in the outer harbour. The shattering rattle of the chains of a steam crane, when the monster iron-arm swung round seeking or depositing its burden and the crank ran out in harsh anger, as it seemed, and defiance. And through all this, as under-current, the confused clamour of the ever-shifting, ever-present crowd, and the small, steady drip of the rain. Squalid, sordid, brutal even, the coarse actualities of her trade and her poverty alike disclosed, her fictions and her foulness uncondoned by reconciling sunshine, Naples had declined from radiant goddess to common drab.

It was in this character that Richard Calmady, driving yesterday and for the first time through the streets at noon, had been fated to see his so-fondly-idealised city. It was in this character that he apprehended it again to-day, waiting in his deck-cabin until cessation of the rain and on-coming of the friendly dusk should render it not wholly odious to sit out on deck. The hours lagged, and into even this bright and usually spotless apartment

—with its shining, white walls, its dark, blue leather and polished, mahogany fittings—the coal dust penetrated. It rimmed the edge of the books neatly ranged on the racks. It smirched the charts laid out on the square locker-table below. It drifted in at the cabin windows, along with the babel of sound and the all-pervading stench of the port. This was, in itself, sufficiently distasteful, sufficiently depressing. And to Richard, just now, the disgust of it came with the heightened sensibility of physical illness, and as accompaniment to an immense private shame and immense self-condemnation, a conviction of outlawry and a desolation passing speech. He looked for comfort, for promise of restoration, and found none, in things material or things intellectual, in others or in himself. For his mind, always prone to apprehend by images rather than by words, and to advance by analogy rather than by argument, discovered in surrounding aspects and surrounding circumstance a rather hideously apt parable and illustration of its present state. Just as this seemingly fair city was proven, on intimate acquaintance, repulsive beyond the worst he had ever feared and earnestly refused to know of it, so a certain fair woman, upon whom, since boyhood, his best, most chivalrous, most unselfish, affections had centred, was proven—herself, moreover, flagrantly contributing to that proving—vile beyond all that rumour, heard and passionately denied by him, had ever ventured to whisper concerning her. Nor was the misery of this revelation lessened by the knowledge that his own part in it all had been very base. He had sinned before. He would sin again probably. Richard had long ceased to regard these matters from a strictly puritanic standpoint. But this particular sinning was different to any that had gone before, or which could come after it. For it partook—so at least, it now appeared to him—of the nature of sacrilege, since he had sinned against his ideal, degrading that to gross uses which he had agreed with himself to hold sacred, defiling it and, thereby, very horribly defiling himself.

And this disgrace of their relation, his own and hers, the inherent abomination of it all and its inherent falsity, had been forced home on him with a certain violence of directness just in the common course of daily happenings. For among the letters, brought to him along with his first breakfast yesterday after that night of secret licence, had been three of serious import. One was from Lady Calmady; and that he put aside with a certain anger, calling himself unwilling, knowing himself unfit, to read it. Another he tore open. The handwriting was unknown to him. He began reading it in bewilderment. Then he understood.

" MONSIEUR,"—it ran,—" You are in process of exterminating me. But, since I have reason to believe that no sufficient opportunity has been afforded you of realising the enormity of your conduct, I rally the profoundness of nobility which I discover within me — I calm myself. I go further, I explain. Living in retirement, you may not have learned that I am in Naples. I followed your cousin here—Madame de Vallorbes. My connection with her represents the supreme passion of my passionate youth. At once a frenzy and an anodyne, I have found in it the inspiration of my genius in its later development. This work must not be put a stop to. It is too majestic, it is weighted with too serious consequences to the whole of thinking France, of thinking Europe. A less experienced woman cannot satisfy the extravagance of my desires, the demands of my all-consuming imagination. The reverence with which a person, such as yourself, must regard commanding talent, the concessions he must be willing to make to its necessities, are without limit. This I cannot doubt that you will admit. The corollary is obvious. Either, *monsieur*, you will immediately invite me to reside with you at your villa—thereby securing for yourself daily intercourse with a nature of distinguished merit—or you will restore Madame de Vallorbes to me without hesitation or delay. Her devotion to me is absolute. How could it fail to be so, since I have lavished upon her the treasures of my extraordinary personality? But a fear of insular prejudice on your part withholds her at this moment from full expression of that devotion. She suffers as well as myself. It will be your privilege to put a term to this suffering by requesting me to join her, or by restoring her to me. To do otherwise will be to prolong the eclipse of my genius, and thereby outrage the conscience of civilised humanity which breathlessly awaits the next utterance of its chosen poet. If you require the consolation of feminine society, marry—it would be very simple — some white-souled, English miss. But restore to me, to whom her presence is indispensable, this woman of regal passions. I shall present myself at your house to-day to receive your answer in person. The result of a refusal, on your part, to receive me will be attended by calamitous consequences to yourself.—Accept, *monsieur*, the expression of my highest consideration,

PAUL AUGUSTE DESTOURNELLE."

For the moment Richard saw red, mad with rage at the insolence of the writer. And then came the question, was it true, that which this letter implied? Had Helen, indeed, lied to him?

And, notwithstanding its insane vanity, did this precious epistle give a more veracious account of her relation to the young poet than that which she had herself volunteered? He tried to put the thought from him. Who was he—to-day of all days—to be nice about the conduct of another? Who was he to sit in judgment? So he turned to his correspondence again, taking another letter, at random, from the pile. And then, looking at the superscription, he turned somewhat sick.

"MON CHER,"—wrote M. de Vallorbes,—"My steward informs me that he has just received your draft for a quarter's rent of the villa. I thank you a thousand times for your admirable punctuality. Decidedly you are of those with whom it is a consolation to do business. Need I assure you that the advent of this money is far from inopportune, since a grateful country, while showering distinctions upon me with one hand, with the other picks my pocket? I find it not a little expensive this famous military service! But then, ever since I can remember, I have found all that afforded me the slightest active pleasure equally that! And this sport of war, I promise you, is the most excellent sport in which I have as yet participated. It satisfies the primitive instincts more thoroughly than even your English fox-hunting. A *battue* of *Communards* is obviously superior to a *battue* of pheasants. To the dignity of killing one's fellow-men is added the satisfaction of ridding oneself of vermin. It becomes a matter of sanitation and self-respect. And this, indirectly, recalls to me, that report declares my wife to be with you at Naples. *Mon cher je vous en fais câdeau.* With you, at least, I know that my honour is safe. You may even instil into her mind some faint conception of the rudiments of morality. To be frank with you, she needs that. A couple of months ago she did me the honour to elope—temporarily, of course—with M. Paul Destournelle. You may have glanced, one day, at his crapulous verses. I suppose honour demanded that I should pursue the guilty pair and account for one, if not both, of them. But I was too busily engaged with my little *Communards*. We set these gentry up against a wall and dispose of them in batches. I have had a good deal of this, but, as I say, it has not yet become monotonous. Traits of individual character lend it vivacity. And then, putting aside the exigencies of my profession, I do not know that anything is to be gained by inviting public scandal. You have an English proverb to the effect that one should wash one's dirty linen at home. This I have tried to do, as you cannot but be aware, all along. If one has had the

30

misfortune to marry Messalina, one learns to be philosophic. A few lovers more or less, in that connection, what, after all, does it matter? Indeed, I begin to derive ironical consolation from the fact of their multiplicity. The existence of one would have constituted a reflection upon my charms. But a matter of ten, fifteen, twenty, ceases to be in any degree personal to myself. Only I object to Destournelle. He is too young, too *rococo.* He represents a descent in the scale. I prefer *des hommes mures,* generals, ministers, princes. The devil knows we have had our share of such ! Your generosity to her has saved us from Jews so far, and from *nouveaux riches,* by relieving the business of commercial aspects. Give her some salutary advice, therefore, *mon cher,* and if she becomes inconvenient forward her to Paris. I forgive to seventy-times-seven, being still proud enough to struggle after an appearance of social and conjugal decency. *Enfin* it is a relief to have unburdened myself for once, and you have been the good genius of my unfortunate *ménage,* for which Heaven reward you.—Yours, in true cousinly regard and supreme reliance on your discretion,

ANGELO LUIGI FRANCESCO DE VALLORBES."

That this, in any case, had a stamp of sincerity upon it, Richard could not doubt. It must be admitted that he had long ceased to accept Madame de Vallorbes' estimate of her husband with unqualified belief. But, be that as it might, whether he were a consummate, or merely an average profligate, one thing was certain that this man trusted him—Richard Calmady,—and that he—Richard Calmady—had very vilely betrayed that trust. He stared at the letter, and certain sentences in it seemed to sear him, even as the branding-iron used on a felon might. This was a new shame, different to, and greater than, any his deformity had ever induced in him, even as evil done is different to, and greater than, evil suffered. Morality may be relative only and conventional. Honour, for all persons of a certain standing and breeding, remains absolute. And it was precisely of his own honour that he had deprived himself. Not only in body, but in character, he was henceforth monstrous. For a while Richard had remained very still, looking at this thing into which he had made himself as though it were external and physically visible to him.

Then, suddenly, he had reached out his hand for his mother's letter. A decision of great moment was impending. He would know what she had to say before finally making that decision. He wondered bitterly, grimly, whether her words would plunge him yet deeper in this abyss of self-hatred and self-contempt.

"My Darling,"—she wrote,—"I am foolishly glad to learn that you are back at Naples. It gives me comfort to know you are even thus much nearer home and in a country where I too have travelled and of which I retain many dear and delightful recollections. You may be surprised, perhaps, to see the unaccustomed address upon my notepaper and may wonder what has made me guilty of deserting my post. Now, since the worst of it is certainly over, I may tell you that my health has failed a good deal of late. Nothing of a really serious nature— you need not be alarmed about me. But I had got into a rather weak and unworthy state, from which it became very desirable I should rouse myself. Selfishness is insidious, and none the less reprehensible because it takes the apparently innocent form of sitting in a chair with one's eyes shut! However that best of men, John Knott, brought very bracing influences to bear on me, convincing me of sin—in the gentlest way in the world—by means of Honoria St. Quentin. And so I picked myself up, dear Dickie,—picked the whole of myself up, as I hope, always saving and excepting my self-indulgent inertia,—and came away here to Ormiston. At first, I confess, I felt very much like a dog at a fair, or the proverbial mummy at a feast. But they all bore with me in the plenty of their kindness ; and, in the last week, I have banished the mummy and trained the scared dog to altogether polite and pretty behaviour. Till I came back to it, I hardly realised how truly I loved this place. How should it be otherwise? I met your father first here after his third term at Eton. I remember he snubbed me roundly. I met him again the year before our marriage. Without vanity I declare that then he snubbed me not one little bit. These things are very far away. But to me, though far away, they are very vivid and very lovely. I see them as you, when you were small, so often pleaded to see a fairy landscape by looking through the large end of the gold and tortoiseshell spy-glass upon my writing-table. All of which may seem to you somewhat childish and trivial, but I grow an old woman and have a fancy for toys and tender make-believes—such as fairy landscapes seen through the big end of a spy-glass. The actual landscape, at times, is a trifle discouragingly rain-blotted and cloudy!—Roger and Mary are here. Their two boys are just gone back to school again. They are fine, courteous, fearless, little fellows. Roger makes a rather superb middle-aged man. He has much of my father—

your grandfather's reticence and dignity. Indeed, he might prove slightly alarming, was one not so perfectly sure of him, dear creature. Mary remains, as of old, the most wholesome and helpful of women. Yes, it is good to dwell, for a time, among one's own people. And I cannot but rejoice that my eldest brother has come to an arrangement by which, at his death, your uncle William will receive a considerable sum of money in lieu of the property. This last will go direct to Roger, and eventually to his boys. If your uncle William had a son, the whole matter would be different. But I own it would hurt me that in the event of his death there should be no Ormiston at Ormiston after these many generations. In all probability the place would be sold immediately, for it is an open secret that, through no fault of his own, poor man, William is sadly em-barrassed in money matters. And he has other sorrows—of a rather terrible nature, since they are touched with disgrace. But here you will probably detect a point of prejudice, so I had best stop!—I look out upon a grey, northern sea, where 'the white horses fume and fret' under a cold, grey, northern sky. The oaks in the park are just thickening with yellow-green buds. And there, close to my window, perched on a topmost twig, a missel-thrush is singing, facing the wind like a gentleman. You look out upon a purple sea, I suppose, beneath clear skies and over orange trees and palms. I wonder if any brave bird pipes to you as my storm-cock to me? It brings up one's courage to hear his song, so strong and wild and sweet, in the very teeth of the gale too! But now you will have had enough of my news and more than enough. I write to you more freely, you see, than for a long time past, being myself more free of spirit. And therefore I dare add this, in all and every case, my darling, God keep you. And remember, should you weary of wandering, that not only the doors of Brockhurst, but the doors of my heart, stand forever wide open to welcome you home.—Yours always,

K. C."

Reading which gentle, yet in a sense daring, words, Richard's shame took on another complexion, but one by no means calculated to mitigate the burning of it. His treachery towards de Vallorbes became almost vulgar and of small moment beside his cruelty to this superbly magnanimous woman, his mother. For, all these years, determinately and of set purpose, defiant of every better impulse, he had hardened his heart against her. To differ from her, to cherish that which was unsympathetic to her, to put aside every tradition in which she had nurtured him,

to love that which she condemned, to condemn that which she
loved—and this, if silently, still unswervingly—had been the
ruling purpose of his action. That which had its origin in
passionate revolt against his own unhappy disfigurement, had
come to be an interest and object in itself. In this quarrel with
her—a quarrel intimate, pre-natal, anterior to consciousness and
to volition—he found the justification of his every lapse, his
every crookedness of conduct and of thought. Since he could
not reach Almighty God, and strike at the eternal First Cause
which he held responsible for the inalienable wrong done to him,
he would strike, with cold-blooded persistence, at the woman
whom Almighty God had permitted to be His instrument in
the infliction of that wrong. And to where had that sustained
purpose of striking led him? Even—so he judged just now—to
the dishonour and desolation of to-day, following upon the
sacrilegious licence of last night.

All this Richard saw with the alternately groping, benumbed,
mental vision and the glaring, mental nakedness of breeding
fever. Small wonder that looking for comfort, for promise
of restoration, he found none in things material, in things
intellectual, in others, or in himself! He felt outcasted beyond
hope of redemption ; but not repentant, hardly remorseful even,
only aware of all that which had happened, and of his own
state. For Lady Calmady's letter was to him little more, as
yet, than a placing of facts. To trade upon her magnificent
generosity of affection, and seek refuge in those outstretched
arms now, with the mark of the branding-iron so sensibly upon
him, appeared to him of all contemptible doings the most
radically contemptible. Obviously it was impossible to go
back. He must go on rather — out of sight, out of mind.
Fantastic schemes of disappearing, of losing himself, far away
in remote and nameless places, among the coral islands of the
Pacific or the chill majesty of the Antarctic seas, offered
themselves to his imagination. The practical difficulties presented by such schemes, their infeasibility, did not trouble him.
He would sever all connection with that which had been, with
that which had made for good equally with that which had made
for evil. By his own voluntary act and choice he would become
as a man dead, the disgrace of his malformed body, the closer
and more hideous disgrace of his defiled and prostituted soul,
surviving in legend merely, as might some ugly, old-time fable
useful for the frightening of unruly babes.

And to that end of self-obliteration he instantly applied himself, with outward calm, but with the mental hurry and restless-

ness of increasing illness. His first duty was to end the whole matter of his relation to Helen,—Helen shorn of her divinity, convicted liar and wanton, yet mistress still for him, as he feared, of mighty enchantments. So he wrote to her very briefly. The note should be given her later in the day. In it he stated that he should have left the villa before this announcement reached her, left it finally and without remotest prospect of return, since he could not doubt that she recognised, as he did, how impossible it had become that he and she should meet again. He added that he would communicate with her shortly as to business arrangements. That done, he summoned Powell, his valet, bidding him pack. He would go down to the yacht at once. He had received information which made it imperative he should quit Naples immediately.

To be out of all this, rid of it, fairly started on the road of negation of social being, negation of recognised existence, infected him like a madness. But even the most forceful human will must bend to stupidities of detail and of material fact. Unexpected delays had occurred. The yacht was not ready for sea, neither coaled, nor provisioned, nor sound of certain small damages to her machinery. Vanstone, the captain, might mislay his temper, and the first mate expend himself in polysyllabic invective, young Penberthy cease to dream, stewards, engineers, carpenters, cooks, quartermasters, seamen, firemen, do their most willing and urgent best, nevertheless the morning of next day, and even the afternoon of it, still found Richard Calmady seated at the locker-table of the white-walled deck-cabin, his voyage towards self-obliteration not yet begun.

Charts were out-spread before him, upon which, at weary intervals, he essayed to trace the course of his coming wanderings. But his brain was dull, he had no power of consecutive thought. That same madness of going was upon him with undiminished power, yet he knew not where he wanted to go, hardly why he wanted to go, only that a blind obsession of going drove him. He was miserably troubled about other matters too—about that same brief letter he had written to Helen before leaving the villa. He was convinced that he had written such a letter; but struggle as he might to remember the contents of it they remained to him a blank. He was haunted by the fear that in that letter he had committed some irremediable folly, had bound himself to some absurdly unworthy course of action. But what it might be escaped and, in escaping, tortured him. And then, this surely was Friday, and Morabita sang at the San Carlo to-night? And surely he had promised to be there, and to meet the famous *prima donna* and sup with her after the performance, as in former days at Vienna? He had not always been quite kind to her, poor, dear, fat, good-natured, silly soul! He could not fail her now.—And then he went back to a chart of the South Pacific again. Only he could not see it plainly, but saw, instead of it, the great folio of copper-plate engravings lying on the broad window-seat of the eastern bay of the Long Gallery at home. He was sitting there to watch for the racehorses coming back from exercise, Tom Chifney pricking along beside them on his handsome cob. And the long-ago, boyish desperation of longing for wholeness, for freedom, brought a moistness to his eyes, and a lump into his throat. And all the while the coal dust drifted in at each smallest crevice and aperture; and the air was vibrant with rasping, jarring uproar and nauseous with the stale, heavy odours of the city and the port. And steadily, ceaselessly, the descending rain drummed upon the roofing overhead.

At length a stupor took him. His head sank upon his arms, folded upon those outspread charts, while the noise of all the rude activities surrounding him subtly transformed itself into that of a great orchestra. And above this, superior to, yet nobly supported by it, Morabita's voice rose in the suave and passionate phrases of the glorious cavatina—"*Ernani, Ernani, involami, all'abborito ampleso.*"—Yes, her voice was as good as ever! Richard drew a long breath of relief. Here, at least, was something true to itself; and amid so much of change, so much of spoiling, still unspoilt!—He raised his head and listened. For something must have happened, something of serious moment. The orchestra, for some unaccountable reason, had suddenly broken down. Yes, it must be the orchestra which disaster had overtaken, for a voice very certainly continued. No, not a voice, but voices—those of Vanstone the captain, and Price the first mate, and old Billy Jinn the boatswain — loud, imperative, violently remonstrant; but swept under and swamped at moments by cries and volleys of foulest, Neapolitan *argot* from hoarse, Neapolitan throats. And that abruptly silenced orchestra? — Richard came back to himself, came back to actualities of environment and prosaic fact. An infinitely weariful despair seized him. For the sound that had reached so sudden a termination was not that of cunningly-attuned musical instruments, but the long-drawn, chattering rush of the coal, pitched from the baskets down the echoing, iron shoots.

The cabin door opened discreetly and Powell, incarnation of

decorous punctualities even amid existing tumultuously discom-
posing circumstances, entered.

"From the villa, sir," he said, depositing letters and newspapers
upon the table.

Richard put out his hand, turned them over mechanically.
For again, somehow, and notwithstanding the babel without, that
exquisite invitation—"*Ernani, Ernani, involami,*"—assailed his
ears.

The valet waited a little, quiet and deferential in bearing, yet
observing his master with a certain keenness and anxiety.

"I saw Mr. Bates, as you desired, sir," he said at last.

Richard looked up at him vaguely. And it struck him that
while Powell was on shore to-day he had undoubtedly had his
hair cut. This interested him—though why, he would have
found it difficult to say.

"Mr. Bates thought you should be informed that a gentleman
called early yesterday afternoon, as he said by appointment."

Yes—certainly Powell had had his hair cut.—"Did the
gentleman give his name?"

"Yes, sir, M. Paul Destournelle."

Powell spoke slowly, getting his tongue carefully round
the foreign syllables, and, for all the confusion of his hearer's
mind, the name went home. Vagueness passed from Richard's
glance.

"He was refused, of course."

"Her ladyship had given orders that should any person of
that name call he was to be admitted."—Powell spoke with
evident reluctance. "Consequently Mr. Bates was uncertain
how to act, having received contrary orders from you, sir, the
day before yesterday. He explained this to her ladyship, but
she insisted."

Richard's mind had become perfectly lucid.

"Very well," he said coldly.

"Mr. Bates also thought you should know, sir, that after
M. Destournelle's visit her ladyship announced she should not
remain at the villa. She left about five o'clock, taking her maid.
Charles followed with all the baggage."

The valet paused. Richard's manner was decidedly discouraging, yet, something further must at least be intimated.

"Her ladyship gave no address to Mr. Bates for the
forwarding of her letters."

But here the cabin door, left slightly ajar by Powell, was
opened wide, and that with none of the calm and discretion
displayed by the functionary in question. A long perspective of

grimy deck behind him, his oilskins shiny from the wet, with trim black beard, square-made, bold-eyed, hot-tempered, warm-hearted, alert, humorous—typical West Countryman as his gentle dreamy cousin, Penberthy, the second mate, though of a very different type — stood Captain Vanstone. His easily-ruffled temper suffered from the after effects of what is commonly known as a "jolly row," and his speech was curt in consequence thereof.

"Sorry to disturb you, Sir Richard," he said, "and still more sorry to disappoint you, but it can't be helped."

Dickie turned upon him so strangely drawn and haggard a countenance, that Vanstone with difficulty repressed an exclamation. He looked in quick inquiry at the valet, who so far departed from his usual decorum as to nod his head in assent to the silent questioning.

"What's wrong now?" Richard said.

"Why, these beggarly rascals have knocked off. Price offered them a higher scale of pay. I had empowered him to do so. But they won't budge. The rain's washed the heart out of them. We've tried persuasion and we've tried threats—it's no earthly use. Not a basket more coal will they put on board before five to-morrow morning."

"Can't we sail with what we have got?"

"Not enough to carry us to Port Said."

"What will be the extent of the delay this time?" Richard asked. His tone had an edge to it.

Again Captain Vanstone glanced at the valet.

"With luck we may get off to-morrow about midnight."

He stepped back, shook himself like a big dog, scattering the water off his oilskins in a shower upon the slippery deck. Then he came inside the cabin and stood near Richard. His expression was very kindly, tender almost.

"You must excuse me, sir," he said. "I know it doesn't come within my province to give you advice. But you do look pretty ill, Sir Richard. Everyone's remarking that. And you are ill, sir—you know it, and I know it, and Mr. Powell here knows it. You ought to see a doctor, sir—and if you'll pardon plain language, this beastly cess-pit of a harbour is no fit place for you to sleep in."

And poor Dickie, after an instant of sharp annoyance, touched by the man's honest humanity smiled upon him—a smile of utter weariness, utter hopelessness.

"Perfectly true. Get me out to sea then, Vanstone. I shall be better there than anywhere else," he said.

Whereupon the kindly sailor-man turned away swearing gently into his trim, black beard.

But the valet remained, impassive in manner, actively anxious at heart.

"Have you any orders for the carriage, sir?" he asked. "Garçia drove me down. I told him to wait until I had inquired."

Richard was long in replying. His brain was all confused and clouded again, while again he heard the voice of the famous soprano—"*Ernani, Ernani, involami.*"

"Yes," he said at last. "Tell Garçia to be here in good time to drive me to the San Carlo. I have an appointment at the opera to-night."

CHAPTER XI

IN WHICH DICKIE GOES TO THE END OF THE WORLD AND LOOKS OVER THE WALL

THE opera box, which Richard Calmady had rented along with the Villa Vallorbes, was fifth from the stage on the third tier, to the right of the vast horse-shoe. Thus situated, it commanded a very comprehensive view of the interior of the house. The *parterre*—its somewhat comfortless seats rising, as on iron stilts, as they recede, row by row, from the proscenium—was packed. While, since the aristocratic world had not yet left town, the boxes—piled, tier above tier, without break of dress-circle or gallery, right up to the lofty roof—were well filled. And it was the effect of these last that affected Richard oddly, displeasingly, as, helped by Powell and Andrews, the first foot-man—who acted as his table-steward on board the *Reprieve*,—he made his way slowly down to the chair, placed on the left, at the front of the box. For the accepted aspects and relations of things seen were remote to him. He perceived effects, shapes, associations of colour, divorced from their habitual significance. It was as though he looked at the written characters of a language unknown to him, observing the form of them, but attaching no intelligible meaning to that form. And so it happened that those many superimposed tiers of boxes were to him as the waxen cells of a gigantic honeycomb, against the angular darknesses of which little figures, seen to the waist, took the light—the blond face, neck and arms of some woman, the fair colours of her dress—and showed up with perplexing insistence.

For they were all peopled, these cells of the honeycomb, and—
so it seemed to him—with larvæ, bright-hued, unworking, indolent,
full-fed. Down there upon the *parterre*, in the close-packed
ranks of students, of men and women of the middle-class, soberly
attired in walking costume, he recognised the working bees of
this giant hive. By their unremitting labour the dainty waxen
cells were actually built up, and those larvæ were so amply, so
luxuriously, fed. And the working bees—there were so many,
so very many of them! What if they became mutinous, rebelled
against labour, plundered and destroyed the indolent, succulent
larvæ of which he—yes, he, Richard Calmady—was unquestionably and conspicuously one?

He leaned back in his chair, pulled forward the velvet
drapery so as to shut out the view of the house, and fixed his
eyes upon the heads of the musicians in the orchestra. The
overture was nearly over. The curtain would very soon go up.
Then he observed that Powell still stood near him. The man
was strangely officious to-day, he thought. Could that be
connected in any way with the fact he had had his hair cut?
For a moment the notion appeared to Dickie quite extrava-
gantly amusing. But he kept his amusement, as so much else,
to himself. And again the working bees, down in the *parterre*,
attracted his attention. They were buzzing, buzzing angrily, displeased with the full-fed larvæ in the boxes, because these last
were altogether too social, talked too loud and too continuously,
drowning the softer passages of the overture. Those dull-coloured
insects had expended store of hard-earned *lire* upon the queer seats
they occupied, mounted as upon iron stilts. They meant to have
the whole of that which they had paid for, and hear every note.
If they swarmed, now, swarmed upward, clung along the edges of
those many tiers of boxes, punished inconsiderate insolence with
stings?—It would hardly be unjust.—But there was Powell still,
clad in sober garments. He belonged to the working bees.
And Richard became aware of a singular diffidence and
embarrassment in thinking of that. If they should swarm,
those workers, he would rather the valet did not see it, somehow.
He was a good fellow, a faithful servant, a man of nice feeling,
and such an incident would place him in an awkward position.
He ought to be spared that. Carefully Dickie reasoned it all
out.

"You need not stay here any longer, Powell," he said.

"When shall I return, sir?"

The curtain went up. A roll of drums, a chorus of men's
voices, somewhat truculent, in the drinking song.

"At the end of the performance, of course."

But the valet hesitated.

"You might require to send some message, sir."

Richard stared at the chorus. The opera being performed but this once, economy prevailed. Costumiers had ransacked their stock for discovery of garments not unpardonably inappropriate. The result showed a fine superiority to details of time and place. One Spanish bandit, a portly *basso*, figured in a surprising variety of Highland dress designed, and that locally, for a chieftain in the opera of *Lucia di Lammermoor*. His acquaintance with the eccentricities of a kilt being of the slightest, consequences ensued broadly humorous. — Again Dickie experienced great amusement. But that message?— Had he really one to send? Probably he had. He could not remember, and this annoyed him. Possibly he might remember later. He turned to Powell, forgetting his amusement, forgetting the too intimate personal revelations of the unhappy *basso*.

"Yes—well—come back at the end of the second act, then," he said.

If the bees swarmed it would be over by that time, he supposed, so Powell's return would not matter much one way or the other. A persuasion of something momentous about to be accomplished deepened in him. The madness of going, which had so pushed him earlier in the day, fell dead before it. For this concourse of living creatures must be gathered together to witness some event commensurate in importance with the greatness of their number. He felt sure of that. Yes—before long they would swarm. Incontestably they would swarm!—Again he drew aside the velvet drapery and looked down curiously upon the arena and its occupants. For a new idea had come to him regarding these last. They still presented the effect of a throng of busy, angry insects. But Richard knew better. He had penetrated their disguise, a disguise assumed to ensure their ultimate purpose with the greater certainty. He knew them to be human. He knew their purpose to be a moral one. And, looking upon them, recognising the spirit which animated them, he was taken with a reverence and sympathy for average, toiling humanity unfelt by him before. For he saw that by these, the workers, the final issues are inevitably decided, by these the final verdict is pronounced. Individually they may be contemptible; but in their corporate intelligence, corporate strength, they are little short of majestic. Of art, letters, practical civilisation, even religion, even, in a degree, Nature herself, they are alike architects and judges. It must be so. It always has been so, time out of mind, in point of fact. And then he wondered why they were so patient of constraint? Why had they not risen long ago and obliterated the pretensions of those arrogant, indolent larvæ peopling the angular apertures of the honey cells—those larvæ of whom, by birth and wealth, sinfulness and uselessness, he was himself so conspicuous an example?

But then clearer understanding of this whole strange matter came to him.—They, like all else,—mighty though they are in their corporate intention, — are obedient to fate. They can only act when the time is ripe. And then he understood still more clearly. Their purpose in congregating here, whether they were conscious of it or not, was retributive. They were present to witness and to accomplish an act of foreordained justice.— Richard paused a moment, struggling with his own thought. And then he saw quite plainly that he himself was the object of that act of foreordained justice, he himself was the centre of that dimly-apprehended, approaching event. His punishment, his deliverance by means of that punishment, was that which had brought this great multitude together here to-night. He was awed. Yet with that awe came thankfulness, gratitude, an immense sense of relief. He need not seek self-obliteration, losing himself among far-away, tropic islands, or the ice-bound regions of the uttermost South. He could stay here. Sit quite still even—and that was well, for he was horribly tired and spent. He need only wait. When the time was ripe, they would do all the rest—do it for him by doing it to him.—How finely simple it all was! Incidentally he wondered if it would hurt very much. Not that that mattered, for beyond lay peace. Only he hoped they would get to work pretty soon, so that it might be over before the end of the second act, when Powell, the valet, would come back.

Richard's face had grown very youthful and eager. His eyes were unnaturally bright. And still he gazed down at that great company. His heart went out to it. He loved it, loved each and every member of it, as he had never conceived of loving heretofore. He would like to have gone down among them and become part of them, one with them in purpose, a partaker of their corporate strength. But that was forbidden. They were his preordained executioners. Yet in that capacity they were not the less, but the more, loveable. They were welcome to exact full justice. He longed after them, longed after the pain it was their mission to inflict.—And they were getting ready, surely they were getting ready! There was a sensible movement among them. They turned pale faces away from the brilliantly lighted stage, and towards the great horse-shoe of waxen cells enclosing them. They were busy, dull-coloured insects again, and they buzzed—resentfully, angrily, they buzzed.

Yet even while Dickie noted all this, greatly moved by it, appreciating its inner meaning, its profound relation to himself and the drama of his own existence, he was not wholly unmindful of the progress of the opera and the charm of the graceful and fluent music which saluted his ears. He was aware of the entrance of the hero, of his greeting by his motley-clad followers. He felt kindly, just off the surface of his emotion so to speak, towards this impersonator of Ernani. The young actor's appearance was attractive, his voice fresh and sympathetic, his bearing modest. But the aristocratic occupants of the boxes treated him cavalierly. The famous Milanese tenor, whose name was on the programme, having failed to arrive, this local, and comparatively inexperienced, artist had been called upon to fill his part. Therefore the smart world talked more loudly than before, while the democratic occupants of the *parterre*, jealous for the reputation of their fellow-citizen, broke forth into stormy protest. And Richard could have found it in his heart to protest also. For it was a waste of energy, this senseless conflict! It was unworthy of the dignity of that dull-coloured multitude, on whom his hopes were so strangely set—of the men in whose hands are the final rewards and punishments, by whose voice the final judgment is pronounced. It pained him to see these ministers of the Eternal Justice thus led away by trivial happenings, and their attention distracted from the main issue. For what, in God's name, did he and his sentimental love-carollings amount to, this pretty fellow of a player, this fictitious hero of the modern, Neapolitan, operatic stage? Weighed in the balances, he and his whole occupation and calling were lighter, surely, than vanity itself? Rightly considered, he and his singing were but as a spangle, as some glittering trifle of tinsel, upon the veil still hiding the awful, yet benign, countenance of that tremendous and so surely approaching event.—Let him sing away, then, sing in peace. For the sound of his singing might help to lighten the weariness of the hours until the supreme hour should strike, and the glittering veil be torn asunder, and the countenance it covered be at last and wholly revealed.

Reasoning thus, Richard raised his opera glasses and swept those many superimposed ranges of waxen cells. And the aspect of them was to him very sinister, for everywhere he seemed to encounter soft, voluptuous, brainless faces, violences of hot

colour, and costly clothing cunningly devised to heighten the
physical allurements of womanhood. Everywhere, beside and
behind these, he seemed to encounter the faces of men,
gluttonous of pleasure, hungering for those generously-dis-
covered, material charms. They were veritable ante-chambers
of vice, those angular-mouthed, waxen cells. And, therefore, very
fittingly, as he reflected, he had his place in one of them, since
he was infected by the vices, active partaker in the sensuality, of
his class.—Oh! that the bees would swarm—swarm, and make
short work of it all, inflict fulness of punishment, and thereby
cleanse him and set him free! In its intensity his longing
came near taking the form of articulate prayer.

And then his thought shifted once more, attaching itself
curiously, speculatively, to individual objects. For his survey
of the house had just now brought a box into view situated on
the grand tier, and almost immediately opposite his own. It was
occupied by a party of six persons. With four of those persons
Richard was aware he had nothing to do. But with the remaining two persons—a woman fashioned, as it appeared, of ivory and
gold, and a young man standing almost directly behind her—he
had much, everything, in fact, to do. It was incomprehensible
to him that he had not observed these two persons sooner, since
they were as necessary to the accomplishment of that terrible, yet
beneficent, approaching event as he himself was. The woman he
knew actually and intimately; though as yet he could give her no
name, nor recall in what his knowledge of her consisted. The
young man he knew inferentially. And Dickie was sensible of
regarding him with instinctive repulsion, since his appearance
presented a living and grossly ribald caricature of a figure august,
worshipful, and holy. Long and closely Richard studied those
two persons, studied them, forgetful of all else, straining his
memory to place them. And all the while they talked.

But, at last, the woman fashioned of ivory and gold ceased
talking. She folded her arms upon the velvet cushion of the front
of the box and gazed right out into the theatre. There was a
splendid arrogance in the pose of her head, and in the droop of
her eyelids. Then she looked up and across, straight at Richard.
He saw her drooping eye-lids raised, her eyes open wide, and
remain fixed as in amazement. A something alert, and very
fierce, came into her expression. She seemed to think carefully
for a brief space. She threw back her head, and he saw uncontrollable laughter convulse her beautiful throat. And, at that
same moment, a mighty outburst of applause and of welcome
shook the great theatre from floor to ceiling; and, as it died

away, the voice of the famous soprano, rich and compelling as
of old, swelled out, and made vibrant with passionate sweetness
the whole atmosphere.   And Richard hailed that glorious voice,
not that in itself it moved him greatly, but because in it he
recognised the beginning of the end.   It came as prelude to
catastrophe which was also salvation.—Very soon the bees would
swarm now !   He rallied his patience.   He had not much longer
to wait.

Meanwhile he looked back at that box on the grand tier,
striving to unriddle the mystery of his knowledge of those two
persons.   He needed glasses no longer.   His sight had become
preternaturally keen.   Again the two were talking—and about
him, that was somehow evident.   And, as they talked, he beheld
a being, exquisitely formed, perfect in every part, step forth from
between the lips of the woman fashioned of ivory and gold.   It
knelt upon one knee.   Over the heads of the vast, dull-coloured
multitude of workers, those witnesses of and participators in the
execution of Eternal Justice, it gazed at him, Richard Calmady,
and at him alone.   And its gaze enfolded and held him like
an embrace.   It wooed him, extending its arms in invitation.
It was naked and unashamed.   It was black—black as the reeking, liquid lanes between the hulls of the many ships, over which
the screaming gulls circled seeking foul provender, down in
Naples harbour.—And he knew the fair woman it came forth
from for Helen de Vallorbes, herself, in her crocus-yellow gown
sewn with seed pearls.   And he knew it for the immortal soul
of her.   And he perceived, moreover, as it smiled on and
beckoned him with lascivious gestures, that its hands and its
lips were bloody, since it had broken the hearts of living women
and torn and devoured the honour of living men.

"*Ernani, Ernani, involami*"—still the air was vibrant with
that glorious voice.   But the love of which it was the exponent,
the flight which it counselled, had ceased, to Richard's hearing,
to bear relation to that which is earthly, concrete, and of the
senses.   The passion and promise of it were alike turned to
nobler and more permanent uses, presaging the quick coming of
expiation and of reconciliation contained in that supreme event.
For he knew that, in a little moment, Helen must arise and
follow the soul which had gone forth from her—the soul which,
in all its admirable perfection of outward form and blackness of
intimate lies and lust, was close to him—though he no longer
actually beheld it—here, beside him, laying subtle siege to him
even yet.   Where it went, there, of necessity, she who owned it
must shortly follow, since soul and body cannot remain apart,

save for the briefest space, until death effect their final divorce. Therefore Helen would come speedily. It could not be otherwise—so, at least, he argued. And her coming meant the culmination. Then, time being fully ripe, the bees would swarm, swarm at last,—labour revenging itself upon sloth, hunger upon gluttony, want upon wealth, obscurity upon privilege,—justice being thus meted out, and he, Richard, cleansed and delivered from the disgrace of deformity now so hideously infecting both his spirit and his flesh.

Of this he was so well assured that, disregarding the felt, though unseen, presence of that errant soul, disdaining to do battle with it, he leaned forward once more, looking down into the close-packed arena of the great theatre. All those brilliant figures, members of his own class, here present, were matter of indifference to him. In this moment of conscious and supreme farewell, it was to the dull-coloured multitude that he turned. They still moved him to sympathy. Unconsciously they had enlightened him concerning matters of infinite moment. At their hands he would receive penance and absolution. Before they dealt more closely with him,—since that dealing must involve suffering which might temporarily cloud his friendship for them,— he wanted to bid them farewell and assure them of his conviction of the righteousness of their corporate action. So, silently, he blessed them, taking leave of them in peace. Then he found there were other farewells to be said.—Farewell to earthly life as he had known it, the struggle and very frequent anguish of it, its many frustrated purposes, fair illusions, unfulfilled hopes. He must bid farewell, moreover, to art as he had relished it—to learning, as he had all too intermittently pursued it—to travel, as he had found solace in it—to the inexhaustible interest, the inextinguishable humour and pathos, in brief, of things seen. And, reviewing all this, a profound nostalgia of all those minor happinesses which are the natural inheritance of the average man arose in him—happiness of healthy, light-hearted activities, not only of the athlete and the fighting-man, but of the playing-field, and the ball-room, and the river—happinesses to him inevitably denied. With an almost boyish passion of longing, he cried out for these.—Just for one day to have lived with the ease and freedom with which the vast majority of men habitually live! Just for one day to have been neither dwarf nor cripple; but to have taken his place and his chance along with the rest, before it all was over and the tale told!

But very soon Richard put these thoughts from him, deeming it unworthy to dwell upon them at this juncture. The call was

31

to go forward, not to go back. So he settled himself in his chair once more, pulling the velvet drapery forward so as to shut out the sight of the house. Bitterness should have no part in him. When that happened which was appointed to happen, it must find him not only acquiescent but serene and undisturbed. He composed himself, therefore, with a decent and even lofty pride. Then he turned his eyes upon the narrow door, there in the semi-obscurity of the back of the box, and waited. And all the while royally, triumphantly, Morabita sang.

During that period of waiting—whether in itself brief or pro-longed, he knew not—sensation and thought alike were curiously in abeyance. Richard neither slept nor woke. He knew that he existed, but all active relation to being had ceased. And it was with painful effort he in a measure returned to more ordinary correspondence with fact, aroused by the sound of low-toned, emphatic speech close at hand, and by a scratching as of some animal denied and seeking admittance. Then he perceived that the door yielded, letting in a spread of yellow brightness from the corridor. And in the midst of that brightness, part and parcel of it thanks to the lustre of her crocus-yellow dress, her honey-coloured hair, her fair skin and softly-gleaming ornaments, stood Helen de Vallorbes. Behind her, momentarily, Richard caught sight of the young man whose face had impressed him as a ribald travesty of that of some being altogether worshipful and holy. The face peered at him with, as it seemed, malicious curiosity over the rounded shoulder of the woman of ivory and gold. The effect was very hateful, and, with a sense of thank-fulness, Richard saw Helen close the door and come, alone, down the two steps leading from the back of the box. As she passed from the dimness into the clearer light, he watched her, quiescent, yet with absorbing interest. For he perceived that the hands of the clock had been put back somehow. Intervening years and the many events of them had ceased to obtain, so that, of all the many Helens, enchanting or evil, whom he had come to know, he saw now only one, and that the first and earliest—a little dancer, with blush-roses in her hat, dainty as a toy, finished to her rosy finger-tips and the toes of her pretty shoes, merry and merciless, as she had pirouetted round him mocking his shuffling, uncertain progress across the Chapel-Room at Brock-hurst fifteen years ago.

"Ah! so you have come back!" he exclaimed, almost involuntarily.

Madame de Vallorbes pushed a chair from the front of the box into the shadow of the velvet draperies beside Richard.

"It is unnecessary that all Naples should take part in our interview," she said. She sat down, turning to him, leaning a little towards him.

"You do not deserve that I should come back, you know, Dickie," she continued. "You both deserted and deceived me. That is hardly chivalrous, hardly just indeed, after taking all a woman has to give. You led me to suppose you had departed for good and all. Why should you deceive me?"

"The yacht was not ready for sea," Richard said simply.

"Then you might, in common charity, have let me know that. You were bound to give me an opportunity of speaking to you once again, I think."

In his present state of detachment from all worldly concerns absolute truthfulness compelled Richard. The event was so certain, the swarming of the bees so very near, that small diplomacies, small evasions, seemed absurdly out of place.

"I did not want to hear you speak," he said.

"But doesn't it strike you that was rather dastardly in face of what had taken place between us? Do you know that you appear in a new and far from becoming light?"

Denial seemed to Richard futile. He remained silent.

For a moment Helen looked towards the stage. When she spoke again it was as with reluctance.

"I was desperately unhappy. I went all over the villa in the vain hope of finding you. I went back to that room of yours in which we parted. I wanted to see it again."—She paused. Her speech was low-toned, soft as milk.—"It was rather dreadful, Dickie, for the place was all in disarray, littered with signs of your hasty departure, damp, cheerless—the rain beating against the windows. And I hate rain. I found there, not you,—whom I so sorely wanted—but something very much else.—A letter to you from de Vallorbes."—Once more she paused. "I excuse you of anything worse than negligence in omitting to destroy it. Misery knows no law, and I was miserable. I read it."

Richard had listened with the same detachment, yet the same absorbed interest, with which he had watched her entrance. She was a wonderful creature in her adroitness, in her handling of means to serve her own ends! But he could not pay her back in her own coin. The time was too short for anything but simple truth. He felt strangely tired. These reiterated delays became harassing. If the bees would swarm, only swarm! Then it would be over, and he could sleep. He clasped his hands behind his head and looked at Madame de Vallorbes. Her soul kneeled on her lap, its delicate arms were clasped about her neck—black against the lustrous white of her skin and all those twisted ropes of seed pearls. It pressed its breasts against hers, amorously. It loved her and she it. And he understood that in the whole scope of nature there was but it alone, it only, that she ever had loved, or did, or could, love. And, understanding this, he was filled with a great compassion for her. And, answering her, his expression was gentle and pitiful. Still he needs must speak the truth.

"Perhaps it was as well that you should read Luigi's letter," he said.

She turned upon him fiercely and scornfully, yet even as she did so her soul fell to beckoning to him, soliciting him with evilly alluring gestures.

"My congratulations to you," she exclaimed, "upon your praiseworthy candour! I am to gather, then, that you believe that which my husband advises himself to tell you? Under the circumstances it is exceedingly convenient to you to do so no doubt."

"How can I avoid believing it?" Richard asked, quite sweet-temperedly. "Surely we need not waste the little time which remains in argument as to that? You must admit, Helen, that Luigi's letter fits in. It supplies just the piece of the puzzle which was missing. It tallies with all the rest."

"All the rest?"

"Oh yes! It is part of the whole, precisely that part both of you and of Naples which I knew, and tried so hard not to know, from the first. But it is worse than useless to practise such refusals. The Whole, and nothing less than the Whole, is bound to get one in the end. It is contrary to the nature of things that any integral portion of the whole should submit to permanent denial."—Richard's voice deepened. He spoke with a subdued enthusiasm, thinking of the dull-coloured multitude there in the arena and the act of retributive justice on the eve, by them, of accomplishment.—"It seems to me the radical weakness of all human institutions, of all systems of thought, resides in exactly that effort to select and reject, to exalt one part as against another part, and so build not upon the rock of unity and completeness, but upon the sand of partiality and division. And sooner or later the Whole revenges itself, and the fine fanciful fabric crumbles to ruin, just for lack of that which in our short-sighted over-niceness we have taken such mighty great pains to miss out! This has happened times out of number in respect of religions, and philosophies, and the constitution of kingdoms, and in that of fair romances which promised to stand firm to all eternity. And now, now, in these last few days,—since laws which rule the general, also rule the individual life,—it has happened in respect of you, Helen, to my seeing, and in respect of Naples."—Richard smiled upon her sadly and very sweetly. —"I am sorry," he said, "yes, indeed, horribly sorry. It is a bitter thing to see the last of one's gods go overboard. But there is no remedy. Sorry or not, so it is."

Madame de Vallorbes looked at him keenly. Her attitude was strained. Her face sombre with thought.

"My God! my God!" she exclaimed, "that I should sit and listen to all this! And yet you were never more attractive. There is an unnatural force, unnatural beauty about you. You are ill, Richard. You look and you speak as a man might who was about to join hands with death."

But Dickie's attention had wandered again. He pulled the velvet drapery aside somewhat, and gazed down into the crowded house. They lingered strangely in the performance of their mission, that dull-coloured multitude of workers!—Just then came another mighty outburst of applause, cries, *vivas*, the famous soprano's name called aloud. The sound was stimulating, as the shout of a victorious army. Richard hailed it as sign of speedy deliverance, and sank back into his place.

"Oh yes!" he said civilly and lightly, "I fancy I am pretty bad. I am a bit sick of this continued delay, you see. I suppose they know their own business best, but they do seem most infernally slow in getting under weigh. I was ready hours ago. However, they must be nearly through with preliminaries now. And when once we're fairly into it, I shall be all right."

"You mean when the yacht sails?" Madame de Vallorbes asked. Still she looked at him intently. He turned to her smiling, and she observed that his eyes had ceased to be as windows opening back onto empty space. They were luminous with a certain gay content.

"Yes, of course—when the yacht sails, if you like to put it that way," he answered.

"And when will that be?"

The shout of the arena grew louder in the recall. It surged up to the roof and quivered along the lath and plaster partitions of the boxes.

"Very soon now. Immediately, I think, please God," he said.—But why should she make him speak thus foolishly in riddles? Of a surety she must read the signs of the approach of that momentous and beneficent event as clearly as he himself! Was she not equally with himself involved in it? Was she not, like himself, to be cleansed and set free by it? Therefore it came as a painful bewilderment and shock to him when she drew closer to him, leaned forward, laid her hand lightly upon his thigh.

"Richard," she said, very softly, "I forgive all. I am not satisfied with loving. I will come with you. I will stay with you. I will be faithful to you—yes, yes, even that. Your loving is unlike any other. It is unique, as you yourself are unique. I—I want more of it."

"But you must know that it is too late to go back on that now," he said, reasoning with her, greatly perplexed and distressed by her determined ignoring of—to him—self-evident fact. "All that side of things for us is over and done with."

Her lips parted in naughty laughter. And then, not without a shrinking of quick horror, Richard beheld the soul of her—that being of lovely proportions, exquisitely formed in every part, yet black as the foul, liquid lanes between the hulls of the many ships down in Naples harbour—step delicately in between those parted lips, returning whence it came. And, beholding this, instinctively he raised her hand from where it rested upon his thigh, and put it from him, put it upon her glistering, crocus-yellow lap where her soul had so lately kneeled.

"Let us say no more, Helen," he entreated, "lest we both forfeit our remaining chance, and become involved in hopeless and final condemnation."

But Madame de Vallorbes' anger rose to overwhelming height. She slapped her hands together.

"Ah, you despise me!" she cried. "But let me assure you that in any case this assumption of virtue becomes you singularly ill. It really is a little bit too cheap, a work of supererogation in the matter of hypocrisy. Have the courage of your vices. Be honest. You can be so to the point of insult when it serves your purpose. Own that you are capricious, own that you have lighted upon some woman who provokes your appetite more than I do! I have been too tender of you, too lenient with you. I have loved too much and been weakly desirous to please. Own that you are tired of me, that you no longer care for me!"

And he answered, sadly enough:—

"Yes, that last is true. Having seen the Whole, that has happened which I always dreaded might happen. The last of my self-made gods has indeed gone overboard. I care for you no longer."

Helen sprang up from her chair, ran to the door, flung it open. The first act of the opera was concluded. The curtain had come down. The house below and around, the corridor without, were full of confused noise and movement.

"Paul, M. Destournelle, come here," she cried, "and at once!"

But Richard was more than ever tired. The strain of waiting had been too prolonged. Lights, draperies, figures, the crowded arena, the vast honeycomb of boxes, tier above tier, swam before his eyes, blurred, indistinct, vague, shifting, colossal in height, giddy in depth. The bees were swarming, at last, swarming upward through seas of iridescent mist. But he had no longer empire over his own attitude and thoughts. He had hoped to meet the supreme moment in full consciousness, with clear vision and thankfulness of heart. But he was too tired to do so, tired in brain and body alike. And so it happened that a dogged endurance grew on him, simply a setting of the teeth and bracing of himself to suffer silently, even stupidly, all that might be in store. For the bees were close upon him now, countless in number, angry, grudging, violent. But they no longer appeared as insects. They were human, save for their velvet-like, expressionless eyes. And all those eyes were fixed upon him, and him alone. He was the centre towards which, in thought and action, all turned. Nor were the dull-coloured occupants of the *parterre* alone in their attack. For those gay-coloured larvæ—the men and women of his own class—indolent, licentious, full-fed, hung out of the angular mouths of the waxen cells, above the crimson and gold of the cushions, pointing at him, claiming and yet denouncing him. And in the attitude of these—the democratic and the aristocratic sections—he detected a difference. The former swarmed to inflict punishment for his selfishness, uselessness, sensuality. But the latter jeered and mocked at his bodily infirmity, deriding his deformity, making merry over his shortened limbs and shuffling walk. And against this background, against this all-enclosing tapestry of faces which encircled him, two persons, and the atmosphere and aroma of them, so to speak, were clearly defined. They were close to him, here within the narrow limits of the opera box. Then a great humiliation overtook Richard, perceiving that they, and not the people, the workers, august in their corporate power and strength, were to be his executioners. No—no—he wasn't worth that! And, for all his present dulness of sensation, a sob rose in his throat. Madame de Vallorbes, resplendent in crocus-yellow brocade, costly lace, and seed pearls, the young man, her companion—the young man of the light, forked beard, domed skull, vain eyes and peevish mouth—the young man of holy and dissolute aspect—

were good enough instruments for the Eternal Justice to employ in respect of him, Richard Calmady.

"Look, M. Destournelle," Helen said very quietly, "this is my cousin of whom I have already spoken to you. But I wished to spare him if possible, and give him room for self-justification, so I did not tell you all. Richard, this is my friend, M. Destournelle, to whom my honour and happiness are not wholly indifferent."

Dickie looked up. He did not speak. Vaguely he prayed it might all soon be over. Paul Destournelle looked down. He raised his eye-glass and bowed himself, examining Richard's mutilated legs and strangely-shod feet. He broke into a little, bleating, goat-like laugh.

"*Mais c'est etonnant!*" he observed reflectively.

"I was in his house," Helen continued. "I was there unprotected, having absolute faith in his loyalty."—She paused a moment. "He seduced me. Richard, can you deny that?"

"*Canaille!*" M. Destournelle murmured. He drew a pair of gloves through his hands, holding them by the finger-tips. The metal buttons of them were large, three on each wrist. Those gloves arrested Richard's attention oddly.

"I do not deny it," Dickie said.

"And having thus outraged, he deserted me. Do you deny that?"

"No," Dickie said again. For it was true, that which she asserted, true, though penetrated by subtle falsehood impossible, as it seemed to him, to combat.—"No, I do not deny it."

"You hear!" Helen exclaimed. "Now do what you think fit."

Still Destournelle drew the gloves through his hands, holding them by the finger-tips.

"Under other circumstances I might feel myself compelled to do you the honour of sending you a challenge, *monsieur*," he said. "But a man of sensibility like myself cannot do such violence to his moral and artistic code as to fight with an outcast of nature, an abortion, such as yourself. The sword and the pistol I necessarily reserve for my equals. The deformed person, the cripple, whose very existence is an offence to the eye and to every delicacy of sense, must be condescended to, and, if chastised at all, must be chastised without ceremony, chastised as one would chastise a dog."

And with that he struck Richard again and again across the face with those metal-buttoned gloves.

Mad with rage, blinded and sick with pain, Dickie essayed to fling himself upon his assailant. But Destournelle was too adroit for him. He skipped aside, with his little, bleating, goat-like laugh; and Richard fell heavily, full length, his forehead coming in contact with the lower step of the descent from the back of the box. He lay there, too weak to raise himself.

Paul Destournelle bent down and again examined him curiously.

" *C'est etonnant!* " he repeated.—He gave the prostrate body a contemptuous kick. "Dear madame, are you sufficiently avenged? Is it enough?" he inquired sneeringly.

And vaguely, as from some incalculable distance, Richard heard Helen de Vallorbes' voice:—"Yes—it is a little affair of honour which dates from my childhood. It has taken many years in adjusting. I thank you, *mon cher*, a thousand times. Now let us go quickly. It is enough."

Then came darkness, silence, rest.

BOOK VI

THE NEW HEAVEN AND THE NEW EARTH

CHAPTER I

IN WHICH MISS ST. QUENTIN BEARS WITNESS TO THE FAITH
THAT IS IN HER

HONORIA divested herself of her travelling-cap, thrust her
hands into the pockets of her frieze ulster, and thus,
bare-headed, a tall, supple, solitary figure, paced the railway
platform in the dusk. Above the gentle undulations of the
western horizon splendours of rose-crimson sunset were out-
spread, veiled, as they flamed upward, by indigo cloud of the
texture and tenuity of finest gauze. And those same rose-
crimson splendours found repetition upon the narrow, polished
surface of the many lines of rails, causing them to stand out, as
though of red-hot metal, from the undeterminate grey-drab of the
track where it curved away, south-eastward, across the darkening
country towards the Savoy Alps. And from out the fastnesses
of these last, quick with the bleak purity of snow, came a breathing of evening wind. To Honoria it brought refreshing emphasis
of silence, and of immunity from things human and things
mechanical. It spoke to her of virgin and unvisited spaces,
ignorant of mankind and of obligation to his so many and so
insistent needs. And there being in Honoria herself a kindred
defiance of subjection, a determination, so to speak, of physical
and emotional chastity, she welcomed these intimations of the
essential inviolability of nature, finding in them justification and
support of her own mental attitude—of the entire wisdom of
which she had, it must be owned, grown slightly suspicious of
late.

And this was the more grateful to her, not only as contrast to the noise and dust of a lengthy and hurriedly-undertaken journey; but because that same journey had been suddenly, and, in a sense violently, imposed upon one whom she held in highest regard, by another whom she had long since agreed with herself to hold in no sort of regard at all. Since the highly-regarded one set forth, she—Honoria—of course, set forth likewise. And yet, in good truth, the whole affair rubbed her not a little the wrong way! She recognised in it a particularly flagrant example of masculine aggression. Some persons, as she reflected, are permitted an amount of elbow-room altogether disproportionate to their deserts. Be sufficiently selfish, sufficiently odious, and everybody becomes your humble servant, hat in hand! That is unfair. It is, indeed, quite extensively exasperating to the dispassionate onlooker. And, in Miss St. Quentin's case, exasperation was by no means lessened by the fact that candour compelled her to admit doubt not only as to the actuality of her own dispassionateness, but, as has already been stated, as to the wisdom of her mental attitude generally. She wanted to think and feel one way. She was more than half afraid she was much disposed to think and feel quite another way. This was worrying. And, therefore, it came about that Honoria hailed the present interval of silence and solitude, striving to put from her remembrance both the origin and object of her journey, while filling her lungs with the snow-fed purity of the mountain wind and yielding her spirit to the somewhat serious influences of surrounding nature. All too soon the great Paris-express would thunder into the station. The heavy, horse-box-like sleeping-car—now standing on the Culoz-Geneva-Bâle siding—would be coupled to the rear of it. Then the roar and rush would begin again—from dark to dawn, and on through the long, bright hours to dark once more, by mountain gorge, and stifling tunnel, and broken woodland, and smiling coast-line, and fertile plain, past Chambéry, and Turin, and Bologna, and mighty Rome herself, until the journey was ended and distant Naples reached at last.

But Miss St. Quentin's communings with nature were destined to speedy interruption. Ludovic Quayle's elongated person, clothed to the heels in a check travelling-coat, detached itself from the company of waiting passengers, and blue-linen-clad porters, upon the central platform before the main block of station buildings, and made its light and active way across the intervening lines of crimson-stained metals.

"If I am a nuisance mention that chastening fact without hesitation," he said, standing on the railway track and looking

up at her with his air of very urbane intelligence. "Present
circumstances permit us the privilege—or otherwise—of laying
aside restraints of speech, along with other small proprieties of
behaviour commonly observed by the polite. So don't spare
my feelings, dear Miss St. Quentin. If I am a bore, tell me so ;
and I will return, and that without any lurking venom in my
breast, whence I came."

"Do anything you please," Honoria replied, "except be run
over by the Paris train."

"The Paris train, so I have just learned, is an hour late,
consequently its arrival hardly enters into the question. But,
since you are graciously pleased to bid me do as I like, I stay,"
Mr. Quayle returned, stepping on to the platform and turning to
pace beside her.—"What a gaol delivery it is to get into the
open ! That last engine of ours threw ashes to a truly penitential
extent. My mouth and throat still claim unpleasantly close
relation to a neglected, kitchen grate. And if our much vaunted
wagon-lits is the last word of civilisation in connection with
travel, then all I can say is that, in my humble opinion, civilisation has yet a most exceedingly long way to go. It really is a
miraculously uncomfortable vehicle. And how Lady Calmady
contrives to endure its eccentricities of climate and of motion,
I'm sure I don't know."

"In her case the end would make any sort of means support-
able," Honoria answered.

Her pacings had brought her to the extreme end of the
platform where it sloped to the level of the track. She stood
there a moment, her head thrown back, snuffing the wind
as a hind, breaking covert, stands and snuffs it. A spirit of
questioning possessed her, though not—as in the hind's case—
of things concrete and material. It is true she could have dis-
pensed with Mr. Quayle's society. She did not want him. But
he had shown himself so full of resource, so considerate and
helpful, ever since the news of Sir Richard Calmady's desperate
state had broken up the peace of the little party at Ormiston
Castle, now five days ago, that she forgave him even his precious-
ness of speech, even his slightly irritating superiority of manner.
She had ceased to be on her guard with him during these days
of travel, had come to take his presence for granted and to
treat him with the comfortable indifference of honest good-
fellowship. So, it happened that now, speaking with him, she
continued to follow out her existing train of thought.

"I'm by no means off my head about poor Dickie Calmady,"
she said presently,—"specially where Cousin Katherine is con-

cerned. I couldn't go on caring about anybody, irrespective of their conduct, just because they were they. And yet I can't help seeing it must be tremendously satisfying to feel like that."

"A thousand pardons," Ludovic murmured, "but like what?"

"Why as Cousin Katherine feels—just whole-heartedly, without analysis, and without alloy—to feel that no distance, no fatigue, no nothing in short, matters, so long as she gets to him in time. I don't approve of such a state of mind, and yet"— Honoria wheeled round, facing the glory of colour dyeing all the west—"and yet, I'm untrue enough to my own principles rather to envy it."

She sighed, and that sigh her companion noted and filed for reference. Indeed, an unusually expansive cheerfulness became perceptible in Mr. Quayle.

"By-the-bye, is there any further news?" she inquired.

"General Ormiston has just had a telegram."

"Anything fresh?"

"Still unconscious, strength fairly maintained."

"Oh! we know that by heart!" Honoria said.

"We do. And we know the consequences of it—the sweet little see-saw of hope and fear, productive of unlimited discussion and anxiety. No weak letting one stand at ease about that telegram! It keeps one's nose hard down on the grindstone."

"If he dies," Honoria said slowly, "if he dies—poor, dear Cousin Katherine!—When can we hear again?"

"At Turin," Mr. Quayle replied.

Then they both fell silent until the far end of the platform was reached. And there, once more, Honoria paused, her small head carried high, her serious eyes fixed upon the sunset. The rosy light falling upon her failed to disguise the paleness of her face or its slight angularity of line. She was a little worn and travel-stained, a little dishevelled even. Yet to her companion she had rarely appeared more charming. She might be tired, she might even be somewhat untidy; but her innate distinction remained—nay, gained, so he judged, by suggestion of rough usage endured. Her absolute absence of affectation, her unself-consciousness, her indifference to adventitious prettinesses of toilet, her transparent sincerity, were very entirely approved by Ludovic Quayle.

"Yes, that see-saw of hope and fear must be an awful ordeal, feeling as she does," Miss St. Quentin said presently. "And yet, even so, I am uncertain. I can't help wondering which really is best!"

" Again a thousand pardons," the young man put in, "but I venture to remind you that I was not cradled in the fore-court of the temple of the Pythian Apollo, but only in the nursery of a conspicuously philistine, English country-house."

For the first time during their conversation Honoria looked full at him. Her glance was very friendly, yet it remained meditative, even a trifle sad.

"Oh! I know, I'm fearfully inconsequent," she said. "But my head is simply rattled to pieces by that beastly *wagon-lits*. I had gone back to what I was thinking about before you joined me, and to what we were saying just now about Cousin Katherine."

"Yes—yes, exactly," Ludovic put in tentatively. She was going to give herself away—he was sure of it. And such giving away might make for opportunity. In spirit, the young man proceeded to take his shoes from off his feet. The ground on which he stood might prove to be holy. Moreover Miss St. Quentin's direct acts of self-revelation were few and far between. He was horribly afraid those same shoes of his might creak, so to speak, thereby startling her into watchfulness, making her draw back. But Honoria did not draw back. She was too much absorbed by her own thought. She continued to contemplate the glory of the flaming west, her expression touched by a grave and noble exaltation.

"I suppose one can't help worrying a little at times—it's laid hold of me very much during the last month or two—as to what is really the finest way to take life. One wants to arrive at that fairly early; not by a process of involuntary elimination, on the burnt-child-fears-the-fire sort of principle, when the show's more than half over, as so many people do. One wants to get hold of the stick by the right end now, while one's still comparatively young, and then work straight along. I want my reason to be the backbone of my action, don't you know, instead of merely the push of society and friendship, and superficial odds and ends of so-called obligation to other people."

"Yes," Mr Quayle put in again.

"Now, it seems to me, that"—Honoria extended one hand towards the sunset—"is Cousin Katherine's outlook on life and humanity, full of colour, full of warmth. It burns with a certain prodigality of beauty, a superb absence of economy in giving. And that"—with a little shrug of her shoulders she turned towards the severe, and sombre, eastern landscape—"that, it strikes me, comes a good deal nearer my own. Which is best?"

Mr. Quayle congratulated himself upon the removal of his

shoes. The ground was holy—holy to the point of embarrassment even to so unabashable and ready-tongued a gentleman
as himself. He answered with an unusual degree of diffidence.

" An intermediate position is neither wholly inconceivable nor
wholly untenable, perhaps."

" And you occupy it? Yes, you are very neatly balanced.
But then, do you really get anywhere?"

" Is not that a rather knavish speech, dear Miss St. Quentin?"
the young man inquired mildly.

" I don't know," she answered, " I wish to goodness I did."

Now was here god-given opportunity, or merely a cunningly
devised snare for the taking of the unwary? Ludovic pondered
the matter. He gently kicked a little pebble from the dingy grey-
drab of the asphalt on to the permanent way. It struck one of
the metals with a sharp click. A blue-linen-clad porter, short of
stature and heavy of build, lighted the gas lamps along the
platform. The flame of these wavered at first, and flickered,
showing thin and will-o'-the-wisp-like against the great outspread of
darkening country across which the wind came with a certain
effect of harshness and barrenness—the inevitable concomitant
of its inherent purity. And the said wind treated Miss St.
Quentin somewhat discourteously, buffeting her, obliging her to
put up both hands to push back stray locks of hair. Also the
keen breath of it pierced her, making her shiver a little. Both
of which things her companion noting took heart of grace.

" Is it permitted to renew a certain petition?" he asked, in a
low voice.

Honoria shook her head.

" Better not, I think," she said.

" And yet, dear Miss St. Quentin, pulverised though I am by
the weight of my own unworthiness, I protest that petition is not
wholly foreign to the question you did me the honour to ask me
just now."

" Oh! dear me! You always contrive to bring it round to
that!" she exclaimed, not without a hint of petulance.

" Far from it," the young man returned. " For a good, solid,
eighteen months, now, I have displayed the accumulated patience
of innumerable asses."

" Of course, I see what you're driving at," she continued
hastily. " But it is not original. It's just every man's stock
argument."

" If it bears the hall-mark of hoary antiquity, so much the
better. I entertain a reverence for precedent. And honestly, as
common sense goes, I am not ashamed of that of my sex."

Miss St. Quentin resumed her walk.

"You really think it stands in one's way," she said reflectively, "you really think it a disadvantage, to be a woman ? "

"Oh! good Lord !" Mr Quayle ejaculated, softly yet with an air so humorously aghast that it could leave no doubt as to the nature of his sentiments. Then he cursed himself for a fool. His shoes indeed had made a mighty creaking ! He expected an explosion of scornful wrath. He admitted he deserved it. It did not come.

Miss St. Quentin looked at him, for a moment, almost piteously. He fancied her mouth quivered and that her eyes filled with tears. Then she turned and swung away with her long, easy, even stride. Mentally the young man took himself by the throat, conscience-stricken at having humiliated her, at having caused her to fall, even momentarily, from the height of her serene, maidenly dignity. For once he became absolutely uncritical, careless of appearances. He fairly ran after her along the platform.

"Dear Miss St. Quentin," he called to her, in tones of most persuasive apology.

But Honoria's moment of piteousness was past. She had recovered all her habitual lazy and gallant grace when he came up with her.

"No—no," she said. "Hear me. I began this rather foolish conversation. I laid myself open to—well to a snubbing. I got one, anyhow !"

"In mercy don't rub it in !" Mr. Quayle murmured contritely.

"But I did," Honoria returned. "Now it's over and I'm going to pick up the pieces and put them back in their places—just where they were before."

"But I protest !—I hailed a new combination. I discover in myself no wild anxiety to have the pieces put back just where they were before."

"Oh yes, you do !" Honoria declared. "At least, you certainly will when I explain it to you."—She paused.—"You see," she said, "it is like this. Living with and watching Cousin Katherine, I have come to know all that side of things at its very finest."

"Forgive me.—It ? What ? May I recall to you the fact of the philistine nursery ? "

The young lady's delicate face straightened.

"You know perfectly well what I mean," she said.—"That which we all think about so constantly, and yet affect to speak of as a joke or a slight impropriety—love, marriage, mother-hood."

"Yes, Lady Calmady is a past-master in those arts," Mr. Quayle replied.—Again the ground was holy. He was conscious his pulse quickened.

"The beauty of it all, as one sees it in her case, breaks one up a little. There is no laugh left in one about those things. One sees that to her they are of the nature of religion—a religion pure and undefiled, a new way of knowing God and of bringing oneself into line with the truth as it is in Him. But, having once seen that, one can decline upon no lower level. One grows ambitious. One will have it that way or not at all."

Honoria paused again. The bleak wind buffeted her. But she was no longer troubled or chilled by it, rather did it brace her to greater fearlessness of resolve and of speech.

"You are contemptuous of women," she said.

"I have betrayed characteristics of the ass, other than its patience," Ludovic lamented.

"Oh! I didn't mean that," Honoria returned, smiling in friendliest fashion upon him. "Every man worth the name really feels as you do, I imagine. I don't blame you. Possibly I am growing a trifle shaky as to feminine superiority, and woman spelled with a capital letter, myself. I'm awfully afraid she is safest—for herself and others—under slight restraint, in a state of mild subjection. She's not quite to be trusted, either in-tellectually or emotionally—at least, the majority of her isn't. If she got her head, I've a dreadful suspicion she would make a worse hash of creation generally than you men have made of it already, and that"—Honoria's eyes narrowed, her upper lip shortened, and her smile shone out again delightfully—"that's saying a very great deal, you know."

"My spirits rise to giddy heights," Mr. Quayle exclaimed. "I endorse those sentiments. But whence, oh, dear lady, this change of front?"

"Wait a minute. We've not got to the end of my con-tention yet."

"The Paris train is late. There is time. And this is all excellent hearing."

"I'm not quite so sure of that," Honoria said. "For, you see, just in proportion as I give up the fiction of her superiority, and admit that woman already has her political, domestic, and social deserts, I feel a chivalry towards her, poor, dear thing, which I never felt before. I even feel a chivalry towards the woman in myself. She claims my pity and my care in a quite new way."

32

"So much the better," Mr. Quayle observed, outwardly discreetly urbane, inwardly almost riotously jubilant.

"Ah! wait a minute," she repeated. Her tone changed, sobered. "I don't want to spread myself, but you know I can meet men pretty well on their own ground. I could shoot and fish as well as most of you, only that I don't think it right to take life except to provide food, or in self-defence. There's not so much happiness going that one's justified in cutting any of it short. Even a jack-snipe may have his little affairs of the heart, and a cock-salmon his gamble. But I can ride as straight as you can. I can break any horse to harness you choose to put me behind. I can sail a boat and handle an axe. I can turn my hand to most practical things—except a needle. I own I always have hated a needle worse—well, worse than the devil! And I can organise, and can speak fairly well, and manage business affairs tidily. And have I not even been known—low be it spoken—to beat you at lawn tennis, and Lord Shotover at billiards?"

"And to overthrow my most Socratic father in argument. And outwit my sister Louisa in diplomacy—*vide* our poor, dear Dickie Calmady's broken engagement, and the excellent, scatterbrain Decies' marriage."

"But Lady Constance is happy?" Honoria put in hastily.

"Blissful, positively blissful, and with twins too! Think of it!—Decies is blissful also. His sense of humour has deteriorated since his marriage, from constant association with good, little Connie who was never distinguished for ready perception of a joke. He regards those small, simultaneous replicas of himself with unqualified complacency, which shows his appreciation of comedy must be a bit blunted."

"I wonder if it does?" Miss St. Quentin observed reflectively. Whereat Mr. Quayle permitted himself a sound as nearly approaching a chuckle as was possible to so superior a person.

"A thousand pardons," he murmured, "but really, dear lady, you are so very much off on the other tack."

"Am I?" Miss St. Quentin said. "Well, you see—to go back to my demonstration—I've none of the quarrel with your side of things most women have, because I'm not shut out from it, and so I don't envy you. I can amuse and interest myself on your lines. And therefore I can afford to be very considerate and tender of the woman in me. I grow more and more resolved that she shall have the very finest going, or that she shall have nothing, in respect of all which belongs to her special province—in regard to love and marriage. In them she shall have what

Cousin Katherine has had, and find what Cousin Katherine has found, or all that shall be a shut book to her forever. Even if discipline and denial make her a little unhappy, poor thing, that's far better than letting her decline upon the second best."

Honoria's voice was full and sweet. She spoke from out the deep places of her thought. Her whole aspect was instinct with a calm and reasoned enthusiasm. And, looking upon her, it became Ludovic Quayle's turn to find the evening wind somewhat bleak and barren. It struck chill, and he turned away and moved westwards towards the sunset. But the rose-crimson splendours had become faint and frail; while the indigo cloud had gathered into long, horizontal lines as of dusky smoke, so that the remaining brightness was seen as through prison bars. A sadness, indeed, seemed to hold the west, even greater than that which held the east, since it was a sadness not of beauty unborn, but of beauty dead. And this struck home to the young man. He did not care to speak. Miss St. Quentin walked beside him in silence, for a time. When at last she spoke it was very gently.

"Please don't be angry with me," she pleaded. "I like you so much that—that I'd give a great deal to be able to think less of my duty to the tiresome woman in me."

"I would give a great deal too," he declared, regardless of grammar.

"But I'm not the only woman in the world, dear Mr. Quayle," she protested presently.

"But I, unfortunately, have no use for any other," he returned.

"Ah, you distress me!" Honoria cried.

"Well, I don't know that you make me superabundantly cheerful."

Just then the far-away shriek of a locomotive and dull thunder of an approaching train. Mr. Quayle looked once more towards the western horizon.

"Here's the Paris-express!" he said. "We must be off if we mean to get round before our horse-box is shunted."

He jumped down on to the permanent way. Miss St. Quentin followed him, and the two ran helter-skelter across the many lines of metals, in the direction of the Culoz-Geneva-Bâle siding. That somewhat childish and undignified proceeding ministered to the restoration of good-fellowship.

"Great passions are rare," Mr. Quayle said, laughing a little. His circulation was agreeably quickened. How surprisingly fast this nymph-like creature could get over the ground, and that gracefully, moreover, rather in the style of a lissome, long-limbed youth than in that of a woman !

"Rare? I know it," she answered, the words coming short and sharply. "But I accept the risk. A thousand to one the book remains shut forever."

"And I, meanwhile, am not too proud to pass the time of day with the second best, and take refuge in the accumulated patience of innumerable asses."

And, behind them, the express train thundered into the station.

CHAPTER II

TELLING HOW, ONCE AGAIN, KATHERINE CALMADY LOOKED ON HER SON

THE bulletin received at Turin was sufficiently disquieting. Richard had had a relapse. And when at Bologna, just as the train was starting, General Ormiston entered the compartment occupied by the two ladies, there was that in his manner which made Miss St. Quentin lay aside the magazine she was reading and, rising silently from her place opposite Lady Calmady, go out on to the narrow passage-way of the long sleeping-car. She was very close to the elder woman in the bonds of a dear and intimate friendship, yet hardly close enough, so she judged, to intrude her presence if evil-tidings were to be told. A man going into battle might look, so she thought, as Roger Ormiston looked now—very stern and strained. It was more fitting to leave the brother and sister alone together for a little space.

At the far end of the passage-way the servants were grouped —Clara, comely of face and of person, neat notwithstanding the demoralisation of feminine attire incident to prolonged travel. Winter, the Brockhurst butler, clean-shaven, grey-headed, suggestive of a distinguished Anglican ecclesiastic in mufti. Miss St. Quentin's lady's-maid, Faulstich by name, a North-Country woman, angular of person and of bearing, loyal of heart. Zimmermann, the colossal German-Swiss courier, with his square, yellow beard and hair *en brosse*.—An air of discouragement pervaded the party, involving even the polyglot conductor of the *wagon-lits*, a small, quick, sandy-complexioned, young fellow of uncertain nationality, with a gold band round his peaked cap. He respected this family which could afford to take a private railway-carriage half across Europe. He shared their anxieties. And these were evidently great. Clara wept. The old butler's mouth twitched, and his slightly pendulous cheeks quivered. The door at the extreme end of the car was set wide open. Ludovic Quayle stood upon the little, iron balcony smoking. His feet were planted far apart, yet his tall figure swayed and curtseyed queerly as the heavy carriage bumped and rattled across the points. High walls, overtopped by the dark spires of cypresses, overhung by radiant wealth of lilac wistaria, and of roses, red, yellow, and white, reeled away in the keen sunshine to left and right. Then, clearing the outskirts of the town, the train roared southward across the fair, Italian landscape beneath the pellucid, blue vault of the fair, Italian sky. And to Honoria there was something of heartlessness in all that fair outward prospect. Here, in Italy, the ancient gods reigned still surely, the gods who are careless of human woe.

"Is there bad news, Winter?" she asked.

"Mr. Bates telegraphs to the General that it would be well her ladyship should be prepared for the worst."

"It'll kill my lady. For certain sure it will kill her! She never could be expected to stand up against that. And just as she was getting round from her own illness so nicely too "—

Audibly Clara wept. Her tears so affected the sandy-complexioned, polyglot conductor that he retired into his little pantry and made a most unholy clattering among the plates and knives and forks. Honoria put her hand upon the sobbing woman's shoulder and drew her into the comparative privacy of the adjoining compartment, rendered not a little inaccessible by a multiplicity of rugs, travelling-bags, and hand-luggage.

"Come, sit down, Clara," she said. "Have your cry out. And then pull yourself together. Remember Lady Calmady will want just all you can do for her if Sir Richard—if "—and Honoria was aware somehow of a sharp catch in her throat—"if he does not live."

And, meanwhile, Roger Ormiston, now in sober and dignified middle-age, found himself called upon to repeat that rather sinister experience of his hot and rackety youth, and, as he put it bitterly, "act hangman to his own sister." For, as he approached her, Katherine, leaning back against the piled-up cushions in the corner of the railway carriage, suddenly sat bolt-upright, stretching out her hands in swift fear and entreaty, as in the state-bedroom at Brockhurst nine-and-twenty years ago.

"Oh, Roger, Roger!" she cried, "tell me, what is it?"

"Nothing final as yet, thank God," he answered. "But it

would be cruel to keep the truth from you, Kitty, and let you buoy yourself up with false hopes."

"He is worse," Katherine said.

"Yes, he is worse. He is a good deal weaker. I'm afraid the state of affairs has become very grave. Evidently they are apprehensive as to what turn the fever may take in the course of the next twelve hours."

Katherine bowed herself together as though smitten by sharp pain. Then she looked at him hurriedly, fresh alarms assaulting her.

"You are not trying to soften the blow to me? You are not keeping anything back?"

"No, no, no, my dear Kitty. There—see—read it for yourself. I telegraphed twice, so as to have the latest news. Here's the last reply."

Ormiston unfolded the blue paper, crossed by white strips of printed matter, and laid it upon her lap. And as he did so it struck him, aggravating his sense of sinister repetition, that she had on the same rings and bracelets as on that former occasion, and that she wore stone-grey silk too—a long travelling sacque, lined and bordered with soft fur. It rustled as she moved. A coif of black lace covered her upturned hair, framed her sweet face, and was tied soberly under her chin. And, looking upon her, Ormiston yearned in spirit over this beautiful woman who had borne such grievous sorrows, and who, as he feared, had sorrow yet more grievous still to bear.—"For ten to one the boy won't pull through—he won't pull through," he said to himself. "Poor, dear fellow, he's nothing left to fall back upon. He's lived too hard." And then he took himself remorsefully to task, asking himself whether, among the pleasures and ambitions and successes of his own career, he had been quite faithful to the dead, and quite watchful enough over the now dying, Richard Calmady? He reproached himself, for, when Death stands at the gate, conscience grows very sensitive regarding any lapses, real or imagined, of duty towards those for whom that dread ambassador waits.

Twice Katherine read the telegram, weighing each word of it. Then she gave the blue paper back to her brother.

"I will ask you all to let me be alone for a little while, dear Roger," she said. "Tell Honoria, tell Ludovic, tell my good Clara. I must turn my face to the wall for a time, so that, when I turn it upon you dear people again, it may not be too unlovely."

And Ormiston bent his head and kissed her hand, and

went out, closing the door behind him; while the train roared southward, through the afternoon sunshine, southward towards Chiusi and Rome.

And Katherine Calmady sat quietly amid the noise and violent, on-rushing movement, squaring accounts with her own motherhood. That she might never see Dickie again, she herself dying, was an idea which had grown not unfamiliar to her during these last sad years. But that she should survive, only to see Dickie dead, was a new idea, and one which joined hands with despair, since it constituted a conclusion big with the anguish of failure to the tragedy of their relation, hers and his. Her whole sense of justice, of fitness, rebelled under it, rebelled against it. She implored a space, however brief, of reconciliation and reunion before the supreme farewell was said. But it had become natural to Katherine's mind, so unsparingly self-trained in humble obedience to the divine ordering, not to stay in the destructive, but pass on to the constructive stage. She would not indulge herself with rebellion, but rather fashion her thought without delay to that which should make for inward peace. And so now, turning her eyes, in thought, from the present, she went back on the baby-love, the child-love which, notwithstanding the abiding smart of Richard's deformity, had been so very exquisite to her. Upon the happier side of all that she had not dared to dwell during this prolonged period of estrangement. It was too poignant, too deep-seated in the springs of her physical being. To dwell on it enervated and unnerved her. But now, Richard the grown man dying, she gave herself back to Richard the little child. It solaced her to do so. Then he had been wholly hers. And he was wholly hers still, in respect of that early time. The man she had lost, so it seemed, how far through fault of her own she could not tell. And just now she refused to analyse all that. Upon all which strengthened endurance, upon gracious memories engendering thankfulness, could her mind alone profitably be fixed. And so, as the train roared southward, and the sun declined and the swift dusk spread its mantle over the face of the classic landscape, Katherine cradled a phantom baby on her knee, and sat in the oriel-window of the Chapel-Room, at Brockhurst, with the phantom of her boy beside her, while she told him old-time legends of war, and of high endeavour, and of gallant adventure, watching the light dance in his eyes as her words awoke in him emulation of those masters of noble deeds whose exploits she recounted. And in this she found comfort, and a chastened calm. So that, when at length General Ormiston—

incited thereto by the faithful Clara, who protested that her ladyship must and should dine—returned to her, he found her storm-tossed no longer, but tranquil in expression and solicitous for the comfort of others. She had conquered nature by grace,—conquered, in that she had compelled herself to unqualified submission. If this cup might not pass from her, still would she praise Almighty God and bless His Holy Name, asking not that her own, but His will, be done.

It followed that the evening, spent in that strangely noisy, oscillating, onward-rushing dwelling-place of a railway-carriage, was not without a certain subdued brightness of intercourse and conversation. Katherine was neither preoccupied nor distrait, nor unamused even by the small accidents and absurdities of travel. Later, while preparations were being made by the servants for the coming night, she went out, with the two gentlemen and Honoria St. Quentin, on to the iron platform at the rear of the swaying car, and stood there under the stars. The mystery of these last, and of the dimly discerned and sleeping land, offered penetrating contrast to the sleeplessness of the hurrying train with its long, sinuous line of lighted windows, and to the sleeplessness of her own heart. The fret of human life is but as a little island in the great ocean of eternal peace—so she told herself—and then bade that sleepless heart of hers both still its passionate beating and take courage. And when, at length, she was alone, and lay down in her narrow berth, peace and thankfulness remained with Katherine. The care and affection of brother, friends, and servants, were very grateful to her, so that she composed herself to rest whether slumber was granted her or not. The event was in the hands of God—that surely was enough.

And in the dawn, reaching Rome, the news was so far better that it was not worse. Richard lived. And when, some seven hours later, the train steamed into Naples station, and Bates, the house-steward—the marks of haste and keen anxiety upon him—pushed his way up to the carriage door, he could report there was this amount of hope even yet, that Richard still lived, though his strength was as that of an infant and whether it would wax or wane wholly none as yet could say.

"Then we are in time, Bates?" Lady Calmady had asked, desiring further assurance.

"I hope so, my lady. But I would advise your coming as quickly as possible."

"Is he conscious?"

"He knew Captain Vanstone this morning, my lady, just before I left."

The man-servant shouldered the crowd aside unceremoniously, so as to force a passage for Lady Calmady.

"Her ladyship should go up to the villa at once, sir," he said to General Ormiston. "I had better accompany her. I will leave Andrews to make all arrangements here. The carriage is waiting."

Then, Honoria beside her, Katherine was aware of the hot glare and hard shadow, the grind and clatter, the violent colour, the strident vivacity of the Neapolitan streets, as with voice and whip, Garçia sprung the handsome, long-tailed, black horses up the steep ascent. This, followed by the impression of a cool, spacious, and lofty interior, of mild, diffused light, of pale, marble floors and stairways, of rich hangings and distinguished objects of art, of the soft, green gloom of ilex and myrtle, the languid drip of fountains. And this last served to mark, as with raised finger, the hush — bland, yet very imperative—which held all the place. After the ceaseless jar and tumult of that many-days' journey, here, up at the villa, it seemed as though urgency were absurd, hot haste of affection a little vulgar, a little contemptible, all was so composed, so very urbane.

And that urbanity so bland, so, in a way, supercilious, affected Honoria St. Quentin unpleasantly. She was taken with unreasoning dislike of the place, finding something malign, trenching on cruelty even, in its exalted serenity, its unchanging, inaccessible, masklike smile. Very certainly the ancient gods held court here yet, the gods who are careless of human tears, heedless of human woe ! And she looked anxiously at Lady Calmady, penetrated by fear that the latter was about to be exposed to some insidious danger, to come into conflict with influences antagonistic and subtly evil. Wicked deeds had been committed in this fair place, wicked designs nourished and brought to fruition here. She was convinced of that. Was convinced further that those designs had connection with and had been directed against Lady Calmady. The thought of Helen de Vallorbes, exquisite and vicious,—as she now reluctantly admitted her to be—was very present to her. As far as she knew, it was quite a number of years since Helen had set foot in the villa. Yet it spoke of her, spoke of the more dangerous aspects of her nature.—Honoria sighed over her friend. Helen had gone, latterly, very much to the bad, she feared. And as all this passed rapidly through her mind it provoked all her knight-errantry, raising a strongly protective spirit in her. She questioned just how much active care she might take of Lady Calmady without indiscretion of over-forwardness.

But even while she thus debated, opportunity of action was lost. Quietly, a great simplicity and singleness of purpose in her demeanour, without word spoken, without looking back, Katherine followed the house-steward across the cool, spacious hall, through a doorway and out of sight.

And that singleness of purpose, so discernible in her outward demeanour, possessed Katherine's being throughout. She was as one who walks in sleep, pushed by blind impulse. She was not conscious of herself, not conscious of joy or fear, or any emotion. She moved forward dumbly, and without volition, towards the event. Her senses were confused by this transition to stillness from noise, by the immobility of all surrounding objects after the reeling landscape on either hand the swaying train, by the bland and tempered light after the harsh contrasts of glare and darkness so constantly offered to her vision of late. She was dazed and faint, moreover, so that her knees trembled. Her sensibility, her powers of realisation and of sympathy, were for the time being atrophied.

The house-steward ushered her into a large, square room. The low, darkly-painted, vaulted ceiling of it produced a cavernous effect. An orderly disorder prevailed, and a somewhat mournful dimness of closed, green-slatted shutters and half-drawn curtains. The furniture, costly in fact, but dwarfed, in some cases actually legless, was ranged against the squat, carven bookcases that lined the walls leaving the middle of the room vacant, save for a low, narrow camp-bed. The bed stood at right angles to the door by which Katherine entered, the head of it towards the shuttered, heavily-draped windows, the foot towards the inside wall of the room. At the bedside a man knelt on one knee; and his appearance aroused, in a degree, Katherine's dormant powers of observation. He had a short, crisp, black beard and crisp, black hair. He was alert and energetic of face and figure, a man of dare-devil, humorous, yet kindly eyes. He wore a blue serge suit with brass buttons to it. He was in his stocking-feet. The wristbands and turn-down collar of his white shirt were immaculate. Katherine, lost, trembling, the support of the habitual taken from her, a stranger in a strange land, liked the man. He appeared so admirable an example of physical health. He inspired her with confidence, his presence seeming to carry with it assurance of that which is wholesome, normal, and sane. He glanced at her sharply, not without hint of criticism, and of command. Authoritatively he signed to her to remain silent, to stand at the head of the bed, and well clear of it, out of sight. Katherine did not resent this. She obeyed.

And standing thus, rallying her will to conscious effort, she looked steadily, for the first time, at the bed and that which lay upon it. And so doing she could hardly save herself from falling, since she saw there precisely that which the shape of the room and the disarray of it, along with vacant space and the low camp-bed in the centre of that space, had foretold — notwithstanding her dumbness of feeling, deadness of sympathy—she most assuredly must see.—All these last four-and-twenty hours she had solaced herself with the phantom society of Dickie the baby-child, of Dickie the eager boy, curious of many things. But here was one different from both these. Different, too, from the young man, tremendous in arrogance, and in revolt against the indignity put on him by fate, from whom she had parted in such anguish of spirit nearly five years back. For, in good truth, she saw now, not Richard Calmady her son, her anxious charge, whose debtor—in that she had brought him into life disabled—she held herself eternally to be; but Richard Calmady her husband, the desire of her eyes, the glory of her youth—saw him, worn by suffering, disfigured by unsightly growth of beard, pallid, racked by mortal weakness, the sheet expressing the broad curve of his chest, the sheet and light blanket disclosing the fact of that hideous maiming he had sustained — saw him now, as on the night he died.

Captain Vanstone, meanwhile, reassured as to the new-comer's discretion and docility, applied his mind to his patient.

"See here, sir," he said, banteringly yet tenderly, "we were just getting along first-rate with these uncommonly mixed liquors. You mustn't cry off again, Sir Richard."

He slipped his arm under the pillows, dexterously raising the young man's head, and held the cup to his lips.

"My dear, good fellow, I wish you would let me be," Dickie murmured faintly.

He spoke courteously, yet there were tears in his voice for very weakness. And, hearing him, it was as though something stirred within Katherine which had long been bound by bitterness of heavy frost.

Vanstone shook his head.—"Very sorry, Sir Richard," he replied. "Daren't let you off. I've got my orders, you see."

The bold and kindly eyes had a certain magnetic efficacy of compulsion in them. The sick man drank, swallowed with difficulty, yet drank again.   Then he lay back, for a while, his eyes closed, resting.   And Katherine stood at the head of the bed, out of sight, waiting till her time should come.   She folded her hands high upon her bosom.   Her thought remained inarticulate, yet she began to understand that which she had striven so sternly to uproot, that which she had supposed she had extirpated, still remained with her.   Once more, with a terror of joyful amazement, she began to scale the height and sound the depth of human love.

Presently the voice—whether that of husband or of son she did not stay to discriminate—it gripped her very vitals—reached her from the bed.   She fancied it rang a little stronger.

"It is contemptibly futile, and therefore conspicuously in keeping with the rest, to have taken all this trouble about dying only, in the end, to sneak back."

"Oh!   well, sir, after all you're not so very far on the return voyage yet," Vanstone put in consolingly.

Richard opened his eyes.   Katherine's vision was blurred. She could not see very clearly, but she fancied he smiled.

"Yes, with luck, I may still give you all the slip," he said.

"Now, a little more, sir, please.   Yes, you can if you try."

"But I tell you I don't care about this business of sneaking back.   I don't want to live."

"Very likely not.   But I'm very much mistaken if you want to die like a cat, in a cupboard, here ashore.   Mend enough to get away on board the yacht to sea.   There'll be time enough then to argue the question out, sir.   Half a mile of blue water under your feet sends up the value of life most considerably."

As he spoke the sailor looked at Katherine Calmady.   His glance enjoined caution, yet conveyed encouragement.

"Here, take down the rest of it, Sir Richard," he said persuasively.   "Then I swear I won't plague you any more for a good hour."

Again he raised the sick man dexterously, and as he did so Katherine observed that a purple scar, as of a but newly healed wound, ran right across Dickie's cheek from below the left eye to the turn of the lower jaw.   And the sight of it moved her strangely, loosening the last of that binding as of frost.   A swift madness of anger against whoso had inflicted that ugly hurt arose in Katherine; while her studied resignation, her strained passivity of mental attitude, went down before a passion of violent and primitive emotion.   The spirit of battle became dominant in her, along with an immense necessity of loving and of being loved. Tender phantoms of past joy ceased to solace.   The actual, the concrete, the immediate, compelled her with a certain splendour of demand. Katherine appeared to grow taller, more regal of presence. The noble energy of youth and its limitless generosity returned to her. Instinctively she unfastened her pelisse at the throat, took the lace coif from her head, letting it fall to the ground, and moved nearer.

Richard pushed the cup away from his lips.

"There's someone in the room, Vanstone!" he said, his voice harsh with anger. "Some woman—I heard her dress. I told you all—whatever happened—I would have no woman here."

But Katherine, undismayed, came straight on to the bedside. She loved. She would not be gainsaid. With the whole force of her nature she refused denial of that love.—For a brief space Richard looked at her, his face ghastly and rigid as that of a corpse. Then he raised himself in the bed, stretching out both arms, with a hoarse cry that tore at his throat and shuddered through all his frame. And, as he would have fallen forward, exhausted by the effort to reach her and the lovely shelter of her, Katherine caught and, kneeling, held him, his poor hands clutching impotently at her shoulders, his head sinking upon her breast. While, in that embrace, not only all the motherhood in her leapt up to claim the sonship in him, but all the womanhood in her leapt up to claim the manhood in him, thereby making the broken circle of her being once more wholly perfect and complete, so that carrying the whole dear burden of his fever-wasted body in her encircling arms and upon her breast, even as she had carried, long since, that dear fruit of love, the unborn babe, within her womb, Katherine was taken with a very ecstasy and rapture of content.

"My beloved is mine—is mine!" she cried,—"and I am his.'

Captain Vanstone was on his feet and half way across the room.

"Man alive, but it hurts like merry hell!" he said, as he softly closed the door.

CHAPTER III

CONCERNING A SPIRIT IN PRISON

UPON those moments of rapture followed days of trembling, during which the sands of Richard Calmady's life ran very low, and his brain wandered in delirium, and he spoke unwittingly of many matters of which it was unprofitable to hear. Periods of unconsciousness, when he lay as one dead; periods of incessant utterance—now violent in unavailing repudiation, now harsh with unavailing remorse—alternated. And, at this juncture, much of Lady Calmady's former very valiant pride asserted itself. In tender jealousy for the honour of her beloved one she shut the door of that sick-room, of sinister aspect, against brother and friend, and even against the faithful Clara. None should see or hear Richard in his present alienation and abjection, save herself and those who had hitherto ministered to him. He should regain a measure, at least, of his old distinction and beauty before any, beyond these, looked on his face. And so his own men-servants—Captain Vanstone, capable, humorous, and alert—and Price, the red-headed, Welsh first mate, of varied and voluminous gift of invective—continued to nurse him. These men loved him. They would be loyal in silence, since, whatever his lapses, Dickie was and always had been, as Katherine reflected, among the number of those happily-endowed persons who triumphantly give the lie to the cynical saying that "no man is a hero to his *valet de chambre.*"

To herself Katherine reserved the right to enter that sinister sick-room whenever she pleased, and to sit by the bedside, waiting for the moment—should it ever come—when Richard would again recognise her, and give himself to her again. And those vigils proved a searching enough experience, notwithstanding her long apprenticeship to service of sorrow—which was also the service of her son. For, in the mental and moral nudity of delirium, he made strange revelation, not only of acts committed, but of inherent tendencies of character and of thought. He spoke, with bewildering inconsequence and intimacy, of incidents and of persons with whom she was unacquainted, causing her to follow him—a rather brutal pilgrimage—into regions where the feet of women, bred and nurtured like herself, but seldom tread. He spoke of persons with whom she was well acquainted also, and whose names arrested her attention with pathetic significance, offering, for the moment, secure standing ground amid the shifting quicksand of his but-half-comprehended words. He spoke of Morabita, the famous *prima donna*, and of gentle Mrs. Chifney down at the Brockhurst racing-stables. He grew heated in discussion with Lord Fallowfeild. He petted little Lady Constance Quayle. He called Camp, coaxed and chaffed the dog merrily—whereat Lady Calmady rose from her place by the bedside and stood at one of the dim, shuttered windows for a while. He spoke of places, too, and of happenings in them, from Westchurch to Constantinople, from a nautch at Singapore to a

country fair at Farley Row. But, recurrent through all his
wanderings were allusions, unsparing in revolt and in self-abase-
ment, to a woman whom he had loved and who had dealt very
vilely with him, putting some unpardonable shame upon him,
and to a man whom he himself had very basely wronged. The
name, neither of man nor woman, did Katherine learn.—Madame
de Vallorbes' name, for which she could not but listen, he never
mentioned, nor did he mention her own.—And recurrent, also,
running as a black thread through all his speech, was lament, not
unmanly but very terrible to hear—the lament of a creature,
captive, maimed, imprisoned, perpetually striving, perpetually frustrated in the effort to escape. And, noting all this, Katherine not
only divined very dark and evil pages in the history of her beloved
one ; but a struggle so continuous and a sorrow so abiding that,
in her estimation at all events, they cancelled and expiated the darkness and evil of those same pages. While the mystery, both of
wrong done and sorrow suffered, so wrought upon her that,
having, in the first ecstasy of recovered human love, deserted
and depreciated the godward love a little, she now ran back
imploring assurance and renewal of that last, in all penitence and
humility, lest, deprived of the counsel and sure support of it, she
should fail to read the present and deal with the future aright—
if, indeed, any future still remained for that beloved one other
than the yawning void of death and inscrutable silence of the
grave !

The better part of a week passed thus ; and then, one fair
morning, Winter, bringing her breakfast to the ante-room of that
same sea-blue, sea-green bed-chamber—sometime tenanted by
Helen de Vallorbes—disclosed a beaming countenance.

"Mr. Powell wishes me to inform your ladyship that Sir
Richard has passed a very good night. He has come to himself,
my lady, and has asked for you."

The butler's hands shook as he set down the tray.

"I hope your ladyship will take something to eat before you
go downstairs," he added. "Mr. Powell told Sir Richard that
it was still early ; and he desired that on no consideration should
you be hurried."

Which little word of thoughtfulness on Dickie's part brought
a roundness to Katherine's cheek and a soft shining into her
sweet eyes ; so that Honoria St. Quentin, sauntering into the
room just then with her habitual lazy grace, stood still a moment
in pleased surprise noting the change in her friend's appearance.

"Why, dear Cousin Katherine," she asked, "what's happened ?
All's right with the world !"

"Yes," Katherine answered. "God's very much in His heaven, to-day, and all's right with all the world, because things are a little more right with one man in it.—That is the woman's creed—always has been, I suppose, and I rather hope always will be. It is frankly personal and individualistic, I know. Possibly it is reprehensibly narrow-minded. Still I doubt if she will readily find another which makes for greater happiness or fulness of life. You don't agree, dearest, I know—nevertheless pour out my tea for me, will you? I want to dispose of this necessary evil of breakfast with all possible despatch. Richard has sent for me. He has slept and is awake."

And as Miss St. Quentin served her dear friend, she pondered this speech curiously, saying to herself:—"Yes, I did right; though I never liked Ludovic Quayle better than now, and never liked any other man as well as I like Ludovic Quayle. But that's not enough. I'm getting hold of the appearance of the thing, but I haven't got hold of the thing itself. And so the woman in me must continue to be kept in the back attic. She shall be denied all further development. She shall have nothing unless she can have the whole of it, and repeat Cousin Katherine's creed from her heart."

Richard did not speak when Lady Calmady crossed the room and sat down at the bedside. He barely raised his eyelids. But he felt out for her hand across the surface of the sheet. And she took the proffered hand in both hers and fell to stroking the palm of it with her finger-tips. And this silent greeting, and confiding contact of hand with hand, was to her exquisitely healing. It gave an assurance of nearness and acknowledged ownership, more satisfying and convincing than many eloquent phrases of welcome. And so she, too, remained silent, only indeed permitting herself, for a little while, to look at him, lest so doing she should make further demand upon his poor quantity of strength. A folding screen in stamped leather, of which age had tempered the ruby and gold to a sober harmony of tone, had been placed round the head of the bed, throwing this last into clear, quiet shadow. The bed linen was fresh and smooth. Richard had made a little toilet. His silk shirt, open at the throat, was also fresh and smooth. He was clean shaven, his hair cropped into that closely-fitting, bright-brown cap of curls. Katherine perceived that his beauty had begun to return to him, though his face was distressingly worn and emaciated, and the long, purplish line of that unexplained scar still disfigured his cheek. His hands were little more than skin and bone. Indeed he was fragile, she feared, as any person could be who yet had life in him, and she wondered, rather fearfully, if it was yet possible to build up that life again into any joy of energy and of activity. But she put such fears from her as unworthy. For were they not together, he and she, actually and consciously reunited? That was sufficient. The rest could wait.

And to-day, as though lending encouragement to gracious hopes, the usually gloomy and cavernous room had taken to itself a quite generous plenishing of air and light. The heavy curtains were drawn aside. The casements of one of the square, squat windows were thrown widely open. The slatted shutters without were partially opened likewise. A shaft of strong sunshine slanted in and lay, like a bright highway, across the rich colours of the Persian carpet. The air was hot, but nimble and of a vivacious and stimulating quality. It fluttered some loose papers on the writing-table near the open window. It fluttered the delicate laces and fine muslin frills of Lady Calmady's morning-gown. There was a sprightly mirthfulness in the touch of it not unpleasing to her. For it seemed to speak of the ever-obtaining youth, the incalculable power of recuperation, the immense reconstructive energy resident in nature and the physical domain. And there was comfort in that thought. She turned her eyes from the bed and its somewhat sorrowful burden —the handsome head, the broad, though angular, shoulders, the face, immobile and masklike, with closed eyelids and unsmiling lips, reposing upon the whiteness of the pillows—and fixed them upon that radiant space of outer world visible between the dark-framing of the half-open shutters. Beyond the dazzling, black-and-white chequer of the terrace and balustrade, they rested on the cool green of the formal garden, the glistering dome and slender columns of the pavilion set in the angle of the terminal wall. And this last reminded her quaintly of that other pavilion, embroidered, with industry of innumerable stitches, upon the curtains of the state-bed at home—that pavilion, set for rest and refreshment in the midst of the tangled ways of the Forest of This Life, where the Hart may breathe in security, fearless of Care, the pursuing leopard, which follows all too close behind.—Owing to her position and the sharp drop of the hillside, Naples itself, the great painted city, its fine buildings and crowded shipping, was unseen; but, far away, the lofty promontory of Sorrento sketched itself in palest lilac upon the azure of sea and sky.

And, as Katherine reasoned, if this fair prospect, after so many ages of tumultuous history and shock of calamitous events, after battle, famine, terror of earthquake and fire, devastation by

33

foul disease, could still recover and present such an effect of triumphant youthfulness, such an at once august and mirthful charm, might not her beloved one, lying here broken in health and in spirit, likewise regain the glory of his manhood and the delight of it, notwithstanding present weakness and mournful eclipse?—Yes, it would come right—come right—Katherine told herself, thereby making one of those magnificent acts of faith which go so far to produce just that which they prophesy. God could not have created so complex and beautiful a creature, and permitted it so to suffer, save to the fulfilment of some clear purpose which would very surely be made manifest at last. God Almighty should be justified of His strange handiwork and she of her love before the whole of the story was told.—And, stirred by these thoughts, and by the fervour of her own pious confidence, Katherine's finger-tips travelled more rapidly over the palm of that outstretched and passive hand. Then, on a sudden, she became aware that Richard was looking fixedly at her. She turned her head proudly, the exaltation of a living faith very present in her smile.

"You are the same," he said slowly. His voice was low, toneless, and singularly devoid of emotion.—"Deliciously the same. You are just as lovely. You still have your pretty colour. You are hardly a day older"—

He paused, still regarding her fixedly.

"I'm glad you have got on one of those white, frilly things you used to wear. I always liked them."

Katherine could not speak just then. This sudden and complete intimacy unnerved her. It was so long since anyone had spoken to her thus. It was very dear to her, yet the toneless voice gave a strange unreality to the tender words.

"It's a matter for congratulation that you are the same," Richard went on, "since everything else, it appears, is destined to continue the same. One should have one thing it is agreeable to contemplate in that connection, considering the vast number of things altogether the reverse of agreeable and which one fondly hoped one was rid of forever, which intrude themselves."

He shifted himself feebly on the pillows, and the flicker of a smile crossed his face.

"Poor, dear mother," he said, "you see again, without delay, the old bad habit of grumbling!"

"Grumble on, grumble on, my best beloved," Katherine murmured, while her finger-tips travelled softly over his palm.

"Verily and indeed, you are the same!" Richard rejoined.

Once more he lay looking full at her, until she became almost abashed by that unswerving scrutiny. It came over her that the plane of their relation had changed. Richard was, as never heretofore, her equal, a man grown.

Suddenly he spoke.

"Can you forgive me?"

And so far had Katherine's thought journeyed from the past, so absorbed was it in the present, that she answered, surprised :—

"My dearest, forgive what?"

"Injustice, ingratitude, desertion," Richard said, "neglect, systematic cruelty. There is plenty to swell the list. All I boasted I would do I have done—and more."—His voice, until now so even and emotionless, faltered a little. "I have sinned against heaven and before thee, and am no more worthy to be called thy son."

Katherine's hand closed down on his firmly.

"All that, as far as I am concerned, is as though it was not and never had been," she answered.—"So much for judgment on earth, dearest.—While in heaven, thank God, we know there is more joy over the one sinner who repents than over the ninety-and-nine just persons who need no repentance."

"And you really believe that?" Richard said, speaking half indulgently, half ironically, as if to a child.

"Assuredly I believe it."

"But supposing the sinner is not repentant, but merely cowed?"—Richard straightened his head on the pillows and closed his eyes. "You gave me leave to grumble—well, then, I am so horribly disappointed. Here have life and death been sitting on either side of me for the past month, and throwing with dice for me. I saw them as plainly as I can see you. The queer thing was they were exactly alike, yet I knew them apart from the first. Day and night I heard the rattle of the dice—it became hideously monotonous—and felt the mouth of the dice-box on my chest when they threw. I backed death heavily. It seemed to me there were ways of loading the dice. I loaded them. But it wasn't to be, mother. Life always threw the highest numbers—and life had the last throw."

"I praise God for that," Katherine said, very softly.

"I don't, unfortunately," he answered. "I hoped for a neat little execution—a little pain, perhaps, a little shedding of blood, without which there is no remission of sins—but I suppose that would have been letting me off too easy."

He drew away his hand and covered his eyes.

"When I had seen you I seemed to have made my final peace. I understood why I had been kept waiting till then. Having seen you, I flattered myself I might decently get free at last. But I am branded afresh, that's all, and sent back to the galleys."

Lady Calmady's eyes sought the radiant prospect—the green of the garden, the graceful columns of the airy pavilion, the lilac land set in the azure of sea and sky. No words of hers could give comfort as yet, so she would remain silent. Her trust was in the amiable ministry of time, which may bring solace to the tormented, human soul, even as it reclothes the mountain-side swept by the lava stream, or cleanses and renders gladly habitable the plague-devastated city.

But there was a movement upon the bed. Richard had turned on his side. He had recovered his self-control, and once more looked fixedly at her.

"Mother," he said calmly, "is your love great enough to take me back, and to give yourself to me again, though I am not fit so much as to kiss the hem of your garment?"

"There is neither giving nor taking, my beloved," she answered, smiling upon him. "In the truth of things, you have never left me, neither have I ever let you go."

"Ah! but consider these last four years and their record!" he rejoined. "I am not the same man that I was. There's no getting away from fact, from deeds actually done, or words actually said, for that matter. I have kept my singularly repulsive infirmity of body, and to it I have added a mind festering with foul memories. I have been a brute to you, a traitor to a friend who trusted me. I have been a sensualist, an adulterer. And I am hopelessly broken in pride and self-respect. The conceit, the pluck even, has been licked right out of me."—Richard paused, steadying his voice which faltered again.—"I only want, since it seems I've got to go on living, to slink away somewhere out of sight, and hide myself and my wretchedness and shame from everyone I know.—Can you bear with me, soured and invalided as I am, mother? Can you put up with my temper, and my silence, and my grumbling, useless log as I must continue to be?"

"Yes—everlastingly yes," Katherine answered.

Richard threw himself flat on his back again.

"Ah! how I hate myself—my God, how I hate myself!" he exclaimed.

"And how beyond all worlds I love you," Katherine put in quietly.

He felt out for her hand across the sheet, found and held it. There were footsteps upon the terrace to the right, the scent of a cigar, Ludovic Quayle's voice in question, Honoria St. Quentin's in answer, both with enforced discretion and lowness of tone. General Ormiston joined them. Miss St. Quentin laughed gently. The sound was musical and sweet. Footsteps and voices died away. A clang of bells and the hooting of an outward-bound liner came up from the city and the port.

Richard's calm had returned. His expression had softened.

"Will those two marry?" he asked presently.

Lady Calmady paused before speaking.

"I hope so—for Ludovic's sake," she said. "He has served, if not quite Jacob's seven years, yet a full five for his love."

"If for Ludovic's sake, why not for hers?" Dickie asked.

"Because two halves don't always make a whole in marriage," Katherine said.

"You are as great an idealist as ever!"— He paused, then raised himself, sitting upright, speaking with a certain passion.

"Mother, will you take me away, away from everyone, at once, just as soon as possible? I never want to see this room, or this house, or Naples again. The climax was reached here of disillusion, and of iniquity, and of degradation. Don't ask what it was. I couldn't tell you. And, mercifully, only one person, whose lips are sealed in self-defence, knows exactly what took place besides myself. But I want to get away, away alone with you, who are perfectly unsullied and compassionate, and who have forgiven me, and who still can love. Will you come? Will you take me? The yacht is all ready for sea."

"Yes," Katherine said.

"I asked this morning who was here with you, and Powell told me. I can't see them, mother, simply I can't! I haven't the nerve. I haven't the face. Can you send them away?"

"Yes," Katherine said.

Richard's eyes had grown dangerously bright. A spot of colour burned on either cheek. Katherine leaned over him.

"My dearest," she declared, "you have talked enough."

"Yes, they're beginning to play again, I can hear the rattle of the dice.—Mother, take me away, take me out to sea, away from this dreadful place.—Ah! you poor darling, how horribly selfish I am!—But let me get out to sea, and then later, take me home—to Brockhurst. The house is big. Nobody need see me."

"No, no," Katherine said, laying him back with tender force

upon the pillows.—"No one has seen you, no one shall see you. We will be alone, you and I, just as long as you wish. With me, my beloved, you are very safe."

CHAPTER IV

DEALING WITH MATTERS OF HEARSAY AND MATTERS OF SPORT

ONE raw, foggy evening, early in the following December, the house at Newlands presented an unusually animated scene. On the gravel of the carriage-sweep, without, grooms walked breathed and sweating horses—the steam from whose bodies and nostrils showed white in the chill dusk—slowly up and down. In the hall, within, a number of gentlemen, more or less mud-bespattered, regaled themselves with cheerful conversation, with strong waters of unexceptionable quality, and with their host, Mr. Cathcart's, very excellent cigars. They moved stiffly and stood in attitudes more professional than elegant. The long, clear-coloured drawing-room beyond offered a perspective of much amiable comfort. The glazed surfaces of its flowery-patterned chintzes gave back the brightness of candles and shaded lamps, while drawn curtains shut out the somewhat mournful prospect of sodden garden, bare trees, and grey, en-shrouding mist. At the tea-table, large, mild, reposeful, clothed in wealth of black silk and black lace, was Mrs. Cathcart. Lord Fallowfeild, his handsome, infantile countenance beaming with good-nature and good-health above his blue-and-white, bird's-eye stock and scarlet hunting-coat, sat by her discoursing with great affability and at great length. Mary Ormiston stood near them, an expression of kindly diversion upon her face. Her figure had grown somewhat matronly in these days, and there were lines in her forehead and about the corners of her rather large mouth ; but her crisp hair was still untouched by grey, her bright, gipsylike complexion had retained its freshness, she possessed the same effect of wholesomeness and good sense as of old, while her honest, brown eyes were soft with satisfied mother-love as they met those of the slender, black-headed boy at her side.—Godfrey Ormiston was in his second term at Eton, and had come to Newlands to-day for his exeat.—The little party was completed by Lord Shotover, who stood before the fire warming that part of his person which by the lay mind, unversed in such mysteries, might have been judged to be already more than sufficiently warmed by the saddle, his feet planted far apart and a long glass of brandy and soda in his hand. For this last he had offered good-tempered apology.

"I know I've no business to bring it in here, Mrs. Cathcart," he said, "and make your drawing-room smell like a pot-house. But, you see, there was a positive stampede for the hearth-rug in the hall. A modest man, such as myself, hadn't a chance. There's a regular rampart, half the county in fact, before that fire. So I thought I'd just slope in here, don't you know. It looked awfully warm and inviting. And then I wanted to pay my respects to Mrs. Ormiston too, and talk to this young chap about Eton in peace."

Whereat Godfrey flushed up to the roots of his hair, being very sensibly exalted. Since what young male creature who knew anything really worth knowing—that was Godfrey's way of putting it at least—did not know that Lord Shotover had been a mighty sportsman from his youth up, and upon a certain famous occasion had won the Grand National on his own horse?

"Only tea for me, Mrs. Cathcart," Lord Fallowfeild was saying. "Capital thing tea. Never touch spirits in the daytime and never have. No reflection upon other men's habits."—He turned an admiring, fatherly glance upon the tall, well-made Shotover.—"Other men know their own business best. Always have been a great advocate for believing every man knows his own business best. Still stick to my own habits. Like to be consistent. Very steadying, sobering thing to be consistent, very strengthening to the character. Always have told all my children that. As you begin, so you should go on. Always have tried to begin as I was going on. Haven't always succeeded, but have made an honest effort. And it is something, you know, to make an honest effort. Try to bear that in mind, you young gentleman,"—this, genially, to Godfrey Ormiston. "Not half a bad rule to start in life with, to go on as you begin, you know."

"Always provided you begin right, you know, my dear fellow," Shotover observed, patting the boy's shoulder with his disengaged hand, and looking at the boy's mother with a humorous suggestion of self-depreciation. Now, as formerly, he entertained the very friendliest sentiments towards all good women, yet maintained an expensively extensive acquaintance with women to whom that adjective is not generically applicable.

But Lord Fallowfeild was fairly under weigh. Words flowed from him, careless of comment or of interruption. He was innocently and conspicuously happy. He had enjoyed a fine day's sport in company with his favourite son, whose financial embarrassments were not, it may be added, just now in a critical condition. And then access of material prosperity had recently come to Lord Fallowfeild in the shape of a considerable coal-producing property in the north of Midlandshire. The income derived from this—amounting to from ten to twelve thousand a year—was payable to him during his lifetime, with remainder, on trust, in equal shares to all his children. There were good horses in the Whitney stables now, and no question of making shift to let the house in Belgrave Square for the season, while the amiable nobleman's banking-account showed a far from despicable balance. And consciousness of this last fact formed an agreeable undercurrent to his every thought. Therefore was he even more than usually garrulous according to his own kindly and innocent fashion.

"Very hospitable and friendly of you and Cathcart, to be sure," he continued, "to throw open your house in this way. Kindness alike to man and beast, man and beast, for which my son and I are naturally very grateful."

Lord Shotover looked at Mary again, smiling.—"Little mixed that statement, isn't it," he said, "unless we take for granted that I'm the beast?"

"I was a good deal perplexed, I own, Mrs. Cathcart, as to how we should get home without giving the horses a rest and having them gruelled. Fourteen miles"—

"A precious long fourteen too," put in Shotover.

"So it is," his father agreed, "a long fourteen. And my horse was pumped, regularly pumped. I can't bear to see a horse as done as that. It distresses me, downright distresses me. Hate to over-press a horse. Hate to over-press anything that can't stand up to you and take its revenge on you. Always feel ashamed of myself if I've over-pressed a horse. But I hadn't reckoned on the distance."

"'The pace was too hot to inquire,'" quoted Shotover.

"So it was. Meeting at Grimshott, you see, we very rarely kill so far on this side of the country."

"Breaking just where he did, I'd have bet on that fox doubling back under Talepenny wood and making across the vale for the earths in the big Brockhurst warren," Lord Shotover declared.

"Would you, though?" said his father. "Very reasonable forecast, very reasonable, indeed. Quite the likeliest thing for him to do, only he didn't do it. Don't believe that fox belonged to this side of the country at all. Don't understand his tactics.

If it had been in my poor friend Denier's time, I might have suspected him of being a bagman."

Lord Fallowfeild chuckled a little.

"Ran too straight for a bagman," Shotover remarked. "Well, he gave us a rattling good spin whose-ever fox he was."

"Didn't he, though?" said Lord Fallowfeild genially.—He turned sideways in his chair, threw one shapely leg across the other, and addressed himself more exclusively to his hostess. "Haven't had such a day for years," he continued. "And a very pleasant thing to have such a day just when my son's down with me—very pleasant, indeed. It reminds me of my poor, dear friend Henniker's time. Good fellow Henniker. I liked Henniker. Never had a better master than Tom Henniker, very tactful, nice-feeling man, and had such an excellent manner with the farmers— Ah! here's Cathcart—and Knott. How d'ye do, Knott? Always glad to see you.—Very pleasant meeting such a number of friends. Very pleasant ending to a pleasant day, eh, Shotover? Mrs. Cathcart and I were just speaking of poor Tom Henniker. You used to hunt then, Cathcart. Do you remember a run, just about this time of year?—It may have been a little earlier. I tell you why. It was the second time the hounds met after my poor friend Aldborough's funeral."

"Lord Aldborough died on the twenty-seventh of October," John Knott said. The doctor limped in walking. He suffered a sharp twinge of sciatica and his face lent itself to astonishing contortions.

"Plain man Knott," Lord Fallowfeild commented inwardly. "Monstrously able fellow, but uncommonly plain. So's Cathcart for that matter. Well-dressed man and very well-preserved as to figure, but remarkably like an orang-outang now his eyes are sunk and his eyebrows have grown so tufty."—Then he glanced anxiously at Lord Shotover to assure himself of the entire absence of simian approximations in the case of his own family.—"Oh! ah! yes," he remarked aloud, and somewhat vaguely. "Quite right, Knott. Then of course it was earlier. Record run for that season. Seldom had a better. We found a fox in the Grimshott gorse and ran to Water End without a check."

"And Lemuel Image got into the Tilney brook," Mary Ormiston said, laughing a little.

"So he did, though!" Lord Fallowfeild rejoined, beaming. And then suddenly his complacency suffered eclipse. For, looking at the speaker, he became disagreeably aware of having, on some occasion, said something highly inconvenient concerning this lady to one of her near relations. He rushed into speech again :—"Loud-voiced, blustering kind of fellow Image. I never have liked Image. Extraordinary marriage that of his with a connection of poor Aldborough's. Never have understood how her people could allow it."

"Oh! money'll buy pretty well everything in this world except brains and a sound liver," Dr. Knott said, as he lowered himself cautiously on to the seat of the highest chair available.

"Or a good conscience," Mrs. Cathcart observed, with mild dogmatism.

"I am not altogether so sure about that," the doctor answered. "I have known the doubling of a few charitable subscriptions work extensive cures under that head. Depend upon it there's an immense deal more conscience-money paid every year than ever finds its way into the coffers of the Chancellor of the Exchequer."

"So there is, though!" said Lord Fallowfeild, with an air of regretful conviction. "Never put it as clearly as that myself, Knott, but must own I am afraid there is."

Mr. Cathcart, who had joined Lord Shotover upon the hearth-rug, here intervened. He had a tendency to air local grievances, especially in the presence of his existing noble guest, whom he regarded, not wholly without reason, as somewhat lukewarm and dilatory in questions of reform.

"I own to sharing your dislike of Image," he remarked. "He behaved in an anything but straightforward manner about the site for the new cottage hospital at Parson's Holt."

"Did he, though?" said Lord Fallowfeild.

"Yes.—I supposed it had been brought to your notice."

Lord Fallowfeild fidgeted a little.—"Rather too downright Cathcart," he said to himself. "Gets you into a corner and fixes you. Not fair, not at all fair in general society.—Oh! ah!—cottage hospital, yes," he added aloud. "Very tiresome, vexatious business about that hospital. I felt it very much at the time."

"It was a regular job," Mr. Cathcart continued.

"No, not a job, not a job, my dear fellow. Unpleasant word job. Nothing approaching a job, only an oversight, at most an unfortunate error of judgment," Lord Fallowfeild protested.—He glanced at his son inviting support, but that gentleman was engaged in kindly conversation with bright-eyed, little Godfrey Ormiston. He glanced at Mary—remembered suddenly that his unfortunate remark regarding that lady had been connected with her resemblance to her father, and the latter's striking defect of personal beauty. He glanced at the doctor. But John Knott sat all hunched together, watching him with an expression rather sardonic than sympathetic.

"There was culpable negligence somewhere, in any case," his persecutor, Mr. Cathcart, went on. "It was obvious Image pressed that bit of land at Waters End on the committee simply because no one would buy it for building purposes. His affectation of generosity as to price was a piece of the most transparent hypocrisy."

"I suppose it was," Lord Fallowfeild agreed mildly.

"A certain anonymous donor had promised a second five hundred pounds, if the hospital was built on high ground with a subsoil of gravel."

"It is on gravel," put in Lord Fallowfeild anxiously. "Saw it myself—distinctly remember seeing gravel when the heather had been pared before digging the foundations—bright yellow gravel."

"Yes, and with a ten-foot bed of blue clay underneath. Most dangerous soil going,"—this from Dr. Knott, grimly.

"Is it, though?" Lord Fallowfeild inquired, with an amiable effort to welcome unpalatable, geological information.

"Not a doubt of it. The surface water and generally the sewage—for we are very far yet from having discovered a drain-pipe which is impeccable in respect of leakage—soak through the porous cap down to the clay and lie there; to rise again, not at the Last Day by any means, but on the evening of the very first one that's been hot enough to cause evaporation."

"Do they, though?" said Lord Fallowfeild. He was greatly impressed.—"Capable fellow Knott, wonderful thing science," he commented inwardly and with praiseworthy humility.

But Mr. Cathcart returned to the charge.

"The hospital was disastrously the loser, in any case," he remarked. "As a matter of course, the conditions having been disregarded, Lady Calmady withdrew her promise of a second donation."

"Oh! ah! Lady Calmady, really!" the simple-minded nobleman exclaimed. "Very interesting piece of news and very generous intention, no doubt, on the part of Lady Calmady. But give you my word, Cathcart, that until this moment I had no notion that the anonymous donor of whom we heard so much from one or two members of the committee—heard too much, I thought, for I dislike mysteries — foolish, unprofitable things mysteries—always turn out to be nothing at all in the finish— oh! ah! yes — well, that the anonymous donor was Lady Calmady!"

And thereupon he shifted his position with as much assumption of *hauteur* as his inherent kindliness permitted.   He turned his chair sideways, presenting an excellently flat, if somewhat broad, scarlet-clad back to his persecutor upon the hearth-rug.—"Sorry to set a man down in his own house," he said to himself, "but Cathcart's a little wanting in taste sometimes.   He presses a subject home too closely.   And if I was bamboozled by Image, it really isn't Cathcart's place to remind me of it."

He turned a worried and puckered countenance upon his hostess, upon Dr. Knott, upon the drawing-room door.   In the hall, beyond, one or two guests still lingered.   A lady had just joined them, notably straight and tall, and lazily graceful of movement.   Lord Fallowfeild knew her, but could not remember her name.

"Oh! ah! Shotover," he said, over his shoulder, "I don't want to hurry you, my dear boy, but perhaps it would be as well if you'd just go round to the stables and take a look at the horses."

Then, as the gentleman addressed moved away, escorted by his host and followed in admiring silence by Godfrey Ormiston, he repeated, almost querulously:— "Foolish things mysteries. Nothing in them, as a rule, when you thrash them out.   Mares' nests generally.   And that reminds me, I hear young"—Lord Fallowfeild's air of worry became accentuated—"young Calmady's got home again at last."

"Yes," Mrs. Cathcart said, "Richard and his mother have been at Brockhurst nearly a month."

"Have they, though?" exclaimed Lord Fallowfeild.   He fidgeted.   "It's a painful subject to refer to, but I should be glad to know the truth of these nasty, uncomfortable rumours about young Calmady.   You see there was that question of his and my youngest daughter's marriage.   I never approved.   Shotover backed me up in that.   He didn't approve either.   And in the end Calmady behaved in a very high-minded, straightforward manner.   Came to me himself and exhibited very good sense and very proper feeling, did Calmady.   Admitted his own disabilities with extraordinary frankness, too much frankness, I was inclined to think at the time.   It struck me as a trifle callous, don't you know.   But afterwards, when he left home in that singular manner and went abroad, and we all lost sight of him, and heard how reckless he had become and all that, it weighed on me.   I give you my word, Mrs. Cathcart, it weighed very much on me.   I've seldom been more upset by anything in my life than I was by the whole affair of that wedding."

"I am afraid it was a great mistake throughout," Mrs. Cathcart said. She folded her plump, white hands upon her ample lap and sighed gently.

"Wasn't it, though? So I told everybody from the start you know," commented Lord Fallowfeild.

"It caused a great deal of unhappiness."

"So it did, so it did," the good man said. He looked crestfallen, his kindly and well-favoured countenance being over-spread by an expression of disarmingly innocent penitence.— "It weighed on me. I should be glad to be able to forget it, but now it's all cropping up again. You see there are these rumours that poor, young Calmady's gone under very much one way and another, that his health's broken up altogether, and that he is shut up in two rooms at Brockhurst because—it's a terribly distressing thing to mention, but that's the common talk, you know — because he's a little touched here" — the speaker tapped his smooth and very candid forehead—"a little wrong here! Horrible thing insanity," he repeated.

At this point Dr. Knott, who had been watching first one person and then another present from under his shaggy eyebrows with an air of somewhat harsh amusement, roused himself.

"Pardon me, all a pack of lies, my lord," he said, "and stupid ones into the bargain. Sir Richard Calmady's as sane as you are yourself."

"Is he, though?" the other exclaimed, brightening sensibly. "Thank you, Knott. It is a very great relief to me to hear that."

"Only a man with a remarkably sound constitution could have pulled round. I quite own he's been very hard hit, and no wonder. Typhoid and complications"—

"Ah! complications?" inquired Lord Fallowfeild, who rarely let slip an opportunity of acquiring information of a pathological description.

"Yes, complications. Of the sort that are most difficult to deal with, emotional and moral—beginning with his engagement to Lady Constance"—

"Oh, dear me!"—this, piteously, from that lady's father.

"And ending—his Satanic Majesty knows where! I don't. It's no concern of mine, nor of anyone else's in my opinion. He has paid his footing — every man has to pay it sooner or later—to life and experience, and a personal acquaintance with the *thou shalt not* which, for cause unknown, goes for so almighty much in this very queer business of human existence. He has had a rough time, never doubt that, with his high-strung, arrogant, sensitive nature and the dirty trick played on him by

that heartless jade, Dame Fortune, before his birth. For the
time, this illness had knocked the wind out of him. If he sulks
for a bit, small blame to him. But he'll come round. He is
coming round day by day."

As he finished speaking the doctor got on to his feet somewhat awkwardly. His subject had affected him more deeply than
he quite cared either to own to himself or to have others see.

"That plaguy sciatic nerve again," he growled.

Lord Fallowfeild had risen also.—"Capable man Knott, but
rather rough at times, rather too didactic," he said to himself, as
he turned to greet Miss St. Quentin. She had strolled in from
the hall. Her charming face was full of merriment. There was
something altogether gallant in the carriage of her small head.

"I was so awfully glad to see Lord Shotover!" she said, as she
gave her hand to that gentleman's father. "It's an age since he
and I have met."

"Very pleasant hearing, my dear young lady, for Shotover, if
he was here to hear it! Lucky fellow Shotover."—The kindly
nobleman beamed upon her. He was nothing if not chivalrous.
Mentally, all the same, he was much perplexed. "Of course, I
remember who she is. But I understood it was Ludovic," he
said to himself. "Made sure it was Ludovic. Uncommonly
attractive, high-bred woman. Very striking looking pair, she and
Shotover. Can't fancy Shotover settled, though. Say she's a lot
of money. Wonder whether it is Shotover?—Uncommonly fine
run, best run we've had for years," he added aloud. "Pity you
weren't out, Miss St. Quentin.—Well, good-bye, Mrs. Cathcart.
I must be going. I am extremely grateful for all your kindness
and hospitality. It is seldom I have the chance of meeting so
many friends this side of the country.—Good-day to you, Knott
—good-bye, Miss St. Quentin.—Wonder if I'd better ask her to
Whitney," he thought, "on the chance of its being Shotover?
Better sound him first, though. Never let a man in for a woman
unless you've very good reason to suppose he wants her."

Honoria, meanwhile, thrusting her hands into the pockets of
her long, fur-lined, tan, cloth driving-coat sat down on the arm of
Mary Ormiston's flowery-patterned, chintz-covered chair.

"I left you all in a state of holy peace and quiet," she said,
smiling, "and a fine show you've got on hand by the time I come
back."

"They ran across the ten-acre field and killed in the shrub-
bery," Mrs. Ormiston put in.

John Knott limped forward. He stood with his hands behind
him looking down at the two ladies. Some months had elapsed

since he and Miss St. Quentin had met. He was very fond of the young lady. It interested him to meet her again. Honoria glanced up at him smiling.

"Have you been out too?" she asked.

"Not a bit of it. I'm too busy mending other people's brittle anatomy to have time to risk breaking any part of my own. I'm ugly enough already. No need to make me uglier. I came here for the express purpose of calling on you."

"You saw Katherine?" Mary asked.

"Oh yes! I saw Cousin Katherine."

"How is she?"

"An embodiment of faith, hope, and charity, as usual; but with just that pinch of malice thrown in which gives the compound a flavour. In short, she is enchanting. And then she looks so admirably well."

"That six months at sea was a great restorative," Mary remarked.

"Yet it really is rather wonderful when you consider the state she was in before we went to you at Ormiston, and how frightened we were at her undertaking the journey to Naples."

"Her affections are satisfied," Dr. Knott said, and his loose lips worked into a smile, half sneering, half tender. "I am an old man, and I have had a good lot to do with women—at second hand. Feed their hearts, and the rest of the mechanism runs easy enough. Anything short of organic disease can be cured by that sort of nourishment. Even organic disease can be arrested by it. And what's more, I have known disease develop in an apparently perfectly healthy subject simply because the heart was starved. Oh! I tell you, you're marvellous beings."

"And yet you know I feel so abominably sold," Honoria declared, "when I consider the way in which we all—Roger, Mr. Quayle, and I—acted bodyguard, attended Cousin Katherine to Naples, wrapped her in cotton wool, dear thing, sternly determined to protect her at all costs and all hazards from—well, I am ashamed to say I had no name bad enough at that time for Richard Calmady! And then this very person, whom we regarded as her probable destruction, proves to be her absolute salvation, while she proceeds to turn the tables upon us in the smartest fashion imaginable. She showed us the door and entreated us, in the most beguiling manner, to return whence we came and leave her wholly at the mercy of the enemy. I was furious"—Miss St. Quentin laughed—"downright furious! And Roger's temper, for all his high-mightiness, was a thing to swear at, rather than swear by, the morning he and I left Naples. With

the greatest difficulty we persuaded her even to keep Clara.   She
had a rage, dear thing, for getting rid of the lot of us.   Oh! we
had a royal skirmish and no mistake."

"So Roger told me."

Honoria stretched herself a little, lolled against the back of
the chair, steadying herself by laying one hand affectionately on
the other woman's shoulder.   And John Knott, observing her,
noted not only her nonchalant and almost boyish grace, but a
swift change in her humour from light-hearted laughter to a
certain, and as he fancied, half-unwilling enthusiasm.

"But to-day," she went on, "when Cousin Katherine told me
about it, I confess the whole situation laid hold of me.   I could
not help seeing it must have been finely romantic to go off like
that—those two alone—caring as she cares, and after the long
separation.   It sounds like a thing in some Elizabethan ballad.
There's a rhythm in it all which stirs one's blood.   She says the
yacht's crew were delightful to her, and treated her as a queen.
One can fancy that—the stately, lovely queen-mother, and that
strange only son!—They called in at the North African ports,
and at Gib and Madeira, and the Cape de Verds, and then ran
straight for Rio.   Then they steamed up the coast to Pernambuco,
and on to the West Indies.   Richard never went ashore, Cousin
Katherine only once or twice.   But they squattered about in the
everlasting summer of tropic harbours, fringed with palms and
low, dim, red-roofed, tropic houses—just sampled it all, the
colour, and light, and beauty, and far-awayness of it—and then,
when the fancy took them, got up steam and slipped out again
to sea.   And the name of the yacht is the *Reprieve*.   That's in
the picture, isn't it?"

Honoria paused.   She leaned forward, her chin in her hands,
her elbows on her knees.   She looked up at John Knott, and
there was a singular expression in her clear and serious eyes.

"I used to pity Cousin Katherine," she said.   "I used to
break my heart over her.   And now—now, upon my word, I
believe I envy her.—And see here, Dr. Knott, she has asked me
to go on to Brockhurst from here.   It seems that though Richard
refuses to see anyone, except you of course and Julius March, he
fusses at his mother being so much alone.   What ought I to do?
I feel rather uncertain.   I have fought him, I own I have.   We
have never been friends, he and I.   He doesn't like me.   He's
no reason to like me—anything but!   What do you say?   Shall
I refuse or shall I go?"

And the doctor reflected a little, drawing his great, square
hand down over his mouth and heavy, bristly chin.

"Yes, go," he answered. "Go and chance it. Your being at Brockhurst may work out in more of good than we now know."

CHAPTER V

TELLING HOW DICKIE CAME TO UNTIE A CERTAIN TAG OF RUSTY, BLACK RIBBON

YET, as those grey, midwinter weeks went on to Christmas, and the coming of the New Year, it became undeniable there was that in the aspect of affairs at Brockhurst which might very well provoke curious comment. For the rigour of Richard Calmady's self-imposed seclusion, to which Miss St. Quentin had made allusion in her conversation with Dr. Knott, was not relaxed. Rather, indeed, did it threaten to pass from the accident of a first return, after long absence and illness, into a matter of fixed and accepted habit. For those years of lonely wandering and spasmodic rage of living, finding their climax in deepening disappointment, disillusion, and the shock of rudely inflicted insult and disgrace, had produced in Richard a profound sense of alienation from society and from the amenities of ordinary intercourse. Since he was apparently doomed to survive, he would go home; but go home very much as some trapped or wounded beast crawls back to hide in its lair. He was master in his own house, at least, and safe from intrusion there. The place offered the silent sympathy of things familiar, and therefore, in a sense, uncritical. It is restful to look on that upon which one has already looked a thousand times. And so, after his reconciliation with his mother, followed, in natural sequence, his reconciliation with Brockhurst. Here he would see only those who loved him well enough—in their several stations and degrees —to respect his humour, to ask no questions, to leave him to himself. Richard was gentle in manner at this period, courteous, humorous even. But a great discouragement was upon him. It seemed as though some string had snapped, leaving half his nature broken, unresponsive, and dumb. He had no ambitions, no desire of activities. Sport and business were as little to his mind as society.

More than this.—At first the excuse of fatigue had served him, but very soon it came to be a tacitly admitted fact that Richard did not leave the house. Surely it was large enough, he said, to afford space for all the exercise he needed? Refusing to occupy

34

his old suite of rooms on the ground-floor, he had sent orders, before his arrival, that the smaller library, adjoining the Long Gallery, should be converted into a bed-chamber for him. It had been Richard's practice, when on board ship, to steady his uncertain footsteps, on the slippery or slanting plane of the deck, by the use of crutches. And this practice he in great measure retained. It increased his poor powers of locomotion. It rendered him more independent. Sometimes, when secure that Lady Calmady would not receive visitors, he would make his way by the large library, the state drawing-room, and stair-head, to the Chapel-Room and sit with her there. But more often his days were spent exclusively in the Long Gallery. He had brought home many curious and beautiful objects from his wanderings. He would add these to the existing collection. He would examine the books too, procure such volumes as were needed to complete any imperfect series; and, in the departments of science, literature, and travel, bring the library up to date. He would devote his leisure to the study of various subjects—specially natural science — regarding which he was conscious of a knowledge deficient, or merely empirical.

"I really am perfectly contented, mother," he said to Lady Calmady more than once. "Look at the length and breadth of the gallery! It is as a city of magnificent distances, after the deck of the dear, old yacht and my twelve-foot cabin. And I'm not a man calculated to occupy so very much space after all. Let me potter about here with my books and my *bibelots*. Don't worry about me, I shall keep quite well, I promise you. Let me hybernate peacefully until the spring, anyhow. I have plenty of occupation. Julius is going to amend the library catalogue with me, and there are those chests of deeds, and order-books, and diaries, which really ought to be looked over. As it appears pretty certain I shall be the last of the family, it would be only civil, I think, to bestow a little of my ample leisure upon my forefathers, and set down some more or less comprehensive account of them and their doings. They appear to have been given to rather dramatic adventures.—Don't you worry, you dear sweet! As I say, let me hybernate until the birds of passage come and the young leaves are green in the spring. Then, when the days grow long and bright, the sea will begin to call again, and, when it calls you and I will pack and go."

And Katherine yielded, being convinced that Richard could treat his own case best. If healing, complete and radical, was to be effected, it must come from within and not from without.

Her wisdom was to wait in faith. There was much that had never been told, and never would be told. Much which had not been explained, and never would be explained. For, notwithstanding the very gracious relation existing between herself and Richard, Katherine realised that there were blank spaces not only in her knowledge of his past action, but in her knowledge of the sentiments which now animated him. As from a far country his mind, she perceived, often travelled to meet hers. "There was a door to which she found no key;" but Katherine, happily, could respect the individuality even of her best beloved. Unlike the majority of her sex she was incapable of intrusion, and did not make affection an excuse for familiarity. Love, in her opinion, enjoins obligations of service, rather than confers rights of examination and direction. She had learned the condition in which his servants had found Richard, in the opera box of the great theatre at Naples, lying upon the floor, unconscious, his face disfigured, cut, and bleeding. But what had produced this condition, whether accident or act of violence, she had not learned. She had also learned that her niece, Helen de Vallorbes, had stayed at the villa just before the commencement of Richard's illness—he merely passing his days there, and spending his nights on board the yacht in the harbour, where, no doubt, that same illness had been contracted. But she resisted the inclination to attempt further discovery. She even resisted the inclination to speculate regarding all this. What Richard might elect to tell her, that, and that only, would she know, lest, seeking further, bitter and vindictive thoughts should arise in her and mar the calm, pathetic sweetness of the present and her deep, abiding joy in the recovery of her so-long-lost delight. She refused to go behind the fact—the glad fact that Richard once more was with her, that her eyes beheld him, her ears heard his voice, her hands met his. Every little act of thoughtful care, every pretty word of half-playful affection, confirmed her thankfulness and made the present blest. Even this somewhat morbid tendency of his to shut himself away from the observation of all acquaintance, conferred on her such sweetly exclusive rights of intercourse that she could not greatly quarrel with his secluded way of life. As to the business of the estate and household, this had become so much a matter of course to her that it caused her but small labour. If she could deal with it when Richard was estranged and far away, very surely she could deal with it now, when she had but to open the door of that vast, silvery-tinted, pensively fragrant, many-windowed room, and entering, among its many strange and costly treasures, find him—a treasure as strange, and if counted by her past suffering, as costly, as ever ravished and tortured a woman's heart.

And so it came about that, to such few friends as she received, Katherine could show a serene countenance. Shortly before Christmas, Miss St. Quentin came to Brockhurst; and coming stayed, adapting herself with ready tact to the altered conditions of life there. Katherine found not only pleasure, but support, in the younger woman's presence, in her devoted yet unexacting affection, in her practical ability, and in the sight of so graceful a creature going to and fro. She installed her guest in the Gun-Room suite. And, by insensible degrees, permitted Honoria to return to many of her former avocations in connection with the estate; so that the young lady took over much of the outdoor business, riding forth almost daily, by herself or in company with Julius March, to superintend matters of building or repairing, of road-mending, hedging, copsing, or forestry; and not infrequently cheering Chifney—a somewhat sour-minded man just now and prickly-tempered, since Richard asked no word of him or of his horses—by visits to the racing-stables.

"I had better step down and have a crack with the poor old dear, Cousin Katherine," she would say, "or those unlucky little wretches of boys will catch it double tides, which really is rather superfluous."

And all the while, amid her very varied interests and occupations, remembrance of that hidden, twilight life, going forward upstairs in the well-known rooms which she now never entered, came to Honoria as some perpetually recurrent and mournful harmony, in an otherwise not ungladsome piece of music, might have come. It exercised a certain dominion over her mind; so that Richard Calmady, though never actually seen by her, was never wholly absent from her thought. All the orderly routine of the great house, all the day's work and the sentiment of it, was subtly influenced by awareness of the actuality of his invisible presence. And this affected her strongly, causing her hours of repulsion and annoyance, and again hours of abounding, if reluctant pity, when the unnatural situation of this man—young as herself, endowed with a fine intelligence, an aptitude for affairs, the craving for amusement common to his age and class—and the pathos inherent in that situation, haunted her imagination. His self-inflicted imprisonment appeared a reflection upon, in a sense a reproach to, her own freedom of soul and pleasant liberty of movement. And this troubled her. It touched her pride somehow. It produced in her a false conscience, as though she were guilty of an unkindness, a lack of considerateness and perfect delicacy.

"Whether he behaves well or ill, whether he is good or bad, Richard Calmady invariably takes up altogether too much room," she would tell herself half angrily—to find herself within half an hour, under plea of usefulness to his mother, warmly interested in some practical matter from which Richard Calmady would derive, at least indirectly, distinct advantage and benefit!

This, then, was the state of affairs one Saturday afternoon late in February. With poor Dickie himself the day had been marked by superabundant discouragement. He was well in body. The restfulness of one quiet, uneventful week following another had steadied his nerves, repaired the waste of fever, and restored his physical strength. But along with this return of health had come a growing necessity to lay hold of some idea, to discover some basis of thought, some incentive to action, which should make life less purposeless and unprofitable. Richard, in short, was beginning to generate more energy than he could place. The old order had passed away, and no new order had, as yet, effectively disclosed itself. He had not formulated all this, or even consciously recognised the modification of his own attitude. Nevertheless he felt the gnawing ache of inward emptiness. It effectually broke up the torpor which had held him. It made him very restless. It re-awoke in him an inclination to speculation and experiment.

Snow had fallen during the earlier hours of the day, and, the surface of the ground being frost-bound, it, though by no means deep, remained unmelted. The whiteness of it, given back by the ceiling and pale panelling of walls of the Long Gallery, notwithstanding the generous fires burning in the two ornate, high-ranging chimney-places, produced, as the day waned, an effect of rather stark cheerlessness in the great room. This was at once in unison with Richard's somewhat bleak humour, and calculated to increase the famine of it.

All day long he had tried to stifle the cry of that same famine, that same hunger of unplaced energy, by industrious work. He had examined, noted, here and there transcribed, passages from deeds, letters, order-books, and diaries offering first-hand information regarding former generations of Calmadys. It happened that studies he had recently made in contemporary science, specially in obtaining theories of biology, had brought home to him what tremendous factors in the development and fate of the individual are both evolution and heredity. At first idly, and as a mere pastime, then with increasing eagerness—in the vague hope his researches might throw light on matters of moment to himself and of personal application—he had tried to trace out tastes and strains of tendency common to his ancestors. But under this head he had failed to make any very notable discoveries. For these courtiers, soldiers, and sportsmen were united merely by the obvious characteristics of a high-spirited, free-living race. They were raised above the average of the country gentry, perhaps, by a greater appreciation than is altogether common of literature and art. But, as Richard soon perceived, it was less any persistent peculiarity of mental and physical constitution, than a similarity of outward event which united them. The perpetually repeated chronicle of violence and accident which he read, in connection with his people, intrigued his reason, and called for explanation. Is it possible, he began to ask himself, that a certain heredity in incident, in external happening, may not cling to a race? That these may not by some strange process be transmissible, as are traits of character, temperament, of stature, colouring, feature, or face? And if this —as matter of speculation merely—is the case, must there not exist some antecedent cause to which could be referred such persistent effect? Might not an hereditary fate in external events take its rise in some supreme moral or spiritual catastrophe, some violation of law? The Greek dramatists held it was so. The writers of the Old Testament held it was so, too.

Sitting at the low writing-table, near the blazing fire, that stark whiteness reflected from off the snow-covered land all around him, Richard debated this point with himself. He admitted the theory was not scientific, according to the reasoning of modern physical science. It approached an outlook theological rather than rationalistic; yet he could not deny the conception, admission. The vision of a doomed family arose before him— starting in each successive generation with brilliant prospects and high hope, only to find speedy extinction in some more or less brutal form of death; a race dwindling, moreover, in numbers as the years passed, until it found representation in a single individual, and that individual maimed and incomplete! Heredity of accident, heredity of disaster, finding final expression in himself—this confronted Richard. He had reckoned himself, heretofore, a solitary example of ill-fortune. But, mastering the contents of these records, he found himself far from solitary. He merely participated, though under a novel form, in the unlucky fate of all the men of his race. And then arose the question— to him, under existing circumstances, of vital importance—what stood behind all that—blind chance, cynical indifference, wanton and arbitrary cruelty, or some august, far-reaching necessity of, as yet, unsatisfied justice?

Richard pushed the crackling, stiffly-folded parchments, the letters frayed and yellow with age, the broken-backed, discoloured diaries and order-books, away from him, and sat, his elbows on the table, his forehead in his hands, thinking. And the travail of his spirit was great, as it needs must be, at times, with every human being who dares live at first, not merely at second hand—who dares attempt a real, and not merely a nominal assent—who dares deal with earthly existence, the amazing problems and complexities of it, immediately, refusing to accept—with indolent timidity—tradition, custom, hearsay, convenience, as his guides.—Oh! for some sure answering, some unimpeachable assurance, some revelation not relative and symbolic, but absolute; some declaration above all suspicion of cunningly-devised opportunism, concerning the dealings of the unknown force man calls God, with the animal man calls man!—And then Richard turned upon himself contemptuously. For it was childish to cry out thus. The heavens were dumb above him as the snow-bound earth was dumb beneath. There was no sign. Never had been. Never would be, save in the fond imaginations of religious enthusiasts, crazed by superstition, by austerities and hysteria, duped by ignorance, by hypocrites and quacks.

With long-armed adroitness he reached down and picked up those light-made, stunted crutches, slipped from his chair and adjusted them. For a long while he had used them as a matter of course without criticism or thought. But now they produced in him a swift disgust. His hands, grasping the lowest crossbar of them, were in such disproportionate proximity to the floor! For the moment he was disposed to fling them aside. Then again he turned upon himself with scathing contempt. For this too was childish. What did the use of them matter, since, used or not, the fact of his crippled condition remained? And so, with a renewal of bitterness and active rebellion, lately unknown to him, he moved away down the great room—past bronze athlete and marble goddess, past oriental jars, tall as himself, uplifted on the squat, carven, ebony stands, past strangely-painted, half-fearful, lacquer cabinets, past porcelain bowls filled with faint sweetness of dried rose leaves, bay, lavender, and spice, past trophies of savage warfare and, hardly less savage, civilised sport, towards the wide mullion-window of the eastern bay. But just before reaching it, he came opposite to a picture by Velasquez, set on an easel across the corner of the room. It represented a hideous and mis-shapen dwarf, holding a couple of graceful greyhounds in a leash—an unhappy creature who had made sport for the household of some Castilian grandee, and whose gorgeous garments, of scarlet and gold, were ingeniously designed so as to accentuate the physical degradation of its contorted person. Richard had come, of late, to take a sombre pleasure in the contemplation of this picture. The desolate eyes, looking out of the marred and brutal face, met his own with a certain claim of kinship. There existed a tragic free-masonry between himself and this outcasted being, begotten of a common knowledge, and common experience. As a boy Richard hated this picture, studiously avoided the sight of it. It had suggested comparisons which wounded his self-respect too shrewdly and endangered his self-security. He hated it no longer, finding grim solace, indeed, in its sad society.

And it was thus, in silent parley with this rather dreadful companion, as the blear February twilight descended upon the bare, black trees and snow-clad land without, and upon the very miscellaneous furnishings of the many-windowed gallery within, that Julius March now discovered Richard Calmady. He had returned, across the park, from one of the ancient brick-and-timber cottages just without the last park gate, at the end of Sandyfield Church-lane. A labourer's wife was dying, painfully enough, of cancer; and he had administered the Blessed Sacrament to her, there, in her humble bed-chamber. The august promises and adorable consolations of that mysterious rite remained very sensibly present to him on his homeward way. His spirit was uplifted by the confirmation of the divine compassion therein perpetually renewed, perpetually made evident. And, it followed, that to come now upon Richard Calmady alone, here, in the stark, unnatural pallor of the winter dusk, holding silent communion with that long-ago victim of merciless practices and depraved tastes, not only caused him a painful shock, but also moved him with fervid desire to offer comfort and render help. Yet, what to say, how to approach Richard without risk of seeming officiousness and consequent offence, he could not tell. The young man's experiences and his own were so conspicuously far apart. For a moment he stood uncertain and silent, then he said :—

"That picture always fills me with self-reproach."

Richard looked round with a certain lofty courtesy by no means encouraging. And, as he did so, Julius March was conscious of receiving yet another, and not less painful, impression. For Richard's face was very still, not with the stillness of repose, but with that of fierce emotion held resolutely in check, while in his eyes was a desolation rivalling that of the eyes portrayed by the great Spanish artist upon the canvas close at hand.

"When I first came to Brockhurst, that picture used to hang in the study," he continued, by way of explanation.

"Ah! I see, and you turned it out!" Richard observed, not without an inflection of scorn.

"Yes. In those days I am afraid I did not discriminate very justly between refinement of taste and self-indulgent fastidiousness. While pluming myself upon an exalted standard of sensibility and sentiment, I rather basely spared myself acquaintance with that, both in nature and in art, which might cause me distress or disturbance of thought. I was a mental valetudinarian, in short. I am ashamed of my defect of moral courage and charity in relation to that picture."

Richard shifted his position slightly, looked fixedly at the canvas and then down at his own hands in such disproportionate proximity to the floor.

"Oh! you were not to blame," he said. "It is obviously a thing to laugh at, or run from, unless you happen to have received a peculiar mental and physical training. Anyhow, the poor devil has found his way home now and come into port safely enough at last!"

He glanced back at the picture, over his shoulder, as he moved across the room.

"Perhaps he's even found a trifle of genuine sympathy—so don't vex your righteous soul over your repudiation of him, my dear Julius. The lapses of the virtuous may make, indirectly, for good. And your instinct, after all, was both the healthy and the artistic one. Velasquez ought to have been incapable of putting his talent to such vile uses; and the first comer, with a spark of true philanthropy in him, ought to have knocked that poor little monstrosity on the head."

Richard came to the writing-table, glanced at the papers which encumbered it, made for an arm-chair drawn up beside the fire.

"Sit down, Julius," he said. "There is something quite else about which I want to speak to you.—I have been working through all these documents, and they give rise to speculations neither strictly scientific nor strictly orthodox, yet interesting all the same. You are a dealer in ethical problems. I wonder if you can offer any solution of this one, of which the basis conceivably is ethical. As to these various owners of Brockhurst—Sir Denzil, the builder of the house, is a delightful person, and appears to have prospered mightily in his undertakings, as so liberal-minded and ingenious a gentleman had every right to prosper. But after him—from the time, at least, of his grandson, Thomas—everything —seems to have gone to rather howling grief here. We have nothing but battle, murder, and sudden death. These become positively monotonous in the pertinacity of their repetition. Of course one may argue that adventurous persons expose themselves to an uncommon number of dangers, and consequently pay an uncommon number of forfeits. I daresay that is the reasonable explanation. Only the persistence of the thing gets hold of one rather. The manner of their dying is very varied, yet there are two constant quantities in each successive narrative, namely violence and comparative youth."

Richard's speech had become rapid and imperative. Now he paused.

"Think of my father's death, for instance," he said.

His narrow, black figure crouched together, Julius March knelt on one knee before the fire. He held his thin hands outspread, so as to keep the glow of the burning logs from his face. He was deeply moved, debating a certain matter with himself.

"To all questions supremely worth having answered, there is no answer—I take that for granted," the young man continued. "And yet one is so made that it is impossible not to go on asking. I can't help wanting to get at the root of this queer recurrence of accident, and all the rest of it, which clings to my people. I can't help wanting to make out whether there was any psychological moment which determined the future, and started them definitely on the down-grade. What happened—that's what I want to arrive at—what happened at that moment? Had it any reasonable and legitimate connection with all which has followed?"

As he held them out-spread, between his face and the glowing fire, Julius March's hands trembled. He found himself confronted by a situation which he had long foreseen, long and earnestly prayed to avoid. The responsibility was so great of either giving or withholding the answer, as he knew it, to that question of Dickie's. A way of rendering possible help opened before him. But it was a way beset with difficulties, a way at once fantastic and coarsely realistic, a way along which the sublime and the ridiculous jostled each other with somewhat undignified closeness of association, a way demanding childlike faith, not to say childish credulity, coupled with a great fearlessness and self-abnegation before ever a man's steps could be profitably set in it. If presented to Richard, would he not turn angrily from it as an insult offered to his intellect and his breeding alike? Indeed, the hope of effecting good showed very thin. The danger of provoking evil bulked very big. What was his duty? He suffered an agony of indecision. And again with a slight inflection of mockery in his tone, Richard spoke.

"All blind chance, Julius? I declare I get a little weary of this Deity of yours. He neglects His business so flagrantly. He really is rather scandalously much of an absentee. And He would be so welcome if He would condescend to deal a trifle more openly with one, and satisfy one's intelligence and moral sense. If, for instance, He would afford me some information regarding this same psychological moment which I need so badly just now as a peg to hang a theory of causality upon. I am ambitious—as much in the interests of His reputation as in those of my own curiosity—to get at the logic of the affair, to get at the why and wherefore of it, and lay my finger on the spot where differentiation sets in."

Julius March stood upright. Richard's scorn hurt him. It also terminated his indecision. For a little space he looked out into the stark whiteness of the snowy dusk, and then down at the young man, leaning back in the low chair, there close before him. To Julius' short-sighted eyes, in the uncertain light, Dickie's face bore compelling resemblance to Lady Calmady's. This touched him with the memory of much, and he went back on the thought of the divine compassion, perpetually renewed, perpetually made evident in the Eucharistic Sacrifice. Man may rail, yet God is strong and faithful to bless. Perhaps that way was neither too fantastic, nor too humble, after all, for Richard to walk in.

"Has no knowledge of the received legend about this subject ever reached you?"

"No—never—not a word."

"I became acquainted with it accidentally, long ago, before your birth. It is inadmissible, according to modern canons of thought, as such legends usually are. And events, subsequent to my acquaintance with it, conferred on it so singular and painful a significance that I kept my knowledge to myself. Perhaps when you grew up I ought to have put you in possession of the facts. They touch you very nearly."

Richard raised his eyebrows.

"Indeed," he said coldly.

"But a fitting opportunity—at least, so I judged, being, I own, backward and reluctant in the matter—never presented itself. In this, as in much else, I fear I have betrayed my trust

and proved an unprofitable servant—if so may God forgive
me."

"It would have gone hard with Brockhurst without you,
Julius," Richard said, a sudden softening in his tone.

"I will bring you the documents the last thing to-night,
when—your mother has left you. They are best read, perhaps,
in silence and alone."

CHAPTER VI

A LITANY OF THE SACRED HEART

RICHARD drew himself up on to the wide, cushioned
bench below the oriel-window. The February day was
windless and very bright. And although in sheltered, low-lying
places, where the frost held, the snow still lingered, in the open
it had already disappeared, and that without unsightliness of
slush—-shrinking and vanishing, cleanly burned up and absorbed
by the genial heat. A sabbath-day restfulness held the whole
land. There was no movement of labour, either of man or
beast. And a kindred restfulness pervaded the house. The
rooms were vacant. None passed to and fro. For it so
happened that good Mr. Caryll's successor, the now rector of Sandyfield, had been called away to deliver certain charity sermons at
Westchurch, and that to-day Julius March officiated in his stead.
Therefore Lady Calmady and Miss St. Quentin, and the major
part of the Brockhurst household, had repaired by carriage or on
foot to the little, squat, red-brick, Georgian church whose two
bells rang out so friendly and fussy an admonition to the faithful
to gather within its walls.

Richard had the house to himself. And this accentuation of
solitude, combined with wider space wherein he could range
without fear of observation, was far from unwelcome to him.
Last night he had untied the tag of rusty, black ribbon binding
together the packet of tattered, dog's-eared, little chap-books
which, for so long, had reposed in the locked drawer of Julius
March's study table beneath the guardianship of the bronze
pietà. With very conflicting feelings he had mastered the
contents of those same untidy, little volumes, and learned the
sordid, and probably fabulous, tale set forth in them in meanest
vehicle of jingling verse. Vulgarly told to catch the vulgar ear,
pandering to the popular superstitions of a somewhat ignoble
age, it proved repugnant enough—as Julius had anticipated—

both to Richard's reason and to his taste. The critical faculty rejected it as an explanation absurdly inadequate. The cause was wholly disproportionate to the effect, as though the mouse should bring forth a mountain instead of the mountain a mouse. At least that was how the matter struck Richard at first. For the story was, after all, as he told himself, but a commonplace of life in every civilised community. Many a man sins thus, and many a woman suffers, and many bastards are yearly born into the world without—perhaps unfortunately—subsequent manifestation of the divine wrath and signal chastisement of the sinner, or of his legitimate heirs, male or female. Affiliation orders are as well known to magistrates' clerks, as are death-certificates of children bearing the maiden-name of their mother to those of the registrar.

All that Richard could dispose of, if with a decent deploring of the frequency of it, yet composedly enough. But there remained that other part of it. And this he could not dispose of so cursorily. His own unhappy deformity, it is true, was amply accounted for on lines quite other than the fulfilment of prophecy, offering, as it did, example of a class of pre-natal accident which, if rare, is still admittedly recurrent in the annals of obstetrics and embryology. Nevertheless, the foretelling of that strange Child of Promise, whose outward aspect and the circumstances of whose birth—as set forth in the sorry rhyme of the chap-book—bore such startling resemblance to his own, impressed him deeply. It astonished, it, in a sense, appalled him. For it came so very near. It looked him so insistently in the face. It laid strong hands on him from out the long past, claiming him, associating itself imperatively with him, asserting, whether he would or no, the actuality and inalienability of its relation to himself. Science might pour contempt on that relation, exposing the absurdity of it both from the moral and physical point of view. But sentiment held other language. And so did that nobler morality which takes its rise in considerations spiritual rather than social and economic; and finds the origins and ultimates alike, not in things seen and temporal, but in things unseen and eternal—things which, though they tarry long for accomplishment, can neither change, nor be denied, nor, short of accomplishment, can pass away.

And it was this aspect of the whole, strange matter—the thought, namely, of that same Child of Promise who, predestined to bear the last and heaviest stroke of retributive justice, should, bearing it rightly, bring salvation to his race—which obtained with Richard on the fair Sunday morning in question. It refused to quit him. It affected him through all his being. It appealed

to the poetry, the idealism, of his nature — a poetry and
idealism not dead, as he had bitterly reckoned them, though
sorely wounded by ill-living and by the disastrous issues of his
passion for Helen de Vallorbes.   He seemed to apprehend
the approach of some fruitful, far-ranging, profoundly-reconcil-
ing and beneficent event.   As in the theatre at Naples when
Morabita sang, and, to his fever-stricken, brain-sick fancy the
dull-coloured multitude in the *parterre* murmured, buzzing
remonstrant as angry swarming bees, so now a certain exaltation of feeling, exaltation of hope, came upon him.—Yet
having grown, through determined rebellion and unlovely
experience, not a little distrustful of all promise of good, he
turned on himself bitterly enough, asking if he would never learn
to profit by hardly-bought, practical knowledge?   If he would
never contrive to cast the simpleton wholly out of him?   He
had been fooled many times, fooled there at Naples to the point
of unpardonable insult and degradation.   What so probable as
that he would be fooled again, now?

And so, in effort to shake off both the dominion of unfounded
hope, and the gnawing ache of inward emptiness which made
that hope at once so cruel and so dear, as the sound of wheels
dying away along the lime avenue assured him that the goodly
company of church-goers had, verily and indeed, departed, he
set forth on a pilgrimage through the great, silent house.   Passing
through the two libraries, the ante-chamber and state drawing-
room—with its gilded furniture, fine pictures and tapestries—
he reached the open corridor at the stair-head.   Here the
polished, oak floor, the massive balusters, and tall, carven
newel-posts—each topped by a guardian griffin, long of tail,
ferocious of beak, and sharp of claw—showed with a certain
sober mirthfulness in the pleasant light.   For, through all the
great windows of the eastern front, the sun slanted in obliquely.
While in the Chapel-Room beyond, situated in the angle of the
house and thus enjoying a southern as well as eastern aspect,
Richard found a veritable carnival of misty brightness ; so that he
moved across to the oriel-window—whose grey stone mullions
and carved transoms showed delicately mellow of tone between
the glittering, leaded panes—in a glory of welcoming warmth and
sunlight.   Frost and snow might linger in the hollows, but here
in the open, on the upland, spring surely had already come.

With the help of a brass ring, riveted by a stanchion into the
space of panelling below the stone window-sill—placed there long
ago, when he was a little lad, to serve him in such case as the
present—Richard drew himself up on to the cushioned bench.

He unfastened one of the narrow, curved, iron-framed casements, and, leaning his elbows on the sill, looked out.   The air was mild. The smell of the earth was sweet, with a cleanly, wholesome sweetness.   The sunshine covered him.   And somehow, whether he would or no, hope reasserted its dominion ; and that exaltation of feeling entered into possession of him once again, as he rested, gazing away over the familiar home scene, over this land which, as far as sight carried, had belonged to his people these many generations, and was now his own.

Directly below, at the foot of the descending steps of the main entrance, lay the square, red-walled space of gravel and of turf.   He looked at it curiously, for there, with the maiming and death of Thomas Calmady's bastard, if legend said truly, all this tragic history of disaster had begun.   There, too, the Clown, racehorse of merry name and mournful memory, had paid the penalty of wholly involuntary transgression just thirty years ago. That last was a rather horrible incident, of which Richard never cared to think.   Chifney had told him about it once, in connection with the parentage of Verdigris—had told him just by chance. To think of it, even now, made a lump rise in his throat.   Across the turf—offering quaint contrast to those somewhat bloody memories—the peacocks, in all their bravery of royal blue-purple, living green and gold, led forth their sober-clad mates.   They had come out from the pepper-pot summer-houses to sun themselves.   They stepped mincingly, with a worldly and disdainful grace ; and, reaching the gravel, their resplendent trains swept the rounded pebbles, making a small, dry, rattling sound, which, so deep was the surrounding quiet, asserted itself to the extent of saluting Richard's ears.   Beyond the red wall the parallel lines of the elm avenue swept down to the blue and silver levels of the Long Water, the alder copses bordering which showed black-purple, and the reed-beds rusty as a fox, against thin stretches of still unmelted snow.   The avenue climbed the farther ascent to the wide archway of the red and grey gate-house, just short of the top of the long ridge of bare moorland.   The grass slopes of the park, to the left, were backed by the dark, sawlike edge of the fir forest ; and a soft gloom of oak woods, grey-brown and mottled as a lizard's belly and back, closed the end of the valley eastward.   On the right the terraced gardens, with their ranges of glittering conservatories, fell away to the sombre pond in the valley, home of loudly-discoursing companies of ducks. The gentle hillside above was clothed by plantations, and by a grove of ancient beech trees, whose pale, smooth boles stood out from among undergrowth of lustrous hollies and the warm russet of fallen leaves. And over it all brooded the restfulness of the sabbath, and the gladness of a fair and equal light.

And the charm of the scene worked upon Richard, not with any heat of excitement, but with a temperate and reasonable grace. For the spirit of it all was a spirit of temperance, of moderation, of secure tranquillity — a spirit stoic rather than epicurean, ascetic rather than hedonic; yet generous, spacious, nobly reasonable, giving ample scope for very sincere, if soberly-clad pleasures, and for activities by no means despicable or unmanly, though of a modest, unostentatious sort. Richard had tried not a few desperate adventures, had conformed his thought and action to not a few glaring patterns, rushing to violences of extreme colour, extreme white and black. All that had proved pre-eminently unsuccessful, a most poisonous harvest of Dead Sea fruit. What, he began to ask himself, if he made an effort to conform it to the pattern actually presented to him—mellow, sun-visited, with the brave red of weather-stained masonry in it, blue and silver of water and sky, lustre of sturdy hollies, as well as the solemnity of leafless woods, finger of frost in the hollows, and bleakness of snow?

And, as he sat meditating thus, breathing the clear air, feeling the tempered, yet genial, sun-heat, many questions began to resolve themselves. He seemed to look—as down a long, cloudy vista—beyond the tumult and unruly clamour, the wayward resistance and defiant sinning, the craven complainings, the ever-repeated suspicions and misapprehensions of man, away into the patient, unalterable purposes of God. And looking, for the moment, into those purposes, he saw this also—namely that sorrow, pain, and death are sweet to whosoever dares, instead of fighting with or flying from them, to draw near, to examine closely, to inquire humbly, into their nature and their function. He began to perceive that these three reputed enemies, hated and feared of all men, are, after all, the fashioners and teachers of humanity; to whom it is given to keep hearts pure, godly, and compassionate, to purge away the dross of pride, hardness, and arrogance, to break the iron bands of ambition, self-love, and vanity, to purify by endurance and by charity, welding together —as with the cunning strokes of the master-craftsman's hammer— the innumerable individual atoms into a corporate whole, of fair form, of supreme excellence of proportion, the image and example of a perfect brotherhood, of a republic more firmly based and more beneficent than even that pictured by the divine Plato himself—since that was consolidated by the exclusion, this by the inclusion and pacification of those three things which men most dread.—Perceived that, without the guiding and chastening of these three lovely terrors, humanity would, indeed, wax wanton, and this world become the merriest court of hell, lust and corruption have it all their own foul way, the flesh triumph, and all bestial things come forth to flaunt themselves gaudily, greedily, without remonstrance and without shame in the light of day.—Perceived, in these three, a Trinity of Holy Spirits, bearing forever the message of the divine mercy and forgiveness.—Perceived how, of necessity, only the Man of Sorrows can truly be the Son of God.

And, perceiving all this, Richard's attitude towards his own unhappy deformity began to suffer modification. The sordid, yet extravagant, chap-book legend no longer outraged either his moral or his scientific sense. He recalled his emotions in the theatre at Naples when Morabita sang, remembering how wholly welcome had then been to him that imagined approaching-act of retributive justice. He recalled, too, the going forth of love towards his supposed executioners which he had experienced, his reverence for, and yearning towards, the dull-coloured working-bees of the *parterre*. How he had longed to be at one with them, partaker of their corporate action and corporate strength ! How he had rejoiced in the conviction that the final issues are subject to their ruling, that the claims of want are stronger than those of wealth, that labour is more honourable than sloth, intelligence more enduring than privilege, liberty more abiding than tyranny, the idea of equality, of fellowship, more excellent than the aristocratic idea, that of born master and of born serf ! And both that welcome of the accomplishment of a signal act of justice, and that desire to participate in the eternal strength of the children of labour as against the ephemeral and fictitious strength of the children of idleness and wealth, found strange confirmation in the chap-book legend.

For it seemed to Richard that, taking all that singular matter both of prophecy and of cure simply—as believers take some half-miraculous, scripture tale—he had already, in his own person, in right of the physical uncomeliness of it, paid part, at all events, of the price demanded by the Eternal Justice for his ancestors' sinning and for his own. It was not needful that the bees should swarm and the dull-coloured multitude revenge itself on the indolent, full-fed larvæ peopling the angular honey-cells, as far as he, Richard Calmady, was concerned. That revenge had been taken long ago, in a mysterious and rather terrible manner, before his very birth. While, in the stern denunciation, the adhering curse, of the outraged and so-soon-to-be-childless

35

mother, he found the just and age-old protest, the patient faith in the eventual triumph of the proletariat—of the defenceless poor as against the callous self-seeking and sensuality of the securely buttressed rich. By the fact of his deformity he was emancipated from the delusions of his class; was made one, in right of the suffering and humiliation of it, with the dull-coloured multitudes whose corporate voice declares the ultimate verdict, who are the architects and judges of civilisation, of art, even of religion, even, in a degree, of nature herself. Salvation, according to the sorry yet inspiring rhyme of the chap-book, was contingent upon precisely this recognition of brotherhood with, and practice of willing service towards, all maimed and sorrowful creatures. His America was here or nowhere, his vocation clearly indicated, his work immediate and close at hand.

How the Eternal Justice might see fit to deal with other souls, why he had been singled out for so peculiar and conspicuous a fate, Richard did not pretend to say. All that had become curiously unimportant to him. For he had ceased to call that fate a cruel one. It had changed its aspect. It had come suddenly to satisfy both his conscience and his imagination. With a movement at once of wonder and of deep-seated thankfulness, he, for the first time, held out his hands to it, accepting it as a comrade, pledging himself to use rather than to spurn it. He looked at it steadfastly and, so looking, found it no longer abhorrent but of mysterious virtue and efficacy, endued with power to open the gates of a way, closed to most men, into the heart of humanity, which, in a sense, is nothing less than the heart of Almighty God Himself. It was as though, like the saint of old, daring to kiss the scabs and sores of the leper, he found himself gazing on the divine lineaments of the risen Christ. And this brought to him a sense of almost awed repose. It released him from the vicious circle of self, of sharp-toothed disappointment and leaden-heavy discouragement, in which he had so long fruitlessly turned. He seemed consciously to slough off the foul and ragged garment of the past and all its base, unprofitable memories, as the snake sloughs off her old skin in the warm May weather and glides forth, glittering, in a coat of untarnished, silver mail. The whole complexion of his thought regarding his personal disfigurement was changed.

Not that he flattered himself the discomfort, the daily vexation and impediment of it, had passed away. On the contrary these very actually remained, and would remain to the end. And the consequences they entailed remained also, the restrictions and deprivations they inflicted. They put many things, dear to every sane and healthy-minded man, hopelessly out of his reach, very much upon the shelf. Love and marriage were shelved thus, in his opinion, let alone lesser and more ephemeral joys. Only the ungrudging acceptance of the denial of those joys, whether small or great, was a vital part of that idea to the evolution of which he now dedicated himself—that Whole which, in process of its evolution, would make for a sober and temperate well-being, formed on the pattern, sober yet nobly spacious, very fair and wholesome, of the sun-visited landscape there without. He had just got to discipline himself into harmony with the idea newly revealed to him. And that, as he told himself, not without a sense of the humour of the situation in certain of its aspects, meant in more than one department, plenty of work!— And he had to spend himself and go on, through good report and ill, through gratitude and, if needs be, through abuse and detraction, still spending himself, actively, untiringly, in the effort to make some one person—it hardly mattered whom, but for choice, those who like himself had been treated unhandsomely by nature or by accident—just a trifle happier day by day.

But, while Richard rested thus in the quiet sunshine, he lost count of time. High-noon came and passed, finding and leaving him in absorbed contemplation of his own thought. At last a barking of dogs, and the sound of wheels away on the north side of the house, broke up the silence. Then a faint echo of voices, a boy's laughter in the great hall below. Then footsteps, which he took to be Lady Calmady's, coming lightly up the grand staircase. At the stair-head those footsteps paused for a little space, as though in indecision whither to turn. And Richard, pushed by an impulse of considerateness somewhat, it must be owned, new to him, called :—

"Mother, is that you? Do you want me? I'm here."

Whereat the footsteps came forward, in at the open door and through the soft glory of the all-pervading sunshine, with an effect of gentle urgency and haste. Katherine's grey, silk pelisse was unfastened, showing the grey, silk gown, its floating ribbons, pretty frills and flounces, beneath. Every detail of her dress was very fresh and very finished, a demure daintiness in it, from the topmost, grey plume and upstanding, velvet bow of her bonnet to the pretty shoes upon her feet. Along with a lace handkerchief and her church books, she carried a bunch of long-stalked violets. Her face was delicately flushed, a great surprise, touching upon anxiety, tempering the quick pleasure of her expression.

"My dearest," she said, "this is as delightful as it is un-expected. What brings you here?"

And Richard smiled at her without reserve, no longer as though putting a force upon himself or of set purpose, but naturally, spontaneously, as one who entertains pleasant thoughts. He took her hand and kissed it with a certain courtliness and reverent fervour.

"I came to look for something here," he said, "which I have looked for many times and in very various places, yet never somehow managed to find."

But Katherine, at once tenderly charmed and rendered yet more anxious by a quality in his manner and his speech unfamiliar to her, the purport of which she failed at once to gauge, answered him literally.

"My dearest, why didn't you tell me? I would have looked for it before I went to church, and saved you the trouble of the journey from the gallery here."

"Oh! the journey wasn't bad for me, I rather enjoyed it," Dickie said. "And then to tell you the truth, you've spent the better part of your dear life in looking for that same something which I could never manage to find! Poor sweet mother, no thanks to me, so far, that you haven't utterly worn yourself out in the search for it."—He paused, and gazed away out of the open casement.—"But I have a good hope that's all over and done with now, and that at last I've found the thing myself."

And Katherine, still charmed, still anxious, looked down at him wondering, for there was a perceptible under-current of emotion beneath the lightness of his speech.

"However, all that will keep," he continued.—"How did you enjoy your church? Did dear old Julius distinguish himself? How did he preach?"

And Katherine, still wondering, again answered literally.

"Very beautifully," she said, "with an unusual force and pathos. He took the congregation not a little by storm. He fairly carried us away. He was eloquent, and that with a simplicity which made one question whether he did not speak out of some pressing personal experience."—Katherine's manner was touched by a pretty edge of pique. — "Really I believed I knew all about Julius and his doings by this time, but it seems I don't! I think I must find out. It would vex me that anything should happen in which he needed sympathy, and that I did not offer it.—His subject was the answer to prayer and the fulfilment of prophecy—and how both come, come surely and directly, yet often in so different a form to that which, in our narrowness of vision and dulness of sense, we anticipate, that we fail to recognise either the answer or the fulfilment; and so miss the blessing they must needs bring, and which is so richly, so preciously, ours if we had but the wit to understand and lay hold of it."

Whereupon Richard smiled again.

"Yes," he said, "very probably Julius did speak out of personal experience, or rather vicarious experience. However, I don't think he need worry this time, at least I hope not. The answer to prayer and fulfilment of prophecy, when they're good enough to come along, don't always get the cold shoulder."— Then his expression changed, hardened a little, his lips growing thin and his jaw set.—"Look here, mother," he added, "I think perhaps I have been rather playing the fool lately, since we came home. I propose to take to the ordinary habits of civilised, christian man again. If it doesn't bother you, would you kindly let the servants know that I'm coming down to luncheon?"

"Oh! my dearest, how stupid of me, I'm so grieved!" Katherine cried. She sat down beside him on the cushioned bench, dropping service books, handkerchief, and violets, in the extremity of her gentle and apologetic distress.—"It never occurred to me that you might like to come down. The Newlands people came over to church, and I brought Mary and the two boys back. Godfrey is over from Eton for the Sunday, and little Dick has had a cold and has not gone back to school yet. What can we do? It would be so lovely to have you, and yet I don't quite know how I can send them away again."

"But why on earth should they be sent away?" Richard said, touched and amused by her earnestness. "Mary's always a dear. And I've been thinking lately I shouldn't mind seeing something of that younger boy. He is my godson, isn't he? And Knott tells me he is curiously like you and Uncle Roger. You see it's about time to select an heir-apparent for Brockhurst. Luckily I've a free hand. My life's the last in the entail."

Then, looking at him, Lady Calmady's lips trembled a little. Health had returned and with it his former good looks, but matured, spiritualised, as it seemed to her just now. The livid line of the scar had died out too, and was nearly gone. And all this, taken in connection with his words just uttered, affected her to so great and poignant a love, so great and poignant a fear of losing him, that she dared not trust herself to make any comment on those same words lest the flood-gates of emotion should be opened and she should lose her self-control.

"Very well, Dickie," she said, bowing her head.—Then she

added quickly, with a little gasp of renewed distress and apology :
—" But—but, oh ! dear me, Honoria is here too ! "

Whereat Richard laughed outright.   He could not help it,
she was so vastly engaging in her distress.

" All right," he said, " I am equal to accepting Honoria
St. Quentin into the bargain.   In short, mother dear, I take
over the lot ; and if anybody else turns up between now and two
o'clock I'll take them over as well.—Why, why, you dear sweet,
don't look so scared !   There's nothing to trouble about.   I'm
not too good to live, never fear.   On the contrary, I am prepared
to do quite a fine amount of living—only on new and more
modest lines perhaps.   But we won't talk about that just yet,
please.   We'll wait to give it a name until we're a little more
sure how it promises to work out."

CHAPTER VII

WHEREIN TWO ENEMIES ARE SEEN TO CRY QUITS

GODFREY ORMISTON scudded along the terrace, past
the dining-room windows, at the top of his speed, and
Miss St. Quentin followed him at a hardly less unconventional
pace.   Together they burst, by the small, arched side-door, into
the lobby.   There ensued discussion lively though brief.   Then,
Winter setting wide the dining-room door in invitation, sight of
Honoria was presented to the company assembled within.—She,
in brave attire of dark, red cloth, black braided and befrogged,
heavy, silk cords and knotted, dangling tassels,—head-gear to
match, dark red and black, a tall, stiff aigrette set at the side of it,
—in all producing a something delightfully independent, soldierly,
ruffling even, in her aspect, as she pushed the black-haired,
bright-faced, slim-made lad, her two hands on his shoulders,
before her into the room.

" May we come to luncheon as we are, Cousin Katherine ? "
she cried.   " We're scandalously late, but we're also most
ferociously hungry and "—

But here, although Lady Calmady turned on her a welcoming and far from unjoyful countenance, she stopped dead ;
while Godfrey incontinently gave vent to that which his younger
brother—sitting beside his mother, Mary Ormiston, at table, on
Richard Calmady's right—described mentally as " the most awful
squawk."   Which squawk, it may be added,—whatever its effect

upon other members of the company,—as denoting involuntary and unceremonious descent from the high places of thirteen-year-old, public-school omniscience on the part of his elder, produced in eight-year-old Dick Ormiston such over-flowings of unqualified rapture that, for a good two minutes, he had to forego assimilation of chocolate *soufflet*, and, slipping his hands beneath the table, squeeze them together just as hard as ever he could with both knees, to avoid disgracing himself by emission of an ecstatic giggle. For once he had got the whip hand of Godfrey!—Having himself, for the best part of an hour now, been conversant with interesting developments, he found it richly diverting to behold his big brother thus incontinently bowled over by sudden disclosure of them. He repressed the giggle, with the help of squeezing knees and a certain squirming all down his neat, little back; but his blue eyes remained absolutely glued to Godfrey's person, as the latter, recovering his presence of mind and good manners, proceeded solemnly up to the head of the table to greet his unlooked-for host.

Honoria, meanwhile, if guiltless of an audible squawk, had been—as she subsequently reflected—potentially, alarmingly capable of some such primitive expression of feeling. For the shock of surprise which she suffered was so forcible, that it induced in her an absurd unreasoning instinct of flight. Indeed, that had happened, or rather was in process of happening, which revolutionised all her outlook. For that the unseen presence, consciousness of which had come to be so constant a quantity in her action and her thought, should thus declare itself in visible form, be materialised, become concrete, and that instantly, without prologue or preparation, projecting itself wholesale, so to speak, into the comfortable commonplaces of a Sunday luncheon—after her slightly uproarious race home with a perfectly normal schoolboy, from morning church too—affected her much as sudden intrusion of the supernatural might. It modified all existing relations, introducing a new and, as yet, incalculable element. Nor had she quite realised what power the unseen Richard Calmady, these many years, had exercised over her imagination, until Richard Calmady seen, was there evident, actually before her. Then all the harsh judgments she had passed upon him, all the disapproval of, and dislike she had felt towards, him, flashed through her mind. And that matter too of his cancelled engagement!—The last time she had seen him was in the house in Lowndes Square, on the night of Lady Louisa Barking's great ball, standing— she could see all that now — it was as if photographed upon her brain—always would be—and it turned her a little sick.—Nevertheless it was impossible to pause any longer. It would be ridiculous to fly, so she must stick it out. That best of good Samaritans, Mary Ormiston, began talking to Julius March across the length of the table.

"Oh dear, yes, of course," she was saying. "But I never realised she was a sister of your old Oxford friend. I wish I had. It would have been so pleasant to talk about you and about home in that far country ! Her husband is in the Rifle Brigade, and she really is a nice, dear woman. I saw a great deal of her while we were at the Cape."

And so, under cover of Mary's kindly conversation, Miss St. Quentin settled down into her lazy, swinging stride. Her small head carried high, her pale, sensitive face very serious, her straight eyebrows drawn together by concentration of purpose, concentration of thought, she followed the boy up the long room.

As 'she came towards him, Richard Calmady looked full at her. His head was carried somewhat high too. His face was very still. His eyes—with those curiously small pupils to them—were very observant, in effect hiding rather than revealing his thought. His manner, as he held out his hand to her, was courteous, even friendly ; and yet, notwithstanding her high and fearless spirit, Honoria—for the first time in her life probably—felt afraid. And then she began to understand how it came about that, whether he behaved well or ill, whether he was good or bad, cruel or kind, seen or unseen even, Richard, of necessity, could not but occupy a good deal of space in the lives of all persons brought into close contact with him. For she recognised in him a rather tremendous creature, self-contained, not easily accessible, possessed of a larger portion than most men of energy and resolution, possessed too—and this, as she thought of it, again turned her a trifle sick—of an unusual capacity of suffering.

"I am ashamed of being so dreadfully late," she said as she slipped into the vacant place on his left, Godfrey Ormiston was beyond her, next to Julius March.—Honoria was aware that her voice sounded slightly shaky, in part from her recent scamper, in part from a queer emotion which seemed to clutch at her throat.—"But we walked home over the fields and by the Warren, and just in that boggy bit where you cross the Welsh-road, Godfrey found the slot of a red-deer in the snow, and naturally we both had to follow it up."

"Naturally," Richard said.

"I'm not so sure it was a red-deer, Honoria," the boy broke in.

"Oh yes, it was," she declared as she helped herself to a cutlet. "It couldn't have been anything else."

"Why not?" Richard asked. He was interested by the tone of assurance in which she spoke.

"Oh, well, the tracks were too big for a fallow-deer to begin with. And then there's a difference, you can't mistake it if you've ever compared the two, in the cleft of the hoof."

"And you have compared the two?"

"Oh, certainly," Honoria answered.—She was beginning to recover her nonchalance of manner and indolent slowness of speech. "I lose no opportunity of acquiring odds and ends of information. One never knows when they may come in handy."

She looked at him as she spoke, and her upper lip shortened and her eyes narrowed into a delightful smile—a smile, moreover, which had the faintest trace of an asking of pardon in it. And it struck Richard that there was in her expression and bearing a transparent sincerity, and that her eyes—now narrowed as she smiled—were not the clear, soft brown they appeared at a distance to be, but an indefinable colour, comparable only to the dim, yet clear, green gloom which haunts the under-spaces of an ilex grove upon a summer day. He turned his head rather sharply. He did not want to think about matters of that sort. He was grateful to this young lady for the devoted care she had bestowed on his mother; but, otherwise, her presence was only a part of that daily discipline which must be cheerfully undertaken in obedience to the exigencies of his new and fair idea.

"Probably it is a deer that has broken out of Windsor Great Park and travelled," he said. "They do that sometimes, you know."

But here small Dick Ormiston, whose spirits, lately pirouetting on giddy heights of felicity, had suffered swift declension boot-wards at mention of this thrilling adventure in which he, alas, had neither lot nor part, projected himself violently into the conversational arena.

"Mother," he piped, his words tumbling one over the other in his eagerness—"Mother, I expect it's the same deer that grandpapa was talking about when Lord Shotover came over to tea last Friday, and wanted to know if Honoria wasn't back at Newlands again. And then he and grandpapa yarned, don't you know. Because, Cousin Richard—it must have been while you were away last year—the buckhounds met at Bagshot and ran through Frimley and right across Spendle Flats"—

"No, they didn't, Cousin Richard," Godfrey interrupted. "They ran through the bottom of Sandyfield Lower Wood."

"But they lost—any way they lost, Cousin Richard," the younger boy cried.—"You weren't there, Godfrey, so you can't know what grandpapa said. He said they lost somewhere just into Brockhurst, and he told Lord Shotover how they beat up the country for nearly a week, and how they never found it, and had to give it up as a bad job and go home again. And—and—Lord Shotover said, rotten bad sport, stag-hunting, unless you get it on Exmoor, where they're not carted and they don't saw their antlers off. He said meets of the buckhounds ought to be called Stockbrokers' Parade, that was about all they amounted to. And so, Cousin Richard, I think—don't you, mother?—that this must be that same deer."

Whereat the elder Dick's expression, which had grown somewhat dark at the mention of Lord Shotover, brightened sensibly again. And, for cause unknown, he looked at Honoria, smiling amusedly, before saying to the very voluble, small sportsman :—

"To be sure, Dick. Your arguments are unanswerable, convincingly sound. No reasonable man could have a doubt about it ! Of course it's the same deer."

Thereupon the luncheon went forward gaily enough, though Miss St. Quentin was conscious her contributions to the cultivation of that same gaiety were but spasmodic. She dreaded the conclusion of the meal, fearing lest then she might be called upon to behold Richard Calmady once again, as she had beheld him—now nearly six years ago—in the half-dismantled house in Lowndes Square, on the night of Lady Louisa Barking's ball. And from that she shrank, not with her former physical repulsion towards the man himself, but with the moral repulsion of one compelled against his will to gaze upon a pitifully cruel sight, the suffering of which he is powerless to lessen or amend. The short, light-made crutches, lying on the floor by the young man's chair, shocked her as the callous exhibition of some unhappy prisoner's shackling-irons might. It constituted an indignity offered to the Richard sitting here beside her, so much as to think of, let alone look at, that same Richard when on foot. Therefore it was with an oddly mingled relief and sense of playing traitor, that she rose with the rest of the little company and left him by himself. She was thankful to escape, though all the while her inherent loyalty tormented her with accusation of meanness, as of one who deserts a comrade in distress.

But here the small Dick, to whom such complex refinements of sensibility were as yet wholly foreign, created a diversion by prancing round from the far side of the table and forcibly seizing her hand. He was jealous of the large share Godfrey had to-day secured of her society. He meant to have his innings. So he rubbed his curly head against her much braided elbow, butting her lovingly in the exuberance of his affection as some nice, little ram-lamb might. But just as they reached the door, through which Lady Calmady and the rest of the party had already passed, the boy drew up short.

"I say, hold on half a minute, Honoria, please," he said.

And then, turning round, his cheeks red as peonies, he marched back to where Richard sat alone at the head of the table.

"In case—in case, don't you know," he began, stuttering in the excess of his excitement—"in case, Cousin Richard, mummy didn't quite take in what you said at the beginning of luncheon—you did mean for really that I was to come and stay here in the summer holidays, and that you'd take me out, don't you know, and show me your horses?"

And to Honoria, glancing at them, there was a singular, and almost tragic, comment on life in the likeness, yet unlikeness, of those two faces—the features almost identical, the same blue eyes, the two heads alike in shape, each with the same close-fitted, bright-brown cap of hair. But the boy's face flushed, without afterthought or qualification of its eager happiness; the man's colourless, full of reserve, almost alarmingly self-contained and still.

Yet, when the elder Richard's answer came, it was altogether gentle and kindly.

"Yes, most distinctly *for really*, Dick," he said. "Let there be no mistake about it. Let it be clearly understood I want to have you here just as long, and just as often, as your mother and father will spare you. I'll show you the horses, never fear, and let you ride them too."

"A—a—a real big one?"

"Just as big a one as you can straddle." Richard paused.—"And I'll show you other things, if all goes well, which I'm beginning to think—and perhaps you'll think so too some day—are more important even than horses."

He put his hand under the boy's chin, tipped up the ruddy, beaming, little face and kissed it.

"It's a compact," he said. — "Now cut along, old chap. Don't you see you're keeping Miss St. Quentin waiting?"

Whereupon the small Richard started soberly enough, being slightly impressed by something—he knew not quite what—only that it made him feel awfully fond, somehow, of this newly discovered cousin and namesake. But, about half-way down the room, that promise of a horse, a thorough-bred, and just as big as he could straddle, swept all before it, rendering his spirits uncontrollably explosive. So he made a wild rush and flung himself headlong upon the waiting Honoria.

"Oh! you want to bear-fight, do you? Two can play at that game," she cried, "you young rascal!"

Then, without apparent effort or diminution of her lazy grace, the elder Richard saw her pick the boy up by his middle, and, notwithstanding convulsive wrigglings on his part, throw him across her shoulder and bear him bodily away through the lobby, into the hall, and out of sight.

Hence it fell out that not until quite late that evening did the moment so dreaded by Miss St. Quentin actually arrive. In furtherance of delay she practised a diplomacy not altogether flattering to her self-respect, coming down rather late for dinner, and retiring immediately after that meal to the Gun-Room, under plea of correspondence which must be posted at Farley in time for to-morrow's day mail. She was even late for prayers in the chapel, so that, taking her accustomed place next to Lady Calmady in the last but one of the stalls upon the epistle-side, she found all the members of the household, gentle and simple alike, already upon their knees. The household mustered strong that night, a testimony, it may be supposed, to feudal as much as to religious feeling. In the seats immediately below her were an array of women-servants, declining from the high dignities of Mrs. Reynolds the housekeeper, the faithful Clara, and her own lanky and loyal North-Country woman Fauistich, to a very youthful scullery-maid, sitting just without the altar rails at the end of the long row. Opposite were not only Winter, Bates the steward, Powell, Andrews, and the other men-servants; but Chaplin, heading a detachment from the house stables, and—unexampled occurrence!—Gnudi the Italian *chef*, with his air of gentle and philosophic melancholy and his anarchic sentiments in theology and politics, liable,—these last,—when enlarged on, to cause much fluttering in the dove-cot of the housekeeper's room. "To hear Signor Gnudi talk sometimes made your blood run cold. It seemed as if you couldn't be safe anywhere from those wicked foreign barricades and mass-acres," as Clara put it. And yet, in point of fact, no milder man ever larded a woodcock or stuffed it with truffles.

Alone, behind all these, in the first of the row of stalls with their carven spires and dark-vaulted canopies, sat Richard Calmady, whom all his people had thus come forth silently to welcome. But, through prayer and psalm and lesson, as Miss St. Quentin noted, he remained immoveable, to her almost alarmingly cold and self-concentrated. Only once he turned his head, leaning a little forward and looking towards the purple, and silver, and fair, white flowers of the altar, and the clear shining of the altar lights.

—" Then shall the righteous answer him, saying, Lord, when saw we thee an hungered, and fed thee? or thirsty and gave thee drink? When saw we thee a stranger, and took thee in? or naked and clothed thee? Or when saw we thee sick, or in prison, and came unto thee? And the King shall answer and say unto them, Verily I say unto you, inasmuch as ye have done it unto one of the least of these my brethren, ye have done it unto me."

The words were given out by Julius March, not only with an exquisite distinctness of enunciation, but with a ring of assurance, of sustaining and thankful conviction. Richard leaned back in his stall again, looking across at his mother. While Honoria, taken with a sensitive fear of inquiring into matters not rightfully hers to inquire into, hastily turned her eyes upon her open prayer-book. They must have many things to say to one another, that mother and son, as she divined, to-day,—far be it from her to attempt to surprise their confidence !

She rose from her knees, cutting her final petitions somewhat short, directly the last of the men-servants had filed out of the chapel ; and, crossing the Chapel-Room, a tall, pale figure in her trailing, white, evening dress, she pulled back the curtain of the oriel-window, opened one of the curved, many-paned casements and looked out. She was curiously moved, very sensible of a deeper drama going forward around her, going forward in her own thought—subtly modifying and transmuting it—than she could at present either explain or place. The night was cloudy and very mild. A soft, sobbing, westerly wind, with the smell of coming rain in it, saluted her as she opened the casement. The last of the frost must be gone, by now, even in the hollows ; the snow wholly departed also. The spring, though young and feeble yet, puling like some ailing baby-child in the voice of that softly-complaining, westerly wind, was here, very really present at last. Honoria leaned her elbows on the stone window-ledge. Her heart went out in strong emotion of tenderness towards that moist wind which seemed to cry, as in a certain homelessness, against her bare arms and bare neck.—" Inasmuch as ye did it unto one of the least of these my brethren "—

But just then Katherine Calmady called to her, and that in a sweet, if rather anxious, tone.

"Honoria, dear child, come here," she said.   "Richard is putting me through the longer catechism regarding those heath fires in August last year, and the state of the woods."

Then, as the young lady approached her, Lady Calmady laid one hand on her arm, looking up in quick and loving appeal at the serious and slightly troubled face.

"My answers only reveal the woful greatness of my ignorance.   My geography has run mad.   I am planting forests in the midst of cornfields, so Dickie assures me; and making hay generally—as you, my dear, would say—of the map."

Still her eyes dwelt upon Honoria's in insistent and loving appeal.

"Come," she said, "explain to him, and save me from further exposition of my own ignorance."

Thus admonished the young lady sat down on the low sofa beside Richard Calmady.   As she did so Katherine rose and moved away.   Honoria determined to see only the young man's broad shoulders, his irreproachable dress clothes, his strangely still and very handsome face.   But, since there was no concealing rug to cover them, it was impossible that she should long avoid also seeing his shortened and defective limbs and oddly shod feet.   And at that she winced and shrank a little, for all her high spirit and inviolate, maidenly strength.

"Oh yes! those fires!" she said hurriedly.   "There were several — you remember, Cousin Katherine? — or I daresay you don't, for you were ill at the time.   But the worst was on Spendle Flats.   You know that long, three-cornered bit"—she looked Richard bravely in the face again—"which lies between the Portsmouth Road and our cross-road to Farley?   It runs into a point just at the top of Star Hill."

"Yes, I know," Dickie said.

He had seen her wince.—Well, that wasn't wonderful!   She could not very well do otherwise, if she had eyes in her head. He did not blame her.   And then, though it was not easy to do so with entire serenity, this was precisely one of those small unpleasant incidents which, in obedience to his new code, he was bound to accept calmly, good-temperedly, just as part of the day's work, in fact.   He had done with malingering.   He had done with the egoism of sulking and hiding—even to the extent of a *couvre-pieds*.   All right, here it was!—Richard settled his shoulders squarely against the straight, stuffed back of the Chippendale sofa, and talked on.

"It's a pity that bit is burnt," he said. "I haven't been over that ground for nearly six years, of course. But I remember there were very good trees there—a plantation at the top end, just before you come to the big gravel-pits, and the rest self-sown. Are they all gone?"

"Licked as clean as the back of your hand," Honoria replied, warming to her subject. "They hardly repaid felling for fire-wood. It made me wretched. Some idiot threw down a match, I suppose. There had been nearly a month's drought, and the whole place was like so much tinder. There was an easterly breeze too. You can imagine the blaze! We hadn't the faintest chance. Poor, old Iles lost his head utterly, and sat down with his feet in a dry ditch and wept. There must be over two hundred acres of it. It's a dreadful eyesore, perfectly barren and useless, but for a little sour grass even a gipsy's donkey has to be hard up before he cares to eat!"—Miss St. Quentin shifted her position with a certain impatience. "I can't bear to see the land doing no work," she said.

"Doing no work?" Dickie inquired. He began to be interested in the conversation from other than a purely practical and local standpoint.

"Of course," she asserted. "The land has no more right to lie idle than any of the rest of us—unless it's a bit of tilth sweetening in fallow between two crops. That is reasonable enough. But for the rest," she said, a certain brightness and self-forgetting gaining on her—"let it contribute its share all the while, like an honest citizen of the universe. Let it work, most decidedly let it work."

"And what about such trifles as the few hundred square miles of desert or mountain range?" Richard inquired, half amused, half, and that rather unwillingly, charmed. "They are liable to be a thorn in the side of the—well, socialist."

"Oh, I've no quarrel with them. They come under a different head."—Honoria's manner had ceased to be in any degree embarrassed, though a slight perplexity came into her expression. For just then she remembered, somehow, her pacings of the station platform at Culoz, the salutation of the bleak, pure, evening wind from out the fastnesses of the Alps, and all her conversation there with her faithful admirer, Ludovic Quayle. And it occurred to her what singular contrast in sentiment that bleak, evening wind offered to the mild, moist, westerly wind—complaint of the homeless baby, Spring—which had just now cried against her bosom! And again Honoria became conscious of being in contact, both in herself and in her surroundings, with more coercing, more vital drama than she could either interpret or place. Again something of fear invaded her, to combat which she hurried into speech.—"No, I haven't any quarrel with deserts and so on," she repeated. "They're uncommonly useful things for mankind to knock its head against—invincible, unnegotiable, splendidly competent to teach humanity its place. You see we've grown not a little conceited —so at least it seems to me—on our evolutionary journey up from the primordial cell. We're too much inclined to forget we've developed soul quite comparatively recently, and therefore that there is probably just as long a journey ahead of us—before we reach the ultimate of intellectual and spiritual development—as there is behind us physically from, say the parent ascidian, to you and me. And—and somehow"— Honoria's voice had become full and sweet, and she looked straight at Dickie with a rare candour and simplicity—"somehow those big open spaces remind one of all that. They drive one's ineffectualness home on one. They remind one that environment, that mechanical civilisation, all the short cuts of applied science, after all count for little and inevitably come to the place called *stop*. And that braces one. It makes one the more eager after that which lies behind the material aspects of things, and to which these merely act as a veil."

Honoria had bowed herself together. Her elbows were on her knees, her chin in her two hands, her charming face alight with a pure enthusiasm. And Richard watched her curiously. His acquaintance with women was fairly comprehensive, but this woman represented a type new to his experience. He wanted to tolerate her merely, to regard her as an element in his scheme of self-discipline. And it began to occur to him that, from some points of view, she knew as much about all that, as much about the idea inspiring it, as he did. He leaned himself back in the angle of the sofa, and clasped his hands behind his head.

"All the same," he said, "I am afraid those burnt acres on Spendle Flats are hardly extensive enough to afford an object for me to knock my head against, and so enforce salutary remembrance of the limitations of human science. Possibly that has already been sufficiently brought home to me in other ways."

He paused a minute.

Honoria straightened herself up. Again she saw—whether she would or no—those defective shortened limbs and oddly shod feet. And again, somehow, that complaint of the moist spring wind seemed to cry against her bare arms and neck, begetting an overwhelming pitifulness in her.

"So, since it's not altogether necessary we should reserve it as an object-lesson in general ineffectualness, Miss St. Quentin, what shall we do with it?"

"Oh, plant," she said.

"With the ubiquitous Scotchman?"

"It wouldn't carry anything else, except along the boundaries. There you might put in a row of horn-beam and oak. They always look rather nice against a background of firs.—Only the stumps of the burnt trees ought to be stubbed."

"Let them be stubbed," Richard said.

"Where are you going to find the labour? The estate is very much under-manned."

"Import it," Richard said.

"No, no," Honoria answered, again warming to her subject. "I don't believe in imported labour. If you have men by the week, they must lodge. And the lodger is as the ten plagues of Egypt in a village. If a man comes by the day, he is tired and slack. His heart is not in his work. He does as little as he can. Moreover, in either case, the wife and children suffer. He's certain to take them home short money. He's pretty safe, being tired in the one case, or in the other, on the loose, to drink."

Dickie's face gave. He laughed a little.

"We seem to have come to a fine *impasse*!" he remarked. "Though humiliatingly small, that tract of burnt land must clearly be kept to knock one's head against after all."

Honoria rose to her feet.

"Richard, I wish you'd build," she said, in her earnestness unconscious of the unceremonious character of her address. "Iles ought to have done that before now. But he is old and timid, and his one idea has been to save. You know this Brockhurst property alone would carry eight or ten more families. There's plenty of work. It needn't be made. It is there ready to hand. Give them good gardens, allotments if you can, and leave to keep a pig. That's infinitely better than extravagant wages. Root them down in the soil. Let them love the place —tie them up to it"—

"Your socialism is rather quaintly crossed with feudalism, isn't it?" Dickie remarked.

He drew himself forward, slipped down off the sofa, stood upright. And then, indeed, the cruel disparity between his stature and her own—for tall though she was, he, by right of make and length of arm, should evidently have been by some two or three inches the taller—and all the grotesqueness of his

36

deformity, were fully disclosed to Honoria. For the second time that day, her tact, her presence of mind, her ready speech, deserted her. She backed a little away from him.

And Richard perceived that. It is not easy to be absolutely philosophic. Something of his old anger revived towards Miss St. Quentin. He shuffled forward a step or two, and, supporting himself with one hand on the arm of the sofa, reached down to pick up his crutches. But his grasp was not very sure just then. He secured one. To his intense annoyance the other escaped him, falling back on the floor with a rattle. Then, instantly, before he could make effort to recover it, Honoria's white figure swept down on one knee in front of him. She laid hold of the crutch, gave it him silently, and rose to her full height again, pale, gallant, stately, but with a quivering of her lips and nostrils, and an amazement of regret and pity in her eyes, which very certainly had never found place there heretofore.

"Thanks," Richard said.—He waited just a minute. He too was amazed somehow. He needed to revise the position.— "About those eight or ten happy families whom you wish to root so firmly in the soil, and the housing of them—are you busy to-morrow morning?"

"Oh no—no"—Honoria declared, with rather unnecessary emphasis.

Generosity should surely be met by generosity. Dickie leaned his back against the arm of the sofa, and looked up at the speaker. Her transparent sincerity, her superb chastity—he could call it by no other word—of manner and movement, even of outline—the slight angularity of strong muscle as opposed to soft roundness of cushioned flesh—these arrested and impressed him.

"I had Chifney up from the stables this afternoon and made my peace with him," he said. "He was very full of your praises, Honoria—for the cousinship may as well be acknowledged between us, don't you think? You have supplemented my lapses in respect of him, as of a good deal else."—Richard looked away to the door of Lady Calmady's bedroom. It stood open, and Katherine came from within with some books, and a silver candlestick, in her hands.

"My dears," she said, "do you know it grows very late?"

"All right," he answered, "we're making out some plans for to-morrow."—He looked at Honoria again.—"Chifney engaged that he and Chaplin would find a horse, between them, which could be trusted to—well—to put up with me," he said. "I promised to go down and have breakfast with dear Mrs. Chifney

at the stables, but I can be back here by eleven. Would
you be inclined to come out with me then? We could ride
over that burnt land and have a poke round for sites for your
cottages."

"Oh yes, indeed, I can come," Honoria answered. Her
delightful smile beamed forth, and it had a new and very
delicate charm in it. For it so happened that the woman in her
whom—to use her own phrase—she had condemned to solitary
confinement in the back attic, beat very violently against her
prison door just then in attempt to escape.

"Dear Cousin Katherine, good-night. Good-night, Richard,"
she said hurriedly.—She went out of the room, lazily, slowly,
down the black, polished staircase, across the great, silent hall, and
along the farther lobby. But she let the Gun-Room door bang to
behind her and flung herself down in the arm-chair—in which,
by the way, the old bull-dog had died a year ago, broken-hearted
by over long waiting for the home-coming of his absent master.
And then Honoria, though the least tearful of women, wept—
not in petulant anger, or with the easy, luxuriously sentimental
overflow common to feminine humanity; but reluctantly, with
hard, irregular sobs which hurt, yet refused to be stifled, since
the extreme limit of emotional and mental endurance had been
reached.

"Oh, it's fine!" she said, half aloud. "I can see that it's
fine—but, dear God, is there no way out of it? It's so horribly,
so unspeakably sad."

And Richard remained on into the small hours, sitting before
the dying fire of the big hearth-place, at the eastern end of the
gallery. Mentally he audited his accounts, the profit and loss
of this day's doing, and, on the whole, the balance showed upon
the profit side. Verily it was only a day of small things, of very
humble ambitions, of far from world-shaking successes! Still
four persons, he judged, he had made a degree or so happier.—His
mother rejoiced, though with trembling as yet, at his return to
the ordinary habits of the ordinary man. Sweet, dear thing, small
wonder that she trembled! He had led her such a dance in
the past, that any new departure must give cause for anxious
questionings. Dickie sunk his head in his hands.—God forgive
him, what a dance he had led her!—And Julius March was
happier—he, Richard, was pretty certain of that—since Julius
could not but understand that, in the present case at all
events, neither fulfilment of prophecy nor answer to prayer
had been disregarded. — And the hard-bitten, irascible, old
trainer, Tom Chifney, was happier—probably really the happiest

of the lot—since he demanded nothing more recondite and far-reaching than restoration to favour, and due recognition of the importance of his calling and of the merits of his horses.—And nice, funny, voluble, little Dick Ormiston was happier too. Richard's heart went out strangely to the dear little lad! He wondered if it would be too much to ask Mary and Roger to give him the boy altogether? Then he put the thought from him, judging it savoured of the selfishness, the exclusiveness and egoism, with which he had sworn to part company forever.

He stretched his hand out over the arm of the chair, craving for some creature, warm, sentient, dumbly sympathetic, to lay hold of.—He remembered there used to be a man down near Alton, a hard-riding farmer, who bred bull-dogs—white ones with black points, like Camp and Camp's forefathers. He would tell Chifney to go down there and bespeak the two best of the next litter of puppies.—Yes—he wanted a dog again. It was foolish perhaps, but after all one did want something, and, since other things were denied, a dog must do—and he wanted one badly.—Yet the day had been a success on the whole. He had been true to his code. Only—and Richard shrugged his shoulders rather wearily—it had got to be begun all over again to-morrow, and next day, and next—an endless perspective of to-morrows. And the poor flesh, with its many demands, its delicious and iniquitous passions, its enchantments, its revelations, its adorable languors, its drunken heats, must it have nothing, nothing at all?—Must that whole side of things be ruled out forever? He had no more desire for mistresses, God forbid—Helen, somehow, had cleansed him of all possibility of that. And he would never ask any woman to marry him. The sacrifice on her part would be too great.—He thought of little Lady Constance.—Simply, it was not right.—So, practically, the emotional joys of life were reduced to this—they must consist solely in giving—giving—giving, of time, sympathy, thought and money. A far from ignoble programme no doubt, but a rather austere one for a man of liberal tastes, of varied experience, and of barely thirty.—And he was as strong as a bull now. He knew that. He might live to be ninety.—Yes, he thought he would ask for little Dick Ormiston. The boy would be an amusement and interest him. And then suddenly the vision of Honoria St. Quentin, in her red and black-braided gown, with that air of something ruffling and soldierly about it, whipping the small Dick up in her strong arms, throwing him across her shoulder and bearing him off bodily; and of Honoria again later, her sensitive face all alight, as she discoursed of the ultimate aim and purpose of life and of living, came before him. Above her white dress, he could see her white and finely angular shoulders as she swept down to pick up that wretched crutch.—Yes, she was a being of singular contrasts, of remarkable capacity, both mental and practical! And she might have a heart—she might. Once or twice it had looked rather like it.—But, after all, what did that matter? The feminine side of things was excluded. Besides he supposed she was half engaged to Ludovic Quayle.

Dickie yawned. He was sleepy. His meditations became unprofitable. He had best go to bed.

" And the devil fly away with all women, saving and excepting my best-beloved mother," he said.

CHAPTER VIII

CONCERNING THE BROTHERHOOD FOUNDED BY RICHARD CALMADY, AND OTHER MATTERS OF SOME INTEREST

IT was still very sultry. All the windows of the red drawing-room stood wide open. Outside the thunder rain fell, straight as ram-rods, in big globular drops, which spattered upon the grey quarries and splashed on the pink and lilac, lemon-yellow, scarlet and orange of the pot plants,—hydrangeas, pelargoniums, and early-flowering chrysanthemums,—set three-deep along the base of the house wall, the whole length of the terrace front. The atmosphere was thick. Masses of purple cloud, lurid light crowning their summits, boiled up out of the south-east. But the worst of the storm was already over, and the parched land, grateful for the downpour of rain, exhaled a whiteness of smoke —as in thanksgiving from off some altar of incense. On the grass slopes of the near park a flight of rooks had alighted. They stalked and strode over the withered turf with a self-important, quaintly clerical air, seeking provender, but, so far, finding none, since the moisture had not yet sufficiently penetrated the hardened soil for earth-worms and kindred creeping-things to move surfacewards.

Within, the red drawing-room had suffered conspicuous change. For, on Richard moving downstairs to his old quarters in the south-western wing of the house, Lady Calmady had judged it an act of love, rather than of desecration, to restore this long-disused apartment to its former employment. Adjoining the dining-room—connecting this last with the billiard-

room, summer-parlour, and garden-hall—this room was convenient to assemble in before, and sit in for a while after, meals.
Richard would thereby be saved superfluous journeys upstairs.
And this act of restitution, which was also in a sense an act of
penitence, once decided upon, Katherine carried it forward with
a certain gentle ardour, renewing crimson carpets and hangings and
disposing the furniture according to its long-ago positions. The
memory of what had once been should remain forever here
enshrined, but with the glad colours of life, not the faded ones
of unforgiven death upon it. It satisfied her conscience to do
this. For it appeared to her that so very much of good had
been granted her of late, so large a measure of peace and hope
vouchsafed to her, that it was but fitting she should bear testimony
to her awareness of all that by obliteration of the last outward
sign of the rebellion of her sorrowful youth. The Richard of
to-day, homestaying, busy with much kindness, thoughtful of her
comfort, honouring her with delicate courtesies—which to whoso
receives them makes her womanhood a privilege rather than a
burden—yet teasing her not a little, too, in the security of a fair
and equal affection, bore such moving resemblance to that other
Richard, first master of her heart, that Katherine could afford to
cancel the cruelty of certain memories, retaining only the lovelier
portion of them, and could find a peculiar sweetness in frequenta-
tion of this room, formerly devoted wholly to sense of injury and
blackness of hate.

And on the day in question, Katherine's presence exhaled a
specially tender brightness, even as the thirsty earth, refreshed by
the thunder-rain, sent up a rare whiteness as of incense smoke.
For she had been somewhat anxious about Dickie lately. To
her sensitive observation of him, his virtue, his evenness of
temper, his reasonableness, had come to have in them a pathetic
element. He was lovely and pleasant in his ways. But sometimes, when tired or off his guard, she had surprised an expression
on his face, a constrained patience of speech, even of attitude,
which made her fear he had given her but that half of his confidence calculated to cheer, while he kept the half calculated to
sadden rather rigorously to himself. And, in good truth, Richard
did suffer not a little at this period. The first push of enthusiastic
conviction had passed, while his new manner of conduct and of
thought had not yet acquired the stability of habit. The tide
was low. Shallows and sand-bars disclosed themselves. He
endured the temptations arising from the state known to saintly
writers as "spiritual dryness," and found those temptations of an
inglorious and wholly unheroic sort. And, though he held his

peace, Katherine feared for him—feared that the way he elected to walk in was over strait, and that, though resolution would hold, health might be overstrained.

"My darling, you never grumble now," she had said to him a few days back.

To which he answered :—

"Poor, dear mother, have I cheated you of one of your few, small pleasures? Was it so very delightful to listen to that same grumbling?"

"I begin to believe it was," Katherine declared. "It conferred a unique distinction upon me, you see, because I had a comfortable conviction you grumbled to nobody else. One is jealous of distinction. Yes—I think I miss it, Dickie."

Whereupon he laughed and kissed her, and swore he'd grumble fast enough if there was anything—which positively there wasn't—to grumble about. All of which, though it charmed Katherine, appeased her anxiety but moderately. The young man worked too hard. His opportunities of amusement were too scant. Katherine cast about in thought, and in prayer, for some lightening of his daily life, even if such lightening should lessen the completeness of his dependence upon herself. And it was just at this juncture that Miss St. Quentin wrote proposing to come to Brockhurst for a week. She had not been there since the Whitsuntide recess. She wrote from Ormiston, where she was staying on her way south, after paying a round of country-house visits in Scotland. It was now September. She would probably go to Cairo for the winter with young Lady Tobermory—grand-niece by marriage of her late god-mother and benefactress—whose lungs were pronounced to be badly touched. Might she, therefore, come to Brockhurst to say good-bye?

And to this proposed visit Richard offered no opposition, though he received the announcement of it without any marked demonstration of approval.—Oh, by all means let her come! Of course it must be a pleasure to his mother to have her. And he'd got on very well with her in the spring—unquestionably he had.—Richard's expression was slightly ironical.—But he did really like her?—Oh dear, yes, he liked her exceedingly. She was quite curiously clever, and she was sincere, and she was rather beautiful too, in her own style—he had always thought that. By all means have her.—After which conversation Richard went for a long ride, inspected cottages in building at Sandyfield, and visited a house, undergoing extensive internal alterations, which stands back from Clerke's Green, about a hundred yards short of Appleyard, the saddler's shop at Farley Row. He came in late. Unusual silence held him during dinner. And Lady Calmady took herself to task, reproaching herself with selfishness. Honoria was very dear to her, and so, only too probably, she had over-rated the friendliness of Dickie's attitude towards the young lady. But they had seemed to get on so extremely well in the spring, and very fairly well at Whitsuntide! Yet, perhaps, in that, as in so much else, Richard put a constraint upon himself, obeying conscience rather than inclination. Katherine was perturbed. Nor had her perturbations suffered diminution yesterday, upon Miss St. Quentin's arrival. Richard remained unexpansive. To-day, however, matters had improved. Something—possibly the thunderstorm—seemed to have thawed his coldness, broken up his reticence of manner. Therefore Katherine gave thanks and moved with a lighter heart.

As for Miss St. Quentin herself, an innate gladsomeness per-vaded her aspect not easy to resist. Lady Calmady had been sen-sible of it when the young lady first greeted her that morning. It remained by her now, as she stood after luncheon at one of the open windows, watching the up-rolling thunder-cloud, the spatter-ing raindrops, the quaintly solemn behaviour of the stalking, striding rooks. Honoria was easily entertained to-day. She felt well-disposed towards every living creature. And the rooks diverted her extremely. Profanely they reminded her of certain archiepiscopal garden-parties; with this improvement on the human variant, that here wives and daughters also were con-demned to decent sables instead of being at liberty to array themselves according to self-invented canons of remarkably defective taste. But, though diverted, it must be owned she gave her attention the more closely to all that outward drama of storm and rain and to the antics of the rooks, because she was very conscious of the fact that Richard Calmady had followed her and his mother into the red drawing-room, and it hurt her—though she had now, of necessity, witnessed it many times—it hurt, it still very shrewdly distressed her, to see him walk. As she heard the soft thud and shuffle of his onward progress, followed by the little clatter of the crutches as he laid them upon the floor beside his chair, the brightness died out of Honoria's face. She registered sharp annoyance against herself, for she had not anticipated that this would continue to affect her so much. She supposed she had grown accustomed to it during her last two visits to Brockhurst, and that, this time, it would occasion her no shock. But the sadness of the young man's deformity remained present as ever. The indignity of it offended her. The desire by some, by any, means to mitigate the woful circumscription of liberty and opportunity which it inflicted, wrought upon her almost painfully. And so she looked very hard at the hungry, anticking rooks, both to secure time for recovery of her equanimity, and also to spare Richard smallest suspicion that she avoided beholding his advance and installation.

"We needn't start until four, mother," she heard him say. "But I'm afraid it is clearing."

Honoria turned from the window.

"Yes, it is clearing," she remarked, "incontestably clearing! You won't escape the Grimshott function after all."

"It's a nuisance having to go," Richard replied. "But you see this is an old engagement. People are wonderfully civil and kind. I wish they were less so. They waste one's time. But it doesn't do to be ungracious, and we needn't stay more than half an hour, need we, mother?"

He looked up at Honoria.

"Don't you think, on the whole, you'd better come too?" he said.

But the young lady shook her head smilingly. She stood close beside Lady Calmady.

"Oh dear, no," she answered. "I am quite absolutely certain I hadn't better come too."

Richard continued to look up at her.

"Half the county will be there. Everything will be richly, comprehensively dull. Think of it. Do come," he repeated, "it would be so good for your soul."

"Oh, my soul's in the humour to be nobly careless of personal advantage," Honoria replied. "It's in a state of almost perilously full-blown optimism regarding the security of its own salvation to-day, somehow."—Her glance rested very sweetly upon Lady Calmady.—"And then all the rest of me— and not impossibly my soul has a word to say in that connection too—cries out to go and tramp over the steaming turf and breathe the scent of the fir woods again."

Honoria sat down lazily on the arm of a neighbouring easy-chair, against the crimson cover of which her striped blue-and-white, shirting dress showed excellently distinct and clear. Richard's prolonged and quiet scrutiny oppressed her slightly, necessitating change of attitude and place.

"And then," she continued, "I want to go down to the paddocks and have a look at the yearlings. How are they coming on? Have you anything good?"

"Two or three promising fillies. They're in the paddock nearest the Long Water. You'll find them as quiet as sheep.

But I'll ask you not to go in among the brood-mares and foals unless Chifney is with you. They may be a bit savage and shy, and it is not altogether safe for a lady."

He stretched out his hand, taking Lady Calmady's hand for a moment.

" Dear mother, you look tired. You'll have to put up with Grimshott. The weather's not going to let us off. Go and rest till we start."

And when, a few minutes later, Katherine, departing, closed the door behind her, he addressed Miss St. Quentin again.

" How do you think my mother is ? "

" Beautifully well."

" Not worried ? "

" No," Honoria said.

" You are really quite contented about her, then ? "

The question both surprised and touched his hearer, as a friendly and gracious admission that she possessed certain rights.

" Oh dear, yes," she said. " I am more than contented about her. No one can fail to be so who, loving her, sees her now. There was just one thing she wanted. Now she has it, and so all is well."

" What one thing ? " Dickie asked, with a hint of irony in his manner and his voice.

" Why, you—you, Richard," Honoria said.

She drew herself up proudly, a little alarmed by, a little defiant of, the directness of her own speech, perceiving, so soon as she had uttered it, that it might be construed as indirect reproach. And to administer reproach had been very far from her purpose. She fixed her eyes upon the domes of the great oaks, crowning an outstanding knoll at the far end of the lime avenue. The foliage of them, deep green shading into russet, was arrestingly solid and metallic, offering a rather magnificent scheme of stormy colour taken in connection with the hot purple of the uprolling cloud. Framed by the stone work of the open window, the whole presented a fine picture in the manner of Salvator Rosa. A few bright raindrops splashed and splattered, and the thunder growled far away in the north. The atmosphere was heavy. For a time neither spoke. Then Honoria said, gently, as one asking a favour :—

" Richard, will you tell me about that home of yours? Cousin Katherine was speaking of it to me last night."

And it seemed to her his thought must have journeyed to some far distance, and found difficulty in returning thence, it was so long before he answered her, while his face had become set, and showed colourless as wax against the surrounding crimson of the room.

"Oh, the home!" he exclaimed, shrugging his shoulders just perceptibly. "It doesn't amount to very much. My mother in her dear unwisdom of faith and hope magnifies the value of it. It's just an idle man's fad."

"A fad with an uncommon amount of backbone to it, apparently."

"That depends on its eventual success. It's a thing to be judged not by intentions but by results."

"What made you think of it?"

Richard looked full at her, spreading out his hands, and again shrugging his shoulders slightly. Again Miss St. Quentin accused herself of a defect of tact.

"Isn't it rather obvious why I should think of it?" he asked. "It seemed to me that, in a very mild and limited degree, it was calculated to meet a want."—He smiled upon her, quite sweet-temperedly, yet once more there was a flavour of irony in his tone.—"Of course hideous creatures and disabled creatures are an eyesore. We pity, but we look the other way. I quite accept that. They are a nuisance, since they are a standing witness to the fact that things, here below, very far from always work smoothly and well, and that there are disasters beyond the power of applied science to put right. The ordinary human being doesn't covet to be forcibly reminded of that by means of a living object-lesson."

Richard shifted his position, clasped his hands behind his head. He had begun speaking without idea of self-revelation; but the relief of speech, after long self-repression, took him, goading him on. Old strains of feeling, kept under by conscious exercise of will, asserted themselves. He asked neither sympathy nor help. He simply called from off those shallows and sand-bars laid bare by the ebbing tide of his first enthusiasm. He protested, wearied by the spiritual dryness which had caused all effort to prove so joyless of late. To have sought relief in words before his mother would have been unpardonable he held. She had borne enough from him in the past, and more than enough. But to permit it himself in the presence of this young, strong, capable woman of the world, was very different. She came out of the swing of society and of affairs, of large interests in politics and in thought. She would go back into those again very shortly, so what did it matter? She captivated him and incensed him alike. His relation to her had been so fertile of contradictions—at once singularly superficial and fugitive, and singularly vital.   He did not care to analyse his own feelings in respect of her.   He had, so he told himself, never quite cared to do that.   She had wounded his pride shrewdly at times, still he had unquestioning faith in her power of comprehending his meaning as she sat there, graceful, long-limbed, indolent, in her pale dress, looking towards the window, the light on her face revealing the fine squareness of the chiselling of her profile, of her jaw, her nostril, and brow.   She appeared so free of spirit, so untrammelled, so excellently exalted above all that is weak, craven, smirched by impurity, capable of baseness or deceit.

"But naturally with me the case is different," he went on, his voice growing deeper, his utterance more measured.   "It is futile to resent being reminded of that which, in point of fact, you never forget.   It's childish for the pot to call the kettle black.   And so I came to the conclusion, a few months ago, to put away all such childishness, and set myself to gain whatever advantage I could from—well—from my own blackness."

Honoria turned her head, averting her face yet farther. Richard could only see the outline of her cheek.   She had never before heard him make so direct allusion to his own deformity, and it frightened her a little.   Her heart beat curiously quick. For it was to her as though he compelled her to draw near and penetrate a region in which, gazing thitherward questioningly from afar, she had divined the residence of stern and intimate miseries, inalienable, unremittent, taking their rise in an almost alarming remoteness of time and fundamentality of cause.

"You see, in plain English," he said, "I view all such unhappy beings from the inside, not, as the rest of you do, merely from the out.   I belong to them and they to me.   It is not an altogether flattering connection.   Only recently, I am afraid, have I had the honesty to acknowledge it !   But, having once done so, it seems only reasonable to look up the members of my unlucky family and take care of them, and if possible put them through—not on the lines of a charitable institution, which must inevitably be a rather mechanical, step-mother kind of arrangement at best, but on the lines of family affection, of personal friendship."

He paused a moment.

"Does that strike you as too unpractical and fantastic, contrary to sound, philanthropic principle and practice?"

Honoria shook her head.

"It is based on a higher law than any of modern organised philanthropy," she said, and her voice had a queer unsteadiness in it. "It goes back to the Gospels—to the matter of giving your life for your friend."

As she spoke, Honoria rose. She went across and stood at the window. Furtively she dabbed her pocket handkerchief against her eyes.

"Well, after all, one must give one's life for something or other, you know," Richard remarked, "or the days would become a little too intolerably dull, and then one might be tempted to make short work of life altogether."

Honoria returned to her chair again and sat down — this time not on the arm of it but in ordinary conventional fashion. She faced Richard. He observed that her eyelids were slightly swollen, slightly red. This gave an extraordinary effect of gentleness to her expression.

"How do you find them—the members of your sad family?" she asked.

"Oh, in all sorts of ways and of places! Knott swears it is contrary to reason, an interfering with the beneficent tendency of nature to kill off the unfit. Yet he works like a horse to help me—even talks of giving up his practice and moving to Farley Row, so as to be near the headquarters of my establishment. The lease of a rather charming, old house there fell in this year. Fortunately the tenant did not want to renew, so I am having that made comfortable for them."

Richard smiled. A greater sense of well-being animated him. Out of the world she had come, back into the world she would go. Meanwhile she was nobly fair to look upon, she was pure of heart, intercourse with her made for the justification of high purposes and unselfish experiment—so he thought.

"I am growing as keen on bagging a fine cripple as another man might be on bagging a fine tiger," he said. "The whole matter at bottom, I suspect, turns on the instinct of sport.— Only the week before last I acquired a rather terribly superior specimen—a lad of eighteen, a factory hand in Westchurch. He was caught by some loose gearing and swept into the machinery. What is left of him—if it survives, which it had much better not, and yet I can't help hoping it will, he is such a plucky, sweet-natured fellow—will require a nurse for the rest of its life. So I am pushing on the work at Farley, that the home may be ready when we get him out of hospital.—By the way, I must go to-morrow and stir up the workmen. Do you care to come and see it all, if the afternoon is fine and not too hot?"

And Honoria agreed. Nor did she shrink when Richard slipping out of his chair picked up his crutches.—"I suppose it is about time to get ready for the Grimshott function," he said. —She walked beside him to the door, opened it and passed into the neutral-tinted, tapestry-hung dining-room. There the young man waited a moment. He looked not at her but straight before him.

"Honoria," he said suddenly, almost harshly, "you and Helen de Vallorbes used to be great friends. For more than a year I have held no communication with her, except through my lawyers. Can you tell me anything about her?"

Miss St. Quentin hesitated.

"Nothing very direct—I heard from de Vallorbes about three months ago. I don't think I am faithless—indeed I held on to her as long as I could, Richard! I am not squeamish, and then I always prefer to stand by the woman. But whatever de Vallorbes may have been, he pulled himself together rather admirably from the time he went into the army. He wanted to keep straight and to live respectably. And—I hate to say so—but she treated him a little too flagrantly. And then—and then"—

Honoria put her hands over her eyes and shook back her head angrily.

"It wasn't one man, Richard."

Dickie went white to the lips.

"I know that," he said.

He moved forward a few steps.

"Who is it now? Destournelle?"

"Oh no—no"—Honoria said. "Some Russian—from the extreme east—Kazan, I think — prince, millionaire, drunken savage. But he adores her. He squanders money upon her, surrounds her with barbaric state. This is de Vallorbes' version of the affair. The scandal is open and notorious. But she and her prince together have great power. Something will eventually be arranged in the way of a marriage. She will not come back."

CHAPTER IX

TELLING HOW LUDOVIC QUAYLE AND HONORIA ST. QUENTIN
WATCHED THE TROUT RISE IN THE LONG WATER

SOME hour and a half later Miss St. Quentin passed down the flight of stone steps, leading from the southern end of the terrace to the grass slopes of the park. Arrived at the lowest step she gathered the skirt of her dress up over one arm, thereby securing greater freedom of movement, and displaying a straight length of pink and white petticoat. Thus prepared she fared forth over the still smoking turf. The storm had passed, but the atmosphere remained thick and humid. A certain opulence of colour obtained in the landscape. The herbs in the grass, wild-thyme, wild - balm, and star - flowered camomile, smelt strongly aromatic as she trod them under foot, while the beds of bracken, dried and yellowed by the drought, gave off a sharp, woody scent.

Usually, when thus alone and in contact with nature, such matters claimed Honoria's whole attention, ministering to her love of earth-lore and of Mother Earth—producing in her silent worship of those primitive deities who at once preside over and inhabit the waste-land and the tilth, the untamed forest and the pastures where heavy-uddered, sweet-breathed cows lie in the deep, meadow grass, the garden ground, all pleasant orchard places, and the broad promise of the waving crops. But this afternoon, although the colour, odour, warmth, and all the many voices praising the refreshment of the rain, were sensibly present to her, Honoria's thought failed to be engrossed by them. For she was in process of worshipping younger and more compassionate deities, sadder, because more human ones, whose office lies not with Nature in her eternal repose and fecundity, but with man in his eternal failure and unrest. Not august Ceres, giver of the golden harvest-fields, or fierce Cybele, the goddess of the many paps, but spare, brown-habited St. Francis, serving his brethren with bleeding hands and feet, held empire over her meditations.—In imagination she saw—saw with only too lively realisation of detail—that eighteen-year-old lad, in the factory at Westchurch, drawn up—all the unspent hopes and pleasures of his young manhood active in him—by the loose gearing, into the merciless vortex of revolving wheels; and there, without preparation, without pause of warning, without any dignity of shouting multitude, of arena or of stake, martyred—converted in a few horrible seconds from health and wholeness into a formless lump of human waste. And up and down the land, as she reflected, wherever the great systems of trade and labour, which build up the mechanical and material prosperity of our day, go forward, kindred things happen—let alone question of all those persons who are born into the world already injured, or bearing the seeds of foul and disfiguring diseases in their organs and their blood. Verily Richard Calmady's sad family was a rather terribly large one, well calculated to maintain its numbers, even to increase! For neither the age of human sacrifice nor of cannibalism is really done with ; nor is the practice of them limited to savage peoples in distant lands or far-away isles of the sea. They form the basis actually, though in differing of outward aspect, of all existing civilisations, just as they formed the basis of all past civilisations—a basis, moreover, perpetually recemented and relaid. And, as she considered—being courageous and fair-minded—it was inevitable that this should be so, unthinkable that it should be otherwise, since it made, at least indirectly, for the prosperity of the majority and development of the race. Considering which—the apparently cruel paradox and irony of it—Honoria swung down past the scattered hawthorns, thick with ruddy fruit, across the fragrant herbs and short, sweet turf, through the straggling fern-brakes, which impeded her progress plucking at her skirts, careless of the rich colour and ample beauty out-spread before her.

But soon, as a bird after describing far-ranging circles drops at last upon the from at-first-determined spot, so her thought settled down with relief yet in a way unwillingly—and that not out of any lingering repulsion, but rather from a certain proud modesty and self-respect—upon Richard Calmady himself. Not only did he apprehend all this, far more clearly, more intimately than she could—had he not spoken of the advantages of a certain blackness ?—Honoria's vision became somewhat indistinct —but he set out to deal with it in a practical manner. And in this connection she began to understand how it had come about that through years of ingratitude and neglect, and of loose-living on his part, his mother could still remain patient, could endure, and supremely love. For behind the obvious, the almost coarse, tragedy and consequent appeal of the man's deformity, there was the further appeal of something very admirable in the man himself, for the emergence and due blossoming of which it would be very possible, very worth while, for whoso once recognised its existence to wait. John Knott had been right in his estimate of Richard. Ludovic Quayle had been right. Lady Calmady had been right.—Honoria had begun to believe that, even before Richard had come forth from his self-imposed seclusion, in the spring. The belief had increased during her subsequent intercourse with him, had been reinforced during her few days' visit at Whitsuntide. Yet, until now, she had never freely and openly admitted it. She wondered why ? And then hastily she put such wondering from her. Again a certain proud modesty held her back. She did not want to think of herself in relation to him, or of him in relation to herself. She wished, for a reason she refused to define, to exclude the personal element. Doing that she could permit herself larger latitude of admiration. His acknowledgment of fellowship with, and obligation of friendship towards, all victims of physical disaster kindled her enthusiasm. She perceived that it was contrary to the man's natural arrogance, natural revolt against the humiliation put upon him—a rather superb overcoming, in short, of nature by grace. Nor was it the outgrowth of any morbid or sentimental emotion. It had no tincture of the hysteric element. It took its rise in conviction and in experiment. For Richard, though still young, struck her as remarkably mature. He had lived his life, sinned his sins—she did not doubt that—suffered unusual sorrows, bought his experience in the open market and at a sufficiently high price. And this was the result! It pleased her imagination by its essential unworldliness, its idealism and individuality of outlook. She went back on her earlier judgment of him, first formulated as a complaint,—he was strong, whether for good or evil, now unselfishly for good; and Honoria, being herself among the strong, supremely valued and welcomed strength. And so it happened that the tone of her meditations altered, being increasingly attuned to a serious, but very real congratulation; for she perceived that the tragedy of human life also constitutes the magnificence of human life, since it affords, and always must afford, supreme opportunity of heroism.

She had traversed the open space of turf, and come to the tall, iron hurdles enclosing the paddock. She folded her arms on the topmost bar of the iron gate and stood there. She wanted to rest a little in these thoughts that had come to her. She was not quite sure of them as yet. But, if they meant anything, if they were other than mere rhetoric, they must mean a very great deal, into harmony with which it would be necessary to bring her thought upon many other subjects. She was conscious of an excitement, a reaching out towards some but-half-disclosed glory, some new and very exquisite fulness of life. But was it new, after all? Was it not rather the at-last-permitted activity of faculties and sensibilities hitherto refused development, voluntarily, perhaps cowardly, held in check and repressed? She appeared to be making acquaintance with unexpected depths of apprehension and emotion in herself. And this, for cause unknown, brought her into more lively commerce with her immediate surroundings and the sentiment of them. Her eyes rested upon them questioningly, as though they might afford a tally to, perhaps an explanation of, the strange, yet lovely emotion which had invaded her.

37

Here in the valley, notwithstanding the recent drought, the grass was lush. Across the paddock, just within the circuit of the far railings, a grove of large beech trees broke the expanse of living green. Beyond, seen beneath their down-sweeping branches, the surface of the Long Water repeated the hot purple, the dun-colour and silver-pink, of the sky. On the opposite slope, extending from the elm avenue to the outlying masses of the woods and upward to the line of oaks which run parallel with the park palings, were cornlands. The wheat, a red-gold, was already for the most part bound in shocks. A company of women, wearing lilac and pink sun-bonnets and all-round, blue, linen aprons faded by frequent washing to a fine clearness of tone, came down over the blond stubble. They carried, in little baskets and shining tins, tea for the white-shirted harvesters who were busy setting up the storm-fallen sheaves. They laughed and talked together, and their voices came to Honoria with a pleasant quality of sound. Two stumbling baby-children, hand in hand, followed them, as did a small, white-and-tan spotted dog. One woman was bare-headed and wore a black bodice, which gave a singular value to her figure amid the all-obtaining yellow of the corn.

The scene in its simple and homely charm held the poetry of that happier side of labour, of that most ancient of all industries—the husbandman's—and of the generous giving of the soil. Set in a frame of opulently coloured woodland and sky, the stately red-brick and freestone house crowning the high land and looking forth upon it all, the whole formed, to Honoria's thinking, a very noble picture. And then, of a sudden, in the midst of her quiet enjoyment of it and a tenderness which the sight of it somehow begot in her, she was seized by sharp, unreasoning regret that she must so soon leave it. Unreasoning regret that she had engaged to go abroad this winter, with poor, pretty, frivolous, young Lady Tobermory— spoilt child of society and of wealth—now half-crazed, rendered desperate, by the fear that disease, which had laid a threatening finger on her, might lay its whole hand, cutting short her play-time and breaking her many toys. Of anything other than toys and playtime she had no conception.—"Those brutes of doctors tell Tobermory I must give up low gowns," she wrote. "And I adore my neck and shoulders. Everyone always has admired them. It makes me utterly miserable to cover them up. And now that I am thinner I could have my gowns cut lower than ever, nearly down to my waist, which makes it all the more intolerable. I went to Dessaix about it, went over to Paris on purpose, though Tobermory was wild at my travelling in the heat. He—Dessaix, I mean, not poor T.—was just as nice as possible, and promised to invent new styles. Still, of course, I must look dowdy at night in a high gown. Everybody does. I shall feel exactly like our clergyman's wife at Ellerhay, when she comes to dine with us at Christmas and Easter and once in the summer. I refuse to have her oftener than that. She has a long back and about fourteen children, which she seems to think a great credit to her. I don't, as they are ugly, and she is dreadfully poor. She wears her Sunday silk with lace *wound* about, don't you know, but wound *tight*. That means full dress. I am buying some lace, Duchesse at three and a half guineas a yard. I suppose I shall come to *winding* that of an evening. Then I shall look like her. It makes me cry dreadfully, and, as I tell Tobermory, that is worse for me than any number of lungs. Darling H., if you really love me in the least, bring nothing but high gowns. Perhaps I mayn't mind quite so much if I never see you in a low one."—There had been much more to the same effect, pathetic in its inadequacy and egoism. Only, as Honoria reflected, that is a style of pathos dangerously liable to pall upon one. She sighed, for the prospect of spending the winter participating in the frivolities, and striving to restrain the indiscretions of this little, damaged butterfly, did not smile upon her. She might have stayed on here, stayed on at Brockhurst, and worked over the dear place as she had so often done before—helping Lady Calmady. Why had she promised?—Well—because she had been rather restless, unsettled, and at loose ends of late—

Whereupon the young lady bent down and unfastened the padlock with a certain decision of movement, closed the gate, relocking it carefully behind her; and started off across the deep grass of the paddock, her pale face very serious, her small head held high. She would keep faith with Evelyn Tobermory. Of course she would keep faith with her. It was not only a matter of honour, but of expediency. It was much, very much, better to go. Yet whence this sudden heat proceeded, and why the Egyptian journey assumed suddenly such paramount desirability, she carefully did not stay to inquire—an omission not, perhaps, without significance.

The half-dozen dainty fillies, meanwhile, who had eyed her shyly from their station beneath the beech trees, trotted gently towards her with friendly whinnyings, their fine ears pricked, their long tails carried well away in a sweeping curve. Honoria went on to meet them. She was glad of something to occupy her hands, some outside, concrete thing to occupy her thought.

She took the foremost, a dark bay, by the nose-strap of its
leather head-stall, patted the beast's sleek neck, looked into its
prominent, heavy-lidded eyes,—the blue film over the velvet-like
iris and pupil of them giving a singular softness of effect,—drew
down the fine, aristocratic head, and kissed the little star where
the hair turned in the centre of the smooth, hard forehead.   It
was as perfectly bred as she was herself—so clean, so fresh, that
to touch it was wholly pleasant !   Then she backed away from it,
holding it at arm's-length, noting how every line of its limbs and
body was graceful and harmonious, full of the promise of easy
strength, easy freedom of movement.   That it was a trifle blown
out in barrel, from being at grass, only gave its contours an added
suavity.   It was a lovely beast, a delicious beast !   Honoria
smiled upon it, talked to, patted and coaxed it.   While another
young beauty, waxing brave, pushed its black muzzle under her
arm, and lipped at her jacket pockets in search of bread and of
apples.   And, these good things once discovered, the rest of the
drove came about her, civilly, a trifle proudly, as befitted such
fine ladies, with no pushings and hustlings of vulgar greed.
And they charmed her.   She was very much at one with them.
She fed them fearlessly, thrusting one aside in favour of another,
giving each reward in due turn.   She passed her hands down
over their slender limbs.   The warm colours and the gloss of
them were pleasant to her eyes.   And they smelt sweet, as did
the trampled grass beneath their unshod hoofs.   For a while the
human problem—its tragedy, magnificence, inadequacy alike—
ceased to trouble her.   The poetry of these beautiful, innocent,
clean-feeding beasts was, for the moment, sufficient in and by
itself.

But, even while she thus played with and rejoiced in them,
remembrance of their owner came back to her, his maiming, as
against their perfection of finish, the lamentable disparity between
his physical equipment and theirs.   Honoria's expression lost its
nonchalant gaiety.   She pushed her gentle, equine comrades
away to left and right, not that they ceased to please but that
the human problem and the tragedy of it once more became
dominant.   She walked on across the paddock rapidly, while the
fillies, forming up behind her, followed in single file treading a
sinuous pathway through the grass, the foremost one still pushing its black muzzle, now and again, under her elbow and
nibbling insinuatingly at her empty jacket pockets.—If only that
horrible misfortune had not befallen Richard Calmady !   If—
if—   But then, had it not befallen him, would he ever have been
excited to so admirable effort, would he ever have attained so

absorbing and vigorous a personality as he actually had? Again her thought turned on itself, to provocation of momentary impatience.—Honoria unfastened the second padlock with a return of her former decision. There were conclusions she wished instinctively to avoid, from which she instinctively desired escape. She forced aside the all-too-affectionate, bay filly who crowded upon her, shot back the bar of the gate and relocked it. Then, once again, she kissed the pretty beast on the forehead as it stretched its neck over the top of the gate.

"Good-bye, dear lass," she said. "Win your races and, when the time comes, drop foals as handsome as yourself; and thank your stars you're under orders, and so have small chance to muddle your affairs—as with your good looks, my dear, you most assuredly would, like all the rest of us."

With which excellent advice she swung away down the last twenty yards of the avenue and out on to the roadway of the red-brick and freestone bridge. Here in the open, above the water, the air was sensibly fresher. From the paddock the deserted fillies whinnied to her. The voices of the harvesters came cheerily from the cornland. The men sat in the blond stubble, backed by a range of upstanding sheaves. The women, bright in those frail blues, clear pinks, and lilacs, knelt serving their meal. She of the black bodice stood apart, her hands upon her hips, looking towards the bridge and its solitary occupant. The tan-and-white spotted dog ran to and fro chasing field-mice and yapped. The baby-children staggered after it, uttering excited squeakings and cries. The lower cloud had parted in the west, disclosing an upper stratum of pale gold, which widened upward and outward as the minutes passed. Save immediately below, in the shadow of the bridge, this found reflection in the water, overlaying it as with the blond of the stubble and warmer tones of the sheaves. Honoria sat down sideways on the coping of the parapet. She watched the moorhens, dark of plumage, a splash of fiery orange on their jaunty little heads, swim out with restless, jerky motion from the edge of the reed-beds and break up the shining surface with diverging lines of rippling, brown shadow. In the shade cast by the bridge, trout rose at the dancing gnats and flies. She could see them rush upward through the brown water. Sometimes they leapt clear of it, exposing their silver bellies, pink-spotted sides, and the olive-green of their backs. They dropped again with a flop, and rings circled outward from the place of their disappearing.

All this Honoria saw, but dreamily, pensively. She realised,

as never before, that, much as she might love this piace and the
life of it, she was a guest only, a pilgrim and sojourner.   The
absoluteness of her own independence ceased to please.—" Me
this unchartered freedom tries."   As she quoted the line,
Honoria smiled.   These were, indeed, new aspects of herself!
Where would they carry her, both in thought and in action?   It
was a little alarming to contemplate that.   And then her pensiveness increased, a strange nostalgia taking her—amounting
almost to physical pain—for that same but-half-disclosed glory,
that same new and very exquisite fulness of life, apprehension
of which had lately been vouchsafed to her.   If she could
remain very still and undisturbed, if she could empty her
consciousness of all else, bend her whole will to an act at once
of determination and of reception, perhaps, it would be given
her clearly to see and understand.   The idealist, the mystic,
were very present in Honoria just then.   She fixed her eyes
upon the shining surface of the water.   A conviction grew upon
her that, could she maintain a certain mental and emotional
equilibrium, something of permanent and very vital importance
must take place.

Suddenly she heard footsteps upon the gravel of the roadway.   She started, turned deliberately, holding in check the
agitation which possessed her, to find herself confronted by
the tall, pre-eminently modern and mundane figure of Ludovic
Quayle.   Honoria gave herself a little shake of uncontrollable
impatience.   For less than twopence-halfpenny she could have
given the very gentlemanlike intruder a shake too!   He let her
down with a bump, so to speak, from regions mysterious and
supernal, to regions altogether social and of this world worldly.
And yet she knew that such feelings were not a little hard and
unjust as entertained towards poor Mr. Quayle.

The young man, in any case, was happily ignorant of having
offended.   He sauntered out on to the bridge, hat in hand, his
head a trifle on one side, his long neck directed slightly forward,
his expression that of polite and intimate amusement — but
whether amusement at his own, or his fellow-creatures' expense,
it would have been difficult to declare.

"At last, I find you, my dear Miss St. Quentin," he said.
" And I have sought for you as for lost treasure.   Forgive a
biblical form of address—a reminiscence merely of my father's
morning ministrations to my unmarried sisters, the footmen, and
the maids.   He reads them the most surprising little histories at
times, which make me positively blush ; but that's a detail.   To
account for my invasion of your idyllic solitude—I learned

incidentally you proposed coming here from Ormiston this week. I thought I would venture on an early attempt to find you. But I drew the house blank, though assisted by Winter—the terrace also blank. Then from the troco-ground I beheld that which looked promising, coquetting with Dickie's yearlings. So I followed on to know—my father and the maids again—followed on to—to my reward."

Mr. Quayle stood directly in front of her. He spoke with admirable urbanity, yet with even greater rapidity than usual. His beautifully formed mouth pursed itself up between the sentences, with that effect of indulgent superiority which was at once so attractive and so excessively provoking. But, for all that, Honoria perceived that for once in his life the young man was distinctly, not to say acutely, nervous.

"The reward will be limited I'm afraid," she replied, "for my temper is unaccountably out of sorts this afternoon."

"And, if one may make bold to inquire, why out of sorts, dear Miss St. Quentin?"

He sat down on the parapet near her, crossed his legs, and fell to nursing his left knee. The woman of the black bodice went up across the pale stubble to her companions. She talked to them, nodding her head in the direction of the bridge.

"I have promised to do a certain thing, and, having promised, of course I must do it."

Honoria looked away towards the harvesters up there among the gold of the corn.

"And yet, now I have committed myself, thinking it over I find I dislike doing it warmly."

"The statement of the case is just a trifle vague," Mr. Quayle remarked. "But—if one may brave a suggestion—supersede a first duty by a second and, of course, a greater. With a little exercise of imagination, a little goodwill, a little assistance from a true friend thrown in perhaps, it is generally quite possible to manage that, I think."

"And you are prepared to play the part of the true friend?"

"Undoubtedly."

"Then go to Cairo for the winter with Evelyn Tobermory. You must take no low gowns—ah! poor little soul, it is pathetic, though—she's forbidden to wear them. And—let me stay here," Honoria said.

Ludovic gazed at his hands as they clasped his knee, then he looked sideways at his companion.

"Here, meaning — meaning Brockhurst, dear Miss St. Quentin?" he asked very sweetly.

"Meaning England," she declared.

"England?—ah! really. That pleases me better. Patriotism is an excellent virtue. The remark is not a wholly original one, but it comes in handy just now, all the same."

The young lady's head went up. She was displeased. Turning sideways, she leaned both hands on the stonework and stared down into the water. But speedily she repented.

"See how the fish rise," she said. "It really is a pity one hasn't a fly-rod."

"I was under the impression you once told me that you objected to taking life, except in self-defence or for purposes of commissariat. The trout would almost certainly be muddy. And I am quite unconscious of being exposed to any danger—at least from the trout."

Miss St. Quentin kept her eyes fixed upon the water.

"I told you my temper was out of sorts," she said.

"Is that a warning?" Ludovic inquired, with the utmost mildness.

Honoria was busy feeling in her jacket pockets. At the bottom of them a few crumbs remained. She emptied these on to the surface of the water, by the simple expedient of turning the pockets inside out.

"I know nothing about warnings," she said. "I state a plain fact. You can make of it what you please."

The young man rose leisurely from his place, sauntered across the roadway, and stood with his back to her, looking down the valley. The harvesters, their meal finished, moved away towards the farther side of the great cornfield. The women followed them slowly, gleaning as they went. It was very quiet. And again there came to Honoria that ache of longing for the but-half-disclosed glory and fulness of life. It was there, an actuality—could she but find it, had she but the courage and the wit. Then, from the open moorland beyond the park palings came the sound of horses trotting sharply. Ludovic Quayle turned and recrossed the road. He smiled, but his superfine manner, his effect of slight impertinence were, for the moment, in abeyance.

"Miss St. Quentin," he said, "what is the use of fencing any longer? I have done that which I engaged to do, namely displayed the patience of innumerable asses. And—if I may be pardoned mentioning such a thing—the years pass. Really they do. And I seem to get no forwarder! My position becomes slightly ludicrous."

"I know it, I know it," Honoria cried penitently.

"That I am ludicrous?"

"No, no," she protested, "that I have been unreasonable and traded on your forbearance, that I have done wrong in allowing you to wait."

"That you could not very well help," he said, "since I chose to wait. And, indeed, I greatly preferred waiting as long as there seemed to be a hope there was something—anything, in short—to wait for."

"Ah! but that is precisely what I have never been sure about myself—whether there really was anything to wait for or not."

She sat straight on the coping of the parapet again. Her face bore the most engaging expression. There was a certain softness in her aspect to-day. She was less of a youth, a comrade, so it seemed to Mr. Quayle, more distinctly, more consciously a woman. But now, to the sound of trotting horse-hoofs was added that of wheels. With a clang the lodge-gates were thrown open.

"And are you still uncertain? In the back of your mind is there still a trifle of doubt?—If so, give me the benefit of it," the young man pleaded, half laughingly, half brokenly.

A carriage passed under the grey archway of the red-brick and freestone lodges. Rapidly it came on down the wide, smooth, string-coloured road—a space of neatly kept turf on either side—under the shade of the heavy-foliaged elm trees. Mr. Quayle glanced at it, and paused with raised eyebrows.

"I call you to witness that I do not swear, dear Miss St. Quentin, though men have been known to become blasphemous on slighter provocation than this," he said. "However, the rather violently-approaching interruption will be soon over, I hope and believe; since the driving is that of Richard Calmady of Brockhurst when his temper, like your own, being somewhat out of sorts, he, as Jehu the son of Nimshi of old—my father's morning ministrations to the maids again—driveth furiously."

Then, with an air of humorous resignation, his mouth working a little, his long neck directed forward as in mildly surprised inquiry, he stood watching the approaching mail-phaeton. The wheels of it made a hollow rumbling, the tramp of the horses was impetuous, the pole-chains rattled, as it swung out on to the bridge and drew up. The grooms whipped down and ran round to the horses' heads. And these stood, a little extended, still and rigid as of bronze, the red of their open nostrils and the silver mounting of their harness very noticeable. Lady Calmady called to Mr. Quayle. The young man passed round at the back of the carriage, and, standing on the far side of the road-way, talked with her.

Honoria St. Quentin remained sitting on the parapet of the bridge.

A singular disinclination to risk any movement had come upon her. Not the present situation in relation to Ludovic Quayle, but that other situation of the but-half-disclosed glory, the new and exquisite fulness of life, oppressed her, penetrating her whole being to the point of physical weakness. Question-ingly, yet with entire unself-consciousness, she looked up at Richard Calmady. And he, from the exalted height of the driving-seat, looked down at her. A dark, cloth rug was wrapped tight round him from the waist downward. It concealed the high driving-iron against which his feet rested. It concealed the strap which steadied him in his place. His person appeared finely proportioned. His head and face were surprisingly handsome seen thus from below—though it must be conceded the expres-sion of the latter was very far from angelic.

" You were well advised to stay at home, Honoria," he said. There was a grating tone in his voice.

" The function was even more distinguished for dulness than you expected ? "

" On the contrary, it was not in the least dull. It was actively objectionable, ingeniously unpleasant. Whereas this "—

His face softened a little. He glanced at the golden water and cornland, the lush green of the paddock, the rich, massive colouring of woodland and sky. Honoria glanced at it likewise, and, so doing, rose to her feet. That nostalgia of things new and glorious ached in her. Yet the pain of it had a strange and intimate charm, making it unlike any pain she had ever yet felt. It hurt her very really, it made her weak, yet she would not have had it cease.

" Yes, it is all very lovely, isn't it ? " she said.

She laid her hand on the folded leather of the carriage hood. Again she looked up.

" It is a good deal to have this—always—your own, to come back to, Richard."

She spoke sadly, almost unwillingly. Dickie did not answer, but he looked down, a certain violence and energy very evident in him, his blue eyes hard, and, in the depth of them, desolate as the sky of a winter night. Calmly, yet in a way desperately as those who dare inquiry beyond the range of permitted human speech, the young man and woman looked at one another. Lady

Calmady's sweet voice, meanwhile, went on in kindly question. Ludovic Quayle's in well-placed, slightly elaborate answer. The near horse threw back its head and the pole-chains rattled smartly.—Honoria's lips parted, but the words, if words indeed there were, died in her throat. She raised her hands, as though putting a tangible and actual presence away from her. She did not change colour; but for the moment her delicate features appeared thickened, as by a rush of blood. She was almost plain. Yet the effect was inexpressibly touching. It was as though she had received some mysterious injury which she was dumb, incapable to express. She let her hands drop at her sides, turned away and walked to the far end of the bridge.

Suddenly Richard's voice came to her, aggressive, curt.

"Look out, Ludovic—stand clear of the wheel."

The horses sprang forward, the grooms scrambled up at the back, and the carriage swung away from the brightness of the open to the gloom of the avenue and up the long hill to the house.

Mr. Quayle contemplated it for a minute or so. Then, with an air of amused toleration, he followed Miss St. Quentin across the bridge.

"Poor, dear Dickie Calmady, poor, dear Dickie!" he said. "He attempts the impossible. Fails to attain it—as a matter of course; and, meanwhile, misses the possible—equally as a matter of course. It is all very magnificent, no doubt, but it is also not a little uncomfortable, at times, for other people.—However that trifle of criticism is, after all, beside the mark. Now that the whirlwind has ceased, Miss St. Quentin, may the still, small voice of my own affairs presume to make itself"—

But there he stopped abruptly.

"My dear friend," he asked in quick anxiety, "what is the matter? Pardon me, but what on earth has happened to you?"

For Honoria leaned both elbows on the low, carved pillar terminating the masonry of the parapet. She covered her face with her hands. And, incontestably, she shuddered queerly from head to foot.

"Wait half a second," she said, in a stifled voice. "It's nothing—I'm all right."

Slowly she raised herself, and took a long breath. Then she turned to her faithful lover, showing him a brave, if somewhat drawn and tired, countenance.

"Ludovic," she said gently, "don't, don't please let us talk any more about all that. And don't, I entreat you, wait any longer. If there was any uncertainty, if there was a doubt in the back of my mind, it's gone. Forgive me—this must sound brutal

—but there is no more doubt. I can't marry you. I am sorry, horribly sorry—for you have been as charming to me as a man could be—but I shall never be able to marry you."

Mr. Quayle's expression retained its sweetness, even its effect of amusement, though his lips quivered, and his eyelids were a little red.

" I do not come up to the requirements of the grand passion ? " he said. "Alas ! poor me "—

" No, no, it isn't that," Honoria protested.

" Ah, then,"—he paused, with an air of extraordinary intelligence—"perhaps someone else does ? "

" Yes," she said simply, " I don't like it, but it's there, and so I've got to go through with it—someone else does."

" In that case it is indeed hopeless ! I give it up," he cried.

He moved aside and stood gazing at the rising trout in the golden-brown water. Then he raised his head sharply, as in obedience to a thought suddenly occurring to him, and gazed at Brockhurst House. The brightness of the western sky found reflection in its many windows. A noble cheerfulness seemed to pervade it, as it crowned the hillside amid its gardens and far-ranging woods.

" By all that's "— Mr. Quayle began. But he repressed the exclamation, and his expression was wholly friendly as he returned to Miss St. Quentin.

" Good-bye," he said.—" I am glad, honestly glad, you have found the grand passion, though the object of it can't, in the first blush of the affair, be altogether *persona grata* to myself. But, to show that really I have a little root of magnanimity in me, I am quite prepared to undertake a winter at Cairo, plus Evelyn Tobermory and minus low dresses, if that will enable you to stay on here—I mean in England—of course."

He pursed up his beautiful mouth, he carried his head on one side with the liveliest effect of provocation, as he held the young lady's hand while bidding her farewell.

" Out of my heart I hope you will be very happy," he said.

" I shall never be anything but Honoria St. Quentin," she answered rather hastily. Then she softened, forgiving him.— " Oh ! why," she said, " why will you make me quarrel with you just now, just at the last ? "

" Because—because "— Mr. Quayle's voice broke, though his superior smile remained to him.—" I think I will not prolong the interview," he said. " To be frank with you, dear Miss St. Quentin, I am about as miserable as is consonant with com-

plete sanity and excellent health. I do not propose to blow my
brains out, but I think—yes, thanks—you appreciate the desirability of that course of action too?—I think it is about time I
went."

CHAPTER X

CONCERNING A DAY OF HONEST WARFARE AND A SUNSET HARBINGER NOT OF THE NIGHT BUT OF THE DAWN

THAT episode, upon the bridge spanning the Long Water,
brought Richard would-be saint, Richard pilgrim along
the great white road which leads onward to Perfection, into lively
collision with Richard the natural man, not to mention Richard
the "wild bull in a net." These opposing forces engaged battle,
with the consequence that the carriage horses took the hill at a
rather breakneck pace. Not that Dickie touched them, but that,
he being vibrant, they felt his mood down the length of the reins
and responded to it.

"Ludovic need hardly have been in such a prodigious hurry,"
he broke out. "He might have allowed one a few days' grace.
It was a defect of taste to come over immediately; but then all
that family's taste is liable to lapses."

Promptly he repented, ashamed both of his anger and such
self-revealing expression of it.

"I daresay it's all for the best though. Better a thing should
be nipped in the bud than in the blossom. And this puts it all
on a right footing. One might easily drift into depending too
much upon Honoria. I own I was dangerously near doing that
this spring. I don't mind telling you so now, mother, because
this, you see, disposes finally of the matter."

His voice contended oddly with the noise of the wheels, rattle
of the pole-chains, pounding of the hoofs of the pulling horses.
The sentences came to Lady Calmady's ears disjointed, difficult to follow and interpret. Therefore she answered slightly at
random.

"My dearest, I could have kept her longer in the spring if I
had only known," she said, a disquieting suspicion of lost opportunity assailing her. "But, from certain things which you said, I
thought you preferred our being alone."

"So I did. I wanted her to go because I wanted her to stay.
Do you see?"

"Ah, yes! I see," Katherine replied. And at that moment,

it must be conceded, her sentiments were not conspicuously pacific towards her devoted adherent, Mr. Quayle.

"We've a good many interests in common," Dickie went on, "and there seemed a chance of one's settling down into a rather charming friendship with her. It was a beguiling prospect. And, for that very reason, it was best she should depart. The prospect, in all its beguilingness, renewed itself to-day after luncheon."— He paused, handling the plunging horses.—"And so, after all, Ludovic shall be reckoned welcome; for, as I say, I might have come to depend on her. And one's a fool—I ought to have learnt that salutary lesson by this time—a rank fool, to depend on any-body or anything, save oneself, simply and solely oneself"—his tone softened—"and upon you, most dear and long-suffering mother. —Therefore the dream of friendship goes overboard along with all the rest of one's little illusions. And every illusion one rids one-self of is so much to the good. It lightens the ship. It lessens the chances of foundering. Clearly it is so much pure gain."

That evening, pleading—unexampled occurrence in her case— a headache as excuse, Miss St. Quentin did not put in an appearance at dinner. Nor did Richard put in an appearance at breakfast next morning. At an early hour he had received a communication earnestly requesting his presence at the Westchurch Infirmary. His mission promised to be a melan-choly one, yet he was not sorry for the demand made by it upon his time and thought. For, notwithstanding the philosophic tone he had adopted with Lady Calmady in speaking of that friendship which, if not nipped in the bud, might have reached perils of too luxuriant blossoming, the would-be saint and the natural man, the pilgrim on the highroad to Perfection and that very inconvenient animal "the wild bull in a net," kept up warfare within Richard Calmady. They were hard at it even yet, when, in the fair freshness of the September morning—the grasses and hedge-fruit, the wild flowers, and low-growing, tangled coppices by the roadside, still heavy with dew—he drove over to Westchurch. The day was bright, with flying cloud and a westerly breeze. The dust was laid, and the atmosphere, cleared by the storm of the preceding afternoon, had a smack of autumn in it. It was one of those delicious, yet distracting, days when the sea calls, and when whosoever loves sea-faring grows restless, must seek movement, seek the open, strain his eyes towards the margin of the land—be the coast-line never so far distant—tor-mented by desire for sight of the blue water, and the strong and naked joys of the mighty ridge and furrow where go the gallant ships.

With the upspringing of the wind at dawn, that calling of the sea had made itself heard to Richard. At first it suggested only the practical temptation of putting the *Reprieve* into commission, and engaging Lady Calmady to go forth with him on a three or four months' cruise. But that, as he speedily convinced himself, was but a pitifully cheap expedient, a shirking of voluntarily assumed responsibility, a childish cheating of discontent, rather than an honestly attempted cure of it. If cure was to be achieved, the canker must be excised, boldly cut out, not overlaid merely by some trifle of partially concealing plaster. For he knew well enough, as all sea-lovers know—and, as he drove through the dappled sunlight and shadow, frankly admitted—that though the sea itself very actually and really called, yet its calling was the voice and symbol of much over and above itself. For in it speaks the eternal necessity of going forward, that hunger and thirst for the absolute and ultimate which drives every human creature whose heart and soul and intellect are truly animate. And to him, just now, it spoke more particularly of the natural instincts of his manhood—of ambition, of passion, of headlong desire of sensation, excitement, adventure, of just all that, in fact, which he had forsworn, had agreed with himself to cast aside and forget. And, thinking of this, suspicion assailed him that forswearing had been slightly insincere and perfunctory. He accused himself of nourishing the belief that giving he would also receive,—and that in kind,—while that any sacrifice which he offered would be returned to him doubled in value. Casting his bread upon the waters, he accused himself of having expected to find it, not "after many days," but immediately—a full baker's dozen ready to hand in his pocket. His motives had not been wholly pure. Actually, though not at the time consciously, he had essayed to strike a bargain with the Almighty.

Just as he reached the top of the long, straight hill leading down into Westchurch, Richard arrived at these unflattering conclusions. On either side the road, upon the yellow surface of which the sunlight played through the tossing leaves of the plane trees, were villas of very varied and hybrid styles of architecture. They were, for the most part, smothered in creepers, and set in gardens gay with blossom. Below lay the sprawling, red-brick town, blotted with purple shadow. A black canal meandered through the heart of it, crossed by mean, humpbacked bridges. The huge, amorphous buildings of its railway station—engine sheds, goods warehouses, trailing of swiftly dispersed white smoke—the grime and clamour of all that, its factory buildings and tall chimneys, were very evident, as were the pale towers of

its churches.   And beyond the ugly, pushing, industrial commonplace of it, striking a very different note, the blue ribbon of the
still youthful Thames, backed by high-lying chalk-lands fringed
with hanging woods, traversed a stretch of flat, green meadows.
Richard's eyes rested upon the scene absently, since thought just
now had more empire over him than any outward seeing.   For he
perceived that he must cleanse himself yet further of self-seeking.
Those words, "if thou wilt be perfect sell that thou hast and
give to the poor, and follow thou me," have not a material and
objective significance merely.   They deal with each personal
desire, even the apparently most legitimate ; with each indulgence
of personal feeling, even the apparently most innocent; with
the inward attitude and the atmosphere of the mind even more
closely than with outward action and conduct.   And so Richard
reached the conclusion that he must strip himself yet nearer to
the bone.   He must digest the harsh truth that virtue is its own
reward in the sense that it is its only reward, and must look for
nothing beyond that.   He had grown slack of late, seduced by
visions of pleasant things permitted most men but to him
forbidden ; and wearied, too, by the length of the way and
inevitable monotony of it now first heat of enthusiasm had
evaporated.   Well — it was all very simple.   He must just
re-dedicate himself.   And in this stern and chastened frame of
mind he drove through the bustle of the country town—Saturday,
market day, its streets unusually alive—nodding to an acquaintance here and there in passing, two or three of his tenant
farmers, Mr. Cathcart of Newlands in on county business,
Goodall the octogenarian miller from Parson's Holt, and
Lemuel Image the brewer, bursting out of an obviously new suit
of very showy tweeds.   Then, at the main door of the Infirmary,
helped by the stalwart, hospital porter, he got down from the
dog-cart ; and subsequently—raked by curious eyes, saluted by
hardly repressed tittering from the out-patients waiting *en queue*
for admission to the dispensary—he made his slow way along the
bare, vaultlike, stone passage to the accident ward, in the far
corner of which a bed was shut off from the rest by an arrangement of screens and of curtains.

And it was in the same chastened frame of mind that, some
four or five hours later, Richard entered the dining-room at
Brockhurst.   The two ladies had nearly finished luncheon and
were about to rise from the table.   Lady Calmady greeted him
very gladly ; but abstained from inquiry as to his doings or from
comment on the lateness of the hour, since experience had long
ago taught her that of all known animals man is the one of whom

it is least profitable for woman to ask questions.   Dickie was here at home, alive, intact, her eyes were rejoiced by the sight of him, that was sufficient.   If he had anything to tell her, no doubt he would tell it later.   For the rest, she had something to tell him ; but that too must wait until time and circumstance were propitious, since the conveying of it involved delicate diplomacies. It must be handled lightly.   For the life of her she must avoid all appearance of eagerness, all appearance of attaching serious importance to the communication.   Lady Calmady had learned, this morning, that Honoria St. Quentin did not propose to marry Ludovic Quayle.   The young lady, whose charming nonchalance was curiously in eclipse to-day, had given her to understand so much ; but very briefly, the subject evidently being rather painful to her.   She was silent and a little distrait; but she was also very gentle, displaying a disposition to follow Katherine about wherever she went, and a pretty zeal in doing small odd jobs for her.   Katherine was touched and tenderly amused by her manner, which was as that of a charming child coveting assurance that it need not be ashamed of itself, and that it has not really done anything naughty ! But Katherine sighed too, watching this strong, graceful, capable creature ; for, if things had been otherwise with Dickie, how thankfully she would have given the keeping of his future into this woman's hands.   She had ceased to be jealous even of her son's love.   Gladly, gratefully, would she have shared that love, accepting the second place, if only — but all that was beyond possibility of hope. Still the friendship of which he had spoken somewhat bitterly yesterday—poor darling—remained.   Ludovic Quayle's pretensions—she felt very pitifully towards that accomplished gentleman, all his good qualities had started into high relief — but, his pretensions no longer barring the way to that friendship, she pledged herself to work for the promotion of it.   Dickie was too severe in self-repression, was over-strained in stoicism ; and, ignoring the fact that in his fixity of purpose, his exaggerations of self-abnegation, he proved himself very much her own son, she determined secretly, cautiously, lovingly, to combat all that.

It was, therefore, with warm satisfaction that, as Honoria was about to rise from the table, she observed Richard emerge, in a degree, from his abstraction, and heard him say :—

"You told me you'd like to ride over to Farley this afternoon and see the home for my crippled people.   Are you too tired after your headache, or do you still care to go?"

"Oh ! I'm not tired, thanks," Honoria answered.   Then she hesitated ; and Richard, looking at her, was aware, as on the

38

bridge yesterday, of a sudden and singular thickening of her features, which, while marring her beauty, rendered her aspect strangely pathetic, as of one who sustains some mysterious hurt. And to him it seemed, for the moment, as though both that hurt and the infliction of it bore subtle relation to himself. Common sense discredited the notion as unpermissibly fantastic, still it influenced and softened his manner.

"But you know you are looking frightfully done up yourself, Richard," she went on, with a charming air of half-reluctant protest. "Isn't he, Cousin Katherine? Are you sure you want to ride this afternoon? Please don't go out just on my account."

"Oh! I'm right enough," he answered. "I'd infinitely rather go out."

He pushed back his chair and reached down for his crutches. Still the fantastic notion that, all unwittingly, he had been guilty of doing Honoria some strange injury, clung to him. He was sensible of the desire to offer reparation. This made him more communicative than he would otherwise have been.

"I saw a man die this morning—that's all," he said. "I know it's stupid; but one can't help it, it knocks one about a bit. You see he didn't want to die, poor fellow, though, God knows, he'd little enough to live for—or to live with, for that matter."

"Your factory hand?" Honoria asked.

Richard slipped out of his chair and stood upright.

"Yes, my factory hand," he answered. "Dear, old Knott was fearfully savage about it. He was so tremendously keen on the case, and made sure of pulling him through. But the poor boy had been sliced up a little too thoroughly." — Richard paused, smiling at Honoria. "So all one could do was to go with him just as far as is permitted out into the great silence, and then—then come home to luncheon. The home at Farley loses its point, rather, now he is dead. Still there are others, plenty of others, enough to satisfy even Knott's greed of riveting broken human crockery.—Oh yes! I shall enjoy riding over, if you are still good to come. Four o'clock—that'll suit you? I'll order the horses."

And so, in due course, the two rode forth together into the brightness of the September afternoon. The sea still called; but Dickie's ears were deaf to all dangerous allurements and excitations resident in that calling. It had to him, just now, only the pensive charm of a far-away melody, which, though no doubt of great and immediate import to others, had ceased to be any concern of his. Beside the deathbed in the hospital ward he had renewed his vows, and the efficacy of that renewal was very present with him. It made for repose. It laid the evil spirit of defiance, of self-consciousness, of humiliation, so often obtaining in his intercourse with women—a spirit begotten by the perpetual prick of his deformity, and in part, too, by his determined adoption of the ascetic attitude in regard to the affections. He was spent by the emotions of the morning, but that also made for repose. For the time being devils were cast out. He was tranquil, yet exalted. His eyes had a smile in them, as though they looked beyond the limit of things transitory and material into the regions of the Pure Idea, where the eternal values are disclosed and Peace has her dwelling. And, precisely because of all this, he could take Honoria's presence lightly, be chivalrously solicitous of her entertainment and well-being, and talk to her with greater freedom than ever heretofore. He ceased to be on his guard with her because, in good truth, it seemed to him there ceased to be anything to guard against. For the time being, at all events, he had got to the other side of all that; and so she and his relation to her, had become part of that charming but far-away melody which was no concern of his—though mighty great and altogether worthy concern of others, of Ludovic Quayle, for example.—And in his present tranquil humour he could listen to the sweetness of that melody ungrudgingly. It was pleasant. He could enjoy it without envy, though it was none of his.

But to Honoria's seeing it must be owned, matters shaped themselves very differently. For the usually unperturbed, the chaste and fearless soul of her endured violent assaults, violent commotions, the origin of which she but partially understood. And these Richard's frankness, his courteous, in some sort brotherly, good-fellowship, served to intensify rather than allay. The feeling of the noble horse under her, the cool, westerly wind in her face, went to brace her nerves, and restore the self-possession, courage of judgment, and clearness of thought, which had been lacking to her during the past twenty-four hours. Nevertheless she rode as through a but-newly-discovered country, familiar objects displaying alien aspects, familiar phases assuming unlooked-for significance, a something challenging and fateful meeting her everywhere. The whole future seemed to hang in the balance : and she waited, dreading yet longing, to see the scale turn.

This afternoon the harvesters were carrying the corn. Red-painted waggons, drawn by sleek, heavy-made, cart-horses, crawled slowly across the blond stubble. It was pretty to see the rusty-gold sheaves tossed up from the shining prongs of the pitch-forks on to the mountainous load.   Honoria and Richard watched this, a little minute, from the grass-ride bordering the roadway beneath the elms.   Next came the high-lying moorland, beyond the lodges.   The fine-leaved heath was thick with red-purple blossom.   Patches of dusky heather were frosted with dainty pink.   Spikes of genista and beds of needle-furze showed sharply yellow, vividly green, and a fringe of blue campanula, with frail, quivering bells, outlined all open spaces.   The face of the land had been washed by the rain.   It shone with an inimitable cleanliness, as though consciously happy in relief from all soil of dust.   And it was here, the open country stretching afar on all sides, that Dickie began talking, not, as at first, in desultory fashion, but of matters nearly pertaining and closely interesting to himself.

"You know," he said, as they walked the horses quietly, neck to neck, along the moorland road, "I don't go in for system-making or for reforms on any big scale.   That doesn't come within my province.   I must leave that to politicians and to men who are in the push of the world.   I admire it.   I rejoice in the hot-headed, narrow-brained, whole-hearted agitator, who believes that his system adopted, his reform carried through, the whole show will instantly be put straight.   Such faith is very touching."

"And the reformer has sometimes done some little good after all," Honoria commented.

"Of course he has," Dickie agreed.   "Only as a rule, poor dear, he can't be contented but that his special reform should be the final one, that his system should be the universal panacea. And in point of fact no reform is final this side of death, and no panacea is universal, save that which the Maker of the Universe chooses to work out—is working out now, if we could any way grasp it—through the slow course of unnumbered ages. Let the reformer do all he can, but don't let him turn sour because his pet reform, his pet system, sinks away and is swallowed up in the great sea of things—sea of human progress, if you like.   Every system is bound to prove too small, every reform ludicrously inadequate—be it never so radical—because material conditions are perpetually changing, while man in his mental, emotional and physical aspects remains always precisely the same."

They passed from the breezy upland into the high-banked lane which, leading downwards, joins the great London and Portsmouth Road just beyond Farley Row.

"And—and that is where I come in!" Richard said, turning a little in the saddle and smiling sweet-temperedly, yet with a suggestion of self-mockery, upon his companion. "Just because, in essential respects, mankind remains—notwithstanding modifications of his environment—substantially the same, from the era of the Pentateuch to the era of the Rougon - Macquarts, there must always be a lot of wreckage, of waste, and refuse humanity. The inauguration of each new system, each new reform—religious, political, educational, economic—practically they're all in the same boat—let alone the inevitable breakdown or petering out of each, necessarily produces a fresh crop of such waste and refuse material. And in that a man like myself, who does not aspire to cure or to construct, but merely to alleviate and to pick up the pieces, finds his chance."

And Honoria listened, musing—approved, enthusiasm gaining her; yet protested, since, even while she admired, she rebelled a little on his account, and for his sake.

"But it is rather a hard life, surely, Richard," she said, "which you propose to yourself? Always the pieces, the thing broken and spoiled, never the thing in its beauty, full of promise, and whole!"

"It is less hard for me than for most," he answered, "or should be so. After all, I am to the manner born—a bit of human wreckage myself, with which, but for the accident of wealth, things would have gone pretty badly. I used to be horribly scared sometimes, as a small boy, thinking to what uses I might be put if the kindly, golden rampart ever gave."

He became silent. As for Honoria, she had neither courage to look at or to answer him just then.

"And you see, I'm absolutely free," he added presently.—"I am alone, always shall be so. If the life is hard, I ask no one to share it, so I may make it what I like."

"Oh! no, no—you misunderstand, Richard! I didn't mean that," Honoria cried quickly, half under her breath.

Again he looked at her, smiling.

"Didn't you? All the kinder of you," he said.

Thereupon regret, almost intolerable in its poignancy, invaded Miss St. Quentin that she would have to go away, to go back to the world and all the foolish obtaining fashions of it; that she should have to take that pre-eminently well-cushioned and luxurious winter's journey to Cairo. She longed inexpressibly to remain here, to assist in these experiments made in the name of Holy Charity. She longed inexpressibly to— And there Honoria paused, even in thought. Yet she glanced at the

young man riding beside her—at the handsome profile, still
and set in outline, the suggestion, it was no more, of a scar
running downward across the left cheek; at the well-made, upright, broad-shouldered figure, and then at the saddle, peaked,
back and front, with oddly-shaped appendages to it resembling
old-fashioned holsters.—And, as yesterday upon the bridge, the
ache of a pain at once sweet and terrible laid hold of her, making
her queerly faint.   The single street, sun-covered, sleepy, empty
save for a brewer's dray and tax-cart or two standing before the
solid Georgian portals of the White Lion Inn, for a straggling tail
of children bearing home small shoppings and jugs of supper
beer, for a flock of grey geese proceeding with aggressively self-
righteous demeanour along the very middle of the roadway and
lowering long necks to hiss defiance at the passer-by, and for an
old black retriever dozing peacefully beneath one of the rustling
sycamores in front of Josiah Appleyard, the saddler's shop—all
these, as she looked at them, became uncertain in outline, and
reeled before Honoria's eyes.   For the moment she experienced
a difficulty in keeping steady in the saddle.   But the horses still
walked quietly, neck to neck, their shadows, and those of their
riders growing longer, narrower, outstretched before them as the
sun declined in the west.   All the future hung in the balance;
but the scale had not turned as yet.

Then Richard's voice took up its parable again.

"Perhaps it's a rather fraudulently comfortable doctrine, yet
it does strike one that the justification of disaster, in all its many
forms, is the opportunity it affords the individualist.   He may use
t for self-aggrandisement, or for self-devotion—though I rather
shy at so showy a word as that last.   However, the use he makes
of it isn't the point.   What is the point, to my mind at least, is
this—though it doesn't sound magnificent, it hardly indeed
sounds cleanly—that whatever trade fails, whatever profession,
thanks to the advance of civilisation, becomes obsolete, that of
the man with the dust-cart, of the scavenger, of the sweeper,
won't."

Once more Richard smiled upon his companion charmingly,
yet with something of self-mockery.

"And so, you see, having knocked about enough to grow
careless of niceties of prejudice, and to acquire an immense admiration for any vocation which promises permanence, I join hands
with the dustman.   In the light of science, and in that of religion
alike, nothing really is common or unclean.   And then—then, if
you are beyond the pale in any case, as some of us are, it's a little
too transparently cheap to be afraid of soiling"— He broke off.—

"Away there to the left, Honoria," he said. "You see the house? The yellow-washed one, with the gables and tiled roofs—there, back on the slope.—Bagshaw, the Bond Street poulterer, had it for years. His lease ran out in the spring, and happily he didn't care to renew. Had bought himself an up-to-date, villa residence somewhere in the suburbs—Chislehurst, I believe. So I took the place over. It will do for a beginning—the small end of the wedge of my scavenger's business. There are over five acres of garden and orchard, and plenty of rooms on each floor, which gives good range for the disabled to move about in—and the stairs, only one flight, are easy. One has to think of these details. And—well, the house commands a magnificent view of Clerke's Green, and the geese on it, than which nothing clearly can be more exciting!"

The groom rode forward and opened the gate. Before the square, outstanding porch Richard drew up.

"I should like to come in with you," he said. "But you see it's rather a business getting off one's horse, and I can't very well manage the stairs. So I'll wait about till you are ready. Don't hurry. I want you to see all the arrangements, if it doesn't bore you, and make suggestions. The carpenters are there, doing overtime. They'll let you through if the caretaker's out."

Thus admonished, Miss St. Quentin dismounted and made her way into the house. A broad passage led straight through it. The open door at the farther end disclosed a vista of box-edged path and flower-borders where, in gay ranks, stood tall sunflowers, holly-hocks, Michaelmas-daisies, and such like. Beyond was orchard, the round-headed apple-trees, bright with polished fruit, rising from a carpet of grass. The rooms, to left and right of the passage, were pleasantly sun-warmed and mellow of aspect, the ceilings of them crossed by massive beams. Honoria visited them, dutifully observant. She encountered the head carpenter, an acquaintance and ally during those four years so great part of which she had spent at Brockhurst. She talked with him, making inquiries concerning wife, children, and trade, incident to such a meeting, her face very serious all the while, the skirt of her habit gathered up in one hand, her gait a trifle stiff and measured owing to her high riding-boots. But, though she acquitted herself in all kindliness of conversation, though she conscientiously inspected each separate apartment, and noted the cheerful comeliness of orchard and garden, it must be owned all these remained singularly distant from her actual emotion and thought. She was glad to be alone. She was glad to be away from Richard Calmady, though zealously obedient to his wishes in respect of this inspection.   For his presence became increasingly oppressive from the intensity of feeling it produced in her, and which she was, at present, powerless to direct toward any reasonable and definite end.   This rendered her tongue-tied, and, as she fancied, stupid.   Her unreadiness mortified her. She, usually indifferent enough to the impression she produced on others, was sensible of a keen desire to appear at her best.   She did in fact, so she believed, appear at her worst, slow of under-standing and of sympathy.—But then all the future hung in the balance.   The scale delayed to turn.   And the strain of waiting became agitating to the point of distress.

At last the course of her so-dutiful survey brought her to a quaint, little chamber, situated immediately over the square, out-standing porch.   It was lighted by a single, hooded window placed in the centre of the front wall.   It was evidently designed for a linen room, and was in process of being fitted with shelves and cupboards of white pine.   The floor was deep in shavings, long, curly, wafer-coloured, semi-transparent.   They rustled like fallen leaves when Honoria stepped among them.   The air was filled with the odour of them, dry and resinous as that of the fir forest.   Ever after that odour affected Honoria with a sense of half-fearful joy and of impending fate.   She stood in the middle of the quaint, little chamber.   The ceiling was low.   She had to bend her head to avoid violent contact between the central beam of it and the crown of her felt hat.   But circumscribed though the space, and uncomfortable though her posture, she had an absurd longing to lock the door of the little room, never to come out, to stay here forever !   Here she was safe.   But outside, on the threshold, stood something she dared not name.   It drew her with a pain at once terrible and lovely.   She dreaded it. Yet once close to it, once face to face with it, she knew it would have her ; that it would not take no for an answer.   Her pride, her chastity, was in arms.   Was this, she wondered, what men and women speak of so lightly, laugh and joke about ?   Was this love ?—To her it seemed wholly awe-inspiring.   And so she clung strangely to the shelter of the quaint, little room with its sea of rustling, resinous shavings.   On the other side the door of it waited that momentous decision which would cause the scale to turn.   Yet the minutes passed.   To prolong her absence became impossible.

Just then there was a movement below, a crunching of the gravel, as though of a horse growing restless, impatient of standing.   Honoria moved forward, opened the window, pushing back the casement against a cluster of late-blossoming, red roses, the petals of which floated slowly downward describing fluttering circles. Richard Calmady was just below. Honoria called to him.

"I am coming, Richard, I am coming!" she said.

He turned in the saddle and looked up at her smiling—a smile at once courageous and resigned. Yet, notwithstanding that smile, Honoria once again discovered in his eyes the chill desolation and homelessness of the sky of the winter night. Then the scale turned, turned at last; for that same lovely pain grew lovelier, more desirable than any possibility of ease, until such time as that desolation should pass, that homelessness be cradled to content in some sure harbourage.—Here was the thing given her to do, and she must do it! She would risk all to win all. And, with that decision, her serenity and freedom of soul returned. The white light of a noble self-devotion, reckless of self-spending, reckless of consequence, the joy of a great giving, illuminated her face.

As to Richard, he, looking up at her, though ignorant of her purpose, misreading the cause of that inspired aspect, still thought he had never witnessed so graciously gallant a sight. The nymph whom he had first known, who had baffled and crossed him, was here still, strong, untamed, elusive, remote. But a woman was here too, of finest fibre, faithful and loyal, capable of undying tenderness, of an all-encircling and heroic love. Then the desires of the natural man stirred somewhat in Richard, just because—paradox though it undoubtedly was—she provoked less the carnal, perishing passion of the flesh, than the pure and imperishable passion of the spirit. Irrepressible envy of Ludovic Quayle, her lover, seized him, irrepressible demand for just all those things which that other Richard, the would-be saint, had so sternly condemned himself to repudiate, to cast aside and forget. And the would-be saint triumphed—beating down thought of all that, trampling it under foot—so that after briefest interval he called up to her cheerily enough.

"Well, what do you make of the dust-cart? Rather fascinating, isn't it? Notwithstanding its uncleanly name, it's really rather sweet."

To which she answered, speaking from out the wide background of her own emotion and purpose :—

"Yes, yes—it's sad in a way, Richard, penetratingly, splendidly sad. But one wouldn't have it otherwise; for it is splendid, and it is sweet, abundantly sweet."—Then her tone changed.—"I won't keep you waiting any longer, I'm coming," she said.

Honoria looked round the quaint, little room, with its half-adjusted shelves and cupboards, the floor of it deep in resinous, semi-transparent, wafer-coloured shavings, bidding it adieu.   For good or evil, happiness or sorrow, she was sensible it told for much in her life's experience.   Then, something delicately militant in her carriage, she swung away downstairs and out of the house. She was going forth to war indeed, to a war which in no shape or form had she ever waged as yet.   Many men had wooed her, and their wooing had left her cold.   She had never wooed any man.   Why should she?   To her no man had ever mattered one little bit.

So she mounted, and they rode away.—A spin across the level turf to hearten her up, satisfy the fulness of sensation which held her, and shake her nerves into place.   It was exhilarating. She grew keen and tense, her whole economy becoming reliable and well-knit by the strong exercise and sense of the superbly healthy and unperplexed vitality of the horse under her.   Honoria could have fought with dragons just then, had such been there to fight with!   But, in point of fact, nothing more aggressively dangerous presented itself for encounter than the shallow ford which divides the parish of Farley from that of Sandyfield and the tithing of Brockhurst.   Snorting a little, the horses splashed through the clear, brown water and entered upon the rough, rutted road, grass-grown in places, which, ending beneath a broken avenue of ancient, stag-headed oaks, leads to the entrance of the Brockhurst woods.   These, crowned by the dark, ragged line of the fir forest, rose in a soft, dense mass against the western sky, in which showed promise of a fair pageant of sunset. A covey of partridges ran up the sandy ruts before the horses, and, rising at last with a long-drawn whir of wings, skimmed the top of the crumbling bank and dropped in the stubble-field on the right.   A pause, while the keeper's wife ran out to open the white gate,—the dogs meanwhile, from their wooden kennels under the Spanish chestnuts upon the hillock behind the lodge, pulling at their chains and keeping up a vociferous chorus. Thus heralded, the riders passed into the mysteriously whispering quiet of the great woods.

The heavy, summer foliage remained as yet untouched by the hectic of autumn.   Diversity was observable in form rather than in tint, and from this resulted a remarkable effect of unity, a singleness of intention, and of far-reaching secrecy.   The multitudinous leaves and the all-pervading green gloom of them around, above, seemed to engulf horses and riders.   It was as though they rode across the floor of ocean, the green tides sweeping overhead. Yet the trees of the wood asserted their intelligent presence now and again. Audibly they talked together, bent themselves a little to listen and to look, as though curious of the aspect and purposes of these wandering mortals. And all this, the unity and secrecy of the place, affected both Richard and Honoria strangely, circling them about with something of earth-magic, removing them far from ordinary conditions of social intercourse, and thus rendering it possible, inevitable even, that they should think such thoughts and say such words as part company with subterfuge and concealment, go naked, and speak uttermost truth. For, with only the trees of the wood to listen, with that sibilant whisper of the green tide overhead, with strong emotion compelling them—in the one case towards death of self, in the other towards giving of self—in the one towards austere passivity, in the other towards activity taxing all capital of pride, of delicacy, and of tact—developments became imminent, and those of the most vital sort.

The conversation had been broken, desultory; but now, by tacit consent, the pace became quiet again, the horses were permitted to walk. To have gone other than softly through the living heart of the greenwood must have savoured of desecration. Yet Richard was not insensible to a certain danger. He tried, rousing himself to conversation, to rouse himself also to the practical and commonplace.

"I am glad you liked my house," he said. "But I hear the aristocracy of the Row laments. It shies at the idea of being invaded by more or less frightful creatures. But I remain deaf. I really can't bother about that. It is so immeasurably more unpleasant to be frightful than to see that which is so, that I'm afraid my sympathies remain rather pig-headedly one-sided. I propose to educate the Row in the grace of pity. It may lay up merit by due exercise of that."

Richard took off his hat and rode bare-headed, looking away into the delicious, green gloom. Here, where the wood was thickest, oak and beech shutting out the sky, clasping hands overhead, the ground beneath them deep in moss and fern, that gloom was exactly like the colour of Honoria's eyes. He wished it wasn't so. He tried to forget it. But the resemblance haunted him. Look where he might, still he seemed to look into those singular and charming eyes. He talked on determinedly, putting a force upon himself, too often saying that which, no sooner was it out of his mouth, than he wished unsaid.

"I don't want to be too hard on the Row, though. It has a

right, after all, to its little prejudices. Only you see for those who, poor souls, are different to other people it becomes of such supreme importance to keep in touch with the average. I have found that out in practice. And so I refuse to shut my waste humanity away. They must neither hide themselves nor be hidden, be spared seeing how much other people enjoy from which they are debarred, nor grow over-conscious of their own ungainliness. That is why I've planted them and their gardens, and their pigs and their poultry—we'll have a lot of live stock, a second generation, even of chickens, offers remarkable consolations — on the highroad, at the entrance of the little town, where, on a small scale at all events, they'll see the world that's straight-backed and has its proper complement of limbs and senses, go by. Envy, hatred, and malice, and the seven devils of morbidity are forever lying in wait for them—well—for us—for me and those like me, I mean. In proportion as one's brought up tenderly— as I was—one doesn't realise the deprivation and disgust of one's condition at the start. But once realised, one's inclina- tion is to kill. At least a man's is. A woman may accept it more quietly, I suppose."

"Richard," Honoria said slowly, "are you sure you don't greatly exaggerate all—all that?"

He shook his head.

"Thirty years' experience—no, I don't exaggerate! Each time one makes a fresh acquaintance, each time a pretty woman is just that bit kinder to one than she would dare be to any man who was not out of it, each time people are manifestly interested —politely, of course—and form a circle, make room for one as they did at that particularly disagreeable Grimshott garden-party yesterday, each time—I don't want to drivel, but so it is—one sees a pair of lovers—oh! well, it's not easy to retain one's philosophy, not to obey the primitive instincts of any animal when it's ill-used and hurt, and to revenge oneself—to want to kill, in short."

"You—you don't hate women, then?" Honoria said, still slowly.

Richard stared at her for a moment.

"Hate them?" he said. "I only wish to goodness I did."

"But in that case," she began bravely, "why"—   ⁤

"This is why," he broke in.—"You may remember my engagement to Lady Constance Quayle, and the part you, very properly, took in the cancelling of it? You know better than I do—though my imagination is pretty fertile in dealing with the situation—what instincts and feelings prompted you to take that part."

The young lady turned to him, her arms outstretched, notwithstanding bridle-reins and whip, her face, and those strange eyes which seemed so integral a part of the fair greenwood, full of sorrowful entreaty and distress.

"Richard, Richard," she cried, "will you never forgive me that? She didn't love you. It was horrible, yet in doing that which I did, I believed—I believe so still—I did what was right by you both."

"Undoubtedly you did right, and that justifies my contention. In doing that which you did you gave voice to the opinion of all wholesome-minded people. That's exactly where it is. You felt the whole business to be outrageous. So it was. I heartily agree."—He paused, and the trees talked softly together, bending down a little to listen and to look.—"As you say, she wasn't in love. Poor child, how could she be? No woman ever will be— at least not in love of the nobler sort, of the sort which if one cannot have it, one had a vast deal better have no love at all."

"But I am not so sure of that," Honoria said stoutly. "You rush to conclusions. Isn't it rather a reflection on all the rest of us to take little Lady Constance as the measure of the insight and sensibility of the whole sex? And then she had already lost all her innocent, little heart to Captain Decies. Indeed you're not fair to us.—Wait"—

"Like Ludovic Quayle?"

Miss St. Quentin straightened herself in the saddle.

"Oh! dear no, not the least like Ludovic Quayle!" she said.

Which enigmatic reply produced silence for a while on Dickie's part. For there were various ways in which it might be interpreted, some flattering, some eminently unflattering, to himself. And from every point of view it was wisest to accept that last form of interpretation. The whole conversation had been perilous in character. It had been too intimate, had touched him too nearly, taking place here in the clear glooms of the greenwood moreover which bore such haunting kinship to those singularly sincere, and yet mysterious, eyes. It is dangerous to ride across the floor of ocean with the whispering tides sweeping overhead, and in such gallant company, besides, that to ride thus forever could hardly come amiss!—Richard, in his turn, straightened himself up in the saddle, opened his chest, taking a long breath, carried his head high, said a stern "get thee behind me, Satan," to encroaching sentiment and emotion, and to those fair visions which his companion's presence and her somewhat daring talk had conjured up. He defied the earth-magic, defied those sylvan deities who, as he divined, sought to enthral him. For the moment he confounded Honoria's influence with theirs. It was something of a battle, and not the first one he had fought to-day. For the great, white road which leads onward to Perfection looked dusty and arid enough—no reposeful shadow, no mystery, no beguiling green glooms over it. Stark, straight, hard, it stretched on endlessly, as it seemed, ahead. To travel it was slow and tedious work, in any case; and to travel it on crutches!—But it was worse than useless to play with such thoughts as these. He would put a stop to this disintegrating talk. He turned to Honoria and spoke lightly, with a return of self-mockery.

"Oh! your first instinct was the true one, depend upon it," he said. "Though I don't deny it contributed, indirectly, to giving me a pretty rough time."

"Oh! dear me!" Honoria cried, almost piteously. Then she added :—"But I don't see, why was that?"

"Because, I suppose, I had a sort of unwilling belief in you," he said, smiling.—Oh! this accursed conversation, why would it insistently drift back into intimacy thus!

"Have I justified that belief?" she asked, with a certain pride yet a certain eagerness.

"More than justified it," Dickie answered. "My mother, who has a touchstone for all that is of high worth, knew you from the first. Like the devils, I—I believed and trembled—at least that is how I see it all now. So your action came as a rather searching revelation and condemnation. When I perceived all that it involved—oh, well! first I went to the dogs, and then "—

The horses walked side by side. Honoria stretched out her hand impulsively, laid it on his arm.

"Richard, Richard, for pity's sake don't! You hurt me too much. It's terrible to have been the cause of such suffering."

"You weren't the cause," he said. "Lies were the cause, behind which, like a fool, I'd tried to shelter myself. You've been right, Honoria, from first to last. What does it matter after all?—Don't take it to heart. For it's over now, all over, thank God, and I have got back into normal relations with things and with people."—He looked at her very charmingly, and spoke with a fine courtesy of tone.—"One way and another you have taught me a lot, and I am grateful. And, in the future, though the conditions will be altered, I hope you'll come back here often, Honoria, and just see for yourself that my mother is content; and give my schemes and fads a kindly look in at the same time. And perhaps give me a trifle of sound advice. I shall need it safe enough. You see what I want to get at is temperance—temperance all round, towards everything and everybody—not fanaticism, which, in some respects, is a much easier attitude of mind."

Richard looked up into the whispering, green tide overhead.

"Yes, one must deny oneself the luxury of fanaticism, if possible," he said, "deny oneself the vanity of eccentricity. One must take everything simply, just in the day's work. One must keep in touch. Keep in touch with your world, the great world, the world which cultivates pleasure and incidentally makes history, as well as with the world of the dust-cart—I know that well enough—if one's to be quite sane. You see loneliness, a loneliness of which I am thankful to think you can form no conception, is the curse of persons like myself. It inclines one to hide, to sulk, to shut oneself away and become misanthropic. To hug one's misery becomes one's chiefest pleasure—to nurse one's grief and one's sense of injury. Oh! I'm wary, very wary now, I tell you," he added, half laughing. "I know all the insidious temptations, the tricks and frauds and pit-falls of this affair. And so I'll continue to go to Grimshott garden-parties as discipline now and then, while I gather my disabled and decrepit family very closely about me and say words of wisdom to it—wisdom derived from a mature and extensive personal experience."

There was a pause before Miss St. Quentin spoke. Then she said slowly.

"And you refuse to let anyone help? You, you refuse to let anyone share the cares of that disabled family?"

Again Dickie stared at her, arrested by her speech and doubtful of the intention of it. He could have sworn there were tears in her voice, that it shook. But her face was averted, and he could see no more than the slightly angular outline of her cheek and chin.

"Isn't that a rather superfluous question?" he remarked. "As you pointed out a little while ago, mine is not a superabundantly cheerful programme. No one would volunteer for such service—at least no one likely to be acceptable to my mother, or indeed likely to satisfy my own requirements. I admit, I'm a little fastidious, a little critical and exacting, when it comes to close quarters and—well—permanent association, even yet."

"I am very glad to hear that," Honoria said. Her face remained averted, but there was a change in her attitude, a decision in the pose of her figure, suggestive both of challenge and of triumph.

Richard was nonplussed, but his blood was up. This conversation had gone far enough—indeed too far. Very certainly he would make an end of it.

"But God forbid," he exclaimed, "that I should ever fall to such a depth of selfishness as to invite any person who would satisfy my taste, my demands, to share my life! I mayn't amount to very much, but at least I have never used my personal ill-luck to trade on a woman's generosity and pity. What I have had from women, I've paid for, in hard cash. In that respect my conscience is clear. It has been a bargain, fair and square and above board, and all my debts are settled in full. You hardly think at this time of day I should use my proposed schemes of philanthropy as a bait?"

Richard sent his horse forward at a sharp trot.

"No, no, Honoria," he said, "let it be understood that side of things is over forever."

But here came relief from the green glooms of the greenwood and the dangerous magic of them. For the riders had reached the summit of the hill, and entered upon the levels of the great tableland, at the edge of which Brockhurst House stands. Here was the open, the fresh breeze, the long-drawn, sighing song of the fir forest—a song more austere, more courageous, more virile, than any ever sung by the trees of the wood which drop their leaves for fear of the sharp-toothed winter, and only put them forth again beneath the kisses of soft-lipped spring. Covering all the western sky were lines of softly-rounded, broken cloud, rank behind rank, in endless perspective, the whole shaped like a mighty fan. The under side of them was flushed with living rose. The clear spaces behind them paved with sapphire at the zenith, and palest topaz where they skirted the far horizon.

"How very beautiful it is!" Honoria cried, joyously. "Richard, let us see this."

She turned her horse at the green ride which leads to the white Temple, situate on that outstanding spur of hill. She rode on quickly till she reached the platform of turf before the summer-house. Richard followed her with deliberation. He was shaken. His calm was broken up, his whole being in tumult. Why had she pressed just all those matters home on him which he had agreed with himself to cast aside and forget? It was a little cruel, surely, that temptation should assail him thus, and the white road towards Perfection be made so difficult to tread, just when he had re-dedicated himself and renewed his vows? He looked after her. It was here he had met her first—after the time when, as a little maid, she had proved too swift of foot, leaving him so far behind that it sorely hurt his small dignity and caused him to see her depart without regret. She was still swift of foot. She left him behind now. For the moment he was ready to swear that not only without regret but with actual thankfulness, he could again witness her departure. — Yes, he wanted her to go, because he so desperately wanted her to stay —that was the truth. For not only Dickie the natural man, but Dickie "the wild bull in a net," had a word to say just then. God in heaven what hard work it is to be good!

Miss St. Quentin kicked her left foot out of the stirrup, threw her right leg over the pommel, turned, and slipped straight out of the saddle. She stood there a somewhat severely tall, dark figure, strong and positive in effect, against the immense and reposeful landscape—far-ranging, purple distance, golden harvest-fields, silver glint of water in the hollows, all the massive grandeur of the woods, and that superb pageant of sunset sky.

The groom rode forward, took her horse, led it away to the far side of the grass platform behind the Temple. Those ranks of rosy cloud in infinite perspective, with spaces of clearest topaz and sapphire light between, converged to the glowing glory of the sun, the rim of which now touched the margin of the world. They were as ranks of worshippers, of blessèd souls redeemed and sainted, united in a common act of adoration, every form clothed by reflection of His glory, every heart, every thought centred upon God.—Richard looked at all that, but it failed to speak to him. Then he saw Honoria resolutely turn her back upon the glory. She came directly towards him. Her face was very thin, her manner very calm. She laid her left hand on the peak of his saddle. She looked him full in the eyes.

"Richard," she said, "be patient a minute and listen. It comes to this, that a woman—your equal in position, of your own age, and not without money—does volunteer to share your work. It's no forlorn hope. She is not disappointed. On the contrary she has, and can have, pretty well all the world's got to give. Only—perhaps very foolishly, for she doesn't know much about the matter, having been rather cold-blooded so far —she has fallen in love."

There was a silence, save that the wind came out of the west, out of the majesty of the sunset; and with it came the calling of the sea—not only of the blue water, or of those green tides that sweep above wandering mortals in the magic green-wood, but of the sea of faith, of the sea of love—love human, love divine, love universal — which circles not only this, but all possible states of being, all possible worlds.

39

Presently Richard spoke hoarsely, under his breath.

"With whom?" he said.

"With you"—

Dickie went white to the lips. He sat absolutely still for a little space, his hands resting on his thighs.

"Tell her to think," he said, at last.—"She proposes to do that which the world will condemn, and rightly from its point of view. It will misread her motives. It won't spare disagreeable comment. Tell her to think.—Tell—tell her to look.—Cripple, dwarf, the last, as he ought to be, of an unlucky race—a man who's carried up and down stairs like a baby, who's strapped to the saddle, strapped to the driving-seat—who is cut off from most forms of activity and of sport—a man who will never have any sort of career; who has given himself, in expiation of past sins, to the service of human beings a degree more unfortunate than himself.—No, no, stop—hear me out.—She must know it all! —A man who has lived far from cleanly, who has evil memories and evil knowledge of life—no—listen. A man whom you—yes, you yourself, Honoria—have condemned bitterly; from whom, notwithstanding your splendid nerve and pluck, so hateful is his deformity, you have shrunk a hundred times."

"She has thought of all that," Honoria answered calmly. "But she has thought of this too—that, going up and down the world to find the most excellent thing in it, she has found this thing, love. And so to her, Richard, your crippling has come to be dearer than any other man's wholeness. Your wrong doings —may God forgive her—dearer than any other man's virtue. Your virtues so wholly beautiful that—that"—

The tears came into her eyes, her lips quivered, she backed away a little from rider and horse.

"Richard," she cried fiercely, "if you don't care for me, if you don't want me, be honourable, tell me so straight out and let us have done with it! I am strong enough, I am man enough, for that. For Heaven's sake don't take me out of pity. I would never forgive you. There's a good deal of us both, one way and another, and we should give each other a hell of a time if I was in love and you were not. But"—she put her hand on the peak of that very ugly saddle again—"but, if you do care, here I am. I have never failed anyone yet. I will never fail you. I am yours body and soul. Marry me," she said.

CHAPTER XI

IN WHICH RICHARD CALMADY BIDS THE LONG-SUFFERING
READER FAREWELL

THE midsummer dusk had fallen, drawing its soft, dim
mantle over the face of the land. The white light
walked the northern sky from west to east. A nightingale sang
in the big, Portugal laurel at the corner of the troco-ground; and
was answered by another singer from the coppice, across the
valley, bordering the trout stream that feeds the Long Water. A
fox barked sharply out in the Warren. Beetles droned, flying
conspicuously upright, straight on end, through the warm air.
The churring of the night-hawks, as they flitted hither and thither
over the beds of bracken and dog-roses, like gigantic moths, on
quick, silent wings, formed a continuous accompaniment, as of
a spinning-wheel, to the other sounds. And Dick Ormiston
laughed consumedly, doubling himself together now and again
and holding his slim sides in effort to moderate his explosive
merriment. He was in uproarious spirits.—Back from school
to-day, and that nearly a month earlier than could by the most
favourable process of calculation have been anticipated, thanks
to development of measles on the part of some much-to-be-
commended schoolfellows. How he blessed those praiseworthy
young sufferers! And how he laughed, watching the two heavy-
headed, lolloping, half-grown, bull-dog puppies describe crazy
circles upon the smooth turf in the deepening dusk. Seen thus
in the half-light they appeared more than ever gnome-like,
humorously ugly and awkward. They trod on their own ears,
tumbled over one another, sprawled on the grass, panting and grinning, until their ecstatic owner incited them to
further gyrations. To Dick this was a night of unbridled licence.
Had he not dined late? Had he not leave to sit up till half-
past ten o'clock? Was he not going out, bright and early, to-
morrow morning to see the horses galloped? Could life hold
greater complement of good for a brave, little, ten-year-old soul,
and serviceable, little, ten-year-old body emulous of all manly
virtues and manly pastimes?

So the boy laughed; and the sound of his laughter reached
the ears both of the elder and the younger Lady Calmady, as they
slowly paced the straight walk between the grey balustrade and
the edge of the turf. On their left the great outstretch of valley

and wood lay drowned in the suave uncertainties of the summer
night.   Before them was the whole terrace-front of the house,
its stacks of twisted chimneys clear   cut   against the sky.
Bright light shone out from the windows of the red drawing-
room, and from those of the hall, bringing flowers, sections of
grey pavement, and like details into sharp relief.   There were
passing lights in the range of windows above, suggesting cheerful
movement within the great house.   At the southern end of the
terrace, just below the arcade of the garden - hall — which
showed pale against the shadow within and brickwork above—
two men were sitting.   Their voices reached the ladies now and
then in quiet yet animated talk.   A spirit of peace, of security,
of firmly - planted hope, seemed to pervade all the scene, all
the place.   Waking or sleeping, fear was banished.   All was
strong to work to - morrow, therefore to-night all could calmly
yield itself to rest.

And it was a sense of just this, and a tender anxiety lest the
fulness of the gracious content of it should be in any degree
marred to her dear companion, which made Honoria Calmady
say presently :—

"You don't mind little Dick's racketting with those ridiculous
puppies, do you, Cousin Katherine?   If it bothers you I'll stop
him like a shot."

But Katherine shook her head.

"My dearest child, why stop him?" she said.   "The
foolishnesses of young creatures at play is delicious ; and laughter,
so long as it is not cruel, I reckon among the good gifts of God."
—She paused a moment.   "Dear Marie de Mirancourt tried to
teach me that long ago, but I was culpably dull of hearing in
these days where spiritual truth was concerned, and I failed to
grasp her meaning.   I believe we never really love, either man
or Almighty God, until we can both laugh ourselves and let others
laugh.   Of all false doctrines that of the sour-faced, joyless
puritan is the falsest.   His mere outward aspect is a sin against
the Holy Ghost."

And Honoria smiled, patting the hand which lay on her arm
very tenderly.

"How I love your heavenly rage!" she said.   They moved
on a few steps in silence.   Then, careless of all the rapture its
notification of the passing of time might cut short, the clock at
the house stables chimed the half-hour.   Honoria paused in her
gentle walk.

"Bed-time, Dick," she cried.

"All right," the boy returned.   He pursued, and laid hold of, the errant puppies, stowing them, not without kickings and strugglings on their part, one under either arm. They were large and heavy, just as much as he could carry ; and he staggered across the grass with them, presenting the effect of a small, black donkey between a pair of very big, white panniers.

"I say, they are awfully stunning though, you know, Honoria," he said rather breathlessly as he came up to her.

"Very soul - satisfying, aren't they, Dick ? " she replied. "Richard foresaw as much. That is why he got them for you."

"If I put them down do you suppose they'll follow ? Carrying them does make my arms ache."

"Oh, they'll follow fast enough," Honoria said.

He lowered the puppies circumspectly on to the gravel.

"They'll be whoppers when they're grown," he remarked. "What shall you call them ? "

" Adam and Eve I think, because they're the first of my lot. They're pedigree dogs—and later I may want to show, don't you see."

"Yes, I see," Honoria said.

He came close to her, putting his face up half shyly to be kissed. Then as young Lady Calmady, somewhat ghostly in her trailing, white, evening dress, bent her charming head, the boy, suddenly overcome with the manifold excitements of the day, flung his arms round her.

"Oh ! oh ! " he gasped, " how awfully ripping it is to be back here again with you and Cousin Richard and Aunt Katherine ! I wish number-four dormitory would get measles the middle of every term !—Only I forgot—perhaps I ought not to touch you, Honoria, after messing about with the dogs. Do you mind ? "

"Not a bit," she said.

" But, Honoria,"—he rubbed his cool cheek against her bare neck—"I say, don't you think you might come and see me, just for a little weeny while, after I'm in bed to-night ? "

And young Lady Calmady, thus coaxed, held the slight figure close. She had a very special place in her heart for this small Dick, who in face, and as she hoped in nature also, bore such comfortable resemblance to that elder and altogether well-beloved Dick, who was the delight of her life.

"Yes, dear, old chap, I'll come," she said. " Only it must really be for a little weeny while, because you must go to sleep. By the way, who's going to valet you these holidays? Clara or Faulstich ? "

"Oh, neither," the boy answered. "I think I'm rather old for women now, don't you know, Honoria."—At which statement she laughed, his cheek being again tucked tight into the turn of her neck. "I shall have Andrews in future. I asked Cousin Richard about it. He's a very civil-mannered fellow, and he knows about yachts and things, and he says he likes being up before five o'clock."

"Does he? Excellently veracious young man!" Honoria remarked.

But thereupon, exuberance of joy demanding active expression, the boy broke away with a whoop and set off running. The puppies lolloped away at his heels. And young Lady Calmady—whom such giddy fancies still took at times, notwithstanding nearly three years of marriage—flew after the trio, the train of her dress floating out behind her to most admired extravagance of length as she skimmed along the path. Fair lady, boy, and dogs disappeared, with sounds of merriment, into the near garden-hall; reappeared upon the terrace, bearing down, but at sobering pace, upon the occupants of the chairs set at the end of it. One man rose to his feet, a tall, narrow, black figure. The other remained seated. The light shining forth from the great bay-window of the hall touched the little group, conferring a certain grandeur upon the graceful, white-clad Honoria. Her satin dress shimmered as she moved. There was, as of old, a triumph of high purity, of freedom of soul, in her aspect. Her voice came, with a fine gladness yet soft richness of tone, across that intervening triangular space of sloping turf upon which terrace and troco-ground alike looked down. The nightingale, who had fallen silent during the skirmish, took up his passionate singing again, and was answered delicately, a song not of the flesh but of the spirit, by the bird from across the valley.

Katherine Calmady stood solitary, watching, listening, her hands folded rather high on her bosom. The caressing suavity of the summer night enfolded her. And remembrance came to her of another night, nearly four-and-thirty years ago, when, standing in this same spot, she, young, untried, ambitious of unlimited joys, had felt the first mysterious pangs of motherhood, and told her husband of that new, unseen life which was at once his and her own. And of yet another night, when, after long experience of sorrow, solitude, and revolt, her husband had come to her once again; but come, even as the bird's song came from across the valley, etherealised, spiritualised, the same yet endowed with qualities of unearthly beauty — and how that

strange and exquisite communion with the dead had fortified her
to endure an anguish even greater than any she had yet known.
She had prayed that night that she might behold the face of her
well-beloved, and her prayer had been granted. She had prayed
that, without reservation, she might be absorbed by and conformed to, the Divine Will. And that prayer had, as she humbly
trusted, been in great measure granted also. But then the Divine
Will had proved so very merciful, the Divine Intention so wholly
beneficent, there was small credit in being conformed to either!
Katherine bowed her head in thanksgiving. The goodness of
the Almighty towards her had been abundant beyond asking or
fondest hope.

She was aroused from her gracious meditation by the sound
of footsteps—measured, a little weary perhaps—approaching her.
She looked up to see Julius March. And a point of gentle
anxiety pricked Katherine. For it occurred to her that Julius
had failed somewhat in health and in energy of late. She
reproached herself lest, in the interest of watching those vigorous,
young lives so dear to her, participating in their schemes, bask-
ing in the sunshine of their love, she had neglected Julius
and failed to care for his comfort as she might. To those that
have shall be given—even of sympathy, even of strength. In
that there is an ironical as well as an equitable truth; and she
was to blame perhaps in the ironical application of it. It
followed, therefore, that she greeted him now with a quickening
both of solicitude and of affection.

"Come and pace, dear Julius, come and pace," she said, "as
in times past. Yet not wholly as in the past, for then often I
must have distressed and troubled you, since my pacings were
too often the outcome of restlessness and of unruly passion, while
now "—

Katherine broke off, gazing at the little company gathered
upon the terrace.

"Surely they are very happy?" she said, almost involuntarily.

And he, smiling at his dear lady's incapacity of escape from
her fixed idea, replied :—

"Yes, very surely."

Katherine tied the white, lace coif she wore a little tighter
beneath her chin.

"In their happiness I renew that of my own youth," she said
gently, "as it is granted to few women, I imagine, to renew it.
But I renew it with a reverence for them; since my own happiness
was plain sailing enough, obvious, incontestable, whilst theirs is
nobler, and rises to a higher plane. For its roots, after all, are

planted in very mournful fact, to which it has risen superior, and over which it has triumphed."

But he answered, jealous of his dear lady's self-depreciation :—

"I can hardly admit that. To begin in unclouded promise of happiness, to decline to searching and unusual experience of sorrow, and then, by self-discipline and obedience, to attain your present altitude of tranquillity and assurance of faith, is surely a greater trial, a greater triumph, than to begin—as they—with difficulties, with much, I admit, to overcome and resist, but to succeed as they are succeeding and be granted the high land of happiness which they even now possess? They are young, fortune smiles on them. Above all, they have one another "—

"Ah yes!" she said, "they have one another. Long may that last. It is a very perfect marriage of true minds, as well as true hearts. I had, and they have, all that love can give," —Lady Calmady turned at the end of the walk. "But it troubles me, as a sort of emptiness and waste, dear Julius, that you have never had that. It pains me that you, who possess so noble a power of disinterested and untiring friendship, should never have enjoyed that other, and nearer, relation which transcends friendship even as to-morrow's dawn will transcend in loveliness the chastened restfulness of this evening's dusk."

Katherine moved onward with a certain sweet dignity of manner.

"Tell me—is she still alive, Julius, this lady whom you so loved?"

"Yes, thank God," he said.

"And you have never tried to elude that vow which—as you once told me—you made long ago before you knew her?"

"Never," he replied. "Without it I could not have served her as I have been able to serve her. I am wholly thankful for it. It made much possible which must have otherwise been impossible."

"And have you never told her that you loved her—even yet?"

"No," he replied, "because, had I told her, I must have ceased to serve her. I must have left her, Katherine, and I did not think God required that of me."

Lady Calmady walked on in silence, her head a little bent. At the end of the path she stood a moment, listening to the answering songs of the two nightingales.

"Ah!" she said softly, "how greatly I have under-rated the beauty of the dusk! To submit to dwell in the border-land, to stand on the dim bridge thus between day and night, demands perhaps the very finest courage conceivable. You have shown me, Julius, how exquisite and holy a thing it is.— And, as to her whom you have so faithfully loved, I think, could she know, she would thank you very deeply for never telling her the truth. She would entreat you to keep your secret to the end. But to remain near her, to let her seek counsel of you when in perplexity or distress; to talk with her both of those you and she love, and have loved, and of the promise of fair things beyond and above our present seeing—pacing with her at times—even as you and I, dear friend, pace together here to-night amid the restrained and solemn beauty of the dusk. Would she not do this?"

"It is enough that you have done it for her, Katherine," he answered. "With your ruling I am wholly, unendingly content."

"Perhaps Richard and Honoria's dear works of mercy and the noonday tide of energy which flows through the house, have caused us to see less of each other than of old," Lady Calmady continued with a charming lightness. "That is a mistake needing correction. The young to the young, dear Julius. You and I, who go at a quieter pace, will enjoy our peaceful friendship to the full. I shall not tire of your company, I promise you, if you do not of mine. Long may you be spared to me. God keep you, most loyal friend. Good-night."

Then Lady Calmady, deeply touched, yet unmoved from her altitude of thankfulness and calm, musing of many matters and of the working out of them to a beneficent and noble end, slowly went the length of the terrace to where, at the foot of the steps of the garden-hall, Richard still sat. As she came near he held out his hand to her.

"Dear, sweet mother," he said, "how I like to see you walk in that stately fashion, the whole of you—body, mind, and spirit, somehow evident—gathered up within the delicious compass of yourself! As far back as I can remember anything, I remember that. When I watched you it always made me feel safe. It seemed more like music heard, somehow, than something seen."

"Dickie, Dickie," she exclaimed, flushing a little, "don't make me vain in my old age!"

"But it's true," he said. "And why shouldn't one tell the pretty truths as well as the plain ones?—Isn't it a positively divine night? Look at the moon just clearing the top of the firs there! It is good to be alive. Mother—may I say it?—I am very grateful to you for having brought me into the world."

"Ah! but, my poor darling"— Katherine cried.

"No, no," he said, "put that out of your dear head once and for all. I am grateful, being as I am; grateful for everything, it being as it is. I don't believe I would have anything — not anything — save those four years when I left you — altered, even if I could. I've found my work, and it enlarges its borders in all manner of directions; and it prospers. And I have money to put it through. And I have that boy. He's a dear, little chap—and it is wonderfully good of Uncle Roger and Mary to give him to me. But he's getting a trifle too fond of horses. I can't break poor, old Chifney's heart; but when his days are numbered, those of the stables—as far as training racers goes—are numbered likewise, I think. I'll keep on the stud farm. But I grow doubtful about the rest. I wish it wasn't so, but so it is. Sport is changing hands, passing from those of romance into those of commerce.—Well, the stables served their turn. They helped to bring me through. But now perhaps they're a little out of the picture."

Richard drew her hand nearer and kissed it, leaning back in his chair, and looking up at her.

"And I have you"— he said, "you, most perfect of mothers. —And—ah! here comes Honoria!"

PRINTED BY MORRISON AND GIBB LIMITED, EDINBURGH